When Gregory the Grey, head of the Magickers, and Brennard, the leader of the Dark Hand, dueled for the future of the world, it split the space-time continuum, paving the way for the Age of Science while at the same time most sources of magic were lost in our world. All the Magickers and the members of the Dark Hand alive at the time fell into a magic-induced sleep from which they did not begin to awaken until the early 1970s. Since then the Dark Hand has hunted the Magickers, determined to steal their power and destroy them. And legend has it that both Gregory and Brennard survived their duel, and are hidden away, slowly regaining their strength and awaiting the moment of their own awakening.

Now the Magickers' only hope for survival is to seek out children with "talent" and train them to use their abilities for the good, and to find the hidden gateways to strongholds where the sources of magic still exist.

THE
MAGICKERS CHRONICLES

DAW BOOKS PRESENTS
EMILY DRAKE'S
THE MAGICKERS CHRONICLES

VOLUME ONE:
THE MAGICKERS
THE CURSE OF ARKADY

VOLUME TWO:
THE DRAGON GUARD
THE GATE OF BONES

THE MAGICKERS CHRONICLES

VOLUME TWO

THE DRAGON GUARD

THE GATE OF BONES

EMILY DRAKE

DAW BOOKS, INC.

DONALD A. WOLLHEIM, FOUNDER

375 Hudson Street, New York, NY 10014

ELIZABETH R. WOLLHEIM
SHEILA E. GILBERT
PUBLISHERS

www.dawbooks.com

First Printing, October 2010
1 2 3 4 5 6 7 8 9

DAW TRADEMARK REGISTERED
U.S. PAT. AND TM. OFF. AND FOREIGN COUNTRIES
—MARCHA REGISTRADA
HECHO EN U.S.A.

PRINTED IN THE U.S.A.

THE
DRAGON GUARD

Dedicated to my lovely family
both the carrot and the stick
for my success.

Contents

BEGINNING

A TALL figure swathed in black stepped out of a corner door, his lean weight barely causing the floorboards to sound. He moved with the agility of a fighter, a ninja, and he knew it. The great room had been an old dance studio once, this cavernlike room with high windows covered in metal mesh, and creaking wooden floor. Mirrors, their silver backing tarnished in blackened streaks along the edges, lined one entire wall, with a barre fastened below them. He took a moment or two to stretch, only the top half of his face revealed by the ninja veil. His dark clothing moved freely with his agile form. The only color on his form at all came from the clear, prismatic crystal pendant hanging about his neck. After a moment or two of stretches, he reached up and tucked the pendant inside his clothing.

"Ready," he said flatly. He moved into a defensive stance, alert, weight balanced slightly forward on his feet, hands in readiness. The room dropped into silence. He stood in anticipation.

Nothing happened. He tilted his head impatiently. "I am waiting."

A breathless voice answered him from beyond the glass

wall. "Just a moment, Jonnard. A difficulty—" The speaker broke off with a pant and a curse, then all fell silent.

"I said, ready! Do you expect me to wait all morning?" His voice broke harshly, impatiently, through the air. He tilted his head, listening for further action.

More curses followed, punctuated by a sharp yelp of pain. Then, mirrored doors shimmered as they moved inward, and then . . . something . . . came through them.

It looked as if it could be his twin, but it moved . . . wrong. More fluidly, as if it had more joints than he did. It glided toward him, at the ready. The eyes revealed above the ninja wrapping over the face were flat, and filled with hunger.

"No weapons," Jonnard said firmly, "but those of your body." As if what he faced would heed rules of combat. He moved into a stance, and smiled, with an inward breath.

It was the only moment of stillness he had. The Leucator attacked, in a swirl of black and pale hands and face, and the two met in a flurry of hands, feet, arms, and legs, punch, parry, kick, block, attack, and retreat, then attack again. The floor accompanied them in muted thunder as Jonnard fought for his very life.

Then, slowly, the attacker began to give. It made little noise other than a hissing and its own quickened breathing. Jonnard made noise enough for both of them. A triumphant "Hah!" when a blow hit hard, a grunt when the other hit him, a curse when a spinning kick missed.

Their shoes squeaked on the varnished floor when they touched, yet many of their movements seemed almost airborne. Thuds of flesh against flesh drove each back and forth. Yet slowly but surely Jonnard began to drive the Leucator back, back from the center of the huge practice area, toward the corner it had emerged from. His ribs hurt. His hands smarted from the lightning-fast boxing blows of the other, but he knew what his foe would do. It was like watching himself fight, the mirrors eerily reflecting four of him.

Exactly like watching himself, for the Leucator was himself, duplicated and thirsting to find him and rejoin him. It was a creation of Magick, meant to be a tireless Hunter and Seeker. It would not cease or stop its Hunt till rejoined with its Soulmate, although no one in his right mind would allow such a joining. It was a corrupt thing, and its very presence prickled the hair at the back of his neck. Even he, who would do much to achieve his goals, thought of the Leucator as sheer evil. But it knew what he knew, in many ways, and made the perfect opponent to practice against.

Jonnard smiled thinly as they met again in another flurry of moves. Hand to shoulder, other hand to rib, leg, spin, kick, balance, jab, punch, spin again, push away. He could scarcely see the moves, but they lay inside, in the memory of his muscles and his training, and if the Leucator was fast, he must be faster!

The thing caught him with a stunning blow to his temple. Jonnard fell back, his eyes swimming with unshed tears from the sting of it, his ears ringing. He shook his head, trying to clear his senses. The Leucator advanced on him, blows pummeling fast and furious, and Jonnard twisted away, his breath caught in his throat for a moment, as he realized his danger.

It would bring him near to death and then claim him, "reuniting" their selves. Then he would be gone forever, absorbed into the fiber of this corrupted being. He played a deadly game . . . and he was losing!

Jonnard touched the crystal he wore inside his shirt. It warmed, even through the fabric, steadying him. He danced back a step, out of range, and breathed carefully, balancing himself. The ringing in his ear disappeared and he rubbed at his eye, clearing it. The Leucator would not land another such blow! Jonnard inhaled deeply, then stepped forward and back into the attack.

He beat the creature into the corner, slowly, step by step, until suddenly it slipped and went down with an exhausted sound. Jonnard shook out his crystal, cupping it briefly, calling it to fiery life. A singular beam sizzled from it, his own personal light saber, and he sliced off the Leucator's head.

The thing curled into hissing black smoke, sucking inward, until it disappeared.

Jonnard grinned in triumph.

The mirrored doors opened and Antoine Brennard stepped forth, frowning. "Another one dead? These are expensive, my son."

"But worth it for training. I need two. I demand two." Jonnard quelled the crystal sword and once again held an ordinary pendant in his hand. "Jason Adrian will not stand against me. I promise that!"

"Do you now? And what if I need him alive?"

Jonnard felt the heat of his triumph in his eyes as he looked at his father. "Then I promise that, as well. But get me two. I need two to continue training." With that, he pivoted away and slipped off through the corner door, with not a look back. His father would obtain the simulations for him. Expensive or not, they could not afford *not* to. Not if he wanted Jason Adrian defeated and helpless in their hands.

THE HURRIEDER
I GO. . . .

"**A**LL RIGHT! All right, listen up! One goal to tie, two to win! And that's how we get them, one at a time!" Coach's voice broke over the huddle, carrying to each of them, the soccer ball tucked under his arm. His voice carried over Jason like a wave of sound, shutting off the rest of the world. Coach broke off long enough to toss the ball to a waiting referee, then returned to his time-out speech. "Here's how we're going to do it . . ."

Jason grabbed a spare towel and mopped up his face, feeling the sweat trickle between his eyebrows, preparing to slide down his nose. He rubbed the towel through his hair, and waited. The towel felt damp in his hands, but he managed to scrub up the back of his neck before tossing it toward the benches. A limp banner proclaiming "Go Chargers" waved in the spring breeze.

Todd, their goalie, muttered, "Easier said than done." Coach grabbed his shoulder and shook him lightly. The agile teen was already beet red from three quarters of a hard-played game, but his face darkened even more and showed through the roots of his black hair. "I know, one step at a time," the goalie amended quickly as the coach nearly growled.

"Exactly! Now the first step is this . . . I've been using Jason lightly . . ."

Jason looked at his soccer coach in surprise. He'd been running his legs off trying to guard the center, making sure their star forward got as many clear shots as he could, and the sweat plastering his jersey to his body was more than proof of that. Coach Wayne didn't seem to notice his look as he continued. "Jason has been passing to Bradley all day, but I'm gonna cut him loose now. He's up there in right wing on purpose, but the other team has relaxed, they don't know what he can do. So . . . pass the ball to Jason. Let's show 'em."

A burst of elation went through Jason, followed by a brief moment of despair. It was all on him . . . all he wanted and yet, all the responsibility. He made a fist and pumped his hand rather than letting the doubt shake him. He could do it. He would! Enthusiasm leaped through him, and with it his Magick awoke, like a lightning flash, though he quickly contained it. No Magick here, just athletic talent, but he might as well have told himself not to breathe. And his Magick called to the others. From the corner of his eye, he caught sight of his cheering section in the warped and faded wooden bleachers. Bailey, her golden-brown ponytail bouncing in enthusiasm, jumped to her feet and waved. Their quiet friend Ting sat next to her, her hands weaving in a silent cheer. There was a flash of something bright and shiny in her hands, and Jason grinned as he recognized the sparkle of her crystal jewelry. He quickly brought his attention back to the huddle and his teammates. The Wingnuts were already dancing impatiently on the line, as eager to bring the game to a triumphant end as they were.

Bradley gave him a nod. "Watch Karcher, the fullback. He's fast and he's rough." He considered a moment, then added, "I've been faking their goalie right all day. Might try something different."

"Gotcha."

Coach gave them a few more instructions, then ended up with, "Don't pass it to Jason till you know he's in the clear. I don't want to tip our hand too early. Their fullbacks are good, and their goalie is . . . well, he's the reason we're behind. But we won't stay that way!"

A sharp whistle signaled the end of their time, and the

boys broke apart, wheeling back onto the field. From the bench, Jason's friend Sammee yelled "Go get 'em!" and snapped a team towel. Hiding his widening grin, Jason trotted back into his position as right wing and looked down the field for the kick. He took a deep breath. This was it. League semifinals. Chargers against the Wingnuts. This wasn't the school team where nearly everyone who tried out had a position somewhere on one of the strings. No, these players were serious, headed to high school and then college and maybe even the pros in soccer, and the competition was intense. They lost here, and they were out of the tournament. They won, and they went on to the finals. You couldn't get much closer to winning or losing it all than this.

He jogged in place a moment to loosen his calves up, then froze into position as the others lined up and the refs readied for the kick. Without seeming to, he scanned the faces of the opposite team. Like his own, they were bright with sun and sweat, a little tired, yet eager. They smelled victory in the air. He grinned, showing his teeth almost like a wolf, facing into the late afternoon breeze. He was going to do all he could to prove them wrong!

He looked to Bradley, though, stifling his impulse to look them in the eyes, and stare them down. The center nodded back at him. His would be the stealth attack, and he'd give it away if he challenged them. So he took one last stretch, and straightened, and waited for the whistle and kick.

It all seemed to happen at once, noise, sound, and movement as the teams both surged forward. His body carried him down the field, angling to both protect and take advantage of an opening, without him even thinking of doing it. Stiles, on the other team, buffeted him, and he dropped back, then cut away, leaving the defender far behind. Bradley glanced his way and darted around the defender Karcher, then saw him clear, and passed the ball to him sharply.

The black and white came at him. Jason considered passing it off, but he was close enough to try a goal and no one seemed to be taking him seriously . . . yet. He could angle it as he received it, to the goalie's left. The soccer ball met his insole briskly and caromed off like a shot.

There was a long moment in which he just watched,

turning his body to match the geometry of the kick, and the goalie, who had been heading the other way in his nets, saw his look but couldn't cut back in time. The ball went cleanly into the corner of the goal and the team and crowd roared. Bailey and Ting jumped up and down, waving in joy, although their voices were lost in the crowd. From the corner of his eye, he saw a man separate from the bleachers, camera in hand, clicking pictures. He seemed to focus on Bailey and Ting, snapping away. Who wouldn't? Their excitement bubbled everywhere. Bailey's golden-brown hair caught the sun as her ever-present ponytail bobbed with every celebrating bounce. Jason didn't try to hide his ear-to-ear grin.

One more to win.

They gathered for the kickoff. "That was quick," Allgood muttered. Bradley said, "He had it clear, why wait?"

Allgood grunted, his square face red with effort. " 'Cause now I've gotta defend again." He butted his shoulder into Bradley's, with another grunt. "Good pass."

The center grinned. "And it was a great goal." He slapped Jason's shoulder. "Now, let's hope they think that was an accident!"

They lined up and kicked off, and there were frantic, jostling, long moments as the Wingnuts drove downfield without mercy and a goal seemed inevitable. Then, suddenly, Allgood had the drive broken and headed down their way. Jason found his way blocked, then when he dodged away, Stiles picked him up, but not close enough to make physical contact. So, they were cautious but not convinced yet. The zone defense still concentrated on Bradley. He let himself run, feeling good, the tiredness feathering away, the afternoon sun slanting across the field. They didn't expect him to try again, and he tried to contain his fierce joy.

The ball went back in the other direction again for a bit and he had a breather as the Chargers defenders moved into position, and held off the challenge. It was long minutes those, before they regained possession and began passing the ball back toward Bradley. He dropped back, fresh and ready, surveying the Wingnuts defenders jostling around the Chargers center.

A long dark shadow fell across the grass. He jerked in reflex, then looked about, seeing nothing. He glanced upward and saw nothing. The moment cost him a step or two against Stiles, so he circled to regain his position. Something blurred at the corner of his eye, and the back of his left hand began to burn, an old scar turning an angry red. Jason rubbed it warily, and circled again, looking. That scar meant many things to him, but mostly it meant trouble.

It meant something was about that should not be, that had no business in his everyday world but to work evil.

He scrubbed the stinging scar again, searching the soccer field as carefully as he might, yet unable to see more than the milling bodies of the other players as the ball shot back and forth, heading toward his end of the field. No distractions! No Magick. And, hopefully, no Dark Hand of Brennard looking for him.

But his scar burned even more fiercely, telling him otherwise. A cold chill passed across the back of his neck. Jason spun about. A black splinter fell across the field and then, as he stared, it elongated and then widened into a figure. A figure through which he could still see goalposts and net and players wheeling about, a dark ghostly presence. His scar gave one last warning, burning pulse as he looked at the figure of Jonnard Albrite.

"Salutations, Jason. Did you think me gone for good?"

Jason had little time to look at the nearly man-sized boy who faced him, as the fullback Karcher came running at him, and he realized that Bradley had the ball, about to pass it to him. The dark apparition stood between them, wavered as Karcher tore through his presence, re-formed, and smiled. Jason dodged and turned about, trying to stay in his zone and trying to keep from being pulled offside. He frowned.

"I've been training," said the deceitful son of the Dark Hand. "I'm waiting for you."

Jason caught the pass and aimed it right back at Bradley, playing for both time and position. A look of surprise shot over the center's face, but he took the pass and dribbled it downfield, toward the goal and the Wingnuts' incredibly tough goalie.

Jason moved after, but as he approached the black ghost of Jonnard, he felt a pressure and an unyielding wall. He could not pass!

He moved to his right, but Jonnard moved that way, too,

smoothly, laughing in a chill voice that no one but himself could hear. Unless, perhaps, Bailey and Ting . . .

Jason tossed a glance over his shoulder at the bleachers and saw the girls watching him, but neither seemed to sense what he faced. He was alone out here, with something that ought not to be and was, and used Magick to do it. The dark side of the Magick he loved, but Magick nonetheless.

He faked to his right and then moved left. Behind him, Karcher gave an exasperated grunt and Jason realized he'd thrown off both Dark Hand and Wingnut pursuers. He bolted into the clear. Bradley saw it and the ball came hurtling his way again.

Iciness ran across his back and down his shoulder, into his arm, a cold that brought a gripping pain with it.

"You'll not get away from me that easily," Jonnard hissed into his ear, and a freezing darkness blew across the back of his neck, ruffling his short hair.

Jason put his chin down with a sprint of speed, forcing his body across the soccer field with a tremendous effort, meeting Bradley's pass and intercepting the ball. His fingers had gone numb, but it wasn't his hands he needed, it was his legs and feet! He zigged away from Karcher and the other Wingnut defender, driving toward the goal and its nets, his jaw clenched in determination.

He could feel a dark cloud descending over him, shading his eyes, sucking away the air he needed to breathe. Jason had the goal in sight though, he knew where it was and just how the kick should be made. He faked the goalie to the left, and watched the other react, heading to the wrong end of the nets. As the aching cold sank through him, into him, through his torso and down into his legs, stealing warmth, breath, and movement, he drew his foot back and sliced his kick to the right.

The Wingnuts goalie caught the change of momentum. With a midair twist, he threw himself, full body length, at the soccer ball, hands out in a desperate catch.

Jason stumbled to a halt, unable to move, let alone run, as the cold took him. The spinning black-and-white ball went through the goalie's fingertips and solidly into the deep corner of the nets, and a shout went up.

Then, and only then, did he fumble at the throat of his Chargers jersey and wrap his fingers about the crystal hanging tucked inside. It flared as he encircled the cage of wire holding it, and with that touch, all cold left him, that quickly.

A low laugh at the back of his neck, and Jason turned.

Jonnard gave a salute. "I will be seeing you soon enough. And when I do . . . all the crystals in the world won't be able to save you!" Still laughing, a black flame enveloped him, and then both were gone.

The game-ending whistle shrieked through the air a second before his teammates found him, and Jason collapsed under their weight as they threw themselves on him, and he should have laughed with the victory, but he could not.

The Dark Hand was reaching for him once again. He had a feeling the real game was just beginning.

2

NUTS AND CHEWS

BAILEY kept standing and watched as the boys trampled from the field, grinning as she turned to Ting. "They did it!"

"Did you doubt they would?" Ting swung her long dark hair from her shoulders as she tucked her crystal necklace back under the curve of her neckline, the second crystal winking from its charm holder on her bracelet.

Bailey turned her attention to Ting, and paused, thoughtfully. The happiness she felt, that the two of them had shared, seemed to have fled Ting quickly. There was a worried look in her almond eyes. Bailey put her hand out. "Ting . . . what's wrong?"

Ting flushed guiltily, and began to make her way down the weathered wooden bleachers. She stopped and looked back to Bailey. "Does it show? I don't want my mom to see."

Bailey gave a nod. "It shows. To anyone who knows you."

Ting sighed. "We had a call last night. It's my grandmother. She's out of remission."

"Oh, no!" Bailey sat down and pulled Ting down beside

her. "But I thought the treatments were successful. You told me she should be in remission for years."

"That's what we all thought." Something very bright shone in the corner of Ting's eye as she sat. She brushed it away quickly.

"Will you be moving back up to be with her again?" Bailey tried not to look at her, not wanting Ting to see that the idea of losing her across the state once again upset her. After all, what was important here was Ting's grandmother, and her battle against cancer. Besides, what with computers and the Internet and all, San Francisco was not nearly as far away from Southern California as it could have been. She slid her hand over to grasp Ting's and hold on. Her friend's skin felt cold. "It'll be all right."

Ting made a small muffled sound. "My mom spent half the night talking with my father. I don't think it's going to be all right." She scrubbed at her face again. "Bailey, she's been working so hard with me on Magick. What if I wore her out? What if it's all *my* fault?"

Bailey squeezed her hand. "Ting! Cancer is not your fault."

"Nooo."

"I mean, you know that, right? Really know that?"

"Well, of course I know that." Ting squeezed her hand back. "But she's been so frail, and the follow-up treatments have been rough, and I just wonder if helping me has kept her too tired. I mean," she looked at Bailey. "I can't help but wonder."

"I know. I would think, if anything, you've helped her. Imagine going your whole life having a talent for Magick, and hiding it, and yet knowing it was your family's legacy. She got to share that with you . . . she's no longer one of the Hidden. I would think . . ." and Bailey took a deep breath. "I would think becoming a Magicker the best thing in the world."

A tiny smile flickered across Ting's face. "And, of course, no trouble at all."

"Well, not much. Except for the Dark Hand and wolf-jackals. Getting lost in your own crystal. Watching Henry set himself on fire trying to focus his crystal. Having to weed FireAnn's herb garden for forgetting homework. Watching Stefan change into his bear shape unexpectedly . . ." Bailey paused, as if thinking of more as she ticked off the obstacles on her fingers.

Ting giggled, and put her hand up to cover it, in a shy gesture that was all too familiar and welcome.

Watching her friend laugh pleased Bailey more than anything. She hugged Ting. "Things," she promised, "will get better!" She considered. "Of course, my grandmother always used to say they had to get worse first. Let's hope she's wrong."

Ting stifled another laugh. "Bailey. You and your sayings." She stood up and dusted herself off tidily. "Let's go home. I'm getting hungry and I bet Lacey is, too." She tickled a fingertip against the pocket in Bailey's sweatshirt jacket, and was rewarded by a sleepy sounding *Meep*. Seconds later, a little kangaroo rat, more commonly known as a pack rat, poked her face out and sleepily wrinkled her whiskers. Seeing the bright afternoon sunlight, she dove back into Bailey's sweatshirt, leaving her tufted tail hanging out, twitching.

Both girls laughed, and climbed down the rest of the bleachers, aiming for the parking lot, where nearly all the cars and vans for the game had already pulled out. From the corner of her eye, Bailey noticed a lone man sitting in a car parked in the shady corner. He seemed totally uninterested in anything till he saw the girls walk by toward the bus stop.

Did she imagine it, or did his head whip around as if he'd just spotted what he was looking for?

The hair on the back of her neck crawled. She hooked her arm through Ting's elbow. "Let's jog to the stop, I'm getting a little chilly."

Always slimmer and colder, Ting broke into a loping step with her, and their speed carried them through the parking lot and out onto the main street. Something flashed in the corner of her eye, but she dared not look back to see what it was. Instead, Bailey searched the busy street and saw, to her joy, the bus going their way. "Just in time!" she cried out thankfully.

Ting brought their bus passes out of her backpack and they climbed on as soon as the bus door wheezed open. Bailey sat down on the other side, drawing Ting with her, far away from the windows facing the park. She didn't want to know if whoever it was watched them. And she didn't breathe a word to Ting about the thoughts running through her mind. After all, she didn't want Ting thinking she'd gone nuts. She ought to know, but she didn't want to. Anyway, it was probably just her imagination. If there was one thing she had plenty of, it was imagination.

Wasn't it?

Jason got out of the shower, dressed hurriedly, and ran downstairs for something to eat, knowing he wouldn't be able to bear it until dinnertime. His stepmother Joanna sat at the nook table, her reading glasses nearly at the end of her nose, as she worked on some note cards and a stack of lists, pen in one hand and paper in the other. Tiny fake sapphires sparkled all over the plastic frame of the glasses, as if they could make having to wear them much nicer and more fashionable.

"Hi, Mom. Anything to eat?"

"I left chicken salad sandwiches in there for you. And there are some Terra chips in the bread box. Just don't eat more than two sandwiches this close to dinner."

Jason yanked the refrigerator door open happily. Someone, somewhen, had had the good sense to sit Joanna down and explain teen appetites to her. A woman who could rarely be seen eating, and didn't particularly seem to enjoy it even when she did so, at least Joanna didn't make him go by the same rules. He retrieved the two allotted sandwiches, found a plate, poured a small mound of the colorful, all vegetable "potato"-like chips next to them, and trotted over.

She made a note on one of her cards. Jason looked at everything curiously and decided she was working on organizing yet another charity function. She pushed her glasses partway up her nose. "How did you do?"

"We won!"

She looked up. "You did? That's great! What happens now?"

"We go to the finals, but I don't know yet which team we're playing. Their game is scheduled tomorrow."

She tapped her pencil thoughtfully. "Would you mind if we came to see the finals?"

"Mind? I'd love it!" Jason wolfed down half a sandwich

and paused, chewing, while trying to think of the details she'd need to know. Where, when, how long, and so forth. He told her what little he knew, which was mainly that it would be one day next weekend, depending on when the park let them play.

Her mouth curved. "William will be so pleased, and I think he'll be able to get the day off."

"How's the new development going?"

She shook her head. "Some sort of trouble with the permits, and you know how he hates paperwork. But he'll get it smoothed out soon, I'm sure." She watched Jason polish off the first sandwich. "You have homework for tonight?"

He crunched down on a bright orange-red Terra Chip. Sweet potato, one of his favorites. His stepmother had this illusion that this variety was healthier than the old-fashioned potato chip, and she was probably right, but at least he didn't have to eat tofu. Too often. "Yup, and I have to finish the packet you gave me for next year."

"Can you finish that for me tonight?"

He didn't want to. It was thick, and dull. She saw him hesitate.

"You really need to get that done, Jason. You've passed the tests, but your high school is a magnet school—it will be attracting students from all over for its programs. You need to sit down, make some decisions, and finish filling out your paperwork. This is a serious time. You have to decide what to study, for what you want to be for the rest of your life."

Jason stopped in mid swallow. There was no way he could tell her he'd already decided what he wanted to be the rest of his life: a Magicker. There was no way she'd believe him, even if he could break the Vow of Silence and get the words out. Finally, he finished swallowing and said contritely, "I know. I'll get it done, I promise."

Joanna smiled brightly. "Good, good. I'm here, and William is here, if you want to ask us anything later. He has lots of good advice he wants to give you, but . . . well, he's waiting until you ask for it."

He gave a crooked smile. His stepfather, big, outdoorsman-looking William McIntire, often known as "the Dozer," had worked in construction all his life. He was a good man, and Jason couldn't ask for more, he supposed, unless it was the advice of his own mother and father, both dead. He dusted bread crumbs off his hand. "What do you think *my* dad would have said?"

Pain shot through Joanna's face. She looked down at her note cards as her right hand twitched slightly. Then she looked back up. "Jason," she said quietly. "I didn't know him long enough to be able to answer that. I wish I could have."

His throat tightened, and he suddenly wasn't hungry anymore. "Me, too," he got out, standing up and taking his plate to the sink where he rinsed it once or twice. When he thought he could talk again, he set the sandwich plate down on the counter and said, "I better go get that stuff done," and headed upstairs without meeting her gaze.

His was the highest room in the house, the attic made into a large, sprawling bedroom reached only by a trap-door ladder. He liked it . . . no, he loved it. It was his and his alone, private and unique. As if sensing his need for ab-solute solitude now and then, McIntire had had this room made for him and drawing the trapdoor ladder up after him and securing it had a medieval sense to it, like pulling up the drawbridge over a castle moat. He retreated into it now, picking up his clothes to be washed later, and stowing them in the laundry bag in the corner before dropping onto his bed.

He took a close look at his left hand. The crescent-shaped scar just under the knuckles along the back of it appeared as a thin white line and well healed. But he knew it could and would flare an angry red and ache beyond rea-son if anything evil approached him. It had before, and it would again. What he didn't know was *why*. Why had the wolfish beast marked him, and why did it never seem to really heal, and why did it hurt whenever they or the rogue sorcerers of the Dark Hand came near? Surely it hadn't meant it to be a warning to him, but it worked that way. Or did it? Sometimes it hurt so badly it made him cry out sharply, betraying his presence if he had been hidden. Did that make it a beacon to those evil things that searched for him? Had the wolfjackal bitten and chewed on him with a purpose, or just to savage him? He had no real answer. From what he'd seen of Magick, it could take a lifetime of study to answer this and other questions.

Jason dropped his hand down and nudged at a file folder

of papers, neatly labeled by his stepmother, JASON'S HIGH SCHOOL FILE. He didn't know what studying to be a Magicker would make him. Gavan and the others said he was a Gatekeeper, but he really didn't know much about that either. Obviously, he found gateways to other realms of existence, but even that was a hit-and-miss occupation . . . and he had no idea what he did to find them. They were just sort of there when a moment came that he needed them. He knew there had to be more to it, and there was no one alive anymore among the elder Magickers who could train him. Their own lives had been torn apart in the war between Gregory and Brennard, and much had been lost.

He couldn't tell any of this to Joanna and William, of course. First, because he'd taken a Vow of Silence not to, but more importantly, it was because they wouldn't want to understand it. McIntire built real cities on solid ground, as he'd no doubt put it, and Joanna would be worried about the social and cultural implications. But is it wise, she'd say, to be involved in something like *that?* And her nose would wrinkle in disapproval. It was the wisdom of things that bothered her. Left with a son by a man she'd been married to all too briefly, she was worried about appearances. What if she neglected him or misguided him in any way? What would people think?

Jason sighed heavily. Actually, he'd never doubted Joanna's desire to make sure he was presentable. He just wished he had his dad, and his mom, back. That's all. Dirty floors and dishes would be fine with him, if he just had his *family* back. Love made up for the lack of many things, but things could never make up for the lack of love.

He nudged his folder again, halfheartedly. It fell open. There were pamphlets of core courses and pamphlets of electives. His core schedule had been arranged so completely that he had room for maybe one elective a semester, if that. And, that was if he got up and went to school early, taking the ever popular Zero Period for honor students, a whole hour before the rest of the school day started. Add after-school athletics to that . . . he'd be gone from six to six nearly every day. When would he have time to do what he really wanted to do . . . to become what he really wanted to be?

Jason flipped the folder shut, unable to look at the paperwork for the moment. Instead, he reached for his crystal, pulling it loose from its wire jewelry cage, and cradling it in his hands. Light flared through his room, cast from the clear part of the stone, its gold and dark streaks fracturing the pattern as if black lightning had struck. After long moments spent just meditating over its inner patterns, Jason reopened the jewelry cage and replaced it.

The room fell back into normal, everyday, electric lighting, and seemed much smaller and dimmer in comparison.

Then . . . something tapped at the porthole window.

3

AS A CROW FLIES

JASON swung open the porthole window. He'd taken the screen out months ago, and worked on oiling the hinges so it moved smoothly—and quietly. His head followed the pathway of his hand, cautiously, into the dusk, as he peered out. Something brushed at his head as it winged past, swift and dark as the soon to fall night. He jerked back instinctively as the crow gave a laughing CAW at him, and circled around the corner beam of the roof.

Jason crawled out of the porthole, finding it a more difficult job than he had many months ago when he'd first left his room that way, and stood on the slanted roof which made up the ceiling and walls of his attic room. A figure sat, knees doubled up, arm out for the crow to land on. With a smile, Jason went to join him at the precarious edge of the house.

"Well met, Jason Adrian," said Tomaz Crowfeather solemnly, his rich deep voice full of the inflections of the southwest American Indian. His crow nibbled a bit on his denim sleeve, before tucking his head under his wing and resting.

"Fine," Jason said as he settled down next to his elder.

"We won in the League semifinals today, going to the finals!"

"That is good. But you sent a message of worry?"

Jason nodded. Quickly and as clearly as he could paint the imagery, he told of the spectral Jonnard who'd challenged him on the soccer field. Tomaz listened with great interest, saying nothing till Jason had finished, and then asking him only a question or two to clarify. Then both fell into deep silence while Tomaz considered what had happened. Finally, he gave a low grunt. The very last of the sunlight caught the silver rowels on his belt and turquoise stone bracelet, as he gestured at Jason.

"Jonnard is not wise. He has given us forewarning that the Dark Hand is prepared to move again. We can use this in two ways: first, to tweak at Brennard that his son is a fool, and second, to ready ourselves. This is good you told us of this. Gavan will have to know as soon as possible."

"I tried contacting him, but I got no answer."

Tomaz nodded. Jason watched his face, noticing for the first time that a bit of gray had begun to show among the straight black strands of the Magicker's hair, and that the weathered lines in his strong face had grown deeper and sharper. A Magicker aging? The thought almost chased away his other concerns. "Eleanora is ill, Jason."

"What's wrong? Cold or something?"

"We don't know what's wrong."

Those words, coupled with his noticing new signs of age on Crowfeather, made Jason grow very cold for a moment, and stopped his words in his throat. He thought of the Magicker Fizziwig, Gavan's classmate, who'd suddenly aged into a white-haired old man, and then into death. . . . He managed to take a breath. "Not . . . that . . ." he said.

Tomaz lifted and dropped a shoulder in a shrug. "We do not know yet." He stood, in a fluid movement that did not even disturb the crow on his forearm. "Jason, I will pass this on, but you must keep trying to contact Gavan or Eleanora or Freyah with this, in case I don't reach them. It's too important to let go."

"You won't be able to tell them."

"Possibly not." Crowfeather looked over the sea of ordinary rooftops, as night began to hide most of them well and truly, and treetops brushed about them in a gentle night breeze. "I have a project I must tend to, and will be gone a while."

"Where?"

Tomaz smiled slowly, and dropped his free hand, large and warm, on Jason's shoulder. "I follow the track of the wolfjackals, Jason. I trust you to keep this between us, but you, more than the others, may understand."

The scar on the back of his hand gave a tiny pulse of pain, and Jason flinched slightly. "Tracking them here?"

Tomaz shook his head. "No. Tracking them to where they came from, and where they go—and to what master they answer."

"But . . . but . . . they belong to the Dark Hand."

Tomaz shook his head again. "No, Jason, I do not think so. Although they seem to thrive on the evil and chaos the Dark Hand stirs up, events suggest that Brennard is no more in charge of them than we are. Then . . . who is? We need to know."

Jason shivered, in spite of himself. It sounded like something very dangerous. "Gavan knows you're going?"

"He alone knows. And now you do. This is not the kind of thing I wish shouted from the mountaintops." Tomaz squeezed Jason's shoulder. "I should be reachable by crystal, but I may not be able to answer, so you cannot depend on me for a while."

"I understand," Jason said quietly. He did understand, but he didn't like it. "Is there anything we can do to help Eleanora?"

"No answer there either. It may just be exhaustion from her working with Jennifer, or it may be . . . something else."

Jennifer was a young Magicker, like Jason, but she'd run into an edge of dark magic that had stunned her, terrified her, and made her shut all of them away. Eleanora was determined to heal the fear in Jennifer, even if she never returned to Magicking. Jennifer was older than all of them, nearly sixteen, and she'd been a summer camp counselor to Ting and Bailey. How far away last summer seemed now.

Tomaz tickled the chest feathers on his crow, waking him, and then turned his wrist and moved his arm, setting the bird into flight. The beat of wings filled the air for a moment, then the crow glided away sullenly to find a treetop for the night. "There is a Council meeting tonight, Jason. I suggest you go and tell them what you told me."

"Ugh. All that arguing."

Tomaz laughed. "That is true. But at least we all have free will to argue with, right?"

"We must have lots of free will, then." Jason shuddered again. "All those objections. I'll do what I can."

"Do that. And even more importantly, do what you are driven to do, as a Magicker. Find that last gate, Jason, that will open Haven fully and anchor it down. We need that, all of us."

Jason dropped his head down, and stared at his feet. "I'm trying," he answered. He felt unsure as a Gatekeeper, knowing little of how it worked or even if that was truly his calling. If every Magicker had a specialty, who was to say that was his? Magick seemed so vast.

"I know that. And I know that if I say to you, try harder, it would not make a difference because you are doing your best. Do not let the Dark Hand distract you. It may well be that that is one of their chief aims right now. Your vision needs to be the clearest of us all."

The house below him seemed to awaken.

"You'd better go," Tomaz agreed. "I think it is nearly dinnertime, and it is not wise for anyone to find you out here on the roof."

Jason hesitated, then gave Crowfeather a hug. "Be careful!"

Tomaz looked surprised for an instant, then pleased. "That I will be, young Magicker."

Jason crept along the eaves of the roof and wiggled back into his porthole window. His shoulders almost stuck for a moment, and he wondered how much longer he would even be able to wriggle through. Everything changes, he thought, as he dropped back into his room.

Joanna's voice sang up the stairwell. "Dinner!"

Had it been that long? His stomach growled impatiently, telling him that it had. Jason dropped his door down and open. Meeting the Magickers Council on anything less than a full stomach would be a terrible idea. Dinner first, definitely!

CHAMBERS OF SECRET

BRENNARD sat and stared at the evening sky over-head. It was not dark yet, but creeping toward it, even as its constellations edged toward those of spring and then summer. Time. Time was eternal and yet of the essence. For all his abilities, it eluded him. He was Time's prisoner, and would have to suffer its punishment the same as any other prisoner. Well . . . not quite the same. He'd already far out-lived most of his contemporaries.

That, of course, had not been entirely his doing. In standing up to Gregory the Gray's tyranny and misguided direction of Magick, he'd set off a backlash of energy that had affected everyone alive with even a touch of Magick in them. There was no way he could have anticipated that. It killed many by stunning them and leaving them vulnerable to the harsh realities of life many centuries ago. Still others, it threw forward through time . . . and a few more were merely cushioned in a kind of void until they awoke now, in this time and place.

He'd been almost as big a fool as Gregory had been. Brennard would admit that, even if only to himself. Still, he had ambitions and a plan to achieve. He steepled his fingers, then heard a faint, escaping sigh from across the room and remembered he was not alone.

The Dark Hand sat arrayed about him, in various postures of meditation and attention, sprawled on their chairs and cushions. Seven of them, the elite of his followers. Four men, three women. And one of them obviously was yawning in his sleeves, tired of waiting for the statement that he'd almost forgotten he'd gathered them to make. He regathered his thoughts.

"It is important, at this time, to know our enemies as well as we know ourselves. I called you all together for an accounting." His gaze swept the room. His words brought alertness back to their faces as they turned to watch and listen. "First . . . Dr. Anita Patel, of Gregory's Council." He put his hand on a staff lying across his knees, a staff carved to look startlingly like a cobra with its hood spread, a crystal held in its fanged jaws. The crystal was fractured beyond repair, and dull, with black streaks coursing throughout it. He lifted the staff. "She betrayed them for us, but I do not trust traitors. I think I can say that she is of no worry to us now, however."

He dropped the staff on the floor. The crystal fractured even more, spidery lines opening up on its dulled surface. The Hand closest to Brennard shuddered involuntarily and looked away from the staff. Their crystals were their magickal life. Seeing one so destroyed was like seeing their own hearts break. Brennard smiled thinly.

He paused as Jonnard came in quietly, folded his long legs, and took up a large silken cushion in the corner of the atrium. His dark hair was slicked back wetly as if he had just bathed, his face tilted to watch the gathering sunset. However, he also watched his father warily out of the corner of his eyes, and Brennard knew he had his attention.

Brennard put a little more strength into his voice as he continued. "We have our enemies numbered, and knowing them as well as we know ourselves is the key to their undoing. Gregory's Council is unraveling, and we need to use that to our advantage."

"Gregory's lot are loyal," observed a quiet voice near Brennard. "Gavan Rainwater is his acknowledged heir, and holds the Council close."

"Are they? Are they now?" Brennard put the toe of his

shoe out and nudged the cobra staff at his feet. "This one was not. She was theirs, then she became mine. What do we know of them now? We know Freyah has retreated to a pocket of her Magick, making a defense there, and that pocket takes most of the Magick she has available. She is Gregory's own sister, but still there is no help there for Rainwater." He looked about the room, hearing a soft murmur of agreement.

"Then there is Rainwater himself ... well, Gavan is young, impulsive, and still lacks a polish to his training and talent, and he knows it. He leads because there is no one else who will do it, and the others know that as well, jeopardizing the very thing he has been forced to do. He won it by default and there are those who can ... and may yet ... take it away from him. He is distracted by his love for Eleanora, and her own well-being, I hear, is not good these days. They argue with me that Magick is not finite, and yet, my argument becomes more and more compelling that it *is*."

"As for the lovely Eleanora, her ailment takes her out of consideration. We will not face much when we face her." Brennard held his hand up, ticking his fingers off. His hands, like his features, were slender with a hint of underlying steely strength. The years of comatose isolation after his sorcerous battle with Gregory the Gray had taken their toll but he seemed, finally, to be regaining all that he had lost. He had begun to look dangerous again, like some shadowed creature just emerging into the light, and he smiled slightly as if prizing that image. He ruled strong people. He needed to be seen as one who could best them.

"There are four others who could worry us. The herbalist FireAnn will take Gavan's side, of that there is no doubt. Her abilities will make up for the loss of the physician Anita Patel was." Brennard put his hand to a thick bracelet wherein a huge, clear crystal was embedded, and he traced it lightly. It flared with a warm light in answer to his touch. "The Moor Khalil has never been transparent to me, and my understanding is that he has brooked some opposition to Rainwater's plans, as well. If I can't see into his motives, neither can Gregory's Council. Therefore, one may assume he has his own agenda. We all know of Isabella's indiscretions and her love of power and money. As for Tomaz Crowfeather ... coming from the Hidden as he does, from talent that has not been nurtured or instructed by any of the Magickers we know . . . he is also unfathomable. He has been involved in activities Gavan Rainwater knows nothing of, and I know little. He is a dark crystal to be examined, and deciphered. These three then, we must watch and know. Isabella, Khalil . . . and Crowfeather." He lowered his hands.

A chorus of voices answered him. "It shall be done."

"Good," he said. "Very good." He stood then. "But first and most important is the One, the younger Magicker, Jason Adrian. He must be used, and if he cannot be used, he must be stopped." Brennard paused, his dark gaze sweeping the room. "My son Jonnard has been training to handle that One, under my strictest supervision. You will cooperate with him if he asks for your assistance." Then Brennard sketched his hand through the air, leaving behind a glowing symbol, stepped into the shadowed corner of the atrium, and seemed to disappear entirely from sight, although the weight of his presence took much longer to fade. No one said anything. Jonnard got to his feet and left by the main door, head thrown back, a slight, knowing smile on his face. Silence followed him.

5

PLANS AND MICE . . . OR PACK RATS

SOMETIMES having dinner at the McIntire house was like running an obstacle course while carrying a hundred-pound cat who knows a bath is waiting for it at the end. Not that baths are a bad thing at all, although Jason preferred showers, but trying to get a big cat into one could be. And that's just how he felt as he tried to get through dinner, every word from Joanna or William an obstacle to be taken carefully, without dropping the cat. Or getting his eyes scratched out.

"Did you get your forms filled out?"

High jump! "Almost," Jason answered carefully as he speared a few green beans. He munched them and tried to look thoughtful. His stepsister eyed him.

"Electives are as important as core classes," she offered helpfully. "They opened up my love of film and arts."

Dodging through cones! "I've looked through the brochures," Jason said truthfully. "There's a lot that look interesting, but I haven't that much time. I think I might have one slot."

Joanna looked fondly at her daughter. "With Alicia's success in filmmaking, we all know how important it is to find something that fulfills you."

Trip and fall! "It's not that I don't want to find something, it's that I ... can't decide." Jason stabbed at a green bean, a little harder than he intended. The fork went squeaking shrilly across his plate. McIntire looked at him briefly, bushy eyebrow waggling up and down, but he said nothing. Jason shoved the captured green bean in his mouth and chewed vigorously, hoping he wouldn't be asked anything else, at least till he chewed and swallowed.

Alicia watched him, too, her fine blonde hair framing her face, and finally she said, "Must be an awfully tough string bean."

His face warmed. *Time for the sprint!* "I'm thinking of photography," he finally managed. He wasn't, but the words just sorta fell out of his mouth. He stared at his plate in slight amazement. Where had that come from?

McIntire cleared his throat. "A nice hobby. Not that many can make a living at it ..."

"He could be a cameraman. Cinematographer. Or even go into digital effects," Alicia said, with a great deal of satisfaction on her face and her expression. Her forte in film work was directing, but she was always complaining she couldn't find anyone to set up the shots the way she wanted them. Jason was never sure if it was because Alicia was so particular or young or just hard to understand. He'd never quite understood her.

Joanna frowned slightly, saying, "Digital?" in a vaguely unsure voice.

"Computerized photography, Mom, or close enough. They use it in all kinds of special effects, like movies, commercials, and so on."

"Oh, my. That sounds as if it could be very promising. Combined with a good business mind and sense, of course." His stepmother beamed at him then, as she refolded her napkin over her lap.

"I was just looking at it like a hobby. Something fun, you know. To break up the day." Jason pushed a few more green beans around. His appetite seemed to have fled although he could almost guarantee it would return with a growl when he went back upstairs if he didn't eat now. Even if he did eat, he'd be back in the kitchen around ten for a snack before bedtime. Something to do with having the constitution of a fast growing weed.

"Sounds like you're into something interesting and fun. A boy needs a bit of fun now and then, along with the hard work." McIntire gave a deep noise of approval.

Jason felt almost trapped. "It's not a done deal," he said. "I might not have room in the right time period. It might fill early. I might not like it."

"Worrywart." Alicia cleared her plate, standing up. "There're other classes, too. Don't be a typical freshman, running around campus with that 'Bambi caught in the headlights stare' on your face."

"Alicia!"

She flipped her lanky blonde hair, as she turned to her mother. "Well, Mom, honestly, you ought to see them! It's pathetic."

"I won't be pathetic," Jason vowed. "Trust me." His words came out strongly, not at all affected by the strange quaver that sometimes hit his voice now and then.

Joanna looked at him a long moment, then smiled gently. "I think you'll do quite well." She stood, with a relieved expression, as if a heavy burden had been lifted from her shoulders.

Jason excused himself, cleared his place, and fled to the sanctity of his attic room. Was raising him really that big a problem? He had never even thought of getting into things some of the other guys did, but Magick now . . . that would be bad enough. He couldn't ever tell her. He wondered as he trudged up his attic stairs if he could have told his real mother. Or his father. His father he still had memories of, though they were getting fuzzy. From what he remembered of his dad, someone tall, with strong arms and big hands, and a bigger laugh . . . he thought he could have. He hoped he could have.

Jason dropped into his chair with a sigh, kicking the rungs as he did. One of the all-important papers he needed to fill out drifted off the desk and fell to the carpet in a slow-motion kind of billow. He stared at it, rather than picking it up.

He already felt bummed. So, maybe now was just as good a time as any to drop into the Council and get that chore over with. After all, things couldn't get any worse, could they? He got his crystal out, focused on it, and found the plane where interminable Council meetings seemed to be taking place, and went there.

He was, of course, wrong.

Isabella swept in at about the same time he did, wearing a red satin hat with a veil across her face and strong nose, and some kind of feathery fan fastened to the brim of the hat that matched the fan in her gloved hands. She sat down at the conference table with a muffled noise rather like a haughty snort. "It would be nice if meetings started on time."

"There is always someone here at meeting," answered Allenby mildly. The gleaming skin of his bald head flushed pink next to the white fringe of hair that was all that he had left, nearly giving him the appearance of a fluffy halo. Allenby, however, wore a pinstriped business suit and a serious expression that Jason would never associate with any cherubs. His briefcase sat on the table in front of him, a calculator nudging it. His sharp-eyed gaze swept the room. "Well, well, young Jason. Welcome!"

Jason pulled out a chair near the end where Gavan usually sat, and perched on it warily, seeing no sign of Gavan or Eleanora, and knowing Tomaz wouldn't be around. "Good evening, sir," he said, and his voice broke slightly, so he cleared his throat and went silent. Aunt Freyah, another with white hair, looked up from across the table, lowering the knitting needles which had been flying in her hands, and smiled kindly at him. She had dimples in apple-red cheeks, smooth but older skin, fluffy hair, and sapphire eyes, and a small cottage full of animated tables, pictures, trays, teapots, and the like. Jason loved visiting her. He didn't know who baked the best fudge brownies he'd ever tasted, but she always had an ample supply of them! She dropped her project (scarf was it? Something long and narrow with lots of bright yarn, at any rate), reached down into her huge purse and pulled out a steaming cup of apple cider. "Here, dear," she said as she slid it across to him. "This should help."

Actually, from what he'd heard and seen and been told in health class, the only thing that would help would be outlawing or outliving puberty, but he took the cup without argument. The cider smelled great, anyway, apple-and-cinnamon aroma in the steam. He sipped at it cautiously.

Khalil sat kitty-cornered from him, his steepled hands masking his face. As usual, he wore sweeping desert robes, making him look like a Bedouin sheikh. "Small group tonight," he observed. "Are we expecting Rainwater and Eleanora?"

"We'll wait a bit longer," Aunt Freyah said, her knitting needles once again tip-tapping in a blur of movement. "My niece has been feeling a bit under the weather, so we'll give them the benefit of the doubt." Her bright blue eyes looked about the table sharply, as if inviting disagreement, but she got none. Allenby turned his attention to some papers inside his briefcase, Isabella fished out a small, neat book of French poetry from her purse, and Khalil merely closed his eyes as if he were meditating. Jason sat back in his chair, bored, and drank his cider, feeling the sweet tart warmth trickle down his throat, bringing a nice satisfaction with it. He wondered what, if anything, really ever got decided at a Council meeting.

Finally Allenby looked up from his stack of paperwork. "I don't believe they're coming."

"Then we might as well get started." Isabella snapped her book shut with a retort that sounded like a gunshot. Khalil's eyes flew open and then he frowned at her. "Some of us have places to be and things to do."

Jason didn't know much about Isabella except for her European background and residence and that she was a businesswoman, he'd heard, of some wealth. She'd taken advantage of her knowledge of the centuries to become rich, which was in a way using her Magick and in a way not. Most of the Elders had an unspoken creed not to use Magick publicly or for ill-gotten gain. There were those who vowed it couldn't be done anyway. It seemed to backfire, and horribly, rather like the Curse of Arkady. A shiver whispered down the back of Jason's neck at the thought of that one!

Arkady had been a Magicker back in the times when Gregory the Gray and Antoine Brennard were elder and student, and all the Magickers were truly young, sometime around the time of Elizabeth I, although Jason wasn't really sure of the year. Renaissance, that much he knew. The Magickers didn't like to talk about the terrible war between Gregory and Brennard which had killed many and sent the survivors hurtling through time and space. The war was why Gavan and the others today refused to face off with the Dark Hand, in hopes of avoiding another tragedy. Arkady, they did talk about, though. Arkady had been a rather talented but hapless Magicker who couldn't control what he did. Everything had backfired or exploded in his face, but mostly because he hadn't the confidence or discipline to learn what he was doing.

They'd all been warned about the terrible Curse, one that only practice, practice, practice, and confidence seemed to be able to avert!

"First thing, then. Eleanora is not here because she has been ailing a bit, and she is feeling quite drained working with young Jennifer Logan. Jennifer's shroud of corruption not only leeches the Magick out of her, but out of anyone near her. As I understand what Eleanora and Gavan have told me, it would be easier to purge the nastiness all at once, but that might damage Jennifer for life. So, at the moment, the going is slow and difficult for everyone."

There was a murmur of sympathy about the table for Eleanora. Jason joined in, but he worried about Jennifer, too. Poor Jenny. He put his empty cider glass down on the gleaming wood table.

At the sound of its thump on the wood, all heads turned to him quickly, eager for a distraction, and it was like a trap snapping shut on its victim! Jason sat back with a momentary feeling of worry over having attracted their attention. It didn't help that Allenby immediately said, "How about a report on Gating, Jason? How goes your training, and how close are you to stabilizing the Iron Gate?"

Aunt Freyah jabbed a pointy knitting needle skyward. "That's it, put the lad on the spit, first thing, and pump up the coals." She let out an unladylike snort and threw herself back in her chair, staring a challenge at Allenby with her bright blue eyes.

Khalil composed his robes a moment, then said, "Has to be done, Freyah. There are things we have to know."

Another snort, one that *pffuffed* her frothy bangs off her forehead. "Much more is kept secret than shared around here." Freyah wrapped up her knitting briskly and stowed it away in her carpetbag. "All right, then, Jason. Looks like you're going to roast till you talk. Anything you can tell us?"

Her kinder words barely took the edge off the question as everyone kept watching him. He shrugged. "I'm doing my best, but . . . it's not so much my finding a Gate as the Gate finding me . . . I think." His face warmed with embarrassment over his uncertainty. He had no one to train him, the only Magicker in this time who'd had the ability, Fizziwig, had died mysteriously before he could help Jason at all.

"Is that how it works, then?"

Jason looked to Khalil. "It seems to. I mean, that's what happened with the Iron Gate at Camp Ravenwyng and then the Water Gate when the Dark Hand tried to trap us."

Isabella shifted. "We cannot wait for happenstance." She touched her face briefly where lines had begun to etch the corners of her eyes.

"I'm doing everything I can. I practice focusing, I travel whenever I can . . . I try to pay attention to everything I see and touch. That's all I can do," Jason finished up, helplessly.

Allenby closed his briefcase with a snap. "And that's all we can ask of you, given the circumstances." He glanced at Isabella. "Surely all that money can buy you a decent eye cream?"

"It's not that," she snapped back, "and you know it."

"I know that we're all going to grow old, sooner or later. It's the way of things."

Isabella opened her mouth to shoot off another retort but Jason quickly said, "That's not the reason I'm here, though."

Again, all eyes turned to him, and he felt their burn, as he tried not to squirm in the hard wooden conference chair and took a deep breath. "I was playing on the soccer field when Jonnard showed up. He was there, but he wasn't. No one else could see him, not even Ting and Bailey who were watching in the bleachers."

"A Sending? That takes a bit of strength." Freyah watched him thoughtfully.

"I don't know what it was. He bumped me around a bit and talked trash."

Isabella frowned until Allenby leaned over to whisper something to her, his words fluttering the feathered fan on her hat, and then she laughed slightly. "Jonnard is more his mother's than his father's son." But she did not explain what she meant by that, as she redirected her attention down the table.

"What do you think he wanted?"

"I think he wanted me to know he was back, and it's war between us."

"This is, of course, not good."

Jason nodded in agreement.

"They could," Khalil said slowly, as if choosing his words very carefully, "end us all by forcing us out into the open. But I cannot feel they want to do that, for it reveals them, as well. And removes us as targets they can drain."

"War between us is what put all of us in jeopardy. You didn't react to him, did you, Jason?"

"I tried not to."

Allenby fussed with his briefcase, then took a handkerchief out of his coat's inner pocket and mopped his head with it. "Surely you know what you did."

"I was playing soccer," answered Jason firmly. "For the semifinals! I got around him as best as I could."

"Soccer is more important than your life as a Magicker?"

"No. Well, this time it was. But I couldn't reveal myself to anyone, and no one else saw he was even *there*."

"This is serious, Jason, and I'd like to think you took it seriously."

"I did!" Jason stood up. "What did you expect me to do? What he wanted me to? He wanted me to use Magick on him. He wanted me to break the rules. What would you do to me then?"

"Don't raise your voice, young man, we understand your point," Freyah said firmly.

"No, I don't think you do. Every night, you come in here and sit down and bicker, and get mad at me 'cause I'm not doing what you think I should, when you guys can't even agree what it is I should be doing. And, I'm out there, every day, trying to be myself *and* be a Magicker, without much help from anyone else. I'm just trying to warn everyone that the Dark Hand is ready to move again."

Isabella stood, with a swish of red satin, and a wavering of the fan in her hand. "Then, I suggest, young man, that you get ready to move us to safety!"

"I'm doing all I can." Jason stared at her.

"I'm too busy for this," Isabella announced to everyone and no one in the room. She pulled one dangling crystal earring from her ear, looked into it, and was gone.

Jason sighed. He stepped back as another argument erupted around the table as to Jonnard's intentions and the strategy for dealing with the Dark Hand. He'd done what Tomaz had asked him to, and what good had it done? No one had really listened. He rubbed his palm over the crystal he still gripped and in a long moment, he was gone, too.

He found himself standing on the fallen page in his bedroom. He moved off it. Photography and computer techniques, the page read. Jason sighed. He tucked his own crystal safely away and took out the lavender one.

After very long moments, he felt Tomaz's presence in it.

"Jason," Crowfeather said solemnly. "I can tell by your expression it did not go well."

"I think everyone is mad at me."

"Did you expect anything else? You brought news of a fight to them. No one in history has ever taken such news well." He smiled, and then behind him, Jason could see a world, in dusk, and it was not the world he'd been born in. "I have many travels before I can return. Will you be all right until then?"

"Oh, I'll be fine. I always am." Jason managed a grin.

"That is good." Crowfeather turned his face a little then, as if listening to something behind him. He frowned. Then he said something very odd. "Whatever it is that happens to me, Jason, I ask you not to tell anyone of it."

"What are you talking about?"

"Do I have your word on this?"

"But—"

"You will keep this secret?"

"I guess, but—"

A howl cut off the rest of Tomaz Crowfeather's words. A great darkness swirled through the crystal and across the landscape where Crowfeather stood. In it Jason saw and could almost smell the running figures of wolfjackals, growling and snarling, their jaws gaping open and their teeth glowing an eerie yellow green. The immense beasts raced through ebony darkness, surrounding the elder Magicker. The cloud encircled Tomaz and then . . . he was gone.

"Tomaz!" Jason juggled his crystal in his hands, trying to locate him, trying to see more clearly.

He heard one last ringing howl, and then nothing.

6

HEAVY SECRETS

A DULL thump hit the carpet by the side of his foot, and Jason jumped. He looked down to see the lavender crystal roll to one side before settling. He didn't remember dropping it, he thought, as he stooped quickly to retrieve it. First law of Magicking was: Never Drop Your Crystal.

Of course, as he learned more, he realized that the quartzes and gemstones were just for focusing his own inner power, so it was really a matter of . . . Never Lose Yourself. And he had, if only for a moment or two, while watching Tomaz being swept away. He stroked his fingers over the faceted stone. He still didn't know much about the minerals, even though he'd always intended to study them. He though this might be a morganite. If so, it was valuable because of its size and nearly flawless planes. Even more valuable was the presence of Gregory the Gray he could sense within, and the power that could flow through it. The crystal was far more powerful than his first bonded stone, and he'd admitted to Gavan that he was a little afraid of it.

Rainwater had teased him mildly about that, and then taught him another trick or two about meditating upon the object. Gavan Rainwater held a bit of showman about him,

acted a little flamboyant. He was very young for the leadership he'd taken upon himself, and that was part of his cover.
He knew the Dark Hand didn't take him as seriously as
they should, and that was fine with Gavan. "Lad, there's
nothing wrong with being underestimated, as long as you
don't underestimate yourself! Know your strengths."

He didn't, yet, Jason thought, as he warmed the stone
between his hands. He did know he wasn't strong enough
to go after Tomaz and help. And he wasn't sure he could
be strong enough to do as Tomaz asked, and tell no one,
although knowing *why* might have made it a lot easier.

Why didn't Tomaz want anyone knowing what he was
doing, and why would he not want help if something happened to him?

Jason shivered. He'd been so close to Tomaz, linked with
him . . . and he'd never felt any fear, even as the beasts swept
around him. Whatever it was, Tomaz seemed to know what
he was doing, for Jason hadn't sensed a single wavering of
the Magicker's strong will. He'd have to find hope in that.
And, perhaps, even in another source.

He sat down at the computer and opened himself up
to a different kind of magic. With a few key taps, he found
Rich online, with Stef almost certainly sitting on the overstuffed chair in the den behind him, probably munching on
something and reading a sports magazine. Rich confirmed
as much with a smiley face as he typed in,

"And Stef says Hi ☺."

Quick as a flash, Henry was on, with a new SN "theSquibbler." Despite his worries, that made Jason laugh aloud. He
could almost see Henry peering at him, then taking notes
as his habit had become. For without notes, his Magick (like
his life) seemed to be in a chaotic jumble which Henry
muddled through with typical good-naturedness, if slightly
worried about the outcome. Quicker than he got in trouble,
Henry greeted Jason and asked what was going on, and had
he heard from Bailey and Ting.

"No," Jason typed back. **"Not recently. I just had to attend a Council meeting, and I want everyone to join me in
a chat."**

"Ick! Council meetings are the pits."

"Tell me about it." Jason then messaged everyone to
follow him to a chat room. As if knowing they were being

thought about, Ting signed on, and then Bailey bounced into the chat room with a *"Hi! Hi!"*

Trent signed on last, his typing in spurts, just like his tendency to whistle or hum song snatches came and went; his fingers often drumming. **"What's happening? Do I sense trouble—fij4 at Bailey. What did Lacey steal now? Heya, Henry. Ever get Lantern under control?"**

Lantern was the ability to send one's crystal into a well-lit glow, like lantern light. Henry often started a fire instead. He used to practice Lantern wearing heat-proof oven mitts at camp.

"Almost, Trent. I only burned my thumb this week! Soon!"

"Rut-roh," broke in Rich. **"Stef wants the keyboard!"**

Jason sat back in his chair as his computer screen filled with smiley faces and all sorts of other symbols and message jargon in a storm of color. He laughed, for Stef was more and more like the overgrown bear cub that was his shapeshifting other self, rather than the bear cub growing more like the teenager Stef. He waited till the flurry of symbols died away before typing, **"Heya, Stef. Okay guys, this is a little serious. I had to go visit the Council tonight."** He waited until they'd all communicated their sympathy for that one.

"So," Trent typed, **"the real question is: what did they want?"**

Jason found himself sighing as he responded. **"They want a Gatekeeper who can actually find Gates."**

"What? Two aren't enough for them!" He could practically hear Bailey's outraged huff.

"I understand what they're saying, though." That was Ting, thoughtful as always. **"We need a place where we can safely go and train. Maybe even hide."**

Amid a cloud of emote symbols, Stef managed to type, **"Ida join the circus."**

"Who's Ida?" asked theSquibbler.

"No one."

"Then how did Stef know her? And why did she join the circus."

"HENRY," wrote Bailey. **"Stef means he would . . . I'd join . . . the circus."**

"Oh."

"This is serious, guys."

"We know, Jason."

"I can't find it!"

"**It's always the last place you look,**" Rich wrote, after successfully wrestling the computer keyboard away from Stef, for the snowfall of colorful smiling faces and other emotes disappeared and words took their place.

"**This is serious, Rich. What if I can make Haven safe enough that any time Stef changed, the two of you could bolt there? And you wouldn't have to worry about being a freak?**"

"**I'm not the freak. He is. I'm just the friend of a freak.**"

"**Yeah, yeah.**"

"**Why can't you find it, do you think? Are you looking too hard?**"

"**Dunno, Ting. Wish I did. It's like the Gate is there, but I can't see it until I need to, or have to. But we can't wait for things to get worse.**"

"**Explain,**" typed Trent.

And so Jason did, telling them all about the ninja-styled Jonnard who'd appeared and challenged him. That stunned them all into computer silence, except for Henry who typed "**Woah**" over and over. Or maybe he leaned on the repeat key by accident.

"**What do you need us to do?**"

"**Anything! Everything.**" Jason stopped, and took a deep breath. What could they do? He didn't really know.

"**First of all,**" Trent wrote, "**we all need to be looking around carefully. Maybe we can spot something Jason can't, because he's blind to it. Second, we need to watch each other's backs if Jonnard and the Dark Hand are getting ready again. Third, we need to stay in touch with each other, no matter what.**"

"**What kind of things, though?**"

"**Anything and everything,**" Trent shot back to Henry. "**Something that is kinda out of place, but not really. Or something that should change, but doesn't.**"

"**Like a broken clock?**"

"**Sorta. Look, we know that Haven is a step out of time with our own world. So, if it has another side to it that has to be anchored by a second Gate, like the elders are telling us, then it has to be somewhere. Sort of another dimension nudging us every once in a while.**"

Ting wrote, and Jason could also see her shy smile as she did, **"Then Bailey had better clean her room so we can see better."**

"Brat!"

"Brat times two!"

"And proud of it! Besides, this is so Lacey will feel at home <ducks>."

Rich wrote in, **"So it's decided then. We keep our eyes peeled, and we leave messages for each other more often, so we know what's up. AND we don't let anyone bag on Jason, right?"**

"Right!"

"Definitely!"

"Jason's our man, if he can't find a Gate, no one can!" And Bailey added a cheerleading pom-pom to that sentence, and Jason found himself rolling his eyes, but he felt better. They understood. They were with him. They'd help.

Now he had to do everything he could, even if it meant walking into Jonnard again.

Trent signed off and pulled back from the computer he and his father shared. From the living room, his father's soft snore sounded—he'd evidently fallen asleep in front of the TV again. Listening for a moment, Trent could hear the distinctive tones of a narrator on the Discovery Channel. The corner of his mouth twitched in a reluctant smile. Something interesting and intriguing but not interesting enough to keep him from falling asleep. Trent stood up in the nook they called a den and walked softly to his own room, the floor creaking slightly despite his care. He'd let his dad sleep until bedtime, then wake him up before doing dishes and going to bed himself.

Taking care of his dad, he knew how to do. Taking care of Jason, he wasn't sure about. Without Magick of his own, the only thing he could consistently offer was his knowledge of things. But that came from books and imagination ... and the borderline between what mythology thought Magic could be and what Magick was ... would soon be crossed. How much help could he be then? Friendship was probably one of the strongest forces he knew, but Jason needed more than that, and he had nothing else to give.

Trent made his room up, laid his clothes out for the next day, found a good book, and sat down to read for a few minutes, but he wasn't really reading. He thought a great deal more, and nothing helpful came up.

The phone rang, incredibly late. Bailey lifted her head from her pillow, half listening, wondering if something had gone wrong. Lacey rattled about in her cage in her usual night-time activity. Bailey had hidden something sparkly in her container and the pack rat was happily nosing it out and reburying it elsewhere, in a different corner, under sawdust curls and shredded tissue paper. After a moment, Bailey's bedroom door pushed open slightly.

"Bailey? It's Henry. Normally I wouldn't let him talk to you, but he usually doesn't call."

"Is there a problem?"

"I don't know, dear. I have him on hold."

"Okay." Bailey wriggled out from her nest of warm blankets, reaching for the phone on her nightstand. "Henry? What's wrong?"

"I'm sorry, Bailey. I can call back tomorrow."

"No, no. I wasn't asleep yet. Quite." She stifled a yawn. Her bedroom door closed itself quietly, and Bailey punched her pillow into a more comfortable position under her head. "What's up?"

"D-did I wake you?"

"Nah, not yet. Lacey's running around her cage and all."

Henry let out a sigh of breathy relief that carried over the telephone.

"What is it, Henry?"

"I was thinking about what Jason said tonight. About Jonnard and all. Has he bothered you? And could you tell if he did?"

"Well . . ." Images of the stalking man went through her thoughts a moment and she shivered. Lacey stood up in her cage, looked her way, and made a soft, chittering noise as if in question. Moonlight dimly filtered through the curtains and she could barely see the tiny pack rat. "Not exactly."

"Maybe but you're not sure?"

She didn't want to cry wolf. That Jonnard might go after Jason, that all the Dark Hand might, she knew. Herself? No way was she that important. "Something like that, Henry. Has he bothered you?"

"Nothing like that."

"Then why did you call me?"

"I just wanted to, you know, make sure you were all right."

Because he wasn't. She sensed it. "You can tell me."

"No, I can't."

"Henry," she said firmly. "If it walks like a duck and quacks like a duck, then we're gonna eat Chinese. Was it Jonnard? You called me because you had to talk to someone, and you knew you could trust me, so spill it!"

"I . . . I'm not sure. I hear this voice all the time. I think it's him. If it's not—I'm going crazy."

"You're not going crazy."

"Then . . . I . . . I think so."

She sucked her breath in. Poor Henry! He'd been Jonnard's victim before. "Noooo, Henry."

"I'm not sure! And, and, if he is . . . I can handle it this time. We're a lot stronger, Bailey, all of us."

So why then was Henry calling her so late at night and sounding so worried? "Sure we can, Squibbler."

He let out a fidgety noise. "I just wanted you to know in case, well, in case you were in trouble, too, or if they decided I was crazy or something."

"You are definitely not crazy. You're a Magicker, and that's a heck of a something!"

"What about you?"

Bailey wrinkled her nose. "I don't have anything I can prove yet. So, no worries, but I'll keep my eyes peeled."

"Okay. Just don't tell anyone, will you?"

"My word on it. You tell everyone yourself when you're ready." Bailey crossed her fingers. That was, until Henry got in trouble and needed help.

"Thanks."

"And Henry—"

"Yeah?" he answered, as if finally very very tired.

"You're right. We're a lot stronger this time. And it's because we're a 'We.' Got that? Like the Musketeers, all for one and one for all."

Henry sounded cheered a little as he said, "Right! Night, then."

"Talk to you tomorrow."

"Okay. And . . . thanks, Bailey."

She hung up the phone, and squirmed around till she could lie on her back and stare up at the bedroom ceiling. Long ago, her mother had painted it a soft sky blue and added billowy clouds. This wasn't a place they owned, but it was their home. Right now, the sky looked awfully dark, maybe even stormy, but there were those beautiful silvery and white clouds. Every one had a silver lining. Her mom had painted them like that.

Ting moving again. Jason challenged. Trent worried about being discovered, as was Stef, although for different reasons, and Rich unhappy at being a Magicker period. Henry with worries of his own, and she with . . . what? Had she seen someone following her or hadn't she? Without proof, she couldn't ask anyone for help. Not yet.

So they all had secrets, all around. Dark, heavy secrets. Would they have a silver lining?

Bailey closed her eyes and tried to fall back into sleep.

7

THINGS UNSAID

THE wind off the lake was mild and yet held a touch of chill from the past winter. Whimsically named for the life it held only in summer for campers, Lake Wannamee-cha was still a beautiful body of water. There would be fog along the rocky shore and pebbled beaches in the morning, Gavan thought, as he stood outside a weathered building and watched the waters. It was a moment of serenity, of peace, but he did not find he could hold onto it. The moment fled and worry filled him again, even with the sound of a door opening, and gold lantern light spilling over him, as someone joined him with a rustle of long skirts and lace. She carried the lantern light with her, cradled in the crystal upon her wrist. Like his heart, she'd filled her crystal with warmth and illumination and it spilled out now, showing the way.

"It's late," Eleanora said. "Come inside, I've just made a pot of tea." She put her hand through the crook of his arm, and drew close to his side.

Gavan Rainwater felt his heart do a quick double beat, and he turned his face, so that he could rest his chin on the top of her head, where her bountiful curls made a soft pillow. He felt overwhelmed by many things, but most especially by what he'd felt for years and hadn't had the nerve to say. It felt right to say it, never more right, in case he might not have another moment like this again. He remarked, very quietly, "You do know that I love you?"

"Yes. I have known that for quite some time." Her hand tightened on the back of his wrist. Then she said, "And I love you."

"Good. I'm glad that's out of the way!" And he let out a sigh of relief at having finally voiced his feelings, so long left unsaid. Now there was no regret.

Eleanora laughed. "Now we can move on to other things?"

"Precisely." He could feel her laughter vibrating through her body as he touched her. "We can't waste time."

"Such a romantic you are!" Eleanora ducked out from under his chin, and swung around to look up at him. She kissed a fingertip and pressed her delicate hand to his mouth.

He grabbed her hand and nibbled on those fingers before she managed to free herself, and he laughed then, as her eyes widened, and then the carefree moment passed, as he noted the silvery glints in her dark hair . . . just a strand here and there, but . . . there were new lines about her eyes. He inhaled deeply at the sight of them. She'd always been older than he, but never old, never would be old, as he hoped not to be. Still, there was that fear that sudden aging, and death, could strike any of them at any time, as the centuries decided to gain their vengeance for the Magickers having skipped through them. A rift in magickal power had thrown many of them through time. Most had slept through the passing years. Some had been hurtled forward through the centuries as if picked up bodily and thrown. What had the war between Gregory the Gray and the Dark Hand of Brennard done to all of them, outside the laws of natural sciences, and what could it yet do? He thought of his friend Fizziwig, young yet silver-haired, young yet dying of old age, like a candle snuffed out. Young yet gone, unstoppably.

She sensed his sudden turn of mind. "Things," she said, "will work out."

"Not unless we work on working them out." Gavan frowned. His words sounded grimmer than he intended, but perhaps that was just. "I can't stand by, Eleanora, and hope. I have to find an action that works."

"War with our own kind, when there's still a chance we can reconcile with them?"

"I don't think Brennard will ever allow that chance. He wants it all or nothing, and if nothing—that will suit him fine. He wants the children, Eleanora. He's sent me a note asking me to turn them over, and if I do not, he will reveal us to the modern world."

"He has to be bluffing." Eleanora's face paled, even in the moonlight which accented her fair skin. "He can't be serious, he'd give himself away, too. That would destroy all of us."

"Don't think he won't. I imagine he has his little bolt-holes, his hidden places, to keep himself and the others safe while we fall prey. He's as aware as I am what revealing us would do. Scientific inquiries, exams, scorn, imprisonment with fancy words, more that we can't begin to imagine, probably. I don't think he really cares if he ends Magick in this world, as long as he survives and proves his point that Gregory was wrong."

"My father," said Eleanora softly, "was wrong about many things."

He put his arm about her shoulder and pulled her close. "Not the important things," he replied to her.

"Let's hope not." She sighed. "We have to do whatever we can to keep the children safe."

"Even more so than ever. It's not a burden that I want to add to Jason's life, but Brennard has given me a deadline to respond, and after that, we'll all be in deadly peril. The sooner Jason can anchor Haven for us, the more chances we'll have. We need a safe place, a sanctuary, to step away to and educate them, give them a chance to know their Talents and use them." He tightened his hold on her. He could feel the weakness running through her. "How goes your work with Jennifer?"

"It goes very slowly. It's like wrestling an octopus of dark energy, and with every tentacle I free from her, one tries to attach to me." Eleanora seemed to repress a shudder.

"Let me help you."

She shook her head. "I don't think Jennifer or her family would let anyone else get close. She is terrified, Gavan."

"I can't blame her for that. We're going to lose her, aye?"

Eleanora nodded slowly. "I can't bring her back. She doesn't want it, and we both think she is probably too damaged."

He rubbed the palm of his hand over her shoulder in soothing motions. "Then we must make sure she is as free as she can be, and that we don't lose you as well."

She leaned on him. "I'm always so tired these days."

"Get Freyah to help you." The moment he said it, he knew he'd made a mistake. Eleanora stiffened.

"My aunt has her eccentricities."

"And helping us seems to be one of them." Gavan made a noise, rather like a huff, in spite of himself. He loved Freyah despite her quackery and sharp tongue—but if only she'd give more! What she'd been through after the magickal battle that had separated all of them, he could not begin to guess, but she had become secretive and practically a hermit, though just as sharp-witted as ever. Dragging her out of her tiny cottage home was a chore he never relished, nor would he try unless it were a necessity but the time had come when they were all needed. "You cannot be a Magicker," he commented, "without reaching out to others."

"She reaches."

"When it suits her. In the meantime, you're exhausted. The Council asks about you, and your absences. If not Freyah, then go to Khalil. Or Isabella. For advice, support, whatever you can get from them!"

"Allies I know very little about." Eleanora moved her hand from his arm long enough to tuck a curling strand of hair away from her face and behind her ear. "I know Khalil cares very intensely about the children, but Isabella's main concern seems to be the money she's put away over the years, money I think there is no doubt her abilities helped her earn. They have agendas, Gavan, which you and I don't understand yet. Until I know their motivations, I don't want to trust my life to them."

"Your health and Jennifer's are at stake. If it meant going to Brennard himself, I think I would."

"Bite your tongue!" Eleanora slapped the back of his wrist lightly. "Neither of us would, and we both know it."

"Not at any cost?" Gavan considered, then nodded in agreement. "But I won't see you suffer, Eleanora."

"The attacks are less frequent now. Either I am coping better or whatever it is loses strength."

He put his hand over hers, and squeezed gently. He had seen her under attack, and known how much it hurt, how hard it hit, seen her reel and gasp for breath and her skin go ashen, as if she fought for her very soul. As, from what she told him, she did. An evil fought to tear her apart from the inside out, and because of it, she refused to leave Jennifer in her dilemma. He agreed. How could you leave a fifteen-year-old to deal with something like that? Yet, despite their vows, they weren't winning, and Jennifer and Eleanora were slowly, painfully, slipping into shadow.

Jason had to find a sanctuary for all of them before it was too late, untrained though he was, alone in his talent though he was. Jason remained Gavan's main hope. "What do you think your father would have said?"

"Gregory," Eleanora answered firmly, "would say, 'stop scaring my daughter with worry about tomorrow, handle today, and, by the saints, it's about time you declared your love for her!'"

He laughed in spite of himself. He brushed his lips against Eleanora's temple. "There will be an answer," he promised. "And soon." He had no idea how, or when, but having made his promise to her, he'd find a way to keep it.

Both fell into quiet then, and looked out over the lake, where a calm night and good weather allowed a few more hours of serenity.

Henry did not sleep well, despite his talk with Bailey. He stared at the second-story window on the far side of his bedroom. Curtains painted with a scene of the elvish kingdom of Rivendell from *Lord of the Rings* covered the window, giving him a view of another land, far away, framed slightly by the bookends on his high bureau, copies of the tall statues on the river. But his thoughts were not in another world, they were mired in great muddy clumps of this one, and he wasn't happy.

He punched his pillow up, then threw his head back into it, and clenched his teeth. He listened. Far off, muffled, he could hear the beagle down the street barking at something, probably an opossum cautiously crossing the backyard fence. He could hear his toddler sister making restless noises in her sleep. All normal late night sounds. What Henry feared to hear were sounds he shouldn't, that no one else seemed to hear, but that he did. And the thing that frightened him most was that he could not tell if it came from within or without. Was he being haunted or was he going crazy? As Rich and Stef would tease him, what kind of freak had he turned into? Yet, after seeing Stef turn from a burly teen into a chubby bear cub, could Henry not expect that his Talents might transform him? Their Magick seemed to affect them all in ways they were still learning about.

Henry turned over with a sigh, burying his cheek into his pillow which had now gone lumpy. He punched it again, and squinched his eyes shut tightly. In a moment, his breathing had deepened and he lay at the very edge of sleep and dreams, and his body began to relax gratefully.

Then . . .

Henry . . . my precioussssss.

The whisper went through him like an icicle. He sat bolt upright in bed. His breath knotted in his chest and he put his hands to his neck as if he could claw it free, pulling at his pajama T-shirt. A gasp or two and he breathed again, eyes blinking through the bedroom darkness at nothing. He grabbed for his spectacles and pulled them on. Still nothing. Then who or what was playing Gollum in his mind? Henry grabbed his blankets, pulling them close as if they were some kind of armor. He stared about his room.

He felt as if every muscle he had was being pulled out of his body, turned to mush. A great weakness swept over him and he fell back limply onto his bed. His eyelids drooped shut, too weary to remain open. What was happening to him? He felt as if he were nothing more than a limp noodle, boneless, heatless. He had but a heartbeat or two to think, then slipped into exhausted sleep. So deep was his sleep he did not hear the whisper come again. *Sssleeep, precioussssss.* Then a hard, dry laugh.

8

MONDAY, MONDAY

STEF groaned as he sat down on the locker room bench and looked about at the battered steel doors, towels thrown everywhere, his sneakers in his hand. "Mom said if I went up another size in shoes, I'd have to go barefoot." He looked at his scruffy athletic shoes in dismay.

Rich sat down opposite him, his red hair sticking out in every direction. He tried unsuccessfully to comb it down with his fingers, even as he looked at his friend's stockinged feet. "You're already a size twelve. How much bigger can you get?"

"Well, that's the point, isn't it?" Stef let out a disgusted grunt. "We don't know!"

"But you're worried about it before it happens."

Stefan tugged on his shoes gingerly, as if fearful they'd rip apart in his great hands. "You don't know my mom, Rich. It's like I'm this big burden to them. All she and my dad talk about is when I can finish high school and get a football scholarship and go off to college and they're on their own. Like they can't wait or something."

Rich sighed. He couldn't dispute that. He did know Stef's mom and dad, and that was exactly their attitude.

As much as his mom fussed over him and his health, the Olsons grumbled over Stefan and the dent the raising of him put into their lives. Personally, he thought that both families deciding to have only one child had been a pretty darn good decision. The Olsons would have loathed more, and his mom would have had a nervous breakdown if she'd had other unhealthy Hawkinses to worry about.

He stared at Stef's shoes. "They'll hold. The only thing wrong with them is their stench. They reek, Stef. Doncha use that foot powder I bought you?"

"Sure I do. It's the bear. He likes to sleep on 'em sometimes. And he's ripe, you know that. That's the way bears are."

Rich half-smiled at the big square face of his longtime pal. He could see the bear in him, even without knowing that was Stef's shapeshifted other form. Stef was big, burly, strong, and grumbly, with a sweet tooth. He often did not know his own strength, and he had to really focus on something to pursue it, but he'd been working on containing his ability to change unexpectedly.

Rich stood up and began gathering towels, part of his job as trainer to the boys' track team, before basketball shooting them into the canvas bins at the far end of the locker room. Most of the towels made it. The rest were close enough to count, he decided. Stef stood up with a grunt, and put his hands to his right knee. Immediately Rich was there, kneeling, his own hands going to the joint.

"Still swollen? Sore?"

"Nah. Just kinda tight."

"Ah." Rich nodded, his spiky red hair bobbing. "Okay. Just make sure to stretch it before you do anything, even walk, but don't stretch too much. Just kinda loosen it up, okay?"

"Gotcha."

"Good, 'cause this is Monday and we've got a track meeting Thursday."

Stef stared at him. "I know what day it is," he said flatly.

Rich flushed. "Well, I know you do. I was thinking, you know, four days to heal up some more."

"Sure you were." Stef's hand shot out and cuffed his shoulder. "I remember things."

Rich hoped Stef did. He'd spent almost the entire weekend

as a bear, and Rich was exhausted trying to dodge parents and other hazards associated with keeping a half-grown bear under wraps. It was a good thing they'd been allowed to go camping by themselves at nearby Featherly Park. Stef's parents had been more than glad to let him go for the weekend, and Rich's mom had been talked into the tonic qualities of an early spring sleepover. "Yeah, well, next time remember bears can't climb eucalyptus trees, okay? Bark is really slippery and just kinda slides off the tree trunks!" He poked Stef in his meaty ribs. "Let's get out of here. I've got homework and you've got laundry and homework."

Stef grunted again, and ambled with him to the locker room door, pawing at his backpack and pulling out a brightly foil-wrapped protein bar that was nothing less than humongous. "Snack," he mumbled, with his mouth half full. "Jus' a little one."

Rich could not help but grin as Stef wadded up the wrapper and stuffed it back into his backpack. He knew that protein bar brand—made of soy and low carb, low sugar. He'd be willing to bet it was his own mom who'd given it to Stef. Health food nut all the way. Whatever worked to keep both Stef and the bear cub inside him happy. Keeping Stef happy meant keeping curiosity at bay, and of all the Magickers, Rich thought the two of them had the most to hide. Stef's family would probably throw him out if he was ever revealed and his mom . . . well, he just wasn't sure what might happen. He closed the school gym doors behind him, as Stef lumbered away, still happily munching.

On Tuesday, Jason dropped off his finally completed packet. He almost asked for a receipt from the guidance counselor's secretary, just so he could take it home and give it to Joanna, and his stepmother could see he'd finally taken care of business. It wasn't necessary, he knew, but the desire to do it seemed to keep him hanging around the office. The secretary took the big manila envelope from him and then looked up curiously as he just stood by her desk.

"Is there something else, Jason?"

"No, I guess not." He hesitated another moment. "When do we hear?"

"Unless you're taking summer courses, you won't hear until early August. That's when our computer sets all the schedules up, to be sent out. Not our computer here, but the district one, and the high school's department."

"What if I change my mind?"

"The first week after schedules are sent, you go into the high school office and petition to add or drop classes. And you'll be having orientation that week too." Cheerfully, she shuffled his envelope into a rather large stack already on her desk. "It's a big step, high school."

"Anyone ever make ... you know ... a really big mistake?"

"What do you mean?" She looked at him curiously from behind her glasses, the crow's-feet at the corners of her dark brown eyes deepening.

"Well. You know." He shifted uncomfortably. "Becoming someone they really didn't want to be."

She smiled. "You have years, Jason, before you're locked in. And anyway, in this country, you're never really locked in unless you want to be." She checked her watch, and without her saying another word, he knew he'd been dismissed. She was busy.

"Thanks," he said, and moved away, through the guidance part of the school office, where the walls were covered with posters of happy, well-adjusted schoolchildren. Not a one of them, he noticed, wore a crystal focus upon them. Not a one of them was worried about dodging a ninja-clad Jonnard or finding an abducted Magicker, and how that might fit neatly into their future.

On Wednesday, Ting sat down to do her homework, with the background noise of her mother making phone calls and arrangements to move back to San Francisco. She tried not to hear the soft, but decisive words that were shaping her future even as they were spoken. She sat at the dining table, her notebooks and books spread out in front of her, rather than in the solitude of her bedroom at her computer desk. The dining room table had more space, and there was something about the deeply polished cherrywood that made her feel good. She'd grown up with this table waxed to a high gleam, and she wondered if it was moving to San Francisco with her, or if her father would stay behind again with the young ones. No one had said much to her about the arrangements.

Not that she would really mind. She loved her grandmother dearly, and the house with the dragon upon the roof, and the city of San Francisco which was altogether different from any place she'd ever been. It was only that she hated changing schools again, and missing Bailey, and it seemed that the Magickers had more adventures when she was away—and without her. *That* she minded. Bailey seemed to be caught up in the thick of things and she was always hearing about it later. Although, Ting reflected, being attacked by wolfjackals and finding a dead body (poor old Fizziwig) were not exactly the kind of things she wanted to be doing. There were times, though, when she knew she could help, and learn, and she wanted to be close to do it!

Ting closed her hand about her crystal charm on her bracelet. The wire cage holding the crystal was flexible, almost springlike, and could be stretched out to let the crystal slip through, freeing it. It was her own design, the bracelet and cage, fashioned like a long, sinuous Chinese dragon holding a lantern. Chinese dragons were old, wise, and not at all prone to eating young maidens. She had been able to make the bracelet and cage quickly once she'd managed to visualize its design in her mind, and she liked the way it turned out. Even through its clever cage, the crystal warmed to her almost touch, and a feeling of well-being flooded her. With it came the tiniest caress of her grandmother's thoughts.

Ting gasped and freed her crystal so that she could cup it closer, peering into it. She looked up into her grandmother's etched face as if seeing her through water, which she probably was. Her grandmother used a teacup and leaves as a focus rather than a crystal, for that was how she'd been taught many, many years ago. Eleanora and FireAnn referred to Ting's grandmother as one of the Hidden Ones, people of magickal Talent who'd never been really found or taught, and yet used their own abilities in mystical ways. Her grandmother's father had been a Chinese magician and acrobat, and a revered performer who had never given out his many secrets. Ting sometimes wished that she could have seen him, as well, but the age difference was just too great. He had passed away long before she had been born. A very few faded and yellowing black-and-white photos were all her grandmother had left, and in those, he was already aged, and had stopped performing.

"Grandmother!" Ting said in soft delight. "How are you feeling?"

"I am feeling well enough. Do you have a moment to come speak with me?"

"Let me tell Mama." Ting got up, slipping from her chair, and walked to the other room. Her mother held up one finger, asking for a moment of silence while she finished talking, then lowered the phone. "I am going to talk to Grandmother."

Jiao Chuu smiled. "Give her a hug and kiss for me, but don't stay too long."

"I won't. I've homework." Ting cupped her crystal, centered herself for a moment, then stepped into the sharp coldness of the jewel and through its door into her grandmother's kitchen. The room smelled of jasmine tea and its well-steeped tea leaves, and she hugged her grandmother tightly before she even had a chance to lower her porcelain cup in welcome. It had only been a few months since she'd gone home, and yet the body she hugged seemed smaller, more frail than she remembered. Even if she hadn't been told, Ting thought, she'd have known the cancer was back. She kissed her grandmother's cheek.

"You have grown!" her grandmother said proudly as she stood back and looked at her.

"A little."

"That is the way it should be." Her grandmother pulled out a wooden chair for Ting, and then they both sat. New porcelain cups were turned over and filled with steaming hot tea and sugar passed around. Her grandmother never used any, as she had grown up that way, and Ting used only a little. For a few moments, they exchanged pleasantries, as was the custom although Ting fought to keep from squirming in her chair. What had been so important she had to visit like this?

At last, her grandmother set her teacup down. "You are patient with an old woman."

Ting felt her face grow warm. Well, she was *trying*. "I'm afraid I haven't much time today, Grandmother. Tests and papers, and homework."

"Then I shall get to the point. First, I wanted to tell you,

alone, that I am sorry you must come back." Her grandmother's face wrinkled even deeper.

"Don't be! I don't mind, and we want to help."

"You are a far greater help than you understand. Just
knowing that what runs in our blood is not lost . . ." Her
grandmother's voice trailed off. Instead, she reached over
and patted Ting's wrist. After a moment, she took a deep
breath. "Secondly, something rare and strange has happened. The dragon that guards my house has spoken."

Ting almost dropped the delicate porcelain cup balanced in her hands. "It . . . what?" She resisted the impulse
to run outside and look up at it.

"It has spoken."

"What did it say?"

"Not in words, Granddaughter. It hissed at me."

She did put her cup down then, even though her hands
were cold and the cup warm. "Are you sure it was not the
wind, or something? Maybe a possum or raccoon up on the
roof?"

Her grandmother shook her head firmly. "It is made, as
you know, to whistle in the wind, or clatter if a great breeze
or earthquake shock rattles it. But no. I was in the garden,
and looked up at it, and it turned its metal head and hissed
down at me. A long, warning hiss."

"Warning you of what?"

Her grandmother shrugged. "I do not know. But I
thought of you and your friends instantly and decided you
should know what little I do."

Ting swung her legs around. "If I went out to look at it,
do you think it would . . . ?"

"Do it again? I doubt it." Her grandmother smiled then.
"But shall we look?"

They went out the door to the kitchen garden courtyard.
The dragon was made so that it could be seen easily from
that side, as well as on the roof ridge immediately over the
entrance to the house. She looked up at it. Sinuous like the
design of her bracelet, it was similar to a weather vane, but
far more clever and sculpted than that. She had never really seen anything like it before coming here. They stood
in silence for a few moments, until her grandmother gave a
weary sigh. Ting put her arm about her shoulders, to steady
her, as night crept close to the garden and she could feel the

dampness of a Bay fog in the air. "When I come back," she said, "perhaps I'll hear it then."

They turned away, toward the golden doorway of the well lit kitchen. Metal creaked overhead. Ting looked up to see the chrysanthemum-holding dragon peering down at her. It let out a long hiss. Then went quiet. She blinked in amazement.

Her grandmother nodded. "Tell them," she said. "Warn them."

Ting's heart beat rapidly. Her younger ears had caught what her grandmother had not.

The metal dragon had not just hissed. It had said, "Jassssssssssssssson."

FRIDAY, FRIDAY

SOMETIMES Thursdays could be so bad, Trent thought, you just wanted them to sink into oblivion forever so you could get on into Friday, which always seemed to be better no matter *what* was happening. That, of course, was just one of his mistakes.

Along with reading Ting's e-mail about a mysterious warning from the roof dragon at her grandmother's to confound himself with, his father came home from work with a box full of personal things from his desk and an overloaded briefcase. He sat down, cradling the box on his knee, and looked at Trent sadly. "Business," he said, "is not going well."

"They fired you?"

"No," his father answered thoughtfully. "Not yet." He shuffled his carton over onto the free part of the couch. "We'll find out tomorrow if the company has found a buyer willing to take on the debt, or if we're all laid off. Laid off," his father repeated, "is not the same as being fired."

"If you're out of work . . ." Trent muttered, and stopped at the expression on his father's tired face.

"Fired means I did something wrong. Laid off means . . .

the company is struggling and there's no work. It means I can get a job with someone else, hopefully quickly."

"A lot of people are getting laid off," Trent pointed out. "It's been on the news for months."

"I know." His father let his briefcase hit the floor. "That's why I started packing tonight. These are things I don't need at the office anyway, and if it comes to the worst, I'm ready to go. I'll know tomorrow."

"And what then?"

"Then, I bring home my good briefcase, and my last check, and I start sending out résumés. I understand it's done over the Internet now, a lot of the time."

And so on Friday night, Trent sat in his room, doing his homework, and listening for the front door. He didn't know when he finally heard his dad's key in the door if being late was good, bad, or worse. Shoving his desk chair away, he rolled across his bedroom floor, neck craned. His dad walked in with his regular briefcase, and Trent couldn't tell just from looking at him. He stood and went to the threshold of his bedroom. "Well?"

His father looked at him. "Well. I got three months' severance pay, which is really quite good, under the circumstances. But they're closed, and it's done." He just stood there for a moment, a rather dazed expression on his face. He added in a low voice, "I worked there for a long time. I met your mother there. Now they're both gone."

Trent got up and went to him, putting his arms around his dad. "It happens," he said, trying not to feel as scared as his father looked. "You needed a job change anyway! Everyone does, sometimes."

His father gripped his shoulder. "Yes, sometimes they do. I have the retirement funds, of course, although that's for ... well, retirement. And you've your college money put away."

"That," said Trent, "is yours if you need it."

His father shook his head. "We should be just fine. I've got a lot of skills, and they gave me some excellent recommendations."

Trent managed a lopsided grin. "You're not the guy who put them out of business, then?"

"Let's hope not." His father looked around the apartment and into the tiny kitchen. "I think I can manage pizza tonight. It's too late to cook, and I think I might be famished."

"And I think I can manage to find a coupon or two. We need to save money!" Trent dashed off to the corner of the room where newspapers and old mail stacked up. He wasn't sure if he had any appetite for pizza, but his dad needed cheering up, and they could always bring home the leftovers. Pizza for breakfast was always nearly as good as the night before. As he rustled through, looking for the coupons he'd seen days ago, he added, "And after dinner, I'll let you get on-line to look that résumé over."

"I appreciate that."

Trent found what he was looking for, and held the flyer up triumphantly. "And I appreciate *pizza*."

His dad smiled briefly, and then they were headed out the door. Sometimes Fridays were even worse than Thursdays.

Friday night, Jason got word that the soccer championship being held the following Sunday afternoon might not have his coach on the sidelines. He'd broken his arm in a car accident and might or might not be able to be up and about, even with a sling on. The assistant coach promised to fill in and told everyone not to worry, but against a top notch team like they were playing, every little bump felt like a major mountain. Jason knew it was his team that had to face the other team, but not having the coach there would make a difference, no doubt about it. It was rather like Magicking, with Tomaz gone and no one training him right now and his not being able to tell anyone or having a backup. There were times when there was no substitute for the real thing.

He sat back on his bed, book across his knees, and looked at his porthole window, which framed the moon just perfectly and would do so for about thirty minutes. Then, as the world turned, the moon's position would change and he would eventually lose sight of it from his window. It was almost like the glimpses he had caught of Tomaz in his crystal once or twice this week. Neither time had the Magicker seemed to be aware of him, and both times, he had been enveloped in a stormy looking mist, his hands up, and his mouth opened as if chanting, with a pack of wolfjackals sulking at his booted feet, as if his chant and strength alone held them at bay.

Did he really see what was happening? Jason didn't know. Was he supposed to go and help? Was that the meaning of Ting's warning?

He rubbed his forehead. He hated not doing anything, but he knew he couldn't; none of them could afford it if he did something wrong. Too much depended on it. He tried not to imagine ruining the lives of people who had somehow lived across centuries only to be done in by him in one afternoon!

He got out his lavender crystal and rolled it lightly between his palms. The feeling of it was only slightly different from his first crystal, a banded quartz, and the only way he could describe it was the way he'd once told Trent: it was like holding an orange and a lemon with your eyes closed. You could tell they were different, but they were also very much the same. The crystal warmed to his touch and he looked into it, hoping for a glimpse of Tomaz and a knowledge of what he should do to help. Not going to Gavan grated on him every day, and he wasn't sure he could respect Tomaz's wishes much longer.

Finding no hint of the Magicker, Jason opened his mind to even harder things . . . Gates. After all, Tomaz had told him that finding the third Gate was the most important thing he could do, and everything might anchor on that. If only he could. Jason looked deep into the gemstone, sinking into its translucent beauty, and his own thoughts. For long moments he felt himself drift, barely aware that his body lay in his bed, propped up by doubled-over pillows, with his stockinged feet tucked into covers folded at the bottom. The distance between here and now and wherever his thoughts were taking him seemed incredibly far. . . .

Something latched onto him. He had just a moment to realize he was no longer moving aimlessly, but he was being tugged, pulled in a certain direction through nothingness. He experienced a moment of worry, as the tug became a yank and he felt himself catapulting through space and then . . . THUD!

He hit something large and transparent and hard, and slid down it as though it were ice. When he hit bottom, he caught his breath, and stared at the other side of the icy window.

A man lay as if in a tomb. Jason felt his whole body

freeze, but it was not the man of his many nightmares, he already knew who that man was ... Antoine Brennard ... no, this was someone else, and he knew this man, too. And he did not lie atop a stone tomb as Brennard had before finally awakening, but he lay on a lounge, covered with a warm brown blanket, with a small pillow for his head, and a blanket tucked over his body except for his outthrown arms, as if he'd been caught falling backward for all time, and then laid down for that moment when he would ultimately hit bottom.

Someone had also left a tray next to the lounge, and there was a mug and a platter of biscuits, and a small vase with fresh flowers. As if someone, somewhere, loved him and waited for him to wake up. As if he had not died in that awful magickal duel.

He had no air to breathe even as he let out a startled gasp, and when he blinked and drew back, everything had vanished, and he lay in his own bed again. No icy panels. No tray or lounge or blanketed Gregory, and he wondered if he had really *seen* it.

But what if he had?

This, after all, had been Gregory's own crystal. Jason held it tightly. But what did it all mean?

Before he could recover, the phone rang, its sound harsh and jangling in his room. He jumped, the open book across his lap falling to the floor in an angry rustle of pages. He picked the novel up, replacing the dust cover carefully and marking his page. The phone stopped abruptly halfway through its second ring and he knew someone in the house had answered it. To his surprise, though, he could hear Alicia's voice filtering down the hallway and up into his attic room.

"Ja-son! It's Trent, for you."

Jason picked the receiver up, said, "I've got it, thanks!" and waited for the click before he said, "Trent? What's up?"

"You don't know?"

"I guess not." He frowned. Gregory's crystal was still pressed into the palm of his hand, despite his having dropped the book and darn near everything else. He opened the drawer of his desk and deposited it carefully.

Words poured out of Trent in a rush. "My dad got laid

off, and I don't know what we're going to do until he gets work again, and I just got e-mail from Eleanora. Jennifer Logan is leaving tonight, and we're all gathering to say good-bye. Were you asleep or something?" Trent stopped.

"No ... I don't think so." Jason flicked a glance at his desk clock. Not even eight o'clock yet. Downstairs the household would be gathering for their favorite TV show. They usually let him have an hour or two of game time upstairs with Trent and Henry. "She's going?"

"She's quitting. She wants to tell me good-bye, and Bailey, and all of us, Eleanora said. Bring me through, please?" With that, the phone line went dead.

He hadn't left Jason time to argue, and if Jennifer Logan was leaving Magick, Jason wasn't sure he wanted to argue. He got his own crystal out from inside his shirt where it always lay against his skin, and centered on it, reaching out for Trent.

10

HELLOS AND GOOD-BYES

JASON pulled Trent through. "You're sure about this?" The clear crystal doorway shimmered like a bubble, stretched, and then popped slightly as Trent emerged entirely into his attic bedroom.

"As sure as I can be without being able to look through my own crystal." Trent scrubbed his hand through his hair, sending it in all directions. "And I'm beginning to wonder if Eleanora suspects about my talent, or lack of it. She sent me e-mail." He frowned. "You don't think Bailey could have let it slip?"

"Never. One problem at a time." It was odd that the Magicker hadn't used her own crystal to reach Trent, but Jason didn't have time to think about that now. He hadn't been reached that way either, but possibly being in Focus with Gregory's crystal had blocked him. "At least they're giving us the chance to say good-bye, and at least Jennifer asked for you, huh?" He punched Trent's arm lightly. His comment didn't seem to erase Trent's unhappiness. Jason cleared his throat. "Are we waiting for anyone?"

"Ting and Bailey are going to go through on their own. Don't know about Stef and Rich," Jason answered with a shrug. He grabbed a windbreaker off the back of his study chair. "Let's go. I can't afford to be missed."

"You know I hate this."

Jason stared at Trent. "Hate Jennifer's leaving?"

"Hate traveling like this." Trent suppressed a shudder. "Doesn't it ever give you the creeps? Stepping into a rock, for crying out loud. Remember when Bailey got lost in hers? Don't you worry about being trapped?"

"Ummm. No." Jason rubbed his crystal a moment. "Maybe you'd prefer a flying carpet?"

"Actually, a flying carpet has mythological substance to it." Trent leaned his lanky body against the bed frame. "If you could manage to conjure one up. But what I'd really, really prefer is a Pegasus. Great white, winged stallion with a bridle of sunlight, and a sword sheath on his saddle."

Jason laughed, then said, "Keep dreaming," and put his hand on Trent's shoulder, gripping tightly. He looked into his crystal, his rock of clear quartz, and gold flecks, banded with one outer wall of dark blue stone, and found a door, an entry to where the Magickers were gathered. Then he pressed through, feeling it stretch as he pulled Trent with him.

They emerged with a faint popping of ears, and for a brief second Jason thought that Trent might be right. Was this any way to travel? His doubt vanished the moment he saw everyone waiting for them on Jennifer's back lawn, illuminated by the porch lights. If he'd any doubt about where they were, the monstrous moving van parked out in the street in front of the house, and the House for Sale—SOLD sign dispelled it.

Jennifer, Ting, and Bailey sat on the lawn, reminding him a little of a pile of puppies . . . wiggling, cute, and excited. Jennifer was very much like his stepsister in that she was a few years older, willowy with long blonde hair, but the difference between the two was like night and day. He wanted to strangle Alicia. Jennifer, well, he didn't feel about her the way Trent did, but he would protect her any way he could. Alicia was quiet and a little calculating. When Jennifer smiled, it lit up her whole face. Although, since she lost her Magick, she hadn't been smiling much.

Gavan Rainwater and Eleanora stood over the girls . . . or rather, Gavan stood and Eleanora floated. Gavan carried his wolfhead cane, the instrument at odds with the soft shirt and jeans he wore, but the crystal gripped in the handle's pewter sculpture was one of his powers and would never be left behind. His dark hair had been brushed back from his face and fell in a wave to his collar, and the night reflected in his intense blue eyes, but he smiled at Jason.

"There you are. Took the long way round?" The wolf's jaws glittered as he swung about to wave at them. His other hand held a goblet with a deep red liquid in it, and Jason's heart did a funny skip beat thing. The Magicker held a drink that would not only wipe the memories clean but take Magick away with them. Jennifer was really, truly leaving them then.

"Is Henry coming?" Jason blurted out, his thoughts immediately full of their friend who'd drunk that brew once, and nearly lost everything, but he had been able to come back . . . well, nearly so. Magick with Henry was an off and on thing, but it had always been like that.

Eleanora put her hand, framed by soft white lace hanging down from her sleeve, upon Gavan's wrist. "No," she said softly. "We thought it kinder not to have him here." She looked . . . well, thin, Jason thought. Worn thin as if she might be looked all the way through. He turned his gaze away quickly to keep her from seeing the surprise in his eyes at the change in her.

Trent approached Jennifer silently and just stood for a long moment. Then he said, "I know you have to go, but do you have to leave . . . everything . . . behind?"

Jennifer looked up at him. She wore a lavender velvet jogging suit, and she had one arm about Ting's waist and one around Bailey's. She had been smiling, but now she stopped. "Eleanora and I talked about this. It seems the best thing to do. I can't hurt anyone this way." A strand of blonde hair curled about her face, catching the lights streaming through the night. It was still too chilly in the year for mosquitoes, yet early enough to feel that spring was definitely here.

"You couldn't hurt me," Trent protested, and then stopped at the surly sound of his own voice.

"I know it seems harsh." Eleanora moved to Trent, in that odd floating way she had, for she used some of her power to keep herself elevated three to four inches taller than she really was. Petite and brunette and altogether lovely in an otherworldly sort of way, with her dulcimer and her lace and long skirts, and the cameo on a ribbon at her throat. It was no wonder Gavan loved her, for she was beautiful. They could all see it on his face as Rainwater looked at Eleanora, and he wondered if she knew it, too. Trent shrugged as she came near; fending off any kind of hug or comfort she might offer. He didn't want a hug. He wanted to know that Jennifer would stay. If not here, in this house, in this city, at least in the ring of Magickers, so that he would still be friends with her. Sometimes life just dealt too many low blows. First his dad, now Jennifer. Not that he ever expected anything to be easy, but at least a breathing space between catastrophes, please?

Eleanora looked at his face, as though reading his thoughts, and shook her head, sadness crossing her features. "I'm sorry, Trent."

"I'm sorry, too," he mumbled, and crossed his arms over his chest and retreated to stay at the edge of the shade where the porch lights did not reach. He didn't even know why they were all there, if Jennifer wouldn't even remember them or their good-byes!

Jason nudged him slightly, but Trent would not look up at him. He had known why they'd come, but he'd hoped it wouldn't happen.

Gavan leaned on his cane. Very quietly, he said, "The heart always remembers a little, Trent. And I cannot tell you that there won't be a day, sometime in the future, when Jennifer will remember us, need us, even return to us. So good-byes are always hard but not necessarily the last time we see someone."

Trent glanced up quickly. He traded a long look with Gavan. Rainwater nodded slowly. Eleanora's body shimmered as she rose even higher on her magickal tiptoes. She whispered in Trent's ear, "And I wouldn't want you to remember that you made her even sadder than she already is."

He took a deep breath, then moved to the group on the grass and sat down behind Jennifer, putting his arm about her shoulder. She smiled at him then, and for a moment, he forgot everything but the warmth that twinkled in her eyes.

Ting passed over a charm bracelet she had dangling from her fingers. Each tiny charm held an even smaller piece of crystal. There was a frog, a bear cub, a mouse, a lightning bug, and a heart. "The mouse," said Bailey, wrinkling her nose, "is really a pack rat."

Jennifer laughed. "As if I could forget!"

In answer to the sudden happy surge in their voices, Bailey's shirt pocket rippled and Lacey stuck her whiskered nose out, sniffing the early evening air. The tiny pet/pest who had stolen whatever she could from their summer camp cottage before being captured and tamed by Bailey peered at all of them curiously. The pack rat's eyes shone with what seemed to be a laugh of her own, before she turned tail and dove back into Bailey's pocket, leaving only her tufted tail hanging out and twitching happily.

Jennifer hugged Ting and Bailey both. "Thank you!" The bracelet chimed and twinkled as she slipped it onto her slender wrist. Jason took her hand and said, "Friends wherever," and she held his hand for a very long moment. The crescent-shaped scar on the back of it burned sharply till she let go, and he sat back, a little confused.

"I haven't got anything," Trent said. "Really."

"That's all right. I do." She smiled faintly with the wisdom of an older woman, leaned around and kissed him, very gently, and very quickly. Trent's face immediately went fiery red.

Bailey, Ting, and Jason laughed.

Jennifer grinned, murmured, "Sorry . . ."

"Oh. I'm . . . I'm not. Kinda." Trent sat back a little, his face staying red hot, and his eyes watching her closely.

Eleanora, however, watched Jason. "What is it?" she asked quietly.

Casually, he moved his hands out of sight. "Nothing. Just the Draft of Forgetfulness and all that."

"Really."

He stood and moved to the side, Gavan giving him a judging look, and nodding to Eleanora. The lovely Magicker stood in the night shadows with Jason, as Rainwater began to weave a spell over Jennifer, to protect her however he might, although with her Magick gone, even the Dark Hand would no longer have an interest in her.

Jason watched. He rubbed the back of his hand. Eleanora touched it.

He took a deep breath as she repeated, "What is it?"

"My scar," he answered softly. "It's burning. Either something is very near or ..."

Eleanora turned her head, in a tumble of brunette curls, and looked toward Jennifer. "Or it's her."

He swallowed. "Yes."

"I know. I've been fighting it with her since that awful night last fall. It's one of the reasons she's leaving. She's convinced something terrible may happen if she doesn't." Eleanora touched him again, and coolness slid over the back of his hand.

Gavan finished weaving his web of Magick, tapped his cane on the ground, and said, "Done." At his word, a spiderweb of incredible lightness seemed to fall like a gentle curtain over Jennifer and then fade away. He held out the goblet, and Ting and Bailey shrank away instinctively as Jennifer reached for it. Lacey gave a tiny squeak, and her tufted tail jerked and disappeared into Bailey's pocket. Jennifer took a deep breath. She said, in a faint, breathy voice that did not quite sound like her, "Good-bye all," before lifting the cup and drinking down the thick, syrupy juice as fast as she could.

The cup fell from her fingers as her face went pale. She swallowed a last time, as if fighting to keep the drink down. Jennifer shuddered, and Jason shivered with her. Ting and Bailey made a sandwich, with Jennifer held close between, and a tear slid down Ting's face.

Trent couldn't bear to watch any longer. He bolted to his feet. He took his crystal out as if to leave, then hesitated, with Bailey and Jason watching him. Only the three of them knew he wasn't going anywhere. Gavan took him aside, saying, "There are harder things to watch, lad, and I hope you never have to."

Jennifer got to her feet. "I must ... I must go inside. I have to finish packing, and Mother and Father are waiting and ... you are all very nice but ... I don't ... quite ... know you. What are you doing here?"

Eleanora tilted her face up, smiling. "We just came by to say farewell, dear, and wish you luck."

"Oh." Jennifer pushed her blonde hair away from one eye. "That's very ... nice of you." She took a step toward her back porch, her charm bracelet jingling. Reluctantly, Bailey and Ting let her go.

"One last thing," Eleanora said.

"Yes?" Jennifer turned to face her, a bewildered look on her face.

"This," said Eleanora firmly. She reached up, spreading her hand, putting her fingers to Jennifer's forehead.

They all felt it. Later, Jason would wonder how it was Trent did, although it was like a lightning strike. You didn't have to be at ground zero to feel the zap, the power, the snap, and smell the ozone. It was almost exactly like that. Something dark and powerful surged at Eleanora, knocking her to her knees and crackling through the air with power and Magick that reeked and promised nothing but ill. She took it from Jennifer. It snaked through the air in smoky dark lines, fleeing the girl and shooting toward Eleanora, sinking into her before disappearing, one line after another. Eleanora put a hand to her chest as if shot as Gavan cried out in alarm.

She put her other hand up, trembling. "Get her into the house quickly, now!"

Trent took Jennifer by the hand, and found it cold as ice. He led her across the grassy lawn, up the porch, and into the house. Packed boxes lay everywhere, and furniture had been piled neatly as well. She sat down on a box, as someone called from another room, "Jennifer, is that you? Are your friends gone yet?"

"We're leaving now," Trent called back.

She looked up at him. "All of you are so very . . . nice." And she smiled.

He smiled in return, though it took all of his strength to do so. He backed toward the screen door, and out it, and pelted down the porch steps before he stopped breathing.

Eleanora lay on her side on the ground, and Gavan knelt beside her. He held both her hands tightly.

She panted. "It will go," she said. "It will."

The Magickers ringed her, crystals in every hand. In their jeweled light, Trent could see . . . see . . . gray sparkling in Eleanora's hair. Lines at the corners of her eyes and mouth. It was as if she had aged ten years in just the few moments he'd been gone.

Trent and Jason looked at each other. "Fizziwig," Jason mouthed.

Gavan heard them. "No! No, she's not going to . . ." His

voice strangled in his throat. He held his cane up, and the moonlight caught the crystal gleaming. "No!"

The beam of light that shot out from the wolfhead cane spilled across the yard, and in the shadows, things fled, scattered, as if they had been gathered watching. He could hear hot breathing, and paws thundering across the street, and feel the disturbance of great bodies leaping through the night. Jason felt something prickle up the back of his neck as two great glowing green eyes winked and disappeared with a low growl.

He whirled about, searching, every hair on his body tingling with the sense of evil and chaos that wolfjackals always brought with them. The night went very still for a moment. He opened his mouth to shout out a challenge, but something moved in the purple shadows. He spun to face it.

And someone stepped out.

Khalil gathered his desert shroud around him, looking at all of them down his hawk-bridged nose, dark eyes narrowed. "Hello again this eve, it seems," he said, in his deep, purring voice.

"Have you been there all the time?" Gavan gritted his teeth as if he wanted to say more, and had to force himself not to.

"More or less. I wanted to see how you were handling the situation." He came to the curled up Eleanora and gently put his hand on her head. "Very well, until this."

"Help her."

Khalil stared at Gavan. "Only one thing can I do."

"No!" cried Gavan.

Eleanora protested softly, weakly, as Khalil cupped her head carefully against his knee, as he joined Gavan beside her. "It's all right," she managed in a barely audible, breathy voice. "I will accept this," she said.

"No, you won't!" cried Gavan. "No."

Khalil murmured a sentence of words neither Jason nor any of the others could catch, but Gavan heard them, for he seemed to flinch with each one of them. When the tall Magicker stopped, Eleanora lay asleep on the ground, the blush gone from her cheeks, and the breath in her body barely moving through her chest.

"How long?" Gavan asked, looking at her.

"Till you find the cure or awaken her to let her die." Khalil lifted her body in his arms as he stood, Eleanora limp in sleep.

"Like Sleeping Beauty." Ting touched her fingers to the lace drifting over one still hand before drawing back, her face stricken with unhappiness.

"And the curse is our very own Magick," Gavan said bitterly.

"Perhaps not. Perhaps the curse is our not understanding. Take us away from here, before we are seen, and so that we may find a place for our sleeping Eleanora to rest safely."

But Rainwater wasn't done, his face tight with emotion. "Was that all you could do?" Gavan demanded of Khalil.

The two Magickers stared at each other in the darkness of the night.

"Yes," answered Khalil. "For now." He shifted, and handed her body to Gavan. "She is lucky. The rest of us . . . may not have a chance to sleep rather than face our deaths." He turned on his heel and disappeared in a crystal flash.

HOT POTATO

GAVAN stood uneasily, Eleanora draped in his arms. A faraway howl sounded through the late night air that might have been from a lonely dog down the streets, or from banished wolfjackals. It was difficult to tell. Bailey stepped close to brush a trailing lock of hair from Eleanora's face, and shivered slightly as her fingers touched.

"She's so cold already."

"It's what's keeping her alive."

"She looks like Sleeping Beauty," Bailey said wistfully. Ting caught her hand and held it between both of hers, as if warming her.

"Maybe that's where the story came from."

Bailey looked at Ting, baffled. "Just think," Ting said. "Magickers asleep, hidden down the centuries. Maybe one of them was the original Sleeping Beauty."

"One way or the other," Jason interrupted, "we have to do something about this one." He didn't like the sound of another faraway howl wavering on the night air and also fretted at the time. He didn't want to risk being missed at the McIntire household.

Gavan frowned. "I can't hold your hands, so hang on to me however you can. Make sure everyone is connected."

They gathered around him, and with a faint feeling of not being anywhere, they were suddenly at the edge of the lawn of Aunt Freyah's cottage, and it was daytime there, although late in the day, with the warmth of the sun still flooding across the green grass. The cottage looked as if it were caught in a ray, its whitewashed walls cozy, and its tiled roof sound, with two crooked chimneys and dark blue shutters swung wide open. A climbing rose covered a trellis by the east wall, and its blossoms of red and copper were everywhere. A picket fence, rather ramshackle, bordered the little haven, but Jason noted it was falling down in places and he wondered if that was just part of the charming atmosphere or if it meant Aunt Freyah's Magick had begun to fail.

Gavan shook them all off gently like a big dog getting out of a bath. He tossed his head back to clear his eyes, and took a deep breath before approaching the cottage. They all shadowed him, more than willing to let him take the lead, because even though they all loved Freyah, her temper could be uncertain, rather like anyone's eccentric but favorite aunt. Her sharp blue eyes never missed a thing, and she was apt to speak her mind. Bailey inhaled as her pocket fluttered and Lacey let out a timid squeak for both of them, poking her little face out of the flap and watching curiously. The kangaroo rat's little soft velvet ears were still all crumpled up from her nap in Bailey's pocket as she began to clean one whisker thoroughly.

Trent stirred. "What're we waiting for?"

"The best way to go in," Gavan muttered.

Jason said dryly, "I think she knows we're here." He pointed, as the apple-red and somewhat fruit-shaped door began to swing open slowly.

With a sigh, Gavan began to move forward, the others following him. Taking their cue from his attitude, they grew quiet, although visiting Aunt Freyah was generally a boisterous time. That he seemed unsure made them unsure. Lacey kept her head poked out, twittering anxiously and blinking in the sun, and Bailey thumbed her head gently a few times to soothe her. Ting made a quavery sound at the back of her throat, and Trent reached out to catch her hand. Jason kept his eyes on the apple door, and thought of the warmth he'd found inside that cottage a number of times, and wondered what he'd find tonight. Or today, as it seemed to be here.

The difference in time nagged at the back of his mind. What if finding a Gate wasn't a matter of *where* but *when*? What if that was why he'd hadn't been successful . . . and why Fizziwig had aged so much? Jason was so busy mulling over these thoughts that he almost stumbled into Gavan's back as the adult Magicker came to a sudden halt just inside the doorway.

Needless to say, the others piled into Jason as though it were a freeway traffic jam.

"Whiplash," muttered Trent, as they all halted abruptly and stood shoulder to shoulder, packed into the relatively tiny doorway.

They peered around Gavan to see what the problem was, and discovered that the problem was Aunt Freyah. She stood with her feet spread, and her cane in her hands, held across her body in a defensive stance that would have done a martial arts expert proud.

"You shall not pass," Trent whispered in Jason's ear. Jason bit his lip on that remark, but Aunt Freyah did look remarkably determined not to let them by.

"Freyah," said Gavan gently, "there was nothing else to be done."

"Nothing? Nothing? There is always something else that can be done!"

"We couldn't let Eleanora take any more . . . damage . . ." finished Gavan, as if he hadn't any other words.

"Don't mince words with me," Freyah snapped. "As far as I'm concerned, this whole matter of students has been bungled from the start. They need to be sequestered and protected, from themselves, each other, and the outside world, until they can master what flows through them. You have failed on all those counts, Gavan Rainwater, and it's my niece who suffers for it."

"I agree. Yet times are not what they were when you taught me, and Gregory taught. We can't just sweep these sons and daughters away from their families and have anyone understand or agree to it."

"So you teach them bits and drabbles and expose

everyone to a great deal of danger. Do you think that even bad Magick is better than no Magick at all?"

Gavan shifted his weight, and Jason couldn't tell if it was because Eleanora was getting heavy in his arms, or if he was getting a better defense against Freyah's sharp, blue-eyed wrath. "Magick," Gavan said calmly, "manifests itself regardless of what I think."

A long moment of silence. Then Freyah straightened with a hmmmpf, lowering her cane a bit. "First sensible thing you've said in a long time." She thumped her cane against the floor, and leaned on it. "Regardless. You cannot leave her here."

"What other safe home does she have, Freyah?"

"What makes you think this is a safe home?" Freyah's voice sounded a little weak, and she swayed a bit on the cane as if she had stood too long without its support and now paid for it.

Two things happened. Jason put his hand in his pocket and immediately the lavender crystal, already warm with power, fell into his palm as if seeking attention, and Jason thought of what Gavan had just said about Magick. Behind him, at his elbow, Jason became aware of a sudden wriggle from Bailey. Something furry darted across his shoulder and then down his leg and disappeared, running along the cottage baseboards. Lacey! And the tiny creature was off and running as though it was entered in a race.

"Cookie!" whispered Bailey urgently, but the pack rat didn't waver at all as she dove into the depths of the forbidden cottage and disappeared. She put her hand out, and then dropped it as Gavan spit out a curse.

"You'd turn down your own niece! And for what, to spite me? To prove me wrong?"

"No," answered Freyah, her lips tight. "To protect her. Understand me well. It is not safe here."

"Then where? Where?"

"That is not my concern right now." Freyah's knuckles were icy white as she gripped her cane. "Leave now, there is no welcome here for you!"

Gavan threw his head back with a roar, and disappeared in front of them. They stood, blinking, taking a step back at his sudden departure. Jason brought his hand and crystal out, as if to take them all with him and follow, but Bailey tugged on his elbow. "Lacey!" she hissed, but even as she did, the tiny fur ball rocketed out of the shadows and scrambled up her leg and dove headfirst into her pocket. After a second, she pulled her tufted tail in with a squeak.

"Hold on, everyone," Jason said. "Aunt Freyah, I hope we didn't bother you too much. Things have been . . . well, a bit . . . unusual."

She snapped him a sharp-eyed look, then her face softened into a smile. "Lad, get along with you. There is adventure waiting for you elsewhere."

Actually, that was something he'd rather *not* have heard, he thought, as he closed his hand about his crystal and sent them all tumbling after Gavan.

They fell out of nowhere, hard, as though someone had opened a sack and dumped them out, like potatoes rolling onto a kitchen floor. Appropriate, he thought, since they seemed to be in a kitchen, and Eleanora had been shuffled around like a hot potato no one wanted to hold.

He sat up, after removing Trent's elbow from his rib cage, and looked around.

"FireAnn!" Bailey blurted out, half a second before he recognized the camp kitchen as well. Of course, Bailey had spent far more time here than he had when they were at Ravenwyng together, but they'd all taken their turn helping the fiery-haired cook. He got to his feet and put a hand down to help Ting. Bailey had already bounded up, and Trent just stayed on his hands and knees, practicing some deep breathing it looked like.

He could hear muted voices around the corner of the kitchen, near the pantry. They all trailed after the sound as if following a delicious scent.

FireAnn already had Eleanora in a cushiony chair, with her feet up on a well-stuffed ottoman, and was tucking an afghan about her still form, as they finally caught up. FireAnn looked like a gypsy in a sweeping long skirt and peasant blouse, with a kelly green kerchief binding back her intensely red hair, as though anything could tame those boundless curls. She looked up and smiled at them all, and Jason jolted to a stop.

She'd always had laugh lines about her eyes and mouth, but in the less than a year he'd known her, those lines had become sharp and drawn. He closed his mouth, about to say something in surprise, and managing to halt the words in his throat. FireAnn mistook the look on his face.

"Now, lad, dinna be worrying. I'll take good care of Eleanora. Gavan will get things righted around, and she'll be up in no time at all!" FireAnn stood and patted Eleanora's limp hand as she settled her arm across her lap.

"No herbs, then?"

FireAnn turned her smile upon Bailey. "No lass, as you've already been guessin'. Herbs willna do it. Only Magick and time, and we've both."

Jason stared at Gavan's back. The Magicker stood at the door to FireAnn's tiny home, which shared a common wall with the mess hall, but little else, and they could only guess that something about Lake Wannameecha held Rainwater's intense attention.

But did they have both time and Magick? The only thing sure in life was that, sooner or later, they were all going to run out of it.

FireAnn smoothed her apron out. "Best get home with you all. I'd invite you to supper, but all I have is mushroom pie, and younguns need more than that!"

"I'll say," muttered Trent. His stomach made a noise as if emphasizing it.

Ting nudged him. "It's hours past dinner."

"Ten o'clock snack." Trent sighed wistfully.

"Right, then." FireAnn smiled brightly. "Along with you, or do you need a boost."

"No," said Jason. "I've got it." The lavender crystal in his hand still burned with an unexpected warmth. "Good night, Gavan. And to you, FireAnn."

"Night my lads and lassies," the Magicker called back, even as Jason sent them stepping into doorways to take them home. Gavan said nothing, and Jason felt that was possibly the most despairing part of the whole evening.

When even Gavan did not know where to go or what to do, the Magickers were troubled indeed.

12

THE NEWS JUST
GETS BETTER

JASON sat down hard on the edge of his bed, his body shaking a little from the night's activities, and his mind reeling a bit from the time changes. Could he get jet lag from Crystaling back and forth? He wasn't sure, but he did know something. He was suddenly, incredibly, ravenously hungry. He listened a moment. The McIntire household seemed very quiet, as if everyone had settled down to sleep, so he got up and lowered his trapdoor silently to make his way down to the kitchen. He crept as softly as he could, and used what little he knew of Magickal stealth to keep the floorboards and doors from squeaking as he passed by.

Once in the kitchen, he breathed a little easier, as he rounded up a sandwich of baked turkey slices and provolone cheese, on fresh crusty shepherd's bread. He wrapped it in a thick paper napkin to take back upstairs, and was making his way back again, when he heard the soft murmur of voices from the Dozer's office study. He had no curiosity at all, his only intent was to get back up the stairs before he was heard, but then they said his name.

He stopped on the first step of the landing, his whole body poised to listen in spite of his intentions. He found his crystal with his free hand, and heard the noises around him sharpen a bit.

"He keeps secrets."

"Anyone that age has secrets, Joanna. He's a good boy. You need to relax and accept that. It would do you both good if you did."

A sigh. Even if he hadn't recognized his stepmother's voice, he'd know the long-suffering sigh. Part of him quailed. He really didn't want to know what he'd done lately that failed some impossible expectation she had of him that he didn't even understand! But part of him dug his heels in stubbornly.

"I just . . . I can't handle his sneaking out. What if he becomes like his father?"

"Jason's father had an enormous burden he didn't know how to carry. The boy is fine. Trust me."

Jason felt his face crease. What was that all about? What was Joanna talking about? All the times he'd wanted her to talk about his dad, and nothing, and now, in the shadows . . . what? What was she *saying?*

He fought to stay where he was, quiet, unseen, unheard, but his heart thumped as loudly as a drum in protest. Surely they'd hear that! And then he could demand to know what she was talking about. His hands tightened.

"As for sneaking out, do you even know if he's back yet? I should think that would be your first concern."

Movement in the study.

"You're right, of course."

Jason unfroze and took the stairs as quickly as he could, both landings, then sprinted up his trapdoor ladder. The sandwich, crumpled now in his fist, he shoved into his desk drawer. Then he shed his clothes as quickly as he could before diving into bed and had time to draw about four steadying breaths before; a knock sounded downstairs in the hallway.

"Jason?"

"Mmmphf?"

"May I come up?"

He rustled around in his blankets, trying to sound warm and sleepy. "Sure."

The trapdoor lowered and Joanna's face appeared as she climbed the first few steps. "Were you sleeping?"

"Yeah. Something wrong?" He scrubbed a hand over his face, trying to smudge his expression. He wasn't a good liar, never had been, and didn't want to try to get better if he could help it.

"In bed early."

"Oh." He made a noncommittal noise. "I fell asleep in the closet earlier, looking at . . . you know. Stuff."

He had a box, small, of a few of his father's things. Not much to remember anyone by, really, but she'd been careful to give it to him. He kept it in his closet. It had been years since he had slept next to the box, but he'd done it quite a lot in those first horribly empty months after his father had died. He hadn't done it but one other time, that he could remember, since moving into this house.

"In your closet, Jason?"

He nodded and stifled a yawn, a real one this time, and felt his face warm.

"Oh, hon." Joanna looked as if she wanted to say something more, but instead closed her mouth.

"I must have been really tired," he added, by way of explanation, sounding as embarrassed as he felt. "I haven't done that in years, you know? I was just looking at some things, and next thing I knew, I was all stiff and curled up on the closet floor."

"It's all the stress," Joanna said gently. "School, soccer, getting ready for high school." The trapdoor stair creaked and part of her face submerged as she took a step downward. "Jason, if you need to talk about anything, you know you can."

Actually, he couldn't, but it was nice to hear her say that. He took a deep breath. "Someday, I'd like to talk about my dad a little."

"How he died?"

Jason shook his head. "Nah, I know most of that. I want to know how he lived. You know, the day-to-day stuff. I'm forgetting."

She smiled sadly. "We all do, don't we? He was a good man to both of us. Someday, we'll talk." She disappeared entirely then, and the bedroom ladder swung back into place. Jason watched it for a long moment, before getting his sandwich out of the desk drawer, and wolfing it down. The crumpling hadn't hurt the flavor at all, although it seemed a bit chewier. Then, he scrunched down into his bed, and tried to find a way to sleep. He didn't know how he could bother Gavan now about Tomaz with Eleanora so ill, but it seemed to him that the longer things went, the worse they got.

Tomorrow he'd have to do something.

Consequently, it took him a long time to fall asleep as if tomorrow were determined never to arrive.

She'd returned about the time she left, Bailey noted on her watch, as she stepped out of the crystal at her front door. She gave a grin and let out an impish cheer. She had tried to imagine arriving just that way, and she had . . . given that time seemed to flow like an unpredictable river through crystal doorways. Of course, arriving outside her apartment instead of inside, was not a good idea. So the experiment hadn't been as successful as she'd hoped. Still, there were possibilities to consider.

She put her crystal bracelet back on and fumbled in her pocket for her apartment key. Behind her, she could hear someone moving in the corridor. Lacey chittered nervously from her pocket as she tried to fit the key in smoothly. A duplicate key, it hadn't been cut quite right and she always had to do a certain amount of jangling around to get the key in and turned. It stuck stubbornly.

The steps drew closer. Bailey looked over her shoulder. A dark-clothed man stood, watching her. He stepped back when he saw her spot him.

Cripes! She was being followed. No doubt about it now. She shoved her key in, hard, and turned it, praying it wouldn't snap off in the lock. The door opened and she flung herself inside, and quickly secured all the dead bolts. Nothing else happened. She waited a very long moment before looking out the peephole to an empty hallway.

A moan from her mother's bedroom answered her outburst, and Bailey tiptoed to the threshold.

"Mom?"

The room light was dimmed to barely on, and she could see her mother lying on the bed, a folded washrag across her eyes. "Mom? You've got a headache?" 'Cause if it wasn't a headache, and something bad had happened— Bailey's blood felt as though it could boil!

"Yes, hon, I'm sorry. One of my migraines. How is Ting?"

"She's fine, mostly. Really worried about her grandmother."

Her mother smiled wearily. "If you're hungry, there's some tuna casserole left. I'm sorry, I need to get over this headache, and I've got to go in to work tomorrow."

"Overtime!" said Bailey brightly. "That's always good." She entered the room quietly, lifted the washrag, and took it to the bathroom where she ran water as hot as she could stand it and wrung it out a few times before bringing it back steaming, and replacing it across her mother's forehead. "There, that should help."

"Thanks, baby," her mother said faintly, and then lapsed back into a limp heap on the bed, as if she could will the headache away by not really existing. Bailey closed the door nearly shut on her way out. Now was not the time to worry her mother further.

Tuna casserole was, like spaghetti, one of those refrigerator items that often tasted better a day or two later. She crunched up a few stray potato chips from a bag in the bread box, and sat down to eat, mulling over the day's events. From a magickal point of view, it hadn't been a good week, so maybe it was just as well it was Friday and nearly over. She thought a moment, then left a note to her mom that Trent's father had been laid off, just in case there were any openings where she worked. It couldn't hurt.

She checked her watch. She couldn't talk to Ting because . . . if her watch was right . . . Ting and she were in Jennifer Logan's backyard saying good-bye. *If* her watch was right. It couldn't be, of course, because how could she be in two places at once? Or want to be, with someone stalking her.

Unsettled, Bailey paced around her bedroom a bit before grabbing up the dullest book she could find. She read ahead in her classic novel assigned for English, found the dreary book putting her to sleep, and decided to settle Lacey in her cage and herself down for the night when the phone began to ring. She grabbed it up before it could rouse her mother.

"Little girl!" someone said at the other end. "Happy Birthday."

Just when she thought Friday couldn't have gotten much worse. She hadn't heard that voice in nearly a year and a half, and in a few ways, had hoped she never would again, even if that made her a really awful daughter.

"Daddy," said Bailey flatly. "It's not my birthday, and you're drunk."

"Is that any way to talk to me, punkin?"

"Maybe not, but it's true. It's late, and I don't want to talk to you."

"But ish . . . it's your birthday!"

"No, Dad, it's not. My birthday was weeks ago." And he hadn't even sent her a card. Too busy with his new wife and probably a new kid by now, too. "Why don't you just leave me alone?"

"I'm your father!"

"Why is it you're drunk whenever I hear from you? Once a year or so, that is." She glared into the dark of her bedroom as if he could see the anger on her face.

"Baby girl, your mother makes it very difficult on me."

"I don't want to talk about it. I am going to bed. Don't call back." And Bailey hung up, hot tears smarting in her eyes, for the things she wanted to say, and couldn't, and for the things she wanted to hear him say, that he never would.

It was the perfect end to a disastrous week, she thought, as she threw herself backward onto her pillow.

13

A TOUCH OF PEPPER

BAILEY staggered to the kitchen table at what felt like the crack of dawn, her alarm clock having gone off with a furious blast of music. Her note was gone, with another in its place. **Don't forget, you have a half day at school for testing today!**

She had forgotten. Just peachy. She had just enough time to bolt down a bowl of cereal, dress, and dash to make the bus. She could use her crystal to arrive, but there was too much chance of her being seen and causing a riot, or at least a lot of questions. She didn't even take time to sit down but ate her cereal right at the counter standing up. Lacey never stirred as she made sure the cage held fresh water, but it seemed best to leave the tiny creature home this morning.

Bailey reflected—when she finally got to the assembly hall, and waited as they passed the tests out and explained the rules about filling in the tiny areas with a number two pencil and not going on to another section till told, and that they'd be there till noon—that on the other hand, having Lacey would keep her from being bored to tears. Still, this was serious business and she swung her backpack between

93

her feet under the tiny dropdown desktop and tried to have
the proper expression on her face when receiving her test
booklet, scantron sheet, and number two pencil.

She sped through the sections and halted where instructed, bored and half asleep, until given the go-ahead to
start the next. Luckily once the last section was begun, she
could leave the minute she finished, and Bailey was one of
the first to hand in her test and bolt from the stuffy hall.
Outside, she took a deep breath. School buses stood waiting, but she hated to just go and sit, for it was obvious they
wouldn't leave till near full. It was a beautiful spring day,
with just a scattering of clouds. Sinking down onto the grass,
she sat cross-legged, and enjoyed the feel of the breeze and
sun on her face.

If she could manage it, she wanted to go to Jason's soccer game tomorrow. That meant a bit of planning on her
part, because Sunday was laundry day, and catch-up day,
and with her mom working today, it also meant a much
needed rest day. She hated to ask her mom to drive her
over and pick her up in the midst of all that. The temptation
to just use her crystal to go back and forth grew stronger.
After all, what could go wrong?

Bailey seemed to have sat on a rock, bruising her left hip,
and so she squirmed about slightly, resettling herself. The
obvious problem, naturally, was knowing where she would
be Crystaling to. She needed to either see it clearly, or have
seen it before well enough that she was fairly familiar with
it. Otherwise, she could get in all sorts of trouble transport-
ing. She could end up in some sort of parallel limbo where
things were almost as she had pictured, but *not quite*, and
she'd be lost forever in that in-between. She'd almost done
that once before!

Bailey shivered despite the warming spring sun beaming down on her. She could count on Jason to anchor her,
though, if he wasn't too busy getting ready to play, and
getting home should be no problem. The other difficulty
would be in getting permission to go without telling her
mom about the mode of transportation. Her mom could be
pretty trusting, but there were days when Bailey thought
she was facing the Spanish Inquisition! And there was no
way she was going to be able to explain this convincingly.

So, if not by car or her crystal, how was she going to get to the soccer game?

Kids had begun to drift out of the assembly hall and down toward the parking lots and buses. Bailey perked up. Hopefully, the downtown bus would fill enough so that the first one could leave. With a grunt as she hoisted her backpack and got to her feet, she noticed the teachers' parking lot beyond the buses. It was, as would befit a Saturday, nearly empty.

But not quite.

It wasn't so much the few cars parked there, but that a man sat in one of them, a nondescript Taurus, over by the treed edge of the lot. Or even that he sat there, when he should have been in the school working, if he was here on a Saturday at all, but that he sat there with great dark sunglasses on and yet he seemed to be watching her. She couldn't be sure of it, actually, except for the tiny fine hairs on her arms that seemed to be standing on edge, or the way his face turned as she paced by the school buses impatiently, and he reminded her of one of those paintings. The creepy kind, where no matter where you stood in the room, the eyes in the painting always seemed to be looking at you.

She darted behind one of the buses and waited a few moments. Then she peered around the back fender to see if she could catch a closer glimpse of the watcher from another angle. She couldn't, really, but she did see him moving restlessly inside the car as if looking over the growing crowd of kids beginning to mill around the quad, his head swiveling back and forth.

Bailey ducked back.

This really couldn't be happening to her. Who could it be? It had to be one of Brennard's Dark Hands, but why. What had she done to attract notice? Was it because of Jason or something she herself had done? Since a wolfjackal had come sniffing at her door months ago and been dealt with, she'd had no other sign, no problems at all. Maybe her luck was just due to run out.

Bailey reemerged, trying to blend into a group. From the corner of her eyes, she saw the watcher in the Taurus stop shifting inside the car, and fix his attention on her, as though she were a target and he'd suddenly been able to home in on her again. He *was* tracking her. Why, she had no idea, but that he was, she was sure.

She wasn't certain how she was going to get home without his following, but she immediately decided a bus was out of the question. Nothing like trying to be inconspicuous on a big fat yellow school bus. Her crystal jangled in its jewelry cage on her wrist. Buffeted by a growing crowd of kids who were now happy to be out of the test and eager to get home to lunch, she found herself carried along in a wave of T-shirts, backpacks, and denims. Bailey tossed a look toward the other parking lot. Whoever sat in the Taurus had opened the door and begun to swing out. Hidden eyes behind the sunglasses searched for her.

She had no time to lose.

Bailey took a deep breath. She darted between buses parked at the far end of the circle—empty buses—and cupped her crystal. *Home*, she thought desperately, as she looked into the amethyst. *Home!*

She had two crystal clear moments. The first was of being drawn into the purple facets of her gem. The other was of looking up, and seeing that what she had thought an empty bus was actually full of passengers looking down at her, their jaws agape as she vanished into thin air.

Bailey put her back to the door, bracing it. What had she done? She could see it now: Local Student Vanishes into Midair, Abducted by Aliens? Film at Eleven!

What to do now? What could she do? She didn't think the Dark Hand itself could have done much more damage. She sighed.

From the depths of her room came a metallic rattling and scrabbling. Lacey, usually nocturnal, seemed to be awake with a vengeance. Bailey went in to see what the matter was. The little pack rat sat on her haunches, vigorously cleaning her face and paws. She looked up with a soft chirr as Bailey appeared.

She undid the latch and reached in. Lacey immediately jumped to her hand and then scrambled up her arm to perch against the curve of Bailey's neck. She knew the small rodent loved cookies and bright objects, but there were many times when she felt as though Lacey also loved *her*. Bailey stroked her silky flank, making Lacey's tufted tail twitch a few times in pleasure. They stayed quiet for a few moments, and then Lacey's tail went stiff in fear. Bailey swung around on one heel.

Something trod down the outside hall. And fiddled with the apartment door, as though trying to decide if it were open or locked or could be opened. Not a knock. But . . . something else.

An intrusion.

Already in trouble or not, she had nothing else she could do. Bailey scooped up the pack rat and dropped her in her shirt pocket, and clasped her crystal tightly between both palms. She dared not call on the elders. Gavan and FireAnn were probably busy with Eleanora. Tomaz had gone who knows where for a while. She reached out wildly for Trent and Jason, and caught Trent in the net of her thoughts. That was no good. Trent had no Talent.

Bailey let her crystal fall from her fingers, its purple facets sending a soft lavender light over the closed door. She had never felt so alone. Lacey peeked out from her pocket, and gave a soft chirp. Bailey stroked her head gently, and the pack rat wiggled her whiskers before diving back to the bottom of the pocket. She could send Lacey out to take a look, if she could get the tiny creature out a side door, but they had none. The apartment door was all the entrance and exit and protection she had.

Why did she feel it wasn't enough?

The hall floor outside creaked, as if someone moved or took a step. Bailey inhaled deeply. This was not the first time she'd had an intruder at the door. Last time it had been a wolfjackal, noisily snuffling and clawing, until scared away. This time . . . this time it might be a member of the Dark Hand itself. She stared into her amethyst, and met nothing. It was as though something blocked her cry. She knew they were out there, but she couldn't reach out. Her call for elder help would go unheeded. That meant it was up to her.

And Jason and Trent and anyone else she could grab. There was no Magick that could ever seal away her friends. She cupped her crystal again, gazing deep into the planes of the rock, sending her thoughts spiraling after Jason. She Focused her gemstone until she found him, his image hazy, intertwined with Trent. The two had to be talking, which explained why she'd had a handle on Trent earlier. It was a package deal.

"Help!" Bailey cried through her crystal.

Trent could never get there on his own. He couldn't Crystal. But if something were setting up a magickal trap or net around her home, that he could see. He'd done it before. The Dark Hand couldn't hide their webs from Trent.

Trent stood blinking in her thoughts, a clear image even though Jason was not. The remains of a peanut butter and jelly sandwich dropped down the palm of his hands.

"Someone's stalking me."

"What the . . . Wolfjackals?"

"No, a man. He's been at school, everywhere, and I think he followed me home!"

"Get Jason! And pull us both through!"

Her hand shook so she could hardly hold her concentration. "I'm trying!" And then Bailey yanked.

14

ONE LUMP OR TWO, WITH A SLICE OF DRAGON

THE air filled with a prism, sparkling and shining in large waves, like windowpanes of color, and then everything went back to normal, leaving the two boys in its wake. Jason caught his balance, but Trent just gave Bailey a very baffled look, then put a hand to his ear and wiggled it, as if trying to pop it.

"This is so not my favorite way to travel," he said, and then gave a barely stifled yawn.

Jason put an elbow to his ribs. "I don't think you were invited."

"True." Both boys stared at Bailey. "How did you do that?"

"I didn't. I focused on Jason. You're just a bonus prize."

The taller and lankier of the two grunted and wiggled his ear again, then made a noise of relief as he half-yawned. He finished his sandwich, wiped up with a napkin that looked as if it had seen other sticky messes, and smiled with well-fed contentment. "There. About time." Trent stuck his hands in his jeans pocket. "What's up?"

Bailey's pocket wiggled. "I need help."

"We heard that coming through the crystal. What's

99

wrong?" Jason frowned slightly. He was still wearing his practice uniform, although he stood in his stocking feet with his regular tennis shoes dangling from one hand.

"The stalker is back. It has to be someone from the Dark Hand. I couldn't get Gavan or any one. My crystal was blocked."

"Blocked?" Trent raised an eyebrow as Jason swiftly bent to pull on his shoes and tie them. "I didn't know Brennard's crew could do that. But then . . ." he flushed slightly at his own reference to being relatively Talentless. "I'm always blocked, huh." He shrugged.

"Something brought you through with me," Jason said pointedly. "I didn't do it, and Bailey didn't. So, enough of that. You've Talent, but just don't know what it is yet." He rubbed his hands together, pausing. "Uhh . . . Bailey. I don't think it's anyone from the Dark Hand." He stared at the back of the apartment door as if he could see through it, then shook his head. "No. If there's someone out there, it's not anyone with Magick."

"How can you tell?" Bailey looked at Jason curiously. Her pocket flapped about vigorously as Lacey appeared, then ran up to perch on her shoulder, and curled up against her neck. The tiny squeaker watched them with shining onyx-colored eyes.

Jason shifted his weight. "I just can. Besides, if there was anything really bad prowling out there, she'd still be hidden in your clothes." He flicked a finger at the pack rat who began to busily groom her whiskers as if she hadn't a care in the world, and hadn't appeared to have been listening.

Bailey stood on tiptoe and peered out the little spy hole in the apartment door. "Someone *was* here. Honestly."

"I don't doubt that." Jason nodded at her. "But you're all right?"

"Outside of being nearly spooked out of my ponytail." Bailey settled back onto her shoe soles. "I think he might have followed me from the bus stop this morning."

"That's not good." Trent scowled.

"What'll I do?"

"Well . . ." Jason scratched his head and from the expression on his face, he had begun formulating some sort of plan. His mouth opened as if he'd finished just as the door rattled under a heavy THUMP!

Bailey jumped back with a muffled squeak and Lacey dove nose first back into her pocket. Perhaps it was Lacey who'd squeaked, no one had the time to decide.

Jason grabbed Bailey's hand, then Trent's. "Whoever it is, we're not waiting around to see if it's trouble!" He grabbed the crystal pendant around his neck and, with a cradle of all their hands, peered intently into it.

No rainbow of color like Bailey's teleportion, just a rush of cold air, and they were elsewhere. Trent stumbled a bit upon the ground as they alit, but he gripped Jason's hand tightly, and then all three were on solid footing, and Bailey let out a soft sigh of relief as she saw where they were. Fresh air, green grass down slopes leading to a green valley and a deep blue pond, framed by the oddly colored and jagged Iron Mountains. Jason was the only one who could bring the younger Magickers into Haven, for the Gate into the valley hadn't stabilized yet, although the Elders could, and had, brought them all there from time to time. Someday, a school would stand down in the valley, with the Iron Mountains as its backdrop.

Trent said, "Bubble, bubble, toil and trouble . . . when will we three be met again?"

Bailey rolled her eyes and laughed at his poor imitation of a witch from Shakespeare's *Macbeth*, but the color returned to her face, and she let go of their hands, though not before they felt her trembling. Trent and Jason traded looks. It was not like Bailey to let anything rock her optimistic view of the world.

She wrinkled her nose. "I really, really, don't like being scared." A toss of her head, ponytail bouncing, punctuated that.

"I can tell that." Jason beckoned down the trail to the clear blue pond nestled in the valley. "Let's go sit and talk a bit, then we'll see if the coast is clear."

The three of them trotted down into the small valley that was all they knew of Haven, and Bailey threw herself on a scoop-shaped rock that lay close to the water, poking out of the fringe of trees that ringed one end. Its bumpy exterior disappeared, moss covered in the darker, cooler grove. As she settled down on the sun warmed rock in a late afternoon that had given the landscape a warm orange glow, Jason looked about.

"Time," he said, "isn't the same here. Ever notice that?"

Trent nodded. He folded up and sat on a patch of dry grass, facing the lake which formed from a long, thin waterfall tumbling out of the mountain, its spray keeping most of the shore a little damp. "It isn't the same and it doesn't pass the same way. If we study here, I don't know if we'll stay younger or grow older. I've been trying to think of a way to test it."

Jason sat down too, checking the ties on his hastily put on shoes.

Bailey blinked. "Not get older?"

"Something like that. Or maybe we get older faster, but I don't think so."

She considered first Jason, then Trent, then shook her head. "I would have noticed that. You'd have sprouted chin hairs or something."

Jason blushed, but Trent put his head back and laughed. A startled pair of birds took wing and flew off as his voice broke the silence of the small valley. Jason hid his reaction by combing his fingers through his hair. "If time does pass differently here, then chances are your stalker will be discouraged and gone if we go back in a few minutes. The trouble is, how do we keep you safe after that?"

"Depends, doesn't it, on what we're dealing with? Dark Hand, someone following Bailey, or . . ." Trent paused and busied himself with picking strands of grass and braiding them into a grass chain.

"Or what?"

"Or something where we can't begin to know what we're dealing with. Maybe she's imagining something. Maybe someone from school is trailing her 'cause they're too shy to say hello. Or something." Trent did not look up from the strands he twisted through his nimble ringers.

Jason stared out over the valley, the pocket of land he'd found when he'd opened a magickal Gate. "That's just not good enough."

"Well, I know *that*." Trent looked up, grass lanyard dangling from his hand.

Bailey said, "You mean I could be scared over nothing?"

"It's not likely, but yeah, you could. Or something we don't want to deal with."

She frowned, her freckles seeming to dance over her nose as she did. "Like what?"

"Like someone who wants to know more about Magick and isn't magickal at all."

Bailey paled.

"I don't even want to think about that," Jason answered Trent.

"None of us do, but it's bound to happen sooner or later. I have less risk than any of you of being cooped up in some super secret government laboratory while they try to find out what makes me tick, but I'm in this as deep as anyone. So. We have to be careful, and we have to stay hidden and . . . we have to have a safe harbor somewhere."

"Someone saw me Crystaling. Maybe him. I'm almost sure." She knotted her forehead. "It may be too late already."

"You didn't."

"I was trying to get away!" Bailey looked at Trent in despair.

"What's done is done. We need a haven, and we need it now." Trent looked at Jason.

"I'm trying!" Jason bolted to his feet. "Don't think I'm not!"

"We all know you are. The point is, none of us is truly safe till that last Gate is opened. Iron Gate, Water Gate, and whatever it takes to stabilize our being here." Trent put his grass chain in his pocket, Bailey watching. He noticed her stare, and indicated the weaving. "It'll deteriorate at a certain rate. I want to see what it looks like when we get back, and how it dries out, and so forth."

Bailey grinned. "A walking scientific experiment."

Trent nodded.

Jason was not so easily distracted. He seemed to be trying to breathe steadily, every once in a while rubbing the back of his left hand. Finally, he let out an exasperated *chuff*, sounding rather like her beloved bulldog friend, Ulysses S. Grunt. "It's not Dark Hand. So, there's no reason why the crystal would have been blocked for calling for elder help, unless you were so scared, you just couldn't Focus."

"That's a possibility." Bailey chewed on the corner of her lip.

"But, on the other hand, Trent has a point. There could

be others out there, even more dangerous to us, people we haven't even been considering. We've all got to be a lot more careful with our Magick. The vows we took won't keep us from our own stupidity."

They all nodded in agreement.

"And ..." Jason took a deep breath. "I need help and I'm going to be asking everyone for it. We have to have some place to go ... and I don't think I can find it alone."

A deep rumble filled the air. Bailey started as if the ground jolted under her, her arms flailing wildly. Jason and Trent stared as her body ... her rock ... began to lift from the ground. She shrieked and grabbed for a piece of it that jutted up sharply next to her and hung on for dear life to the sun-warmed ... no, hot! rock.

"My ear!" a thunderous voice complained, and the rock tossed about, and then sent Bailey tumbling head over heels in a somersault to the ground, her mouth wide open in a soundless cry. The scoop-shaped granite wavered a bit, morphing into the triangular shaped head of a lizard. A very large lizard.

"A ... a ... dragon!" Bailey got out. She scrambled backward, stopped only by Trent's stunned and frozen body.

Jason stood, one hand still out in gesture, the great lantern eye of the dragon now fixing on him. "Don't move," he said. "Really. Just ... don't move."

The dragon's now sunrise orange-red body revealed itself, looped into the forest, his chin resting on the edge of the watery pool, a serpentine grin opening his toothy jaws. "It would be too late to move, anyway, if I were hungry." The beast flexed one taloned paw which moments before had looked like a tree's dead roots reaching down into the mud at water's edge. "Which I am, but not that hungry."

Bailey let out another shriek as if her throat had finally unfrozen. The dragon immediately swung his gaze on her, and hissed, steam boiling up, with the smell of sulfur. "Enough of that."

She snapped her mouth shut, her eyes getting very big. The dragon stared into her.

Trent managed to say, "Don't look in his eyes! Don't!" but it was too late. Bailey felt herself being drawn into those jewellike saucers, and for an eerie moment, she felt as she did when experiencing what it was like to be Lacey.

Only this was not Lacey. This was an immense, wise, and very old bescaled body lying upon what used to be a very pleasant area to sun oneself.

It is not that you should not be here, but that you should not be here NOW. Take yourself away to whence you came, and that other one with you, or great harm could come to all three of you.

Bailey gulped down a deep breath. There were more words, like a roaring surf breaking over the beach, but she didn't hear them, she experienced them, and she knew she wouldn't understand any of it till later, when she could be still and remember it. But that she did hear. *Leave now. Leave now and take Trent with you, or there will be disaster.*

And there was the picture of her apartment building hallway, and her apartment piercing her mind, and it was safe and clear and empty, and she knew it was all right to go. For now.

She cupped her amethyst. She held her hand out to Trent. "I have to go. We have to go." She looked into her crystal, wrenching her eyes away from the sight of the great orange-red dragon.

"But—" was all she heard Jason say, and then she whisked Trent and herself away.

Jason watched his friends disappear. He looked to the dragon.

"Hasty friends," the other said. "Too bad. I was going to invite them to tea." The beast laughed, forked tongue flickering in and out. "Just a light snack really."

"I never know," Jason said, "quite how to take you."

"Then sit a moment, and talk, for right now I am quite serious. And I cannot talk long, for I *am* indeed getting hungry and might forget myself."

Jason sat, taking the dragon's advice. He also took Trent's advice not to look the firedrake directly in the eyes. He wondered what dragons used to sweeten their tea with . . . one lump of Magickers, or two?

15

WARNING SHOTS

THE dragon put out a talon, stretching it from the scaled toe of its paw, rather like a cat might extend a claw lazily, stretching, yet still reflecting menace with its grace. So much power hidden, and yet a hint of it revealed to him with that movement. Jason caught himself staring at the highly polished surface, thinking that it must be able to cut and slash as if it were diamond. And maybe it was. He had no idea what dragons were made of.

The dragon settled then, putting his chin on that self-same paw, his eyes on a level with Jason's head, making it even harder not to look directly at him. Jason could feel the heat radiating from the orange-red scales. It was rather like sitting next to the fireplace, when the logs had gone to crimson coals, and were best for marshmallow roasting. He rather hoped he couldn't be considered a marshmallow.

"Now, then," said the dragon. "Insofar as I can read the expressions of one of your sort, you look a bit troubled to me."

Of the three of them, he thought he'd probably looked the coolest, what with all Bailey and Trent had been through. Jason sneaked a look at the mirrorlike surface of the pond, saw creases etched deeply across his forehead, and blinked in surprise. He looked . . . well, old. Like McIntire. Or his faint memories of his father. Yes, his father had had a knifelike wrinkle just like that across his forehead. He put his hand up and rubbed, just to check, and to see if he could rub it away. He saw himself do it, and felt his rough fingers, and the wrinkle stayed and obviously belonged to him.

"So it seems," he agreed, although sharing with a hungry dragon bothered him more than he'd let on, friends or not. Never was there a time when they visited that he was not aware that he sat with a vastly bigger and wiser and mostly unknowable being who tolerated him.

"And you come here looking for . . ." The dragon let his question dissolve into a low rumble, rather like a drawn out purr.

"Haven."

A muted thunderous chuckle. "I look safe to you?"

"Safe is not a word I'd use." Jason gazed along the serpentine body which now revealed itself threaded throughout the forest edging the pool, and he wondered how he could not have seen the dragon before. "You are awesome. But this place . . ." He beckoned along the valley's horizon. "I opened the Gate here, and it must have been for some reason. We need a corner of our own, and I think this is it."

"Forgive me if I do not quite get the history right, but isn't that rather like what the pilgrims thought when they came to the New World? All that land, and theirs for use as a Haven?"

Jason nodded.

"But let us not forget that continent was previously occupied, shall we?"

"Well. Um, yeah."

The dragon kneaded his claw a bit, pleased with himself, echoing the catlike image in Jason's thoughts. "So what threatens you?"

"The Dark Hand, for one."

"Sorcerers of opposing ideals?"

"In a nutshell, I guess that describes them."

"A balance of the Universes, Jason, my lad. For every up, a down. For every Light, a Dark. And so forth."

"Does that mean we have to tolerate them? Accept the fact they want to drain us dry even if it kills us?"

"Did I say that?"

"Well, no." Jason felt for a moment as if he sat on a slippery hillside and was trying unsuccessfully to keep from sliding down.

"Your own lands cannot stop this?"

"My own lands." He paused, then took a deep breath. "My own lands would probably crack us open like an eggshell so they could see inside to find out what Magick is."

"My." The dragon's forehead moved, as a scaly eyebrow rose. "You're sure?"

"Fairly sure. Nothing like Magick exists, except in dreams and fairy tales and wishes, for most people. Getting discovered is one of our biggest worries, I guess."

"I see." The dragon lifted its snout, and looked back to the pass where Jason came down from the Gate he had secured there. "Anyone follow you?"

Jason laughed. "No. Of course not." Then his laughter died in his throat, as he realized that was an honest question, not a dry remark from the beast. "No," he repeated quietly. "No one can follow." He left *yet* unsaid.

"You are a warrior?"

"Me?" Jason glanced down and then saw that he still wore his grass-and-mud-smeared soccer uniform, stained and sweat-marked from the day's practice for the big game the following day. He grinned. "Not exactly."

"Explain, then."

And for long moments, Jason tried to explain to the dragon the game of soccer, and for that matter, football and baseball, and sports in general. The dragon rumbled his questions back and forth. It knew about golf, to Jason's surprise, but the games had little comparison and so the two of them did not find much of a common ground. The dragon insisted that the sports Jason described was stylized warfare, with winning and losing sides and hostage taking (and sacrifices), and followers and alliances and so forth until Jason felt like surrendering himself.

"Maybe," Jason finally agreed, and sat back.

"Then," the dragon said firmly, "you are a warrior."

"Maybe."

"But for justice, not mayhem. There will be dark times

ahead, Jason, when justice may be all that separates you from the very forces you think you are fighting. Very, very dark . . . perhaps even fatal times."

"But justice will stand?"

"One hopes."

That sounded better than he'd expected, so Jason let the argument drop at that. He lay back on the grass, staring at a fluffy cloud that seemed to be wandering overhead, and felt the tension go out of his body. A warrior for justice. Yeah, he could accept that, both in soccer and against the Dark Hand. It might call for a lot from him, but he thought he was prepared.

"It is time," the dragon said. "You must go. I hunger, and for you, your world turns."

He sat, then stood. "Did I miss much?" Anxious, then, having forgotten how different time could be from one place to the next.

The dragon tilted its great head. "Lunchtime," it said thoughtfully. "And perhaps an afternoon snack." Its stomach growled in confirmation.

"Not food!"

"Is there anything else?" The dragon gave him a wide, sharp-toothed grin.

He supposed that there were times when even a great intellect gave way to a great hunger . . . and so should he!

The dragon got to its feet, and shook itself, scales rattling, as if loose armor plating, its body shaking with a tremendous clanking and clattering. "A game," it suggested. "Why don't you run as fast as you can back to Iron Gate and see if you make it before I . . ."

"Before you what?"

The dragon's eyes glinted sharply. "Get hungrier!"

Jason sprinted across the grass and up the slope to Iron Gate. He could feel the ground tremble and the heat wave across his back as the dragon chased him, and its laughter, as he dove headfirst through the Gate.

Dark Ties

HENRY stood by the washing machine, feeding in pairs of jeans, checking the pockets as he went and finding loose coins and even a dollar bill as he did. He piled up the booty on top of the dryer as he added detergent and softener, then started his wash. Not that he'd ever admit it to the guys, but he felt pretty good that he could do his own laundry. It was a big help around his busy house, where everyone had to pitch in or they'd all be buried inside of a week, he figured. With any luck, and if his toddler sister went down for a nap when she was finished with lunch, he could find a corner and read a bit or work on his D & D strategy for the next session with Trent and Jason.

And, with any luck, he'd stop hearing voices.

Henry leaned against the washing machine, letting its cheerful noisy intake of water and its chugging about fill his mind, instead of that whisper . . . that sly, cold whisper, he heard so often.

He felt tired. He felt like . . . was it Bilbo Baggins in the books and movies who said, he felt thin . . . stretched out? He felt like that. It was not a good feeling, and he'd tried to tell others about it who might understand, but there was no one who could help. How many people could he tell that he felt like a hobbit, huh?

Henry rubbed his eyes at that one, laughing at himself, then replacing his glasses carefully. That made him feel a bit better. He couldn't laugh at himself if he was going crazy now, could he? Could he?

Henry.

He gripped the edge of the washing machine. It was scientific. It didn't use Magick, couldn't think, couldn't do anything but mechanically churn and swish away. It didn't use crystals to work, and move through air, and light up dials . . . or hiss cold thoughts through his mind. Oh, no!

Henry. Don't think you can ignore me, Henry.

His blood felt icy. Why would he ever think that?

"Who are you?" he muttered fiercely. "What do you want from me?" He grabbed his glasses off his face again, the weight suddenly too heavy on the bridge of his nose.

You can't get away from me, Henry. I have you like a fish on a hook.

A weakness hit him, as if something had ripped him open and was draining everything out of him. He felt it flowing out and grabbed at his stomach, crushing his glasses. Barely standing, he leaned against the laundry room wall and felt everything begin to spin around him.

"What are you? Who are you?" he cried out desperately.

He couldn't be crazy. Because he remembered feeling like this before . . . at Camp Ravenwyng. Before, when Jonnard sucked all the Magick out of him and left him . . . almost like this!

He unclenched his fists. His glasses fell to the floor. He frantically dug his hands into his pockets, searching for his crystal. Gavan, someone, had to help him.

No crystal. Henry searched himself frantically even as his movements got more and more feeble. He could barely stand. Then, desperately and with blurred eyes, he spotted his crystal sitting atop a pile of loose change and crumpled bills on the dryer. He stabbed his fingers at it, and caught it up, sharp quartz edges digging into his fingers. Afternoon sunlight streaming through the laundry room lit it up like a fiery prism as he curled his hand about it tightly. Strength surged through him. He felt warm again suddenly.

For a moment he felt safe. Then he knew he wasn't, as

the strength and weakness warred inside him, a tug-of-war, moving back and forth until he could hardly think. He wasn't going to lose this time . . . he couldn't! The crystal alone would not save him.

Nice try, but worthless.

No, not worthless, it couldn't be. Henry shot his mind through his gemstone, calling to anyone who could hear him for help. He sensed Gavan slipping past him, as though too far away to reach, and Tomaz became a black yawning canyon in his mind, but there was Bailey, and then Jason, and he reached eagerly for them. He found them both, and Trent, too, in that place he knew as the Iron Gate Haven. Then he lost Bailey and Trent and had only Jason to try to anchor on, but his attacker wrapped around his thoughts tightly. *Speak of this and they will take your Magick again. Stay silent, my little Squibb. Silent.* Helplessly, Henry gave up. He sank back, unshed tears in his eyes, his fists clenched.

Jonnard sat back and felt Henry's despair as he tried to elude the bond between them. He braided and unbraided a tiny coil of golden rope he held in his fingers, his strong but slender hands busy as he tied Henry ever closer to his wishes. It was only a Focus, but an apt one. He had Henry tied forever to his powers and there was nothing the other could do, no matter how he twisted and turned. Jon had never thought when he first bonded with Henry to take his power from him, that there could ever be more to it, but he'd discovered that they were still synchronized, and that Henry's slowly returning Magick was just as vulnerable and easy for him to drain as ever. It gave him potential that even his father did not have. *That's it, little Squibb, go and find Jason for me. Find him because now is the hour of my first attack. . . .*

With that, he stood, and a shadowy figure behind him stood as well, radiating the icy coldness as a Leucator will do. Jonnard smiled thinly. He had Jason now, had him at the Iron Gate, and he should have known his rival would be there, probably trying yet again to find the third gate he needed to anchor that tiny Haven. Just as Jonnard obsessed about Jason, Jason obsessed about the Gates.

Jonnard's mouth twisted in a shallow smile. He crooked a finger at the Leucator. "It's time," he said.

The other looked at him with eyes that might as well be dead. It reacted little as Jonnard pocketed his golden rope and took the Leucator by the wrist as he summoned his crystal.

A door opened at the end of his rooms. Brennard's aura filled the room with power and anger before he himself appeared. Jon looked up.

"What are you doing?" Brennard's face looked like a storm cloud, his eyes dark with fury.

"I am, Father dear, doing what you need done. Jason Adrian will be mine, one way or another." He felt his crystal warm to his summoning and the channeling of his energies through it.

"We're not ready yet."

Jon felt his father's unspoken anger rumbling through the room, his aura spiking. So much more powerful than Henry or a Leucator, Jon mused. If only he could bottle it. Or tap it himself. Very quietly, very carefully, he reached a thought toward it and savored the pulse of it. His father neither noticed nor stopped him as he drank of it. The action both fed Jonnard and seemed to calm Brennard.

"Perhaps you are not, but I am. And with Jason out of the way, don't you think our paths will be much easier?"

"Fool! Destroy him, and you destroy my options."

"I don't intend to do that. I merely intend to . . . how do they say it today? I intend to own him."

"Stop."

A tingle spread through Jonnard's body. He melted into transport even as he answered his father, "Too late."

Jason tumbled headfirst through the Iron Gate, body surfing thin air, driven by the heat and laughter of the dragon behind him. The ground and grass and dirt brought him to a skidding stop, out of breath and laughing himself. He sat up, looking back, but there was nothing to see beyond the Iron Gate. It looked like a rusted, old metal gate hanging between two derelict posts, at the far edge of the Raven-wyng campgrounds. Except, of course, Jason knew that if he stood and opened it with Magick, he would see a dragon with flames dancing about, its merrily opened jaws laughing back at him.

He stood up to dust himself off. His stomach growled

slightly, reminding him that lunchtime, wherever he was, had been missed. His left hand let out a tiny throb, and Jason spun around. He saw nothing odd, yet—

He rubbed the pesky scar on his hand. It was rarely wrong. It wouldn't be the first time he'd been attacked at Ravenwyng, by the Dark Hand or wolfjackals.

Without word or other sound, with nothing more than an uncanny feeling, Jason suddenly knew he was no longer alone at the edge of the campgrounds. The skin on his hand prickled, as did the fine hairs at the back of his neck, and he turned around very very slowly . . . to find himself staring at . . . himself.

A rushing filled his ears. For a moment, he felt himself back at summer camp, with the hot sun overhead tempered by a slight breeze off the lake, as they sat on the ground and various benches, log stumps, what-have-yous, as Tomaz paced in front of them. "Magick," he said in his slow, deliberate voice, "has many shapes, and many shapes can hold Magick. And Magick can shift shapes. Of all those who can and do, shapeshifters, skinwalkers . . . the one you never want to face is yourself. We call those Leucators and they are splinters of your soul. They have but one dark desire, and that is to become one with you again, but because they are evil, corrupt, you must never allow that."

Bailey's hand had shot up, waving. Tomaz had looked to her, a slight smile tugging at the deep etchings in his weathered Navajo face. "What is it, Miss Landau?"

"Where did they come from?"

"They were made," Tomaz answered, "to hunt Magickers down."

Jason had shivered then, as he shivered now.

Jonnard Albrite, too, stood there, a chilling smile across his face, his arms crossed over his chest, as he leaned back against the Iron Gate rails. He lifted one hand slightly, and gestured. "Our battle begins," he said. "Now."

He had only a moment to notice the Leucator was dressed in jeans and a shirt, like and unlike him, with cold eyes that seemed to see nothing, yet fixed on him. As Jonnard moved his hand, the thing darted at him.

Jason did the only thing he could think of. He ran.

The lakeshore was knotted with scrub grass and loose dirt, and evergreens sprawled and twisted by wind. He took off through them, cupping his hand around his crystal and sending out a call of alarm to any who could hear. At his heels the Leucator slowly caught up, so near he could hear his own breathing, doubled as the other echoed him. He pivoted and cut back, and he could hear the Leucator slip on the loose dirt, go to the ground, roll, and get back up, sprinting after him. Jason grinned. It knew his moves, yes, but . . . it didn't have his heart. If this were happening on a soccer field, he could outrun him, outplay him, out heart him! It would take a pack of Leucators to corner Jason.

He circled around, not eager to let Jonnard out of his sight, not knowing what the other might be up to while the Leucator did his dirty work for him. The Iron Gate sparkled like a rusty jewel in his eyes as he raced back toward it, marred by the dark-clothed figure of Jonnard leaning against it. Although there was no way Jon could get the Gate open, the thought of him that close to it, of the possibility of his using it, made Jason grit his teeth in determination.

Stall.

Stay away from both the Leucator and Jonnard till help could get there. Surely Magickers would arrive at any moment.

A movement in the corner of his eye warned him. The thing reached for him, catching him, running chilled hands down his arm and Jason let out a yelp. It felt as though something cold squeezed his heart. He swerved sharply, out of range, and the Leucator gave a howl of disappointment. Jason dipped his head to run faster, anything, before that thing could touch him again! He felt as if it had tried to tear a hole into him from the inside out and attempted to crawl in—this thing that seemed as loathsome as last week's garbage, foul and slimy.

Get Jonnard and the Leucator out of here, and away from his Gate. Away from Ravenwyng and the sleeping Eleanora. Away from here and now.

Jason tripped over a hummock of tangled grass. The Leucator dove at him, his body brushing past him, and he gasped at the pain of the coldness sweeping through him. He sprang to his feet and dashed the other way, suddenly afraid. What if he couldn't shake it? What if it caught him?

Jonnard straightened, smiling widely, as they ran past, as if reading the expression on his face.

Was he going to allow that? No!

Jason doubled back and sprinted right at the Leucator, then went into a sliding tackle, both feet aimed high at the knees. Dirty soccer. He'd had it done to him, he knew how it hurt. There was a cold shock as they touched, and then the thing tumbled over, hitting the rocky shore of Lake Wannameecha headfirst. It flopped and then lay very quiet. Jason rolled to his feet, catching his breath, after a look at it, realizing it wasn't dead but knocked cold.

He spun about to face Jonnard as the other boy moved forward, still smiling, his hands coming up.

"I never figured it would do my job," said Jonnard lazily. He attacked.

A blur of punches and kicks drove Jason back. Some hit hard, but he kept dodging, and mostly flesh grazed flesh, although he grunted with the impact. He ground his teeth to Focus, to stay within himself, and do what he knew he could do, despite the fact that Jon was nearly a man grown, taller than Jason, with greater reach and strength.

And another Magicker.

He brought his shield up, a flare of light from the crystal hanging about his neck. It came without his touch, but in mere answer to his thought. Was it his imagination or did Jonnard's expression widen with surprise at that? No time to really think about it. He whirled away from the next assault, and brought a lance of Light into his hand as he did. It flattened into another shield, sizzling as Jonnard connected, and the other let out a yelp of pain and surprise, leaping away.

The moment of surprise gave no advantage. Jonnard dove back in, a dark rippling light now filling his own hands. He closed on Jason and as their shields touched, lightning sparked across them with a nose-burning smell of ozone and a deafening hiss. Both of them sprang apart, shaken.

Jonnard circled him slowly. Jason watched him. "Not as easy as you think," he said tightly.

"Nothing ever is." The black shield came up again, reaching out toward him like a razor sharp pincer.

Jason moved with him, dodging and striking back only when the other struck first. The Magicks screamed whenever they touched, an earsplitting howl that kept him flinching. And then Jonnard jumped him, carrying him to the ground. The breath went out of him and he lay, looking into a shower of sparks, light, and darkness all about him. He could feel Jonnard pressing down on him, but Jason held him back and it was easier than he thought. His shield spit in cat-like fury as he sat up and got to his knees, then his feet, Jonnard moving with him, but it was Jon now on the defensive. What could Jason hope to do? Drive him back somewhere . . . but where?

The sky split over them. Gavan roared in wordless fury, his wolfhead cane in his hands like a wizard's staff, sending both boys flying back and into the dirt and grass. Jonnard's shadow-dark light sputtered and went out, even as he reached out and put a hand up.

"Touch me and everyone here dies," managed Jonnard, his voice stronger than the expression on his face, his chest heaving with exertion.

"No doubt," said Gavan dryly. "I can feel your father's presence. But is it worth it? You'd be as dead as the rest of us. And your father, too, I wager." Gavan settled to the ground, cape behind him floating into soft folds about his form, and the crystal ball his wolfhead cane held muted to a steady white glow.

The thing behind them, the being Jason had dropped, stirred then, and made a mewling noise like a small, blind kitten. The Magicker's head snapped around.

"God's blood, a Leucator." Gavan's eyes narrowed at Jonnard. "You brought that abomination here? I will call an accounting for this—from your hide and your father's!"

"All's fair in love and war," hissed Jonnard. He stood then, and half-turned, then his booted foot shot out, catching Jason across the chest.

Jason doubled over in searing pain. He looked down and his eyes met those of the Leucator as it crawled toward him, hands gnarled in a greedy reach for him.

Jason rolled back, his shoulder rattling against the framework of the Iron Gate. *Haven*, he thought. *Safety*. And with that thought, the Gate opened and he fell through.

Not through, actually, he realized later. Into but not in, up against, but yet not across the threshold. He had no chance as the dragon came roaring out of the gate, Jason cradled against its chest.

Flame licked the air and everyone froze.

The dragon dropped Jason unceremoniously. It picked up the Leucator and tossed it . . . into nothingness. A slit in reality opened up and swallowed it whole, without a yelp or a scrap of cloth to show it had ever existed. Gavan raised his cane defensively, but made no other move, his face gone white as if knowing they had all roused some great, eternal fury.

"You shall not pass. Not again. The Gate is forbidden to you, to all of you!" the dragon thundered. "I am the guard and none shall pass me by. Now this. Your petty fighting, your petty wars will never cross my boundaries!" As it opened its jaws to roar its fiery anger, Jonnard made a pass with his hands and disappeared into his crystal, leaving only Gavan and Jason there.

Flame gouted and the dragon pointed his snout at the sky, painting the heavens with his fury, pouring forth anger in heat and fire until he was quite done, and then, and only then, did he lower his head to look once more at them.

Sadly, it repeated to Jason, "You shall not pass again."

Then it was through the Iron Gate, with a clank and a roar, and everything went still.

Gavan rocked back on his heels.

"What have you done?"

17

PACTS

"WHAT did I do?" Jason repeated, then inhaled sharply at the pain in his side, reeling back against the Iron Gate in an effort to keep standing.

"Aye, what did you do? Jonnard here, and the dragon." Gavan looked around, his shoulder length hair stirred by a wind caused by the passage of the angry beast, and only now settling down upon his neck. His eyes blazed fiercely crystal blue. "Ravenwyng is warded. Was warded. I threw everything I had into it to protect Eleanora, and the wards are shattered, worthless. It will take me, if I can even do it, quite a bit of effort to rebuild them."

He gazed into the sky as if he could see Brennard in front of him as well. "And what brought Brennard? I doubt if he needed to protect Jon. What were you meddling with? Had you opened a Gate that did all this?" He gestured wildly, then took a deep breath and folded both hands over the wolfhead of his cane, set it to ground and leaned on it, the emotion in his face slowly coming under control.

"How could I break a ward?" Uncomprehending, Jason stared, first at Gavan's face, then around him, as if he could see the shattered Magick lying about them, like splinters from a broken crystal. He could see nothing, of course, but he had almost expected to. "Gavan, I didn't try to do anything, except bring Bailey here for safety. We've come here before, the wards pass us by."

"Not this time. No one should have passed lightly, or without alerting me." Gavan took a deep breath as if still gathering himself, and rubbed his eyes wearily. "With Fire-Ann's help, I repaired the two immediately over Eleanora, but the others . . ." he shook his head.

"I'll help. Me, Bailey, Henry, Ting, we'll all help." Too late, he realized he'd left out Trent, but it didn't matter, Gavan gestured him away, dismissing his offer. Jason felt his jaw tighten. It was as if none of them were of any real use to the adult Magickers, nothing but a burden.

"Building a ward is a difficult task, Jason. It's a layering of Magicks, one over the other, and requires precision—"

"How would I know that? How would any of us? Have you taught us that yet? Do you let us work with you?" Words tumbled out of him, hot and angry. "Do you ever let us help? There are things we can do, you know, if you'd only let us try. And you keep things from us all the time, so how can we even know what we're capable of? You won't let us!"

They stared at each other, jaws clenched, angry, almost toe to toe. Then Gavan rocked back on his heels. "Magick is newly come to you, lad," he said slowly, as if trying to force a calm he did not feel. "A little patience would help."

"I don't think any of us have time for that." Jason caught a breath and forced it down, feeling almost shaky with spent anger.

"You're right, we don't." Gavan spun on one heel. He rubbed the wolfhead of his cane, and the crystal it held in its jaws flared with light. "Khalil. Isabella. I want you here, *now*."

And before Jason could say another word or take another breath, he stood with Gavan in the Gathering Hall of Camp Ravenwyng, with Isabella and Khalil both appearing at his heels.

Isabella gathered up the sweeping hem of a red satin skirt, glaring at Gavan. "Rainwater, your youth is exceeded only by your extreme rudeness. What is the meaning of this?"

Khalil still held an orange in one hand, and a small knife in the other, a neat ribbon of orange peel hanging down from the ripe orange fruit. He pocketed both objects in his robes and looked about, eyes narrowing. "Have you no sense, Gavan? This place is barely protected. What's happened to the wardings?" He pulled up a chair at the conference table, and sat down, staring at Gavan.

"I just quelled an altercation," Gavan answered, both hands wrapped tightly about his cane as if he'd rather they were wrapped about Isabella's neck.

"You don't summon me for an altercation." The elegant woman stretched her neck where her pulse ticked angrily as she put her chin up in disdain. "This is the height of arrogance, to pull me through whether I wish it or not. Surely you could handle a petty argument on your own."

Rainwater looked at her. He opened his mouth as if to retort, but Khalil interrupted him. "Quiet down, Isabella. You know better than that, and although it's obvious you had plans for the evening—" Khalil gestured a hand at her fancy gown and attire—"it's just as apparent something here has gone wrong. I suggest we listen a moment."

She looked daggers at Khalil then, and even raked her angry gaze over Jason who took a step back in reaction. "You have about two minutes and then I am leaving."

"I'll have as much time as it takes," Gavan answered her. "The attack was on Jason, by Jon and Brennard, and Leucators were brought to the Iron Gate. Less than a handful of us can create a Leucator and I've two of them standing in front of me." He looked from Isabella to Khalil and then back to Isabella. "I want to know why someone is working with the enemy."

"Strong words if true," Khalil murmured, but Isabella's face paled and she seemed at a sudden loss for words.

She groped for a chair, sitting down heavily. "He wouldn't have been so stupid."

"You did this? You worked with those who've sworn to see us dead to the last one of us?"

"What of it? I saw a chink in their armor. What can any of us do against the Dark Hand? Open warfare? Send us all through horrible agony like the last time? No, I used my wit and talent to infiltrate them." She glared back at Gavan.

"A Leucator is a hunter, not a spy. And all this time,

we've had no way to strike back at them because we did not know where they hid, but you did. You do business with them."

"They contact me through one of my investment addresses. I still have no inkling where Antoine calls home, nor is he likely to tell me. As for betraying you—"

All of them looked at her. She made an impatient movement of her hands. "Of course I made them for him, he paid quite well."

"Who paid?"

"Both of them, father and son. Brennard and Jon. I had no idea what they wanted Leucators of Jonnard for, but I figured if they would risk such foolishness, why not profit by it?"

"How can money be so important to you?"

Isabella shot a look at Khalil. "What? Do you think it's easy maintaining the estates I have about the world? Do you think time stands still while Magickers sleep? Time erodes all things, all havens, all monuments, all flesh. Who do you think hid most of us after the disaster, who paid for bribes and families to act as caretakers?"

"Your contribution is unquestioned, Isabella."

She glared back at Gavan. "And unappreciated, as well. No matter. I profited by it, and I enjoy the fruits of that profit." She beckoned with one hand, her fingers flashing with rays of color from a number of very expensive gemstone rings. "As far as the Leucators go, Brennard ordered one of Jonnard, for Jonnard's use. I didn't ask him how it was to be used, nor did they tell me. It expired. They ordered two more. It seemed harmless to me, and why not drain money away from them? Less mischief for someone else later."

"The Dark Hand never does anything harmless." The wolfhead gleamed in Gavan's hold. "The Leucator we killed was of Jason."

Isabella sat back in amazement. "No. That cannot be. I would not make a Leucator of one of us and give it to the Dark Hand."

"Someone did." Jason fought a shiver. "It tried to kill me."

"That's what they do," said Khalil quietly. "If allowed to get hold of you. Otherwise, they're rather like a hound running quarry to ground. They will hunt endlessly and tire-lessly, till they find their other half, and are most commonly used this way and only out of desperation. This is serious, Isabella, and I have to say I am disappointed you dealt with Brennard in any way, for any reason."

Isabella made a noise that could only be described as French scorn, and settled down to tapping her polished nails on the conference table's gleaming wooden top. Her perfume had settled over the room like a cloud and it tick-led at Jason's nose. He rubbed it to keep from sneezing, trying not to draw any notice as he did so. His calves ached from soccer practice and the fight, and he could smell him-self under the fancy aroma of the scented cloud. He had no idea what time it was at home, but his stomach knew he'd definitely missed a major meal and who knows how much time at home, or how much trouble that would cause. He'd almost forgotten that and now it gnawed at him.

"Where is the Leucator now? Does Jason need to worry about facing it again?"

Gavan shook his head at Khalil. "Dead, as far as I could tell."

Khalil stood, his desert robes rippling about him. "Good. I'd like a look at it."

Gavan cleared his throat. "It's gone."

"Hmmm. Too bad. A body might have been most useful."

"For what?" Jason felt the fine hairs standing up in goose bumps along his arms at the thought of it. He had no desire at all to see what he'd look like dead!

"To find out where it came from and who made it," Khalil told him. "If Isabella here admits to making them of Jonnard, why not of you? So it came from elsewhere, and that might be extremely important to know."

"Next one I face," Jason answered dryly, "I'll save for you."

A grin blazed across the Magicker's face, rather like the desert sun from the lands he lived in, and he raised a hand in salute as he stepped into his crystal and left.

Gavan frowned. "I wasn't done."

"It seems you are, for now." Isabella stood, the fabric of her gown rustling. "I won't take a dressing-down from you, Gavan, so don't even think of trying."

"And don't be so foolish as to think I'm not furious."

She put her chin up. "You need my support."

"Your support is one thing, your out-and-out betrayal is another!"

"Don't try my patience, Gavan." She rubbed a fingertip across her crystal in preparation for leaving.

"Isabella."

"Yes?" She paused in the act of using her crystal, to look back at Rainwater.

"You will let us know if you make any more, won't you?"

"Of course. As Khalil said, it will be important to know if another of us is making them. It might be even more important to know if any of the Dark Hand is capable of turning one Leucator into another." With that, she disappeared as well, in a swish of satins, leaving only her perfume behind her.

Gavan closed his mouth firmly.

"What did she mean?"

Gavan sat down, his face creased in thought. "I think, Jason, that she meant the thing can be twisted from one into another. I've never heard of such a thing before. If she's right . . ." He shook his head. "She can't be. The very existence of a Leucator is a mirror image of the soul. A truly evil twin. It can't be shaped into the twin of another. That flies against all Magick I know." He tapped his cane on the floor.

"I need to get home. I've a game tomorrow and parents worrying."

He took out his own crystal.

"Jason."

He looked at Gavan Rainwater, who seemed measurably older than he had that first day when they'd met only a year and a few days ago.

"Most of what you said was true. We've been neglectful, and I will try to . . . when things get sorted out . . . make it all up. And you are part of a family, here. A strange family, but a family nonetheless." Gavan smiled ruefully. He stood, and straightened his cloak. "It won't make everything perfect, but things will be better once we get the academy built. There's much to learn, but it's difficult to teach Magick since it comes from within, and it's as individual as each and every one of us is different. Do you understand what I mean?"

"A little. I suppose you mean that Magick can't really be taught, but has to be guided."

"Guided," Gavan repeated. He nodded. "You've got a good mind. That's probably an almost perfect way to describe it."

"About the school." Jason shifted his weight from one foot to another. "I don't know if we can ever go back. The dragon said we couldn't."

"It's your Gate. That gives you a power the beast doesn't have, whether it likes it or not. He may guard the Gate with all he has, but it's yours to open and close."

"You're sure of that?"

"Well." Gavan fidgeted a little. "Pretty sure." He put his hand on Jason's shoulder. "Watch out for Bailey if you can. My hands are full here with Eleanora. Be careful. Isabella hasn't betrayed us—yet—but that any of us would deal with the Dark Hand at all . . . I just don't understand it. There are pacts here, my lad, we know nothing of. The rest of us will help whenever we can, but we're stretched thin, and Tomaz has picked a bad time to be gone."

A pang of guilt arced through Jason, and he wanted to tell Gavan, but didn't. Instead he cupped his crystal tightly and went home.

18

STRANGERS IN
THE NIGHT

NO ONE missed him. For once, all the fuss over Alicia's
budding film career didn't bother him, for it seemed
she had received some important mail, setting off a frenzy
of activity in the McIntire household. The Dozer was at
work on-site, but Joanna and Alicia had taken off for parts
unknown, and his only clue was a torn-apart priority mail
envelope, large-sized, that lay on the kitchen counter and
had once been addressed to Alicia; kitchen dishes still out
from lunch; a plate of covered sandwiches in the refrigerator for him; and no sign whatsoever of the two females of
the house. Looking at the envelope, he noted that it came
from some organization that called itself Young Filmmak-
ers of America. Curiosity sated but not hunger, he poured a
large glass of milk and sat down at the nook and devoured
three sandwiches, the first so quickly he wasn't even sure
what kind of sandwich it had been.

The other two were turkey, avocado, and Monterey Jack
cheese and very good.

He cleaned up after everyone except for the remnants
of the envelope, in case the address needed to be saved.
Upstairs, he took a shower, wincing at the black-and-blue

marks emerging on his body. He'd taken a beating from Jon and the Leucator, that was certain. The only good thing about playing soccer the way he did, was that no one would notice the bruises. Then he dressed in some old worn jeans and a shirt and sat down, barefooted, at the computer to talk to Trent. His usually unruffled friend sounded aghast at all that had gone on after Bailey spirited him away.

Keep your friends close, and your enemies closer, Trent wrote. **Sounds like really good advice about now. And what about Tomaz?**

I don't know, Jason responded. **His family was one of the Hidden Ones. I don't even know how he found Gavan and the others, but I'd trust everything I have with him.**

Me, too, agreed Trent. **It's scary though. First Anita goes wrong, and now Isabella, maybe. Everyone seems to have their own agenda. We have our own pact, the handful of us, like the Musketeers. You, me, Bailey, Ting, Henry ... one for all, and all for one.**

Jason and Trent batted some ideas back and forth and came to no conclusion. Trent fretted about his dad and then signed off, saying they were working on résumés and he couldn't stay on the computer much longer. Jason sat back in his chair. He wondered if his dad were still alive, what they might be doing. He couldn't really remember what kind of work his father did. He'd worked in a large company, but doing what, Jason had never really taken the time to understand. It wouldn't be any help at all to say to Trent, "At least you've got a dad to worry about," because it wasn't the same, and he knew it. Just like he couldn't say to Bailey, "Don't make your mom worry about you so much!" He knew how lucky, and unlucky, they both were.

He rocked away from the computer and went through his closet, to make sure he had his gear all set for the game tomorrow. The late afternoon sun slanted heavily across the house, steeping part of his attic room in shadows. His meal sat in his stomach in a warm, comforting lump, and he fought being sleepy. One step at a time, one thing at a time. Time ... if only he had enough Time. If Fizziwig had had the Time to teach him, to tell him what secrets he knew about the Gates.

He fell asleep thinking about Ting and her grandmother

who was running out of time, and whose house dragon had hissed his name.

He woke to a quiet house and a dark room, his body all stiff and cramped in his chair. Yawning, Jason scrubbed a hand over his face. He stood and made his way to his bed. Moonlight caught the edge of a white object shoved through the crack of his trapdoor, and he leaned over to pull it loose. He had to squint in the dim light to read the words: DINNER IS IN THE REFRIGERATOR. WE DECIDED TO LET YOU SLEEP. A flowery "J" signed it.

Wow. He'd slept through everyone coming home, all the excitement, whatever it was, and dinner. And, from the sound of it, it was late enough that everyone had gone to bed. He eased his door open and down, taking the creaking stairs with quiet caution. A funny thought hit him as he did so. As he grew, and growing he was . . . would this door still fit him? When he went away to college, would this still be his room? It was an odd thought to have, and he shook it off. Dinner seemed more important than philosophical ramblings at this hour, because after he'd eaten, he had something he needed to do . . . and he needed the strength and alertness to do it.

The microwave told him it was nearly eleven, not awfully late on a Saturday but McIntire worked hard on construction sites, and so it made sense that they were all asleep by now. He ate his dinner cold rather than send the microwave into peeping fits as it reheated it for him. It wasn't bad, cold meat loaf was nearly as good as warm, and he liked the smoky sweet tomato sauce Joanna always made it with. The potatoes and green beans he ignored, but he scarfed down the chunky applesauce. For good measure, he cut himself another slice of meat loaf and made a thick sandwich out of it, wrapped it in a baggie, and carted it back upstairs.

Upstairs, he dressed warmly, pulling a thick sweatshirt over everything, and shoved a small flashlight into his pants pocket just in case he couldn't use the Lantern spell with his crystals. Jason patted himself down. What had he forgotten? Ah.

He sat down at his computer which still hummed quietly on his desk, and sent a quick message to Trent, informing him of his intentions . . . just in case. Then he turned the machine off entirely. He thought for another few long moments about what he was going to do, and if he should, and came to the same decision he had earlier, and pulled out the lavender crystal.

He'd found this crystal on a world where wolfjackals roamed freely. With it, he'd seen Tomaz, at least once. Now, he was determined to find Tomaz. Jason held the quartz tightly and opened his mind in search.

Bailey felt very alone after she took Trent back, but there was no changing it, so she caught up on homework and cleaned Lacey's cage, and then her room, making time till her mother got off work. The stalker seemed to be gone, and she tried not to look out the window or the door peephole more than six million times to check. Nothing and no one, and even Lacey had settled down, although nighttime was her active time. They played chase the cookie which was one of the pack rat's favorite games, although she preferred chase the sparkly barrette more. Tomaz, who trained her in animal senses, thought it funny a creature would prefer a colorful yet inedible treasure to food. It went against the grain of survival needs, he'd explained.

Bailey tickled the little rodent's chest. Lacey seemed quite plump, so she guessed she wasn't missing any meals! Lacey's tufted tail twitched as if she read Bailey's thought, and the pack rat gave a tiny *chuffing* sound. Bailey laughed. The little kangaroo rat sounded almost like Isabella on the Council when she got irritated!

A faint warmth and purr seemed to flow out of the amethyst Bailey wore and she touched her crystal in answer. Ting's face and voice sprang into her mind as she did so. "Bailey!" A smile spread over her features, erasing what looked to have been a worried expression. "I've been trying all day to reach you. I have to leave tomorrow morning. I was so afraid I wouldn't get a chance to talk to you."

"So soon?"

"I know, I'm going to miss Jason's game and, and, well, everything. But Mom has everything set up."

Focused exclusively on her crystal, Bailey stepped into that plane where Ting was and just wasn't, and hugged her. "You won't be that far away."

It was like hugging a ghost. Something was almost there and yet not, for both of them, and Bailey tried not to shiver.

Ting brushed a long strand of shimmering coal-dark hair from her temple. "It's the worst possible time for me to go."

"There's never a good time," Bailey said. "I know it seems worse, because of Jennifer and Eleanora, and stuff, but there's never a good time to say good-bye to friends. At least we have a way of staying really close. Lots of people don't have that."

"I know." Ting put her hand out, palm up, and touched it to Bailey's matching hand, briefly. The bracelet on her ankle shimmered. "Oh! I made you something. Father said he'd mail it for me."

"What is it?"

Ting grinned. "I can't tell you, it's a surprise!"

"You know I can't wait for a surprise."

"You're going to have to," teased Ting gently. "All right then . . . one hint. Keep it away from Lacey."

"Oh, you made me some jewelry!" Bailey gave a little bounce.

"I hope you like it."

"I know I will. I'll Crystal to you soon as I get it."

"All right." Ting frowned again. "Grandmother went into the hospital yesterday for her treatment and felt so ill they kept her overnight."

"You see? She needs you."

"I know she does. I know. But, Bailey . . ." Ting's voice trailed off.

Bailey looked at her, and saw her friend's lower lip quivering a little as if she couldn't get the words out. "What if she's dying?" Bailey said for her.

Ting nodded.

"First of all, she's not. Not yet. She's got years, even as sick as she is. And second, well, she's got Magick, too, and that's a gift the two of you can share with each other. It'll mean a lot, and probably give her strength right now."

"You think so?"

"Well. I can't promise it, but yeah, I think so!"

Ting smiled. "I guess that's good enough for me."

"Half a cookie is better than none, as my grandma always used to say. And twice as good as a bundt cake."

"Oh, Bailey!" Ting broke into laughter then. They

hugged again, and then Bailey let her concentration on her crystal go, and both of them faded back into their own realities.

Bailey tucked her legs under her and curled up, one shoulder next to Lacey's cage. She turned the TV on, clicking the remote over and over. It wasn't fair that Ting had such awful things to worry about, and Bailey didn't dare tell her about any of the strange things she'd been experiencing. That would have been asking too much of Ting's gentle nature. Bailey finally settled on the Discovery Channel, with one of its wildlife programs, and she sat watching until a key rattled in the apartment door lock and her mother finally walked in the door.

"Why such a long face?"

"Ting's leaving tomorrow. She's going to miss Jason's game, and everything."

"Ah." She gathered Bailey into a warm hug. She smelled of the office, faintly of cigarettes, and coffee, and ink from the copying machine, and she sounded tired. But her arms felt strong around Bailey, and she whispered into Bailey's ear, "I received two free movie passes today, and I thought we could go tonight . . . if you want to."

"What movie?"

"*Kiss Me Again, Kate.* It's a remake of an old musical. Should be funny, with lots of good singing and dancing." Rebecca Landau fished out two colorful pieces of cardboard and waved them through the air as proof.

"That would be great!" And welcome. Anything to get her mind off things. "Are we eating there?"

"We can grab a sandwich across the way at that tea shop, okay?"

"And popcorn?"

"Definitely popcorn. And . . . Junior Mints."

"Wahoo!" Bailey ran to get her jacket. Lacey made a lot of rattling noises in her cage, and Rebecca stuck her finger in, and stroked the animal's side softly. "You get her all day, don't fuss at me."

Lacey dove headfirst into her pile of shredded tissue and wood chips, jerking her tufted tail in after as if insulted. Her mother stifled a laugh as Bailey dashed back in, carrying two jackets.

"Ready?"

"Am I!" Bailey bolted to the front door, and her mother followed after, still chuckling.

For dinner, they split a meatball sandwich with melted mozzarella that hung in strings from their mouths no matter how daintily they tried to eat, and an iced tea that came with two cherries and a slice of orange on a toothpick floating on the top.

"*Two* cherries," beamed Bailey and promptedly claimed one of the maraschinos as her own. "How did they know?"

"How indeed," Rebecca answered, and winked at the girl who had set the sandwich down in front of them.

The movie unfolded in marvelous color and song and dance and costume, and the two of them sat enchanted for nearly two hours till it was over, and Bailey slumped back in her comfortable movie seat and hid a yawn. Rebecca tried to hide her own, but couldn't. She leaned over and kissed the top of Bailey's head.

"One of the best Saturday night dates I've had in a long time. But I think the best thing now would be to go home and snuggle into bed."

Bailey yawned a second time. "I second that," she said. Then, "Any Junior Mints left?"

"Enough for you to have one on your pillow."

"Ew. They were getting kinda warm and gooey."

Rebecca Landau broke into laughter as they strode through the theater lobby and out into the cold, brisk early spring night. Car headlights blinded both of them slightly as they rounded the corner to the theater parking garage. Bailey thought she saw something, a shadow, behind them, but when she turned to look, another car cruised past and she could barely see anything beyond it, except the brilliant neon marquee for the multiplex.

Rebecca reached down and caught her hand. "Just think if everyone sang everything." She cleared her throat. "Baaaaailey. Where do you think we parked the car-aaar?"

Bailey turned two shades of red as other moviegoers passed them by, but she sang back, "Motheeer. I believe it's over heeere!"

They rushed the car and got inside it before anyone else could think them crazy, laughing so much they could hardly get their seat belts buckled. The car eased out of the garage, its engine chugging away and its heater soon pumping in warmed air. Bailey hunched into her jacket, feeling the cheer bubble over her, most of the past week's worries gone away.

They parked in their reserved spot at the apartment building, and Bailey bounced out first, calling dibs on the last of the Junior Mints.

"Not fair!"

"All's fair in candy and war!" Bailey informed her mother. She grinned mischievously over the car at Rebecca.

"Don't I get even one?"

"Oh, all riiiiight, most excellent motheeer," sang Bailey. "Just one!" Bailey did a little pirouette for emphasis. She stopped, gasping, rooted to the ground, as a dark, lanky figure reared out of the shadows. Her breath stuck in her throat as the man reached for her, and then she jarred her voice loose. "Run, Mom! RUN!!!"

The stalker was there, right there, closing on her. Bailey couldn't get another word out, couldn't breathe, as his hand stabbed through the air after her.

Rebecca Landau stood in shock. "Bailey—"

She dodged from the man at the last possible second, slamming her hip into the car fender. The pain wrenched her voice loose. "It's the stalker, Mom! *Run!*"

Rebecca Landau's face sank into fear and worry. "That's not a stalker, hon. That's . . . your father."

19

SURPRISE!

SHE ought to learn to listen first and use her crystal later, Bailey thought a moment too late, as she grabbed her mother's hand, rubbed her amethyst, and suddenly the two of them landed in the hallway outside their apartment door. Sometimes there just wasn't time to think like that! But she had to have been wrong, that couldn't have been her father. Her father wouldn't have *stalked* them.

Her mother paled. "Bailey . . . what on Earth just happened. . . ." She looked around in disbelief, nearly stumbling back a step.

"You blinked."

"I blinked?"

"You blinked and missed it. We ran for it." Bailey let go of her mother's suddenly cold hand and dug through her jeans to fetch her key out. The door key seemed to have a mind of its own, much like her little pack rat, and kept disappearing into deeper and deeper folds in her pocket. Finally she curled fingers around it stubbornly and got it out and in the lock. There it resisted her even more and managed to jam once or twice before turning smoothly and clicking the lock chambers into place.

Bailey put her hand on the door to push it open.

"Stop right there!"

Bailey froze, her heart bouncing inside her chest as if it were jumping rope.

"I don't know what's going on here," came a harried voice from behind them. The stalker slid to a stop in the hallway, polished floorboards squeaking under the soles of his shoes, and he pointed a shaking hand at Rebecca. "What have you done to her?" He paused to catch his breath. He must have taken the stairs in two-at-a-time leaps.

Bailey could almost see her father in the stranger. But she heard him clearly in the voice, loud, unhappy, accusing. She shrank back against the apartment door.

"Get inside, Bailey," her mother said tightly.

"Witch! You've made a damn witch out of her!" The shaking hand settled into a point, aimed right at Bailey's forehead.

"What are you talking about?"

"I don't know what else to call it."

"Inside," Rebecca ordered her firmly.

"Not without you."

"This isn't a democracy. I'm your mother, now go."

Bailey set her chin, and shook her head. The apartment door began to swing in anyway, creaking open behind her.

"I'm taking her back," Jerry Landau told them. "Before it's too late. I don't know—I can't explain what I've seen—but you've made a witch out of her."

Her mother looked down at Bailey, one eyebrow quirking in an unasked question.

"I'm not a witch. I'm ... I ... I ... I ..." Bailey's throat locked up. She couldn't get another word out, and she clenched one hand in fierce frustration. The Vow of Silence! She couldn't tell even loved ones, let alone enemies, what she was! She had no defense.

Rebecca put her hand around Bailey's. The crystal in her palm flared slightly with renewed warmth, and that made Bailey jump slightly in surprise. Her mother and father stared at each other from across the apartment building hallway, but Bailey had the feeling it might as well be across the world's deepest chasm. She'd never seen them fight when they were still a family, but she'd seen many nights of her mother crying, alone, after he'd stormed out.

"I have a restraining order," Rebecca told him. "I want you to leave."

"I have an order in process to take custody," he answered. "I've had her watched, followed, and I've seen it myself as well. She leaves here at all times of the day and night, while you're at work, while you're sleeping. Do you even know where she goes? She goes to hang out with boys, several of them. And I've seen her disappear into thin air. Not once but a number of times." Her father narrowed his eyes at her. "I don't know what you've been teaching her, or maybe it's those friends of hers, but she'll be better off with me, before it's too late."

"Too late for what?"

"To be a decent person. She's a freak, Rebecca, like you."

Bailey started to lunge forward, but her mother's hold stopped her, but couldn't contain the words tumbling out of her throat. "Don't talk to her like that! She's the best mom in the world. We don't need you here, we don't want you here!"

"Ssssh," said Rebecca soothingly, and pulled her back against her body, her free hand brushing Bailey's hair back from her forehead. "I won't argue with you in the damn hallway. You want to try to get a court order, go ahead. I'll fight you every step of the way. Bailey's an outstanding student, and she has good friends, and there isn't anyone who can say otherwise. So bring it on, if you're going to. Otherwise, stay out of our lives. You wanted one of your own; you went and got it, and you're not welcome here." Rebecca took a deep breath, and Bailey could feel it shuddering all the way through her mother's body as they leaned close together. "Get out of here before I call the police. I've still got a restraining order."

"We'll see about this."

Bailey could feel the air crackle, as her mother began to draw her back into the apartment doorway, repeating, "Like I said, bring it on. If you can. Now go!"

The crystal went hot in her hand, in their clasped hands, and Jerry Landau reeled back as if shoved out of the way, freeing them to fall into the apartment and slam the door shut. Through the wood, they could hear his muffled shout. "I'll go, but I'll be back!"

Rebecca fumbled at the dead bolts, and the main lock, then stood, her face whiter than white, as she looked down at Bailey. She rubbed her hands together, the palm of one pink as if sunburned.

"What was that? And you have to tell me, tell me now, or I don't think there's any way I can protect you from your father."

Bailey stood, her jaw slowly dropping, as she stared back into her mother's shocked face. She didn't know what it was either, but the crystal had answered, to both of them. "I . . . don't know what you mean."

Rebecca Landau, her back to the now barred apartment door, slowly slid down it to the floor, and put her face in her hands. Voice muffled, she said, "Bailey. I haven't got the money to fight him in court, not if he really makes a fight out of it. Honey, I'm gonna lose you!"

"No, you won't. We'll think of something."

Rebecca looked up. She wasn't crying, not yet, not quite, but her nose had reddened slightly, and her eyes were very bright with unshed tears. "We always do, right?" She paused. "The boys he talked about?"

"Jason and Trent. Mom, you know them!"

"You know you're not supposed to leave the apartment when I'm at work."

Embarrassment flooded her face. "Things . . . happen. It wasn't anything bad, all right?"

"Then what was it?" Rebecca reached out, took Bailey's chin in her fingers gently and tilted her face up, so they could look into each other's eyes. "I've seen things, too, honey. Strange things I can't explain, but because I know you're good, I never worried. I have to worry now, because if I can't fight your dad, I'm going to lose you."

"I haven't done anything wrong!"

"I don't think you have, but I don't think you've told me the truth, either. Now, you and I both know I didn't take a long blink. How did we get up here?"

"We . . . ran?"

"I don't think so." Her mother leveled both eyebrows into a frown, drilling her gaze into Bailey's.

There was no way she was going to be able to answer, no matter how badly she wanted to. Oh, to be like Ting with a grandmother of the Hidden Blood, and with whom she could share some of her wonderful secrets. Bailey swallowed, as if that could loosen the throat lock she was going to feel.

"I can't tell you."

"Can't or won't?"

"Can't."

"You're sure?"

Bailey tried not to squirm. "Pretty sure. I've tried to tell you before."

"Anything to do with your tutor from school?"

Eleanora had dropped in once or twice, under the guise of a school tutor. But Eleanora looked far from ordinary, and although she and Rebecca Landau had hit it off, Eleanora had decided that she could not risk drawing any more of Rebecca's attention. "Mom, I can't tell you, but it's nothing bad!"

"It's bad if it allows your father to take you away."

"He called a few days ago, late. He was really drunk again. It's not the divorce that makes him a terrible father, it's just the way he is. He wasn't good when he lived with us, and he's not good now." Bailey sighed. "I don't want him to have custody. If he gets it, I'll run away."

"Then they'll put you in a foster home, eventually. You can't run from this problem."

"Oh, yes, I can. They'd never know where to look." Once Jason had Haven open, she would never be found if she went there. Never. Not unless she wanted to be found.

Rebecca lost control of her tears then, and they cascaded slowly down her face.

"I wouldn't run from *you*!"

"Oh, Bailey!" Rebecca put her arms around her daughter and pulled her very close in a comforting hug. "Promise me you won't run away."

"It won't be running away. It'd be another home, only for Magickers—" Bailey stopped in shock.

"What did you say?" Rebecca pulled back and looked at her.

"I didn't—" She couldn't have, could she? "I didn't say anything."

"Magicers? What on earth do you mean?"

"Magickers," corrected Bailey, and took a deep breath. Her mouth didn't snap shut and stay that way, her lips didn't feel like they were glued shut. She blinked. "Magickers! Mom . . . I can say it. That's what I am, I found out last summer at camp, I'm a Magicker." She paused a moment, waiting for the world as she knew it to end. Nothing happened.

"What are you talking about?"

"It's what I do, it's what I am. I can . . . I can talk to Lacey." Bailey bolted to her feet, skidded around the corner to her bedroom, and came back, pack rat in hand. "It's part of my Talent, animal sense. I can make friends with them." She put Lacey down. The furry little rodent twitched her tufted tail once or twice, then sat up and looked at them, in between grooming her long, slender whiskers. "Lacey, go run to the kitchen and bring me back something shiny."

"Bailey . . ."

"It's okay, Mom." Bailey quirked a finger at the pack rat. Lacey twisted away from them, running along the baseboard of the apartment, and disappeared in the general direction of the kitchen. "She'll be back in a few minutes, soon as she finds something."

"What if she doesn't find anything?"

"Mom! She's a pack rat! She can find stuff we don't even know we've lost."

"All right. Now. The long blink?"

"Oh, that! That's Crystaling." Bailey held up her bracelet, with the cage dangling, and her amethyst shining through the thin, spiraled bars. "It's like a . . . a wand in Harry Potter, I'd guess you say. Only I don't have to waggle it and say something in Latin. It's a Focus for energy. I can teleport short distances, if I know exactly where I'm going, and I've trained well enough. Beam me up, Scotty!" Bailey finished with a wide grin.

"And you brought me with you?"

"Yeah. That was hard, made me kind of dizzy. I guess it helps when the person with you knows what you're doing and can't fight it, even self-consciously."

"Unconsciously."

"Whatever."

The sound of claws on the wood flooring interrupted them, and Lacey came barreling around the corner, a flashy piece of tinfoil in her mouth. She skittered up to Bailey, climbed into the hand held down to her, deposited a silvery gum wrapper in her palm, and made a satisfied chitter, as if she'd found a great treasure. Which, to a pack rat, she had. "Good girl," Bailey said, and rubbed her chin. The pack rat grabbed back the foil and tucked it against her body before climbing up to Bailey's shoulder and resting in the curve of her neck, holding on tightly to both her treasure and the shirt collar.

Rebecca leaned back against the wall as if even it might not be strong enough to support her. "And a Magicker is . . . someone who works . . . magic?"

"Exactly."

"That's not possible."

Bailey pursed her lips and made a guppy mouth for a moment in thought. "Well, Gavan explains it this way . . . Magick is derived from rarer laws of physics, many of which are incompletely understood or not discovered yet. Rather like genetics. A family of brown-eyed people can have a blue-eyed child, but it's a recessive gene and you might have to go back several generations to find the parent who had it originally, but it's still in the bloodline."

"Like that?"

Bailey nodded, her ponytail bouncing enthusiastically. "Something like that."

"Is there any limit to what you can do?"

"You mean, like, what's my kryptonite?"

"Sort of, yes."

"Oh, there's a lot we can't do. It depends on our individual Talents, and our stamina and energy, and concentration, and training."

"Ah." Rebecca let out her breath, and rubbed at a faint wrinkle across her forehead. "For a moment, I was hoping you could conjure up a lawyer to get us out of this."

"No. And I can't tell anyone I'm a Magicker either. We took a Vow, to keep the others safe. I mean, who wants to be dissected to find out how we do it, right?"

Rebecca shuddered. "Right." She put her hand on Bailey's knee. "Honey, somehow I think we just jumped from the frying pan into the fire. There could be a lot worse problems than your father trying to get custody."

20

MOONDANCE

HENRY slowly thawed. He had no other way to describe it. The feeling of thawing out crept over his body, leaving behind it the pins and needles of muscles and nerves awakening, and the awful chill of having been colder than he could ever remember. The terrible moment of anchoring to Jason had been followed by a near total nothingness. He remembered dragging himself upstairs to his room, complaining of a headache, then collapsing onto his bed. Night veiled it now, and he must have slept or been unconscious for hours. He hugged himself for a moment, then reached for his crystal, the citrine of yellow-red colors, and brought up the Lantern spell, bathing his darkened room in warm orange color. And it *was* warm, too, although his Focus should have only been for light, but he'd always had trouble keeping heat out of it.

He remembered with embarrassment the times in study when he'd worn one of FireAnn's oven mitts just to avoid burning himself whenever his crystal had exploded into flame as he'd tried for simple illumination. Now though . . . now the flame-warmed depths of his gemstone felt heaven sent. He held it tightly to his chest, feeling the delicious heat

141

bathe him until his teeth finally stopped chattering and he could wiggle around, trying to stomp out the funky pins-and-needles feeling. He gestured his hand over his crystal then, shutting off the Lantern spell, as he sat up.

That *had* been Jonnard in his mind. Had to have been, couldn't have been anything else, unless he was crazy, but now Henry wondered. Being crazy didn't leave you limp as a rag and frozen, did it? But having your *Magick* drained from you did. *That* he remembered. Jonnard had done it before. And somehow, Henry thought frantically, he was doing it again! Squibb, you're not insane! Not yet, anyway.

That made him feel a little better. Not as good as the Light and Warmth spell, but better. The well-being didn't last. A sharp, sickening cramp seized him, like a fist grabbing him and squeezing him. He couldn't tell anyone. They wouldn't be able to help him and they might take what little Magick he had away from him again. He wrestled with that horrible thought. He *had* to be able to tell someone, didn't he?

He scrubbed a hand over his thick black hair, sending it in every direction, no doubt. He had to *think*. He should tell the older Magickers what was happening. They might be able to shield him. They ought to. On the other hand, if Jonnard had managed to reconnect to Henry, it made Henry a possible spy within Gavan's group. What if Jonnard had found a way, not only to tap Henry's Magick whenever he wanted, but to look around through Henry's eyes? Hear through his ears? To *spy* on the others anytime he wanted, without being caught, until Henry dropped in his tracks.

No. No, no. If Gavan and the Council knew that, they'd never trust Henry again. Not as long as Jonnard and the Dark Hand were a threat.

He had to tell them, didn't he? They'd be furious with him if he didn't.

And suspicious.

Henry sighed. He scratched his head. One of them might be able to help. Maybe FireAnn had a potion or something he could drink and it would block his thoughts from Jonnard. Or maybe Gavan could put a damper on his crystal. Or maybe Tomaz could fix him one of those neat fetish bag charms to wear like Jason often wore.

Or maybe they'd just make him drink that awful stuff again and shut him away from ever Magicking.

Neither prospect sounded good, but they might be better than letting Jon pick at him, unravel him, till there was nothing left, like some bony old scarecrow in a raggedy outfit. He needed to think about it, what he wanted to do, what he should do, and what he might expect. He hugged himself tightly, fighting off the last bit of cold.

He wanted to remain a Magicker. He just didn't know right now if anything he did would allow that. After being forced to give it up once, he didn't think he could stand to go through that again. He couldn't ask Bailey or Ting what to do, because he'd be putting them into the same dilemma he was facing, whether to tell or not, and how to handle it. He couldn't put them in jeopardy. Jason or Trent might be more helpful, but they always seemed up to their necks in trouble with the Dark Hand as it was.

He had the eerie feeling that anchoring on Jason, rather than protecting Henry from that awful thing that was happening to him, had led the Dark Hand to the Iron Gate. What if he had somehow sent great trouble to Jason? What if the thing in his mind had left him only because, linking to Jason, it had found better, more important prey?

No, for the moment, he was in this alone. Till he knew what he was dealing with and how to strike back at it, Henry decided.

Somewhere outside his room, the world returned to normal. He could hear his toddler sister fussing in her bedroom. That he could handle. He got up and padded down the darkened hallway to her room, so his mom could sleep a little. It was either a diaper or bottle emergency and after what he'd just been through, he had no doubt he had the answer to *that* problem.

Jason felt a cold wind shear past him even as he stepped through his lavender crystal. It burned at his ears and nose and exposed throat and as soon as he could, he put the hood of his sweatshirt up and shoved hands and crystal deep into waiting pockets. The time shift here was not as obvious as expected, it was the dead of night on this world, too, color and shadows in shades of grays, blacks, and purples, and he wondered if there was ever a daytime here for he'd never seen one. But then, he'd only been here two or three other times, and all of them when he could sneak away, so if they ran in parallel, it would be nighttime here too. Still, it gave him the creeps. The moon overhead was not the moon of his time and place. It hung like a silver-bladed scimitar, low and curved and remarkably large in the sky, as though it could slice out and behead him.

Jason turned on his heel. This was the world where he'd found Gregory the Gray's crystal. The world where wolf-jackals seemed to roam freely and, indeed, the place which might be their home. The world where, when he tried to contact Tomaz, he seemed to see him. All of which did not make him feel particularly good or safe. He hurt where the Leucator had grazed him. His skin burned with an icy cold-ness, and his body ached where Jon had pummeled him.

He'd had worse bruises and injuries in soccer, and he'd garner more the next day, but he hated to go into a game already aching. He'd no choice and it wouldn't slow him down, not with his teammates depending on him, and the fierce joy of the game awaiting him, but he moved deliber-ately and carefully now. In the darkness, he couldn't afford to slip on an unsteady stone and wrench a leg or knee, lam-ing him. That would be unthinkable.

He picked his way down a slope where what looked like grass crackled under his feet like brittle frost, and from the sharpness on the evening wind, just might be. A tree reared up with stick branches hung with icicles and black skin wood, looking far more dead than alive. Surely this world had a spring awaiting it . . . didn't it? It would have to have a cycle of life and rest and seasons, wouldn't it? The wolf-jackals, if they ranged here, would have to have food, and that prey would have to have food or vegetation to support it and so on. Nothing just existed.

Or did it?

Jason picked his way over a frozen brook, little more than a stride wide, cut into the bottom of the slope. He stepped onto a vast, open field, and imagined what it might be like at the height of springtime. It was nearly the size of a soccer field. Would it be filled with grass and grazing ani-mals? Flowers? Small rodents tunneled into freshly turned soil, and birds pulling worms out of the ground, and bees drawn close by nectar. Now it was nothing more than a darkness around him, flat and almost mirrorlike as if frozen like black marble.

Jason slowly turned about, casting his gaze over the desolate scenery. He could see from where he stood now, far in every direction, which was what he wanted. He had no wish for a wolfjackal to be able to spring upon him, unseen. If anything approached him now, he'd spot it.

He took his crystal out again. Jason looked into it and sent a call out for Tomaz. He put every fiber of his being into it with such force that when he finished, the spell flung him back a step, arms outstretched for balance, and he hung there a moment as if caught in midair. He fought to be centered before realizing his feet had never left the ground. Feeling as if he were a giant hawk either lifting into flight or swooping in to settle, Jason lowered his arms and just stood. The power of his call for Tomaz washed around him. His ears buzzed with it.

Gregory's crystal stayed warm in his hand, about the only warmth that could be found in the bleak landscape of this world. He brought both his hands together just for that heat and it flashed with an eerie glow as he did. Jason did a slow turn, looking about, listening to . . . nothing, yet the hair at the back of his neck prickled as if he sensed that he was being watched.

And he could be, anything could be possible. As bare as the landscape seemed to be, there were scraggly shrubs and winter-browned grasses, a boulder here and there. Yet anything that watched him could hardly be big enough to threaten. Unless it spied.

Jason finished his circle and took a deep slow breath. The Magick enveloping him from the call began to ease away. It left him with a faint tingle over his skin, making him want to scratch inside his heavy shirt and sweatshirt and unable to get at it. His ears stayed cold even inside the thick hood. The wind plucked at him as if knowing he hadn't really dressed for whatever winter and nighttime this world could hold. He danced in place to warm his legs up.

Then, a faint something reached his hearing. He could not quite identify it at once. Perhaps the thin, high screech of a hunting owl or the wind whistling through a skeletal branch. Jason turned to face it, trying to catch it better. He reached up and lowered his sweatshirt hood. After a long moment, he heard it again. Pitched almost too high for him to hear, something wailed in the night air. He did not think it could possibly be Tomaz answering his call. The Magick or perhaps his very presence seemed to have attracted something else. He shivered as much from the eerie sound of it as the cold. He could not identify it, but whatever it was, it sounded like it was headed his way.

He readied himself by stowing Gregory's crystal and getting out his own, because he knew how to Shield really well with it. If pressed, he could also bring up a sword of energy which, for lack of any other description, seemed to be something straight out of the *Star Wars* movies. But he did not come to fight, he'd come to find Tomaz. If he were attacked, he'd retreat and head home the same way he'd come. He'd come for answers, though, and he didn't want to leave until he had a few, and Tomaz needed to know about recent events. Crowfeather seemed to have blocked everyone from him but Jason, and that made his burden that much heavier.

The howling suddenly filled the air, keening, rising and falling in pitch, and sounding from all about him like a whirlwind of noise. Jason spun about, seeing nothing but dark clouds boiling in the sky. A tongue of silver lightning licked through them, yet it brought no thunder. He knew that sound now, and he did not wish to face it. As he recognized it, the scar on the back of his left hand twitched painfully.

Wolfjackals, running in the storm of their own chaotic Magick, rushed toward him. The last thing he wanted to meet here and now, and yet he'd expected it. Every time he'd glimpsed Tomaz, wolfjackals had been there. Lightning split the sky again and in its glare he could smell both the power of the natural phenomenon and the Magick it carried. With howls louder than thunder, the wolfjackal pack leaped out of the sky, eyes glowing like green moons, as they bounded to the ground and raced toward him.

He brought his Shield up immediately in expectation but nothing in his wildest thoughts prepared him for what he saw next.

Tomaz rode the pack leader, astride its powerful wolfish shoulders, his own dark mane of shoulder-length hair loose in the wind, a gleam in his eyes. Jason rocked back, steadied himself for anything, as the Navajo shouted words to him in his native tongue that Jason could barely hear above the wind and the howling. The wolfjackals swung about in a wide circle, racing about him, drawing closer with every pass until he could smell their hot breath, and their sharp claws flung pebbles and bits of frozen grass at him as they churned to a halt, growling low.

Jason faced most of them, although one or two snarled at his flank. He could not keep them all to the fore of him, and the beasts knew it, but it was Tomaz he wanted to look in the face.

Crowfeather raised a hand, and said only, "Jason."

What he wanted to answer boiled through his mind. What was Tomaz doing with these beasts, and why, and when was he coming back, and did he have the answers he was seeking and did he have any idea at all how badly things were going in his absence. But he said nothing for a long moment. Then he said, "Eleanora is in a deep sleep. Something dark attacked her, and it began to take her. Aging. Other stuff, and the only thing Gavan and Khalil could do was put her to sleep."

Tomaz frowned. Here, in the barest of moonlight, Jason could see silvery streaks in his dark, unbound hair. The conchas on his belt and bracelet rattled, disks of silver studded with turquoise and other stones, little mirrors of light pooling about him. "How is Gavan taking it?"

"Not well. We tried to find sanctuary for her with Aunt Freyah and she turned us away. We need you, Tomaz. The Council is falling apart. Isabella has been making Leucators for Brennard." Jason gestured with one hand, realizing the spill of words held a sense of hopelessness. "And I can't find the Gate. There's only one of Gavan."

"I am not done here." Tomaz stroked the bristling neck of the beast he rode, and its growling stilled slightly as if soothed by his touch. "I can't come back yet, Jason, but I can, and will, send some strength with you for Eleanora's sake. Come here." He lifted a hand and reached out for Jason.

Jason hesitated. To approach Tomaz would be to enter the pack, for the beast he rode was now surrounded by its smaller pack mates, all growling hotly at him, their teeth gleaming whitely and drool falling to the ground in such warm drops that the frost melted where it touched. What if he saw an illusion? What if only wolfjackals awaited him? He felt his scar tighten and throb. *You are mine*, the wolf-jackal who'd bitten him had said. Was he?

Jason stepped forward. The nearest wolfjackal spun on its haunches and snapped at him. Teeth clashed against his Shield and sparks flew with a stink of Magicks meeting. Jason looked at the beast as it cowered back, red slash of a tongue licking its chops in wounded surprise.

"Hurry," urged Crowfeather. "I cannot hold them long, if at all."

Jason leaped two strides, carrying him to Tomaz's side. The Magicker leaned out, and his rough callused finger traced a sign on Jason's forehead. "See clearly," he said as he did so. Molten heat singed Jason's skin, and then cooled as fiercely.

"It's all I can do," said Tomaz. They traded a long look.

"Hurry," answered Jason.

"I will. Send me word if things worsen." Tomaz paused. "Jason, I would never try to turn you against anyone, but be wary of Isabella. This is a bad thing she has done, and it may not be the worst of her actions. She is dealing with Chaos and every action swings the balance more and more out of control. Promise me you will stay clear of her."

"I will."

Tomaz dropped his hand and thumped the wolfjackal on its flank. Turning its head, it snarled at Tomaz's booted foot, but whirled about in answer and flung itself across the ground, bounding away from Jason. The other wolfjackals yipped and howled in disappointment, then raced after their pack leader, leaving Jason alone in their wake.

He let his Shield drop and put his hand to his forehead. *See clearly.* If only he could!

Jason rubbed his crystal and thought of home.

21

BIG TROUBLE

"I DON'T know whether to commend you or punish you." Antoine Brennard sat in his great fan-backed chair which framed him rather like a throne, and let one hand drop over the arm of the chair as if pondering his own statement.

Jon stood in front of him, unimpressed at the moment because he knew his father's temperament. If he were going to have been rewarded or beaten, both would have happened on the spot, at Iron Gate itself, or a heartbeat away. Brennard was quick to anger and strike or shout, and just as swift in any other emotion, though few emotions ever held him for long. Jon knew it well, for he was just like his father, with a few exceptions.

He held his silence, watching his father's face. The weariness that had driven his breath clean away was gone, and he knew that he had but to reach out for Henry Squibb again and he would be charged. But from the way Henry had tried to fight him, he also knew he should not try again too soon, lest the bird figure out just how caged he was and how to escape as well. It would take Jon too long to find another Magicker to draw from as easily.

149

Unless . . . The temptation to drink from his father's aura again bathed him. Why not? It had been even easier the last time than draining Henry was, and Brennard had not even known. Jon felt spent, old, and so he reached out. He made contact so easily, because they were father and son, he supposed, and his father's angry energy rushed into him. Even as Jon felt its incandescence fill him, his father sat back with a calmed sigh. Perhaps, thought Jon, this was a thing that was good for both of them.

His father stirred from his thoughts. Brennard raised a finger. "None of us was prepared to do battle, yet we almost had them."

Jon gave a slow nod.

"The Leucator was a mistake."

"Perhaps." He would not admit more than that. He could not, and his father would be suspicious if he did. Turning a Leucator from one thing into another had never been done before, yet he *had* done it, if imperfectly, and he knew his father must be mulling that over in the back of his mind. How much effort, how much of a draining would such a thing take, and would it be worth it? Perhaps. Perhaps not. He waited. It was past his bedtime and although he didn't have a very great need for sleep, as he could easily get by on four or five hours, he looked forward to a rest this evening. The fight had taken more out of him than he'd wanted.

"I propose this to you: The best time to hit an enemy is when they are most vulnerable."

"That would seem obvious."

"Obvious, but not always possible." Brennard steepled his fingers and looked over them at Jon. "But if it can be done, we can break them, and once broken, the children will scatter. Once scattered, they will realize they are alone in a dark and hostile world and they will need aid. They might even be willing to accept it from us openly or by guile. Do you not agree?"

It seemed Brennard had been doing a lot of thinking in the past few hours. Openly? Never. But offered in disguise? Maybe. "I do," answered Jon cautiously.

"Good. Because it will tax you, and I want you to be prepared." Brennard then told him how and when and where he intended to strike.

"That soon?"

"If we are tired, they will be exhausted. There isn't a better time, for the moment."

Jon listened solemnly, bowed in understanding, and then left his father's presence for much needed rest, his thoughts tumbling in eagerness, even as he fought for the calm he needed to sleep.

Stef woke curled up around his battered sneakers, their overripe scent filling his nose. "Yuck." He groaned and rolled away. The room stank of bear cub and he knew he'd spent at least half the night in the furry hide of his other self. He sighed. They'd catch him one of these days, and what would he do then? Rich had told him just to say it was a big old dog, a stray, he took in sometimes and which followed him around, but jeez. How blind did his parents have to be to mistake a bear cub, half grown, for a dog? Not to mention the stench. Or the noise, if his cub self decided to start bawling for food. He had a sweet tooth in either form. Impossible, Stef thought, and sighed. They'd never think it was a dog.

Especially since neither animal had permission to be living at their house.

Stef rolled to his knees and then his feet. The smell of hotcakes and coffee filtered into his bedroom, the standard Sunday morning breakfast. His stomach rumbled loudly, in a familiar bearish way, and he decided he was starving. He pulled on pants and shirt, ran a comb through his hair and lumbered to the kitchen, ready to devour as big a stack as his mother could pile on a plate.

"Stefan! Sleepyhead! Ready to eat?"

"Smells great, Mom." He poured himself a glass of milk as his dad winked at him, and tugged a chair away from the kitchen table with his foot so that Stef could sit down.

"All American breakfast, eh? Bacon and pancakes."

He forked himself a few crisp pieces while she took a plate warmed on the stove and heaped it up. She set it down in front of him, saying, "Have you been using that foot powder I bought for you?"

He ladled syrup over the pile and watched the caramel stickiness drip everywhere. "Yes, ma'am."

"It stinks in there, Stefan."

"I'll clean it up tonight, Mom, after Jason's game, okay?

I've got laundry to do and stuff. And . . . and . . . I'll get one of those stick-up things, okay? It's just the football gear, it gets sweat in it, you know. I know it smells. I try to keep it clean."

She ruffled his hair. "You're a good son, Stefan. Don't worry. Someday you will be big football star and we can retire to Florida and watch your games on the TV." Her accent came out a little as she said that, wiping her hands on her apron, as she returned to the stove and poured a new batch of hotcakes onto the griddle.

"College first, Mom."

"Of course. Always the school. You must grow a little more, too. Eat up!" She gave the order with a wave of her pancake turner.

"If he grows any more, Mama, we'll have to buy more shoes," his father said, grinning as he stuffed a forkful of light, fluffy pancakes into his mouth. His eyes twinkled at Stef as he said that, and Stef just grunted at his father's teasing.

His mother let out a little huff, and said, reluctantly, "If he needs them. Only if he needs them!"

Now that she mentioned it . . . "I will soon, Mom," Stef said. He snapped a piece of bacon in two and devoured both halves at once.

"Fine, fine. It goes in the budget. Two weeks your father gives up beer and has liverwurst for lunch sandwiches, and you have new shoes."

His father opened his mouth to protest that, and stopped in mid-word as she turned and waggled the pancake turner menacingly again. "Made of money we are not," she scolded. "But we are your parents and will sacrifice for you. Those two weeks, I will skip bingo at the church, too. Everyone must give up something."

Whatever it was his father had intended to say, it had been stomped flat by the second flood of words from his mom. Instead, his father mopped his face with a napkin and said, "Not the bingo, Mama. I'll make do, but you go to bingo. Who knows? You could win the shoe money!"

Besides which, bingo nights were the only nights of peace at home for his father. Stef hid his grin by polishing off the last of the pancakes on his plate and asking for more. His mother's face flushed with pleasure. "You like my cooking?"

"It's the best, Mom." And it was, nearly.

"Good, good. You say there is a soccer game today?"

"Yup. Jason's team is in it. We're gonna go watch, if that's okay."

"As long as everything is cleaned later." She nodded, and fussed with the bow on her apron before pouring out yet another round of pancakes. "And as long as it is okay with your father."

"It's a big game, Stef?"

"Yup. Part of the championship."

"We should all go. Spring is outside, and we should go." His father stole a pancake off Stef's plate, winking again, his good humor recovering a bit.

"Oh, that might be fun." His mother wiped her hands on her apron. "I'd better start on some sandwiches for lunch!" Humming tunelessly but quite happily, she began to plan her assault on world hunger at lunchtime.

It wasn't quite what Stef had planned, but what could the harm be? Rich's parents never went anywhere with him, his mother worried endlessly about germs and public exposure, so it wouldn't be too crowded.

Stef reached over and plucked a piece of bacon from his dad's plate, grinning, and winked at him. "Sounds like fun."

The early morning flight to San Francisco Bay landed in light fog, bathing the whole area in soft gray mist draped everywhere she could see from the plane window. The gloom held a beauty of its own, but Ting also found it saddening. She had had plans for the day, but they didn't matter, really. Jason would play super with or without her in the stands, and Bailey would cheer loud enough for both of them. It's just that she didn't think . . . she didn't believe . . . that her being with her grandmother would help. Magick couldn't fight cancer, as far as she knew. Being there seemed to be all she could do, and she would. It's just that she felt as if they were all fighting a losing battle. She didn't want to face that.

Ting touched the airplane window as if she could trace a pattern through the mist, to see things better. Jiao Chuu hugged her shoulders gently. "It'll be all right," she said softly, as if reading Ting's mind.

"I hope so." Ting felt the brush of her mother's kiss across the top of her head.

"We don't know if everything will turn out the way we want it to. But I do know that anything done in love will turn out all right."

Ting put her hand out and held her mother's, tightly. Her mother was thinking the same thing, then. They might lose Grandmother, even after all they'd been through, and all they were going to try. She sighed, as the plane lurched downward and bumped on the landing strip and began to brake hard and fast, and her ears popped faintly. Sometimes you had to do things for the past and the present, and not think about the future, she guessed.

Bailey slept soundly all night despite the worry, and she only woke when she heard her mother making an early morning, hushed-voice phone call. She only caught a word here and there which sounded more like she was leaving a message than talking to anyone. Bailey punched her pillow back up and drifted off to sleep again for a little longer until a tiny fuss from the pack rat's cage woke her for the last time.

Lacey appeared to have eaten every tiny morsel of food in existence in the pack rat world. She lay in her empty food cup, her tail tucked around her body, with the tuft under her chin, and looked up with the saddest eyes imaginable.

"Like I would let you starve," Bailey scoffed at her. The fluffy rodent managed a faint chirp.

"Oh, really." Bailey rolled her eyes as she shuffled to the corner of her tiny bedroom where she kept the various packages of seeds and grains and pellets. Lacey got to her haunches at the familiar rattle of food packs. The black tufted tail twitched in eagerness. She barely waited for Bailey to lower the refilled cup into the cage before diving in nose first.

"You must be a stress eater," Bailey observed. Lacey did not make a noise other than rattling through the food till she found what she wanted, stuffed her little cheeks full and then went into her sleep ball filled with freshly shredded tissue and chips. Then came the noise of sunflower seeds being noisily cracked open. Bailey grinned.

Bailey was dressed and halfway through her own breakfast when her mom called out, "What's the agenda for the day?"

"Jason's game, homework, laundry."

"Fun stuff." Rebecca yawned as she sat down opposite Bailey.

"Speak for yourself. I find homework and laundry kinda groadie, myself."

Her mother laughed. "That's why I'm the mom and you're not." She pulled over the teapot that Bailey had made up and poured herself a cup of tea. The teapot looked like the character teapot from Disney's *Beauty and the Beast,* but it reminded Bailey more of Aunt Freyah than anything. If Aunt Freyah ever became a teapot, which of course, she didn't, to Bailey's knowledge.

"Bailey?"

"Hmmm?" She looked back to her mother.

"I called Legal Aid this morning, but they were closed, of course, it being Sunday. So, I won't have any idea what we can do until tomorrow or even Tuesday."

"Okay." It wasn't really quite okay, and they both knew it, but it was all that could be done. From here on out, it was a "wait and see" deal. See what damage her father tried to do, and see if they could counter it somehow. She put a spoon in her teacup and stirred it around, a lot, before adding, "I don't want to live with him."

"He might be able to offer you things I can't."

"If he'd changed, maybe, but from what I can see, he hasn't changed at all. He's gotten worse." Bailey waggled her spoon at her mother. "Some people just shouldn't be parents. There ought to be a license or something where you apply before they let you, like driving school. And I don't want him to be a parent of *me.*"

"You're sure?"

"He may walk like a duck and talk like a duck but that doesn't make him a good father."

"Mmmm," said her mother, the corner of her mouth twitching. "Right." She stood up. "I guess I'd better get going, then. Big day ahead of us."

Bailey finished her breakfast, got up, and loaded the small apartment dishwasher quickly while her mother ate, standing up, as she often did. Trent liked to tease her, "Mrs. Landau! All that food will go to your ankles!" whenever he and Jason came over and joined them. That would be the bright spot in her day, seeing Trent and Jason. She could tell them what had happened and they would tell her they'd help however she needed it. Things would be okay.

"Oh," said her mother, as if she'd remembered something she'd almost forgotten. "About that ... other thing. Maybe you could ... not do it? Just for a while, till this problem with your dad is resolved."

"Not do Magick, you mean?"

Rebecca nodded.

"I can try. I mean, most of the time, you have to really concentrate on it to do anything, you know? It's like hard mental work. Sometimes, though, it just ... pops out at you."

"No one's going to believe you're a witch, but I don't want anyone to be able to prove you do unusual things either."

"Understood." Bailey nodded vigorously, her ponytail bobbing.

"Although ... if you could manage the laundry?" her mother added hopefully.

"Sorry. Magickers don't do laundry. We just summon up new clothes." Bailey fled the kitchen, followed by her mother's laughing disappointment.

In her room, as she sorted through her hamper and laid out various piles of clothes for the wash, she thought about that. She wondered if Gavan or Aunt Freyah were ever tempted to use their power for everyday things. Freyah did, in a way, in her little cottage, but Bailey thought she did what she did to make people feel at ease and taken care of. They all knew picnic hampers didn't really have personalities or dancing food trays really have names, even if they did in Freyah's corner of the world. Did they? Or did Freyah have so much power in her, and so much experience under her hat, that such things were second nature?

Wow. She might *not* have laundry in her future! Wait till she told Jason and Trent that.

Trent steered his father by the elbow the moment they neared the soccer bleachers, and he could see Jason's step-father getting ready to be seated. "Mr. McIntire!"

The big man turned and smiled, laugh lines going deep around his heavily sun-tanned face. "Trent."

"You remember my dad, Frank Callahan?"

"Once in a rare while." McIntire smiled affably and put his hand out. Trent's father looked rather like a string bean next to him as they shook hands.

"Good to see you, sir. We both put in long weekends, these breaks are nice."

"Dad's gonna have a lot of long weekends," Trent interjected. "The company's laying everyone off."

McIntire frowned. "Are they? That's not good. A man of your experience shouldn't have too much trouble getting placed. Sit with me, and catch up."

"Well . . ." Frank traded a look with his son.

"I'm sitting with Bailey," Trent said firmly.

McIntire chuckled. "Jumping up and down cheering, is more like it. It'll be quieter here with us." He motioned to Callahan to sit, as he settled himself next to his wife. Before his dad could protest, Trent escaped.

"You've got the whole fam damly here, looks like," Trent said, as he sat down on the benches and watched Jason lacing up his shoes tightly. The soccer field rang with the noise of people ascending the aluminum bleachers, and kids shouting as they raced around on the spring grass in the midst of the teams trying to warm up a bit. The midafternoon sun shone down brightly, but there was a crisp spring breeze that would keep it from being too hot. All in all, it looked like a good day. "Joanna, Alicia, and the Dozer."

"No kidding. Alicia wanted to film it, and then splice some of the shots into this project she's been invited to do."

"Little Miss Spielberg, huh?"

"Looks like it." Jason straightened his shin guards. "I kinda like having everyone here to watch, though. I hope we give 'em a good game."

"Think you're gonna win it?"

"Hope so, but they're a tough team. They've won before, and we haven't. Depends if we get nervous and if we're good enough and want it enough."

Trent grinned at him. "Going to work for ESPN later, huh?"

Jason cuffed at him, and missed.

"Good thing you don't use your hands in soccer," Trent teased. He waved back at the bleachers.

"Brought your dad?"

"Yup. Thought he might talk to your stepdad, maybe do a little networking."

"Hey." Jason tucked his shirt in. "You know, that's not a bad idea. McIntire might know of some jobs."

"That's what I thought. He could do worse than find Frank Callahan a job." Trent nodded confidently.

"Always thinking." Jason leaned forward, after gazing up into the stands. He could not help but feel tremendously happy seeing his friends gathering there. Henry sat next to Bailey and her mother, his round face very pale in the afternoon sun. Rich and Stefan sat a few rows down, with Stefan's foreign-born parents looking overly American and proud, and even Rich's parents, his mother with a tissue to her nose and trying not to get too close to people. "Rich's parents are here?"

"How can you miss that red hair?"

"I can't, but I thought his mother never went out." Mrs. Hawkins was a notorious hypochondriac, dreadfully afraid of catching some exotic disease or other.

"She doesn't, usually. I guess there's a health fair or something at the other end of the park, so they thought they'd come for the game and then go over and get their blood pressure taken." Trent's eyes sparkled with amusement as he speculated.

The only ones missing were Ting and Gavan. Gavan occasionally sneaked in a soccer game, although professing he knew now that even soccer was out of his time, but quite popular now in England and Europe of course. Jason liked to rib Gavan that only golf and jousting had been invented when Gavan grew up, and for all he knew it was nearly true. Maybe croquet. He'd have to look it up on the Internet sometime, just to see. Ting would be in San Francisco now, so he'd catch her up on the news later either through his crystal or computer.

"Tell 'em, Trent," Jason said suddenly. "No Magick, no matter what happens to me."

It was something that never came up. "We wouldn't—"

"I know. Just . . . in case."

"Right. I'll pass the word." Trent backed away from the benches as more of the team began to gather, and the coach started barking out drills. "Luck." He touched his knuckles to Jason's shoulder.

Luck, indeed.

Trent wove his way through the now crowded bleachers, tapping the others on the shoulder and conferring with each of them the same way before sitting down next to Henry and Bailey. To them all, he whispered, "Hero boy says don't do anything, but we all know what to do if Jonnard shows up, right?"

They all gave him a nod and a wolfish grin of agreement.

Trent settled on the aluminum bleacher. Beautiful day for a championship game. He noticed his father sitting down with the McIntires where he and the Dozer seemed to be having a good conversation. Yup, a good day where a lot could go right.

22

FRIENDS aND OTHER ENEMIES

JASON bloodied his lip sometime in the second quarter. He couldn't quite remember when. It might have been when he tried to head the ball and missed, or it might have been when he got caught in a rundown or it might have been someone tossing an elbow during a throw-in. He didn't remember getting it, and he didn't mind it at all. It only hurt when he needed to suck down some water and he wouldn't even have noticed it at all except for Rich calling down from the bleachers, "Better get some ice on that, Jason!" Only then had he realized he'd split his lip.

He didn't feel it, any more than he felt the tiredness in his legs or the bruising in his ribs from the fight of the day before. He didn't feel anything but the sheer, fierce joy of running down the field, the ball in his control, the goal net in sight. The rush of other bodies flying with him and the jostling contact with others, all intent on controlling that ball and scoring, filled his mind. Like a sharp-eyed eagle, he watched for the hand and body language signs of his teammates, knowing when and where to wheel about, and weave around, and take the pass or kick it off himself. They played like what they were ... a team ... and as the min-

160

utes ticked away and sweat darkened his shirt, the goals added up, three for each side.

As it should have been, he thought. They were all fighting hard and playing well, and he hadn't seen any mistakes. Sometimes a team got to the finals accidentally because it won on a freak day, but not these two teams. Both had earned it. His own Chargers against the Wolverines. Their banner held a depiction of the fearsome beast, a soccer ball being torn to shreds in its great jaws, while his team's showed a white charging medieval warhorse on a field of blue. He felt a keen sense of pride just being there, and a sharp jabbing wish to be the one who made his team the winner. They'd been all over him, though; word had gotten out since his last game, and he found himself bottled up regularly with little he could do but play decoy and defense. Everything he did helped, though, like a puzzle piece fitting in for a greater picture, or that was what the coach had told all of them at the break. Teamwork.

Sound broke over him with a roar like that of waves from the ocean. He could only make out a word now and then from the bleachers as the only voice he was really listening to was that of Coach Wayne bellowing as he paced them up and down the sidelines. Bailey would chide him later. She would say, "Didn't you hear me tell you that a Wolverine was on your heels?" Or, "Didn't you hear us yelling, 'Go, Jason!' for the umpteenth time?" She'd know it if he said he had, she always knew it when he lied, which he rarely did. Maybe that's how she knew it, he hadn't enough practice.

A whistle blew sharply as the Wolverines called a time-out, and Coach Wayne waved at them to come in. He trotted off the field with Sam, his longtime friend, and headed for the big plastic tubs of water. Sam got little play time compared to Jason, but he'd been in for most of the fourth quarter to give other players a break. Coach Wayne pointed a finger at him.

"Good work, Sammee. Bench yourself now, and I want you to watch the defense carefully. See if you spot a chink, and let me know."

Sam tossed a grin. "Sure thing, Coach!"

Benched but with an important assignment. That was the way to do it, Jason thought. He grabbed one of the stiff white towels lying in a heap on the ground and scrubbed off his head and neck. Now that he was not running, he could feel a thin edge of ache along his shins, and his breathing burned a little in his lungs. He took a proffered cup of sports drink and chugged it down, even as Coach said, "All right, boys, gather round. I have something I want you to take a look at."

Without further notice, he lifted his clipboard and began to draw on it, his felt tip pen squeaking as he drew diagrams and line defenses on it. Jason grabbed a second, smaller white cup of sports drink and began to sip it slowly, feeling the mildly flavored fruit punch go down his throat.

"This is what they're doing," explained the coach, "and this is how we're gonna beat 'em while they do it."

Behind them, he could hear chanting. Without really listening, the words sounded a bit like, "The Chargers are cool, the team is gonna rule." He wasn't sure of the wording though, but he could hear Bailey's voice in loud enthusiasm. Jason found himself grinning even as he tried to concentrate on the coach and his assistant as they laid out strategy for this second part of the very last quarter. All too soon, their brief moments of recess were over.

Bradley and Todd bumped fists with him as they trotted back onto the field for the throw-in, Todd dropping back into his place as goalie and Bradley pacing him on the offensive line. The Wolverines joined them, looking appropriately sinister in their black and silver colors and frowning faces, having a much rougher time than they'd figured on. Everyone jogged in place impatiently. Game time was running out.

A dark cloud skittered across the brilliant blue California sky and gusted away as quickly as it had appeared. Its shadow grazed Jason and he looked up briefly. The ref's whistle blew, jerking his attention back just as the throw-in hurtled right at him. He headed it to Bradley and away they went.

Bailey sat back down, and glanced overhead. The dark splinter of cloud that pierced the afternoon brightness was gone, yet another followed on its heels, and a third. They gathered and hung low as if the bright sun and brisk spring breeze had no power over them. Trent followed her glance upward.

"Too late to rain the game out," he said. " 'Sides, soccer is like rugby. They play in anything, till it's over."

"No one said anything about rain though," Bailey muttered. She rubbed her bare arms. Lacey twittered in her shirt pocket, as though aggrieved by the motion or the coolness rapidly descending on them.

"Give her a cookie."

"She's had one whole one already. My pocket is full of oatmeal crumbs." Bailey wrinkled her nose. She spotted something on the field and jumped to her feet, yelling, "Go, Jason! Go!"

Rebecca Landau popped up at nearly the same time, the two so alike they might almost be thought twins. The bleachers rumbled with their excitement. A row or two forward, he could hear Alicia tell her mother confidently, "I'm getting great video of Jason. The automatic focus on this thing is following the action just great."

Dozer's heavy voice followed. "Good thing to have. Jason's in the thick of it now, he'll want to see it later."

"Got it," muttered Alicia, somewhat distractedly as she angled her camcorder through the shoulders of other watchers in the stands. "This should go great with my project, too." Joanna put a hand on her blonde daughter's shoulder, as much to steady her as she filmed, as to encourage her.

Trent frowned, though. He looked back at the sky. A storm front gathered at the edges of the sky with incredible speed, yet the breeze barely ruffled the treetops. Charcoal clouds began to peak, like breakers gathering for high tide. He felt an uncomfortable prickling along his scalp as he often did when Jason or one of the others was working the Magick he didn't have. He shifted as a nervous edginess ran over him. Bailey would have said someone was tripping on his grave.

Trent looked about. The bleachers on this end were packed with families and friends of the Chargers. Parents he rarely saw were here, even ... Rich's nervous mom and dad, his mother with a handkerchief to her nose as if trying to prevent inhaling any germs. Bailey's mom who often worked on weekends. His dad, who was now out of work indefinitely. Joanna and William McIntire and Jason's step-sister Alicia, her fine blonde hair tucked back from her face as she kept her attention intently on the miniature camcorder in her hands. Stefan's thick, rather dowdy look-ing parents who were immigrants and looked it, in an odd, 1950s sort of way. Henry Squibb sat on the other side of Rebecca Landau and he seemed to be the only one there without a parent in tow. Still, that didn't answer Trent's cu-riosity about the Magick he felt adrift. None of his friends had their hands on their crystals, essential for Focusing and using them, just as Jason had asked—for now. Still, just as Shakespeare had written, "By the pricking of my thumbs, something wicked this way comes."

He smelled, in his own unique way, the tainted power of the Dark Hand reaching out toward them all. The others might have Magick, but there were times when he could *see* it and they could not, and now was one of them. As he glanced overhead again, gloom covered the sky and he could see lightning, dark green and blue, lancing above. Henry Squibb's face went white as a sheet. His face twitched toward Bailey. His lips moved as he mumbled something inaudible and then slumped to his side, hands jerking.

Bailey cried out, "Henry!" but no one heard her but her mother and Trent as the Chargers bleachers rose in a roar as someone in white and blue drove in a goal, sending the score to 4 and 3. From the corner of his eye, Trent thought the kicker might have been Jason who punched the air once or twice, but his friend was a team guy and his joy could have been for any one of his teammates who'd done a good job. Trent grabbed Bailey's arm.

"I see Magick," he hissed in her ear.

"What?" She blinked at him, confused, torn between Henry and Trent. Her mother had her arm about Henry and was trying to sit him up.

"Magick!" he repeated hoarsely at her ear, her tangle of golden-brown hair muffling his words.

"No one here . . ." Bailey plowed to a halt. She beck-oned her hands helplessly. "Jason said we couldn't. Not to help him or endanger ourselves."

"I can see it!" Trent insisted. "If it's not us, then it has to be the Dark Hand."

Clouds overhead crackled now, their stormy charcoal depths sparkling with levin fire, and they could hear the sound of lightning bolts sizzling past, without seeing them clearly, and then the low rumble of thunder danced about them. Someone screamed.

"Lightning!"

In panic, people began to clamber from the aluminum bleachers. Trent rose, to protect Bailey and her mom, and Henry, as they did. No rain struck his face, but the sky had gone storm black and he stood, waiting, the hairs on the back of his neck standing up like an angry dog's. He could feel, however, the hot splatter like sparks of Magick falling. Pure, malicious Magick, directed at them. Stef turned to Rich. Trent could see the heaviness on his face blur, his expression rippling as if he were underwater, and the current obscuring him. Had he begun to shapeshift? Not a chance, no, not here, not now! Could he see that Magick, too?

The players on the field lined up for the kickoff, seemingly unaware of the unnatural weather, or perhaps uncaring as the Chargers moved ahead by one goal and the Wolverines swore to get even.

"Shields," Trent called out, knowing no one but themselves would understand. They were under attack!

He should have known that it was too much of a coincidence, too unusual, that all their families had decided on the same Sunday to be here and now. Everyone but Ting and her fragile grandmother was here. Bailey gripped her crystal. "Henry's fainted."

"Shield Stef."

"But—"

Trent tugged on her elbow. "Bailey, he's *shifting.* Shield Stef!" He drew her down the bleachers with him, through the crowd as people settled again, muttering, looking at the gathering storm.

Rich hurried Stef out of their row and onto the ground, behind the team benches. Trent could see the glow of crystal fire playing over both of them and knew Rich had sensed the same thing, and was trying to give Stef the control he needed to keep from morphing into the bear cub. Henry poured out of the bleachers like a wet noodle, still shaking and pale, barely able to stand, his crystal cupped in one fisted hand.

"It's like a ... tug-of-war ..." he managed, breathily, gasping for strength.

"What is?"

"They're pulling on me. We've got to ... get out ... of here!" Henry's eyes flickered, as if they might roll back in their sockets. Bailey threw an arm out to his shoulders to steady him.

Stef bleated. His bear voice rolled out of him, like a belch, and he turned desperately to Rich.

"Shields up, everyone, gather, and concentrate."·

"Everyone is watching!" hissed Bailey, but she did as Trent ordered.

A sharp whistle sounded the end of the game. They could hear the shouts and yells, some happy, some outraged, as the teams wheeled across the field and turned back to their benches. Jason came running toward them, his face decorated with an ear-to-ear grin of sheer joy that turned stark as he saw them.

Lightning crackled overhead. A piercing scream set the crowd to running, pushing and scrambling to get clear of the metal stands. Jason immediately gathered his own crystal, and the sky flared with the white-gold of its shield. His power hung over the spectators like an unearthly umbrella, raining tiny sparks. Trent thought of a glorious fireworks display, exploding, flowering, and then drizzling out of the night sky. Jason had power, more than any of them, and to spare.

But not enough.

Stef bawled and fell to the ground, rolling under the crowded bleachers. Rich and Trent immediately went to his side, without hope of hiding much. The bear cub reared on its haunches, shredding clothing about it as it stood and pawed at its nose, in bewilderment and ursine anger. In seconds, nothing was left of Stef. Rich inhaled deeply and dove at his shape-shifted friend, hitting him in the shoulder and bowling the bear cub over, knocking him under the benches and out of sight.

The sky opened up. Jonnard's laughing voice echoed over them, mocking their pain, as the screams of their friends, family, and teammates surrounded them. Lightning sizzled and struck within inches of them. They could feel the Magick dancing off their skins painfully.

"Hold on a bit longer," Jason grunted. Sweat already darkened his jersey and smeared his hair to his head, and his arm trembled as though the weight of his crystal might be more than he could bear.

The roof of the sky became a field of lightning sparks. It exploded over and over, as if frustrated in reaching its targets on the ground. It drowned out the screams of the stampeding people getting out of the stands and to their cars, to safe places across the open field, away from those gathered in a closed circle and trying to protect them. Henry moaned softly and swayed on his feet. Then he gritted his teeth and said, "No!" as if arguing with someone.

One last lightning stroke blasted the edge of the bleachers with a deafening noise. The air stank with the melting of the aluminum. It ran white, and then melted into a blackened mess at the corner of it. The frightened bear cub let out a bawl of pain and terror, and crawled out from underneath, its fur singed, dragging Rich with it, his hand knotted in its hair. Into the crowd of fleeing people it bolted, Rich stumbling after his friend, yelling, "Stef! Come back!"

The duo raced with the crowd before veering away into the shrubbery and trees guarding the parklike edge of the soccer field. There was a loud noise, and one of the portapotty buildings toppled as the bear cub ran into it, full tilt. Rich shouted, "Stef! Leave the dog alone!" as if he could disguise what they were all seeing. Both boy and bear cub disappeared headlong into the shrubs.

Then, all went silent.

It lasted only a moment before Mrs. Olson cried, "What have you done to my son? What is that animal?"

"Just a stray dog," muttered Trent, somewhat helplessly. Jason looked up, to the flashes of cameras, and to his stepsister's face as she lowered her camcorder, and saw the expressions on the faces of those few left who now began to draw near. They all of them had been exposed. *Film at Eleven*, he thought in despair.

"Oh, my," said Bailey.

23

WHICH WITCH IS WHICH

"IT'S a setup," said Jason. He lowered his aching arm slowly, the light from his Shield dimming as he released the power. He couldn't explain the soaring feeling he'd experienced for a moment, the sense of another figure standing with him, strengthening him. He could name that figure, the lost wizard Gregory, whom he'd never met except for an occasional fleeting glimpse in the lavender crystal.

All he knew was, when he'd tapped for power, both of the crystals on his body had answered, even though he'd only held one. And now, that power was diminished. He felt very alone. The pearl-and-gold glow which had covered them like an umbrella faded as he did, then disappeared with a sharp snap of energy. The soccer field, nearly empty, suddenly drained of its menace. "We were totally set up," Jason repeated.

"No kidding." Trent spun around on one heel, surveying the area, looking for the Dark Hand. He saw no sign of them now as the unnatural electrical storm rolled back, clouds tearing to wispy shreds and dissipating. As quickly as it had been called, it seemed to be blowing apart. Rich bolted into the park grounds at the edge of the soccer field, hot on Stef's furry heels.

Henry muttered, "It's like a tug-of-war." He rubbed his eyes, confused looking, unaware he'd been repeating that over and over.

Bailey rubbed his shoulder. "Stay together." She moved closer, trying to use her body to shield Stef-cub from the sight of anyone still standing in the bleachers. The cub had lit out for the bushes, moving so quickly that it did look like a terrified big golden dog. Of course, nearly having been hit by lightning might have helped its speed, she thought, as the smell of burned hair stung her senses.

Jason realized from his heartbeats that only seconds had passed, though it felt much, much longer, as the remaining spectators came down from the bleachers, their attention fixed on them. Joanna stared at him, her face sheet white, one arm about Alicia's shoulders protectively while his stepsister held her camcorder to her chest as if someone might think of grabbing it away. McIntire's huge body seemed to frame them.

It's on tape, Jason thought, his heart sinking.

"Nobody move," called Trent's father, descending to the trampled earth at the foot of the stands. "That's ball lightning that struck them, and they could still be charged with static electricity."

Trent gave a lopsided grin, trading a look with Jason. Help where they hadn't expected any.

McIntire moved away from his wife and stepdaughter. "It's like Saint Elmo's fire," he agreed. "I've seen the same thing, Frank. Rare as hell but scary. Still . . ." he shrugged heavy shoulders and looked overhead. "Freak storm. You kids okay?"

Someone had been repeatedly letting out high yelps of terror and Jason finally got a look at who—Stefan's mother. She stood with her purse clutched tightly, her frizzled hair practically standing on end. "Where is Stefan! Vhat have you done with him?"

"We're fine. He went after that stray dog." Jason cleared his throat uneasily.

"My boy!" Her hands went white-knuckle on her purse. "I saw no dog . . ."

"Liars. All of you, liars!"

Rebecca and Bailey both swung about, jaws dropping. Jerry Landau stood defiantly, camera in his hands. "It's witchcraft. I've got everything in pictures. The court's going to see everything!"

"Jerry," said Rebecca with forced calmness. "I hope you haven't been drinking. What you think of me is one thing, but let's not do this in front of the kids."

He shook his camera violently. "It's all on film! I've got all the evidence I need, and the court will get it first thing in the morning. You're not keeping Bailey."

Rebecca answered grimly, "I have attorneys, too."

"Oh, no, you don't," muttered Bailey. Her hand, clutched around her crystal, started to swing up.

"No." Jason caught her wrist, putting his body between her and her father. "Not here."

Bailey shot him an angry look, then sighed. She lowered her arm but not before Jason could feel the emotion trembling through her body.

McIntire and Callahan both moved to frame Bailey's father. "I think," said the Dozer slowly, "the kids have been through enough for one day, don't you?"

Trent's dad echoed with, "We need to find out who's been hurt and who's all right, first." Frank Callahan's gaze swept across them, then, a slight puzzled look on his face which he quickly shed for a neutral expression.

"You're all either blind or crazy." Jerry Landau swung about in a circle. "I know what I saw. So do you!"

The Wolverines defender who'd given Jason most of his trouble hung at the edges, listening, although most of his team had been hustled off the field as the storm had threatened. Frowning, he jerked his head toward his coach who also stood, watching. "Does that mean the game gets called? We won?"

"You lost, bud." Trent straightened and his voice went deep with menace.

"Not if he's a witch or something. That would be cheating."

The Wolverines coach suddenly looked as if he might be really interested. He nudged his player. "Don't hang around. Game's over. For now." He trotted off in the direction of the van where two of the black-and-white started refs were standing, papers in their hands, nervously glancing up now and then at the sky.

Jason throttled down the anger he felt, hard words bitten back behind his clenched teeth as Landau started again. "I saw what I saw. You've made some kind of witch out of her, and I'm taking her back. I'll have her exorcised if I need to!"

McIntire moved with astonishing quickness for a big, hefty man. He stepped in, blocking and overshadowing Bailey's father. "I think it's time for you to leave."

"It's a free country!"

"It's never been free for harassment. You've got a lawyer, let him handle it. Now get in your car and go before I call the police."

Landau managed a gesture around McIntire. "This isn't the end of this!"

"No," said Rebecca quietly. "I don't imagine so." She watched as her ex-husband loped off the soccer field and disappeared into the parking lot. Moments later, a car peeled rubber.

McIntire rubbed his hands together and then reached for Joanna. "I'm sorry."

Joanna shook visibly, but the color began to return to her face. She kissed his cheek gently. "Thanks for getting rid of him." McIntire gave a satisfied rumbling which sounded almost like a purr. She said, in a dazed voice, "I don't know what I saw either."

Alicia looked down at her camcorder and up at Jason. She said nothing, but he could see a glint in her eyes.

She knew she had it on film. And he knew it, too.

Jason took a deep breath, trying to think what he could do. Before an answer came to him, Frank Callahan suggested, "Isn't pizza the order of the day? After a victory like this?"

"I'm starving."

"You're always hungry." Henry stared at Trent with very round eyes behind his glasses. He took them off and rubbed his eyes carefully. He looked as if he wanted to say more but did not.

"We all have to talk," said Frank firmly.

Mr. and Mrs. Hawkins had said nothing, but she took her

handkerchief down from her face at that. She shuddered as she got out, "Tell Rich that if he has so much as touched that filthy beast, he's not welcome home till he cleans up." She turned about smartly and marched off. Mr. Hawkins gave them an embarrassed shrug before trailing after his wife.

Mrs. Olson's eyes narrowed. "My son is not filthy. What he is, I am not sure. But not filthy."

"This conversation belongs elsewhere," echoed McIntire. "My home, I think." He beckoned toward the last remaining cars and vans in the parking lot. Jason realized bleakly that his team and coach had left without him.

"We're not freaks," Jason said flatly. Although the living room of the McIntire house was crowded, his voice seemed to echo all about those gathered. The muted, tasteful tones of Joanna's decorating in ivory and golds seemed overwhelmed by the people crowded in now, occupying every sitting space available and then the floor.

"Then what are you?"

"What happened out there was some kind of paranormal power, wasn't it?" Frank Callahan leaned a shoulder against the wall, slouched comfortably, both hands in his pockets.

Henry sat curled up on the end of the couch, his arms about his knees, looking rather like an overstuffed sofa pillow. Some color had finally returned to his face. "We can't say what it was. But it wasn't us."

"Can't or won't?"

"Can't." Trent rubbed his nose. He reluctantly closed the last lid of the last empty pizza box. Rebecca had brought Rich and Stefan with her, after Bailey finally called Stef in with her Talent of animal sense, luring the bear cub close. Messages had been left for the Squibb family that Henry was with them and not to worry. Ravenous as usual, Stef had eaten nearly a whole pizza by himself. He tried to stifle a burp while licking a finger. No one else had had much appetite.

Joanna gazed at him. "I'm so sorry, Jason. All this time, all this time, I thought your father worried about you because of your heart, like your mother. Never did I think anything like this could . . ." Her voice trailed off, and she shook her head.

He stared at his stepmom a moment, struck by the realization that all her worry, all her care for him, had come out of her promise to protect and nurse a potential time bomb, as his mom had been with her heart defect. No wonder she'd practically suffocated him.

"I want an answer from this Rainwater," McIntire offered. "And I want it now." Joanna put her hand on her knee and shook her head.

"Actually," said Bailey, "so do I." Her usually cheerful expression was knotted in unhappiness. "I think he owes us that."

Jason got his crystal out. "Maybe he can say what we can't." He concentrated with the little strength he seemed to have left, and it was barely enough to bring Gavan to his mind. But the Magicker looked at him, and turned away, with a faint whispering thought that Eleanora had worsened, and he could not leave for the moment. He caught a shadowy vision of Eleanora lying cold and still as death, and he thought of his many nightmares of finding a body just like that. "Gavan, come back!" He clutched at the elder and found coldness blocking him, as Henry rolled back against his chair and grabbed at his temples. He tried to force the block, only to hear Henry moan loudly.

"Jason," said Trent, holding his wrist. "You're hurting him. Trouble?"

"Seems to be blocked." Jason retreated in his efforts and Henry sat up, forcing down a deep breath. "Henry's feeling it, too. I can't force it." Henry gave him a look of desperation, then hid his face in his hands.

"So. No help there, at least not yet." Jason rubbed his eyes. "We've got to buy some time."

Stefan's mom sat across from her rumpled son, looking at him with mournful brown eyes. "You cannot stay, my son."

"Mom . . ."

She shook her head. "You won't say what happened, but something did. All here saw it. Do you think I have no eyes? You will be a freak. American television will hunt you down, until someone makes up a crazy story about what happened. Then it will get even worse." She held her hand up, as he protested. "You know this is true! You know it."

"You've all been freaks since you got back from summer

camp," stated Alicia. She balanced her camcorder on her knee.

"Alicia!"

She tilted her head at her mom. "Well, it's true." She turned back to Jason. "So what happened? Some kind of government experiment? Did you guys all get shot up with ESP or something? I mean, we all thought it was strange you guys got all rounded up as talented and stuff. Not that you aren't. But looking back, it's obvious you were recruited."

Rich's mother had taken up a guarded stance in the far corner of the living room, handkerchief to her nose, pausing only to pull out a horribly antiseptic smelling spray and spritzing it every ten minutes or so. She had only come because Rich had called and begged her to, and she'd acted as if they could all contaminate her the moment she'd walked in the front door. Now she let out a choked warble, and grabbed for her husband's arm. "Germ warfare!"

"Oh, don't be ridiculous," Joanna snapped. She blushed then, and leaned back against her sofa, unaccustomed to such outbursts. Jason grinned at her, thinking, *Way to go, Mom!*

"Obviously not," rumbled McIntire. He stared keenly at Jason. "But there have been odd happenings. The old house that burned down last Halloween, for instance."

"Nothing we did," Trent offered.

"Today looked like an attack." Trent's father straightened and walked across the room, as if not wanting to face his son. "In which case, there was nothing you started in October, or today. Would I be right in saying that?"

"We can't tell you," answered Bailey, Henry, and Trent in unison.

Rich bit his lip and Stef decided to check a different pizza box, on the off chance he'd overlooked a slice or two.

But Jason drew himself up. "Something like that," he got out, and waited for his throat to tighten and his jaws to lock, as the Vow of Silence promised it would. Other than the vague uneasiness of being in front of everyone, and in deep trouble, he felt nothing. Immediately, everyone's eyes seemed to be on him. He took a step back involuntarily. "We haven't started anything," he said, feeling a bit lame, and the cords in his neck did tighten then and he wasn't sure if he could get another word out or not.

Rebecca Landau made a small movement with one hand. "I know what it is they're facing, sort of, and they can't tell you, and I've promised not to, but yes . . . they're extraordinary, and they do have powers which will draw attention to them, and may be very dangerous for them. We live in a world which—" She paused. "Well, frankly, it may want to take them apart to see how they do what they do, and they don't even know for sure what they can do. Not to mention people who might want to use them for warfare or covert activities, or just misuse them altogether. I don't think any of us want to risk that."

Mrs. Olson stared at her son, a large tear sliding down her cheek. "You must go," she said in her accented voice, words growing thick.

"Mom."

She shook her head. "No football here. But better than life in a cage."

"We don't know this," started Frank Callahan.

"Yeah, Dad, we do," Trent interrupted. "That's why we can't talk about it, for our own protection. It's *not* witchcraft. There's a good side and a bad side to this and we're on the good, and the others have come after us a couple of times. We don't know what to expect."

"They need a safe place," Rebecca said, drawing Bailey close to her and holding one of her hands tightly.

Henry squirmed. He ran a hand over his head, sending up a thatch of dark hair, but he remained silent.

"There isn't any place." Bailey bit her lip and fell silent.

"I can only think of one place to go," said Jason slowly. Haven was out. But he had places he could go where he wouldn't take no for an answer.

Trent looked at him. "Where?"

Jason shook his head slowly. There wasn't a lot he could say, in front of everyone.

"Richard!" cried Mrs. Hawkins.

The redhead made a gesture with his hand. "Forget it, Mom. You'd be better off without me, if people come hunting around, you know?"

Henry said, "They'd all be b-b-better off."

McIntire stood. "You're all leaving together, then?"

"I think we have to." Jason nodded at his stepfather.

Rebecca said fiercely, "You're not going without me."

Bailey looked up at her mom, and began to cry, softly, silently. "I mean it. Not without me. I know, anyway, so I have to go, right?"

"That would probably be wise." Trent shifted uneasily. "Do you have a plan for all this, Jason?"

"Not yet. I don't know how to cover our tracks." He pulled his crystal out. "But I don't think we can wait around to see who else filmed us or took pictures."

"You just can't disappear," Rich's mom stammered. "There will be questions asked."

"We're not going forever. Just a few weeks or so, and nobody will ask questions."

"The schools . . ."

Trent flexed his fingers. "Schools have computer systems. They might think they know we're gone, but they won't be able to prove it."

Callahan cleared his throat. "If my son just mentioned hacking, I didn't hear it."

"I think," noted McIntire mildly, "that computer manipulation may be the least of his abilities right now. Is there a way we can get hold of you, wherever it is you're going?"

"Not easily, but there's a way." Jason looked at Bailey who turned red. "Some people have already popped in and out a bit."

"No." Joanna rubbed her slender hands together. "I can't do this. I can't just let you go, Jason."

"I think it's gone beyond your wishes or mine," McIntire told her.

She shook her head briskly, elegantly coiffed blonde hair flying. "I promised his father. There's a trust there that I have spent a lot of time making sure was met."

"You've been a great stepmom," Jason told her. *A little too great*, he thought to himself.

McIntire put his hand on Joanna's knee. "Honey, they all leave, sooner or later. This is sooner, and necessary. You've done what you promised Jarrod."

Joanna looked at him, her face with that brittle look that meant intense, held back emotions. He wasn't sure if she was going to cry or not. "You make sure," she said to him, "that you take care of yourself."

"I will." He took his crystal out. "Everyone who is going, join me."

"Wait." Alicia stood, and held out her camcorder. "Take the tape. Just in case, you know." She tucked a blonde wing of hair behind her ear.

Trent looked over her elbow. "What's it show, anyway?"

She lifted a shoulder and dropped it, then pushed a few buttons, and the camcorder whirled faintly as if rewinding the tape, and she pushed Preview Play, so that the tiny screen could show her what she'd filmed.

She fast forwarded through standards scenes of the soccer game, including Jason's winning goal, and then the tumble of the Magickers one by one out of the stands. The sky looked dark and very threatening.

Then her camcorder screen went white gold and showed nothing. Frame after frame of . . . nothing. Trent let out a low whistle, and glanced at Jason.

"The energy appears to have wiped the tape out. And, I'll bet Krispy Kreme Doughnuts the cameras don't have a decent picture either."

"I . . . I didn't do that." Jason looked at the tiny camcorder screen.

"You can't wipe out memories, though. We still gotta go." Stef stood reluctantly, the last one to gather at Jason's side. He stared at his mother.

She nodded. "Go, Stefan. You must do this."

He made a noise that sounded as if the bear cub inside him mourned. "Awww, Stef!" Bailey cried and put one arm around him. The other she held tightly onto her mother with.

One by one, the Magickers linked hands.

"We'll be back," Jason told them, "when we can."

"When it's safe," Trent added.

If it ever would be.

24

CLEAN CUP, MOVE DOWN

THE moment of crossing from one door in the crystal to another only took seconds. Usually. Even in those seconds, he might feel a chill and a darkness as he traveled a strange *between* that did not quite really exist, nor Jason suspected, did he. That last thought would have raised the hair on his arms, but he didn't have time for it. Or rather, he had way too much time. He didn't bring the group through the way he thought he would. They seemed to hang in the void, the iciness and bleakness creeping in until he feared someone would let go, and he'd lose them.

Being lost inside his crystal was nothing he'd wish on anyone, but you wouldn't be lost permanently. At least, Jason didn't think so. On the other hand, it wasn't something he felt like testing. It had been bad enough when Bailey had fallen into her crystal those many many months ago and not only had she disappeared physically, but in time as well. Her disappearance had baffled every one of the Magickers for days and days, until he'd finally picked up on clues she was leaving them, and managed to find her.

Jason started to take a deep breath at the memory, and

all that had changed for them, but the void held no air. There was nothing to suck in, and he panicked for a moment, gripping his crystal tightly and forcing them through and beyond.

The void fought back. It did not want to give him passage or let him go. Bailey let out a small noise, almost a whimper, and he realized they must all be feeling what he did. No light, no air.

The sharp edges of his gemstone cut into his palm as he punched his way through, forcing the void to let them go. He could feel the *between* give way suddenly, and then they emerged, his ears popping, his step settling onto solid ground. They all stepped down onto the lawn, shaking themselves like a dog after an unwanted bath, jostling each other around.

"Wow," said Bailey. "You take the scenic route?"

"I really, really hate traveling this way," muttered Trent. He tapped his fingers on his jeans pocket, his hand moving to a musical beat only he could hear, betraying his nervousness.

"I hate planes," Stef said. He scrubbed at his eyes, and then his crew cut, and it looked for a moment as if the bear cub looked out, too, unhappily.

Jason's stomach growled. They'd all been too nervous to eat more than a single slice of pizza, and now, after Crystaling, his stomach seemed to know what his mind could only sense. They'd been in the void a good deal of time. He was *starving*.

Rebecca Landau just stood there as they regrouped, her mouth half-open as if she wanted to say something, and couldn't. Bailey joggled her mother's arm.

"Mom? You okay?" She frowned. "Jason didn't leave your brain back there, or anything, did he?"

Rebecca moved. "Not . . . quite. This is how you travel?"

"Sometimes. Most of the time, we just get in a car and have a parent drive us."

Rebecca looked at her daughter as if she'd sprouted a second head. Then she shook her own, dispersing thoughts. "How we could have missed this, I'll never know."

"We're not supposed to do it in public," Bailey told her.

"I guess not." Rebecca hugged her. "I can see I have a lot to learn."

Bailey nibbled her lip. "Ummm . . . I don't think I can teach you this."

Rebecca laughed. "That's not what I meant, and I think I agree with Trent. I don't think I want to travel this way."

Jason looked about at the midsummer night sky. Early spring in Irvine, step through a crystal to this place, and the seasons had changed. Possibly even the hemisphere, if this place was even on Earth. "Hopefully, we won't have but one or two more Crystalings to go." Even more hopefully, this would be the last one for a while, but he didn't know if he'd brought them to sanctuary or not.

Henry took his glasses off and cleaned them before putting them back on with a sigh. "I don't think this is a good idea. I shouldn't be here. I shouldn't be here at all," he finished, sounding miserable.

Rich elbowed him. "Course you should, Squibb."

"I didn't get to say good-bye."

"You can Crystal back as soon as we have everyone settled. I'll go with you if you want company," Bailey told him.

He nodded, his face still knotted with unhappiness.

"We'd better get inside," Jason said, "before we attract any more attention." He beckoned at the cottage.

"She didn't welcome us last time. What makes you think she will this time?"

"There's no other place to go. Either she's a Magicker, or she isn't," stated Jason flatly.

They straggled through the sagging picket fence and across the grass, with a keen sense of the hour being very late as a high, bright summer moon shone down on them from overhead. Stars twinkled blue and white in the sky, and the aroma of night-blooming flowers lay about them, although he could not see the hedges where they grew. The other side of the cottage maybe. It occurred to him that Freyah's cottage was very like the moon in that he'd only ever seen the one face of it. Did it have a face toward the sun and one toward the dark side? Had anyone ever seen the other side of that cottage?

The door snatched open just as he reached his hand to knock. Aunt Freyah looked out, her blue eyes flashing with intensity, her silvery hair fluffed about her face, her apple cheeks blazing with blush. "Come in, quickly, don't dawdle.

I've got the teakettles whistling." She counted briskly as they walked past her into the cheerful abode. "Seven of you, altogether? An auspicious number. Sit, sit, find chairs and pull ups. We'll have a bite to eat first, and then we'll talk about why you're pounding on my door at midnight on the summer's eve. And yes, yes, I know it isn't midsummer's eve where you're from, but it is *here*, and that makes it a bit of an omen, don't you agree?" Without waiting for agreement, she beckoned them briskly inside.

Jason lowered his hand. He hadn't pounded, but he wasn't about to dispute the elder Magicker. Everyone filed past him quickly, Bailey saying to her mother, "She has this picnic hamper that makes meals, and a serving tray, his name is George, who serves them. George likes company and will dance for us, I hope."

"Oh, really?" answered Rebecca faintly. She tossed Jason a somewhat desperate look as she moved into the depths of the cottage sitting room.

Trent came through the doorway last. His chest still thumped a bit from Crystaling, and it made no difference whether he liked to travel that way or not, because he couldn't, and he knew he was at the mercy of the others who could. It was not a big deal to any of them to leave their homes or their family because if they wished, and the coast was clear, they could just pop back for a few. He couldn't. Their flight had cut him off from his dad totally, and he felt that loss inside him now. What would his dad do without him? Would he go out and get that new job he needed, or would he fall into a depression as he had years ago when it had first been just the two of them? How would his father get along without him, and how would he get along without his dad? Everyone else here had the ties of Magick which not only linked them to each other, but to every other Magick user across the years, known or unknown. He was alone.

He sat on the ottoman and watched as Aunt Freyah cleared a small table, bistro size, and snapped a fresh white tablecloth over it. A metallic rattle came from the corner leading to the kitchen and George strode out, his burnished surface gleaming, fairly dancing with happiness at the presence of company, his tray laden down with teacups and spoons and sugar jars, and two teapots. For all his skittering about, he spilled not a drop as he settled into place, and well, for lack of a better description, Trent thought, kind of percolated in place. Rather like a car idled, moving yet not going anywhere, just vibrating loudly.

Trent waited for everyone else to serve themselves. Freyah bustled off to the kitchen, leaving them to themselves, but her business around the corner was punctuated with the clatter of crockery and the tinkling of more silverware. He wondered if her famed picnic hamper no longer worked and she was making food the old-fashioned way. As he touched George to retrieve his own cup and saucer, he noticed the aura about the tray. Silvery like the metal tray itself, it sparkled about the serving tray as if dusted lightly over it, but he could see it.

Trent turned to Jason and said softly, "See that?" He poked his finger at George's aura. The tray quivered a little, then settled back to its idling.

Jason tore his attention away from Bailey and her mom, as Bailey tried to explain Magick in her usual tangle and enthusiastic spill of words. "See what?"

"That." Trent rubbed the edge of the serving tray. George let out a catlike purr as if stroked.

"It's George," said Jason.

"I know that. Do you see this?" And he tapped the aura a third time. George made a little move, scooting over toward Trent, still like a cat getting a good ear rub and enjoying it thoroughly.

"I don't see anything but George."

"Surrounding him. This. It's like a ring of color."

"Not a thing."

"You're sure."

"Trent."

"Okay, okay, I was just checking. Don't see anything, huh?" Trent finished.

Jason just shrugged in bewilderment and turned back to Bailey, who flourished her hands and said, "And that's how I had a whole herd of frogs in a chorus after me!"

"And that's how you tamed Lacey, undoubtedly," her mother said. She glanced at the tiny pack rat who'd ventured from Bailey's pocket and now sat perched on her knee, awaiting treats.

Freyah bustled back into the room, demanded introductions all the way around and sat down amid a great deal of loud conversation. She seemed delighted to meet Bailey's mother and not at all perturbed that Bailey's plight had drawn in Rebecca.

Trent leaned forward a little, observing the cottage, trying to do it without attracting attention. He'd gone for a very very long time without any of the Magickers noticing that he had no Magick. For that time, he'd thought it was because of his cleverness and his reading. He loved the idea of magic and mythology and fantasy. He'd read everything on it he could get his hands on, and some of his favorites he read over and over. So when the Magickers had held their little tests to ferret out ability, he'd passed easily. They'd never questioned him in camp or after. He'd finally told Jason about it when they'd been backed into a corner and he'd had no choice, but Jason had never rejected him over it, nor had Bailey later when she'd learned.

Jason once pointed out that Trent had a crystal after all. He'd been bonded to it, even if it was not a clear crystal as they all used; it was a translucent, mingled gem and mineral chunk. Nor had Gavan and Eleanora taken it away from him or tried to change it for another, as they had Jason's. Jason's was flawed, badly, and they seemed to worry about that, but they'd never fussed over Trent's choice. So what did that mean, if anything? He was great at lying and posing? Or did he have a buried Talent as Jason thought and they knew that, and had the patience of saints waiting for it to surface.

In the meantime, he could see Magick where the others couldn't. He couldn't manipulate it or create it, but he could see it from time to time. Was that enough of a Talent to be of any worth? He didn't think so. You could see the effects of the wind, but unless you could harness it, as in sails or windmills, what use was it to see it?

Freyah called out, "Eat hearty, dears!" just as the picnic hamper came waddling out, its woven sides bulging here and there as if laboring to contain every dish stuffed into it. It huffed and chuffed and came to a stop at the foot of the bistro table, and its lid flew open with a loud BANG! "Serves 10 or more" read the sticker on its inner label.

Stef reached in and started to pull out plates of food beginning with a platter heaped with chicken pot pies no

bigger than the palm of Bailey's hand, steaming with a
mouthwatering aroma. A plate of strawberry tarts followed
that, and a third plate of wafer thin cheese pizza slices. Then
a kettle of stewed apples fragrant with cinnamon came after, and with a hiccup from the hamper, a pan of frosted
chocolate brownies. After that, Trent rather lost count of
the goodness overflowing, but he thought he managed to
get at least two of everything on his plate.

When he'd finished, he brushed George a last time, done
and satisfied. He felt a tingle, and the tray lost both its aura
and animation, slowly, like a tire leaking out air until it inevitably became flat. Trent stared at the serving tray in fascination as no one else seemed to notice. He slid his empty
plate onto the tray. It was odd, and he wanted to point it out
to Jason but since Jason hadn't seen it in the first place, well,
there you were. How do you say something is gone that no
one else knew was there but him?

He cast a glance about the cottage. Was Freyah's Magick
fading? He knew that this bit of existence came out of her
creation and she held it together by Talent and strength of
will. He could see the signs of Magick here and there, but
nothing seemed to be nickering or fading. Other than poor
George who'd gone quite to sleep.

Stef let out a belch. He sat on the floor, his back to the
ottoman Rich perched on, and stretched. "Man. That was
good."

"Just think." Rich stared at his friend. "He'll be hungry
again in a few hours."

"Then, by all means," Freyah said, "we'll pack him some
food to go."

"Go?" Jason looked at the elder.

"You're not staying here, dears. Surely you didn't think
you were." Freyah balanced her teacup on her palm. "It's
out of the question."

"Maybe for Eleanora, but there's no place for us now,
and you haven't a choice," said Jason. His voice broke a
little on the last of his sentence and he flushed.

"There is always a choice, Jason, my lad."

"Not if you're a Magicker."

"Now this is just what I've been arguing with Gavan
about. This is no time to be gathering a gaggle of students
and hoping to educate them. Taking one in at a time would

have been the best we could do. Educate and protect that student among ourselves. Now we're strung out so thin we can't help any of you."

"If you'd only taken one of us," said Bailey quietly, her eyes on Freyah, "what would the rest of us have done?"

"We would never have known we were Magickers, that's what," stated Rich. "And, frankly, that sucks." His red hair made him look a tad angrier than perhaps he was.

"Perhaps, but that one Magicker would have been safe, and none of you are now, to my read." Freyah put her teacup down on George. She frowned a moment as she touched the dormant serving tray, then tapped the surface three times and George woke up a little, although greatly subdued. Trent thought it safer to say nothing and just observe.

"Wrong. That one Magicker would have been with one of you, but the rest of us would have been pursued by the Dark Hand. They want us, even if you do not."

"Jason, is that fair?" Bailey blurted out.

He didn't take his eyes off Freyah. "I don't think we're talking fair here. We're talking survival."

Freyah glared back at him. "There are many of us who survived without help."

"So you pass it on? Are you trying to get even with someone? And you had your power. From everything I see here, you were fully grown into it."

Her mouth tightened. It made sharp knifelike wrinkles in her face. "I won't discuss that with you."

"Gregory the Gray couldn't handle Brennard, what makes you think any one of us alone could? But we're not alone. We have each other. And you're not alone either, Freyah, and you know it. You choose to live here alone, but you can reach out and touch a dozen Magickers in a wink if you wish." Jason took a deep breath then, and Trent saw his left hand tremble a bit. The scar on the back of it looked angry and pink although it had healed last summer.

"I'll get Gavan." Freyah stood. "You need to go now."

Jason stood as well. "Get him then, but we're not leaving. You say we'd drain you. I say we can help sustain this place."

Freyah ignored him. She pulled a long hairpin from her silvery coif, glaring into its gemstone butterfly decoration, and Gavan appeared with a blink.

He looked a bit rumpled as if he'd fallen asleep with his clothes on, a faint shadowy beard on his cheeks, his hair mussed, and deep lines across his face. "Auntie dear," he said, bemused. Then his eyebrow went up as he caught sight of everyone gathering around him. Four or five voices broke into explanations. He did not listen but raised a finger, and as everything became quiet, he said, "Now I understand. As a popular movie once stated, 'There was a great trembling in the force.' "

Gavan straightened a little. "I felt it, of course, but not in the way you did. The dark curtain that shrouds Eleanora suddenly got stronger. Deadlier. It took everything Fire-Ann and I had to hold it back."

The teacup in Freyah's hand rattled in its saucer. "Is she all right, then?"

"She is holding. Not better than that, but at least, not worse. I am beginning to think there is much about Magick we all don't know, and that the ignorance of it could be fatal."

"All the more reason they cannot hide with me."

Bailey had jumped to her feet, dumping little Lacey unceremoniously to the cottage floor. The wee pack rat scampered here and there, gathering flaky crumbs from dropped food and then bolted off altogether, disappearing into the unknown depths of Freyah's abode as she had once before. Bailey's jaws opened and shut, and she looked desperately at Jason who merely shook his head. She wrung her hands and stood still as Freyah and Gavan yelled at each other a bit.

"I have important work going on, not the least of which is warding Eleanora."

"They are your charges, and it was your headstrong decision that put them in jeopardy."

"For pity's sake, woman, I cannot be everywhere all the time!"

"If not Ravenwyng, then perhaps Tomaz can take them. Surely he has a hidden nook or two in the desert." Freyah drew herself up stubbornly.

"Tomaz is missing and has been for days." Gavan ran his hand through his hair. He looked much older than Trent remembered, with lines in his face and weariness about his eyes. The care of Eleanora had taken a toll on him.

"Nonetheless, they are not staying here." Freyah folded her arms over her chest and looked stubborn.

"No," answered Gavan sadly. "It is apparent they are not. I don't know what happened to you, Freyah, or when, but a great selfish thing has crept into you and taken possession. Eleanora loves you, and I have always respected you, but turning the children out is an act I can't forgive."

Freyah's expression hardened. "There are reasons, Gavan, you know nothing of."

"I know only that you used to be a pillar of the side we thought was good." Gavan held his hands out. "Gather round, everyone. Time to go."

"I can't!" wailed Bailey.

"Of course you can," snapped Freyah. "And the sooner the better."

"Not without Lacey."

Rebecca put her hand on her daughter's shoulder. "Honey, I don't pretend to understand most of this, but we can't stay where we're not wanted."

Freyah sighed, and sat down heavily. "It's not that I don't want you." She waved a tired hand. "I can't possibly explain, but someday maybe all of you will understand. Even you, Gavan," and she looked at the other sadly.

"A little late to get the sympathetic vote, Auntie." He rubbed the pewter-and-crystal head of his cane. "Leave the beast. As I noted, the trembling in the force could be felt by many, and I for one do not want to see what reaction it may bring. There are other things besides the Dark Hand and wolfjackals to fear."

Bailey closed her eyes tightly. "Just one minute more. Please! I can call her back."

"She's a little wild thing," her mother soothed. "You were bound to lose her sooner or later." She patted Bailey's shoulder.

"Mrs. Landau, I don't think you quite understand," Gavan began, but Bailey's squeal interrupted him.

"She's coming! Hold on, wait!" She bounced in place a moment as the others gathered in a circle, holding hands as they needed to. With a frantic skittering of nails on the wooden floorboards, the pack rat scampered into sight and then up Bailey's leg.

"Now!" she cried out triumphantly, clasping Lacey's furred body close.

"Now, indeed," said Gavan and waved his cane before Trent could even take a gulp and pray he wouldn't lose his meal.

How he *hated* Crystaling.

25

ANTIQUES AND
OTHER VALUABLES

THE step through with Gavan was barely more than a blink. It left only a moment of disorientation, and his stomach did not seem to notice it as it stayed pleasantly full from Freyah's midnight supper. If that gave him a hint of the relationship on other planes of Ravenwyng to Freyah's cottage he didn't trust it. More likely, Jason thought, it was sheer skill and experience on Gavan's part.

They stood outside the Gathering Hall of Camp Ravenwyng, and he felt for a moment as though it were a year ago and they were all just arriving for a summer of unknown adventure. The bright blue wooden cutout of Lake Wannameecha hung on its nail below the camp emblem. Some things never seemed to change, and some things he could barely recognize.

Bailey said quietly, "Ting should know." She stroked Lacey between her hands and was rewarded with a contented chirping. The pack rat's tufted tail hung between Bailey's fingers and swung back and forth in a slow wag, the little black knot of a tuft emphasizing each swing.

"We'll have some time to tell her. In the meanwhile," Gavan rubbed his face. "I think a good night's sleep is in order. The cabins and cottages aren't ready for summer campers yet, so we'll have to rough it in the Hall."

"Just like old times." Trent grinned. He nudged Henry. "Remember that down sleeping bag you had? The one that kept exploding like an air bag and swallowing you whole."

Henry managed a smile for the first time. "Yeah," he said. "Rolling that back up . . ." he shook his head at the thought.

"All I've got are blankets, but you'll be inside the wards, and nothing will disturb you." Gavan glanced at Stef. "Unless someone cannot keep control of himself."

Stef muffled a belch. Rich thumped him between the shoulder blades. "I've noted," offered Rich, "that being well fed seems to help."

"Well, that's something, then. I think Stef polished off most of the hamper all by himself."

Stef's face reddened. "Did not!" He pointed. "Trent helped."

Trent grinned, and straightened his lanky body. "Prove it." Of all of them, he had a body type that would probably never exhibit what he ate.

"Inside, all of you!" With a roll of his eyes, Gavan waved them inside. He touched Rebecca on her arm. "And you, dear lady, are welcome to have the chair in my office or the cot near Eleanora in FireAnn's cottage, if you wish."

"She's in a coma?"

"She's lovely," breathed Bailey. "Just like Sleeping Beauty."

Rebecca shifted uncomfortably and then said, "I think I'll stay with the kids, if you don't mind."

"Extra blankets, then. You should not have to sleep on floors." Gavan frowned slightly, as he unlocked the great doors to the Gathering Hall and flung them open. The air inside smelled a little of old wax and old stuffiness, having been shut away for a long time.

Jason rubbed his crystal, murmuring the Lantern enchantment, and it set off a warm yellow glow that illuminated all of the Hall. There were chairs pushed to one side of it, but basically it was just a large, wooden-floored room, rather like a dance hall or some such, with a small stage at the far end. Gavan left and returned with an overflowing armful of blankets and began handing them out to everyone.

They were suddenly, eye-drooping, bone-aching tired. Stef plopped down first, hugging a blanket to his chest, and settling in rather like a big dog. He let out a wide, pink-mouthed yawn and fell immediately into sleep. Bailey blinked at him.

"Is it just me, or . . ."

Rich shook his head. "He gets more bearlike every day." He sighed, and unfolded his blanket neatly. "I think, even if things settle down, he might not ever be able to go back home. Medically, it's fascinating, but realistically, he doesn't want a life as a freak."

"We'll cross that bridge when we come to it." Gavan handed the last three blankets to Rebecca. "Rest well. Fire-Ann will be around in the morning, with shower towels and breakfast call. I'll be here if you need me." He rubbed his eyes. "Even if you don't."

"Good night, and thank you." Rebecca Landau paused, then added, "Eleanora is very lucky, I think."

Gavan cleared his throat and looked a tad embarrassed before striding out of the Hall. His cloak, so much a part of him, as were the blue jeans, swirled about and then hid his passing.

After a few trips to the lavatories down the passageway and some muted talking while Stef began to snore as soon as his eyes closed, everyone seemed to settle down except for Bailey who had developed a rather odd eye twitch every time she looked at Jason.

Finally he stood up and gave a twitch of his own to the corridor, went out and waited for her.

She bounced in.

"What is it? We're all tired."

"I . . . we . . . that is, Lacey . . . saw something at Aunt Freyah's."

He stared at her. "I'm tired."

"You're tired, I'm tired, we're all tired. But she saw something."

"What?"

"That's just it, I don't know."

He leaned against the wall. "Give me a little hint.

Something big and furry with fangs or maybe a human or what." Lacey was more than a pet, she was a familiar to Bailey's budding Talents, but the two of them were far from sure what their partnership could do.

"Well, it was downstairs. Down into a creepy cellar like. Lots of stuff was stored down there, old vases, trunks, lamps, you know. A wine rack, I think."

"Like antiques and stuff put away?"

"Exactly. And something else, something big, something that scared her a lot. It had power to it. She ran off before she could give me a clear look at it, but even then, I don't know that I could be sure what it was. Seeing what a pack rat sees is kinda difficult."

"It's not like you've had a lot of practice at it yet, anyway." He rubbed his nose which felt as though he was on the verge of a sneeze or snort. "That does explain why she doesn't want us, or anyone, there. She might have a power source or something to keep her little place going. From what I've seen, most Magickers would love to have some sort of battery that boosts power."

"You think?"

"I only think, I don't know what it is she's hiding down there. What I do know is that she doesn't care if it costs Eleanora her life or hurts us to keep it secret." He let out a short breath of disappointment. "So it must be pretty important to her, at least." And something that the Dark Hand might well kill for.

"I wouldn't normally believe in blackmail," said Bailey, frowning. "But the next time one of us needs help, I'm gonna pull her chain."

"Not yet, Bailey. You don't know how strong or desperate Aunt Freyah is, and I don't think you want to learn."

"She should be helping us!"

"Bailey, we can't make someone feel that kind of obligation. You know that. There's a lot of that going around in the world, and nobody's been able to solve that problem yet." He put a hand on her shoulder. "What you found might matter later, but we have to see how without hurting her. Let's keep it quiet for now and see what tomorrow brings."

"What will tomorrow bring?" She looked at him. The Lantern spell on his crystal had nearly worn off, and the glow it cast was down to a faint, but steady gold. It brought out the gold in her hair and made the dusting of freckles across her nose look like pixie dust.

"I wish I knew," he said. "But then again, the way things have been going, maybe it's a good thing we don't!" He turned her around and pointed her back in the direction of the Hall. "One disaster at a time."

He trotted down to the bathrooms where he scrubbed himself as clean of the soccer game and all that had followed as best he could. He'd changed his clothes at his home, but there'd been no time for a shower. Coming back to the Hall with his hair still wet and plastered to his skull, he could see Bailey sitting up, her amethyst cupped in her hand, an intense look on her face and her mouth moving a bit as if she whispered to herself.

Telling Ting, no doubt, most of what had gone on. She finished as he settled down on his spread blanket, waved at him, and curled up next to her mother's back.

He settled back on his blanket, which did little or nothing to pad the hardwood floor underneath. If he weren't so tired, he didn't think he'd ever be able to sleep, but the last few days had made him feel worn and edgy. If he'd learned anything, it was that he had to trust himself. He had to trust his instinct that Tomaz knew what he was doing, and it was vitally important, despite the fact they all desperately needed him. He trusted Trent, after all, had never doubted his friend's value as a Magicker. He trusted Bailey, with her boundless enthusiasm for everything, and quiet Ting who was often Bailey's shadow—yet so much more. He trusted Gavan's vision for an academy to both hold Magickers secure and educate them. His instincts, surely, were guiding him where he needed to go. Jason dropped into dreams, wondering what he could do next.

In the morning, he knew. The sound of FireAnn's percussion on pots and pans and yelling, "Breakfast, come and get it, lads and lassies!" permeated the dawn. He waited until after they'd all eaten and stood in the cafeteria kitchen, washing and cleaning up.

"I'm going back to Haven," he announced, "and opening the last Gate there. It's where we need to be."

"But you said we were cut off."

He nodded. "We were forbidden."

"Then ..." Henry stopped cleaning the pot he held and stood, dish towel in one hand and pot in the other.

"And we're going. Everyone but Rebecca."

Bailey's mother frowned. "If it's something dangerous—"

"It is, but I need you here as an anchor for Bailey. The two of you are very close, and if we get in trouble, she'll be able to reach and get you, and ..." he paused. "It's like throwing a line to someone, and having them pull it over, see?"

"I see," she answered slowly. "What is it that could be that dangerous?"

"Just a dragon," answered Trent.

Stef grunted and rolled his shoulders. "Big one, too."

"A ... dragon." Rebecca sat down on a kitchen chair, her face pale.

Jason hesitated. She'd taken everything so well up till now.

"Mom, really, it's okay." Bailey hugged her mother tightly about the neck. "If Jason says it is, it will be."

"Well, I don't know ... that much ..." Jason faltered. "I just know it's what I have to do." He looked round the kitchen. FireAnn, her bounteous red hair bound back in a soft green bandanna, stood at the kitchen doorway, twisting bundles of herbs to dry on the many hooks about the kitchen walls and beams.

"Sounds dire, lad," she said, in her soft Irish voice. She wiped her hands on her apron. She was thin and wiry and had a strong nose, and her love was in her herbs and cooking. "He closed the Gate, as I hear tell. Ye're not to trespass there, ever again."

"But that's just it." He faced FireAnn and then swung about to look at all of them. "He had no right to close the Gate. I opened it. I opened the Iron Gate and the Water Gate, there. Twice I was led there, and all of you said I had to find the third way there to stabilize it. It's the only place Magickers can go to be safe right now. And I belong there. It's where my senses, my thoughts, take me. And I have to trust that. I have to trust myself."

"Think he'll listen to reason?"

Jason shrugged at Trent's question. "I have no idea.

We've had a lot of conversations. I used to think he was my friend. But I just don't know. You all can come with me, and help—and I do need your help—or you can stay and wait to see if I do it. Either way, I'm going."

"Count me in," said Bailey.

"Me too, bro." Trent waggled his fingers against the thigh of his pants, tapping out a heroic ballad of some sort, heard only by himself.

"The two of us, of course," Rich said, putting an elbow into Stef who seemed a bit stunned by the idea of facing the dragon.

"And me," Henry finally offered, although he seemed to have gone pasty white again.

"Should I get Ting?" Bailey started to uncage her amethyst.

"No. She can anchor us, if needed. Ting and your mom. Best that way, I think."

Bailey waggled an eyebrow. "She's gonna be so peeved. She keeps saying she is missing all the excitement."

"Ye'll be creating a backwash here," FireAnn stated. "The best I can do is to stay and try to dampen that, so nothing comes to feed on th' energy or any of ye in a weakened state."

"Ummm . . . thanks."

"Think nothing of it, lad." She winked at Jason.

"Ready, then?" Jason fingered his crystal. He wasn't sure he was, but he didn't think it was the kind of moment anyone could actually be ready for. You either took a deep breath and plunged in or you didn't. Sometimes the things you did were life altering and they had to be handled that way, because if you thought about it too much, you'd never do anything. You'd freeze in indecision.

"Go for it," Trent told him. He looped an elbow with Jason and reached for Stefan.

In moments, he could feel them all joining him. As he opened the Iron Gate and brought them through, he could hear Rebecca Landau cry out softly, "Bailey, I love you!"

Her gentle words were drowned out by the roar of the beast bearing down on them, jaws open, huge eyes glaring.

"You shall not pass!"

·

26

DRAGON EYES

THE orange-red guardian of the Gate rushed them. Its scales glittered brilliantly in the morning sun, but not as brightly as its bared fangs. Jason fought not to back up as he said, "Steady," to his friends. He could feel the molten breath of the dragon as it flew down upon them.

All hope for a talk first fled. So many times he had come here, just to talk, and now there seemed no chance of it. It would be war between them. He brought his gemstone up, readying to Shield.

"Hold it," muttered Trent. "Something's not quite right."

They had maybe two heartbeats before the dragon would be upon them.

"What is it?"

"Illusion. I think."

"You think?" Rich countered, his voice breaking off on a high-pitched note, as he and Stef jostled their elbows.

"Note to self: illusions difficult to perceive under pressure," cracked Trent, even as the beast swooped directly overhead, its passage buffeting them with a hot wind as it ... disappeared.

They blinked.

"Gone." Jason turned in his tracks, surveying the area.

"Told ya."

Bailey let out a quivery breath. "What do we do now?"

"Do you have a p-plan?" asked Henry as he pushed his glasses squarely back onto his nose with a nervous gesture.

"I think his plan is to use us all as dragon bait while he finds the Gate he needs," Rich told Squibb. He steadied Stef who'd gone to his knees, body torn between staying human and going bear, at the sight of the menacing dragon.

"That works for me," Jason said lightly. He looked down the pass into the valley where they'd always hoped to build Iron Mountain Academy. Bailey punched him in the arm.

"You wouldn't!"

"Of course he wouldn't," said Trent. "I would, but he wouldn't." He ducked as Bailey swung a nudge his way.

"Seriously," Jason told them, leading them down into the valley. "I haven't much to go on but a gut feeling, and that means unless I find the Gate right away, we may all become dragon bait. It will know we're here, if it doesn't already."

"Think that illusion would be tripped by anyone here in the pass?"

Jason nodded. "Probably."

"Wouldn't a doorbell be just as good? Or maybe a big brass door knocker?" Bailey swung her head about vigorously, ponytail bobbing.

"I think a two-thousand-pound dragon can pretty well use anything it wants for an alarm."

Lacey let out a few sharp chitters as if feeling as disagreeable about the whole matter as Bailey did. "It's not like we've ever done anything to *it*." Bailey rubbed the little creature's nearly transparent pink ears.

"Guys," Jason began and then stopped.

"What?" They all halted in their footsteps, turned, and looked at him.

His face flushed with a slight embarrassment. "Well. It's kind of hard to concentrate with everyone talking and arguing."

Trent put a hand up. "Pipe down, everyone. Shaddup, in other words."

Stef grunted, ducking his big square head down between his shoulders. Rich, though, did not grow still. "Just tell us what we're looking for here, okay? I mean, I could stumble over buried treasure here or something and not know it."

"I'm not sure what we're looking for. All I know is, I'll know it when we find it."

Trent gestured. "How about everybody spread out a little bit, like we did when we had to find the ley lines?"

Stef groaned. He scrubbed both hands up the sides of his head and over his crew cut. He rolled his shoulders from side to side and began a reluctant, lumbering walk. Rich caught up with him and thumped his back. "It's all right, big guy. I've got you covered."

"It's not that I can't find 'em," Stef muttered. "It's because they make me itchy all over, like a spiderweb, you know? And I *hate* that." He scratched his head again.

"They do?" Trent stared with obvious fascination.

"Yeah, they do."

"That's great!"

"It is?" Stef stopped in disbelief and squinted at them.

"It has to be. Ley lines are natural energy lines of Magick running over the Earth, right? And we're all in tune to them, but if you can feel them without any dowsing rods or gear like that, you're really sensitive. Call me stupid, but I think what Jason needs here is probably going to be at the center of a nest of ley lines. Power, you see? And if you can feel it that well, you can lead Jason right to it!"

Stef grunted. "It'll be like a beehive," he muttered. "Stinging me all over. The bear won't like it."

"Then we'll keep a grip on him, Stef," Rich promised his friend. Steering his friend down the grass and rock slope to the valley below, he chanted football plays and facts back and forth, keeping Stef's mind off the unseen power that webbed the area. They trotted slowly away from the rest of the group.

Henry shadowed Bailey. He still looked uncertain of events as he did. Trent fell into step with Jason. "Stands to reason, doesn't it?"

"It does. I should have thought of that."

"Not bad for a guy with no Talent." Trent gave him a grin.

"You've got tons of Talent," Jason told him. "We just don't know what it is yet." He rubbed his crystal.

"It has to be here, right?"

"It has to be," agreed Jason. "All the time I've been looking, every time I was worried or tired or whatever, this is where I came. It's like part of me knows instinctively what the rest of me is fighting to figure out. It *has* to be here."

Trent nodded in agreement as he agilely negotiated the downslope with Jason. "Have any idea how big it is, here?" He surveyed the valley. "Is it just a tidy little land basin or are we looking at a continent here? Or an entirely new world?"

"I don't know. Not sure if it'll make a difference. The Gate, till it's anchored, probably exists everywhere and nowhere. It's like a . . . a shadow. All I have to do is catch a corner of it . . ." Jason's voice trailed off in thought as he trotted closer to the clear blue pool of water, the lake that took up much of the valley's area. He wondered how close he was to that description. Could something as important as a Gate begin as insubstantial and wispy as a shadow? Or had he already seen the Gate and just not recognized it for what it was?

Jason made a fist about his crystal and stumbled to a halt. No. No, it couldn't be. He looked around at the spine of the Iron Mountains edging the valley, and the faint spray off the long waterfall that fell from it into the pool, and across the rolling slopes of soft, green grass.

What he'd said to Trent wasn't quite right. Every time he sought the gate, he came to the valley—and the dragon.

No. And yet . . .

"Everyone stop," he called out. "I've found it. Or rather, I know what it is."

The Magickers halted. Rich and Stef perched on one of the big broken boulders at the foot of the mountains, while Bailey delicately chose a patch of clover and sat down cross-legged. They all found a place to rest and turned to look at him.

"I need the dragon," Jason told them.

"Frankly, Jase, I thought our strategy here was to avoid the dragon, and maybe not get eaten or flamed while we did it." Trent watched him.

"I'm serious."

"I don't think this is a good idea." Henry took his glasses off and cleaned them vigorously. "I'm with Trent. I thought we wanted to stay away from it."

"Things change. Look, I know what I know, when I know it. And what I know is that, just like it's right coming here to find the Gate, it's right to find the dragon."

"If it has closed off the Iron Gate to you, what makes you think it'll let you open another?"

"That, I don't know. Yet." Jason shaded his eyes to scan the horizon.

"Any way you can call it?" Bailey paused to tighten the laces on her sneakers. Lacey perched on her thigh, and nibbled on what looked like a bit of raisin scone. Breakfast from that morning, courtesy of FireAnn.

Jason watched the two of them, a thought nibbling on the edge of his mind, much as the pack rat did on her crumb of scone. "Nooooo," he said, finally. "But . . ."

Trent's attention snapped to him. "But what?" He followed Jason's stare. "Oh. Ummm."

Bailey scratched her pet's chin with a fingertip. "Umm, what?"

"Remember how you called the frogs? And Lacey? And Stef as a bear cub?"

"Cut to the chase," Trent told him. He pointed at Bailey. "Jason wants you to call the dragon."

"Oh." Bailey rocked back on her elbows.

"I don't think you want to do that," offered Henry.

Both Rich and Stef grabbed Henry up, mock growling at him, "Shaddup!" Henry made an aggrieved growl of his own and the three of them rolled around on the grass.

Bailey stuck her foot out and nudged at all of them. "Honestly. As if I can't make up my own mind."

"Look," said Jason to her. "This is what we came for. Now, I can't promise that the dragon won't eat every one of us, because I don't know what it'll do. But we've been talking for months and it should know what I won't do, and I won't harm it, not on purpose. Or any of you."

"That," said Bailey, "is good enough for me." She uncaged her amethyst from its wire cage. "What do you think a dragon answers to?"

"Probably something sharp and scaly with fire-breathing jaws," Trent noted.

"You think?"

He nodded sagely. Bailey snorted, *pfuffing* her bangs off her forehead as she did. "Give me a few minutes." As she concentrated, her face knotted more and more. Lacey scampered back into the pocket of her shirt, but hung there, looking out, resting her chin on her tail tuft.

"Now is probably a really good time to work on your Shields," reflected Trent.

Instantly other hands came out, gripping crystals, and light flared around them.

"Not that anything we can put out yet will stop a dragon," added Trent, and he grinned. The Shields stayed up, sparkling in the daylight like some vast soap bubble.

Long moments crawled past. A cloud of gnats flew by after darting once or twice at Stef, circling, and then leaving as they all flailed about and waved their hands frantically to chase off the flying pests. A cloud drifted over and scattered in the bright sun. Rich wandered off to "visit a private bush" and came back and still nothing had happened.

Jason sat down, his knees under his chin. His rib cage still hurt from the various attacks and the soccer game, but not as much as the knowledge that he could never go back and be the same Jason he'd been before. He hadn't noticed it at the time, but, thinking about it later, he'd realized that his coach and Sammee had just walked away from the soccer field while everyone was still ranting and raving, as if he'd done something wrong. The memory was tucked in the corner of his mind and he hadn't even really seen it till he was trying to go to sleep on the Hall's wooden floor. That and other things had circled round and round in his mind, but the dragon had ruled everything.

Sun beat down on his sneakered feet in a warm band. He looked down and saw a small orange lizard lying comfortably across the laces on his right foot. A salamander, a tiny fire lizard, like he'd seen a few times at camp. He looked at it, smiling. It, too, seemed to enjoy soaking up the sun. Then the reptile lifted its head and looked right at him, and Jason froze.

"Nobody move," he said quietly. "It's here." He put his hands back, debating over standing or not.

"What is?"

"Dragon."

"Oh-kay. How invisible is it?"

But Bailey followed his glance downward to his shoe. "Jason, that's a lizard, and it's not any bigger than Lacey."

The pack rat gave a chirp as if insulted. "Not that there's anything wrong with that, but . . ."

"It's not the size." Jason looked at the salamander. "I know what I know." He stood slowly. The lizard uncoiled, yawned lazily, and crawled off Jason's shoe. It stretched, catlike, in the grasses, and it began to grow.

And grow.

And grow.

Until it dwarfed all of them by ten or twelve times, its head alone bigger than two or three of them put together. It cocked its head, and rattled the spiny plates on its back. "Smart, lad." Its crimson forked tongue slithered in and out of its teeth a few times, testing the air.

"Not smart enough, sometimes. Anyway. It's like this. I want the Gate."

"You cannot pass."

He shook his head. "Not good enough. This isn't a game anymore. Our lives depend on it."

"You cannot pass." The dragon's eyes glared a bit, but he did not dare look straight into them, wisdom passed on from Trent and the tricky ways of mythological beasts.

"You cannot stop me. I opened the Iron Gate, and the Water Gate, and I'll open the third Gate, too."

The dragon bellowed. The noise shivered off the very mountains, sending clusters of rocks tumbling down, and thundering off their eardrums, all but Jason throwing their arms about their heads to shut the sound away. He took a deep breath.

"I know what I know."

"You know nothing if you do not understand what you are opening this time."

"A sanctuary, a haven, a school."

"Think that, do you?" The dragon shifted around, coiling its tail across its haunches. It hunkered down, chin on the ground before Jason. "Are you a warrior or a guardian?"

"We've talked about this before. I'll fight if I need to." He rubbed his hand across his ribs. "If I need to," he repeated.

"Find the Gate if you can," hissed the great beast. "And my wrath if you cannot, because a Gate is the only way you'll escape me." His gemlike eyes blazed with defiance, and heat rolled off the creature's body like a cloud of steam. The dragon could be deadly, and left no doubt of that.

Jason opened his mouth to retort again, then closed it. His crystal felt hot in his hand. He turned his head slightly. "Get back, all of you."

"What are you going to do?"

"Open a Gate." He stepped forward. He put his hand out, on the Dragon's head to steady himself, as he leaned in and looked deeply into the gleaming eyes of the beast. "You, my friend, do not only guard the Gate. You *are* the Gate." And he fell into its depths.

SMOKE AND MIRRORS

H E FELT the heat. Amber color swallowed Jason whole, and it carried the warmth of a fiery forge with it, shimmering off his skin like the sun off a sandy beach. That was the first essence of the dragon he perceived. Hidden inside the warmth came a sharpness like that of knives, slicing against him, not deep enough to cut but enough to feel their many edges. The dragon's talons and teeth, he thought. And more than that, he felt the profound intellect surrounding him, weighing him, judging him. He walked carefully forward, making sure not to slip, for any false move would drop him into the fire, into the sharp edge, into trouble.

He walked into an inner chamber and stood inside the lanternlike glowing amber, and stopped there. He could hear the thunderous yet slow and steady beat of a faraway drum. It pulsed with a steady sureness. Jason listened, baffled a moment, and then realized it was the dragon's heart he heard.

He wondered what was happening outside. Had he disappeared to them or did he stand paralyzed next to the beast, drawn in by its glorious eyes? And were they safe? Had he abandoned them?

Jason frowned and turned around slowly, looking all about the honey-gold cavern. He had not a clue what to do next, but he knew he had to be right. The dragon was the Gate itself, or at least so deeply wound into it that he could not separate one from the other. The rightness of it seeped into him.

Golden-orange coils began to separate from the wall facing him. In a moment or two, the sinuous beast extracted itself to face Jason, just a little taller but a Chinese dragon of length and grace as well as strength, its jaws and claws no less impressive as it studied him.

"You cannot pass."

"No matter how many times you say it, it doesn't make it true." Jason looked at the dragon.

"Then you will have to fight your way through." The dragon had whiskers, not at all catlike, but fine, strong whiskers for all that, and they bristled as it looked at Jason.

Jason shook his head. "I can't do that."

"Why not?"

"You're my friend. At least, I always thought you were. But even if you weren't, I can't just attack something. I fight if I have to, not before."

"Warrior or guardian," the dragon stubbornly insisted.

"There's no right answer there."

"There is more of an answer than you think." The dragon reared back, then struck at him.

Jason threw himself to his right. He slid on his elbow and came up rolling. As soon as he could get to his feet, the beast struck again. He dodged in the other direction. Its fang caught his sleeve as he did, ripping through. Pain scraped him as he landed on one knee and thrust himself out of range as the dragon recoiled and then snapped at him again. Its scaly body cut the air with a sharp hiss. It missed him again and again and again, every strike closer and faster until he panted.

He couldn't do this all day until it caught him. Jason rolled over and gathered himself, watching, waiting for the next snap. When it came, he leaped, not away but at it, catching the beast at the back of the head and wrapping his arms and legs about its body with all the strength he had left.

The dragon reacted like a bucking bronco. It reared and

flung him back and forth to shake him off. Jason clung with everything he had. He pushed his voice through clenched teeth.

"This . . . is not . . . about fighting! If it were, you'd . . . have me . . . beat!"

The dragon rattled him as though he were a rag doll. He couldn't let go now. If he did, he'd be thrown across the cavern with such force, he'd break in two when he hit the wall. "Listen! You win!"

The dragon reared up, balancing on its haunches, panting a little itself, its blood racing like fire through its scaly body. Jason felt as though he were hugging a furnace. "But it is you who has me."

"I'm just holding on, trying not to get hurt." Jason sucked in a breath. "You're my friend! There has to be a way to make you see what I have to do."

"Get down," the dragon ordered quietly.

After a moment of hesitation, Jason let go and slid down. His arms and hands felt as though they had been sandpapered with a thousand small, stinging cuts. He'd read once that a shark's skin was like that . . . tiny scales that were miniatures of its dangerous teeth.

"Tell me." The dragon settled then, curling up in front of him.

Jason fell onto his butt, too weary to stand. He tried to sit cross-legged. "This Haven feels right. I can't explain it better than that. It's like when you walk into a room, and you know you belong there. Not because you own it, but because you . . . created it. And you love it, and you care for it. Does that make any sense?"

The dragon pulled at a whisker, curling it against its sharp obsidian claw. "And?"

"And whether you try to deny me or not, you can't deny the rightness of it, do you see?"

The beast lowered its head until their chins were nearly level. It said quietly, "Warrior or guardian?"

Jason rolled his eyes. "How should I know? You're the being with an ancient mind, full of riddles and history."

"Ah!" It drew back, grinning in a draconic way. "A riddle then? I win, you go, you win, you . . . go through. Agreed?"

Jason rubbed his eyebrow. He could almost hear Trent in the back of his mind saying, "Careful!" Maybe he did hear Trent. And Bailey, too, saying, "You can do it." He nodded. "Okay."

"Good. This riddle is a story." The dragon rubbed his claws. "Centuries ago, in a land you may or may not have heard of, a mighty emperor was told by his astrologer that his days were coming to an end. He was a great ruler, and a great warrior, and had lived long, so he was not sad. But he had a burden in picking someone to rule after him, as he had no family. He had built an empire that was good for its people, and he wanted that to live on after him. After thinking long, he devised a test. He picked six candidates for this test. One of his generals, one of his priests, one of his accountants, two of his mayors, and the sixth, a common man who had been in his army and was now his gardener.

"All were humbled at being summoned to the emperor's court. Even more humbled when told why. 'But,' he said to them, 'I have a test and the one who passes best will be my successor,' and they all agreed to abide by it.

"To each man he gave a nest with an egg in it. 'Take care of this egg, and hatch it, and return in six months' time with what you have nurtured.' And he sent each man away, even the gardener who was named Ding.

"Ding had traveled far and been a soldier and knew the ways of the civilized world before returning to the land and becoming a gardener. He knew how to care for his nest. He kept the egg just warm enough and turned it as a mother bird would, and yet it never hatched. Long day after long day passed and nothing emerged from the emperor's egg. The dawn came when all the candidates were summoned back to the emperor's court, and each was to present his nest with its bounty."

The dragon looked keenly at Jason. It indicated him with a toe claw. "Think of what you would do if you were Ding.

"The general came forth. He showed the emperor a mighty falcon, hooded and resting on his wrist. 'Young but eager for the hunt,' the general said proudly. The emperor nodded and waved the general to one side.

"The accountant approached next. He held a woven cage of small size, efficient and neat. A sparrow sat inside, picking insects out of the air. He said nothing, but put the cage on the floor at the emperor's feet, bowed deeply and backed away. Sparrow and emperor looked at one another a moment.

"Beautiful birdsong came through the air, as the third candidate brought in his cage, far bigger and prettier, containing a lovely canary who sang as if for the gods themselves, or so the priest maintained. He too set his cage on the floor.

"The mayors came in together. They presented a large clay pot. 'We both hatched ducks,' they said proudly. 'And in alliance with one another, have butchered them and cooked them, in a dish fit for an emperor. Thus may all eat and prosper.'

"Indeed, smell from the clay pot was wonderful!

"Ding waited to go last for his turn. The emperor turned expectantly to him."

The dragon motioned to Jason. "You with your empty nest. What do you do?"

Jason blinked.

"Quickly," said the dragon. "What do you do?"

"I enter, and put the nest on the floor and tell the emperor I failed," said Jason finally. There were a thousand clever things that came to mind, but he did not like lying, never had, and not even as the humble gardener could he see doing it.

"Nothing else. Excuses?"

"I have none. I did my best, but I failed." Jason shrugged.

"And that is what Ding did, and said," the dragon told him. "The mayors told him out of the sides of their mouths that he was a fool, and could have described a mighty phoenix, but that the bird had escaped him. The others just stared. The emperor rose to announce, 'I have chosen my heir, and it is Ding. The eggs I gave you all were infertile. He presented no grand illusions or imposters, but told the truth and showed no fear in presenting it. I wished to choose an honest man, and a man who is not afraid to judge himself.' And so, in due time, Ding became an emperor."

"I guessed the riddle?"

"Not quite." The dragon tapped his claws together. "Warrior or guardian?"

Impossible! thought Jason. Would the dragon never give up? "Guardian," Jason finally, reluctantly, told him. "I would only fight if I had to, and to protect those I needed to, I guess."

The sinuous serpent drew back, coiling, as if for one last fatal strike. It looked at Jason, its eyes gleaming.

"The Gate is Open," the dragon said. "Pass it if you dare."

28

WHOOPS

LIGHT blazed around him. Jason lost his vision as he fell through it. The air smelled of fire and copper, burning away all his senses as Magick roared past him, over him, *through* him. He tumbled in midair, as though caught up in the winds of a hurricane, all the power swirling around him. It made him want to scream in fear and shout for joy and roar in triumph, all at once, and he could not make a sound. Instead, he seized it. Jason spread his arms and rode it, surfing across the Magick as if it were a vast, curling wave.

He had never felt anything like this before, and knew his world had changed, and as it bore him through the void, it began to lose strength, and he realized he would probably never feel anything so fierce, so pure again.

And it was his. He was part of it, braided into it, held up by it.

He threw his arms up, fists clenched in sheer joy. The Magick carried him through forever, then began to lower him, and his voice came back, shouting aloud in victory, as it washed onto an edge of now, and deposited him gently there.

Jason dropped his arms. He felt incredibly weak from

the rush, and his heartbeat surged in his throat painfully, subsiding slowly as he took a few great breaths. He stood in a dirt cave and he walked out of it, ducking his head to avoid sharp outcroppings of rock. Outside, the sunlight made him squint as he turned back around to see where he'd come from.

He'd walked out of the Iron Mountains, through a cave he'd no idea had existed. Or maybe it hadn't, before. He'd opened a Gate, after all. Jason stood, swaying, his knees still weak, his whole body feeling limp with the effort, but he put his chin up and looked at the Gate.

Chiseled out of the rough, rust-red stone of the mountain, was a pouncing dragon, jaws opened wide to gather up any who dared to enter, with sharp teeth of stone. It looked awesome. Jason grinned broadly.

"Jason!" Bailey tackled him and he went to the ground, laughing. The others dog-piled on, all screaming and pummeling him.

"Did you see that? A Dragon Gate! Did you see what you made?"

"We didn't know! You disappeared and then the dragon, and then everything got really quiet. Then we could hear the mountain moaning."

"We all thought, 'Earthquake!' "

Jason rolled over, still grinning, and trying to protect his ribs from the hugs and pinches and nudges of his buddies. "And then what?"

"Don't you know?" Bailey stared at him, aghast.

"I," Jason told her, "was on the inside, don't forget."

"Oh!" She tossed her head.

"Whole mountain shook," Stef grumbled. "Dust and pebbles poured down. We figured it was all over, place was coming apart. We figured you were done for."

"Woah." He rubbed his face. He hadn't thought of that, of what might happen to the unstable Haven if he failed.

Rich sat back on his heels, his normally pale face reddening from being out in the sun so long, his freckles standing out as though he'd been hit with chocolate chips. "So you killed the dragon?"

"I don't think so. I hope not. We were friends." Jason struggled and managed to sit up. Everything looked as if it was going to spin around, and he closed his eyes.

"Friends don't eat friends," Bailey said firmly.

"Did you get eaten?"

"Noooo."

"Well, then." Jason opened one eye to peer at her.

Trent leaped to his feet. "So. We're good here?"

"Should be."

Stef let out a bearlike grunt. "We'd better be, because you let off so much power, it's like attracting flies."

"Or something like that." Rich stood, too. "Is it always like that when you open a Gate? I don't remember feeling anything before."

"Never," vowed Jason, "like that." And it probably never would be again, and that was fine with him. Some things should be a once in a lifetime experience. He still felt overwhelmed. He tried to stand. "I think you guys need to . . ." He paused. He wobbled to his feet.

Henry put his arm out to try and catch Jason. "Do what?"

"Camp. Or something." Jason swayed on his feet, and his ears roared, and blackness threatened to gobble all his thoughts. He pulled Rebecca Landau through and knew he had to shut the Gate because of the backlash crashing down on him. He left a tiny crack open for Ting and only hoped she could find it, and them. Jason felt the weakness surge back through him, and fell into darkness. Something squeaked and he hoped it was Bailey in surprise and not the pack rat as he fell.

Ting sat in the client lobby, waiting for both her mother and grandmother. Her mother had gone to move the car around, and her grandmother was being wheeled into the reception area even as Ting shifted restlessly, trying to ignore the other outpatients and their families. It was like a library in that no one wanted to speak above a whisper, and the marble flooring held a chill that the sun glinting through the corridor couldn't warm, and there was a feeling that several of those waiting held little faith in the treatment they'd received that morning. Waiting for the end, her grandmother had told her, walking in. "They have no faith!" She'd swung her cane about vigorously. "Even if I go, I live on. In your mother, in you. That is faith enough."

And now, just a bare hour later, she was being wheeled back out, the color behind her naturally tanned and Asianpigmented skin gone pale, her arm bandaged where the IV had been, and one of those paper cup masks over the lower half of her face. She raised a hand to grasp Ting's firmly as the nurse said, "I'll be back when the car is here."

Ting's grandmother hardly took up any room at all in the wheelchair. Ting slid in next to her, pressing against her so she could lend her own body's warmth. "How do you feel?"

Ting's grandmother wrinkled her nose. "Bad taste in my mouth. Even my best tea leaves will taste awful for days." She rubbed Ting's hand in her own. Her hand held strength in it still, although it was wrinkled and somewhat shrunken by her illness and age. "But what can one do?"

"Mom'll be out front in a minute. Then we'll go home and you can rest." Ting leaned her head against that of her grandmother's. She smelled of medicine and antiseptics and it would be good to get her home where she could brew ginger tea against the nausea and she would smell of that goodness instead. They were sitting that way when the wave of power hit them.

It rippled through the clinic lobby like a shock wave. Ting sat back in the wheelchair with a smothered gasp as it lanced through her as though it were pure sunlight, almost blinding. It gripped them both so strongly neither one could move and they could hardly breathe—and it continued to just pour through them. Ting's eyes stung with the brilliance that no one but the two of them seemed to see!

Her grandmother's hand curled tighter over hers. "What is it?" she managed.

"I don't know!" Ting wanted to shout with joy though as it soared around her. She tasted Magick in it. In fact, it *sang* with Magick. But where it came from, or what caused it, she had no idea. She put her chin up to face it, seeking it as a flower did the sun. It felt glorious, and her grandmother gave a soft sound, rather like a purr, as they clasped hands.

"Someone is a master," her grandmother said. They breathed in the Magick for another few, long moments before it began to fade and then was gone.

Ting blinked and realized someone had honked a car horn out front, at the doors. She let go of her grandmother's hand and went to the back of the wheelchair to push it out in answer. "I wonder what happened."

"We must go there."

"Where?"

"You can find it," her grandmother said confidently.

"But Mom . . ."

"She will understand." Her grandmother got to her feet. She wore silk trousers and a black silk jacket quilted in gold thread with a small tiger embroidered over her left pocket. She tugged her clothes into place. "Leave a note."

Ting fished around in her purse, scribbled something quickly, and left it on the wheelchair seat. She took her grandmother into the empty corridor, got her crystal out and Focused. After a shaky try, she found the trail of Magick and, gripping her grandmother's hand firmly, took her there.

Gavan woke with a jerk. He leaped to his feet, dismayed at having slept so soundly or so late, and being awoken so abruptly. He swung his cane about, searching for intruders, for trouble. Then he stopped, puzzled. Nothing or no one to sense. He took a deep breath, and sat back down by Eleanora's side. "Alarms over nothing." He touched her cold, still hand, then added, "Not nothing if it's over you, that's not what I meant." He rubbed the wolfhead on his cane as if gathering his thoughts. "Aunt Freyah kept me awake half the night raving over the kids. Worry over you kept me awake for most of the rest of the night. I am up against a rock here, Eleanora, without any answers. I keep asking myself what your father would have done, and yet I cannot help having angry thoughts that Gregory put us in this position. If only he'd dealt with Brennard instead of seeing him get stronger and darker every day . . ." Gavan paused. He traced a finger down the side of Eleanora's sleep-frozen face. "Of course, that wasn't his way, nor yours. I'll admit my position varies from day to day. There are days when I'd seek Brennard out now just for the satisfaction." He took a deep breath, which was good, because when the wave hit him, it was so strong, such a lash of power, that he could not breathe again for many long moments. It flared through the diamond gemstone gripped by the wolf's pewter jaws of his cane, and shone through like a laser beam, sharp and glaring white, and he'd no doubt if he Focused it, it would cut through steel. He sat pushed back in his chair with the force of it, felt it part every fiber of his body and flow through him unstoppably. When it had gone and he could finally breathe again, he took two or three whooping gulps of air, then knelt down beside Eleanora.

Its passing had tousled her long brunette hair into a jumble, but other than that, she seemed untouched. Perhaps not entirely untouched. The lines on her face seemed to have relaxed, and she wore more of a serene expression in her deep rest. Nothing untoward, though, and for that he gave many thanks.

He stood and shook his cane. He had no idea what had just happened, but he *would* find out.

Khalil paused in his study, his hand stretched out to take down a dusty leather book fastened with cords of twisted gold, and felt the power sweep over him. He considered it for a moment until he had absorbed its strength, its flavor, and its portent. He smiled slowly. The act would have come sooner or later, but the consequences of the chaos it would rip loose by its doing ... He shook his head. They had no consideration about what it was they were doing. He had some research to conduct, then he would look into the matter.

He continued smoothly reaching to take his book down, and opened it carefully, for the pages were greatly aged and written many a century ago. He sat down under a strong electric light and began to read.

In dark chambers halfway across the world, Brennard jumped to his feet. The power that had swept through left him chilled and shaking in his chair. He put his hands to his face, cupping his eyes a moment, for the Magick had nearly blinded him, and it took him a while to recover. Then he threw his head back and let out an angry roar. He flung his hand out, swiping a Ming vase aside and smashing it to the floor where porcelain centuries old and valuable beyond compare shattered into a thousand pieces.

At the sound of the crash, Jon ran in, and stopped amid the rubble, his face chalk white. He looked down. "What happened?"

"Did you not feel it?"

Jon looked as though searching for an answer, then said,

"How could it not be felt? It roared through here like a typhoon or cyclone."

"Backtrace it."

"I cannot. It recoils from me as if knowing my power and its are opposite from each other."

"Find someone who can!" Brennard bellowed. "I want to know who unleashed that kind of Magick on the world."

"Want to . . . or need to?" asked Jonnard quietly, studying his father's face.

"You can be a fool."

"We are both fools if you think you can chase that down, and triumph against whomever sent it."

"I do not think it an attack."

"But you do not know for sure."

"No." Brennard clenched one hand. "It could have been deliberate or the residue from some deliberate act, a backlash they had no idea would occur. Either way, I need to know who did it."

Jon inclined his head. "I will find out." His ties with Henry Squibb had been very weak the last day or so, but only because he hadn't tried to reinforce them. Squibb had been fighting him, and it seemed wiser to conserve his strength for other problems. Now he had other priorities and Squibb could be useful again. "Anything else?"

"The vase," Brennard answered, looking down on the floor as if in sudden recognition of the accident.

Jon waved his hand. A thousand fine pieces of porcelain rose in the air, circling about aimlessly and then more and more into a maelstrom pattern that grew closer and closer together until the vase re-formed itself. Jon dropped his hand and the Ming vase settled to once again to rule a corner of his father's desk in dark blues and milky whites and incomparable porcelain. "Please be careful, Father," Jon noted mildly. "You could have cut yourself." He turned and left the inner offices of his father's domain.

An excitement woke in him. He could do something Brennard could not. The days of his father's unlimited power seemed to be drawing to a close. He would need Jonnard more than ever, and perhaps even finish his training, and confide in him.

And then the day when Jon could take over entirely

would be that much nearer. He wanted the power, and he wanted it now.

He'd had a taste of his father's strength, and knew the rest of it could be his any time he wanted. When he had it, he could then command the army his father had assembled over the years, mercenaries from lost wars over the centuries, lean and hungry men who slept in the catacombs below their estate, ready to be awakened and used however necessary.

They had not been born in modern times. Like Brennard, like Jon, they did not have a fondness for modern sensibilities. They had all sprung from eras in which survival of the fittest was the highest code. Thanks to Isabella's unwitting help, Jon could now make Leucators of any of them, not to hunt down its twin, but to hunt with it. Unstoppable.

Jon smiled slowly. They had the means to make the world theirs, whether by might or Magick. It was up to him to make sure that the time was now theirs as well.

29

NOT IN KANSAS

GAVAN bent over his crystals, sifting, searching, and finally found the thread he looked for. He seized it with a shout of joy, bounded to his feet, and ran through the corridors of the Gathering Hall and out to FireAnn's cottage where the herbalist sat in a rocking chair, making notes in a cookbook the size of a massive dictionary as she watched Eleanora.

"It's the kids," he announced.

"We thought as much, since they were gone."

"True, but now I can locate them."

FireAnn had her kerchief off, and her luxurious red hair had fallen to her shoulders in a fiery mass of curls. "And the power, lad? Either they got the dragon or it got them."

"Possibly."

"Ye're not about to go charging in there by yourself, are you?"

"Not that I want to, but it seems wisest."

FireAnn put her fountain pen in her book and closed it thoughtfully. " 'Tis a sad day when we canna trust our allies, Gavan."

"I know. But who on the Council would you call in? Other than Tomaz."

"I'd have to say, we're pretty much it, as it stands. What do you expect to find?"

"Trouble, one way or the other. An unleashing of power like that could mean anything, although I hope not what it might mean."

FireAnn raised an eyebrow over her sparkling green eye. "Not the Forbidden."

"We have no idea what resources Brennard has hidden, although Gregory told me he feared the worst when Antoine turned." Gavan rubbed his wolfhead cane. "To my way of thinking, I don't see how Brennard could hope to get away with it. This is a different world. We balance on science instead of superstition. Our shadows are too well lit. And anything he could raise that was Forbidden would bring attention to him he wouldn't want. My real fear is that he would stop at nothing to expose us, and then flee to leave us facing the consequences, as he has already tried with the children."

"Then he has to be stopped. Am I going or staying with our lass?"

"Staying. Here's the thread of power I'm following . . ." Gavan let it graze FireAnn's mind and thoughts till he felt she could grasp it herself if needed. "I'll send word one way or the other. If I can't come back." He stopped.

"She'll know how much ye loved her, and I'll see to her. We'll beat this, I promise." FireAnn rubbed her hands together lightly, wincing at the pain of the arthritis-swollen joints. "Perhaps it's only right that time catches up with some of us, eh? We've been a tricksy lot."

"Not like this, FireAnn, not like this." He kissed her forehead, then bent down and kissed Eleanora's mouth gently. Standing, he grasped the thread he intended to follow and Crystaled out of the existence of Camp Ravenwyng.

Ting's grandmother leaned heavily on her, as they burst through the plane of her crystal, and emerged in a green valley she knew well. "Haven!" cried Ting happily as her feet touched ground, and she tightened her arm about her grandmother's waist. A rainbow of color met their eyes from the grove at the edge of the deep blue pond, where shirts appeared to have been knotted together. From under their canopy, Bailey burst out, shouting, "Ting! Ting!"

She ran across the ground and gathered both of them in joy, her ponytail bouncing. "What are you doing here!" Into her ear, she whispered confidentially, "This place is awesome. We are definitely not in Kansas anymore."

Ting shook her lightly before letting go and giving a little, formal bow. "Bailey Landau, I wish you to meet my grandmother, Qi Zhang. Grandmother, this is my best friend, Bailey."

Bailey gave a little bow back, saying, "I am honored to finally meet you, Ting's esteemed grandmother." She tilted a glance at Ting as if asking if she'd done it properly.

Ting grinned. "Qi means fine jade, Bailey."

"Cool name! Are you feeling better?"

Ting's grandmother lowered the paper mask from her mouth, and took a deep breath. "Much better," she announced. "Can you not feel the power in the dragon bones of this earth?"

"Not exactly," Bailey admitted, "although we did see the dragon. He seemed pretty well fed, too, not at all bony, mostly teeth and claws and bright shining eyes. That was just before Jason opened the Dragon Gate."

"And I missed it!" Ting gave a hop. "Is that what hit us? We felt it all the way in San Francisco!"

"It was incredible," Bailey said to her, as Lacey poked her head out of her pocket, whiskers shaking as she gave a pack rat squeak of agreement.

"Tell us about it! But first, we need a place for Grandmother to sit. She had chemo this morning, and sometimes . . ." Ting gave her grandmother a worried look.

Qi, however, shook her head as she leaned on her bamboo cane. "I am fine, Granddaughter. However, I want to listen to this tale being told, and I see others waiting for us."

Bailey took each by the hand and led them to the canopy under the treetops, where Rebecca sat beside a sleeping Jason who looked pale even in the shade. Ting came to an uncertain halt. "Ooooh . . . what happened?"

Qi leaned over and touched his forehead. "He is fine. Much power went through and out of him." The tiny Chinese woman frowned. "I shall have to teach him the ways of Wu Shu. He must be a fighter inside and outside of his body."

"Wu Shu?"

"Martial arts. You Westerners have many names for it, but in northern China, I was taught the Wu Shu. It disciplines your mind and soul and health as well as your body. It makes one a whole person, in order to live well, not just fight a little better." She winked.

She sat down on a small, flat rock, tucking her silk trousers around her, and laying her cane across her lap. She put her hand on Rebecca Landau's knee. "You must be the mother of Bailey. I see a resemblance of face and soul."

Rebecca smiled. "Thank you. Are you one of ..." She stopped helplessly and made a gesture.

Qi inclined her chin. "I am honored you think so, but my abilities are small compared to the others gathered here."

"Not true!" Ting protested. "Eleanora calls her a Hidden One, one of Talent although untrained."

"Blood runs true to blood, do you not think so, Mother of Bailey? She favors you in Talent as well as heart."

"Oh, I'm not." Rebecca paused, and got a thoughtful expression on her face. "At least, I never thought I was." She leaned back and grew very silent.

Qi smiled at her granddaughter. Her paper mask hung about her neck now, like an odd necklace, and her dark eyes snapped with humor. "I am trained," she corrected softly, "although perhaps not in the way of the long noses." Her wrinkles creased deeply with her silent laugh at that. "So, now, the tale."

Ting sank onto the grass and pulled Bailey down with her. "Spill it! Everything."

Bailey opened her mouth to say something, interrupted by the bawling of a bear cub as it barreled past them, Rich chasing in hot pursuit. No one but Ting's grandmother seemed to think it odd, as the two raced past and into the woods, Rich yelling, "Stef! Darn it! Come back here!"

Three or four paces behind them trotted Trent and Henry. At the sight of the girls, they stopped their pursuit and dropped to the grass as well, both boys a little out of breath. No one wore shirts because it was their garb that made the canopy overhead that shaded them without being deeper in the colder woods. "That cub can run!"

"Maybe he'd stop, if he were not chased?"

Trent thought over Rebecca's statement before shrugging. "Stef is out of control right now. I think it's the surge we had through here. He went bear and can't get back, and he's terrified."

"Another who could use training in the ways of Wu Shu," said Ting's grandmother wisely.

Squibb said nothing, except that he gave Ting a beaming smile. He sat back uneasily, braced against a tree trunk. "I think we're safe here," he told Ting.

"If Jason opened the Gate, we are."

Bailey pointed at the Iron Mountains, with the massive dragon carved out of rock at its foot, darkness in its yawning jaws.

"Wow." Ting stared in unabashed amazement. "Okay, now I *have* to know what happened." She scooted over to her grandmother's knee, and touched her, as if checking to see all was well. Qi smiled down on her.

Trent grinned at Bailey. "You tell it and I'll fill in the blanks when you get excited."

Bailey turned blazing pink, but that did not stop her from flinging herself headfirst into the tale, starting at the soccer game. No one spoke for long moments after she finally finished, with occasional explanations inserted from Trent in a strictly helpful way. "And then he keeled over, nearly squashing Lacey, and that's it."

"Exhausted," said Rebecca. She nodded. "I don't think it's anything worse than that."

Ting stood and dusted herself off. "We should get back, then. We can leave, can't we?"

"No one's tried yet. We all seem kinda burned out for the moment. I can't reach anyone, but it's coming back. I think we just have to wait."

Qi put her hand out to Ting. "I am staying, Granddaughter. Tell your mother that I love her and gather up my things."

She blinked. "What?"

"My father, the magician and acrobat Jinsong, had a prophecy when I was born. It was told that I would spend my last days in the shadow of the red dragon. He feared it meant the communism that gripped our country and sent me to the United States when he could. I was a woman grown then and he old and dying, and we did not understand the prophecy at all, and so feared it. But now I believe . . ." Qi looked at the rusty cliffside with its sculpture. "I believe that this is my destiny, and a worthy one. There is work to do here, am I right? A haven, a school to be built. And I have strength here, Ting. I can feel it."

"Grandmother, your medicine . . ."

"My medicine works by killing me little by little and hoping that my body can survive it longer than the illness. But it cannot give me more than a few more years, even if it works. Here, I feel strength. My soul has purpose rather than merely surviving."

"Yes, but—"

"I wish to stay."

Ting stammered a bit. Her eyes sparkled brightly. Bailey jumped to her feet. "You'll be back!"

"I will?"

"How could you not? You're a Magicker!"

"But . . . my mom . . . but . . ."

"Jiao is a wise woman," her grandmother told her. "She knows I will need you, and she knows you have your own growing to do. Trust her, trust yourself. You will be back."

Ting looked down at the ground, her wings of lustrous dark hair hiding her face for a moment, before she put her chin back up. "I will see you soon, then, Grandmother!" She hugged Qi fiercely, cupped her crystal and disappeared before anyone could say another word.

She found the Gate open only a tiny splinter, and it frightened her for a moment. Would she even be able to return? She brushed Jason's thoughts as she tried to Focus. *Go*, he whispered wearily. *I will try and let you back through*. Then he faded a little, as if tired even beyond the help of sleep and dreams, and she Crystaled anyway, for if Jason did not keep his word, who would? She trusted him.

Qi settled back as her granddaughter shimmered out of sight. "Now," she stated, "I am old and have been through a great deal. I must rest my body. Do not disturb me or the boy, as I have much teaching to do, and he much training."

"In his sleep?" Rebecca stood gracefully.

"For now, yes. It is best for the two of us. He has much to learn. If his mind knows how to do it, his body will follow." Qi nodded sagely. "We shall see if the bones of the dragon in this earth aid him as they do me." She leaned back against the tree trunk, put her small hand on Jason's forehead, and closed her eyes.

"Wonder where your ex-wife and daughter went to?"

Jerry Landau slowly slid upright in the seat of his car. The upholstery creaked under him, papers from fast food dinners crackling under his feet as he moved. He rubbed his eyes. Everything felt crusty. Late afternoon sun arced through the dusty windshield, and the street had begun to pick up traffic, heading into the hour when nearly everyone got off work.

He looked at the slender, dark-haired man leaning against the fender of his car. "Who in the hell are you?"

"Maybe someone who wants to help."

"Yeah? Or maybe not. No one knows where they went, least of all me." He eyed the apartment building which he'd been waiting outside of since Sunday afternoon. Several days now. "The w-w-w-" He cursed and gave up trying to say witch. He hadn't been able to speak about anything straight since he'd seen it. And it hadn't been on the news or in the papers. It was as if everyone who'd witnessed it had been cursed. No pictures, nothing. As if a hurricane had hit the county and no one knew or admitted anything about it. He rubbed his jaw, which ached with the effort of trying to get the word out.

"Too bad," the stranger said smoothly. "Here you are, a father, just trying to see your kid get raised properly, despite the ex. And she runs out on you again."

"Got that right. The school won't even tell me anything. She's got a restraining order against me. All the rules and lawyers in a row on her side." Jerry leaned on his elbow, against the rolled down car window. He didn't remember having left it down, but it was electric and couldn't have come down on its own. The restraining order had been in effect for a few years, but Landau saw no reason to muddy the waters here. He was the victim, after all.

"So that's why I'm here. Figured we could help each other."

Jerry looked at the man. Well dressed. Hadn't seen a lot of sun, or hard work either, for that matter, but probably had money. Never hurt to have money on your side. Once he had custody of Bailey, his new wife could raise her however she wanted, religious freak that she was, and he could get the support payments off his back. That would be a miracle in itself. "How's that?" he asked.

The stranger smiled. "Ever notice how we all saw something but none of us can talk about it?"

Jerry nodded.

"I think it's a kind of mass hypnosis. A crowd hysteria kind of thing, you know? Controlling what we saw or thought we saw."

Jerry wasn't quite sure, but he wouldn't admit he couldn't keep up with the dark-haired man, so he nodded again. The stranger smiled again, slowly. "Now, some of us are harder to hypnotize than others. Stronger wills."

Now that, Jerry understood. He had a will of iron. Except maybe when it came to wanting a drink now and then, but that was different. That was because he deserved it, for all he went through. It wasn't easy working and providing.

"So what's that mean?"

"That means that one of us is going to be able to break the control. Could be any minute now, could be a few days. Those kids are missing. No one seems to know anything about it, but—" His new friend paused. He rubbed his gloved hands together. "Someone has to know something. And I want to be there when everything cracks open. My kid deserves that."

"So . . . what do we do?"

"All I ask of you is that when you learn something, anything at all, you share it with me. And in return, I'll use all my resources to see you get your daughter back."

Jerry's eyes narrowed. "She's not supposed to take Bailey out of state, restraining order or not."

"There you go. You're in the right, and you know it."

The stranger stepped away from the car, into a dark shadow cast upon the street.

"But how do I get hold of you—"

"Don't worry. You will."

Jerry sneezed suddenly, grabbing for a paper napkin on the dashboard, and when he'd finished mopping up, the man had gone. Jerry wadded up the napkin and tossed it out the window. About damn time someone had listened to his side. He glared out at the apartment building. There wasn't a place Bailey could hide now.

FORGOTTEN and FORBIDDEN

GAVAN knew the moment something went wrong. The thread he followed twisted and then turned on him, as though it were some great snake coiling and fighting with him. He growled back at it and yanked, then immediately felt a chill of fear. The void he tried to enter shut on him. Jason's thread snapped and disappeared. Gavan often likened Crystaling to jumping from an airplane. There was that moment of plunging off and then just hanging, before reaching for the parachute cord and deploying it. His cord had just broken away and he had no place to go. He drifted in the cold nothingness of *between* and tried to search out a true path. That which he had sensed before stayed as if it had never existed at all. Instead, he found Eleanora, faint and weak, beckoning him. He concentrated on her then and even as he emerged, he knew he was not at Ravenwyng.

Nor was it truly Eleanora who'd caught him.

Something waited for him, wanted him, hungrily. Too late to stop Crystaling, Gavan went through. He landed at the ready, eyes narrowed, weight balanced, awaiting anything. A faint, damp breeze lifted the cape on his shoulders and let it drop as quickly as if sulking.

He murmured a word to Lantern the darkness. Gavan looked about, not sensing Jason or Bailey or any of the others, but the hungry presence hovered nearby, and Gavan juggled a thought of leaving as quickly as he'd come, but curiosity got the better of him. He'd felt Eleanora calling. He couldn't be wrong about that. Had she been taken? Had she led him here? Or did something dark and sinister mock his love for her? His thread had been tangled or captured, his journey detoured and he wanted to know by what.

The glow from his crystal fell on cave walls and crude drawings jumped into sight. He stepped closer to look at renditions of hunters depicting the hunt of thousands of years ago, paint fading yet still preserved. He put a hand up, and then dropped it, knowing his touch could disintegrate that record of a struggle immemorial. The caves led deeper into stillness and Gavan followed the cave wall cautiously. "Eleanora?" he called lightly, quietly, not expecting an answer, hoping fervently there would be none. She did not belong here. Yet a small sense of her lingered, and it bothered him, drove him deeper into the caverns. Lichen growing here and there seemed to glow with its own phosphorescence as his Lantern light touched it. He trod carefully, making as little noise as he could, yet knew that would not help. Whatever it was he approached knew as well as he did that he sought it even as it sought him.

Gavan brushed the essence of Eleanora again and recoiled from it. It couldn't be her and yet it was, and he feared that she had fallen into true darkness. It was as though nothing had been left of her but an aching need.

So hungry it was! And tired and cold, but most of all thirsting for him. It pulled him nearer and nearer relentlessly and Gavan had no doubt that it would savage him if they met. Yet though he sensed he was moving nearer to it, he could not feel that it was moving toward him. Did it wait in shadowy ambush? Was there a Gateway here he had no knowledge of? Had that been a Gate he felt opening? Yet, if it had been, it should not have led to this.

Gavan slipped through the caves into a labyrinth, a catacomb passage that he could see had been carved both by hands and time. There were traces along the way of what it had once been. A broken crate, old and weathered, rotting away. Old rope. Rutted wheel marks ground into the dirt and stone below his feet. He could smell, faintly, the dampness of a river or perhaps a seacoast. A smuggler's passageway.

The cave drawings brought Lascaux, in the south of France to mind, although he doubted that these drawings had ever been found by those of archaeological academia. He had a pretty good idea whose domain he trespassed in. He had to be underneath an estate, a manor house or perhaps what might even pass for a castle in these days, built over hidden caves and passages and the smuggling trade along the waterways. He could not imagine why the remnant of his Eleanora would be here in the shadow of another Magicker except that it had to be a trap or worse, and he could not turn back now.

He rounded a corner, and lantern light bounced back at him, dazzling him for a moment as the catacombs opened into an immense cavern, studded with oil burning sconces and hung with prisms to reflect and increase the meager light. Heavy chain rattled amidst teakettle loud hissing at his stumbling entry and Gavan halted, and stood, surrounded.

Dead eyes watched him from all around the cavern. The captives tried their chains and shackles, reaching for him and failing, their faces hungry to touch him. He shuddered as he turned about slowly, taking the horrible sight in. Leucators filled the room. Their mouths *sissed* at him in anger and need. They clawed the air trying to reach him, their white-gray bodies clothed in the crudest of rags, gnawed bones scattered at their feet, and everywhere felt icy cold.

"Eleanora!" He raised his cane, letting light fall on her, but it wasn't her. The Leucator reared back in its chains, its brunette hair in greasy disarray about its face, like the youthful Eleanora when he'd first fallen in love with her but horribly, terribly wrong. And yet the Leucator retained the youth she herself had lost. The bitterness of it filled his mouth, and he spat. It raised a shaking hand at him in entreaty, then dropped it, and its eyes looked at him hopelessly. He would have wept but something tugged viciously at his ankle nearly pulling his leg out from under him.

Gavan spun about. Another Leucator crawled back, whimpering, and slyly covered its head with one arm, and he stared in shock. "My God," he whispered. "Fizziwig." It couldn't be, but it was. His study partner, his colleague, his best friend from days he could hardly remember anymore looked back at him. His friend from before the battle, before the great jump across time, before he'd become old and cheerful and spritely and then had suddenly died. No, this Fizziwig had the mop of unruly golden curls which had later gone to shocked white, and his unhealthy Leucator skin remained free of wrinkles. The creature grinned back at him mockingly. If only it knew how terrible it was.

Unable to face either it or the doppelganger of Eleanora, Gavan turned again, slowly. He looked into parodies of faces he recognized and felt bile rise at the back of his throat in disgust and fear. Someone had made doubles of them all, as well as doubles of strangers.

This had been Forbidden. Gregory had made it clear in no uncertain terms. Leucators should not be created but if they were, a Magicker should never fall into the delusion that it can be fed from.

Yet, as Gavan swung about, it was clear someone had. Like a vampire with its own herd of cattle hidden in these caves, someone had been feeding. He clenched his teeth. No wonder Eleanora lay near death, her soul being drained through the Leucator and its Maker. And perhaps that had killed Fizziwig as well, or at least haunted him all the days he'd had left after the disaster, for a Leucator was a mirror, and this one had been made *before* the War of the Wizards. Fizziwig had been doomed even before the rest of them. As for Eleanora, did she sense it? She had pushed him this way, and then the Leucator had drawn him the rest of it. She must have! She must lie in her sleep and know that she was being fed upon and drained and helpless. Anger shot through him.

The sound of a chain rattled in his ear. Gavan jerked away, shuddering at the thought of being touched by one. A pebble rolled under the heel of his shoe and he went to one knee. A shadow fell over him.

Gavan twisted his head to look up, and his heart stilled for the barest of moments.

Not all the Leucators were chained.

He pushed himself away, rolling, and came up, back to part of the cavern wall. Three closed in on him. Their howls of hunger filled the air and the chained ones added their own hissing excitement. Gavan put his Shield up and waited, his heartbeat having recovered and now racing in his throat. Cornered and likely outnumbered, he was not sure if he would have time to Crystal elsewhere or not.

Silence filled the cavern. Dead silence. The Leucators all retreated a step, their mouths writhing in unuttered distress as someone entered the cavern.

"Well, well, my beauties. Look what you have found."

Bailey woke. She didn't know why, because she'd been in such a deep sleep that she'd forgotten she was on the ground in a strange place. Everyone around her appeared to be lost in dreams, too, their breathing deep and strong. Stef, back in human form, snuffled a bit in his sleep.

Bailey rolled to her knees and got up quietly. She went to Jason and stood at his side a long moment, listening. He appeared to be in regular sleep now. Before he had been fitful and hot, as though fighting a cold or something, and they'd finally put damp cloths across his forehead to bring down his temperature a bit. He looked better now though, his face turned to one side, lit by the low silvery moon.

Madame Qi opened one eye and smiled at Bailey. "Let him sleep," she said. "He is still learning much."

"How do you do that?"

"Teach? Tell me, when you learn something new, something important, do you not dream of doing it?"

Bailey looked closely at Ting's grandmother. "Sometimes. Yeah, I do." She grinned in sudden realization.

"So, you see." Qi smiled and closed her eye, leaning back securely against the tree once more.

Bailey thought everything was going to be all right. She walked quietly to the edge of the pond and pulled up the bucket Ting's grandmother had woven for them out of green sticks and lined with mosses. It didn't stay full of water, about half would drain through but it made for a good catch and drink. When it was safer, Rebecca and Bailey had already decided to sneak back for their camping things and extra clothes and other necessities.

She drank deeply of water that tasted more heavenly than anything out of a faucet or fancy plastic bottle before dropping the bucket back into place at the shore. With a hand covering her yawn, she made her way back to the little hollow on the ground next to her mother's sleeping form. Then her eyes opened wide in surprise.

Where she'd been sleeping but a few minutes before now rested . . . well . . . things. Bailey sat down. She combed through the items. Three onions. A small cloth bag with a dozen eggs in it. Three applelike looking fruits. And a stack of four crudely woven but ever so soft blankets. She unfolded one and a tiny bunch of herbs fell out. She picked them up and sniffed. The sachets smelled faintly like flowers and cinnamon.

Bailey looked around. Leaves shifted and twigs cracked in the grove but she saw nothing.

Obviously the items were presents and welcome ones, too, for it meant a breakfast awaited them in the morning. She thought a moment, then slid her bracelet off her wrist, jewelry Ting had made, and she laid it out on a flat rock nearby. "Thank you," she said softly to the evening air. Quietly Bailey took out the blankets and covered those she could, before crawling back next to her mother and taking a corner of the last blanket. Its scent drifted over her as she fell back into sleep, wondering who had visited them.

Gavan still could not see who approached, but he rubbed his wolfhead cane and said, amiably, "Well, then, Isabella. I was wondering how long before you would know I was here."

"Always astute." With a rustle of satin, Isabella stepped out of the shadows. She lifted a gloved hand, and the Leucators slunk away, sinking onto their haunches, still watching him avidly but cowed by her presence. "A little too late, but a very clever lad nonetheless."

"This is an abomination," Gavan told her. "And it *will* be stopped."

"Stopped?" She paused, in her elegant designer gown, its hem dragging the filthy floor, jewels sparkling at her throat, ears, and wrists. "By whom? You?"

"Me and the Council. Whatever it takes."

Isabella laughed softly. The sound of it was colder than the flesh of the Leucators about her. "I see no Council. In fact, I barely see a Magicker." She rustled a step nearer. "Do you really think you need a Shield between us?"

"I'll stand with it," Gavan said.

She moved again, imperceptibly nearer. He watched her face. Could he tell, with a master of Magick such as she, if this were really Isabella or yet another Leucator? He stared at her eyes. He thought he could. His life might well depend upon it. The problem with dueling another Magicker is that the power they wielded carried more chance of destroying whatever it was they fought for, and themselves, than of saving it. It was best never to come to blows at all.

He didn't think he'd get out of here without a fight, however. His mouth went dry.

Isabella put her hand up, and made a small, elegant gesture with her gloved fingers. The Lantern light from his crystal dimmed.

It could be coincidence, because the spell only lasted so long once cast or it could be that she drained it away. Amusement danced over Isabella's face as she read the expression on his.

"I wouldn't want to be down here in the dark," she observed.

He had no intention of lingering that much longer. To his flank, he could hear the creatures stirring, growing restless in their chains once more. "How could you have done this?" he asked of her.

She made a noise of scorn. "And why not? It is Magick, to be used whenever it is necessary. I could help Eleanora, you know." She inched forward again.

"Eleanora?" That did catch him by surprise.

"They have their uses, Leucators, besides running their prey to the ground."

"I can see how you used them," he answered stiffly.

"Bah. You see nothing!" She gathered her hem up with her left hand, freeing her legs a bit from the sweeping folds of her dress gown. "Do you think we all slept after Brennard defeated Gregory? Are you really that naive, Gavan? Some were physically hurtled through the centuries but some of us," and her voice dropped to a low hiss. "Some of us had to live the decades."

Her sibilant voice echoed in the cavern about her, picked up and hissed softly by the Leucators.

"What are you talking about?"

"This." Isabella beckoned. "The Forbidden. Yes, I create them and then I draw on them. They have no life but what

I give them, and so it is only just that I take it back! Look at me!" She cried out, and dropped her Magicks and he saw her then . . . saw her aged but proud face, deeply lined by the years, the true color of her vibrant hair turn to thinning gray, liver spots multiplying along her porcelain flesh to muddy it. He saw an antique, an old woman of great strength who had once been young but was no longer, even with her powers.

Yet Isabella stood triumphantly, for she might look every day of ninety years old, yet she had lived four hundred years or more getting there.

"Now do you see? Think on Eleanora, Gavan. Do you wish her to sleep forever? I can give her a century or two, even without glamour to hide her years. I can save her for you!" And Isabella laughed again, her voice rising until it sounded shrill.

"At the cost of her sanity? Her soul? Like yours? And the Leucators you gave to the Dark Hand. Do they feed on them as well, or just use them to harass us? Do you even know or care?"

Isabella waved her hand. Her glamour rose again, concealing her, and she became once again the handsome woman he knew. But now, as if she wore a transparent mask, he could see the truth beneath it, if he tried. The illusion was eerie.

Gavan gathered himself. He put the thought of Eleanora away, for even if Isabella told the truth, and he doubted that, he knew his beloved would never choose to stay alive that way. He would find another answer for Eleanora. But first, he had to get out of here *alive*.

He threw his hands up in summoning. The Lantern spell flared out in a brilliant, crystalline burst even as Isabella moved to counter him. "If I die here, you and your works are going with me," he said grimly.

31

CLEVER IS as CLEVER DOES

JASON'S eyes flew open. He sucked down a deep breath feeling as if he had been drowning. For a moment, he thought he really *had* been as something very wet and sloppy slid off his face and plopped onto his chest as he sat up. The sodden rag looked (and smelled) as though it had lately been part of one of Stef's T-shirts. Jason held it up and off to the side, puzzled. Water ran off it into a little puddle.

"Young master awakes."

Jason swiveled around. Ting's grandmother sat, a bamboo cane across her knees, watching him, a twinkle in her deep-set eyes as if she saw something that gave her great pleasure. "Grandmother," he smiled. "Am I still dreaming?"

"Do you think so?"

"I don't know." He rubbed the bridge of his nose. Sunlight glanced off deep blue water and he winced at its brightness even as he yawned. A look at the Iron Mountains told him he was where he remembered, great stone dragon crouched and roaring out of the cliff side. He hadn't done that, the dragon had, as a reminder he supposed of what they had shared and what it expected out of Jason. Warrior or guard. It looked as awesome as the dragon itself. He stood.

"Where is everyone?"

"Rich and the one known as Stefan-cub are off gathering wood, with Trent guiding. Henry, Bailey, and her mother are trading."

"Trading?"

Ting's grandmother inclined her head. That made no sense to Jason, but then he wasn't sure if he were truly awake yet and into that state where anything would make sense.

"And Ting?"

"My granddaughter is making arrangements to return. She brings my things and things of her own. Much work to do here." The wizened Chinese woman looked about.

"Bringing your things?"

Grandmother stood as he did. She planted her feet firmly on either side of the bamboo cane. "I stay. The bones of this earth are powerful, and give me strength."

"That's great!"

She winked at him. "So you say now. When I am done with you, you may not feel the same."

"Ummm . . . why?"

She raised her cane and tapped him on the side of his leg, lightly slapping his calf. "Great power means great discipline. You must learn it inside and out, or the power will use you rather than you it. With what you know comes great responsibility. I will teach you Wu Shu, the martial art of my province, which is more than fighting. It is a discipline for the mind and soul."

"I can use all the help I can get." He stretched gingerly, still feeling sore from the soccer game.

"You will have more help from me than you want," Ting's grandmother promised him. She gave a giggle that reminded him intensely of Ting. "Here. We saved a bit of breakfast for you."

She passed him a speckled brown egg and part of what might have been an apple on a broad green leaf and motioned for him to sit again. He did so. The egg was hardboiled, so he peeled it and found it chewy and good. The fruit wasn't quite an apple. It reminded him how near and far from home they were. He chased it down with a few swallows of water. She watched him intensely, then leaped to her feet. The gold threads in her black silken outfit glittered. "Now. I am Madame Qi Zhang. You will call me Master Qi."

He bowed back. "Pleased to know your name, Ting's grandmother."

That mischievous grin flashed. "So we hope."

He remembered his dreams. Without more than a touch of thought in introduction, she'd appeared to him. Very soon, he thanked his soccer coaches for making him run circuits all day long, for she had him trotting about the valley of Haven till the breath knotted in hot little pinches in his lungs and he staggered to a stop, hands on his knees. Madame Qi would give him five breaths, before stamping her cane, and he'd bolt off again feeling like a skittish thoroughbred colt in its pasture. When she'd run his legs off, she made him stand and just center himself.

With legs like rubber, he wondered that he could stand at all. She spoke to him as he stood, with a voice barely audible, until it was as much a part of him as the racing pulse that slowly calmed to where it should and then quieted even more. He could feel the blood river inside him, cleansing and feeding his body from within, and Qi's words helped him look inside to see that. He stood so long he felt as if he were part of the Iron Mountains itself: tall, still, quiet, and strong.

It was sometime in that moment when he felt the bones of the earth, as Qi called them, the natural power of merely being that sank deep into this corner of the world. Sank deep and strong, yes, and allowed him to touch and draw from it. He opened his eyes then, to see Qi sitting on the grass watching him yet again. The sun slanted steeply across the sky.

She smiled, deepening the many lines in her face. "You are a good student."

"You are a masterful teacher."

She winked. "Ready for more?"

"I . . . think so."

"Good." She tapped her cane and stood. "Show me."

Jason took a deep breath, then let his mind drop his body into a nimbleness he didn't know he had, somersaulted and tumbled his way across the grass with such speed and vigor he couldn't stop himself in time and bowled into the small Chinese elder. She wobbled a bit and paled, then caught herself.

"Master Qi!"

She held her hand up. "I will be fine. It is true that this old body would prefer not to be an acrobat. Yours, however, should not argue with you."

Jason readied himself. "Tell me and I'll do it."

He was limper than a noodle when she finished and let him fall to the grass. She stood over him.

"Tomorrow," she promised, "you will do better."

Jason managed a groan.

The valley filled with voices.

"Jason! Jason, you're awake!"

He got up on one elbow to see Bailey racing toward him. He threw his hand up. "Don't touch me. I hurt all over."

"And you smell all over, too." She came to a stop, ponytail bouncing, and wrinkled her nose.

"That is good all-American sweat." He straightened. "I think Ting's grandmother used to build pyramids in a former life." He stretched carefully, muscles aching where he didn't know he had muscles. Even his toes hurt.

Madame Qi smiled. "This one has enough strength left to complain. Tomorrow I should work him harder." She giggled before ducking her head and retreating back to the canopy which seemed to be their camp. After a few strong steps, her body seemed to cave and she leaned heavily on her cane, as Rebecca came to her aid and helped her.

"I missed a lot. What's going on? And what did she mean when she told me you were trading?"

Bailey shrugged a large sack from off her shoulder. "Trading." She opened her sack. "We're not alone."

That hit him harder than anything Qi had instructed him in. He felt it like a kick to his gut. "What?"

"We're not alone. I haven't actually seen anyone yet, but we've been trading things back and forth. I've gotten blankets, food, and these tunic things . . ." She pulled a shirt-tunic out of her sack. "Maps."

"Let me see that!"

She pulled out a scroll. The paper looked like papyrus of some sort. He unrolled it carefully.

He'd unlocked the Gate to a world. Not just a corner, a small haven, a tiny place where they could be safe, but a world. His breath stuck in his throat for a moment. Why hadn't the dragon told him?

Or had that world existed only from the moment he unlocked the Gate? Numbly, he handed the scroll back to her.

"We can't stay here."

"Why not? I think it's cool other people are here. Otherwise this would be like, what, I dunno . . . *Gilligan's Island* or something."

Henry caught up to the two of them, dragging a much larger bundle. He dropped it. "This is supposed to be a tent or something if we can put it together. Bailey tell you?"

"Some of it. See anyone at all?"

"Nothing but squirrels and birds and a few skittery things in the bushes, but those tunics look like they'll fit most of us." He scratched his chest, and Jason realized Henry had no shirt. "Where is your shirt?"

Henry thumbed at the canopy hanging across several tree branches. "Same place the other guys' shirts are. And I, for one, will be glad to be wearing something." He took the tunic Bailey was waving about and shrugged into it.

She hid the look on her face a moment. Henry combed his fingers through his hair. "All right, I look like a refugee from a Renaissance Faire, but it's warm and clean." He glanced at Jason. "And you smell like you've been wrestling in a mud pit."

"That good, huh?"

"I think even Stef would be offended."

"Thanks. I think." He took a tunic Bailey pushed at him. Before the day got any cooler, he'd better go for a swim.

"I'll sit as lookout," offered Henry. "And then, I want to go home, Jason."

Jason peeled down to his jockeys. He threw himself into the pond, knowing it would be nearly ice cold, and it was. He came up gasping, and scrubbing at himself. The cleaner, the sooner, the better. "Home," he repeated then, as he sank back to his chin for a soak. "Are you sure?"

"Everyone got to say good-bye but me. They've gotta be awful worried."

"Time is different here."

"Not different enough."

"Are you coming back?"

Henry's mouth worked back and forth a bit. "I can bring some food and supplies back. I'm not sure if I should come back and stay, though."

Jason ducked under, and washed his head as thoroughly as he could with only water. He came back up, spitting. Finally he climbed out and got his jeans back on and the tunic that Bailey had given him, roughly cut and sewn but of a soft, blue-green fabric. He scrubbed his socks out and then trudged back to the campsite with Henry. "You're one of us. You've always been one of us."

"Oh, it's not that!" Henry shook his head vigorously, sending his glasses sliding down his nose. He caught them before they did a ski jump off his face. "It's just that—"

Whatever it was he was going to say got interrupted by the other boys sliding into camp. Actually, it was Trent who slid, chin down, for he had been riding Stef-cub rodeo style and lost his grip just as they came around the corner. Rich staggered after them laughing so hard he had to hold his ribs, as Stef-cub let out a growling bawl, sat back, and grunted in satisfaction. A ripple and Stefan sat there, grinning ear to ear.

Bailey wrinkled her nose. Silently, she pointed at the pond. All three turned around and trudged back.

Jason hung his socks over a tree branch. With any luck, they'd be dry by midday tomorrow. In the meantime, he'd have to suffer cold feet or wear his shoes without, and for right now, with a fire going, he could do without either. He sat down. "Mrs. Landau, whatever that is you're cooking, it smells great."

"It's stew. Hopefully, it'll be edible although how we're going to eat it, I'm not sure. Bailey traded for a pot, but we've no dishes or utensils."

"There's always fingers."

"I suppose. Feeling better?"

"I was." He grinned. Madame Qi looked to be napping under the canopy although with the others just roaring through, he doubted she actually slept. "I have a new Master and she is tough."

"Sometimes that's what you need."

"And sometimes you need all the help you can get."

Jason lapsed into silence and heavy thoughts until everyone had returned. Then he looked up. "You all felt it. Even Ting felt it. Madame Qi here said she felt it, and insisted Ting bring her."

Rich nodded. Stef rubbed his nose which looked as if it had been bee stung and it probably had.

"Then why aren't any of the elders here? This is what we were all aiming for, and it's happened . . . and no one's here. Unless one of you has heard, and I don't know?" Jason looked from face to face. Each of them shook his or her head slightly.

"Not a nudge, nothing?" He felt stunned. How could Gavan and the others not know or care? After all he'd gone through. Up until that moment, he'd assumed they'd looked in while he recovered, and made plans to return.

Qi opened one eye. "Clever boys, but not clever enough." She swung the tip of her cane about, indicating the area. "It is blocked. Use your senses. Nothing in, nothing out."

"But Ting felt it . . ."

"Ting is one of us," Bailey protested. "We're like sisters, always connected."

"It's never been able to block before." Jason frowned. Trent traded a look with him before surveying the surrounding valley and mountains. Then he nodded in confirmation.

"You're the Gatekeeper here, Jason. That's your magic, all about, except for a tiny sliver of an opening, more like a contact . . ." Trent hesitated, then looked at Henry.

Henry lost all color and bolted to his feet. "I told you I was bad luck! I shouldn't even be here!" He cupped his gemstone with a citrine flare of heat and power.

He was going. Or he was trying, but Jason could feel him bouncing against the walls that *he'd* set up. Only Henry couldn't stop himself. In a dead panic, he flung himself against the blockade a second time, and Jason knew he had to let Henry go through or his friend would kill himself trying.

He let the Gate swing, and Squibb disappeared in a brilliant golden flash.

32

RIGHT PLACE, WRONG TIME

HE SHOULDN'T even be here, Gavan thought, as he turned away another attack, a trickle of sweat sliding down his temple and his arm trembling slightly. His beam flared and spit, spinning Isabella away with a sharp cry. She recovered and bared her teeth to face him. He retreated again, his back coming up against the cave wall. His left arm hung all but useless, flesh ripped from a Leucator attack, and worse, chilled to the bone. The cold made it useless. Even the blood that slowly dripped to the floor seemed barely thawed enough to ooze from the wound.

He could not Crystal unless he dropped the remnants of his Shield, but that Shield was all that kept the three Leucators from falling on him. They moaned at the smell of his blood and pain and hung at the edges of their Maker's skirts, waiting for an opportunity to lunge. Isabella's eyes shone with a fierce triumph as she closed in on him.

The only thing he could do was Call, and so he sent it out, knowing that few if any could hear or would answer. FireAnn would not answer, being held to her promise to stay with Eleanora, and he did not even know how powerful a Call for help he could project.

He had one last resort. He could step into his crystal, imprisoning himself. Isabella would not be able to destroy him but neither would she probably ever allow his crystal to see the light of day again with any hope that another Magicker might be able to free him. Eventually, inside the gem, he would go crazy or die.

"One last offer," Isabella said. "Save yourself and the fair Eleanora, too."

"My opinion of you has not changed in the past few hours."

"I am wounded." Isabella allowed herself a bitter smile. "I offer you my wisdom, Gavan. I struggled for decades for it, while the two of you slept like babes, unworried, unknowing. I can't give her back the time she's lost, but I can show her how to seize another century or two. Living is sweet compared to the alternative."

"It doesn't appear to have sweetened you."

She gestured and tried his Shield again. It shuddered but held.

Gavan dug deep for more stamina and taunted her a bit more. "Backing Gregory against Brennard would have avoided all of this."

She made another noise of disdain. "Two men in a pissing contest. What else could be expected but that they would destroy everything for the rest of us. Stubborn and combative. And you, my dear boy, are showing the same traits." She lashed out, her power shoving his.

He stumbled. He fell on one knee, and a sharp pain went through it as he did. He glanced down to see a rock piercing his skin, nailed into his kneecap. That was going to hurt even worse later.

Gavan expanded his Shield to protect his suddenly open and vulnerable back. A Leucator hit him from the flanks, hard, and bounced off, but Gavan felt it, deep in every bone as the tackle rattled his teeth and knew, Shield or not, he was about done for.

He could retreat into his crystal or he could explode it. Exploding it might take out most of this cavern and the horrid things that resided within it. It wouldn't touch Isabella, for she had her own Shielding up although most of her energy was aimed at the offensive, at him. He hadn't much of a choice left.

A howling arose. It started thinly, at the edge of his nerves, and he struggled to stand. He made his mind up what he would do, and began to marshal the last of his energies to accomplish it. The keening grew. It came from without the caverns, and Gavan paused. He knew that sound.

Isabella dropped the hem of her gown, turning slightly. Then she let out a string of curses that would make a French stevedore blush. Perhaps even a cabbie. Gavan managed to get his back to the wall again, even as a wind swirled inside the cave and the lanterns in the sconces flickered wildly. Chaos flooded in, with the beasts that always rode it.

Wolfjackals. Drawn by their duel and the Magick unleashed, the beasts would tear them both apart. Gavan did not know if he welcomed the distraction or had simply attracted a new way to die. He dug his heels in as the pack came in, snarling and slavering, and going after the Leucators with savage teeth.

Gavan braced himself for the new battle, then looked up and saw in surprise that Tomaz Crowfeather was riding the lead beast. Tomaz raised one palm, and a clear, blue light from the many turquoise stones on his wrist cut the air. Isabella turned and ran.

At the threshold of the great cavern, Isabella halted. She let out a series of sharp, arcane words, and the shackles on the Leucators shattered. They shook themselves free of the chains with a low groan of eagerness that grew louder and louder. In a great swirl of colorful satin, the Magicker turned and fled, her Leucators in her wake, crying her name as if she promised them life. Only the one he knew as Eleanora hesitated, turning back for one last, longing look at him, before fleeing the caves as the wolfjackals went after them. Amid snarls of attack and hideous screams of the unfortunate few caught behind, Tomaz dismounted and caught Gavan up.

Rainwater nearly fainted as Tomaz took his arm and tucked it inside his shirt, before lifting him onto the back of a wolfjackal. The creature turned its head, hot drool falling from its gleaming fangs, but allowed Gavan to remain. Gavan knotted his hand in the thick-furred ruff, wondering how he was going to manage to stay on.

"Where in hell did you come from?" He looked at his friend.

Tomaz grinned. "I always wanted to be the cavalry come to the rescue." He swung up on the pack leader. "Let's get you out of here, and then we have much to explain to each other."

Henry landed in his kitchen. He immediately sank to the floor with a sob of relief and happiness at being home, his gemstone dropping from his hand. It rolled around and then lost its faint glow, and came to a stop against his leg. He picked it up and pocketed it, sighing. *Never drop your crystal.*

He looked about. The big family-style kitchen lay swathed in darkness. It must be the middle of the night. What night, he wasn't sure. A day or two or three after they'd left. Hopefully not longer. The trouble with Crystaling is that he was never quite sure when he was coming or going.

He never wanted to go back to Haven, but he knew he had to, if only long enough to drop off what supplies he could. The Squibb family believed in being prepared and the garage had boxes of powdered and freeze-dried foodstuffs against earthquakes or whatever other disasters might hit. His mom would go through once a year and donate the older stuff to the homeless shelter and restock, so he'd just be saving her that job. Not that freeze-dried beef stroganoff was the best stuff in the world, but it was better than stir-fried grass and onions. At least, he thought that's what Ting's grandmother had been cooking when he'd left.

He scrubbed away a tear with the heel of his hand. He couldn't be around any of them for long, he was too dangerous to them. He didn't know how or what was happening to him, but he feared that anything he could and did do might betray them. Henry vowed he'd never let that happen, even if he had to give up Magick again. Where he would go or what he would do, he didn't know. He had no idea what he wanted to tell his mom. So he'd get the supplies together, and while he did that, he'd think of something. Surely.

Gathering himself, he made his way out to the garage, fumbling here and there a bit, not wanting to snap on a light or even use his crystal. He found the mesh booty bags they used in camping and the cardboard boxes of supplies. The stainless steel storage unit held the newer cartons to the left, so all he had to do was go down to the right and pull a carton open. He gave up and cast a small Lantern spell on his crystal and set it on the top shelf where it glowed like a tiny harvest moon so that he could see what he was doing. He shoveled the packets into the bag as his eyes adjusted and nearly had the sack full when the side door creaked open farther.

He froze, spotlighted by the glow from his gemstone, as someone hesitated in the doorway.

"Henry?"

"Mom!" Caught, but he almost didn't care.

She rushed to him and gave him a great hug, her comfortable chenille robe surrounding him. She made one of those noises that mothers make when they're very very happy and trying not to cry and scare you because of it, and held him tightly.

"I'm sorry, Mom, I'm sorry, I didn't want you to worry."

She kissed the top of his head. "I wasn't too worried." She took a deep breath and made a little sniffling noise. "Joanna McIntire called me. I don't understand what's going on."

"Me neither," he said with heartfelt truthfulness. "And even if I did, I'm not sure how much I could tell you."

She held him away then, and searched his face. "But it's nothing bad?"

"I don't think it is. I mean, we don't mean it to be. It's not gangs or drugs or anything like that."

She glanced at the bulging mesh bag lying on the floor. "Are you leaving again?"

"I think so."

"Come into the kitchen and talk with me a moment or two." Her gaze rested then on the glowing crystal. She didn't say anything but led the way back into the house. He had to grab his crystal and drag the heavy bag back behind him.

"Is Dad awake?" he asked, as she fixed him an English muffin with peanut butter and jam.

"Your father could sleep through anything." She sat down on a breakfast chair and folded her hands on her lap. "I want you to know we love and trust you."

That made his eyes smart. He didn't deserve it, especially

not with the battle he was having with himself. Henry shook his head. "I'm just trying my best, Mom."

She nodded. "But you can't tell me what's happening?"

"Can't. I want to, but . . ."

She put her hand out, smoothing his hair away from his forehead. "Does this have anything to do with summer camp, Henry?" She took his crystal from his hand gently, examining it. "And your powers?"

"Mom!"

She gave the crystal back. "Unlike your father, you are a restless sleeper. And you talk in your sleep." She touched his cheek lightly. "I couldn't help but listen, you were so sick with poison oak when you came home, but more than that, you were so unhappy. You'd lost your abilities, your talents, that you'd been so proud of."

"You never said anything to me!" He stared at her.

"And you never said anything to me."

"I couldn't! There's this Vow of Silence, you see, and it just locks you up, keeps everything bottled in, and then I had this drink to make me forget everything cause they had to send me away, but it didn't work right, and then I started remembering, and then the Magick came back and—" He plowed to an astonished halt. "And I shouldn't be able to tell you now."

"Maybe it's one of those protective things, that only works when there's danger." She laced her fingers together, watching him.

"Maybe." He rubbed his citrine. "Something happened and we had to run."

"Bailey? Jason? You? And the others?"

He nodded.

"Where can you go?"

"We're back at the camp, sorta. The trouble is . . ." He didn't quite know how to tell her. Henry stared down at the kitchen floor a moment.

"The world never understands people who are different."

He looked up. "Did I ever tell you I think you're the best mom in the whole world?"

She smiled slightly. "Yes, you did!" She held her arms out. He hugged her again. Her voice fell to a near whisper. "I'm very proud of you, Henry Squibb, and don't you ever forget that! Take whatever you need, and come and go as often as you can." She let go of him then. "Maybe someday you can tell everyone who and what you are."

"I don't know if that will ever happen."

"When it does, you be the first ambassador. Now, it looks like you have breakfast, lunch, and dinner to deliver!"

He rubbed his crystal. "Watch this," he said with pride as he took hold of the booty bag and disappeared from her sight.

Through the *between*, Henry searched for Jason. *Please, please, please, let me back.* He had to tell them what he could, and help however he could. It was the only way he'd ever be proud of himself, no matter what they thought, or his mom thought. He held to the hope that the tiny swing in the Gate Jason had given for him might yet be there. He searched so intently, he never felt the tiny nibble at the back of his mind.

Ah, there you are, my little Squibb. Where have you been and what have you been doing, and where are you going?

He never felt a thing as Jonnard sifted through his mind and then sat back with a gloating laugh as, for the first time, he saw all and knew all that Henry did. Henry, in his eagerness to Crystal, had left his mind totally open. Even the delicious moments of stealing his Magick had never peeled the boy's thoughts open like a ripe fruit. And now, Jon knew all he could ever wish. He let Henry slip through, felt him bursting through the Dragon Gate into Haven, even as he stood with a triumphant yell for his father.

33

BATTLE STATIONS

TRENT eyed Jason. "You're taller than I am."

"I'm what? When did that happen?" Jason looked himself over.

"I have no idea. I think it happened overnight . . . about the same time that tunic last fit you." Trent jabbed a thumb at him.

Jason tugged on his tunic. It did, indeed, hang shorter and feel a lot tighter around the shoulders than he remembered which was sometime yesterday when he'd gotten it. His chin itched. He scratched it with one finger thoughtfully. He would have thought more of it if they had been anywhere but where they were. Rich and Trent were already tired of Haven, with little to do but try and set traps for Bailey's sight unseen trader friend: "Don't worry, it's capture and release," they told her when she found out and got upset. They'd tied Stef's sneakers to the top of the highest tree they could find, but the bear cub had merely scaled it and knocked them down. They'd hidden Madame Qi's cane at least three times but given it up when she had placidly opened her hand and called it back to her each time. Jason was of the opinion they would have tried something on Rebecca Landau, too, but as she seemed to be doing most of the cooking, they'd changed their minds. It had only been a few days and they were itching to explore.

Still, idle hands and minds . . . Jason came to the conclusion that it was obviously his turn. "I'm not falling for this," he said to Trent.

Trent widened his eyes innocently. "Falling for what?"

"Whatever."

"Okay, we'll call Miss Bundle of Enthusiasm herself over. Bailey! C'mere."

She looked up and wrinkled her nose before trotting over curiously. "What are you two up to?"

"Me, nothing. Trent here is trying to—" He never got a chance to finish.

"Jason!" Bailey let out a squeal. "You've got chin hairs." She stared at his face in fascination.

"Okay, now I'm P.O.'d. Taller than me with chin hairs." Trent squinted at him.

"Cut it out, you two!" Jason tried to yank his tunic into place about his body.

Trent put his hand on Jason's shoulder. "I'm not kidding, bud." He looked at Jason closely.

Bailey crossed her heart. Well, actually, it was Lacey she crossed who grumbled sleepily in her pocket as the gesture disturbed her. The little pack rat kicked about and bumped around a bit before resettling. Bailey tilted her face to look up at him. She wrinkled her nose again. "And taller."

"He is, isn't he? Am I right, or am I right?"

"You're right. The question is: why?"

"We're guys. We have these spurts of growth."

She shook her head. "Not in just a few days. And if we were all doing that, well, we'd all be taller or something. But we're not. Just you, Jason." She looked a bit worried.

"You're aging." Trent glanced at him.

"I don't feel older."

"I don't think Eleanora does either," said Trent quietly.

The impact of his words hit both Jason and Bailey. She paled. "From . . . the Magick?"

"Probably. His aging doesn't seem to be as drastic as Eleanora's, but still." Trent swallowed. "This can't be good."

He didn't feel different. His shoes were cramped and his tunic too small, and his chin scratchy, but he really didn't feel different. He walked over to the pond and looked down at its glassy surface. He didn't look more mature to his eyes, but the water didn't give him that clear a picture back. "It is what it is," he said, finally. He touched the image as if reassuring himself of what he saw.

Something rippled across the water as he touched it. Looking into it, he saw a pack of wolfjackals in the sky, circling, coming closer, riding a storm of black chaos as they always did. He looked back over his shoulder. Nothing behind him. The sky seemed a clear blue and undisturbed. Yet, as he stared back into the water, the vision became more and more distinct. To his surprise, the wolfjackals bore riders. At first, he saw Tomaz and Gavan. Then, as the water rippled, he saw Jonnard and Brennard and others. He rubbed his eyes. Who came? What was he seeing?

"What is it?"

"The water," he murmured, thinking.

Bailey leaned over. "Water mirrors are for prophecies."

"So?" Trent nudged her.

"So, Jason is a Gatekeeper."

They jostled each other, Jason barely aware of their bantering.

"You've got a peephole in your apartment door, right?" Bailey eyed him suspiciously before nodding.

"All right then. This is Jason's peephole through the Gates." Trent jabbed his thumb at the deep blue water.

"You think so?"

Jason heard that last. He wondered himself. But a pounding inside his ears like the rolling thunder of a faraway storm told him he wouldn't have long to think about it.

"Get ready," he warned.

"What's wrong?"

He didn't have time to explain. He stood and yelled, his voice ringing over the small valley. "Get ready!" His crystal flared.

If they were going to attack, it would be on his terms. The vision of Tomaz and Gavan shimmered across the lake again. They looked caught, trapped within the maelstrom of chaos. The wolfjackals ran raggedly, their jaws dripping with foam from exhaustion. Did the creatures bear Tomaz and Gavan willingly? Possibly. If so, from what did they run? And why did the storm hold them against their will? If he blinked, he saw the Dark Hand commanding wolf-jackals. They rode as warriors, bearing down on him, teeth bared. Who came after them? He wanted the true Seeing, and knew he would have to make a decision. He reached into the water and shook an image free. Power raged up his arm as he did.

They burst out of the lake. Water spewed up in great, foamy waves carrying the intruders on them. Wolfjack-als heaved themselves onto the bank, their heated bod-ies steaming off the water, Tomaz clinging to the massive leader and Gavan trying in vain to hold to the second with one arm. He fell to the shore at the beast's second leap onto solid ground, three or four pack-mates on its heels.

"Thank the gods," Gavan said weakly, and closed his eyes.

Tomaz threw his leg over and landed lightly. Before any-one but Jason could react, he had Gavan up on his feet and one arm over his shoulder.

Wearily, Jason lowered his crystal to watch the wolfjack-als circle. He waited for the familiar throb from his scar, but it stayed flat and cool. No menace came from them, this time.

"Good instincts, Jason," Tomaz said to him. "Let them go. They were as trapped in that burst of Chaos as we were."

In the wink of an eye, he opened a Gate and tossed them through, their howls of joy echoing back before the sound cut off abruptly, and it was as if the wolfjackals had never come to Haven.

"You're bloodied," Jason said to Tomaz.

"Been in a fight, and a fire would be good." He nodded to Jason.

Later, Gavan would say, "I'd have been here sooner, lad, but I was a bit busy."

"Hold still," Rich muttered. He dabbed on some more peroxide and began wrapping gauze again. Gavan gave him a bemused look. "It'll scar," Rich told him, "but it's mostly just surface damage. You didn't bleed out much ei-ther, from the looks of it."

"Good news and bad news, aye?" He flexed his arm gin-gerly when Rich finished. "A handy kit you carry about."

"Won't do much if anyone gets really thrashed, but it's good for a cut or sprain." He clipped it back onto his belt.

"You've a talent there."

"Thanks. I mostly thought my Talent consisted of bear herding."

Stef snorted and dropped a load of deadwood onto the ground. He ignored everyone as he carefully fed another log into the fire. Gavan had finally warmed judging by the color in his cheeks, but he still leaned close to the flames.

Tomaz squatted across from them. He looked tired and worn, himself. His jeans sagged a bit about his body, and his bracelets seemed loose when he moved, as if he'd lost weight running with the wolfjackals. He'd said little about them, only that they were torn from Chaos and sought it to go back where they belonged. Jason had the feeling that there were volumes to be learned from the shaman but nothing he wished to tell at the moment. It was surprising enough to know that the wolfjackals could be entrapped by Chaos, and it was a near thing that he had freed them all.

Gavan straightened. He gave Jason a look of sheer pride. "You've opened the last Gate, lad. Good job. If Iron Mountain ever gets built, it'll be because of heroic acts like that."

"If? Not when?" Trent drummed his fingers on his knee.

Tomaz said quietly, "There are other matters at hand."

"We're going to be under attack." Everyone looked to Jason.

"Possibly," agreed Gavan slowly. "What makes you say that?"

"When I looked in the pool, I saw wolfjackals. Some bore the two of you . . . others bore the Dark Hand."

Bailey whistled. Rebecca reached out and grabbed her daughter's hand. Madame Qi tightened her grip on the cane across her knees. "It is a good thing," she said, "I have been able to teach Jason a few things."

"Very good," Gavan said to her. "As for what detained me . . ." He took a deep breath, wincing as if it pained him. In slow, halting words, he told them of the caves and the Leucators. "We've got to rally what's left of the Council, and Tomaz and I have to bring in Eleanora. I couldn't get through before."

"I've got it blocked."

"Can you open the Gates, Jason? Open and hold them, till we get Eleanora and FireAnn and what others we can in?"

"Jason won't be alone." Trent stood. A small piece of kindling snapped in his hands.

Gavan gave them a tired, lopsided smile. "From the first, none of you have ever been alone. You've always had each other. You are Magickers, more than we could ever have hoped for." He got to his feet carefully, his right arm tucked against himself like a broken wing. He held Jason's chin with his good hand, and looked into his eyes. "We will be back."

Jason shifted his weight. He said quietly, "I'm waiting for Ting and Henry, too. So I'll swing the Gates open every now and then, looking for you. We'll hold each as best we can."

"The Dark Hand will have tried the moment they felt the wave of the Dragon Gate being opened. Your blocking must have shut them out, as it nearly did me, and as it did Tomaz. I'm guessing they don't know where you're to be found."

"They will." Jason held an intense belief in the danger he'd seen in the lake.

"Then you'll have no choice but to guard the Gates carefully once they're open. When I get the Council in, we'll be able put up permanent wards, with pass runes." Gavan clasped Jason's hand. "Outstanding work, my lad. I can't wait to get Eleanora here."

After they left, it got very quiet. Bailey said, "It's not right without Ting and Henry."

"Ting will be here," Qi told her. "She is on the way now."

"I think Henry will be back, too."

"They'll be here," Jason said with certainty. "But this is what we have to do. There're three Gates in. Iron Gate, Water Gate, Dragon Gate. They'll have to be watched whenever I open them."

"Battle stations," agreed Trent. The Magickers all stood and walked to Jason and they slapped their hands in the air.

*   *   *

Ting tried not to fuss as her mother strapped together the last bundle and loaded it into her backpack. She didn't know how long she'd been gone from Haven, but it had been two days while lawyers drew up papers and made arrangements since Qi Zhang had said she would not be back. Jiao finally looked into Ting's face. "I know, I know," she said in soft answer to the rebellion on Ting's face. "You can go back and forth, but these are things she will need." She paused.

"And when everything is settled, I'll bring you to visit," Ting promised.

"You can do that?"

Ting nodded.

"Then I am content." Her mother held her a moment. "We'll stay here at the house until you can bring the papers back, and we know how she's really feeling. Sometimes, the health is a false promise."

"I know, Mom. We've been over this."

"Have patience with me, Ting. It's hard to lose a mother and a daughter in the same day."

"You won't lose either of us!" Ting promised fervently, and threw her arms around her mother's neck. "Now, I really have to go."

"I will wait," Jiao Chuu told her, and her mother's calm face was the last thing she saw as her crystal took her. She felt Jason's Gate waiting as if just for her, and slipped through quietly.

"It's time, my friend," the stranger said, and tapped lightly on Jerry Landau's car window. Jerry woke with a start. Sleeping again? He stretched, then groaned. He felt as dried out and crusty as an old mummy. How long had he been sitting there, watching the apartment building? He rubbed at his eyes.

"I never saw her," he muttered in disgust.

"It's all right. You should go home and wait. But before you go, I would like something small and insignificant from you to help in our quest."

Jerry looked at the man with a little bit of suspicion. He had little enough of anything to give away, and he thought uneasily that this man had never really been clear why he was at all interested in Bailey or Jerry's difficulties with her. As partnerships go, he hadn't really benefited one way or another. He brushed a paper off his dashboard and tried to straighten a bit in his seat, pins and needles in his legs from hours of not moving.

Antoine Brennard smiled thinly. "Don't worry," he reassured. "You'll never miss it. Just a touch of your soul." He reached through the half-open car window and ripped it away.

Jerry Landau gasped. He shoved his legs out and went rigid against the driver's seat, his heart pounding, his body stiff as a board, his ears roaring. Heart attack! He had to be having a heart attack.

Brennard pulled his hand back filled with shadow. "Trust me. I can do much better things with this than you can. We'll have your daughter, one way or another." He stepped away from the car. "Now go home and forget." He made a gesture.

Landau's mouth moved open and shut like a fish caught ashore and trying to breathe dry air. Brennard stepped back and into the shadows before Landau could move at all and hurriedly started his car. He burned rubber getting away from the curb as the automobile screeched into motion. Brennard cupped the essence in his hands. A Leucator from this subject might come in very handy indeed.

Henry had forgotten how to breathe. The *between* held him gripped in its jaws and the plane of Crystaling stretched into a long black forever, and he knew he was doomed.

Suddenly, a tiny crick of light fractured across it. With a grateful sob, Henry dove toward it headfirst. The Gate! He'd finally found the Gate! He could feel Jason's presence, warm and welcoming, and clutched at it. Something broke inside of him, and he hurtled through with a grateful yell.

Henry landed on top of Stefan. Both boys let out shouts of surprise, Stef's breaking into the cub's voice as they rolled away from each other. With a bang and a clatter, they woke everyone else.

"Henry!" cried Ting in delight. "You came back!"

His head throbbed and Stef shoved him away with a

good-natured grunt, and someone lit a Lantern spell, bathing the campsite in soft light. His booty bag had spilled open and Rich had already grabbed out a foil wrapped package of Rice Krispies treats and broken it open to share.

"Back, with treats," Rich noted.

"And that's not all," said Henry miserably. He dusted himself off. "Jason, Trent, I need to talk to you. If I can." He took a deep breath as they followed him off to a quiet place, and he said, "I've had Jonnard in my head." To his surprise, it came out, and he sobbed in gratitude.

Jason listened quietly as Henry spilled his guts. Trent did as well before putting in, "It isn't your fault. You didn't even know for sure what was going on, and I'm willing to bet he wasn't going to let you tell."

Henry puffed up his cheeks and then let his breath out slowly. "If only there was some way I could make it up." He looked at Jason.

Jason waved a hand. "Actually, I think you just gave us an unexpected advantage."

"I did? How?"

"Okay, Henry. This is what I need you to do. I need you to drain Jonnard."

"Me? But . . ." Squibb took his glasses off and cleaned them deliberately, thinking. "You're not going to just shut me off?"

Jason shook his head. Trent put his hand on Squibb's shoulder and shook him lightly. "Think about it, man. We may have a huge advantage here."

Henry looked at both of them, his round face slightly puzzled. "I've been a mole, and you guys are happy about it?"

"Not really, but . . . like Trent said, think about it. You've held the key all along. You kept muttering, tug-of-war, when Jon drained you. Henry, it *is* just like a tug-of-war. Only, this time, you pull back."

"I pull back."

"That's the plan."

Realization hit him. Henry put his glasses back on and pushed them into place. "How hard?"

"As hard as you can. Incapacitate him."

"I can do that?" Without waiting for an answer, he inclined his chin. "Of course I can. It goes both ways." Henry gave a delighted grin.

"It's not going to be quite that easy," Jason warned him. "We don't want Jon to know what you can do. You have to be light and quick about it."

Trent nodded vigorously. "No bull in a china shop," he added. "Got that?"

"I can do it." Henry's grin widened even more. "This is going to be fun."

"This is going to be dangerous."

"Oh, I know that. But it's still going to be fun. When do I do this?"

"Now," Jason told him. "Tomorrow may be too late."

"All right. It may be a long night."

"Not as long as it will be tomorrow."

Henry squinted up at him. "Did you get taller?"

"You think?"

Despite the pain in his arm, Gavan felt more alive and full of hope than he had in weeks, as Tomaz brought him to Ravenwyng. His feet touched the ground, and he could feel the spring air with the promise of summer on his face. He forced himself to think of unpleasant things, even though his heart sang with the hope he could bring to Eleanora at last.

"We'll have to deal with Isabella. Strip her of her powers forcibly, if need be, and then neutralize every one of the Leucators."

"That will take time but we shall get it done," agreed Tomaz. "Do you think there is any possibility at all Eleanora could be helped by that?"

"I think," Gavan said firmly, "she is being killed by it. As was Fizziwig and who knows who else? Isabella has to be stopped."

"Then that we will do." Tomaz paused. He stopped at the edge of the Gathering Hall building. "Did you not say you left the camp warded?"

"I did . . ." Gavan stepped around him. A haze of smoke and stench of burning hung like a fog. "Gods, no!" He broke into a shambling run for FireAnn's cottage, Tomaz on his heels. The front door lay in splinters. Inside, the smell of crushed herbs filled the air where they'd been trampled.

The inside of the cottage looked thrashed as if a hurricane had hit it. It stood empty of all life. Gavan dropped into a squat by the empty bed where Eleanora had lain. He put a hand on the cold covers. He stared up at Tomaz helplessly.

"FireAnn didn't let her go easily."

"No." Gavan scrubbed the heel of his hand across his eyes. "What do they want of her?"

A shadow in the corner of the cottage shuddered and undulated and Brennard stepped out. His Shield of deep obsidian sparkled about him, carrying the shadow with him as he moved.

"Tell your boy to open the Gates and keep them open. If you want Eleanora alive. Otherwise, I shall leave her in Isabella's untender care."

"And FireAnn."

"And the redhead as well." Brennard waved his hand. "We will take Haven."

Gavan got to his feet. "And if I say no?"

Brennard crossed the cottage. With a word, he reduced the wall to rubble, and through its broken framework, they could see a convoy forming. Gavan managed a breath in spite of the emotion gripping his chest. He rubbed the head of his cane, and Tomaz's thoughts sprang into his own.

Let them pass. We will gather those we can and follow.

"Rainwater," said Brennard impatiently. "Get us passage."

"You shall have it," Gavan said, his voice dull, even though his mind churned with thoughts, and plans. "The boy is a Gatekeeper. I can ask him to open the Gates. I cannot keep him from defending them."

"I'll deal with him then."

"Leave Eleanora!"

"You'll have the two once we're safely across the borders. Don't do anything, Gavan, that you will regret later."

Too late, he thought. He'd already brushed Jason's mind and told him to throw the Gates open and why, and what he and Tomaz planned to do.

He wondered if he'd put too much on Jason's shoulders, boy, not quite man.

He had no choice.

34

GUARDS AND WARRIORS

"REMEMBER," whispered Qi's voice inside his ear. "Wu Shu is an inner defense as well as an outer. Even more true for one such as yourself with the power. The enemy will press you on both fronts, but you will succeed." Ting's grandmother sounded confident and proud.

Jason drew himself together with those thoughts ringing through his mind. He knew he'd grown in just these few days, for the mysterious aging factor had only matured him, not weakened him. Not yet. Even more importantly, although he looked very much alone, he was not. Locked inside were the strengths of every Magicker he had ever touched, and every friend he'd ever shared with. The only thing he doubted was if his own strength would be enough, but it wouldn't be because he hadn't tried.

The corner of his mouth crooked up a little. He wondered what kind of brownie points against the Dark Hand he'd get for just trying.

He shifted his weight on the rock outcropping. From where he stood, he could see the four corners of this tiny pocket of Haven, which he'd once thought was the entire face of it. Now Jason knew better. A wind came through the valley, faint and clear, playing against his face and carrying the scent of spring on it, of green grass, a hint of faraway rain, and blossoms he had no names for because they were of Haven and no place he had ever been to before. After this was all over, he made a note, he'd ask FireAnn about some of those herbs and flowers. Or maybe he and Bailey could go on a walking tour.

He wondered about what the dragon had hinted at. As he fought here, when the battle came to him, would it be reflected elsewhere? Were all great battles in his world and Haven ripples of battles somewhere or somewhen else? And did the battles they started on their own create ripples that in turn carried grief and strife? Somehow he had always thought when war came to him, he'd be wearing a uniform and carrying a weapon of another sort, rather than a Chinese grandmother's cane.

Jason ran his hands over it. "Good, Chinese bamboo," Qi had said. "Nothing harder, not even a stubborn boy's skull." He wasn't sure what he'd do with it, other than what she'd shown him. His version of Wu Shu would have moves in it no master could have envisioned.

A trembling came on the wind. He felt it, more than heard it. Magic was even harder to define or see than the wind that carried it, but it pricked at his nerves. A storm rode the wind now. Jason swallowed. He was as ready as he could ever be, he hoped. He was to keep the Gates open, yet hold them here while Gavan and Tomaz gathered their allies and came from the rear. He was to let them in, but not to let them pass.

Or, as Bailey put it, "We're the cork in the bottle," which made sense in a Bailey sort of way. Jason hadn't thought to ask her whether the Dark Hand was breaking out of, or into, that bottle. He wasn't sure he really wanted to know. All that mattered was that he stood there, his face tilted to the wind, trying to catch the first glimpse of the attack.

He heard it first. Borne on the wind came an eerie howling that he knew all too well, the battle song of the wolf-jackal. He shaded his eyes as the horizon darkened with clouds of storm gray and the wolflike beasts seemed to rip the very sky apart with their flashing teeth as they raced toward him. The back of his left hand twitched in pain from the long-ago scar, and he rubbed it slightly to distract himself. From Chaos itself, the wolfjackals seemed to obey no rule of time or space as they raced across the building clouds, descending to earth only when they drew near. That did not surprise him.

What immobilized him for a long moment was the sight of riders upon their shaggy backs. To see the Dark Hand mounted shot defiance into his heart. The dark powers would feed upon each other, making both more powerful than they would have been alone! Tomaz must have known this, even as Jason could sense it. Had he betrayed them to the Dark Hand as well, as Henry had, as Isabella had, some in lesser ways, others in far greater? Had he shown them this fact unwillingly or willingly? Dare he trust Tomaz now, at Gavan's side, planning a rescue?

Jason narrowed his eyes after one fierce blink to chase away a bitter tear. He had no way of knowing and no time to guess. *I know what I know. Doubt brings weakness, and is the way of the enemy.* Tomaz had never failed him before. He would not believe the Magicker had failed him now!

He placed both hands on his bamboo cane once more and centered his thoughts. The crystal pendant at his throat answered with a flare of warmth. Strengthened by his exercises, he no longer had to cup it for Focusing. It answered him by sheer thought and will with a beacon of light that enveloped him in a luminous glow that muffled the ever sharper howling. The bamboo seemed to mold to his grip on it as he eyed the wolfjackal riders.

Jonnard moved to the fore, brandishing a black sword. Behind him rode Brennard and two of the Dark Hand he had seen before but whose names he'd never known or he'd forgotten, young men, pale, angry, wearing long duster coats straight out of the *Matrix* movies, and the fifth rider of the Hand was a Leucator of himself. Jason inhaled deeply, his breath hissing through his teeth. Isabella had always thought herself so clever.

The galloping wolfjackals covered leagues of ground in bare minutes, coming toward him at a dead run. He could hear their hot breath between howls and snarls and the sound of the men riding them urging them after him. Jason stood on high ground, but that wouldn't protect him, and he bent his knees slightly for the force of the first physical attack even as he readied for the mental unleashing of power they would send against him.

The glow of his Shield took on a rainbow-edged hue as Ting and Bailey and Rich and Stef bent their own powers through the clever gemstone pendant Ting had fashioned. They were out of his sight, in strategic corners of the green vale, protecting the other Gates, like him, trying to hold an invisible line. Like linking hands, Ting had said hopefully, and he could feel it now as if they did and prayed it would continue to hold the bond she'd forged for him. Only Henry did not filter through his crystal for obvious reasons. Trent, for less obvious.

The wolfjackals and riders leaped up below him. He moved, raining tiny pebbles and sand downward, and scarcely felt the first stings of power they sent against him. His Shield made tiny spits as it repelled each attempt to touch him. He felt as though he wore a great suit of armor and they could not touch him. If only it would last!

The Leucator dropped to the rear of the pack, watching him with eyes that would have looked like his own, but they were flat with the lack of expression. Dead eyes, Bailey would say. Something odd caught his attention as the Leucator raised his hand to guide his surly wolfjackal into submission but exactly what it was escaped him.

Jonnard stretched upward on his wolfjackal mount. "Give us passage."

"The Gates were open. That is all we promised." His voice sounded braver than he felt.

"We don't need promises to take what we can take." Jonnard threw his hands up, lightning shivering between them. Jason reeled back, as he threw his hands up in response, barely holding onto his cane.

He let his Magick talk for him. He swung around, aiming his gaze at one of the dark riders he barely knew, and the power swung with him and shot out with a sizzle. A wolfjackal dodged with a yelp and snarl, nearly unseating its rider. The smell of burned dirt filled his nostrils.

He brought his attention back to Jon and Brennard.

Brennard cuffed his wolfjackal to a crouching standstill. "So," he noted. "The boy becomes a man."

"Not man enough." Jon spit out a curse and gestured. Jason's feet went out from under him as the earth moved, tossing him, and he landed, rolling, on the sharp rocks. He came up on his knees and catapulted into a back flip, courtesy of Qi's teaching, twisting his body into balance as he did, settling firmly onto his feet.

The look of satisfaction on Jonnard's face bled away.

A rumble like thunder cut through the stormy sky and Jason looked up toward it. None of the Dark Hand did, and that meant they expected it. He frowned. Out of the depths of dark clouds great forms rolled forward and then halted, waiting.

Huge wagons with black canvas tarps over them appeared, with hooded drivers, their dull brown draft horses stamping on the dirt restlessly, the fittings on their harnesses jingling like bells. He could not imagine what they carried but was afraid they would all find out before this fight was over. Behind them, he could see human figures, also waiting. An army. Brennard had brought an army with him. Jason shook his head as though he could clear his vision of that sight.

On the seat of the leading wagon, Isabella sat brazenly, and she held a limp Eleanora across her lap as if she were a rag doll or already dead.

Just hold them, Gavan and Tomaz had said. *Hold them until we arrive.*

Jason tightened his hands on his cane, feeling as though caught in some heroic movie and knowing the outcome couldn't possibly be the same. He might stand against the five drawing nearer and nearer to him as though they were a noose and he the neck they would tighten around, but an army?

Panic shot through him. He considered the options they'd planned beforehand, getting Ting, and Grandmother, and Bailey and Rebecca to safety if anything happened. His hand jerked in a reflex upward to grasp his crystal and signal a retreat.

How could he hold against an army?

A bamboo splinter came off in his palm, sharply, as he moved. Jason bit off a cry at the surprising hurt, then stifled a second exclamation. Qi's voice cut through his memory. They will fight you inside and out, Jason. Remember that!'

Yes. He had forgotten that . . . momentarily. He bit his lip against the sting of the splinter and gazed at one of the wolfjackals who paced and snarled, and then Jason took aim. A shard of white fire exploded at its feet and the beast bolted with a howl of dismay. It took to its heels. The Hand riding the wolfjackal thrashed and whipped it, unable to halt it, and no one moved to help him as the beast whirled about. They disappeared back into the storm that had brought them. Jonnard put a heel firmly to the side of the shaggy beast he rode, reminding it who was in charge, and it paced sideways to flank Jason. The Gatekeeper moved to watch Jonnard. That was a mistake.

In a flash, they were on him from two sides. He felt a claw rip at him and the heat wave of a power surge. Jason ducked his head and let his body soar as Qi had shown him, diving into a tumbling somersault and coming up, swinging his cane. He connected even as he kicked about, pivoting out of range as a wolfjackal snarled at his ear. No time to look, just react. Let his body avoid the danger. His spirit sensed the blows before they would hit and carried him away.

He waved a hand, crying out for Light and the Magick gave it to him, flaring in the eyes of the beast snapping at him. The wolfjackal veered away yelping and stumbled down the small hill, pawing at its blinded eyes. It dumped its rider who put a hand out, then pulled back his duster coat and stood his ground. Jason shrugged a shoulder and sent a lance of song at him that vibrated through him. He stared in astonishment at his hand, at the spear he held, as it shook harder and harder and then disintegrated into metal dust and rained out from between his fingers.

Jason turned away from the backlash on that spell but it hit him anyway, the noise of drums bursting in his skull until his own Shield rattled under the turmoil and he could hear Ting gasp softly in her own pain as she tried to protect him. He brought his Focus back on himself to dispel the sonics and then stood, panting, feeling something wet drip down the side of his jaw.

Jason touched fingers to his face and brought them away crimson. Someone had marked him, Shield or not, Magick or not. How badly was he cut? Was it a gaping wound that would drain him of all his blood? The thought of flesh opening to his skull, exposing nerves and muscles, made him shake and he stared at his fingers.

Jason, stop it. That's what they want you to think. It's a surface wound, minor, or I'd be out there bandaging you! Rich's voice echoed faintly in his head. Jason shook himself. He couldn't take his eyes off the blood dripping from his hand.

Two of them jumped him at once. He went down between them, rolling and kicking, feeling his flesh tear and his soul shiver. He kicked them apart and got back to his feet, battered, and wondered how much more he could take.

Trent watched from his position beside Henry, and saw Jason sway with pain. He muttered to Henry, "Now." Jason hadn't yet given the signal, but he wasn't sure Jason could even think clearly. He saw his friend struggle to remain standing.

"Now?" repeated Henry. His own face had gone deathly pale, as Jonnard leeched power from him. Tiny drops of sweat beaded his forehead.

Trent gripped his shoulder hard. "If you're going to do it, Henry, it's now or never! Finish him!"

"Tug-of-war," Henry muttered with determination. He squeezed his eyes shut. "He shut me down earlier, but he won't this time!"

Trent watched anxiously. Jason traded more blows, as the wolfjackals and riders circled up the small hill toward him. He wouldn't have much of a defense left on the high ground when they reached him in another jump or two.

Trent pulled his crystal from his pocket. Of all of them there, he was the least. He knew it, they knew it. It was of no help at all to be able to see the Magick raging around Jason now. There were no subtle traps. He would either stand or he wouldn't, and the rest of them had the other Gates to hold. The only thing he could do was help Henry a bit, and damnit, he was tired of being the cheerleader.

He thumbed his rock. Beautiful but obscured, a clouded white crystal it had been when he picked it and that was the way it stayed. Yet, it had been out with all the others gems for bonding with the new Magickers. Surely someone should have seen it was a dud and cast it out, just like him. He rolled it between his fingers even as Henry groaned.

"Hang in there, Henry! You're stronger!"

He didn't even know if Henry could still hear him. They crouched in the Y of a tree, Henry having made cheerful comments about being in the arms of an Ent, one of Tolkien's fantasy tree people. Trent had tied him to the main trunk just to make sure he wouldn't fall out. He guessed it was just the way he saw things. He didn't trust the fantasy the way Henry did.

A wolfjackal howled as Jason let go with a mighty blow, the bamboo cane KER-AKing as it hit. Rider and mount fell heavily on the hill and slid down to a quiet heap at the bottom. Trent could see the effort trembling in Jason's torso as he stood, and steadied, and readied himself for yet another assault from Brennard and Jon. And the Leucator that was Jason's double waited to the rear, an eerie apparition. It was so like Jason that it had already fooled Trent once or twice at a glance.

Where were Gavan and Tomaz and whatever others they could reach?

Henry let out a sharp cry as he bit his lip and crimson ran down his chin. Trent gripped the other's shoulder again. Henry opened his eyes and said weakly, "I've got him!" He managed a grin.

Trent didn't think it would be enough. "Good man, Henry," he answered in spite of his apprehension. "Just don't let go!"

Stef fought himself. He could feel the bear cub trying to burst through the seams of his body, and he shook with the effort to stay human. The Magick rolling about him tore away his control and he could not help himself. He let out a deep, groaning sound from the very depths of his body, before turning a helpless look at Rich. "Rich . . . I'm sorry . . ."

"It's all right, man." Rich's face stayed pale against his freckles, his shock of brilliant red hair standing disheveled about his head, all his thoughts bent on the Water Gate. He could feel the caravans rolling into the valley, feel the sting of their corruption as it pierced the goodness that had been Haven's heart. The bear cub stood on its hind legs, weaving, and growled heavily. Then it dropped to all fours and lumbered to where Jason had chosen to take his stand.

"Stefan!" cried Rich after his friend, but the burly bear

cub never looked back. His growling rose in intensity, sensing a fight.

Brennard looked down the vale and saw the half grown bear shambling toward them. He gave a chill smile. "We've broken the first," he said to Jonnard. "Now after the others." He circled his wolfjackal about, riding back to the black wagons and waving his hand in a signal. The tarp rolled up. A single Leucator got down, and looked about, nostrils flaring for a scent. Then with a low hissing, it loped away.

Qi collapsed with a tiny sound and fell to the grass. Ting immediately knelt at her side, pulling her grandmother to her, feeling her face. Qi took Ting's hands in hers, saying weakly, "This battle is not for the old. I am very, very weary."

"I'll take you home!"

"This is my home now. Only let me rest. Do what you must, Granddaughter, or . . . or I'll never forgive you!" Qi tried to squeeze her hands hard, but the effort proved too much for her, and her fingers just trembled about Ting's.

"You can't stay here."

"I can and will." Qi struggled to sit up, pulling her black, quilted jacket and pants straight.

"Back in the grove then," Ting insisted, getting her grandmother to her feet. "I'll be back!" she called to Bailey as she helped Qi hobble toward the safety and shade of the trees.

Bailey had felt the weakening of their Shields the moment Ting let go, but she said nothing. She bit her lip in concentration, knowing that somewhere beyond this curve of Haven, a battle to keep the Dark Hand at a standstill raged. She could feel it in her crystal and in the jewelry Ting had fashioned.

Lacey let out a series of worried chirps, ran out of her pocket, and climbed onto her shoulder, nestling against the curve of her throat. Her tiny furred body felt incredibly warm and comforting as the pack rat clung to her. Rebecca gently laid her hand over Bailey's, saying, "I don't know what I can do."

A strengthening surged into Bailey where her mother touched her. "Wow! Mom . . . you're a battery!"

"A battery?"

"You're like stored energy. I can feel it!" Bailey grinned at her mother, the moment of uncertainty when Ting left her gone. She felt its glow and goodness wrap about her, helping to fill in the gap Ting had left behind. She beamed her power to Jason, feeding him, feeling the tremendous need he had for whatever help she could give him. Her eyebrows lowered.

"What is it?"

"I don't think it's going well," said Bailey quietly.

"It will," Rebecca told her with a fierce pride in her voice. "You've got to believe the others are coming to help."

"If they can."

Rebecca leaned against her daughter, trying to will belief and hope into her, not truly understanding the battle they were waging except that much of it came from inside, and that could surely be encouraged by positive thoughts.

Neither of them heard the third person approach until his voice rose around them.

"Wife and daughter."

Rebecca swung about. "Jerry!"

"They told me you were hiding here. They told me they'd help me find you." He put a hand out, walking slowly toward them, but his chest heaved as if he'd been running. "It's time to be a family again."

Bailey turned wildly toward them, and then began backing up. "Mom! Mom, that's not Daddy. Don't let him touch you!"

Rebecca put herself between them. "Jerry?"

"Mom, don't!" Bailey's hand jerked. "It's not human."

"Is that any way to talk about your father? Who carried you around when you had colic? Who took you to your first pony ride? Baseball game?"

Bailey's mouth twisted. "You took me to the ball game because it was Nickel Beer Night."

"A man deserves a little reward now and then." The thing stopped, mouth working at a smile.

"Bailey, stay behind me."

"Look at its eyes, Mom. That's a . . . a Leucator. It's a made thing."

"All you've done is twist her against me, Becca. What a horrible, horrible thing for a mother to do. You should be punished!" He lunged at her.

He grabbed Rebecca. She screamed at the chill pain that jolted her at his touch, her arm going numb, as he pulled her away from their daughter. "Come to Daddy," he said to Bailey. He threw Rebecca away, on the ground, where she went limp with shock and lay there, dazed.

"Mom!"

He batted at her. Their hands connected even as Bailey tried to dart away, and her amethyst went flying. *Never drop your crystal.* She fell backward and scrambled to get away from the thing that looked like her father. Her Shield, her power, winked out, leaving her very much alone. Lacey squeaked in her ear and then bit her earlobe, *hard.* "Ow!" Bailey shot to her feet and the Leucator lunged past her, just missing. The chill of its body passing felt as if someone had opened a freezer door.

Bailey danced back. She removed Lacey from her neck and gently tossed her to the grass. "Go get it!" The fuzz ball squeaked off, tufted tail twitching in her quickness.

It wasn't quite alive. Therefore, it couldn't be quite as fast as she was. Bailey dodged and danced, staying just out of its reach, drawing it away from her mother who lay quite still below. She was wrong.

The Leucator was deadly quick, like a striking cobra. It came after her again, and she twisted out of its hold, icy hands leaving white brands on her wrists as she got clear. Both arms screamed with the pain and hot tears blurred her eyes. She dodged again, barely escaping it. She felt the soft ground give as it leaped at her again and Bailey fell.

It knocked the wind out of her. She lay gasping a second, then heard the panting and frantic chirping of her tiny familiar as Lacey hobbled toward her, laboriously dragging the amethyst. She caught both up and swung about, just as the Leucator came at her with a deadly embrace.

Purple fire split the air. It sizzled deep into the being, and her father's double opened its mouth, crying wordlessly. Then it began to melt into itself, and the sight made Bailey stumble away, choking. Her father's face looked at her, crying out, "Baby gurrrlllll," the voice melting with it. When it was done, and nothing left but a heap of smudge on the ground, she turned her head and vomited.

"Oh, Bailey!" Rebecca crawled to her and stood, wavering, one arm and shoulder limp as she pulled her child close with all the strength remaining in her uninjured arm. Lacey let out a squeak of protest then quieted as both mother and daughter cried. Then Bailey made a strangled noise and looked up. "Jason!"

She took off at a run, headlong into the fray of the battle on the other side of the hill.

Jason staggered back, spent. He took a moment to spin around, as if looking uselessly for his supporters scattered about Haven, and finding no reserve, turned back to Jonnard. Trent could see the despair in his face. Stef-cub barreled into the wolfjackals with a bawl, sending them wheeling about, dumping their riders to the ground. With a deepening bear yowl he ran around the lupine beasts, chasing them back into the inky pass of the Iron Gate.

Trent rubbed his stone again. He looked into its useless depths. The milky white cloudiness reminded him of the energy he'd seen surrounding George, Aunt Freyah's dancing service tray.

Jason let out a sharp cry. Trent's head snapped up to see Jason and Jon locked in deadly combat, hand-to-hand, toe-to-toe. They traded blows, somersaulted away, and drove back in, their hands and feet moving like blurs. It was more brutal than anything he'd ever seen before, and he knew it would kill one of them.

Brennard made a pass with his hands, and darkness ribboned the valley. He could feel its oppression, its workings. The Dark Hand had begun to block Haven off as the Gatekeeper failed.

Trent shoved at the dead stone in his hand with all his anger and frustration. Nothing! He was worth nothing, he could do nothing to help!

The gemstone warmed and then its interior swirled. A nova of a thousand stars spun in the palm of his hand, then cleared away. A transparent quartz rested within his fingers, marked only by a few mica and pyrite flecks along one facet.

Trent's jaw dropped.

He stood up in the tree. His gaze scanned the bowl of the valley. He could see the bright, shimmering band of energy that surrounded it. He always had seen it, since they'd tumbled in desperately looking for the dragon. He tapped into it.

The sky ribbon shimmered. Then it filled him. It shot through the darkness of the gathering storm, blazing it away, with a Light of its own, and a fierce kind of singing filled him.

Noise sounded in his ear. He could hear Bailey's whoop and Ting's excited squeal, in his thoughts, *in his freaking mind!*

Trent stood in amazement, his crystal clenched in his fist. He pushed against the darkness being wrought by the Dark Hand, and he could feel it give!

Jonnard reeled back. Sweat slicked his black cloth to his body and he panted heavily. His hands moved in defensive mode, and welts striped his face.

Jason pressed forward. "Henry isn't there anymore," Jason said. "You're on your own."

"No!" Jon reached out, and a charcoal lash of power rayed out from his hand, striking the ground wildly. "Father!"

"Fight as you've been trained. You have him!" Brennard raised a fist in rage, crystal flaring, missing Jason as he swung on him.

Jonnard sank to his knees, sucking breath through clenched teeth, gone so pale his skin was gray. Jason drew near, prepared to take him out. Jon hissed and raised a hand toward his father. A snake of energy roped through the air, latching from one to the other. Antoine Brennard, who sat at the bottom of the crest, looked up in sudden surprise as his son took everything he had from him. He raised his hand to his chest, where the energy snake was sucking his life from him, and then looked at Jonnard in anguished surprise.

Jon roared in rage and leaped at Jason.

Jason met every blow with pain jolting through him. The bamboo cane took one last hit and then shattered in his palms. Splinters sprayed everywhere. He somersaulted backward and landed for a split second before kicking out and letting his crystal's power loose.

It knocked Jon down. The other rolled off the crest,

screams of hatred and anger spewing as he fell. He flailed in vain to get up and could not, quivering like a broken animal. Jason dropped to his knees and tried to breathe. His crystal flickered at his chest and went dim.

He kicked out. He caught Jonnard in the side of the head and the youth fell as if axed. He rolled over and over and over and came to a limp halt. He flailed once. He put his hand up, and cried, "Mother."

Someone shouted a command and the great wagons rolled forward. Isabella sprang down from the wagon to haul Jonnard into the shelter of the wagon bed. Then she snapped out a command, and rough hands gathered Brennard's body and heaved it up, so that he, too, disappeared into the depths of a wagon.

She snapped off a word. Jason blinked, and then rolled to his side, as his Leucator fell on him. He shrieked at the cold fire as it tried to devour him. He stared into his own face, as it put its hands to his neck, and began to choke him.

She threw a great cloaking over the caravan, as it rolled past him and disappeared into the depths of Haven. The other black, long wagons followed, and three troops of grim faced soldiers after. They stared at him as they marched past. He could not stop them.

He wrestled with the Leucator, feeling the strength in his body drain away, heartbeat by heartbeat. He could feel the hands on his throat grow stronger and stronger.

"Which one?"

"Take them both out."

"No!" Bailey cried. "One is Jason, one is not."

He struggled and tried to kick free. His hand throbbed on the other's neck. The very touch of the Leucator sent burning chills deep into him. He could feel his neck bruising, collapsing, his breathing slowing.

Suddenly Bailey cried out, and the amethyst in her hand arched into a sword blade and she swung with all her might, and one of the Jasons stopped moving.

He sat up, gasping, after a very long moment.

"What . . . took you . . . so long?" He crouched, shivering uncontrollably.

"I had to know which was which." She reached down and tapped his hand. "His scar was on the right hand. And his was all white and flat."

His hand throbbed. The crescent scar flared red and angry, as it always did when evil came near. Jason tried to stand, and couldn't, and flopped down.

Trent climbed the hill, took Jason by the elbow, and helped him up.

"You won."

Jason looked at him a moment, trying to comprehend the two simple words. Then he shook his head.

"Brennard is dead."

"Jonnard lives. And they got through." Jason leaned heavily on his friend. Bailey came up and gently bolstered him from the other side. "They still have Eleanora and FireAnn."

Trent said quietly, "We lived. They didn't expect that. They used their hostages to get passage. And they've paid a heavy price."

"So did we!" He could barely stand. He could feel the pain and hurt in every fiber of his body.

"We'll get them back."

He had failed, ignoring what the dragon had tried to tell him. He thought he'd understood it all, and now he realized he understood nothing. Yes, the others who stood with him were safe, and for that he could be thankful, but he'd failed himself and Gavan. He had become the warrior instead of the guard, and had let war into a world he scarcely even knew.

"Whatever it takes," he told Trent. "I will get them out of Haven."

Trent held him up. "Then that's what we'll do. Tomorrow."

THE
GATE OF BONES

I'd like to dedicate this book to friends and family who have enriched our lives tremendously.

Wayne Allen
A tall, lanky and self-made man whose hard work and thirst for knowledge continues well into his nineties. A man who never fails to share his insight and advice, with sincere thanks.

Uncle Sam Stein
Another self-made man whose hard work is exceeded only by his generous heart and inventive mind. May we toast your one hundredth!

Bernard Couch
A plain-spoken gentleman who brings light to our home every time he crosses the doorstep, with sincere gratitude for the pleasure of knowing him.

Larry Stone
A gentle giant with a sense of humor exceeded only by his sense of fair play.
Thanks for the opportunities he's bestowed upon our family.

To Alexander, Tyler Jo, and Adrian
With a thank you for being young readers and magical people yourselves!

And to my mother Barbara and my aunt Criss, for sharing with me their love of books, reading and adventure. You shall both be greatly missed and your memories treasured.

Contents

CONTENTS

1

Night Raid

A FULL HUNTER'S MOON rose over the fields and forest of Avenha, its golden shine almost as clear as the sun through the cloak of night. Avenha itself slept, the villagers weary from days of busy harvesting and storing for the coming winter. Signs all around them had warned of a long, harsh season awaiting them. Like villages all over, they prepared as well as they could. Now, as the moon rode the evening sky, the hunters it had been named for were out to catch those unwary creatures who grazed under its brilliant light. Newly harvested fields brought them all in: deer, boar, hill sheep. The next weeks would be spent curing meat and tanning hides as the days of autumn trekked toward winter.

Renart shifted uneasily at the chieftain's gate, trying to stretch his long legs without disturbing the others as he sat silently. He did not know why he'd been summoned and wondered if he was finally back in favor. He rubbed his hands together, the tattoos dappling the curve of his thumb and index finger marking him as a member of the Trader Guild. All he'd ever done was what he'd been born and trained to do, barter and trade.

Except he'd chosen invaders to do it with.

But how could he not? They'd seemed so harmless, so confused when they'd first arrived. Defenseless, even. Renart had rarely been more wrong. Of course, there were those who later understood his attraction to them. The new arrivals did seem somewhat out of the mists of tall tales, people who'd just awakened to the world. Yet the others who'd followed them had none of the helpless charm of the first group. He'd made friends with invaders. Traded with them. Given them knowledge and supplies through which they survived . . . and some of them survived well enough to hunt down his own people. Renart couldn't blame any of the chieftains who had later refused to deal with him when the Trader Guild pulled his license and demoted him to the lowly position of clerk for his mistakes. No, even if there hadn't been trouble, he could see the problems he'd caused. He'd established trade with a new people, without the consent of his own master and guild. Now, he realized, it looked like a shameless grab for power on his part. It hadn't been, though, it had been done out of curiosity and pity. He'd testified to that, over and over. Surely, they would eventually realize the truth, and he would regain their trust.

Surely? He stared at his shoes, odd things, invader things . . . *sneakers* he was told they were called. Certainly, their strange soles made walking very quiet. He wore them like a badge of honor despite all the trouble they had caused him. He didn't think he was truly wrong for what he'd done. He could never have predicted that the invaders would be the same people, yet two distinctly different groups. Like good and evil, two sides of the same coin.

Torches at the gate burned low. In the chieftain's hut, glowing coals were banked against the growing chill of the night, and a hooded lantern cast little illumination beyond its immediate circle. The chieftain sat on a sagging hide chair, his legs folded comfortably, the dappling of the tattoos across his cheekbones and forehead that marked his line and position little more than shadows in the room. He tapped a pipe against the stones banking the coals, and tiny sparks flew out. Renart gathered his wits about him.

A guardsman stirred in the gatehouse. "How much longer do we wait?"

"Night after night," Mantor answered. "Until the trap is sprung."

"And if they do not come?"

"Then our ambassadors have greatly misunderstood our new guests. But I think not. And I think our wait will end tonight. What do you think, Renart?"

The young trader flushed. "I—I wonder both how I can help and why you called me. Chieftain Mantor, there is no one better than you at what you do, but . . ." Renart shuddered in memory. "The Dark Hand is unstoppable. They use sorcery. I can only advise one way to meet that."

"Good thoughts. I need a scribe to help my daughter with the warehouse records. As for it being you, specifically, well . . ." He paused for a long moment. "I do not wear the tattoos of chieftain because I am a good painter, eh? I look at people and judge them. At seasons and harvests, I judge them. I think you deserve a second chance." Chieftain Mantor looked across the tiny flames licking up now and then from the red-hot coals, gazing at his daughter, her faced marked the same as his, as she took notes on the conversation, her hands busy with ink and paper. Her eyes were better than his in the dim light.

Another man stirred in the gatehouse. "What if we've misjudged?"

"I do not think we have. We know of the laziness of these invaders and the outlaws they have gathered to them. We know the other villages they have hit, just as the harvests have been laid down for store. Shall we wait for the Holy One to return as Warlord, or protect ourselves with the skill he passed down to us? I vote we fight." The chieftain's attention returned to rest on the questioner. "Nervous or eager, Flameg?"

"Both. Waiting is never easy." Flameg shifted his burly frame, and wood creaked under him as he moved. He stilled immediately. They had wanted to draw no attention. No one knew they waited. No one knew a snare had been laid. His hand brushed across his longbow.

"Do not even think it." Mantor traded looks with his head guardsman.

"No." Flameg nodded. "I will think it, but not act it. The council has agreed with your guidance, and for that matter so do I, but—" He had no time to finish his sentence. A call sounded from the gatewalk, and even that could barely be heard over the low rumble, the sound of hoofbeats approaching.

Many hoofbeats.

The group got to their feet. Trader Renart had said little, his wiry frame wrapped in a tartan cloak against the chill of the autumn night, his hair in a mouse's nest of disarray, his eyes still sleepy from a hastily caught nap. He was not a fighter, not like the chieftain and Flameg or even the chieftain's heir and daughter, Pyra. His tattoo marks sprinkled the backs of his hand and his clever fingers, like a craftsman. Once he was back in the graces of his guild, and far in the future when he became a master trader, he'd gain a single dot at his temple, to indicate his knowledge and experience. Flameg's markings were across his powerful shoulders, not to be seen unless he took off his tunic. Renart flexed his hands now. He wondered again if he should have regretted it, those first tentative trades, especially with the second group, who his keen senses soon told him were vastly different from the first people he'd met. Yet he'd not hesitated to barter and trade with them. Not until they'd caught and tortured him. They were mortal enemies, these Magickers and Dark Hand, and it had been his ill luck to discover them both.

Did they bring war with them, war such as only the Warlord had once fought? His far-flung kingdom now lived in peace, in cities and villages across the lands, ruled only by councils which took the Warlord's words from the writings of his time, and from the words and visions of his Holy Spirit now. Even the Warlord's fortresses were now little more than dry, rotting piles of wood, barely more than a wall here, a guard tower there. He was neither a warrior or a counselor who heard the spirit, but he was a trader and scribe. So, as the others prepared, he reached out to Pyra.

He took the paper and ink from Pyra, and the leather pouch she tossed to him, as she drew her curved cutlass to join her father. Trying not to show the tremor that ran through him, he stowed the writing instruments and implements, and then slung the pouch over his shoulder. The rumbling thunder grew louder until it broke into hoofbeats.

Unmistakably, it roared into the noise of horsemen charging down the valley toward Avenha's gates.

Mantor gave a quick nod and a grunt of satisfaction. "They come. Now the trap awaits." He crooked a finger. "Follow me."

Orange flame trailed down the hill as the riders swept through the night, torches in the hands of the outriders. Renart held his breath. He had heard the tales, and hoped them exaggerations, but he knew now they were not. He turned his gaze away. He had not brought them to his world, but had he helped them thrive? Barely more than three dozen at first, they'd attracted the lazy and outlawed who would rather steal than work themselves. He looked at a charge of nearly fifty riders, and it took his breath away.

In a cloud of smoke and dust and chaff from the newly shorn fields, the raiders swept up to the barred gates, barely slowing. Riders at the front threw up gloved hands. Crystal gems grasped in their palms caught the gleaming light of the Hunter's Moon and threw it back at the wooden gates. Gemstones flared, emitting great bolts of power. Lightning cracked, and the air stank of scorched wood as the gates exploded into fiery splinters.

Above and to the side, the chieftain's gatewalk trembled, and Mantor cursed under his breath. Renart looked quickly at him. Had he thought the gates would hold against sorcery? His guardsman caught the chieftain's elbow. "Now?"

Mantor shook his head. At his flank, Pyra's face paled, but she kept her stance at the ready. "Not yet," Mantor answered quietly. "Not yet."

Renart kept his balance, his strange shoes gripping the narrow wooden gatewalk with ease, but he hardly noticed. Below, riders swept into the town, hammering down doors and heading with precision toward the longhouses where the food stores were kept. It made him ill to watch. Despite the carefully laid plans of the chieftain, a door was suddenly flung open and a shouting man ran out. He brandished his scythe, sharp and hooked, and his square body blocked the narrow street. Then he sank with a cry of pain, an arrow buried in his thigh, and the raiders rode over him without a second thought.

"Stubborn man," grunted Mantor. "He wouldn't leave

and let me handle these raiders. They'll pay for that, even so."

Pyra let out a muffled sound. Renart watched her put her wrist to her mouth, stifling her emotion. Chieftains had to be made of stern stuff. Her free hand tightened about her cutlass, her wrist like a mask over the expression on her face. Renart thought for a fleeting moment he'd never seen anyone more fierce or beautiful.

"It won't work," said Flameg.

"We shall see." Mantor pulled his own longbow off his shoulder and nocked a wicked-looking black arrow. His body blocked them all into the shadows of the gatehouse. His dark eyes narrowed as he looked down into the village that was the trust of his guardianship.

Renart found himself breathing again, shallow, quiet inhalations. The raiders raced to a storehouse and, with shouts and gestures, surrounded it. Six men dismounted and gathered up a battering ram, taking aim at the stout double doors. Wood groaned and then cracked, but stood up to the assault.

"Enough!" A woman's voice split the air. Curbing her mount with a strong pull on the reins, she kneed the others aside and raised her gloved hand. In it, the crystal gleamed. A ray of power blazed from it, her horse rearing under her in fright, as the warehouse door shattered. She pivoted her horse around, her great skirts swirling about her and covering the animal. With a look of disdain, she lifted her hand, and again Lightning swept out of her palm. The remains of the door blew apart in splinters that caught fire and drifted through the air in orange curls.

"We can't fight blades against Lightning fire."

"Not this way, no." Mantor lowered his longbow. He pulled back into the shadows even farther, drawing all of them with him. "Take Pyra and go, Flameg."

"Chieftain—"

"There is nothing you can do here, now, tonight. Take her and go."

The guardsman's mouth clamped shut, his lips thinning in protest, but he lowered his head and then made a fist of obedience, bringing it to his shoulder. Pyra threw a kiss at her father, before scampering after Flameg as he swung down from the gatewalk and the two disappeared. Renart tried to watch her leave, but the hidden gate worked all too well, and she was gone without a trace.

Mantor hissed.

Shouts of anger rose, and the warehouse shook as the horsemen pounded inside and . . . and discovered the structure was empty. Torches dipped and flared, and wood crackled up into reluctant, smoky flame, for the wood had been green, on purpose. Eventually, it would burn, but slowly.

Mantor had left them an empty village to ransack. Only a few stubborn old men had refused to go, and one of them now lay dead in the street. The chieftain ground his teeth angrily. Renart heard him murmur something to the Warlord under his breath.

In fury, the raiders bashed down stores, homes, guild houses, the other two empty storehouses, and burned all they could, looting what few goods had been left behind. They destroyed everything they touched.

Empty, Avenha had been, but not unlivable. Now, it was. Renart sighed, then choked as smoke filled his nostrils, his throat. His eyes watered fiercely. With screams of hatred and anger, the horsemen swept back to the gate, and milled about, shaking their hands and throwing the last of their torches on the broken walls of Avenha. Then, with the horses crying in pain as spurs and whips lashed their sides, the raiders thundered back into the night.

They waited until only the noise of the fire could be heard, then Mantor stirred. He swung down from the gatewalk, and held up his hand to help Renart.

Once outside, trotting across a newly harvested field, heading for the hillside caves where he had sent his people, Mantor said, "You were right. They're unstoppable, this Dark Hand. You were also right about how we must fight them." Under the Hunter's Moon, Chieftain Mantor halted and put his hand on Renart's shoulder. The trader suppressed a shiver, suddenly realizing just why the chieftain had brought him to Avenha that night.

"Send for the Magickers."

Dark Roads

MORE USED TO RIDING in a caravan than on a horse, Renart took the night road cautiously, following a ribbon of trampled and rutted dirt that seemed ominously dark despite the Hunter's Moon at his back. He needed speed, but riding at night called for caution lest he lame or lose the horse altogether and be stranded on foot. On foot, he would never get to the Magickers before the cold of the mountain passes got to him.

He wondered if his suspension would get worse for seeking them out again, without his guild's direction. But then, how could it? The chieftain had sent him, and who would argue with Mantor, a leader of Avenha as well as a councillor of the Holy Spirit? If one who followed the Warlord in all ways of his life told him to do something, Renart was bound by the laws of the land to do it.

If it brought him trouble this time, he'd bear it. Or perhaps he would become a wanderer, one of those itinerant workers who always seemed unwelcome wherever they traveled, beyond laws and civilization. He didn't think the wanderers had a good peddler among their groups; he could probably teach them quite a bit and learn a bit himself. He

288

could travel again, then, something his ink-stained hands and mind longed to do. Being a clerk for the warehouses was *not* what he had in mind when someone said "Trader." Not in the least.

Then again, he was traveling, his saddle-sore legs reminded him, and riding on a very dark road. The only good thing about it was that he could tell it clearly led away from the direction in which the raiders had ridden. Renart murmured a word of thanks to the Warlord's Holy Spirit for that happiness. He had no idea if the spirit of that long-ago warrior heard him or not, but the lands had lived long and in prosperity after his death, due to the strength of the Spirit he left behind to keep it so. The councils prayed to him and received answers, or so they claimed, and they also had written volumes well stocked in libraries everywhere of the sage advice the Warlord had given while he was still alive. Yet, even the old Warlord had been quiet about this latest menace in his countries. Did he sleep? And if he did, would what Renart was about to undertake wake him?

The countries he would leave behind him, the Warlord had explained, were like a chain of clasped hands, an impenetrable wall of spirit and knowledge that could hold back any foe . . . as long as it remembered it was a chain composed of many and acting for the good of many but never at the expense of a few unless so willed and offered in sacrifice. Simple enough. It had kept them safe for centuries, once the living Warlord had turned back the enemies from across the great sea. It was said it was not only his might that had turned back those enemies, but a massive plague, and many worried that those times could return. Yet the Spirit of the Warlord seemed to keep them safe.

Now, Renart wondered, how the Warlord's words would stand against these strange enemies from much, much farther away than that. With thoughts weighing heavily on his mind and his eyelids, he traveled the dark road slowly into the night, finding no answer and only the immediate danger of being a fool alone on this journey. He hoped morning would find him safe and well along his way.

As the night's darkness thinned and even the light of the moon paled before the dawn, Renart swung down off his horse, and found a good place to pasture it for a bit of rest and grazing. He squatted in the damp grass and debated on making a fire for warmth, but the thought of night raiders still about made up his mind for him. Why take chances?

He stretched gingerly, feeling muscles protest being on horseback for so long, and the scarred welts from his torture also protested, although with far less pain than he'd ever hoped. It was something he tried not to think about, knowing that he could have been beaten far worse than he was, and that the healing ointment applied by Tomaz Crowfeather's deft hands could have helped far less than it did. That Magicker was an elder, one with a great sense for the land and its beasts, and had a presence about him that had reassured Renart from the first time he'd spied him. Tomaz had remarked at the time, that the beating was not too bad, and that Renart was lucky. The Dark Hand had ways of knowing whether he spoke truth or not, in answer to their questions, and if he held back. They must have decided early on that Renart knew little.

And so he had, then. The questions Isabella and the quietly menacing Jonnard had put to him, between blows, made no sense. Were there other Gates? How often was the Gate opened? Who came through? How had Haven gathered people? And more . . . more that, despite the beatings, he could never have answered. They'd finally thrown him out on the road in disgust, where he'd made it back to his little peddler's cart, crawled onto it, and let the old horse draw him where it would. Luckily, it had taken him to Iron Mountain.

Until then, he'd not realized that the two groups of newcomers were like night and day; although the Hand had made him a bit uneasy at first, they'd concealed their true nature with guile. He hadn't seen much of the Magickers since then, for upon returning to his home city of Naria, his master discovered Renart's healing condition and the Trader Guild put him through a verbal inquisition to which he *did* know the answers, and he'd had his ranking and license taken from him while they discussed his actions. How naive he'd been, he realized now, not seeing that his actions had made many traders uneasy, as a grab for power and influence. He'd only seen it as a charity.

Renart rubbed his hands together. He should have brought gloves, he knew that. It was autumn now and the nights and even days would grow damper, colder, and any trader knew how important it was to be prepared while out on the road. It was just that he'd been clerking in warehouses for weeks now and hadn't thought about being on the road again. He wondered if Chieftain Mantor would be able to influence the councillors as he promised he would. Oh, to be established again, doing what he loved. . . .

He'd get a firsthand sight of how the academy was coming along, and how the wanderers he'd sent there were working out, as well. Wanderers were a strange people, outcast by most towns and villages for their refusal to accept rule by the councils and the Warlord's Holy Spirit. No Spirit, they claimed, no matter how powerful and influential in this life, could help being tainted by evils on the spiritual side, and therefore was not trustworthy in a Spirit life. Never mind that the Warlord had proven Himself time and again. They refused to accept him, and so the rest of Haven refused to accept the wanderers.

Still, a people had to live, did they not? They were not harmful, just strange. Strange and often poor and bedraggled, as if punished for their beliefs. Perhaps they had been. Renart closed his eyes a moment in thought.

He awoke with the sun's rays striking his face, the morning fog completely gone from the meadowland, and his horse still cropping grass contentedly. He leaped to his feet, let out a groan as his whole body began to ache, and quickly made ready to ride again. To save Avenha and the other peoples he had grown to love, and to redeem himself. Traders got few chances to be heroic, and this was his! To ride! He snapped the reins and his horse raced forward on the road.

"Trent, if you don't stop asking for stuff, I am never going to get Henry Gated out of here." Jason sat cross-legged on the top floor of the academy, his face shadowed by a corner beam, but nothing could quite hide the intensity that gleamed out of him. The power that he would use to open a Gate between two worlds already hummed through his body, in preparation for being loosed.

Tall and wiry Trent stopped in mid-sentence, and swung around to look at Jason, his fingers still clenching a handful of white paper. His jaw worked as if the words couldn't quite come out, then he said, "Don't you get it, Jason? You,

Henry?" He turned toward Henry, who also sat with an apologetic expression over his round face, black hair unruly, and caught in mid-yawn. Henry put his hand over his mouth as heat flooded his face.

The long summer and mild autumn so far had turned the boys lean, grown them tall as they had hit that time of life when boys became men, almost overnight it seemed. Only Henry wore clothes like they'd all worn when they first came to Haven, but that was because he was going back. Back for supplies and news and to reassure families at home that the Magickers were doing fine, and Haven was indeed a Haven. Henry, the ambassador between two worlds and showing diplomatic grace, would not mention the growing menace of the Dark Hand. He scrubbed his face now and widened his round eyes, then put his glasses back on.

"I am listening," he vowed.

"Well, good. Because you need to. This stuff is important." Trent tapped his papers. "I need these books or articles, Henry. Anything you can pull out of a used bookstore or off the Internet, okay? Because Haven is full of people almost like us, but not us, and these myths . . . these tales they tell . . . hold the answer to their beginnings. I need as much research done as you can manage. Now, I know what Gavan and Tomaz told you to do is more important, I'm just asking for a little help here." It went without saying that the wishes of the elder Magickers, the headmaster and the beastmaster, would rule all of Henry's actions.

Henry reached out and took the lists. "I'll do it," he said confidently.

"Good." Jason stood. "Are we settled, then? I can Gate now, but after the day's work, I'll be too tired to do it. So I need to get Henry out of here now, and get the passage closed again before the Hand senses anything."

Trent made a gesture which had as much to do with the music that always seemed to be thrumming inside him as it had to do with what he and Jason and Henry were talking about. "Look . . . remember we talked about the Gordian knot and Alexander the Great? The wise men and prophets said only someone who could undo the knot would fulfill their prophecy about a great ruler . . . and Alexander, instead of trying to untie the knot, just took up his sword and sliced through it."

"Yeah." The list of things needed crackled a bit as Henry folded it carefully and put it in his pocket.

"That's a myth. The reality is that the Gordian knot was most likely a complicated political arrangement of alliances and religions that opposed anyone who would unite that part of the world. Rather than deal with them and get caught up in their politics and bribery and self-interest, Alexander just took his armies and conquered them. That was the sword slicing through the knot, see? So . . . we hear things from the wanderers and Renart and others, and somewhere in the myths we're hearing is a little bit of truth about Haven."

"Right."

Trent rolled his eyes and threw up his hands. "No one listens!"

"We all listen. And you're right. But what we have to do now is get the academy built before the rains start, and then winter hits us. If for no other reason than we need a way to keep our butts warm and dry. Then, when that's done, we can sit around a desk and talk about your theories. On long winter nights it might even be a fun thing to do." Jason stood, folding his arms, and tilting his head at Trent.

Trent's mouth snapped shut and he settled for a mild punch to Jason's shoulder. The other boy rocked back with a soft grunt, still grinning.

"Hey! Don't punch the Gatekeeper. I have a date to go home!" Henry scrambled to his feet, gathering up his empty backpack. He'd bring it back brimming with items all the exiled Magickers had requested. Foremost on his list seemed to be chocolate, requested by Bailey and Ting.

"I'll look for you in a week's time," Jason promised.

"Just remember, time is different here than there."

"Right. Which is why I won't just open the Gate. You're going to have to tell me if you're ready yet. I think we can touch thoughts that long. Don't give me big explanations—just a 'yeah, let's go, or no, see me next week,' got it?"

Henry's head bobbed. "Got it."

"Good." Jason gripped his friend's shoulder. "Say hi to everyone for us, right?"

"First on all my lists." Henry took a deep breath. "Okay. I'm ready."

Trent turned his back on them, his face creased with a

kind of sorrow, and Jason knew he was thinking of his father, left behind and sorely missed. Jason filled his hands with his crystals and gripped them tightly. With a deep breath, he opened his mind, and found that essence which was the Dragon Gate, and swung it open. He literally tossed Henry through it, and slammed it shut, hoping that the Dark Hand had not sensed the abrupt flow of energies.

He stood for a long moment, feeling the surge of great power running through him, and ebbing away, as though it sank into the very floorboards of the unfinished building about him, as if the academy grounded him. Then his heart did a double beat, and he inhaled again, and his crystals stilled in his hands.

Trent waited another moment before saying gruffly, "C'mon. We've got a lot to do today."

"Always," Jason agreed. He looked up at the sky. "Maybe a roof in a few more days?"

"Maybe. Although I think I'd rather have hot water."

Jason snorted. "What do you think I am? A magician?"

Trent tackled him and they wrestled with laughs and snorts and grunts until the sound of shouting for them drew them apart and into a long day of hard work.

Sparklies

WAKING MEANT more than just prying the eyes open. It also meant finding the nerve to stick one's arms out from under the covers into the cold morning air and then putting one's bare feet on chilly wooden planks. So Bailey eased out of her warm cocoon of a bed gingerly, her face all screwed up in an expression of intensity as she woke and then dashed to the cupboard, flinging clothes every which way till she found the warmest combo she could find and dove in headfirst. Once dressed and with her feet shoved into a pair of fleece-lined boots, she could work on the niceties of dressing . . . like ties and belts and tucking in her blouse. She turned around, pulling on her lacings, to see Ting's brown eyes peering over the tops of her blankets with amusement sparkling in their depths.

"It's cold," muttered Bailey.

"And likely to get much colder!" Ting agreed. "Do you realize we might get snow?"

While snow had sounded like the epitome of winter fun in sunny Southern California, here . . . far away and someplace strange . . . it sounded . . . well . . . *cold.*

"I dunno," answered Bailey dubiously.

"You'll love it! We'll have the chimneys working by then, and this place will heat up. Gavan and Tomaz promised."

Bailey arched her back and looked at the wooden structure encompassing them, and their sleeping room just a small part, one day to be a classroom. Iron Mountain Academy (IMA wizard school, she added mentally) was no longer a dream, it was nearly a reality. One without a top floor and roof and indoor plumbing, as of yet. "First," she commented, "we have to finish building it."

"Not on an empty stomach!" Ting threw herself out of bed then, scrambling for her clothes in much the same hurried fashion as her best friend. Bailey would have crawled back into her still warm blankets to wait, but her boots hadn't been cleaned, and she had no intention of pulling them off just to sit on her cot. So she paced back and forth until the vibration of her boot heels set off an irritated chattering in the corner. A small whiskered mouse face poked out of a wooden barrel that had once been a nail keg but had now been appropriated for her home. As if also anticipating the return of the Ice Age, the little pack rat had promptly filled it with as many scraps of paper and fabric as she could find and drag in for her nesting.

Bailey squatted down and put her hand out, palm up. "Morning, Lacey."

The little creature stopped chittering, put her paws to her whiskers for a quick scrub, then hopped into the hand. Bailey swept her up and deposited her in her bodice pocket as Ting gave one last brush through her gleaming blue-black hair.

They looked at one another and said, in unison and emphatically, "Breakfast!"

As they headed down the inner, spiraling stair, they could hear the sounds of others who were already awake and about. Workmen's voices rang through the air, along with the thump of hammers and the noise of handsaws. The smell of a wood-burning fire as well as cooking food filled the air, while a thin fog curled away from the ground. Breakfast was always served in the outdoor camp, to feed the wanderers who helped with the construction, for Gavan and Bailey's mother Rebecca couldn't help but take pity for the thin, tense faces of those who'd come to help build the academy.

The hardest part of leaving home and coming to Haven was trying to understand the new people they eventually met.

Quiet and wary and seemingly shy, it had been months before they'd actually met anyone face-to-face—and that first one had been Renart, the young trader who'd bartered items with them from the shadows. Some days they'd find a shirt folded up on a rock, for which they left small things of their own, the next they'd find a basket of eggs. Eventually, one day, Rebecca had been startled to find Renart himself, sitting cross-legged, awaiting them, his six-fingered hands folded in his lap, his eyes bright with curiosity, with a new sack of trade offerings at his side. They taught him to shake hands and he taught them how to "sketch a bow." Gavan and Tomaz painstakingly made "Talker" crystals, crystals that they had imbued with a kind of translating ability, and they'd shared their first words with the native of a new world the Magickers had, basically, invaded.

Rebecca Landau turned from a great pot, hung on a cooking rod, and waved her spoon in the air. Bailey beamed at her mother in pride. "Who'd have thunk," she whispered to Ting, "that someone who hates camping would be doing so well in Haven?"

Indeed, Rebecca glowed. Or maybe it was just reflected heat from the campfire which kept her cauldron of oatmeal bubbling. One tiny streak of charcoal etched the side of her face and Bailey grinned, wondering if she should tell her mom or not. Old, naturally, and a mom, of course, but Rebecca still looked slender and pretty, her light brown hair pulled back from her face in French braids, and her long skirt swirling down to sweep the ground. Yup, old Mom looked pretty good in Haven gear.

Over the hubbub of the workmen, Madame Qi's imperious voice could be heard, and the thump of her bamboo cane. "Shoulders straight, arms out, eyes closed . . . I want you to breathe deep!"

Ting's mouth opened in a soft laugh at her grandmother's drill sergeant tone. She nudged Bailey. "She's got them at it already."

"Our turn will come tonight," Bailey groaned. She was still sore after yesterday's exercises.

"It's good for you," Ting protested.

"So is cod liver oil, but that tastes like tuna fish gone bad, very, very bad, and you don't see me taking it!" Bailey wrinkled her nose, freckles dancing.

"Oh, you shush." Ting put up her hand and ran to the small, wrinkled Chinese woman who held a line of young men at her command with nothing more than the crack of her voice.

Bailey veered away to the campfire. "Need help, Mom?"

"No, no. Qi and I got everything going this morning." Rebecca pulled at her shirtsleeves, then dished out a bowl of steaming oatmeal, or what passed for oatmeal, and gave it to Bailey. "I have a little bit of brown sugar and raisins saved aside for you . . ."

"Wow!" She beamed at her mom. "Is Henry going to bring back more?"

"If he has the money. It's difficult for him and his family . . ."

Bailey sat on a stump, wooden spoon in hand. Actually, it was more like a miniature pancake turner than a spoon. Someday she'd have to explain the concept of spoon bowls to a Havenite and see what they could come up with. "Being an ambassador between two worlds isn't all it's cut out to be, huh?"

"One could say that." Rebecca frowned. "He's also worried about being watched."

"Ummm." Bailey nodded slowly. No wonder Henry's visits between were getting more and more unreliable. Watched! That could ruin everything . . . She carefully sprinkled only a few pinches of brown sugar over her hot cereal, and doled out half a dozen raisins or so. The idea of rationing had been with them since day one, but sometimes it was hard. Still, it was far, far better than living in a world which now promised to hunt them down like dogs and then observe them like laboratory rats.

Bailey stirred her oatmeal thoughtfully. Lacey gave a hopeful squeak from her pocket, so Bailey dipped in a fingertip and then offered a dollop of the creamy cereal to the pack rat who delicately nibbled it away.

Ting came over, got her own bowl and slid in next to Bailey saying, "Move your big rump," with a wicked grin on her face. Bailey moved over with a roll of her eyes. They ate quickly while the heated breakfast could still warm their insides, and that was a good thing because a commotion broke out among the boys.

"Stefan," said Madame Qi firmly, standing ramrod stiff, her cane outstretched in her hands. "You must try."

"I tell ya, this isn't working for me. It isn't. It's like . . . it's like trying to make a silk whatever out of a bearskin." Big, square Stefan frowned, his face grimacing in frustration. He punctuated his remark with a wave of a beefy arm, leaving the quad and coming over to the campfire. "Ready for breakfast," he said with a grunt. Effort and emotion reddened his face as he grabbed up a bowl and waved it near Rebecca.

"Stefan, you are not dismissed."

He grunted again. "Yeah, I am. 'Cause I *quit*." He waved his bowl again, and Rebecca hesitated, looking toward Madame Qi.

Her bamboo cane slashed the air like a sword. "Stefan, you must train both your mind and your body."

With a roll of his shoulders, he turned his back on her. "It's not working."

For a moment, Madame Qi looked like what she sometimes was . . . a very aged, small Chinese woman, with great concern written across her wrinkled features. Then she straightened and the weakness fled, even as Ting drew in her breath and held it. "Think on it, Stefan. I will be here when you are ready." She turned her attention back to the others who were jumping up and down in the cold morning air, trying to keep their bodies warm and limber. Her voice cracked out instructions and the three still in a line bent to follow.

Rebecca spooned out a hefty dish of oatmeal but said nothing to Stefan who took his meal and retreated around the corner of the building to eat alone.

Ting sighed then.

"Do you think she's afraid of him?" Bailey eyed the corner of the building where Stef had disappeared.

"Maybe. More likely, she just doesn't want to provoke the bear coming out. Every time it does, he loses more and more control, unless he wills it, you know?"

Bailey nodded. She stood with her empty bowl and dropped it into a second cauldron of bubbling hot water, readying the dishes for a good cleansing. Before she could offer her services for cleanup, another hubbub of voices roses, this time from the wanderers who were grouped together, voices rising, arms waving, and then they swarmed on Gavan Rainwater, the Magicker on whose shoulders many burdens were carried.

Gavan listened a moment, his cape swirling about his young, strong body, his dark blond hair curled to his shoulders, his wolfhead cane sheathed by his side the way some might carry a sword, and when he turned about in answer to the protests, his piercing blue eyes fastened on Bailey.

Uh-oh, she thought, even as she wondered what she could have done this time.

Gavan moved toward them with a dramatic swing of his long cape, wanderers in his wake, their babble diminishing to a quiet murmur. He stopped by the outdoor kitchen fire. "It seems we have a thief."

"Thief?"

Everyone stopped in their routine then, whether it was cooking, eating, or dancing to Madame Qi's barked instructions, and looked at the headmaster. The wanderers stayed at Gavan's heels, their eyes wide with curiosity, their wandering status tattooed in a single dot over their right eyebrow, their six-fingered hands shoved in as they crossed their arms over their chests. The headmaster nodded solemnly, then pointed his cane at Bailey.

"M—me?" squeaked Bailey.

"One of the Lantern crystals is missing. Dokr here has checked everyone, and among his tents. The crystal isn't crucial till afternoon falls, but their work depends on illumination. It seems most likely, Miss Landau, that you know the perpetrator of the crime. You were visiting their camp yesterday, I believe?"

"But . . . but . . ." She stared helplessly at Gavan. She had no need for a Lantern crystal, she could focus the light into her own any time she concentrated. What, then . . .

Gavan raised his eyebrows and stared into her face. She felt as if she should know the answer, and had no idea. Why would he think she'd stolen . . . ?

Lacey poked her head out curiously. The little pack rat saw the gang of people nearby and gave off a mousy squeak of fear, diving back into Bailey's pocket.

"Oh . . . no," breathed Bailey. "Lacey!" She bowed to

Gavan and the workmen. "I'm so . : . so sorry. Sparklies, you know? Let me go check her nest."

Gavan's mouth twitched as he tried to maintain a stern expression and nodded his permission.

Oh, that Lacey! How she'd even gotten into their tents . . . it must have been when she and her mom had gone through yesterday, distributing apples to the children. Good thing Gavan had remembered! Bailey took the stairs to her room in great leaps and then picked the nail keg up off the floor and dumped out its contents onto a table-top. The nest came tumbling out, mats of fabric and tissue and pack rat treasures. Sure enough, a bright citrine crystal rolled out from the other clumps of useless broken bits of this and that.

"Thief!"

Lacey chittered from the depths of her bodice pocket, as Bailey swept up the crystal. She ran downstairs, breathless, and put it into Gavan's hand.

The Magicker made a show of it, examining the gem-stone, concentrating on it, letting its brilliance rain through his fingers as he cupped it closely, then solemnly returning it to Dokr.

"My apologies, Foreman. The little beast knows only that it is pretty, and not that it is part of your hard-earned wages."

Dokr clicked his heels as he bowed, accepting back the Lantern crystal. "Master, we who are poor know the value of many things thought useless to others. With these, we can work when and where we please, and our craft is our only way to keep our families secure."

The Talker crystal at Gavan's belt flared slightly as it translated the words almost effortlessly, although Bailey sometimes wondered if that was really what was said. Dokr didn't seem the flowery or overly diplomatic type, to her. But grateful, yes. She dipped a curtsy at him, adding her own apology. Without the workmen, the academy would never be finished before winter storms made building impossible.

Gavan nodded at her, turning away, and dropping his hand on Dokr's shoulder. "Perhaps, for your trouble and dedication, we could add, oh . . . six more Lanterns to your end wages? You can do that, can't you, Ting?"

Ting shifted her weight and frowned in thought, her almond eyes slanting a little. "Six would be difficult. I think I could manage three, however. Would three be all right?"

Dokr lit up like one of the crystals he coveted. "Oh, master, mistress, that would make us wealthy indeed! Blessings on you!" He turned to his men and added a few more sentences, and they all scattered to their jobs once more, their drawn faces now happy.

Gavan nodded in approval at Ting and crooked a finger at Bailey. "Next time," he said, "keep an eye on that pet of yours. We can't afford to lose the construction crew!" His laugh belied his scolding words as he sauntered off.

"Win some and lose some," Ting said, as Bailey sagged in relief. Her gaze indicated the sullen Stefan who'd come out to listen a moment, before isolating himself again.

"Yeah." Bailey rubbed her nose. Who said coming to a brand-new world was going to be easy?

4

Planners and Dreamers

"**P**SSSST! TING, are you awake?"

A silence followed, then a sleepy answer came from the darkness of the room. "Do you mean . . . lately? Or now?"

"Now."

"No." The response came accompanied by the rustle of blankets and the squeak of the uneasy sleeping cot as Ting burrowed back into its depths.

That was silly. Of course she was awake if she was talking. Bailey tried again. "Ting?"

A pink shimmering answered her as Ting stretched out one hand and touched a fingertip to a crystal lying in the night between them; at her touch it began to glow with a soft radiance that lit the whole room. "Bailey," said Ting, sitting up, pushing her long dark hair from her eyes, and smiling slightly, her almond-shaped eyes tilting a little more. "What is it?"

Their voices echoed slightly in the room, because it was huge, and nearly empty, a big bare wooden dorm room meant to hold a class of students someday in the near future. Now it held only the two of them, two spindly cots,

303

and an assortment of three-legged stools that they used for tables and dressing stands and whatever other use they could be put to. One even held a few things washed out and draped over its upside-down position, as a drying rack. The three-legged stools had been constructed by hand, from rough branches of wood they found, and Bailey was proud of them, primitive as they were. Things were not in Haven as they'd been at home.

This was their home now, more than home, their sanctuary. It was the place they'd come to, escaping discovery and more persecution in their own world, and both girls felt more than a little like pilgrims come to the new lands. Magick was reality, and reality had morphed into another world altogether, a world with new peoples and places, hopes and dreams.

"I can't sleep."

"I noticed. Why not?"

"I keep thinking about tomorrow. Where we can go, what we might find."

"The great search for chocolate," noted Ting, her face lighting with amusement.

"Why not?" Bailey bobbed her head in agreement. Her sun-tinged golden-brown hair fell in soft waves to her shoulders. Normally she wore it pulled back in a ponytail that danced with every lively move she made. "Tomaz has found wild turkeys...horses...we don't know what's wandered across Gates in the past. Cacao trees could be growing somewhere!"

Ting grinned. "We can only hope."

"Always."

"Think you can find a pizza tree?"

Bailey made a sound of pleasure. "Don't make me hungry. I don't want to get caught trying to get a midnight snack."

"As if the boys don't go into the kitchen at least once a night." Ting looped her slender arms about her knees. "What would you do if we did find cacao trees?"

"Oh, Henry has orders to bring back to me everything he can find on the Internet about growing cacao and making it into chocolate!" Bailey made a little face. "And, of course, we'd have to plant sugar beets for sugar."

"Renart would love that. Sugar beets would be something he could trade anywhere!"

"He'd make a fortune on them." A solemn expression crossed Bailey's face as she considered their first friend in Haven, the six-fingered trader who'd risked much to barter with them, and found trouble for doing it. He'd approached her mother first from the shadows, leaving food and clothing for barter, and it had been months before they even met him face-to-face. It seemed as if he had sensed how different they were from him. Yet, as he'd put it more than once, they were all the same in souls. He'd suffered for his deeds, though, shut out by his own people. "If the Trader Guild ever gives him back his license to trade. Do you ever think what it means for us to be here and changing this world?"

"Every day, Bailey. Every day."

"We couldn't have made it without Renart." Bailey pulled her blankets closer about her, aware that the room had grown chilly as night steeped heavy and close about them and the half finished building. She took a shivery breath. "I've got this map."

Ting smiled. "So that's it. I knew you had something you've been hiding every day, for weeks. Is that what made you think about chocolate?"

Bailey shook her head slightly. "Not exactly. I mean, yes and no . . . Henry can bring back chocolate chips, but what if I run out? No. There's other things that have to be here. I've been reading it and looking it over, and this is where I'd like to go tomorrow. I can't wait any longer. Well, today," she amended, looking at their shuttered window. She pulled a scroll from under her pillow and unrolled it beside the glowing crystal. She tapped it. "Here."

Ting peered at it. The trader's hand markings and scratchings were impossible for her to decipher, but she knew Bailey had been working at it for weeks. It wasn't so much a different language barrier, as that traders used guild-taught secret marks on their maps, often hiding their findings from outsiders. Secret routes to caches of spices, furs, precious metals were meant to stay secret. But Bailey, like Renart and her mother Rebecca, had a nose for other curiosities. The richness of the world did not rest in gold or diamonds. Ting smiled at her. "I'll go," she said. "I still don't know where or for what, though! You know I can't read that."

Bailey let out her breath. "Actually . . . I think these are unicorns. I'm not sure, but . . . it seems like it."

"Unicorns! Bailey, that's not possible."

"Think about it! Really think about it. See, this is our world." Bailey took out her crystal. At her touch, it lit softly, with a violet glow. She picked up Ting's crystal and moved them close. "And this is Haven. Now we know they're the same, but not the same. Some *when,* they separated. But they still touch in places, for moments." Gently, she clicked the two crystals together. Their glows seemed to merge into a third, hazy glow. "Look what's crossed over! We know that happens. Jason has his dragon—"

"Actually," corrected Ting, "I think the dragon has him. If it is a real dragon." She paused thoughtfully. "Sometimes I think it's just a mass of energy, and a dragon is the way it appears to us, you know?"

Bailey didn't know. She had only the barest idea of what Ting was saying. She frowned. "People have crossed over. And dogs. And horses. And other things."

"The people here have six fingers."

"Well . . . that is odd, I'll admit, but Anne Boleyn had six fingers. Some people do!"

"And have been called witches because of it, but that's something different altogether. Maybe it's just a genetic thing that happened and stayed." Ting hugged her knees tighter. "But unicorns. What if that's just some wild rumor, some trap set by the Dark Hand to get us to go wandering?"

"What if it isn't? What if it could help your grandmother and . . . and everyone else?"

"My grandmother is doing fine here."

"I know that. I know she looks stronger, but it's cancer, Ting. You don't know what we can do to fight it here."

Ting pulled on a strand of her blue-black hair. "She won't go back. She says she can feel the bones of the earth here, and it strengthens her. I can't make her go back."

Bailey leaned forward intently, her hands full of the glowing crystals that cast a dancing light through the entire room. "What if what she feels are unicorn bones?"

The two girls sat in a long silence. Then Ting said, "How did you get permission to go look?"

"I told them I thought I could find chickens, wild chickens. From what Renart told me, anyway, there might actually be. And we could use a steady supply of good eggs, rather than just what we can steal from the nests around here." They were careful about what they took, not wanting to diminish the natural population around the academy grounds.

"True! Oh, yum ... scrambled eggs with cheese! That sounds even better than unicorns, at the moment." Ting shivered hopefully. She lay down, and as if in answer to her growing quiet again, the light from her crystal began to dim as Bailey set it back down on the stool between their cots. "But sleep first, right?"

"All right," Bailey agreed, if somewhat reluctantly. She rolled her scroll map and tied it before stowing it back under her pillow. "Sleep sounds good. But not as good as chocolate," she added firmly, before diving into the depths of her blankets. She smiled as she pulled her covers tightly about her. Ting thought her a bit crazed about the unicorns, but she was willing to go for the adventure anyway. That's what friends were about. And maybe they'd find something wonderful.

Three floors upstairs, a deeper voice with a growly under rumble to it, stated, "Rich. I'm hungry."

Another squeaky cot shuddered in the nighttime as its occupant rolled over with a groan. "Stef. Man. You're *always* hungry."

"I can't help it. I'm eating for two here."

"The way that bear cub side of you is growing, I'd say you were eating for a whole flock of bears. Flock? Herd? What do you call a bunch of bears?"

"Other than hungry? I dunno."

The two boys lapsed back into silence. It sounded almost as if Rich's heavy breathing verged on the edge of a mild snore when Stefan said, again, "Rich. I'm *starving* here."

A sigh. Then a crystal flared white, sending the room into near daylight brilliance as Rich sat up. "All right, all right," he muttered, combing his fingers through his wild red hair which stood up at every angle. "Let's go get you something to eat."

"Thanks, Rich!" said Stefan happily, as if it had been Rich's suggestion all along. He heaved himself to his feet, all stocky and square and looking not unlike the bear he morphed into when he willed it and often when he did not. His stomach growled as if seconding the wisdom of Rich's suggestion.

Downstairs, they found a wheel of cheese and pulled it out of cold storage, along with a slender knife, and a loaf of bread, and sat eating simple sandwiches. Rich had one, eaten slowly and deliberately, after cutting off the crusts and making sure nothing was out of order. Stefan gobbled down four big-fisted sandwiches before letting out a contented sigh that turned into a belch, and reaching for one last slice of cheese, without the bread, declaring he was full. He frowned a bit then, golden-brown brows knotting between his blue eyes.

"I miss FireAnn."

"So do we all." Rich had his heels up on the rough kitchen table and immediately dropped his feet to the floor as if the fiery Magicker with the thick Irish brogue might come in and berate him for his manners.

"She could cook anything," mourned Stef.

"She still can. She's just not with us, that's all. Jonnard and his crew dare not touch her. Or Eleanora. Especially," Rich added darkly, "Eleanora."

Both boys lapsed into silence at the thought of the young and beautiful Eleanora, stricken by the sudden aging that mysteriously hit users of Magick and who had been sent into a coma so she would not age. Then her sleeping body had been stolen by Jonnard and his followers of darkness to keep her hostage, along with FireAnn. Rich wrapped up the remains of the wheel of cheese almost fiercely. To his relief, there was a great deal left. He knew that they had to manage their rations and yet Stefan always seemed to be hungry, always seemed to be needing more than his share.

"Things," Stef said, "aren't always what they seem."

Rich straightened up the table and cleaned the cheese knife. "No? What was with you and Madame Qi today?"

He shook his head. "I can't study her way. I try, but I feel like I have to fight it. I do try, Rich."

"I hope so. I mean, they're just trying to help you." Rich stopped eating for a moment, and watched his friend's face. "We can't have you breaking into your bearskin at the drop of a hat. It's hard on you, and all of us."

"I know," he said heavily. "But her way isn't working. So . . . well, I haven't given up."

"No?"

"No." Stef's heavy voice sounded even deeper than usual and more firm. "I'm going out scouting tomorrow."

"On free day? I thought you'd sleep or something."

Stef shook his head. "No. Scouting. And then lessons."

Rich put his hand on the back of a chair. "Lessons? In what?" He blinked.

"I've been learning how to swing a sword."

"You what?"

"Yup." Stef colored slightly but with pride. The warmth flooded his big, square face.

"You're kidding me? And you go where to learn that?"

"Renart's town. There's a lass. . . a girl. . . there. Her father's the swordsmith. She's giving me lessons whenever I can get there. And, hmmm." Stef cleared his throat. "She's pretty. She thinks I'm . . . well . . . they've heard of other shapeshifters, skinwalkers, see? She thinks I'm heroic. Someone who could be a great warrior, you know?"

"Well. I'll be." Rich sat down, and looked at his friend. "That's great, Stef! But don't be taking this hero thing too seriously yet. You have to learn what you're doing! You could cut off a toe or something until you know, you know?"

"I know," rumbled Stefan glumly. "Bear doesn't take to lessons well, but we're trying."

"So, it's better than Madame Qi's way?"

"Much better. Bear wants to fight, not flow like a river. Or something like that."

"And she's pretty."

"Yup!" Stef brightened again.

"Wow." Rich considered his friend. Stef was not a rocket scientist, but he had good common sense, except when the bear had control of him body and soul, and . . . well, he guessed they were all growing up. Stef was as big now as most college fullbacks. The Magick seemed to bring growing spurts to all of them. "That's great," Rich added. "Really great."

"It's nothing much." Stef looked closely at him. "Don't go making it out more than it is. I just like her, that's all, and the bear doesn't scare her."

"And she's pretty."

He grinned foolishly. "That doesn't hurt either."

"Anyone else know?"

"Gavan knows I go. I Crystal there and back. He watches, makes sure I do it right, so I don't get lost. He promised not to tease or anything."

Rich crossed his heart. "I won't tell anyone."

"Good. Come with me tomorrow, then?"

"Gee. Well. I . . . hmmm. Swords aren't for me, Stef."

"I know. Go to the market, look at the herbs and stuff, scout around. You might hear something I don't." Stef folded his great hands, faint scars across the knuckles from years of playing football. He leaned forward. "There has to be word of 'em, somewhere, Rich."

Rich thought a moment. While he wasn't into mingling with strange crowds . . . who knew what germs and fevers they carried . . . still, the allure of new herbs and intriguing gossip drew him. He nodded his head. "All right, then. Tomorrow we go adventuring!"

Stefan beamed. He lumbered to his feet. "Now," he announced, "I'm sleepy!" He made his way to the back stair without waiting, and Rich scurried to catch up, crystal in hand, lighting their way.

And still the night wore on uneasily.

5

The Beginning

JASON KNEW HE WAS dreaming. He moved through it as though striding through real life, yet knowing he wasn't and unable to break the dream and awaken. It gripped him like a tiger with steel-trap teeth. He walked through a fortress or castle, its stone walls leaning in on him, his footsteps hammering on the floors and the hairs on his arms standing up as nervousness ran through his body. He did not know the place, but it felt as if it knew him and had been waiting.

He walked alone, but he was a Magicker and knew he was no longer ever truly alone except, perhaps, in his dreams. Somewhere nearby his friends slept . . . Ting, Rich, Stefan, Bailey, Trent, and Henry, although Henry slept in another world that night, off on a mission for them all. Somewhere, farther off, his enemies slept as well. Hopefully. Things Magickal were far more mysterious and dangerous than even he had ever dreamed.

Everyone dreamed, of course. Some remembered their nights and some did not, and he usually did not worry about his except that, once in a blue moon, his dreams were achingly clear. This was such a time. Jason would have awakened, rolled over, punched his pillow, and ignored it if he could. Where he slept now was not the comfort of his old bed, and what he used for a pillow probably wouldn't take punching very kindly, and the fact that he dreamed in spite of it all told him it was important. Maybe he was a Prophet instead of a Gatekeeper. So, with both fear and curiosity, he continued to walk into the dream.

A pair of immense wooden doors, lashed together with black leather and ornate bronze nails, loomed at the end of the stone passage. With no idea of what he would face beyond them, dread filled him. Jason raised his hands in readiness to push them open, and found his fingers clutching his crystals, one in each hand . . . the lavender crystal in his left and his gold and blue accented crystal in his right. No dream yet had been so real. He could feel the faceted edges of the gems cutting into his palms. Should he wake or should he stay? What faced him behind those doors? He thought he'd made the decision to go forward and find out, but now he found himself hesitating yet again. Wake up! Or could he?

The doors creaked open, swinging inward before he even touched them. The thought struck him that, gripped by the dream or not, he should take the chance to turn back. It was, after all . . . only a dream. Wasn't it? But curiosity prickled at him, as much as fear, and so he took a deep breath. After all, he'd seen a great many strange things since he'd become a Magicker. Jason marched into a great hall; a group of people swung around to face him, the clamor of talk dropping into a low murmur, a ripple of acknowledgment rolling toward him. The cavernous room, with its elaborate stone arches, seemed like the interior of some great, aged castle or fortress—except that it wasn't. Aged that is. It looked fairly new, the stone raw and clean rather than worn and stained with time.

Someone stamped an iron staff onto the stone floor with a harsh ringing sound. The man stood tall and straight under his sweeping robes, the staff of black iron firmly in his grip, and nearly as tall as he was. The noise cut into his ears and Jason suppressed a grimace.

"The accused is here. Court is convened!"

He knew he shouldn't have gone in. Panic tingled through him for a moment, like a lightning strike. Just as quickly, it left him. He was, obviously, the accused, for he was the only one who'd just arrived. Jason lifted his chin, sizing up the crowd of strangers as he used to check out an opposing soccer team. A good defense or a good offense depended on knowing and understanding what and who he faced.

"Accused of what?" he sang out, and his voice carried just as strongly as he hoped it would. There were lapses these days when it would fail him at the oddest times, sending Bailey and Ting into fits of giggles and Trent looking the other way, clearing his own unpredictable throat and drumming his fingers to a music track only Trent could hear.

Jason squared his shoulders as the men facing him broke away from their groups and sat down in stern-looking wooden chairs. He did not assume they were human, not as he was, for they did not come from the world he'd come from, although he was now a part of their world. They were dressed much as he was now, in clothing he'd come to know as Haven garb, jerkins and tunics and short coats, pants tucked into leather boots and so on, with formal looking robes over that. Bailey referred to it as styles from the Princess Bride Shop of the Realms.

One man raised his hand, and the murmuring ceased entirely, all gazes drawn to Jason. Jason looked back at the man, his white hair braided back neatly, his chin beard neatly clipped, his dark eyes with a slant that resembled Ting's Chinese ancestral features, and his six-fingered hand lowered to rest on his knee. So like and yet unlike.

"You are accused, Jason Adrian, of bringing war and death to Haven."

The words fell into silence, and then the fellows sitting around the speaker burst into talk again, agitated and overriding each other in bursts of sound. This was it, then, what he knew had to come, and what he'd feared. Condemnation for his actions. And yet, was it fair? Was it at all fair? Words tried to bubble out, all at once, so he kept a lid on all of them until he could sort through them and choose the right ones. What did they expect him to say? Did any of them really want to bother listening to his story of how and why they arrived?

What would he answer? What could he? "I am the Gatekeeper," he agreed slowly, "who opened the Dragon Gate to Haven."

"Plead you guilty, then?"

He hadn't said that! Jason shifted uneasily before the assembly. How unfair could they be? He wondered if he were indeed dreaming or if he saw something that awaited him in the future.

Finally, he said, "If death never existed here before, if war never existed here before, then, yes."

"You mince words like a cook chopping for a stew. You deny your actions?"

"People do different things for different reasons. Do the reasons matter to any of you?"

The assemblage turned to stare at the white-haired man, as if he alone had a voice and could speak for them. He shook his head, his eyes creasing in a sad expression. "Not in this court, I fear."

"But sometimes things happen because they have to, because bad as they are, worse things would happen if something else were done. . . ."

"It makes no excuse, Jason Adrian. Are you guilty or not?"

Jason bit the inside of his cheek to stop his words, and to create a different kind of pain than the guilt he felt. Oh, yes, he'd opened the Gate to his enemies as well as his friends, and he could never deny that. And he would never find peace in himself until the day when he found a way to drive Jonnard and the Dark Hand out of Haven, or died trying. He wouldn't lie. "I don't deny what I did, but you must understand—"

"We do not have to understand anything!"

"But you do. You have to try to . . . I didn't know anyone was here. I had no idea there were people and villages and problems. My Gate didn't show me that, I didn't know!"

"And if you had known?"

Jason tried to meet the other's piercing gaze, unflinching. It was the toughest stare down he'd ever done, besides the dragon.

"I would have asked," Jason said.

"Do you think that would have made a difference? Giving us a choice?"

It would have made a difference to *him*. Having a choice seemed to be a great and wonderful thing. Like in being asked if he'd wanted to be born a Magicker, or losing both his parents, or being yanked out of his own world, or . . . the list went on too long. This was beginning to sound like a debate class in high school. Did choice make a thing less evil because it chose to be evil? Not Jonnard. Not the Dark Hand! "It would have made it easier on all of us," Jason said. "We could have been ready."

"There was nothing to be made ready for," the judge told him, "till you brought disaster amongst us."

With a deep breath, he raised his arm. The iron staff struck the flooring again, and rang like a bell throughout the immense room. The sound stabbed through his ears, making Jason wince. "The accused accepts the charges!"

Jason made a stammering sound and stopped, before he could feel any more idiotic and guilty under their stare. He managed a deep breath. "Then," he said, a lot more evenly than he felt, "since you're so determined to have me guilty . . . what are you going to do with me?"

"Not just you, Jason Adrian. All of you. The Magickers."

"Oh, no. Huh-uh. You brought just one of us here for trial, and that was me, and no one else. I'm the Gatekeeper, anyway. So . . . what are you going to do about it?"

"You insist on standing alone?"

"You're not going to try the others without their being here! That's bogus! Where's the justice in that?"

"The justice in that," said the white-haired man quietly, "lies in the oath all Magickers swear to one another. But it is you, and you alone, who puts that oath aside now. So be it." He inclined his head, deep in thought for a moment, both hands wrapped about the staff.

For a very long, cold moment, Jason had the feeling that he'd just failed some sort of test. But he couldn't think how he could have done that, or what else he might have said. Nor did he think it was very fair that he was being given the sense of all this *after* it was a done deal! Where was the fairness in that? But it was a dream, he told himself, just a dream, and when he thought about it later, it would make about as much sense as a certain young lady falling down a white rabbit's hole into a tea party.

"This is serious business," the judge finally said. He wrapped and unwrapped his hands about his staff. "Remember you this."

It was as if he'd just read Jason's thoughts. . . . Jason took a deep breath, then swallowed, and nodded. Serious business. He'd keep that in mind, for later.

Their gazes locked. "Guilt being undeniable, then, the punishment is mine to give. I charge you with undoing what you have wrought."

That was the trap, then. From the frying pan into the fire. "I can't take them back," Jason said. "Not my friends. It's too dangerous to go back. You don't understand what our world would do to us for our Magick. As for Jonnard and the others, I'll do what I can." He tightened his left hand into a fist, gripping his crystal so tightly it slashed into his skin. "I'll either send them back or make it so they can't do any harm here."

"The undoing is your punishment. No more, no less."

"But I can't do that."

"You stand, Jason Adrian, with a foot in each world. To undo what you have done, you must choose!"

"Choose?" He stared back at the other in disbelief, feeling his jaw drop slightly. What did choice have to do with any of this? It had already been made . . . did they think he could back up time? What did they expect of him? Did they make fun of him because he hadn't given them any choices?

"Choose!" The white-haired man raised a hand and chopped it through the air, and at his signal, the staff rang out sharply yet again. This time, the stone floor cracked under its impact. A huge line began to open up, and then widen, snaking its way toward Jason, spreading between his feet and zigzagging onward. Jason looked down.

The rift began to yawn, a chasm opening up, and he was straddling it. A mist began to swirl about each booted foot and he would have moved, but he could not. He seemed rooted in place. And the chasm widened and deepened until he could see that he would soon fall in, and indeed, the whole room would collapse into its unseen depths. Perhaps even all of Haven might be swallowed up.

"You must choose, Jason Adrian." The white-haired man waved to his fellows and, cautiously skirting the doom that was splitting the hall, they began to leave. "Or you will destroy both worlds in which you stand."

"Wait!" Jason struggled to raise feet that felt as if they'd grown roots and anchored themselves into the stone, even as they pulled apart, and his position grew worse and worse. "It's not just my world, it's yours, too. Things can't just rest on me!"

They passed him relentlessly, just out of reach, until the last man stood next to him, the white-haired judge. "Do you see your dilemma?" he asked Jason, softly.

"I can't do what you want. Don't *you* see? What's past is past. All I can do is change things that may happen."

The judge shook his head slowly, the creases about his eyes deepening them into even sadder folds. He bowed deeply, turned on his heel, and followed the others out of the great room.

The doors slammed shut. "Wait!"

His voice bellowed, echoing, in the hall. Below, the chasm growled as if it had a voice as well, earth and stone groaning in movement as the crack deepened. And he couldn't do anything about it!

He grasped his crystals tightly, feeling the Magick surge through them. "Help, trouble, danger!" he cried, and the crystals sang with his need, his last and only chance. *Alarm! Warn the Magickers! Alarm!*

Darkness yawned under him. The edges of the abyss crumbled, and he began to fall. He looked down into the crevice and saw orange flame and heat rising to meet him as if he'd opened the gates of hell itself. Then it rushed toward him with a roar, and he realized he looked down into the mouth of a dragon. Eyes glared up at him as the snout snapped shut and massive black claws gripped him, snatching him up. The beast winged out of the abyss, Jason tight in its hold. Pain pinched him even as the icy nothingness of the void tried to reach out and swallow him. The dragon had him and would not give him up. Its claws tightened without mercy.

6

Alarms and Other Considerations

ANGRY DRAGONS make the sound of a hundred hissing teakettles, Jason had a moment to think. Maybe a thousand, but then, that would be a Bailey exaggeration. A hundred would be sufficient, all whistling at eardrum-piercing sound and strength. The pain of the claws hooked around him, and the shrill of the hissing woke him from his dream, for once and for all. Cold night wind shrieked past his ears till his nose turned icy cold. For good measure, the dragon shook him once, as they soared out over the Iron Mountains, leaving the framework of Iron Mountain Academy and the work camp of the Magickers in tiny relief below them.

He was awake now, well and truly, and what good did it do him? One of the biggest, most dire beasts he could dream of had him in its grip.

Unceremoniously, the dragon swooped low over a plateau, barely visible in the near dawn sky, and baited its wings as it settled to land, dropping Jason in a heap.

Jason rolled and got to his feet, dusting himself off. Plucked both from a dream and a sound sleep, he was nonetheless suddenly wide awake, as the dragon lowered its immense snout to look at him.

"Do I look angry?"

Steam boiled off his orange-red scales like steam off one of those teakettles Jason had been thinking about, and firelight danced deep in his amber eyes. Smoke curled out of his sooty nostrils in a slow, deliberate flow.

"Do I look sleepy?" Jason shot back, trying to comb his fingers through his hair.'

"What would I know of sleep, with the nightmares of Gatekeepers keeping me awake day and night?" the dragon grumbled back, his voice deep in his chest and sounding rather like a freight train laboring uphill. He settled next to Jason and wrapped his long tail about him rather like a blanket against the still chilly night.

"Truce?" Jason asked.

"Truce," the dragon rumbled. They paused for a very long moment, watching the edge of dawn flirting with the deep of the autumn night, with the Hunter's Moon still riding high in the sky. It would no doubt be there till nearly midday, Jason decided.

He'd been asleep on the seventh floor of the now distant Iron Mountain Academy, the unfinished but final floor, awaiting beams and roofing, but a rather fine place to sleep. A solid floor underneath, the only roof that of the sky . . . he and Trent enjoyed it. He wondered what Trent would make of waking up and finding him gone. Or if he'd even seen the dragon snatch him up. Trent slept deeply, whatever troubles he gathered during the day usually banished by nightfall.

"Deep thoughts," said the dragon, flexing a paw and then stretching it out, to curl his talons gently about Jason's body. Jason sat back into the embrace of a deadly yet oddly comfortable chair. There was a brilliant dark blue sky overhead framing the dragon's orange-red form, and soft, sweet grass under Jason's legs, and yet there was nothing peaceful about Haven this morning. He wondered that grass grew so far up in the mountains, and decided that when the frosts hit, the grass would probably die off for the winter. His sanctuary, and far removed from the world he'd grown up in, and yet he could not find what he looked for.

"I was thinking," he said slowly, his voice catching up with a mind that had, indeed, been sunk in thoughts as deep as the ocean, "that it seems to be awfully easy to start a war, and impossibly hard to stop one."

A vibration rolled through the dragon's body, warming it, and Jason felt the amusement in the beast. "And this revelation just occurred to you?"

Jason scrubbed his hand through his hair again. It was growing, and he needed a haircut, he realized, and the family barber was ... what, a whole world away? He wondered if any of them, exiled as they were, had bothered to bring scissors. Maybe Trent or Henry could invent them.

As for family ... he hadn't any, not really, except his stepmother and his stepfather, his own parents having died, but his world, he realized, had been his family. And now that was gone. He'd given it up, fleeing willingly to this world of Haven to which he'd opened a magical Gate, and it seemed that his action, like so many others, had been taken without much thought to the consequences. Like scissors being left behind. And hamburgers. Computers. Television. Laws and lawmakers. Soccer. Or as Bailey would add, her freckled face quirked in a longing smile, *chocolate*.

The dragon, he realized, was waiting.

"I guess I never thought about it that much. I mean, we're always fighting about something at home, terrible fights that go on for generations and people do what they can to stop them, but there always seemed to be ... I dunno ... hope." He sighed at that.

"And you've no hope here?"

"Not yet." He would have scratched his nose, but he realized he'd been fidgeting, and the dragon talon chair that wrapped about his lean form could grow impatient with him. "It's my fault for drawing Jonnard and the Dark Hand after us, and I've got to do something about it. I didn't know who else shared Haven, but I've brought in something terrible, and I'm the one who has to deal with it." The realization that he had personal enemies who would stop at nothing had finally sunk in.

Another hot rumbling passed through the dragon's scaled body, and Jason realized the creature was laughing noiselessly. The dragon lowered his immense muzzle to Jason and eyed him with one of his great, glowing eyes.

"Then let me make your acquaintance," he said. "It is an honor, if dubious, to meet the young man who single-handedly invented war and conflict."

Jason pushed at the dragon's nose, turning the muzzle a little away from him. "You know what I mean!"

"And you know what I mean. You're no more responsible for war than I am for rain. Nor are you culpable for Jonnard's actions. I agree that you must find a way to deal with him, and soon, or he and Isabella will cause much misery here in Haven. Yes." The dragon's gaze deepened a moment, and he lifted his head and looked off over the Iron Mountains ringing the valley, as if he could see very, very far away. "Misery and death, and more."

Jason didn't want to think how anything could be more than death. A shiver danced its way down his arms. "What should I do?"

"Sometimes, the best and hardest thing to do is . . . wait."

"Wait? I can't wait—"

"There are other fates in play besides yours, Jason. I did say it might be the hardest thing to do."

Jason shook his head. Every day meant the Hand grew bolder and stronger, and the towns and villages about Haven suffered. He didn't know what he could or should do, but he did know he couldn't wait much longer to do something. "No other advice?"

"Don't you mean, no better advice?"

A blush heated his face. "Kinda, I guess."

The dragon belched a puff of smoke, its version of a snorting laugh. Jason waved the cloud away from his face, coughing. Now Bailey was going to complain till he bathed! Nothing worse than a nonsmoker around a dragon-smoked person. Before Jason could venture much else, alarms began to sound, faintly heard up on their plateau but heard all the same, just as he'd felt in his dreams.

Jason jumped to his feet. Before he could grasp his crystal and focus on returning, the dragon shoved his nose between Jason's knees, dumping him back onto his neck, even as the beast ran forward and launched himself off the mountaintop.

Alarms. Death, and other things, Jason thought, as he wildly grabbed for a hold on the scaly neck and they descended at breakneck speed down into the valley.

Wills and Ways

BAILEY WOKE to noise, rolling over in her cot as Ting groaned. "There have got to be quieter ways to wake up," her friend said. Horns wailed and howled like the famed hound of the Baskervilles.

Bailey rubbed her face. It seemed like she had just closed her eyes. She stared at the rough ceiling of the sixth-floor east wing dorms, marveling for a moment that there *was* a ceiling overhead, and feeling a bit of chill in the air, "Is the sun even up?"

"I don't know," answered Ting sulkily. She stood, and began to braid her long black hair away from her face. "I will rise, but I won't shine!" She reached for her clothes, folded in a neat pile on a three-legged stool in the corner. Bailey's things hung in a helter-skelter fashion from a hook on the wall. Well, three hooks, actually . . . and one had slipped down to rest across her boots. As she reached for her blouse, it stirred and the little kangaroo rat, the pack rat Lacey, poked her whiskery face out curiously.

Above them, the roof sounded like a pack of goats stampeding over them. "Boys are up," she commented, as she laced her tunic and pulled her boots on.

Bailey dressed quickly, her pulse beginning to race. "This is serious," she said. "I think there's real trouble." She could feel an uneasiness dancing in the air. "You don't suppose they found out about my map. . . ."

Ting nodded. "Me, too." She rubbed her fingertips across the crystal charmed-bracelet she wore. The gems woke at her touch, gleaming softly with all the colors of the rainbow. The two looked at each other. "They wouldn't sound the alarms for that. They'd just pull us in and lecture our hides off."

"True!" Bailey wrinkled her nose and tried to lighten the mood. "I can't decide if we look good, or if we look like refugees from an old Renaissance Faire." She tugged on the hem of her blouse.

Ting nudged her. "We look good!" She sprinted for the staircase. Bailey was hot on her heels, Lacey tucked securely in a pocket of her bodice, chittering as they raced downstairs. The clattering of their hard-soled boots seemed a dim echo of the thundering of the boys across their ceiling, but all emerged, at the same time, into the yard of the Iron Mountain Academy where Gavan Rainwater and Tomaz Crowfeather awaited them.

Tomaz still dressed as the modern Navajo he was, but Gavan had reverted to the clothes of the age he knew best, breeches and boots, vested shirt, and flowing cape. He had been trained in magic in the golden years of the true Renaissance, even though a magical war had ripped him out of time and sent him forward to the twenty-first century. Now he'd returned. Somewhat. None of them were quite sure *what* the world of Haven was, or could be, or had been, except that Jason had found safety for them there. Yet it was neither safe nor their home, really.

The wooden-framed building that would be their academy and home was still far from finished, yet enough had been built to provide shelter that thundered with the running footsteps of the others. It had been built in two wings, like a giant V against the rust-colored Iron Mountains, and only its seventh and final floor gaped open, unfinished and unroofed. The wanderers who labored on it would return soon, to get the job finished before the autumn rains started. Then, Gavan had more plans for the academy, before winter's cloak flung itself over all of them, but pride etched his face as he looked at the structure and the teens tumbling out of it.

Only Jason didn't appear. Stef came thudding down the back stairs last, shrugging his vest into place. He never wore shirts anymore and only the last few days had he even started, reluctantly, to wear a vest over his fuzzy-haired chest. His great feet stayed, mostly, in thickly strapped sandals. He looked almost as furry in his human shape as he did in his bearskin shape when he changed, and a summer of sun had tanned him a rich golden-brown all over. Rich was the only one of them to have stayed in his original clothes. The others had either grown or just worn their regular world clothes to bits. Rich had stayed in beige cargo pants and a sleeveless sweat top, but he wore a deeply pocketed tunic over it.

Trent looked almost piratelike, having hit a growth spurt which made him taller once again than Jason. His hair had darkened to a sandy brown, and he wore it in a single braid at the back of his head. He stayed in his jeans, but their length had shrunk and shrunk on him till they hit nearly mid-calf. His ankle boots were cuffed under the bells of his pants, and Bailey always fought the urge to say "arrrr!" when she saw him.

She didn't expect Henry; he was on one of his brief trips back to their own world, the only one of them who could slip back and forth without causing much of a stir. She could only pray he'd bring some chocolate back with him although there were so many important things they needed. Her mother and Ting's grandmother leaned out of a second-story window, watching. They waved but stayed up in what would one day be real classrooms, keeping an eye on the horizon. It was Magickers who gathered anxiously about Gavan and Tomaz, young Magickers, in answer to the alarms at dawn.

And that was not all. A weary, lathered horse carrying a bedraggled rider stood there, Gavan's hand on the bridle and Tomaz murmuring soft words to the animal who looked as if he could drop in his tracks. As the rider unfurled his dirty cloak, and the sun brightened from dawn into daylight, Bailey could see his face.

"Renart!"

"Indeed," said Tomaz gently. "It has been long, my friend, since you've visited." He took Gavan's hand from the animal's harness and pressed the reins into Bailey's fingers, as he helped Renart swing down. "He needs walking, Bailey, slow and sure."

"But . . . but . . ." The leathers felt cold and stiff in her hand from the night weather, and the horse snuffled at her mildly. She didn't want to miss the excitement, and shifted from foot to foot.

"Here," Tomaz said, "would be fine. In small circles. You'll not miss a word." He winked at her, the expression deepening the creases in his own southwestern-marked face. With a blush, she began to lead the tired horse about.

"I think I broke his wind," Renart managed, his own voice hoarse and cracked.

"No. You used him hard, but these mountain horses of yours are sturdy. The question is: why?" Gavan brushed his hair from his piercingly blue eyes, and peered at the Haven trader.

"Dire need, and I was sent here."

"After being forbidden to see us and having your Trader Guild license pulled?" Gavan folded his arms and sat down on the step of the academy. He gestured for silence as the boys ranged around.

The alarms blew one last, quavering call, clarion trumpets in the wind, and Jason appeared from the mountainside of the academy, looking disheveled and wind rumpled, and smelling of hot metals like copper and brass. He always smelled like that, Bailey thought, when he'd been with the dragon. His hair had streaked light blond from the summer in the wilderness, and he had made a headband out of his old blue-and-white soccer shirt, to keep it pulled back. Pants of dark indigo dye were tucked into his boots, and he wore a long-sleeved white shirt under a matching indigo vest. He spent a moment tidying himself up, before flashing a sheepish grin at Gavan who muttered something about dragons and alarms.

And Bailey thought it had been Renart who'd set off all the noise! She pondered the skies behind the Iron Mountains but saw no sign of the beast, except for the massive stone gate carved in its likeness leading into the mountain and nowhere, unless Magick opened it. Yet its presence had set off the elaborate warding system the elder Magickers had ranged about the valley.

Renart's horse, exhausted as it was, tossed its head, letting out an anxious whinny as it rolled white-rimmed eyes at Jason. The dragon scent put it near the end of its endurance and it trembled. Bailey put her hand to its soft nose, and spoke gently, her voice unconsciously imitating that of Tomaz.

Renart collapsed on the step beside Gavan. The boys said nothing, but grouped together, waiting. Rich, ever on the alert for illness of any kind, fished through a large hide pouch he wore over his shoulder, and drew out a small bottle, and a cup. He half-filled the battered cup and handed it over. "That will help," he said.

"Many thanks, young Magicker," the trader said, grasping it and pulling it close with his six-fingered hands.

Rich blushed to the roots of his fiery red hair. "Any time!"

Gavan waited till Renart had emptied the cup. Then he coaxed the story from the trader. "Our success here came from you, my friend, from those early days of bartering and trading that kept us going. You were blamed and banished for that, and we owe you much. You say you were sent here? Or are you risking further punishment for coming? And what drove you so hard?"

Renart took a deep breath, the color coming back to his face. "Sent," he said quietly. "By Chieftain Mantor, of Avenha."

Gavan's brows arched. His deep blue eyes lost the last smudge of sleepiness at the trader's words, and he sat back, awaiting the rest of Renart's explanation, keen interest crossing his face.

"I was asked to attend the Hunter's Moon," Renart continued. "Surprised, since few talk to me, and I lost my guild status with my license."

Trent made a noise of outrage, but Renart gestured, dismissing the tall boy's indignation. "It's all right. It's temporary, and like the tides, a trader's life is full of highs and lows. We all expect it. I would not have done any differently, even knowing that. You were outlanders and most intriguing." Renart paused, smiling faintly, as if remembering. He plowed ahead again. "At any rate, I could not refuse Mantor. He's a shrewd man and holds much power, not only within his lands of Avenha but in many neighboring areas. His word even carries to the high steppes and the capital. If he traffics with me, others will follow. So I went. Mantor was expecting raiders."

"Ah," murmured Tomaz. He hooked his thumbs in his silver disk belt, the conchas gleaming like small, hammered suns, a work of his homeland. "And did they show?"

"They did. They were displeased at the decoy storerooms Mantor set up, and avoided the catching pits he had dug in the surrounding streets and fields, and used their crystal lightning to smash gates and set the walls on fire. They vowed to be back, and take their vengeance for his trickery."

"And that's the good news," commented Jason dryly.

"Almost. Even better, after the many times I suggested it, it was he who said . . . 'Send for the Magickers.'"

Big, burly Stefan stomped back and forth behind Rich. He grunted. "Fight fire with fire."

"Just so." Renart nodded at the boy who could, and often did, change into the bear he was coming to resemble more and more.

It was Tomaz who voiced the comment, "We were all branded as enemies. Does this signal a change of mind?"

"I believe it does. And with it, a change of fortunes for us all. He's a proud man, the chieftain, but smart. You have to go. You have to."

Bailey watched Jason who paled as Gavan said, "We are not proud of the countrymen who followed us through the Gate, Renart. I don't know what we can do to help, but help we will. Understand, though, that Jonnard and his Dark Hand have hostages of ours . . ." Gavan paused and breathed slowly, as if fighting for words or to contain something within, "And our hands are tied on many levels."

"This is a breakthrough," Renart protested. "You must go. Not for me, but for yourselves. If you intend to stay here and finish your school and live your lives, then you have to be accepted. Otherwise, you have traded one prison for another, my friends."

"How many raiders?"

"A goodly number. I think I counted fifty or so. There

are more. I've heard of two groups that size hitting the winter stores. She gathers them every week ... there are always those who find working the land too hard, and taking from others easier. They flock to her side, this Isabella and her son."

The Magickers looked at one another, remembering Isabella as one of their own, once ... tall, haughty, in sweeping gowns and jewels, and with unbridled ambition. In the centuries following the magical split that set the Dark Hand against those who followed Gavan and his leader, Gregory, she had worked both sides, building her fortune and holding herself timeless and aloof, or so it had seemed. She had a depth to her powers they could only guess at, and an evil will to keep going. "She and Jonnard are building a kingdom," Tomaz said slowly, and no one argued against that.

Gavan stirred restlessly but said nothing, his expression one of intense thoughts.

"I'll go." Jason spoke up.

Trent traded looks with him evenly, before adding, "If Jason goes, I go."

"There are masters here, and students. There is little wisdom in division." Tomaz paused, as if he thought to say more, and instead dropped back into silence. Jason lifted his chin but also held his silence.

Renart wrung his hands. "It's not just an opportunity for me. These are my people. We cannot stand against the winter if we are stripped bare." He stared at his six-fingered hands, knuckles white.

"We will go." Gavan stood. "Bailey with me. Boys with me. Tomaz, stay with the others. Make sure that Jonnard has not thought we would rush off and leave this place unattended."

Ting frowned. She hid her disappointment, like her hands, in the pockets of her long skirt and would not look at Bailey. Gavan traded looks with Tomaz, and then reached out to Ting.

"I need you here," he said, "because of your rapport with Bailey. If anything happens, it'll be easiest and quickest for you to draw us back, through Crystal."

"Oh," said Ting. "Oh!" Then she brightened, her eyes widening with the realization of his words. She would anchor for Bailey as Bailey would anchor for her.

Bailey began to walk about again, the trader's horse smelling of sweat and heat and bruised heather from its run over the hills. It seemed to be breathing a little easier, although its gait was far from easy. She shot a sidelong glance at Ting, a little upset about her own plans for exploring being delayed, but this seemed far more important. Ting nodded back at her, eyes crinkling in understanding.

Renart looked at his mount. "Should I ask how we're going to get there?"

Gavan took his wolfhead cane from the staff harness at his back, and leaned on it, the great diamond crystal in its jaws winking in the morning light. "Now, Renart," he said easily. "How did you think?"

Renart swallowed. "I had hoped . . . not that way."

"We've few horses here, certainly not enough for all of us. As long as you can picture part of Avenha for us, and hold it, we can get there." Gavin rubbed his palm over his crystal focus in the wolf's jaws. "Everyone going, link up." He waited till Bailey passed the horse's reins back to Tomaz and linked arms between Jason and Trent.

"The one thing you absolutely must remember, Renart, is that as much as we may wish to fight the Dark Hand, as much as it is our will to do so . . ." Gavan frowned. "We may not have a way." He cleared his throat. "But we will answer the call!"

Renart swallowed tightly again. He linked an arm through the crook of Gavan's elbow.

"Now think of Avenha," Gavan ordered, "something you can see no matter what, and hold to it, tightly."

The Stars help him, Renart tried to think of something else but all he could concentrate on was the lovely face of Pyra. His stomach lurched and there was a whistling in his ears as they winked out of *then* and went somewhere *else*.

Mud

SO THE SEVEN of them appeared abruptly in the sleeping quarters of the chieftain's daughter of the prosperous and important holding of Avenha. Bailey reflected that there was nothing like an actual demonstration to learn a good defensive kick and put-down hold, although Renart's red, bulging face indicated that Pyra's reaction was more than a mere demonstration as he squirmed in discomfort under her foot. And, as far as alarms went, Pyra's and her sisters' screams more than equaled any of the wailing windhorns from the Iron Mountain Academy. When all was said and done (and much was, in the confusion), their arrival was met with a great deal of fuss.

Bailey stared at the wiry chieftain's daughter with unabashed admiration. "That was some move."

"Like it? I'll teach you later. Every woman should know how to defend herself," Pyra said frankly. Her cheeks had flushed a bit, and her dark eyes flashed with an inner amusement, as she glanced over at Renart who had finally recovered some composure but wouldn't look back at them.

"That," answered Bailey, "would be terrific!"

"Good. When Chieftain Mantor has spoken, and matters have been handled, I will meet up with you and show you a few of my tricks." Her solemn words did not chase the hilarity from her eyes as she turned away then, and began to bring order to the shambles of her tent, which had nearly caved in around them during the tussle. All of Avenha's city proper had been sent into the hillside with its many caves, and tents dotted the hill about the caves as well, for additional housing while the night raiders were expected.

Wrapped in the shreds of his dignity, Renart escorted them all out, as the booming voice of Chieftain Mantor could be heard. He'd been one of the first to respond to the brawl in his daughters' tent, had taken a quick survey, and left when he was certain things were under control. He sat on horseback now, a small herd of similar mounts crowded around him, shaking their heads in the early morning, chomping their bits and stamping their feathered legs on the dewy ground.

"Dibs on the gold one with the white face," Bailey said.

The ruler of Avenha turned his gaze on her, a slow smile creasing his face. "Because of the pretty color, outlander?" His hands opened and closed on the many lead reins bunched in his hold.

Bailey leaned back a little, unsure of what was really being asked of her, yet instinctively knowing there was much more to the chieftain's question than there appeared to be. When in doubt, the truth seemed best. Still, she picked her way through her answer, much as one of these sturdy horses might pick its way across uncertain terrain. "I have a sense, a Talent, for animals. It's pretty, yes, but more than that . . . I can feel a soundness in its legs, a curiosity but not fear of us, and a pride in its . . . well, how it carries a rider. How it performs." Bailey stammered to a halt, and stood nibbling on the corner of her lip. She cupped her crystal pendant, her focus, and let its well-being flood her.

Mantor stared at her closely for a long moment, then nodded. "A useful Talent." He sorted out the gold's reins and passed them to Bailey. "Anyone else have this . . . dibs?"

No one else had the Talent Bailey did, but it seemed unlikely that the chieftain would have brought ill-suited mounts for the expedition they had planned. The only clear choice was the large, broad-backed bay which seemed destined to carry Stef's bulky weight. Everyone else just shrugged and took whatever horse Mantor assigned to them.

Once up, Renart looked a lot more composed. He flushed deeply when Pyra appeared at her tent flap and gave a wave which could have been directed at any of them, and almost lost his seat when his horse sidestepped suddenly. He grabbed for its mane with both hands, and suffered the snickers with grace. Mantor leveled his consideration on Renart. Finally, he said, "A trader would be an asset to the family line."

That remark made Renart blush even deeper and Mantor swung his horse about and into a trot before the flustered man could stammer out a reply of any kind. His garbled words were lost in the thunder of hoofbeats as the horses broke into a trot, following their leader.

True to her Talent, Bailey had chosen well. The gold moved with steadiness and a smooth gait that made it easy for her to sit the saddle, although she had rarely had a chance to go riding. Southern California, a world and a lifetime away, with its bustling, ever growing cities, had few stables left, and riding had become more and more the hobby of those with time and money to burn. She had neither.

The others rode much as she did, with flapping arms, legs ramrod stiff in their stirrups, trying to maintain as comfortable a seat as possible. Mantor moved among them, giving hints, reaching out and adjusting lanky frames when he felt like it. Trent rode as he walked through life, as though he heard an inner music and moved to it. His horse seemed to trot to the same rocking beat. Stef didn't ride his horse so much as conquer it, and Rich seemed about to fall off at any given minute, his attention far more on the plants dotting the ground about them. It was only a matter of time, Bailey thought, till he dove into those selfsame plants nose first. Only Gavan showed any horse sense at all, settling into his saddle, his cape flowing like a stormy ocean behind him. Of course, he'd probably been on a horse or in a carriage far more than any of them. Bailey watched him, thinking of the times he'd come from. All of the older Magickers had adapted quickly. But was Haven almost like home for him—or just as eerily strange as she found it?

By late morning, her bottom was sore, her stomach and her pack rat were reminding her noisily that they hadn't had breakfast, and she was pondering bringing all those subjects into public knowledge when they came to the top of a rocky crag and Mantor halted his horse.

"Down there," he said. "Although they're making no attempt to hide their whereabouts." He crossed his wrists, resting them on the pommel of his saddle and looked down into a valley crisscrossed with darkness. "That was an old fortress belonging to a warlord who died of a terrible disease, so his troops abandoned it many years ago. They have gone in, rebuilt much of it, added new outbuildings, most of it for barracks and stabling. To attack them directly would be to risk much, especially with their sorcery."

Gavan dismounted. He tapped Trent on the knee. "What do you see?"

Trent stood in his stirrups. Bailey gazed at Trent. He couldn't work Magick but he could see it, and that was more than they could, because the working of it seemed to blind them to subtle underlying traps and strands. It wasn't a Talent exactly.... He shaded his eyes as he stared across the encampment of the Dark Hand, and then nodded to Gavan. "There are ward lines everywhere, that's the shadowing you see. Add that to the sentries positioned about, and they're armed to the teeth for trouble."

"Which we won't give them today." Gavan smothered a faint sigh. He pulled his staff free and ran his hand over the crystal diamond in the wolfhead. It flared, then clouded.

Stef grunted. He scrubbed a thick hand over his brushy golden-brown hair. "I came to fight," he said flatly.

"We all did," Rich told him.

"No," Jason put in. "That's stupid, Stefan ... did your football team ever go to a game without some scouting first? Think about it."

Stefan made a face, then dropped into sullen silence.

"Nothing yet. At least we know where they are, and that they're confident about being able to hold it. That will make a big difference on how we approach things." Gavan twitched, his feelings transmitted almost instantly down the reins to his horse, and his mount sidestepped quickly with a nervous snort.

"Then what are we going to do?" Rich, his face paler than ever, even under the Haven sun, stared at the headmaster.

Trent jabbed a thumb down toward the valley. "Figure out how to get a lot closer without getting tangled in that web." He stretched in his stirrups, surveying the dark weaving, an intense look on his face as if memorizing it. "I think it can be done," he finally finished.

"Good lad." Gavan swung his horse about to face Renart and Mantor. "Eleanora and FireAnn are down there." He stared gloomily into the encampment. "You understand, Chieftain Mantor, that they hold hostages of ours."

"As I am certain you understand that their raids threaten the lives of many people."

"Winters have never been easy to survive."

Mantor's horse stomped a hoof as if reflecting his rider's mood. The chieftain looked from Gavan to Renart who stayed remarkably silent now, though his fine brown eyebrows seemed knotted in protest. "All of you—" and Mantor gestured across the band of them and down across the valley fortress. "Are interlopers here, bringing much with you that is new, strange . . . and evil. We sift for the good, as we sift through our grain, sorting the wheat from the chaff. Many have voiced that all of you are alike, but I say . . ." And Mantor paused a moment. He cleared his throat. "I say that you are no different from any men, that you must be judged one at a time." His six-fingered hand flexed on the reins, and his horse tossed his head. "Renart and I agree in this. It has led to Renart losing his license, and the respect of many. All of you know better than we do, what needs to be faced down there, and what the cost of that will be." Mantor leveled his gaze at Gavan. "Are you telling me that you will not help us?"

"No." Gavan shook his head emphatically. "I'm saying, right now, they have a knife to our throat." He smiled, grimly. "We have to figure out how to blunt the blade before it cuts. But, there is no denying, we intend to fight what we're responsible for, and now we know where they are . . . and what we're facing. Magickers, mark this valley. We'll be back." He swung up then, and with a sharp kick, sent his mount back down the crag the way they had come, in a rattle of loose pebbles and stones.

Mantor let out a primal sound, but whether of agreement or disgust, no one could be sure. He wheeled his horse about to plunge after Gavan. With a sigh, Renart kicked his horse into a trot. Bailey's horse turned to follow without the slightest tug on the reins from her to signal it, and the boys' mounts did the same. Halfway down the crag, her horse veered off the trail and picked its way to the left, down what she could only describe as a goat's trail. She tugged on the reins, but it swung its head back determinedly, and she finally let it go. At the hill's bottom, though, she could not spot the others, only a faint dust cloud from their passing.

"Uh-oh," said Bailey quietly. She pulled on the reins and kicked her horse in the flanks, putting it into a trot in what she could only hope was the right direction. A rustling came from the brush behind her, and she turned in the saddle, expecting to see Stefan or Rich trailing.

Something did indeed trail after her. Brush crackled and pebbles flew from its headlong passage. Jaws carried low, hide of black-streaked silver, ears pricked and eyes catching the sun with a glint of green, a wolfjackal ran after her, mouth curled in a vicious snarl. Neither wolf nor jackal but the worst of both, she'd seen enough to fear them. They'd savaged Jason once. He still bore the scars on his left hand, and she hated to count the near escapes she'd had! Bailey leaned low over her horse, and kicked harder. "Where there's one, there's more," she cried out, urging the animal. "We're in trouble."

The horse didn't seem to catch the scent of the wolfjackal, but broke into a shambling run as the beast let out a long, quavering howl and was answered by three more close by. The horse let out a shivery whinny of fear muted by the thunder of its hooves. "Big trouble," shouted Bailey, as she took up the ends of her reins and tried to snap them against her horse's shoulders. Memories of old cowboy movies spurred her, and her shout seemed to inspire the horse. It laid its ears back, stretched out its neck and pushed into a run, sprinting low across the rough countryside. "Faster!"

The tough little horse was built for mountains and walking all day, not running. It had speed but precious little, and she could tell from its panting that it couldn't run much farther or faster.

Bailey grasped her crystal in desperation, and twisted in

her saddle. She pulled back on the rein, bringing her horse around in a circle, slowing it. Her crystal warmed in her hand. She had plans in her future, and she wasn't going to let anything or anyone stop her from them.

Time to make a stand!

9

Crystal Shields

BAILEY RUBBED her amethyst gem, its answering warmth filling her hands. It wasn't her power, but a focus for it, and she bent her head in concentration to conjure up what she wanted. A Shield of light and energy between her and the enemy. *Think, Bailey, think!* A shimmering leaped into the air and, like a bubble, seemed to settle about them. Her horse whickered anxiously, its golden flanks lathered from the hard run. It stamped in fear as the Shield surrounded it, but it settled under her hold. *Arrooooo! Aroooooo-ah!* Their throats full of noise, the pack of wolfjackals crested the hill and raced toward them. Five in all, from shadow gray to dun to coal-black, their eyes blazed down at her. Their throats swelled with growls and yips. Bailey swallowed. Was she making a mistake trying to put up a Shield here . . . or taking the only chance she had, alone?

She rubbed her crystal a second time, in hopes of sending out a Beacon, a shard of power to alert the others. The Shield dimmed. Her hand shook, and she narrowed her eyes. *Concentrate.* But her mind strayed as the wolfjackals charged at them, their howling broken only by heated snarls, and she dared not look up from her gemstone to see how close they really were. The Shield would hold. Now she needed a Beacon!

She would have dropped her crystal if it had not been cleverly trapped and hanging from its chain. As it was, it bounced out of her grip and dangled for a second before she caught it back up again. Lacey chittered nervously at her from her bodice pocket, and Bailey could only mutter, "Quiet, I'm thinking!" back at the little pack rat.

She clutched her amethyst tightly, feeling its edges bruising her fingers. It felt warm now, but she knew well its cold panes and facets, the geometric precision of its inner secrets. She had trapped herself inside the crystal once, and if Jason had not rescued her . . . an icy shiver ran through Bailey at the thought. She nearly dropped her amethyst again. *Don't think! Don't fear it—just focus!* Her horse shifted under her, putting its ears flat back and baring its teeth, ready to fight. Bailey drew its reins tighter, fearing now that even if she could hold the Shield, the horse might charge through it, breaking the Magick. The way her crystal fought her now, or she fought it, she might not have the strength to put up a new one. Even now, her body shook as though she lifted a tremendous weight.

Bailey bit her lip. Hold on . . . just hold on! Someone was bound to notice the energy surge in this small dell. Someone was bound to notice that her endless chatter had stopped . . . weren't they?

The wolfjackals ranged about her. They began to circle. She could smell the strong odor of their heated bodies. Curved ivory teeth cradled lolling red tongues that dripped with eagerness to taste them. Bailey snugged her legs deep into the saddle's stirrups and wondered if they might yet have to try outrunning the beasts. Her horse had caught its breath, and now stomped defiantly as the lupines circled. One of the wolfjackals bumped another, and they snapped and snarled at each other, their harsh cries shattering in the air. The pack leader turned to face her, head on, eyes glowing, ruff silvery about its neck as it stared boldly, unafraid.

No normal animal meets a human gaze like that. Bailey hefted her crystal a little higher, and the Shield wall shimmered, growing a bit stronger. Tomaz had worked with a wolfjackal pack, accepted by them somewhat, claiming that they were chaos torn free, but their natures were neutral. They sought Magick's overflow, but Bailey felt here and now that they were evil. Pure, vicious evil. She didn't know how the elder Magicker could think otherwise!

And if anyone doubted her, they could trade places with her *right now,* and watch the wolfjackals grin as they imagined her sliding down their gullets for an afternoon snack!

Her horse shivered as if sharing the same thought. Lacey gave up chittering at her and dove headfirst into the depths of the bodice's pocket, with not even her black tufted tail hanging out. "Coward," muttered Bailey. Not that she blamed the little creature one bit.

A wolfjackal lunged at them. The Shield exploded in fiery purple-and-red sparks where it hit. It shrieked in fear and pain, rolling away, paws scrambling in the dirt. It cowered low, glaring at her, and then growled deep in its throat. The Shield healed itself immediately, and Bailey let out a low sigh of relief. It had held. It would hold . . . though for how long, she could not be sure.

She could see them thinking. The pack leader paced about her, its legs moving in the easy swinging gait of a wolf, and it touched muzzles with each of its pack, even the injured one. Then a second wolfjackal drew close. It did not charge as the first attacker had but rather swiped a paw.

The Shield crackled and spat, sparks flying again, but to a lesser degree. Then, slower than the first time, it healed itself where the wolfjackal had torn an opening.

Bailey blinked. Did they see that, too? Did they sense it or know what it could mean? She'd never seen a crystal's Shield gape open like that, or heal back. In all the times she'd had to use a Shield, it had never, ever, behaved like that. Anything could dart through those tears. Anything. . . .

The wolfjackals pulled back, circled, eyeing her closely. She could feel the strain in her arm as though she held a great weight in her hand, the crystal warm enough to nearly burn. She tried to splinter off a thought to Jason, Gavan, anyone, everyone, but the crystal resisted her as if it needed all her power for the Shield and nothing else mattered. As if it were too weak to channel any other magic. Or as if she were too weak . . .

The wolfjackals sank into a crouch, haunches tensing.

Her horse stamped and rolled the bit in its teeth. They were thinking beasts. Had they reasoned out what she feared? Or worse ... had they somehow *read* her thoughts? She had animal sense. Maybe she could push them away. She settled in her saddle, digging her heels in, bracing herself, and opened her mind to see if she could touch them as she often did Lacey. It wouldn't, couldn't, be pleasant, but she had to try.

For a moment, she felt nothing. She relaxed back on the mountain pony, feeling its flanks heaving under the saddle blanket as it fought both its tiredness and its fear of the beasts crouched before them. She could feel the burn of air in its lungs ... but no, no, she was touching the horse, not the wolfjackals. Bailey wrenched her thoughts away from the beast she rode to the beasts who faced them.

Her hands shook. She felt tired, so very tired. She didn't know if she could even hold onto her crystal another moment ... her eyelids fluttered. No! No! She shoved back, and the leader of the pack opened his jaws in a huge, wolf-ish laugh at her.

She hadn't touched them, but he had touched *her*.

Bailey shrank back as if burned and almost threw her crystal with the jolt of her feelings. She clamped a lid down on her fear quickly, and held on with everything she had. A searing caress along the edge of her thoughts, and she almost thought she heard "Magickersssss cubling." But she couldn't have. Wolfjackals could not speak. Could they?

What was it the one wolfjackal had said to Jason? *You are mine.* Bailey swallowed tightly. She wasn't about to become a shaggy snack if she could help it! She might be here till night fell and hell froze over, but she would keep that Shield up.

Jaws snapping at air, the pack leader slashed a wolfish snarl at her, as if in answer. Heart sinking, Bailey clenched her crystal and felt its angles cut into her skin. Looking down, she saw that its purple color had bleached away to nearly silver white. Fool! Why couldn't she have remembered the Avenha outcamp well enough to Crystal back? She'd never tried Crystaling anything as large as a small horse, but how could that be different from a gaggle of Magickers? But she didn't dare try it without a clear inner picture of her destination, and that she did not have.

What she did have was Ting and her mother, and the bare bones beginning of the Iron Mountain Academy, much farther away. There, there was her haven. Distance shouldn't really matter, the theory of crystal teleportation was merely the folding of distance. But it did matter, at least to one as young and newly trained as she. She knew that. This time, though, it couldn't. Bailey cupped both hands tightly about her amethyst. Home, she thought. Channel all her will to bring them safely home....

The crystal flared in her hands with icy cold light. Not the warmth of power, but a deep cold chill that frightened Bailey to her very bones. She felt a brief touch of Ting, a jolt of surprise and a gut-wrenching kick as if repelled, and then ... nothing.

The crystal made a noise as if fracturing deep inside.

No! Oh, no, not that! Bailey let her power go, felt it drain immediately as if barely held there, and the Shield shimmered down to mere sparks before restoring itself, slowly. She dropped her eyes to her hands, examined the crystal quickly before leveling her gaze back at the pack. She narrowed her eyes, willing herself to maintain a steely gaze as if that, and that alone, would keep them from her. Her amethyst seemed whole. She had to believe that it would continue to hold her focus. Without that belief, she had no defense left.

Nor enough power left to try it again, last chance or not. No, their last chance would rest on the mortal power of the little horse to try to outrun the pack when it broke through her faltering Shield.

And it would. If not on this leap, then on the next, or the one after. Bailey knew it in her bones.

Two sprang as one. The first yowled in pain as the Shield threw it back amid a shower of hissing sparks, the power of it dancing about the wolfjackal's fur like bits of fire. The second leaped low, and pierced the tear in the Shield. Bailey's horse squealed. It whirled about and lashed out, hooves striking the wolfjackal solidly. A howl of pain cut abruptly in two, and the limp body sailed through the air, landing outside the Shield's shimmer, and lay still.

The pack leader nosed it, and made a low growling sound as if to promise revenge for the fallen. Bailey curbed her pony to bring it about, to face the enemy again. Magick or not, they wouldn't be easy to pull down! She sat straighter in her saddle.

"Well. Well, well. The little Magicker has teeth. And more."

She hadn't heard a sound, nor had the wolfjackals, but with low growls, they slunk back, curling back and forth among one another, snarling. Bailey twisted in her saddle and saw Jonnard of the Dark Hand watching her from horseback, a faint smile twisting his pale face. Dark cloth and a darker cape, seemingly wrought of shadow, wrapped him from head to toe, revealing only his face and hands. His horse, an immense steed of the deepest midnight color, stood far taller than her own rugged mountain horse. It arched its neck, and an unseen hand or wind stirred its mane and unfurled its tail like a silken coal-black banner. Leave it to Jonnard to ride only the finest horseflesh he could find in Haven.

"Oh, yes," he added. "It is true that the female blooms sooner than the male, is it not? And look at you. You make Eleanora look so . . . old."

"Get out of here." His words, though she didn't quite understand them, still brought an angry flush to her face. He was taunting her, that she knew. Well, she wasn't helpless. Yet. She'd show him that! Her hand clenched her crystal so tightly she thought its one sharp edge might draw blood.

He quirked a finger at her. "How long do you think that Shield will hold? Or . . . that crystal?" He smiled at her, without humor in his eyes. What did linger in his eyes was something she didn't recognize, but it made her afraid. "Let me take you from this peril, Bailey. Rescue you, if you will."

"It will hold long enough," Bailey shot back at him.

Jonnard gestured at the wolfjackal pack, and sent them racing away, after a short snapping disagreement from the leader. They left their dead pack mate behind them. Moments after they were gone from view, a green fog boiled up from the ground about the wolfjackal body, and as it leeched away, thinning, the carcass disappeared with it. The tiny vale seemed deadly quiet, with only the snort of his warhorse and the quieting pant of her sturdy pony.

Jonnard considered her. "I could take you to . . . join . . . Eleanora and FireAnn."

Bailey lifted her chin. "You could *try*."

Jon laughed. "You've grown, Bailey. Not as tall as Jason or Trent, but ... aye, you've grown." He leaned forward in his saddle and his fine dark horse paced forward proudly. "Not enough to withstand me."

"Maybe not, but I bet I could put a big dent in that ego of yours."

"Or die trying, I imagine." He reined his horse to a prancing stop. "What can I do to convince you to visit with me? Just a while? We haven't talked in many a month, yet I remember mornings at camp. Do you still rise in the morning, Bailey, as bright and sunny as the dawn?"

She felt flustered. He was up to something, but she had no idea what. Jonnard had tricks within tricks. "I wouldn't go anywhere with the likes of you."

"No? How sad. And here I had hopes you'd put me on your dance card. And you so charmingly unaware of your ... charms." He paused suddenly, quirking his head, as though aware of something else. His tone changed abruptly. "Then I shall simply give your regards to the lovely ladies already guesting with me." He flicked his reins, and his horse threw his head up, about to bolt into movement.

"They'd better be safe!" Bailey called out, even as he put his heels to the dark horse. A cloud of dust and turf was all the answer she got as Jonnard raced from view, back the way the wolfjackals had fled, and she had no time to wonder why, as a thunder of hooves from the other direction told her the lost had finally been found.

Bailey lowered her aching arm in relief, and let the shield go, its purple sheen flooding back into her amethyst, its color returning a bit. Like her, it looked exhausted and nearly bled of every morsel of strength. Lacey climbed out of her pocket, and onto her shoulder, where she wove her tiny claws firmly into the fabric and took up a determined perch.

"Oh ... now you make a showing," Bailey said to her fondly, and tilted her head to rub her cheek against the small bit of fluff. Lacey chittered back. She looked up at Gavan and Jason and the others as the small herd of horsemen surrounded her, and she said, "It's about time."

10

Mulberry Bush

JONNARD STRIPPED off his riding gloves as he strode up the crude stairwell toward the chambers his mother had claimed as her own. He could smell the aroma of her perfume before he even arrived at the doorway and threw the door open, and her scent washed over him even more heavily, a wave of roses and jasmine and something darker, more mysterious than mere flowers. Perhaps nightshade, he thought. Perhaps something even more deadly. He smiled faintly to himself as he stepped inside her apartments. So different from Bailey who used no wiles but beguiled.

Isabella sat at a writing desk, her dark vermilion gown almost completely enveloping the chair, her graceful neck bent forward as she perused the many volumes stacked upon the desktop. Thin, spidery spectacles rode the bridge of her strong, prominent nose, the delicacy of the one setting off the harshness of the other. The hammered satin of her deep red gown made faint rustling noises as she turned a page and said, without looking at him, "Teasing Gregory's lot, were you?"

"Assessing them." Jonnard tucked his gloves away in his cape, and took up a perch on a tall stool not too close and not too far from her writing desk. His mother looked at him then, a careful nonexpression on her imperious face. If anyone, he thought, had the strength to rule this motley world, it would be her . . . or himself. Then he revised his estimation. He was not ready for the discipline of ruling . . . yet.

"Assessing," repeated Isabella. Her voice still held the faint trace of a French accent, that country in which she had hidden and lived for many many decades. It added to her charm. She closed the book she was reading, taking care to place a pewter bookmark in it first. "I was wondering when they would take the bait we've been laying so carefully." She removed her spectacles carefully, folding the bows, and putting them down on top of a stack of other books. "Have you looked in on our guests to see if anything untoward has occurred?"

"Not yet. I came to you first."

"I see." Her legs moved, the satin dress sounding again with its music of the fabric, and he guessed she probably crossed her legs beneath its skirts. "Tell me what transpired."

"The wards told me we had trespassers. I saddled up to take a closer look. The impulsive one, Bailey, had already separated from the others." Jonnard made a gesture with one hand. "I sent the pack out to keep her cut off and hold her."

"And what, if anything, did you learn?"

"That they have not yet learned what we know." Jonnard smiled with that.

"Good. It's to our advantage, obviously. Anything else?"

"She or her pony killed one of the pack, so I will have to make amends there." That brought a frown to his face, which evaporated quickly. Things happen, and he was not particularly worried or inconvenienced by the loss of a wolfjackal, but he would have to compensate the pack, a trivial nuisance. "As for the others, they saw what you wanted them to see, and I would say from Bailey's state of mind, that you've accomplished what you wanted."

"Did I?" Isabella's mouth twitched slightly. She moved her hands, so that they formed a blockade. "Jon, when is a gate not a gate?"

He looked at her quizzically. "I . . . I don't know."

She looked down at her hands. "When it is a wall." She then flexed her hands, opening them as if they were the aforementioned gate. "He has us locked in. What I want, is that Gate open and free-swinging, so that we can move back and forth at will. I thought I sensed a trembling in that force the other day, but nothing I could pinpoint. But if we could move as we need, Jonnard, then both worlds would indeed be open to us. I would be warm again, and lodged in comfort. . . ." Her gaze became distant, as if she looked into her past, or perhaps another world. She stirred after a moment. "We can use the one, and rule the other, but not until we have a Gatekeeper."

He could sense that her energy seemed down. "He has us bottled up and he is the cork."

Isabella nodded to Jonnard. He made a fist, then turned it, so he could view the strength of the cords across the back of his hand and wrist, the width of his knuckles. "I will break him, Mother. He will either open that Gate for us as you need it, or there will be another Gatekeeper to take his place."

"Can you do that, do you think?"

He could feel the answer blaze deep in his eyes before he put it into words. "I can, and will."

"Good." Isabella stretched out her hand, picked up her spectacles once more, and retrieved her book. "See that you do."

He hesitated a moment, then said, "Perhaps you should draw a bit from the Leucators. You need your strength."

Isabella looked at him over her glasses. "I am fine."

Corrected, he bowed. Dismissed, Jonnard stood, leaving his mother to her study, and went to visit the hostages. Housed in another, quieter wing, with far fewer amenities, he felt a chill brought in with the wind that seemed to know how to wriggle its way through the wooden structure. If they were to stay, he would see plastering invented. Along with indoor plumbing. Jonnard brushed the hair from his forehead before stepping into the guard's hallway, and sketching a gesture at them that he wanted entry.

The two relaxed their vigilance. They were hard men, from a time in the past, when death was both more frequent and less objectionable than it was in current times.

He'd instructed them in just enough magic to keep the wards about the prison rooms safe, to open and close them, and nothing more. They had enough Talent for that, little more, nor did they have ambitions for anything more. They knew that would sign their death warrant, for Jonnard kept his Magick close, and they had been chosen for their duty because of their loyalty and their deep suspicion of anything enchanted. Devil's work, they called it, and they did it only to keep the greater Devils . . . those two women . . . locked safely away.

He passed through the first threshold, coming to a locked and barred door to which he held the key in a small leather pouch cinched tightly to his belt. He fetched it out and unlocked the crude brass lock, hearing the tumblers grind as he did so. Then he set aside the lock, moved the bar it secured, and put his shoulder to the door. The weight of the door alone would deter most women from escape. But, as the power of his own mother often reminded him, a Magicker woman was not an ordinary woman.

As he stepped in, an herb-scented mist greeted him. He sneezed and waved the steam away with one hand, raising his eyebrows at the seated woman and the woman standing by her, waving a towel over a basin of steaming water.

"Another cure-all, FireAnn?" Jonnard asked, with more than a touch of mockery in his tone.

"Whatever it takes," the red-haired woman replied tartly, "to get rid of a pestilence like yerself."

Jon grinned in spite of his anger, and leaned against the doorjamb. "She takes good care of you, Eleanora, but are you sure she isn't dosing you to death?"

The seated woman lifted her face to him. She had been beautiful, once, but now care lined porcelain skin with deepening wrinkles, and silver streaked her lustrous brunette hair. "Even over this smell, I could catch your stench, Jonnard. Been rolling with the wolfjackals again?" Her voice, still low and pleasant, nevertheless held a stinging tone.

"Wolfjackals make excellent household pets. Perhaps I should send one or two up to bunk with you." His grin widened as FireAnn shrank back a little, in spite of herself. "How delightful to come and trade barbs with you. Too bad it will end someday. Not today, of course. Your men rode up to the gates, and looked, and left."

"Left?" Before he could see the expression on Elea-nora's face, FireAnn whisked the towel over her charge's head and shoved the basin under her nose, and the only response he could read to his word was that of a muffled sneeze from under the towel. But he could see the surprise on FireAnn's face before she turned away and continued fussing over Eleanora, the redhead's hands swollen and distorted with the painful symptoms of acute arthritis. Their time in Haven had not been kind to them, nor had he intended it to be.

Magick was not a renewable source, despite what they had been taught by Gregory. It did not flow in every be-ing or in every living thing about them. It could not be tapped or restored, unless from another Magicker, and that only with great difficulty. It came from one source, from within themselves and when they burned it out, that was it. It could be banked, like a smoldering fire, or stoked till the blaze reached the skies, but when all the timber was burned, it was nothing more than ashes, and these two women were part of a movement that squandered the pre-cious commodity that gave them superiority. He could not forgive them that.

If they but knew it, they would thank him for cutting off their use of their Magick now, saving it for the years to come. But of course, his mother's and his work on the fortress hadn't damped all magic use, not entirely. He could smell it here in these rooms. FireAnn, no doubt, using that part of her that came from her background in herbcraft and witchology, and healing. There was Magick in every move she made on behalf of her charge although very little now, yet some seeped in. She could help it no more than he could. He wondered if Eleanora even knew or, if know-ing, was grateful. He doubted it. She would believe, as she had been erroneously tutored by her father, that Magick renewed itself, like wind, air, water. . . .

Jon's face settled into a grimmer expression. He stee-pled his fingers, watching FireAnn carefully. She looked the Irish witch, with her fiery hair all in curls, captured but not tamed by the kerchief she always wore, and her dress with its over apron of many pockets. Even with her back now to him, he could see the stiffness in her posture, the sign of her hatred for him. He made no attempt to hide the disdain he felt for them either.

"Yes, left. No rescue being plotted today, I fear." He paused, after drawing his words out, then added, "Oh, forgive me. I did not mean to put a damper on the news."

"You meant exactly such a thing, you little shit," Eleanora muttered, her voice muffled by the towel about her head. "I hope to be around when someone wipes that smirk off your face."

"I hope you will be around. Alas, you seem to grow ever weaker, even with the tender care of FireAnn."

A loud, less muffled curse answered him. FireAnn removed the towel as she turned about, and both women stared at him with venomous hatred.

Jonnard returned their stares. "Don't blame me," he stated, "if your training has been erroneous these many years and now you suffer the consequences."

"Consequences?" Eleanora's mouth twisted as if she fought not to hiss the word at him. "Your mother is a parasite and those Leucators . . . those *parasitic constructs* . . . are what takes the life from me breath by breath and gives it to her."

He straightened, with a yawn. "Fun time is over. You would do well to remember you are here by Isabella's sufferance, and should be accordingly grateful."

"Grateful?" FireAnn spat on the wooden floor. "You sided with a viper, lad. Take care it doesn't bite you in the ass as well!"

Eleanora reached out a slender hand, trying to keep it from trembling, as she laid it on the other's arm. "FireAnn," she cautioned.

"Yes, FireAnn, you should listen." He started to turn away, but bitter words brought him abruptly about face again as FireAnn cried out, "Oh, yes, fine advice from the son who murdered his father for his mother's sake."

"You know little of us, I see, for all the time you've spent here." Jon drew his chin up. "My father was burned out, done, and he would rather have died than have lived a day without Magick coursing in his veins. I did him a kindness, like putting an old, crippled dog to sleep. He knew that, and she and I know that."

"I'm certain you tell yourself that on nights when you cannot sleep." Eleanora looked into his face, and held her gaze firm.

He smiled again, coldly. "I sleep quite well, thank you. Let us pray you do."

He slammed the huge door into place at his exit, using strength from outside his own body to do it, feeling the very timber shake at his touch as he dropped and then locked the bar down.

Fool! He'd let them get to him, after all.

Who would have guessed that there were days when he missed his father Brennard keenly? Who would have guessed?

Jon tossed the key in his pouch and tied it away again, and left the prison wing.

Gavan frowned at Bailey. "At this point, I doubt I need to say how dangerous that was."

"I was trying to keep up." Bailey shifted her weight from one foot to the other, patted her pony's neck, and tried to look contrite but didn't quite succeed. "It's not my fault you guys went off and left me."

His rainwater eyes darkened to a stormy blue, and his mouth opened to drop a scathing reply when Trent called out, "She's right—it wasn't her fault. Look here," and he traced a line along the hillside only he seemed to see. "This was laid here, and it's only Bailey's luck she's the one who was misled by it."

Gavan's mouth snapped shut. He traded a look with Jason, who said quietly, "What is it you see, Trent? We can't see it."

"Ah. Well," and he snapped his fingers. "It's like a fence, a low one. Probably the horse sensed it and just started trotting alongside it, not willing to cross it. It's not a real barrier, more like a ..." He frowned and drummed his hand on his thigh. "More like a nudge. It's fading now, even as we speak."

"So, someone would have been singled out, regardless, if they ran into it."

Renart shuddered. His hands went white-knuckled on his reins. Gavan thumped his shoulder. "Not meant for you, my friend. One of us."

"I've seen the wolfjackals," the young trader said tightly. "I didn't like it."

And he must not have, to be so blunt, Jason thought. He nodded. "It isn't a deadly trap, or it would have been."

Bailey tilted her head at him, and made a scoffing sound.

"Sure, you defended yourself, I'm not saying *that*. I'm saying, he probably wanted another captive, if anything. So you foiled that plan." Gavan regarded her. "But what did he say to you?"

She shrugged. She'd already recounted most of the conversation. "That I was blooming and made Eleanora look old. Something about being on my dance card."

Gavan frowned. Renart coughed and looked at the ground, studying something there he found fascinating. The boys stared at her. Then Jason said, "Well . . . he is right."

"Nah." Rich shook his head, and traded a glance at Stef. "You think?"

"It's Bailey," Stef protested loudly.

"Right. It's Bailey."

Jason watched her a moment longer before saying, "But Bailey has always been kinda . . ." He muttered something as he kicked his pony in the ribs and trotted off across the terrain.

"What did he say? What?" Bailey looked around.

No one answered. Then Renart gave a little bow and said, "I believe, little miss, he said beautiful. I could be mistaken, though."

Bailey tossed her head, ponytail flying, a pleased look on her face as she turned away.

Gavan twitched in his saddle. He looked over the horizon. "That settles that," he muttered.

"Settles what?"

"Everyone mount up. I'm going to knock on their door, rather hard, before we leave." Gavan swung his wolfhead cane out, and tucked it under one arm, like a lance or spear, as he put his heels to his horse's flanks and the beast galloped forward with a tiny squeal of eagerness.

"What are you doing?" Rich called out.

Gavan looked over his shoulder, his cloak flowing about him. "There are times when you have to let a snake know that you know it is a snake." He caught up with Jason and cried, "Follow me!"

"Oh, boy!" grunted Stefan, and thumped his sandals on his sturdy pony's sides. The horse grunted, too, before breaking into a spine-jolting trot after Gavan. One by one, they wheeled around to follow. They crested the hill in a line, ready to follow Gavan in whatever he planned, but he reined up hard and looked down, then pointed a hand across at Renart.

"Are we at the right spot?"

The trader had come chugging up the terrain last and reined to a weary halt, his face pale. He blinked at Gavan, unthinking for a moment, then looked down across the valley and shock dawned across his face.

"They're gone. It's . . . it's empty."

An evening wind had arisen, growing autumn cold as it swept over them, and down into the valley, where the broken ruins of an old wooden fort lay abandoned.

Gavan's jaw tightened, then he said slowly, "We saw it less than an hour ago. They couldn't have pulled out in an hour. Even with crystals. That would have been a massive operation, and we'd have *felt* it, if nothing else."

"They can't be gone."

Trent stood in the stirrups of his saddle, as if he could gain a sight the others couldn't, his gaze sweeping the valley. He said nothing.

"Don't bother," Gavan said harshly. "Your Talent is to see Magick where the rest of us cannot. Not to see what isn't there at all." He looked at Renart. "Are there other forts in the area? Any at all . . . within a week's ride, say?"

Renart thought hard, then nodded slowly. "At least two, I'd say. This is a boundary here, of the Warlord's old kingdom. There would be ruins of fortifications across its old borders. There was no need to keep the forts, because now we have the Holy Spirit to protect us."

Gavan ignored the last of Renart's information. He made a chopping gesture at the valley. "Then we saw a projection. A trap, far more elaborate than that set for Bailey. It's a good thing we didn't ride into it." Gavan pivoted his horse around. "They've grown strong. Far too strong." He put his horse into a slow canter, back the way they had come, as the sun showed signs of lowering toward evenfall.

Trent shook his head and caught Jason by the elbow as their horses jostled close. "It's *there*," he said quietly.

Jason looked back. "Think so?"

"I know so."

"But then . . . how . . . why?"

Trent shook his head. "He wouldn't believe me. Even you aren't quite sure. That's some Talent I have, isn't it?" He bit his last words off bitterly, shoved his boots into his stirrups, and rode off, leaving Jason alone for a moment on the hillside.

There or not . . . if Jonnard and the Dark Hand had accomplished anything, it was to make them all doubt themselves a bit. Jason frowned heavily before turning for home.

Sticks and Stones

AFTER AN APPEAL from both Rich and Stef when they turned in their mounts to the Avenha strongholding, Gavan let the boys Crystal on their own to Naria, the town where Stefan had found a weaponmaster. Gavan defended his decision by commenting, "Stef is more than a shapechanger, he's a berserker, and that energy has to go somewhere. Better he should use it in the training arena rather than pacing about us restlessly. He'll come home tired and bruised and happy, and Rich will keep him from trouble."

Trent's hand twitched, drumming thin air, but he merely shrugged. Bailey gave Renart a hug which made Lacey squeak indignantly from her bodice pocket and the laughter broke the tension a little. Jason rubbed the back of his neck in relief, not liking the unhappiness shadowing his friend's eyes.

Not to be believed . . . he knew how that felt. Or rather, not being able to walk in the truth of his own life. That was what he'd left. Trent still struggled with it. Admitting he had no Magick, that his crystal was dead and stayed dead . . . had been hard. But in that admission to everyone around him, Trent had also discovered he did have Talent. Just an obscure and difficult one to understand, let alone train. He could see what they did, or the trails, the remnants of it. He could see just what it was he lacked. A blessing and a curse, as he'd often told Jason.

Jason understood that well. He put his hand on Trent's shoulder, and gripped it, waiting for Gavan to draw the rest of their group together for Crystaling back to the academy grounds. It was dark, and late, and a chill wind had risen with a hint of fog to come later. This was a land of seasons, and discovery, and danger.

"What do you think Gavan meant by berserker?" Bailey asked, as the headmaster lingered for a moment to talk to the chieftain and his daughter, and Renart. Their hushed voices and turned backs shut out the younger Magickers, and she had joined the boys with a toss of her ponytail in protest.

"A berserker is a warrior." Trent shrugged. "He uses his anger to fuel his fighting, lets nothing get in his way. Old legends had them turning into bears and other large creatures. Maybe it wasn't legend."

"You think?"

"It's a possibility," Jason told her. "Maybe it only happened once or twice, but the witnesses remembered and related it, and hundreds of years later, we think of them as folktales. But now we have Stef. So maybe."

Bailey stroked Lacey's head thoughtfully, looking over the hill and caveside encampment of Avenha. Campfires dotted the area like smoldering orange eyes, and the smell of woodsmoke stung their noses. The actual city below lay shrouded in darkness, still abandoned for the moment. "I just can't . . . you know . . . I can't imagine Stefan killing anyone."

"None of us can, but it may come down to it. I don't think Jonnard is going to give up Eleanora for anything less."

"No. I guess not." She let out a soft sigh.

"Out of the frying pan, into the fire, huh?" Jason kidded her softly.

Bailey nibbled on the corner of her mouth before nodding slowly. "Sometimes it feels like it." She became very quiet as Gavan broke off talking, and moved to rejoin them. He linked them all together with his large hands, and murmured in a voice only Jason could hear, "Work with me," as he brought up his wolfhead cane, and the crystal in its jaws glowed. Jason added his Talent to Gavan's, and the crystal flared like a newly minted silver coin. A stomach-jolting swoop, and then they were home.

Bailey shook herself. Lacey let out a rattle of scolding clutters before diving nose first into her pocket and refusing to come back out, apparently upset by the teleportation.

Trent's stomach growled, as they all dusted themselves off. "Dinner," he said emphatically.

"Washing first, we all smell like horses." Gavan cuffed his charge lightly and sent them off to the primitive wash stands built by the waterfall off the Iron Mountain. The cold water may have made them smell better, but they all stood shivering as they regrouped to make their way to the kitchens.

Warmth and light from the rooms flooded over them, however, along with the rich aroma of stew and freshly baked bread. Ting and Bailey's mother Rebecca busily set steaming bowls on the table while Ting's grandmother sat with her snapping dark eyes, and watched all of them. She had brewed tea and the kettle sat in front of her, with its row of cups; she would serve them once they all sat.

So dinner went, as it had been going for months, familiar and yet different, and Trent ate as if famished, and made a sandwich out of thick bread slices with stew ladled between them, to take back to his room for "later on." No one said anything, but Jason grinned. The only one in the group who could outeat Trent was working off his bearlike aggressions elsewhere that night.

And the difference between the two was that one could see Stefan bulking up over the months, but Trent stayed wiry thin as always. After dinner, the boys cleaned while Ting and Bailey dashed upstairs "to talk" and Rebecca and Madame Qi went out to the lecture hall to talk and work on darning clothes at their leisure.

Gavan disappeared to find Tomaz; the other hadn't shown up for dinner, but they could all feel his presence about, and that left Trent and Jason elbow-to-elbow at the great tubs for cleaning up.

"Did you mean what you said?"

Trent looked at him. He thought for a moment, then twitched one shoulder. "Sometimes I do, sometimes I don't. I mean, how do you handle the pressure of being a Gate-keeper? Hard as you study, you can't turn that on and off, right?"

"True. But that's not the point. It's that you thought Ga-van wouldn't listen to you. That he wouldn't think you told the truth."

"He wouldn't have. And maybe he's right . . ." Trent paused, scrubbing bag in hand, elbow-deep in the foam-ing tub. "Maybe it was an illusionary trap, laid by the Dark Hand. But I don't think so. What we saw was there, and it's still there, only he can't sense it. And you can't. And no one else could but me. And I've got no Talent, virtually, so, how can I be right?"

"But if you are, you are," answered Jason flatly.

"It's that black and white? Look, Jason. Nothing in life is that black and white. Nothing."

"Some things are. I trust you."

"But if I were wrong a lot, you wouldn't. I might have been wrong about the old fort, but I don't think so." Trent rubbed at his nose, leaving a soap bubble on it. It left a glis-tening spot as it popped.

"We should go back, then."

"After what happened to Bailey, I don't think so. Not just the two of us."

Jason finished up his stack of crockery and slid it care-fully into the rinsing tub. "You need to talk to Gavan."

"You think so?"

He nodded. "Don't you think so?"

"I suppose you're right." Trent slowly finished his own stack of crockery, before adding, "I think I'll talk to Ma-dame Qi first."

Jason smiled a little. Ting's grandmother had a kind of no-nonsense philosophy that was welcome to them all, which she sometimes thumped into place with her bamboo cane, and sometimes slipped into their heads with just a wink of her dark eyes. Either way, Qi was old and very, very learned, and her strain of Magick went deep in her blood, although she was untrained by Magicker standards. "Good idea." If anyone could get past Trent's wariness, she could.

They raced each other then, through the last of the

kitchen cleanup before tumbling outside to check the perimeter wards and stargaze and see if they could find Tomaz before bedtime. They were successful in all.

Ting pulled Bailey into their room quickly and shut the door before hugging her so hard that Lacey had no choice but to climb out of her pocket with a squeak and clamber onto Bailey's shoulder as if in fear of being crushed.

"I thought you weren't coming back!" Ting paused as the words tumbled out of her and she stood breathless for a moment. "I felt your touch, a tug and then . . . oh, Bailey. All my crystals went dark!"

"What?" Bailey blinked at her in astonishment.

"Every one of them. I couldn't find you. I knew you were trying to get back somehow. I went frantic. And Grandmother couldn't help and I was afraid to let anyone else know. My crystals!" Ting flung her slender hands in the air, where they made movements like lost, startled birds.

"But . . . but . . ."

"No, wait, that's not all. I heard the wolfjackals howling." Ting sat down then, gazing up at Bailey, her eyes intent. "I knew they weren't around here. I was so frightened for you. I knew you were trapped, Bailey! What happened? Tell me everything!"

Bailey sat down. She pried Lacey off her shoulder, and put her down where the tiny pack rat scampered across the wooden flooring, looking for interesting and sparkling bits of treasure. Distracted, both girls watched as the clever creature found something and skittered into the corner, climbed into her cage, and stowed it away.

"So that's where my barrette went," muttered Ting. "Such a troublemaker."

"I'll fetch it out later," Bailey promised. She sat back, clasping her arms about her knees as she folded her legs under her on the cot. "We Crystaled to Avenha. The whole city is in retreat, up in the hills and caves behind it. I guess years ago, they wintered there during really hard times or attack or something. Renart got us horses and we rode out to an old fortress where they said the raiders camped."

"Was it the Dark Hand?"

"Oh, yes. As if there were any doubt." Bailey let out a tiny snort. "A long ride, though. I think my legs are going to fall off by tomorrow morning. Something odd about the fort, but I'll tell you that later. Gavan looked it over, and then turned around. We thought we were going to, well ... I dunno ... attack or something, but he didn't."

"He can't."

"Still. We rode all the way out there."

"Maybe he was hoping to get a trace of Eleanora."

"Maybe. He should have. We were close enough, but I don't know." Bailey frowned, trying to remember. "If he did, he didn't show a sign of it. We turned back then, noting to Renart that we couldn't do anything now, but that we *would*. I think he understood that. And I got lost heading back."

"Lost! Oh, no."

Bailey nodded at Ting. "That's when the wolfjackals hit. They galloped over the low hills and surrounded me. It's like I couldn't decide what to do first, and I tried to do it all at once, Shield, reach you, Crystal back, Beacon Gavan and Jason—and only the shield held. Everything else I couldn't do. I know I get flustered sometimes, but ... it was scary, Ting. Really, really scary."

"I know," said Ting quietly. She reached her hand out and grasped Bailey's wrist. "I was so frightened."

"They circled closer and closer. My little horse kicked one of 'em to pieces. I didn't know how much longer I could hold out, and then he showed up."

"Gavan? Jason?"

Bailey shook her head, ponytail bobbing vigorously. "Jonnard!"

"No!" Ting's eyes widened. "That snake!"

"He laughed at me. I don't know how I managed, I kept the Shield up and finally, someone felt the energy, and I could hear the hoofbeats pounding over the hill. He could, too, so he talked some trash and then rode off as fast as he could."

"Wow."

"Then Gavan got mad. So we went back to the fort. I don't know what he was going to do, but he was going to do something ... and the fort wasn't there! Not a sign of it. Just old ruins. Before, it had buildings and wagons and we could see the raiders training, working. Now, nothing. As though it had all been a bad dream."

"That couldn't be."

"No, it couldn't." Bailey leaned back and stretched her tired legs gingerly. "Gavan said it had been a trap, some kind of illusion, he thought. I don't know. If that's true, then they're strong. Very, very strong." She shook herself, as if shaking off an unspoken thought. "Jason and Trent were muttering at each other the whole time, so something is going on. I just don't know what."

"Bailey," said Ting softly. "My crystals finally started coming back, but it took hours. And I'm thinking ... I'm thinking that the power here is very strange. I think we get depleted easier and recover a lot slower. Maybe don't recover at all, if we're not careful."

"You think so?"

"I think when you reached out for me, you drew on me. I know I felt this surge, and then everything went dark. I don't think you meant to, but if you hadn't, you might not have kept that Shield up. And it could explain a lot of things."

"Such as?"

Ting flipped her long dark hair over her shoulders. "Why the building is taking so long. They're pacing themselves. They can feel the power drain, too, but they're not telling us that. You know they don't tell us a lot of stuff."

"True. But this is serious, then!"

"Very serious. The internal structure of this whole academy is laced with Magick, for one reason or another. To protect against fire and rot, and to ward against other Magicks. It has to be difficult to do, and they're going slowly because they have no choice."

"Then Eleanora's time could be ... running out."

Ting nodded, and both girls fell silent.

After a long moment, Bailey said, "Well. This makes it a whole new ball game, doesn't it?"

"What do you mean?"

"If we're weaker, they're weaker. And if they're not, then we need to find out why. You and I, my girl, have some experiments to run. When we have some more answers, then we can tell Gavan and Tomaz what we've discovered. I think you're right. We don't have much time!"

12

Wind Beneath My Wings

JASON WOKE WITH THE certainty that something was wrong. He rolled over in his cot, smothering a groan from sore muscles that had been used to ride a barrel-bellied short horse all day, and put his face back in his pillow. In a way, he welcomed the soreness. He used to ache all over after a bruising soccer game, and it was a way of reminding him he'd done something fun and great at the same time. He'd have to get the Havenites together in soccer teams as soon as he could figure out how to make good balls. The rest of the game would be fairly easy to re-create, and he thought they'd take to it. Maybe even the wanderers could put together a team to compete as they went from town to town, gaining acceptance on a level no one could predict or prevent. Athletics had a way of bringing people together.

But those thoughts didn't smooth down the hairs on the back of his neck. Jason peeked to the side and saw, in the early morning darkness, Trent sitting bolt upright on his cot, eyes squeezed tightly shut, his body gyrating and jerking as he performed what Jason could only call "air drums," his hands and arms beating out rhythms on an unseen drum and cymbal set. His head bobbed in time to a hard rocking beat that Jason could all but hear himself as he watched. Jason sat up slowly to face his friend, who seemed to have no idea of time or place, so lost was he in his song. Trent's mute musical performance grew in fervor until suddenly he stopped, drained, and just sat, his hands on his knees, breathing as hard as if he'd been on stage for a driving drum solo.

His eyes opened slowly to find Jason watching him.

"I'd ask what that was," Jason told him, "but I think I know."

Trent lifted his chin. "Sometimes you feel like you've gotta do something."

"And sometimes it feels like you can't do anything right."

Trent shrugged then. "Look, I can't blame Gavan or Tomaz or any of them. I faked all of you guys out for a long time. So who says I'm not faking now?" He fetched his crystal out, his opaque, dead-looking crystal. "They should have known it when I picked this one out. Everyone else's is transparent, or nearly so. You can't focus your energy into something you can't see into." He tucked it away. "We might as well both be useless."

That time at summer camp near the still blue waters of Lake Wannameecha, when they'd been called to pic- nic tables, their tops covered with trays of glittering gems and crystals, and told to pick a crystal, seemed incredibly long ago, although it had only been a few years. His life had changed immeasurably since that time, as had Trent's. Jason pointed at his friend.

"I think the whole point is that you see differently than we do. That crystal was on the table with all the others because, like all the others, it had something. It offered a conduit the elders could sense, even if they couldn't un- derstand it. Our crystals are chosen just like we are, even if they never find a user to bond to. They're just gems, after all. Even if most of us can't see or feel what you do, we can tell your Talent is there, and growing. Yesterday was a fluke. Gavan wasn't thinking about you or any of us. He was try- ing to find Eleanora and couldn't."

"So in a stable of racehorses, even a pack mule has value?"

"I didn't say that! And you're no mule, even if you're as backassward as one, sometimes."

Trent gestured through the air before dropping his hand back on his leg, and beginning to tap out the unheard rhythm again. "Look, I appreciate the effort. I do, really. But you're not me, and you wouldn't understand. I know you're trying, but you're not me."

"That's right. I'm not. I know that I couldn't be myself without you around. Look at you. Really look. You kept almost everyone fooled for months about your Talent. You're so damn smart, none of us knew any different, and if we wanted to know anything, if we didn't understand anything about the myths and power behind magic and all the new stuff we were learning, there you were with an answer. How much cooler is that?"

"Almost anyone," Trent said somberly, "is better off than I am. Look at you."

"You want to know the worst part about being me?" Jason said suddenly.

"Worst part? How can there be a worst part? You're the golden Magicker, Jason. You're the Gatekeeper." Trent looked at him sideways, then swung around to face him, his fingers still moving in a drumbeat on his leg to the music only he could hear.

Jason shrugged. "It's only good because no one else is, right now, but no one can show me what to do either. Yet that's not it. I don't mean being a Magicker, I mean being *me.*"

Something flickered in Trent's eyes. "You mean, like being an orphan?"

"Yeah, like that."

"It never seems to worry you. Look at your stepparents. Joanna is great, and McIntire is way cool. They let you come here, they made things easy."

"But they're like that to anybody, Trent. The dirtiest, mangiest stray cat could wander in, and they'd clean it up, and bathe it, and feed it royally, and then find the best home in the world for it . . . and it's like . . . it's like I was never any different to them."

"You can't mean that! Of course you're different."

Jason shook his head. "Maybe, but I never felt it. I can't say it, exactly. Joanna never talks about my dad, you know? It's almost as if he never existed, or she never wants to say anything imperfect about him. So I don't know what he was, and I'm forgetting what I knew. I'm forgetting my dad. My mom was already forgotten, except in a dream now and then." He looked away for a moment, and swallowed hard. "So I'm growing up, and I feel like I'm never quite part of anything, you know? But I get along, and it could be a lot worse. They treated me well. I didn't have to live in a cupboard under the stairs or anything—but I never know quite who I'm supposed to be. Suddenly, I find out I have a temper—"

"You? A temper?" Trent wrinkled his nose in disbelief.

"I am being serious here. I wake up at night, with my fists clenched, and I'm so mad I'm just sweating it out, and my teeth hurt 'cause I'm biting down so hard on it. That angry."

"Wow." Trent shifted. "Is it at me or something?"

Jason shook his head. "It's at myself. Maybe someone else sometimes, but it's like finding out you have a volcano inside of you. I feel like I'm going to explode with all this anger and I can't go to Joanna and say, did my dad have a temper? And if he did, what did he do about it? Did he go walk it out or did he sit in front of the TV set for hours and punch the remote, or did he yell and scream at someone? 'Cause she would never tell me. She has this code about making sure I have this perfect impression about my dad, and all it does is make him a nonperson, like he never existed. But he did, and it's the warts I need to know about, it's the . . . the wrinkles that make him real!"

"Did you ever tell her that?"

"I tried. Once. It was right after I overheard something." Jason paused. He scratched the corner of his eye. "McIntire had said something I wasn't meant to hear. Something that made it sound as if my dad had been drinking the night of the car crash. That maybe, once in a while, he did that. I tried to ask her. She wouldn't say a word about what McIntire had spilled, just told me, 'Jason, don't worry about anything, you'll be fine.' But I'm not. I want to know. At the same time, I don't dare be less than perfect either. How would she deal with me then? How badly would I disappoint her? Would she look at me and compare me with this loser she never talked to me about? I felt like I couldn't breathe sometimes."

"Jeez." Trent let his breath out slowly. "I think she just

wanted to make things smoother for you. Losing your mom so young, and then your dad, too, I think she is always worried about how hard it is for you."

Jason nodded slowly. "Like the stray that doesn't have a family, or not a real one, anyway."

"Cut that out! We're your family!" Trent's expression blazed.

The corner of Jason's mouth twitched. "Exactly. So when I say to you, don't take it so badly, you know what I mean."

Trent blinked slowly, then a smile crept over his face. "Did you walk me into that?"

"Like Bailey into a wall." Jason nodded again, firmly. He stood up. "Anyway, you're coming with me."

"Where?"

"Somewhere," Jason said firmly, "you've never been before."

He left a note for Gavan about missing the morning of the workday, that he and Trent had work to do. Then they grabbed some food from the kitchen pantry before the sun had begun to crack open the sky, and Jason took Trent climbing up one of the easier slopes of the Iron Mountains. They scaled it slowly at first, muscles awakening and stretching, and then warming even as the sun warmed their backs as it dispersed the clouds of night. They emerged on a wide, flat plateau.

Trent cast his gaze about.

"Looks like a plane could land here."

"That's about the size of it." Jason stepped back, took a deep breath, and opened his mind, sending out an appeal he was not even positive would be answered. He was not sure what would happen.

A cloud drifted through the brilliantly blue sky, a sky that looked as if it had been washed clean just for today's appearance, and the sun dimmed for a moment. Before he could look around, sound rushed at him, and a keening shriek not unlike that of an eagle, only this came from a fire-rimmed throat coated in shimmering orange-red scales that looked as if they had just been pulled from a heated forge.

The dragon circled lazily once or twice before diving

sharply and swooping down on them. Trent stood absolutely still as though not wanting to attract anything by movement. He'd seen the dragon a few times, but there was no way anyone could be nonchalant about its appearance, awesome and demanding. The dragon curled his talons under him, taking on the appearance of a rather large cat, and looked down with huge lanternlike eyes.

"Greetings, young Magickers. Note that I said Magickers and not appetizers." The dragon rumbled at himself in amusement.

"Always nice to hear," Jason responded. He took a few steps and leaned in, and scratched the scales just under the curve of the reptile's jaw, being careful not to ruffle the edges. Not only could he hurt the dragon, but the edges were sharp enough to slice through his fingertips, quite painfully. "I never ask, but I must today. Trent and I have some scouting to do and I wondered if you'd take us."

"Two hearty lads on my back?" The dragon managed to raise a ridge of scales over one eye, much like an eyebrow. His long, spiny whiskers quivered as well, but he did not sound insulted.

"If you would allow it."

"What sort of scouting?" Both spoke at once, Trent's higher voice underscored by the low rumbling of the dragon.

"Anywhere you want to take us." He had hopes, of course, where he wanted to go but knew if the dragon agreed to carry them anywhere, it would be where the dragon wanted to go. And, truthfully, flying anywhere on dragonback would be glorious.

"Get on and hold tightly then. Have a soft belt, do you?" The dragon tilted his triangular face curiously at Jason.

"Two," answered Jason softly, pulling them from the inside of his vest. He kept one on him at all times and had stuffed the second one in before hauling Trent out the academy doors. He looped them about the dragon's neck and mounted quickly, then put an arm out to help Trent up. "Mind the scale edges. They're sharp and if you dislodge them, he gets sore. Use the belt to hold onto, and watch me."

Trent took a deep breath before grabbing Jason's forearm and leaping up. He settled behind Jason and secured himself within the looping belt, leaning over once or twice to see how Jason did it.

"Everyone set?"

Jason could feel the dragon's voice rumbling throughout his body, vibrating against his calves. "Looks like it."

"Good, good! A fine, brisk day for flying!" The last roared out as the dragon broke into a run and launched himself with a bellow off the edge of the plateau into the bright blue sky. For a dizzying moment, it felt as if the whole world fell away from under them. Trent gasped in Jason's ear, echoing Jason's moment of stomach-dropping sensation. Then the dragon's wings beat strongly, one, twice, thrice, and they caught a current stream and soared along it, climbing slowly but steadily.

They banked, and below them could see the small dale where the academy and the Dragon Gate lay, and the small encampment. Trent pointed as they wheeled over it, the dragon's body heat warming them from the inside out, it seemed, even as the cool morning air whipped past them.

Trent let out a yip of sheer joy as they skimmed the Iron Mountains, and the small corner of Haven that they knew fell away. Even Jason had never seen this part from dragon-back, as the dragon generally kept to the valley and dale of their refuge. But it seemed as if the dragon knew his mind today, his wings dipping into the air and pushing them farther and farther over the unknown. Indigo and silver rivers crossed below them like lacy ribbons. Dark green forests looked impenetrable. Small roads cut across the terrain in determined manner, linking one small patch of community to another, marked by their quiltlike squares of fields and groves with a town square in the center. Trent bumped Jason's shoulder with his chin.

"Look at that," he said, his voice snatched out of his mouth, the words whipping away almost before Jason could hear them. Trent pointed. "See the Magick. I can. It follows that edge of the area. It's as if it were a river of its own."

"You'd see more on the ground, though, right?"

"Sure. Like energy lines. But that. That's one massive band of power, for me to see it up here!"

Jason tried to note its position and wondered if it had anything to do with the old Warlord's spirit presence and the forts that had made up his border, but he couldn't see well enough to know if there were more ruins about or not. The dragon seemed to be carrying them high enough to remain unnoticed, even if their noses and ears and fingers felt like they might freeze off!

"Hold on!" the dragon commanded.

Jason laced his numbing hands deeper into the woven belt. Trent did the same, his body stiffening behind Jason in apprehension.

With a defiant bellow, the dragon did a wheel and roll, and came across an immense lake, his belly barely clearing the surface even as Jason let out a dizzy groan and Trent a whoop of excitement.

"Did you feel that? Out of nowhere, from the clouds to the water!"

The dragon extended a taloned paw, slicing through the water, and coming up with a handful of large, wiggling fish. He swallowed his meal in one gulp and belched contentedly, before turning about on a wing tip and launching himself skyward again.

It felt like riding a rocket. Up, up, up, straining, straining, straining, till he thought his eyes might pop out, and then the beast leveled off again, and a loud vibration thrummed through their bodies. The dragon, it seemed, was humming in contentment.

"Sushi does a body good," Trent laughed in his ear.

Jason grinned at that, then, his stomach settling down from the loop-the-loops. Trent had more of a Talent for dragon riding than he did! Or at least, the stomach.

They slowly circled back toward the Iron Mountains and although the ride seemed too short, Jason found himself shivering, the only warm parts of him wherever he was in contact with the dragon's body. When they landed, both boys slid off and leaned against the beast for a moment, shaking and laughing and grinning.

The dragon tented his wing about them. "Enjoy that, did you?"

"That was great! That was ... incredible!" Trent's nose was bright red with the cold, and joy sparkled in his eyes.

"Thank you," Jason managed. He quickly untied the soft belts from the dragon's neck and stowed them away inside his shirt and vest, then ran his hands over the creature, careful to ensure that he had not damaged the scales or leathery skin in any way. The dragon purred a moment as Jason stroked and massaged him.

Then he cocked an eye at Trent. "Seeing power?"

"I was, yes."

"Do you look for it?"

"Ummm." Trent thought about it. "I guess not. It's either there, or it isn't, right?"

"Not always," the dragon said, his voice booming deep in his chest. "But it is best not to search for the hidden powers. They are that way for a reason, and many are unpleasant to deal with. You see the brightest, and that is best for you, I think."

"I'll take that as a positive, then." Trent hugged himself a moment, and the momentary hesitation caused by the dragon's words fled his expression, replaced by exuberance. "Man, that was great!"

"Good. You can stay up here all day and talk about it, but me . . . I think I'm going back down where it's warm, even if I have to work for it!"

Trent grinned at him. He found the trail they'd hiked up and disappeared over the edge. Jason ducked out from under dragon wing to follow, but found himself stopped by one obsidian claw.

"Watch him," the dragon said. "He sees too much and knows too little."

Jason bit his lip, then nodded. "Okay. I'll remember that."

The dragon inclined his head. "And next time, bring warmer clothing." He laughed, his hot breath washing over Jason, as he drew his foot back, freeing the Gatekeeper.

"You'd better believe it!" Jason threw one arm about the dragon's snout, hugging him, and then he hurried to catch up with Trent.

If there was still a hot breakfast waiting down below, he wanted to be sure he got his share.

13

Button, Button

BAILEY PLUCKED Lacey out of her pocket, rubbing her thumb over the sleepy rodent's head. If Lacey could have snored, she would have, as the pack rat's eyelids reluctantly fluttered open. "Time to work," she crooned softly. Lacey nicked her tufted tail, catlike, as if answering and then gave a half chirp.

"Must be hard on her," Ting offered, leaning over to pet the small creature herself. "She's nocturnal by nature, but we keep her up all day."

"Don't fool yourself! She does a lot of sleeping in my pocket." Bailey flashed a grin. "Besides, keeping her awake during the day means *we* sleep better at night. She does a lot of rattling around otherwise."

Ting wrinkled her nose. That was too true. Because the pack rat was more than a pet, Bailey kept her close, but the tiny rodent's nighttime habits of rambling, searching, nesting, bug hunting and so forth made sleeping really difficult for others. She gave Lacey one last head rub between Bailey's fingers and said, "Put her to work, then! I need my sleep." She leaned over and picked up a small basket of glowing crystals, each one imbued with energy that Gavan

370

Rainwater and others had flooded into it, each one able to do a variety of small enchantments. Some of them she could read easily if she tried, others were too intricate and powerful for her to decipher. Ting would like nothing better than to sit down and sort through the tiny gems, pondering each of them and its inner mysteries, but she knew that would be frowned upon. If the elder Magickers had wanted her to know, they'd have told her. Still . . . she ran her fingers through the basket's contents, letting the crystals rain through her slender touch. She trailed after Bailey as they climbed into the inner workings of the unfinished academy wing.

Their footsteps echoed in the hollow rooms of the building. Bailey knelt down, placing Lacey on the floor. She held her hand out to Ting, who gave her a crystal. "White ones in the ceiling ducts," she repeated, although they'd been doing this for days.

"Right." Bailey handed the small crystal to the pack rat who took it eagerly with a chitter and promptly stuffed it in a cheek pouch, then sat and cleaned her whiskers as if she hadn't a hidden treasure on her. She fed her several more before sitting cross-legged on the floor, closing her eyes, and reaching for Lacey's thoughts.

Whiskers. Dirty and dusty, must groom. Lacey sat, combing her paw through her long, silky whiskers with pride. Beautiful whiskers, and useful, too! Bailey gave the creature's thoughts in her head a little nudge. Treasures must be placed on rafters and in ventilation ducts, in nooks and crannies all over and then *left* there, unnested. Lacey flipped her tail in irritation at such unpack ratlike behavior. Gathered, yes, and put away for safety!

Bailey nudged her thoughts again. "No cookies," she muttered aloud and Ting muffled a giggle at that. Bailey opened one eye to stare at Ting. "She's being stubborn."

"Imagine that." Ting hid her grin behind one slender hand.

Bailey shut her eyes again. Tomaz wouldn't approve of this way to work with the beast, but she found it easier. When Lacey moved, she dashed and hopped around so quickly, that Bailey got motion-sick trying to look through two pairs of eyes. This way, she could concentrate on the pack rat's movements without feeling like she was going to

hurl doing it. That, of course, made her less in charge but
more in tune with the animal. Sometimes she wondered if
Tomaz Crowfeather knew what he asked of her, but then
remembered him with all his crows and ravens about him,
and knew he knew exactly what he was trying to teach and
ask of her. He could brush thoughts with almost any animal, if he tried. She wondered if her Talent would someday
be as great as his. She shivered at the thought. There were
many animals she had no desire to share with! Starting with
wolfjackals and working her way down to cockroaches!

Lacey dashed off with a squeak. The thought of cockroaches had pushed her into action. As much as they made
Bailey shudder, they made Lacey hungry. Crunchy and good
to eat. Not as good as cookies (what was?), but almost. This
building had a disturbing lack of such good things to nibble
on, although crickets could be found now and then. It was
not the season for crickets as evenings got cold, but they
would be back in the spring. Lacey scrambled up beams
and dove nose first into the heating ducts. She found a good
niche for the crystal in her cheek, took it out and placed it.
Sniffing for insect goodies and not finding them, she dashed
deeper and deeper into the ducts, placing crystals whenever Bailey poked at her to do so, until her cheek pouches
had emptied. Luckily, she found a lazy, sleepy cricket and
munched it down before scrambling out of the ducts and
returning to Bailey's outstretched hand.

Bailey had just pinched off a piece of oatmeal cookie,
more health food than cookie, but the pack rat didn't care.
Bailey opened her eyes as the whiskery face nuzzled all
her fingers thoroughly, mopping up every possible bit of
crumb.

Ting ran her hand through the basket again. Not many
crystals remained for placement. "I could do this," she said,
voicing her thoughts aloud.

"All of them?"

"Well, not all, but most! And I can tell that Gavan has
enchanted some of these a couple of times, as if he didn't
get them strong enough the first time."

"Why?"

Ting shrugged. "No idea. Unless he's just doing too
much. Which is why I said, I could do this. We can help, you
know, more than they let us."

Bailey looked about. "We have been helping! We've built almost this entire academy." She stood, dusting her fingers off on her breeches. "I want to know where the secret passages are."

"Secret passages?"

"Sure! Don't you think they're in here? I'm willing to bet they are. For escaping and hiding."

"They built them when we weren't looking?"

"Something like that." Bailey made a soft fist and tapped experimentally on a wall, listening. She moved a few paces down and tapped again.

Ting watched her for long moments, then said, "Well, far be it from me to suggest that if I had a creature who could wiggle inside almost any passageway to look ..."

Bailey shot her a glance. "Use Lacey?"

Ting shrugged.

"She knows the inner ways well enough, but she's not smart enough to know if it's a regular passage or a secret one, you know?"

"But you are."

"Of course! Now, give me some more crystals and let's move a room over."

Ting picked up her basket with a soft laugh, and shadowed Bailey to the next lecture hall.

Bailey waited for Lacey to fill her cheek pouches with a few crystals, then put her down and directed her scampering off. She sat down cross-legged again, shoulder to shoulder with Ting, feeling her senses reel again as Lacey ran across flooring, ducked into an opening, and then scaled the inner walls to the ventilation passageways. A darkness covered her eyesight for a moment, then cleared as Lacey's own acute sight adjusted, although it was the sense of smell which enveloped her. The wood had keen smells to it, and the nails another, and the bracketing and fixtures another. She could see how animals saw the world in a kaleidoscope of patterns that humans did not. It used to muddle her terribly when she first felt Lacey's thoughts, but now she knew how to both embrace and filter it. Of course, there was a part of her that vigorously rejected the idea of hunting down crunchy crickets, or rolling along colorful balls of lint if found for a wonderful pocket of nesting material in a corner, or any number of things that flitted through the pack rat's small mind.

It took most of her concentration to keep Lacey moving and placing the crystals where the diagrams she and Ting studied indicated they should be. One, two, three crystals from Lacey's cheek pouches, laid in a mitred crevice or put atop a beam, from which the rodent jumped and swung about like an acrobat.

Then Lacey took out the last crystal. A stray bit of light hit it from a crack through the joints, and the gem piece dazzled in her paw. Bailey felt the flash of emotion in the beast. Pretty!

And Lacey was off, dashing away through the vents and along the beams, crystal in her mouth and hoarding in her thoughts. Nudging her back to her job lost its possibility. The rodent flung herself into headlong flight and disobedience.

Bailey leaped to her feet. "She's off!" she cried to Ting.

"What?"

"She's stolen the crystal. I've lost her completely." Bailey pulled Ting to her feet. "You go that way. I'll go this!" And she dashed off as well. Ting picked up her basket before running in the other direction, not a clue in her head as how to find one tiny pack rat in one huge, rambling, unfinished building.

Bailey ran till she was out of breath, upstairs and down, and skidded to a halt, her heart thumping in her chest. This was ridiculous! And most of the panting and excitement she felt came from Lacey, through the barest of connections, as the little furball tried to run and hide.

"Poor thing," Bailey muttered to herself. "She knows she's been bad, but she can't help it!" She stood for a moment. If she were a pack rat, where would she go?

Button, button, who's got the button? Bailey turned in a slow circle. She could almost hear Lacey panting. She'd run in the same direction, however wildly it seemed she'd been going.

She had to be somewhere about, and close. Maybe … Bailey slid her palm along the wall in front of her, looking for a crack or unfastened panel. Somewhere about here …

The wall clicked.

Bailey blinked as it suddenly swung open into darkness in front of her, and at the same time, something swung into the back of her, knocking her through!

She went headlong into nothingness, and the wall solidly thudded into place behind her.

"I think," said Bailey quietly, standing very still, "I found that secret passage."

And worse, as she strained her magickal senses, it was blacked out, warded, against any kind of magic whatsoever.

She was trapped, with no way for anyone to hear her!

14

Chutes and Ladders

BAILEY DISAPPEARED from Ting's thoughts as abruptly as a door slamming shut. She skidded to a halt in a corridor, putting her hand to the wall, and listening. She wondered for a moment if it was her, if she'd suddenly gone deaf or something, because everything about her seemed to stop as well. Then she realized. No Bailey. No best friend of her life. Even when Bailey wasn't cheerfully chattering about something, she put out this vibration, this lively electricity that let Ting know she was awake and about somewhere. Now a void stretched across Ting's life. She hadn't felt anything like it since . . . well, since the last time Bailey had disappeared! Then, new to crystals and focusing, Bailey had projected herself inside her amethyst and it had taken days and days for them to find her, because she'd managed to toggle time itself, as well. Leave it to Bailey to get lost in a way no one else could!

And then there was now. Ting rubbed her arms which suddenly danced with goose bumps. "Bailey?" she called softly, even though they had run in opposite directions. In the new empty corridor, even her quiet call echoed a little.

If not Bailey, then, what about Lacey?

She hadn't the Talent Bailey had, for sure, but she knew Lacey almost as well! Ting wrapped slender fingers about the crystal cage on her bracelet and sent her thoughts casting about for the stubborn, fleeing little furball. She felt nothing at first and concentrated harder. Something feathered against her thoughts before rushing off. Lacey! Ting went after that brushing presence before losing it entirely.

Whatever rabbit hole Bailey had fallen down, Lacey hadn't. That much, she knew.

Ting sighed. What should she do now? Get Gavan? Hope that Bailey would get unlost any moment? She leaned against the wall, trying to think. How serious could this be? Did she just lose track of Bailey or was Bailey really and truly *lost* somewhere and somewhen again? And . . . could it have anything to do with Jonnard?

This last worry sent cold chills through her, making the goose bumps dance even harder, and Ting shivered all through her slender form. She had better find Gavan, and now. Grasping her crystal to find her direction within the walls of the academy, she set her focus on the headmaster, and let her crystal lead the way.

Bailey caught her lower lip in her teeth and tried to think, for a moment, where she could possibly be. That gave her pause, for—d'oh—where else could she be? Trouble was, as nobody knew better than she did, she could be almost *anywhere*.

In the blanketing darkness, her eyes slowly adjusted, and she reached out for thoughts of Ting or her naughty little Lacey and found . . . nothing. It was as if nothing existed but herself and this space beyond the revolving wall. Surely, if she ducked her head and took a step or two, she'd run into the Three Stooges or *Dumb and Dumber* or *someone* as stupid as she was!

"No, no," she said to herself, happy to hear her voice if nothing else. "Think of it as charmed, not stupid. Serendipity! Look what I fell into, Watson." Bailey took another deep, steadying breath. She slipped one foot ahead cautiously, almost swearing she could feel a slant in the floor, stepping ahead slowly in case everything should drop out from under her. Nowhere in her thoughts could she sense Lacey in her frenzy to hide the sparkly she'd stolen, or even

Ting, who was usually buzzing about somewhere close to Bailey's mind, even when they were separated by great distances.

This did not bode well.

"All's well that bodes well?" Bailey muttered to herself, as she inched cautiously through the dark room. She raised her voice a bit. "Hello? Ting? Anyone here?"

Her voice sounded dead and muffled. Bailey brushed her fingers across her crystal and tried to awaken it, but something took the Magick out of the very air, and nothing happened. It couldn't be, but it was. She cupped her amethyst tightly. It still warmed to her and yet not a thought, not a bit of Magick could she send through or take from it. She was well and truly lost, and trapped, by everything she could tell.

"Okay." Bailey inhaled slowly. "What goes up, must come down . . ." If the wall had swung in, there must be a way to get it to swing back out. All she had to do was find the tripping mechanism. That meant she had to find the wall and search every splinter of it. Moving as cautiously and slowly across the floor as if she wore ice skates on a skating rink, Bailey slid and glided back to a wall. She ran her palms over it. Smooth, polished paneling, with no end and no beginning. She thought another moment.

Kicking off one boot, she pushed it up against the base, to mark where she began her search, for as her eyes got used to the near total darkness, she could see a little but not much more, and the wall looked endless. She didn't want to be searching the same area over and over. And as for places taller than she could reach . . . Bailey tilted her head back and looked up the wall at the shadowed ceiling . . . she'd have to hope that whoever wanted to get out hadn't put the levers out of reach!

She knocked, thumped, and rubbed every inch of wall she could touch from her outstretched arms down to the tip of her toes . . . one booted, one in a sock, down the room she inched. A snail would have made faster progress, she told herself, but then, would a snail have gotten itself into this predicament? She didn't think so!

Down the long, dim corridor she went without success until she found herself in a corner. She moved across the end panel to the other wall and thought of marking it with the second boot, then thought again. After all, it was a corner! How many corners could there be in this room? She started off again, swearing that her fingertips were beginning to get blisters as she stroked and poked every square inch of the very odd room. Then, just when she had decided to give up and take a nap, she found something. A small inlay of wood that wiggled a bit.

"Eureka!" Bailey readied to do whatever she had to, to open, turn, poke, and prod it.

"Okay," Gavan said patiently, his clear blue eyes fixed on Ting, his brows furrowed as he tried to understand. "Take it a little slower, and someone explain to me what you mean by 'Off the radar,' please. Am I to understand that Bailey is missing?"

Rich shifted his weight, his tool belt slung low on his hip, but the pockets of his belt, crudely stitched and put together, held herbs and bandages and ointments, not tools. "Bailey missing? Oh, that's new! What's the likelihood of that, hmmm? She was only missing . . . what, twenty-four hours ago?"

Ting wrinkled her nose at him. "Stop it. Yes, she's missing."

Stef had sat down on a tree stump, and he crossed his thick arms over his chest. "How lost can she be? I mean, it's what, a seven-story building with two wings?"

"I mean she's lost, Stefan, really, really lost."

"As in off the radar," Gavan said quizzically, watching her face. "What did you mean by that?"

Ting looked at him, and could no longer hide the stricken feeling inside her. "As in, I can't feel her at all. She's gone."

"Mmmmm. You're usually connected a bit, then?"

"Always. Aren't we . . . supposed to be?" A little defiantly, Ting brushed a soft wing of black hair from her eye.

Gavan smiled gently. "We had hoped, but one never knows. It is a camaraderie some of us never feel, and some of us feel almost instantly." He put his hand out and patted Ting. "And, as Stef so aptly put it, how far could she have gone?"

"Then you don't think it's Jonnard or anything?"

He shook his head vigorously. "Not with the wards we

have set about. We'd have heard an intrusion, believe me. No, it's more likely to be ..." Gavan paused, and then a thought seemed to cross his mind. His mouth twitched. "Yes, I think I know just where Bailey might be."

"Where's that?"

"Where the most trouble is. I can only hope she didn't pull *that* lever ..." Gavin motioned to Rich and Stefan. "I want you two up and down the north wing, and we'll take the south. Crystal me if you find any sign of her, or that pesky little rodent of hers." He swung around, his cloak swirling like a great wing about them. "Ting, come with me, and hurry. I have a suspicion. I just hope we can find her in time!" Concern colored his words.

A broken nail and long minutes later, Bailey figured out how to pry out the end of the small piece of wood. It took not one but three different pressure points, pressed in exactly the right combination, to pop it out of place. That, she found out quite by accident, and by listening carefully. She could hear clicks when she pressed on one corner or the other, but nothing seemed to loosen the inlay properly. It was rather like half unlocking a door with a key.

She found a wooden ring secured into the space behind it. It had a metallic feel to it, as if it might be bronze or an alloy, but it was definitely circular and big enough for her to curl two fingers into. A ring which she then pulled out. It seemed to snap into place. Bailey thought a moment, then twisted it. A noise of tumblers turning and inner workings working and other ominous sounds followed immediately. With a *whoosh!* the floor under her disappeared. Bailey let out a shriek and dropped into space.

The whole building rumbled. Timbers shivered and groaned, and the stairs vibrated heavily underfoot. Ting immediately thought of an earthquake, having grown up in an area where the earth moving was a fact of life. But they weren't anywhere near the San Andreas fault! "What is that?"

"That," said Gavan grimly, "is what I feared." He abruptly switched directions, from heading upstairs, to thundering down. Ting flew along in his wake, the stairs booming around them like cannon fire. They flung headlong down, down, down, as Ting wondered if the academy had a dungeon hidden somewhere (and if so, why?) and then they burst into the vast root cellar storage room where her grandmother and Rebecca were preparing shelves and barrels to store goods in, and Qi was patiently saying, "This dust will keep ants and most other insects out, very old but very good remedy," as she sprinkled a whitish powder around the edges of the room.

Both women looked up in surprise. "Ting!" Rebecca's eyes widened. "Is something wrong?"

Gavan took them both by the elbows, saying, "Move *here* NOW," and looking up with a face creased in great worry.

"Yeeeeooooooowwwww" echoed all about them, descending out of the ceiling, and with the shriek, a corner of the ceiling opened up and Bailey slid through, landing with an unceremonious thump and grunt where her mother and Ting's grandmother had just been standing.

Gavan nodded his head. "I think I need to work on the landing site a bit." He extended his hand to Bailey. "Congratulations, lass, I think you've broken the all-time Magicker curiosity mark."

Bailey sat up, coughing, the wind knocked out of her, and blinked. Finally she managed, "What was that?"

"That, if what happened is what I think happened, was my panic room, where all sounds and Magick are nullified in case of extreme attack, and my escape chute." Gavan stood patiently, waiting for her to grasp his hand. "I had planned a field trip there when everything was worked out, but you seemed to have jumped the schedule."

"Bailey, hon, are you all right?" Rebecca grabbed her daughter by the shoulders and stood her up, then began dusting her off. Any answer Bailey might have made was interrupted by an outraged piping and as they all looked up, a tiny ball of fur fell out of the ceiling chute and into Bailey's quick-thinking grasp.

Lacey let out an aggrieved sneeze and promptly hid her face in her paws. "Troublemaker," Bailey said affectionately, looking down at the pack rat, not seeing much the same look on her mother's face as she looked at her daughter.

"All's well, then. I'd better call off the boys before someone else stumbles onto something."

Bailey rounded on Ting. "See? I told you!"

The headmaster stopped abruptly in the root cellar doorway, and looked back over his shoulder. "Told her what?"

Both girls smiled innocently and chimed together, "Oh, nothing."

"I can only imagine." Gavan made a gesture that trailed sparks through the air as he left. Words lingered behind. "That should also help keep the cellar free of insects." The sparks rained down upon the ground and lay twinkling, dewlike for a moment, before being absorbed.

15

Plans and Plans Gone Awry

WHAT YOU'VE TOLD me about the wolfjackals saddens but does not surprise me," Tomaz Crowfeather said heavily. He squatted by a ward fire, warming his thick hands carefully, the fire's light adding much depth to his already time-carved face. Gavan sat on one of the three-legged stools the children . . . no, not children anymore, he corrected himself . . . delighted in making. The day's ride had tired him more than it should, and he chided himself for that, as well. To go and then do nothing chafed at him like a badly fitting and overly starched shirt. He wanted to pull and then rip the other day away from him, but could not.

"I didn't think the Dark Hand was making use of them anymore."

"They are torn from Chaos and have a need to return to it. Can you think of any force more chaotic than that which Jonnard and Isabella use? No?" Tomaz nodded to himself as if answering his own question when he heard nothing from Gavan. "So. They will go where they must just as we go to fire for warmth, regardless of its danger. We, however, know how to control fire. Usually." He stood, and hooked a thumb in the loop of his hammered silver belt. The conchas, the round disks of metal from which it was made, rattled faintly at his touch. "Do you condemn them for that?"

"Condemn, no, but I'd gladly corral them if I could. I think somehow the Dark Hand feeds off them as well."

Tomaz raised a squared eyebrow. "In addition to the Leucators?"

"Just a theory. One I was hoping you could solve."

Tomaz grunted. "I was, as well." He reached for a crude poker and stirred the ward fire up a bit, watching the shower of orange sparks shoot upward hike fireworks, and sputter out. "What else bothers you?"

Gavan halted in mid gesture of rubbing his eyes. He dropped his hand. "Shows, does it?"

Tomaz shrugged. "We know each other well."

"I couldn't *feel* her, Tomaz. If she was there, and she should have been, both her and FireAnn, I couldn't feel her! I had no lingering touch, no sense, no . . . hope."

"Yet you went back and found the fortress a decoy, did you not?"

"So it seemed."

"So you told Renart and the boys."

"I hadn't the strength left to try and pierce the curtain if it had been hidden. So I decided it was an illusion, and I think it is. I think Isabella has taken the actual workings of her little garrison and laid it over the ruins of a similar one, in a ruse to hide their location. Eleanora forgive me if I'm wrong." Gavan looked away from the firelight, into the night.

"How does that explain Jonnard cornering Bailey?"

"That's the question, isn't it? How does that explain that? He could have sensed someone tripping the trap's perimeter and come to take a look. He's capable of Crystaling for long distances, I should think."

"But why would he? Unless he were already in the region."

"Damnit!" Gavan's left hand gripped his cane tightly. "I don't know! I don't know."

Tomaz looked at him almost mildly and raised his index finger. "We have to remember that things are often more simple than they seem. If not, they would have attacked us before now and driven us off, or even killed us. They cannot do it any more than we can attack them as long as they're holding hostages. The question is . . . what is holding *them* back?"

Gavan shook his head wearily. Then he raised his head, brushing his hair from his eyes and locking his gaze onto Tomaz. "That's it! We have a Gatekeeper. They don't."

Tomaz nodded. "I should imagine that's it. It always has been. Brennard and then Jon have been after Jason from the very beginning. After Fizziwig, too, although poor Fizzi hadn't the skill to open many Gates or keep them open. They killed Fizziwig in their haste. But Jason. Jason has a great deal of ability he hasn't called on yet."

"In other words," Gavan said dryly, "Isabella has no intention of staying bottled up here on Haven."

"I don't think she does."

"Neither would I, if I wanted to be an empress, I suppose. Well, that's it then. Jon came after his trap was sprung, hoping to find Jason. He did not. He caught Bailey instead. He retreated as soon as he discovered that. So. We keep Jason as far from them as we can."

"Even so far as to send him back home?"

They traded looks. Gavan shook his head slowly. "Let's hope it doesn't come to that. Going home for Jason could be even deadlier than having Isabella get her hands on him. She will value the Magick in him. Back home, they'd tear him apart trying to figure out how he ticked."

"Then," commented Tomaz, "we know what we have to do."

"Aye. But no idea how in hell we're going to manage it." Gavan laughed at himself, and the humor did not reach his blue eyes. "The improbable just became more impossible."

Tomaz dropped his hand on his friend's shoulder. "We'll accomplish it one step at a time. It will be like skirting quicksand. We'll need to plan each step carefully."

"Jason won't go to them easily, if at all."

"Not for himself. So we must watch the others carefully. I suggest you get Stefan and Rich back to the academy tomorrow, and keep them here. Isabella is a cold one, but it won't take long for her to realize that Jason's great vulnerability lies not in himself, but in his friends."

"Done." Gavan stood up, leaning slightly on his cane.

Its support felt comforting, and worse, necessary. He was exhausted, he thought. "Shall we tell them?"

"Not quite yet. I want to find out a bit more about our wolfjackals first. If you permit it, I think I need to visit Khalil and talk with him."

Khalil had stayed in their world, where he'd always been, lost in the deserts of what was now known as Dubai. His estates were hidden and yet substantial, and his Talents as well. But he was a Magicker, and an ally, and Tomaz was probably right in seeking him out.

Every time Jason opened the Gate, the world of Haven trembled. Isabella and Jon would feel it. Let them feel it! He thought. Let them wonder what it is we're doing. They'll think it an attack on them, somehow, as if all worlds revolve about them.

Sometimes, they did.

16

Swinging Gates

ISABELLA STUDIED her journals, with a growing irritation buzzing around her, rather like an irritating fly. But she could see nothing as she glanced up. She took a moment to extend her senses about her, wondering what the problem could be, and then a sharp knock at her door interrupted the investigation. She frowned, and rubbed at the bridge of her strong nose. A good, imperious nose, at that.

"Come in."

Tormun, one of her head guardsmen, came in, smelling of the barracks and whatever else such men smelled of, his thumb tucked into his heavy weapons belt, and an apologetic look on his rough face. "I . . . I beg pardon, madame, but . . . well, downstairs . . . the chains are rattling. It's spooking the men, madame."

"Spooking them? Are they men or nervous beasts?" Isabella let out a tiny snort of disdain and got to her feet with an immense rustling of her vast gown. "They know what the sound is."

"That doesn't make 'em any easier about it, madame. That's not why I'm here, though. I just thought you would want to be aware. Those t'ings are restless, mighty restless."

"Perhaps I should send some of the men down to keep them company?"

Tormun went white. He stiffened, rather than taking a step back, and his body hunched as though in disagreement with his mind about what action to take. Then he got out, "If it pleases you, madame."

"It does not. Those *things* as you call them are powerful sorceries, not to be trifled with. I am grateful you alerted me to the problem. I shall attend to it." Isabella scooped up a heavy ring of keys at the corner of her desk and swept past Tormun at the doorway, the hem of her gown catching for a moment on his boots and then drawing free.

It wouldn't do to let the guardsman see her concern, but she had no more real understanding of her constructs than most people did. She made them, they flourished to some extent, she fed off them, and they continued to flourish or they died. She descended into the far basement levels of the fortress, found the cumbersome key to the padlock, and entered the dark realm where she kept her Leucators imprisoned.

Most of them were on their feet, pale faces gleaming in the Lantern light she viewed them by. Their shackled ankles and wrists shook in agitation, as they moved, paced, within the tiny confines of each individual prison. Restless, indeed. But why?

She knew their faces as she passed by them. Some had decayed to absolute ghoulishness, but she knew them. Old friends, old associates, an old Magicker . . . one or two more old husbands. A Leucator had been created, with a bit of stolen soul and flesh, as a hound. It would not rest till its twin, the rightful living being, was found and it was reunited. Unfortunately, like many hounds, it had a tendency to destroy its prey when caught. Leucators, early on, had been decreed to be used only in desperate, desperate need, and never to be made lightly.

Isabella would not be where she was if she had followed rules. She had discovered a far better use for Leucators in her experimentation with their creating. They could, when fed off of carefully, maintain the reserve of Magick within her, and extend her own life greatly. She was one of the few who had survived the magic duel between Brennard and Gregory the Gray without being stunned into a centuries-long coma, or thrown forward through the ages. She had lived the entire time, and lived long, and thanks to her efforts, many of those who were alive now, owed their continued existence to her.

She did not expect them to thank her. In fact, she had already been condemned for it. Isabella grasped the hem of her gown, skirting her way through the whining golems carefully, searching, looking for the core of the unrest. It was true that she had plundered the assets of many, with no one to stop her, and she'd built a fortune doing so. She'd also spent a fortune cocooning those in comas, making crypts to shelter their slumbering bodies, hiring watchers, bribing their families to bear what could only be called witchcraft. In some cases, she'd moved the bodies altogether, knowing if she did not, there would never be peace.

Had she done it to save the Magickers? Not really. It was more in the line of further experimentation. What had magic done to them? When would it wear off? Had it cleansed them of all Talent, or preserved it . . . and why?

Everything was useful to know. And those in slumber rarely knew that they contributed to her Leucators, or that she fed off their state in many ways. It was all in line with Antoine Brennard's beliefs that Magick was not renewable, that when it burned out, it was gone, and so it must be used carefully, weighed out miserly, stolen from others if necessary to avoid harming oneself . . . when magic was gone, it was gone. Gregory had argued that Magick was a Talent for harvesting and bending the natural powers abundant all about them. One could lose the Talent to fear, fatigue, illness, death, but if one knew oneself, it could be renewed. Perhaps not overnight, if greatly taxed, but inevitably, like great tides of the vast oceans, Magick existed and always would. So far, it appeared Brennard was correct. At least, that was Isabella's belief and it had helped her to prosper.

A ghoul hissed at her, as her crystal's Lantern light fell across it. It had been working at the manacles about its wrists, nearly had its slender limbs freed, blood slick on its skin and aiding in the escape effort, as it tried to slide loose. Isabella drew herself up, and studied the Leucator of Eleanora.

"Now," she said quietly, "that won't do. You injure your-self and her . . ." Isabella gazed up, where her captive, no doubt, was equally restless. "You'll have your time, my pet, I promise you." She stretched out her free hand and stroked the lanky brunette strands of the Leucator's hair. It hissed again, shrinking away from her, chains rattling fiercely as it tugged sharply over and over, trying to free itself. The mere nearness of Eleanora's presence obviously tortured it. Isabella wanted to draw from it, but she could feel the weakness in it, and knew that she dared not. As for the other Leucators in the dungeon, most were even weaker. They should be recovering from her tapping of them, but they were not. The raids had drawn much from her, and her resources were growing unreliable, for reasons she did not yet understand. Isabella withdrew her hand. Not tonight. Perhaps in a day or two.

Instead, Isabella veiled a mild calming spell over it and watched it sink down to its knees, then into a cross-legged pose, hunched over as its breathing deepened and it fell into slumber. She smiled thinly. "I promise you, little Leu-cator, your hunt will be successful before this is all over."

She made her way back through, the Leucators subsid-ing into silence as she did, as if the Eleanora duplicate had been the instigator of all their unhappiness, and perhaps it had. Isabella did not feel the shimmering wave of unleashed energy till she stood at the threshold, stepping out.

It hit her. Rolled over and immersed her, a wave of un-mistakable power, and it caught her for a moment, blinding her.

Somewhere, a Gate opened. She could feel the mighty breath the world took in and the even mightier exhalation as it swung back and forth. Isabella knotted her fists. That Gate! Hers. The one she needed and rightfully should have power over. That Gate. That damned Gate the boy had opened.

Isabella closed her eyes against the shiver of power dancing along her skin with sparklike touches. This, this likely had brought the Leucators to their feet. They could sense great Magicks. She opened her eyes slowly, renewed in her determination that a Gatekeeper would be hers.

She turned and left the dungeon.

*   *   *

Jon's head jerked back as he awoke from an unintended nap in his room, his boot heel falling to the floor with a thump from the chair seat he'd propped it on. Books and papers in his lap shifted abruptly, and he grabbed for them, even as he felt the ripple of power. He frowned. Jason was opening and then slamming shut the Dragon Gate, a wash of power reaching him like a ripple effect. Yet, the touch was unmistakable, almost a taunt. In fact, Jon thought, as he stood slowly and gathered himself, it was a taunt. The Magicker wanted him to know he had the power, and had used it, and done it so quickly they couldn't act on it. Jon gritted his teeth together. It was an intentional slap in the face, warranted perhaps by his encounter with Bailey.

Jon brushed his hair from his face, and paced his quarters. There had to be a way he could rein Jason Adrian in . . . and then a thought occurred to him. A smile slowly spread over his face. He'd have to think it through, and put it to paper before he suggested it to Isabella, but yes . . . yes, he might have a way to bend the Gatekeeper to their needs.

Yes, indeed.

17

Ouchified

HENRY FOUND the best way to let his mother know he was home, without kicking up a huge fuss, was just to show up for the next planned meal, as if he'd never been away. So he grabbed his baby sister out of the playpen, took her into the kitchen, and slid into his usual place at the table for lunch. The toddler didn't seem to have grown too much since he last saw her, and after a frowning look as if reassuring herself as to his identity, she settled in his arms and resumed banging her handful of plastic keys against the edge of the table and babbling in a language only she knew.

Time flowed differently between home and Haven. He could see that most decidedly every time he came home and looked at his siblings. The toddler grew in leaps and bounds, but then most children did . . . still, he could see it in her. His other brothers and sisters seemed to lag behind, but he himself . . . Well, it was apparent that he was growing faster than anyone except his baby sister.

Henry hugged her, glad that she'd decided she knew him as the same old familiar big brother who did most of the babysitting for her . . . when he was around. He couldn't help being a little sad at missing her, something that even the mysteries of Magick couldn't quite offset.

He was more than happy going back and forth, though. He nudged the empty backpack at his feet, and listened to the rustle of paper inside it. Lists, and more lists, of things he was to get. The oddest things were the sets of sewing and embroidery needles, but both Rebecca Landau and Madame Qi had been very insistent. These, he'd been told, are the best bartering kits . . . high quality needles of stainless steel absolutely do not exist in Haven and probably never will. Consider them as priceless as gold or diamond gems, and bring back as many packets of them as you can!

Maybe his mother would make more sense of it when she took him shopping. The needles, at least, were relatively cheap. Trent's needs might cost money and would definitely eat up his time. Research, research, research! As for what Gavan and Tomaz had asked him for, he was nearly clueless. They had pressed their scraps of paper into the palm of his hand at the last instant, and he wondered if he were meant to keep his efforts secret. Probably, he should. Seemed best. Better safe than sorry, and all that—

"Henry!" A blur swooped down on him, smelling of soap and lavender water, and hugged him tightly, and he grinned ear to ear with happiness.

"Mom!" He hugged her back.

"I wish I'd known! I'd have baked cookies."

He rocked in her arms and his toddler sister, sandwiched between them, let out a coo of squished happiness. "I'll be here a while, so you've got time."

"Really?"

He nodded. "Probably four or five days, from the looks of it. We've shopping to do, and I've got to look some stuff up."

His mother loosed him, and sat down. She'd highlighted her hair with tints of ginger blonde since he was last home, and she looked good, if tired. Laura Squibb was what everyone else would probably call a beautiful woman, although Joanna McIntire was, without a doubt, the prettiest of all the moms, as slender as a feather, with short fluffy blonde hair that was never out of place. Joanna didn't look a bit like Jason and that was because she was Jason's stepmom, and of course Jason didn't look like the big bulldozer of a man, McIntire himself, because that was his stepfather and Jason was basically an orphan being raised by two strangers. But at least they were two nice strangers.

Now, Henry didn't look like his mom but when you saw Robert Squibb, you'd know right away whose son Henry was. They both had the same thick, wavy brown hair and round face, and need for glasses, and a slightly bemused look on their faces as they contemplated the many things going on around them. His dad could wear contacts but didn't, and Henry couldn't, so the glasses stayed perched on his nose. No, sir, there was no doubt Henry was Robert Squibb's son. Although, last time he looked, there were two or three graying hairs in the sideburns on either side of Robert's oval face.

Laura took her daughter from Henry's lap. "What kind of shopping?"

"Food and seeds and . . . sewing needles." Henry shook his head as if baffled at the last.

"Oh, good!" Her face brightened. "I thought those would go over well."

"You did?" He blinked at her and adjusted his glasses.

"Oh, yes. Good needles would be worth a great deal in preindustrial times. Why, a set used to be a valuable part of a dowry centuries ago." She winked at him. "Women know these things."

"Who'da figured," Henry muttered, as she got up and briskly began to set a lunch, leftovers from dinner, which looked to be plump, juicy pot roast sandwiches, chilled applesauce, and a few other good things. He brightened. He wondered if needles went over well, how good would some decent pots and pans go? Of course, they'd be a lot heavier and bigger to drag around. Maybe he'd best leave things alone, till he was asked for them.

Instead, he wrapped his hands around a sandwich full of steaming beef and managed a smile at his mom before chowing down.

Jason reeled back, his limbs gone weak and his mind buzzing as he released the energy and firmly shut the Dragon Gate after Tomaz. The scenery spun around him and he had a wild thought that he was going to pass out; then the moment slithered past him, and the ground felt firmer under his feet. What the heck? All he'd done was open and shut the Gate. Twice in one week, true, but Henry had been a lot earlier. He had used far more energy than needed this time, and he clenched one hand because of it, knowing he'd wanted to shove the fact down Jon's throat that he'd opened the Gate and the Dark Hand could do nothing about it. The backwash of weakness was just revenge for that, he thought, and he put a hand out to steady himself.

A sharp splinter sank into his palm, and he yelped. The pain brought him back instantly, as he hopped on one foot, holding his hand, and trying gingerly to pinch the long sharp offender out. The thing was nearly two inches long and half of it was buried in the meat of his hand. Jason pulled it out as Gavan eyed him.

"Academy bit you?"

"Feels like it!" Jason shook the splinter and dropped it, then stomped on it. The other laughed softly. Jason sucked at the fiery wound, feeling the sting subside. "Man," he muttered, as the pain ebbed slowly, and the tiredness hit him again.

"Tired?"

He nodded.

"Off to bed with you, then. You've done a full day's work and then some." Gavan paused. "You let a lot of energy wash out with that last Gate."

Jason felt his defiance spring up again, and he ducked his head, wondering if it could be seen in his eyes. "Still a little hard to know exactly how much push it's going to take to open the Gates and close them, you know?"

"And sometimes, it's fun to kick a little dirt at the bad guys."

Jason's gaze shot up. Gavan was watching him with a kind of curious, deliberate nonexpression on his face. "I don't want him messing with Bailey."

"Of course not. None of us do." Gavan looked away then, out into the night, and the faint wrinkles at the corners of his eyes pinched slightly, as if in pain, and Jason wondered if he thought of Eleanora. Of course, he was thinking of her. They all did, and would, till they got her safely back!

Gavan shifted his weight. "All the same, Jason. We cannot give them more power over us than they already have, do you understand?"

"He won't touch her!"

"Let's make sure he doesn't. But you can't do it by expending your power just when you might need it most." Gavan dropped his hand on Jason's shoulder. "Don't forget, lad, I've seen you play soccer. I know what a competitive spirit you have. I know it hurts to hang back, to deliberately let the enemy underestimate you all the time, but in this case—we've no choice. It has to be that way. They already have a good inkling of your abilities, I don't want them to know any more about you. Understand?"

Jason met those hard blue eyes unflinchingly. "I'll do what I have to."

"As you always have." Gavan smiled quickly. "I couldn't ask for more from you, but this time I am. Lay low, Jason. Learn about yourself each day, and do it quietly, because right now we can't afford to attract more attention from the Dark Hand than we already have."

"Why don't you go after Eleanora?"

"Oh, I will. First, I need to see what they can be up to. There are wheels within wheels, I think. If I go charging in, and get taken myself, what happens to the academy? To all of you? I'm not the only one who can take care of you, but each loss weakens our chance of succeeding, of having what we want and need for Magickers yet to be found and trained. So, I wait. But don't think it doesn't stab at me, like a mortal wound." Gavan took a deep breath. "When I left her with FireAnn, I thought there wasn't anyone better I could leave her with, unless it was Tomaz. FireAnn, you see, has a prodigious Talent few are aware of, and it's not for cooking and herbs. Her Talent is Fire."

Jason let his breath out slowly. "Wow."

"Yes. And she's a bit afraid of it, and very, very careful. Too careful, it seems, or they would never have been captured, but Fire is a very dangerous element to go throwing about, eh? I think she hesitated and in that weak moment, they got her. Otherwise . . ." Gavan's voice trailed off. "Otherwise it could have been a totally different outcome."

"So why are you hesitating now?"

"Because I must. Because we need a plan to get in *and* a plan to get out. If we cannot get out, then there is no sense in going at all. It will take all of our strengths, and weaknesses, before this is over." Gavan squeezed his shoulder lightly. "Now go and get some sleep. I need you and Trent up early in the morning. I want Trent to review the wardings we've set into the frame. We need a roof, and soon, and it looks like the wanderers will be ready to start on it in about two days."

Jason nodded. Walking away, it took all of his strength to keep his legs straight and moving; they felt as if they had turned into wet noodles. Sleep sounded wonderful. More wonderful even than chocolate, although he didn't have the craving for it that Bailey did.

His hand still hurt a bit, but as he climbed the stairs to his open air bed, he realized that nothing must hurt as deeply as Gavan knowing he had failed to protect Eleanora.

Nothing could hurt that badly.

Nothing.

18

Journals

STEF WOKE SORE, BRUISED, and happy. His stomach rumbled the moment he rolled over on the floor, blankets shifting and knotting around him. His stomach had probably been rumbling before he really woke, he thought, as he kneaded his belly. He ate a lot, and sometimes it embarrassed him. He wasn't a fat guy, but he knew he was no slim jim like Rich either. Trouble was, his body seemed to have to feed both him and the bear which was no longer a cub but nearly full grown, as he was himself. If he'd stayed in football—oh, man. Stef's face cracked a grin at that thought. He'd have other players peeing in their pants at the thought of going up against him!

He got up, trailing rumpled blankets like a second skin. Rich was still asleep, curled peacefully on one of the small, rush mats the healer Kektl had left down for them. During the night, Stef could see he'd managed to toss and turn halfway across the floor of the small drying shed the healer of Naria used for a guest room. He didn't mind. Kektl was good to them, always happy to see Stef, and had the use of a bathing area off the hot mineral waters for which the great trading city of Naria was famous. All Stef knew was that a good, hot soak after the sword work was very, very welcome. Beryl, the swordsmith's daughter, fought hard and taught hard, and he had great purple welts where her wooden sword had struck him through his defenses. But he didn't mind.

He also had a spot, right below his right cheekbone, where she'd given him a kiss for doing well and out of happiness he'd come to visit her. That hadn't left a bruise, but he could feel it burning his skin all the same.

Stef pulled his blankets off, folded them neatly, and cleaned up his part of the shed. Then he set off to the bathing pool to clean up again for breaking fast with Kektl who seemed to be already up and cooking, a variety of tempting odors drifting through the air. No wonder his stomach growled! He scrubbed himself again, and pulled a shirt on, then his vest, for this was a city town and his going bareskinned under his vest wasn't proper. It also hid the purple welts. Stef grinned as he pawed at his hair and headed toward the healer's croft.

Rich, to his surprise, already sat cross-legged at the healer's table, ladling out hot tea into wooden cups. The two broke off their conversation about the merits of steam-infused herb therapy and bad coughs as Stef sat down. There was something Japanese about the way Kektl ate and lived, he realized. Low tables, sitting on the floor, sleeping on mats. He wondered about the things Trent was always talking about—who the Havenites were and how they got there. Stef wasn't normally philosophical and as his stomach growled again, he gave up the idea for a big trencher of eggs and shredded meat, and dove in.

Kektl grinned, then turned back to Rich. "As I was saying, that is part of the legend of our hot pools, I think. The steam naturally loosens many ills of the lungs."

Rich nodded. He shoved a wooden cup of tea over to Stef as he picked up his own, to sip at the rich, flavorful drink. Not quite like home, but close enough to make him happy. After a long, wonderfully warming swallow, he opened his mouth to add to the discussion again, when he felt a tingling along his skin. With a frown, Rich set his cup down. He stood and bowed to Kektl. "I thank you for having us, but I think we're being called back."

"Oh?" Kektl was a tall, sticklike man, with a spiky brush

of gray-brown hair that stuck out in every direction despite his frequent efforts to comb it down. His eyebrows were an echo of the hair and now wiggled in puzzlement.

Rich tugged at Stefan's arm. "Come on, I think Gavan is coming after us."

"Mmmpf?" Stef swallowed a mouthful hastily, shoveled another one in, and got to his feet reluctantly. He bowed to Kektl even as Rich pulled him out the croft doorway.

Gavan appeared in a shimmering aura of color, his cape swirling about him, then settling about his ankles. Bruise marks under his eyes showed that he had not had much sleep. "Time to go," he said, holding out his free hand.

"But . . ."

"No time to argue. Rich, make your Talker crystal a present to your host, and we must be off."

Rich pulled the crystal from his belt loop and hurried back to where Kektl stood at the doorway. He rubbed the tiny crystal, set in a nice metal cage of Ting's making, and pressed it into Kektl's hands. "A good luck stone," he said. "It will help with the dialects of all your visitors."

The healer smiled broadly. "Rich! Many, many thanks. Sometimes it is all I can do to figure out what hurts them!"

"I know." Rich folded the man's long-fingered hands about the jewelry. "It won't last forever, but I should be back with a new one before it wears out. Thank you for having us."

The man bent stiffly at the waist. "Any time, young healer. Return soon with your ideas. I enjoy talking with you."

Pleasure at the compliment flooded Rich's face with warmth. A master healer finding value in his training? Wow! He broke away as Gavan cleared his throat impatiently. They linked arms and left in a whoosh and a stomach-unsettling haste and landed to a growl of Stefan's unhappiness.

"Whaddaya mean I can't go back?"

"Not for a while, Stef, I am sorry. The training is good for you, I won't argue that—"

"Then I'm goin'! And you can't stop me."

"I can if I must, but I don't want to have to use force. Trust me on this, Stefan. This goes beyond you all the way to the Dark Hand. I can't leave you and the others out there, where they can get to you."

Stef's face had gone dark red, and he clenched both hands into white-knuckled fists. "I'd like to see them try!"

"Trust me," Gavan repeated again, his voice thinning a little, and his gaze darted to Rich.

Rich put his hand on Stef's well-muscled forearm. "Stef..."

He shoved Rich away. "I'll go back when I want to."

"It's not about you, Stef, or Beryl." Rich shifted his weight and touched his friend again. "Am I right?"

"Very right. We think the Dark Hand means to get Jason any way they can. They almost had Bailey. They'll go after any of you. That, with Eleanora and FireAnn already hostage ... well, that would break me." Gavan sat down abruptly. "I can only take so much." The crystal in the wolf-head cane flickered, as if affected by his mood.

Stef let out a low grumble. Then he sighed. "All right. For now." He pushed away Rich's hand and strode off toward the academy larder, intent now on finishing an interrupted breakfast.

Rich hesitated a moment. "It's that bad?" he asked softly.

Gavan gave him a nod. "It could be. So we need to be cautious."

"We need to get Eleanora and FireAnn back."

"Aye. And that, too. I'm working on it." Gavan stood heavily, leaning on his cane.

Something about that bothered Rich, but he shut his mouth instead and went in search of the kitchens himself, for he'd had almost no breakfast at all, and there seemed to be a very long day ahead of them.

Gavan watched them leave. He realized, like yet another weary burden settling on his shoulders, that they were not the boys he'd welcomed to summer camp just a few years ago. These were young men. Still awkward, still gangly, still growing into their own, but he no longer looked down on them ... they met his gaze straight across or, in one or two cases, Gavan had to look up to see into their eyes. They had grown, all of them. It was that time of their lives when they did. He smiled ruefully. It seemed like only yesterday he'd been such a new-made man, coming into his own as a Magicker and falling in love with Eleanora, the head Magicker's daughter. What a time that had been.

She'd scarcely noticed him, for she'd been older, and wiser, and had many suitors to choose from, if she had been interested. Devoted to her father Gregory and to the schooling of their Talents, she had never seemed very interested in courting.

And then had come that day, after losing everything, and fighting to gain it back, step by step, when she'd looked at him, and slid her hand into his, and he'd realized he'd finally caught up to her. Or perhaps she'd waited for him. No matter. Their hearts were finally in step.

Now, though. Now he could not tell if hers still beat or not. He closed his eyes tightly. If this were true, he could not wait to go after her. As soon as Tomaz came back from his investigation of the wolfjackals, they would have to strike. The Dark Hand would hold him at bay no longer. The day was upon them. Trent woke with a hum, as he usually did, although that day's melody held a slightly mournful note which he changed as soon as he recognized the melancholy. He missed his father, but knew that with the adventure he had dived into, his father would be upset if he did not go after it with all he had. So he would. Then, he would go home and tell Frank Callahan of the wonders of another world where Jason talked with dragons and he ... he could see Magick. Not as good as working it, to be sure, but he could see the miracles others worked around him, something that, till they got to Haven he didn't realize only he could do. He'd seen it from time to time before that, but never realized it was nearly impossible for the Magickers to see what they were actually doing. Jason might gesture at an object to move it, but only Trent could see the colored wave of energy moving through the air and affecting the rock or whatever it might be. It was cool beyond words. He thought his dad would appreciate that.

The problem was in finding the words to describe it. Words didn't fit. Music did. Maybe something composed by John Williams, like for the *Star Wars* movies, or *Indiana Jones*. Something that built and built and became a stirring crescendo of music as the magic hit and its force shattered everywhere, doing its will. Maybe that.

Trent drummed his fingers against the washbasin as he cleaned up his face and made an effort to scrub at his teeth. He wondered if Gavan would send them all home now and then for dental exams and cleanings. He ran his tongue over a rough filling. Maybe even . . . ugh . . . something more.

Jason let out a soft groan as Trent tossed dirty water over the side of the building wall, and refilled the basin for him. From the mussed condition of the cot, Trent guessed that Jason had had a fitful night. He'd gone to bed glowering over something which he wouldn't discuss.

Looking over the side of the unfinished floor, the chill of the morning hit him. As much as he liked sleeping on the top floor of the Academy and seeing the tips of the Iron Mountains and the sharply blue sky, Trent didn't relish the idea that soon he would be waking up to a face full of rain if the roof didn't get put on. Trent grinned at that thought. He broke into a hummed rendition of "Singin' in the Rain" as he waved at Jason and hit the stairs to get a warm piece of toast or coffee or something before doing the work Gavan had assigned them. Jason would soon follow him down, making notes as Trent did the survey.

Dokr had left the wanderers' camp early, and sat squatting by the cook fire, a heavy mug of his own brew in his hand. He nodded respectfully at Trent. Regardless of the boys' age, the wanderers seemed to have this innate courtesy and, since the building had begun, Trent felt they had earned it even more. The wanderers were building the academy, of that there was no doubt, but all of the Magickers had thrown their backs and their will into it, and although clumsy at first, soon they'd become sure at following the building plan and helping. Even Ting could miter a board to be jointed neatly, and Stef used his bearish strength in putting huge beams into place that might take the muscles of three other men.

Dokr motioned to the academy. "You checking the frame again today?"

Trent nodded. Madame Qi was already up, her wrinkled face a little pinched as if the foggy morning hurt her aging joints, but she deftly drew him a cup of oolong tea. With a wink, she palmed a bit of sugar and sweetened it for him. Trent flashed her back a thankful grin.

"Always checking the framework," he said to Dokr. "Not for your craftsmanship, but for the alignment with the energies and stars."

The Havenite acknowledged his words with a sage nod

of his own head. The two groups had not discussed Magick. Gavan thought it prudent not to, and Trent agreed. The wanderers were outcasts even among their own people, but why add to their burden by making them work with Magick they might consider devilry? The wanderers reminded Trent of someone back home. Not Gypsies, though, although they had that nomadic quality. They were not carefree and colorful in the least. No, not Gypsies . . . perhaps . . . he blew on his tea and drank it. Puritans! If the Puritans had become homeless followers of the road, they would be like Haven's wanderers!

Pleased with himself, Trent was still humming "Turn, Turn, Turn" by the Byrds when Jason showed up, grabbed a hunk of corn bread and a slate and motioned to him that he was ready.

Trailing corn bread crumbs, the two went over the building from the buried basement and foundations upward, going over the old warding as always to make sure it held, before going onto the new. Trent could see the lines of energy laid into the wood and stone as clearly as if they'd been drawn by Day-Glo markers, and often marveled that Jason couldn't. But Jason could sense them, and their strength, so he used both his own Talents and his note taking, to double-check Trent's work. So far, in all the weeks they'd been doing this, they'd only found one failed ward. Trent wasn't sure how Gavan and the elders did what they did, but he knew the outcome was to keep the wood sound against termites and dry rot and other effects of time, to keep it fireproofed, and to provide a thin layer of magickal protection against outside harm, and to prevent the magic used inside from leaking out. It wasn't strong enough to hold against an fall-out attack, but it would discourage almost anyone from ordinary sabotage and trifling. And, from what Trent gathered, no one could magickally eavesdrop on those inside either. Not unless one knew the frequency.

He'd tried to explain that to Jason. The warding Gavan guided into place was like a broadband radio wave. It sealed Magick on all those frequencies. But there was still leakage above and below the normal band of frequencies. He couldn't quite put together what he saw and heard, though. Either it was sealed or it wasn't.

Trent pointed at the new workings. "Looking good," he said. "As far as it goes."

"Are you on that again? Gavan knows this isn't a fool-proof fortress, we don't have the resources, but he thinks it's guarded pretty well."

"Oh, it is, it is." Trent pondered. "I guess it doesn't really matter, most people can't see what I do. I doubt the Dark Hand will see the problem with it either. But it's there all the same."

Jason shook his head. He finished sketching the addition, and indicating where the warding lay, according to Trent's pointing finger, and how strong it was. "Either it is or it isn't."

"Jason, my man, the world isn't black and white. Neither is Magick." He pursed his lips. "It's like . . . like dog whistles! Just because you can't hear the frequency doesn't mean a dog can't."

His friend raised an eyebrow, then stopped as the analogy hit him. "Dog whistles," he repeated.

"Exactly."

"And you think Magick works on frequencies like that."

"From what I've seen, it does. I mean, I feel magick differently than you do, and it's hard to explain, but that does it. Imagine, too, Jason, that there are colors and sounds I can't see or hear. Maybe your dragon can, though."

Jason finished sketching in the ward lines as Trent had outlined them to him. "Interesting idea. So you think this place is protected well enough for the average Magick user."

"Oh, yeah, sure. It's just not as impregnable as Gavan seems to think it is."

"That could be very important some day. I'll talk to him about it. Later, though, I think. He was up early bringing Stef and Rich back, and everyone seems a little edgy."

"You caught that, too?" Both had been conspicuous by their absence. Now, as they worked, and could see off the upper floor wings, Stef was visible working the big, two-man saw with some of Dokr's men, and his grunts could be heard drifting upward. He seemed to be full of angry energy, which they both felt like a buzz of bees shaken out of a beehive. Stef was no one to be around in that temper because the bear could erupt, and no one but Rich was certain what that bear might do.

Jason lowered his slate. "We're done up here."

Trent held up a finger. "Not quite. I want to look at the chimney shaft again."

"Thought we caught that?"

"Yesterday, not today. They added some more rocks and mortar and a new vent to it."

Jason nodded and trailed after him. Trent caught the new stonework immediately, with its spidery net of runework throughout it, and gave his approval after showing Jason the ley lines of the warding. Jason sketched it quickly, and held it up for Trent to view.

"That's it." Trent wet his lips. "I think second breakfast, and then back to work?" He gave his friend an appealing look, which wasn't necessary because neither had really had a first breakfast.

"Sounds good to me." Jason folded his sketches carefully into the slate cover and trotted down the staircase to Gavan's office where he dropped the slate on a pile of similar slates. Then the two raced each other for "second breakfast."

It was not foggy when Jon awoke, but a black-frost wind had swept over the fortress grounds as he dressed and ate quickly, after first giving the order for a mount to be groomed and saddled for him. He penned a note to Isabella that he was riding out to check the Mirroring at the fortress site before leaving. He had other reasons, of course, that he did not wish his dear mother to know. She was not the maternal type in many senses; she had abandoned him as a baby on Brennard's doorstep and not bothered to introduce herself as his mother till he was nearly eleven, but she had her qualities and he could see many of them in himself, like it or not.

She did not need to know that what he really sought at the other fortress site, the one near Avenha, was the essence of Bailey's short visit there. He wondered if he could still taste, smell, touch it. He rode off the grounds of their home fort to a secluded glen where he would Crystal the remainder of the way. The icy ground crunched under the horse's hooves, smelling of winter, and his breath frosted on the morning air. Forget fall; winter seemed nearly here. Avenha, farther south and lower in the hills, would be much more amenable to his spirits.

The horse shivered as he Crystaled them through, and shook his head nervously, not liking the teleportation, but he had been schooled by Jon for this, and so bore it. As he kicked the animal into a canter, the difference in weather and terrain enveloped them. Grass was still green here, although not the lush grass of spring and summer, and fog dewed it in heavy drops. They splashed through the morning dew like riding through a brook, and the horse whickered as he stretched out into a canter.

Jon did not rein him up until they reached the hollow where he had had Bailey trapped. Then he stretched in his saddle and looked about, letting his senses fill the air as the horse put his head down to greedily crop up the last summer grass.

Oh, yes. He could feel her. Much as when, walking into a room where Isabella sat, he was overwhelmed by musk and jasmine, he could smell and taste Bailey. She was different, though—cleaner, lighter, a fragrance as much of crisp lemon and apples as well as heavier roses—and her touch lingered on the air like something fine and wonderful. It did not leave behind a feeling of dread.

Jon let out a small sigh. He did not want Bailey in his thoughts. She was the enemy, a waster of Talent, a . . . a . . . he let his thoughts go for lack of focus on what she was, exactly. She was a problem if he kept her in his mind.

He picked up the reins after a few moments, moving his horse away from the patch of grass and guiding him over the knolls and down toward the fortress ruins where they had a Mirroring spell set to make it look as though this were their place of operation.

It triggered, faintly, for him, but then it was not meant to impress him, just the locals and any Magickers who might run across it. It had done its work admirably. Jon smiled widely as he rode the perimeter of the grounds. He'd suggested it and Isabella had implemented it, and it only took the efforts of two or three of their Leucators to keep the spell empowered. Thus, it did not drain them unduly, and he calculated it would stay as set for at least several years. He checked the areas where they had discreetly buried prisms, to make sure nothing had been disturbed and nothing had. Evidently, Gavan had kept his group far from the actual grounds, and had not pierced the illusion.

Riding past the guard tower for a second time, sweeping the area with his senses, trying to touch the hot spots of magick here and there, he caught something. Something out of place and intensely different.

Jon reined to a halt. His horse bowed his neck, and shifted uneasily, as if feeling his rider's tension.

What did he feel? Where did it come from? And why?

He turned the horse slowly about, casting. Had he felt anything, even?

No . . . no, there it was! He and the horse now faced it dead center. He looked at a corner post of the guardhouse, one of the only really solid posts left in the fortress. Jon eyed it a moment. Then he swung down and approached it, whatever it was, cautiously.

The closer he got, the stronger it got, until it burned at his mind like a brand, and a tear stung the corner of his eye in spite of himself, for it was Antoine Brennard he felt, his father. His father whose ashes now sat in a gold-and-silver casket at the corner of Isabella's writing desk. His father who had fought to bring them this far, and then failed, whose final contribution was for Jon to drain the remaining bits of his Magick so that he and Isabella could survive.

He did not think anyone else would feel this Magick. It was as though it were pointed at him, and him alone. Perhaps even Isabella would not notice it, though he doubted that.

Jon reached out a gloved hand, at the base of the post and began to dig at the ground. It crumbled under his fingers, surprising him, for this piece of the structure was solid. But this one spot crumbled and gave way, and under it, about a foot into the soil, was a leather trunk. Small, as if a jewelry box or some such, and burned into the top of it . . . his father's initials and magickal sigil.

Jon's breath hissed through his teeth. He wrestled the item out of the ground and sat down abruptly, trunk in his lap. There he opened it and found two slim journals, musty smelling but intact.

He sat, his palm hovering over them. His father had been there before. Obviously. He couldn't have been, but he had. If he had been there, what Gatekeeper had sent him through, past the Dragon Guard?

Jon opened the top journal carefully, listening to pages crackle faintly, but they held, and words struck him.

Here, by my own will and Talent, I walk through a new world.

Jon shut the book. Brennard had opened a Gate! Something he hadn't done often, or he wouldn't have sought Fizziwig and Jason so hard or intensely, but . . . the Talent had been in his blood.

Jon scrambled to his feet, closing the trunk tightly. This would require more examination, and authentication. He dared not let Isabella know any of it till he was sure.

If she'd hunted Jason for his Gatekeeping, she would have no compunction about draining Jonnard dry for his. If he had any such ability.

He was not ready to be so used, by Isabella or anyone else but himself.

Hugging the journals to his rib cage and hidden by his shadow-dark cloak, Jon mounted his horse and headed for home.

19

Words and More Words

MIDAFTERNOON, the sweat poured off Jason and Trent. Despite beginning in a chilly morning, the autumn sun seemed determined to show that it still could pack a punch. Hard work didn't hurt either, so when they finally took a break to share a bucket of cold water and some apples, Trent stared at Jason curiously over his apple core.

"Give it up. Something's bothering you."

Jason shrugged. "A little bit of everything. I don't like the feeling of having my hands tied, and I don't like the idea of Jon stalking Bailey. I know we can't do anything, but that doesn't mean I'm happy about it."

"Why can't we do anything? I mean, from a certain standpoint, not much else can happen. I truly doubt they would harm Eleanora and FireAnn any more than they already have . . . so what have we got to lose?"

"It's more than that."

Trent stood up and lobbed his apple core as far as he could throw it, muscles honed by American baseball rippling across his back and shoulders as he did so. The debris went sailing and disappeared into a fringe of woods where

410

some birds or rodents would no doubt happily peck it to bits. He was surprised to see some of the wanderer children dart after it, diving into the forest as if he'd thrown a gold nugget out there. Jason watched over his shoulder.

"What're they doing?"

Jason thought a moment, then said, "Seeds. They're gathering the seeds."

"They're not allowed to have land for growing, I thought."

"They're already outlaws. Crops mean survival. I couldn't blame them for breaking one more law." Jason looked a few more minutes, then crunched down on the last of his own apple. He waited till one or two of the children emerged, then tossed his apple core to them. With a flash of teeth and a smile, it was caught neatly and tucked away. "Can you imagine," he said to Trent, "a place where seeds have to be stolen? It's this whole warlord thing."

Trent sat down and looped his arms about his knees. Looking like nothing more than a pirate, he sounded more like a schoolteacher as he began to talk. "It seems unlikely to us, but look at it this way . . . we had a great warlord too, sounds pretty much like their old guy. Only ours was named Chi'in and he built the Great Wall of China and united all those provinces into a country named China, after him. We don't know why he had those terra-cotta statues made of all his armies and buried, but suppose it was to . . . I dunno . . . guard and protect his empire? Is that any different than what this guy did?"

"Leaving a good deal of yourself behind as a Spirit would be a little hard for the average person to do." Jason wiped the apple juice off his fingers. He paused at the crescent-shaped scar at the back of his left hand. Thin, healed, barely more than a line now, it still ached sometimes when it had no reason to. His life was not like others, he remembered. It hadn't been since he discovered he was a Magicker. He rubbed the mark made by a wolfjackal as if testing it for sensitivity now. Nothing.

"Don't make me compare this warlord to a dragon," said Trent, his eyebrow going up in a mock threat.

"Don't even go there." Jason threw his handkerchief at the other. "Seriously, what we know almost makes me wonder if these are alternate worlds. As if there was a big split. What if the warlords are the same guy?"

"Not likely. No one here really has an Asian cast to their looks. More Eastern European, but not even that, really. I've thought about it, though. Some of the reference material I asked Henry to find for me goes over that. If there was a split between our worlds, there are three or four different times I think it might have occurred."

"You're serious?"

Trent's head bobbed. "I want to know. Don't you?"

"I don't think it's a mystery we can solve in a few weeks or even a few years. Creation mythology is like . . . like a lifetime of work."

"Mythology is more than just words, though, Jason. There's a kernel of truth inside every one, even if the centuries of storytelling wrap around it. Like the Spirit here. It's not just words that his spirit stays and protects them. They believe it, and although we haven't seen it, there are strong signs now and then that indicate it *is* doing just that."

"But a Spirit? How could that even be?"

"I don't know. It's more than tales, though, we know that. It could even be watching us, trying to decide what to do about us."

"It'll take more than words, then. And it looks like you're going to be awfully busy. I've not run across a Havenite who didn't have days' worth of stories to spin."

"Everyone has to have a hobby!" Trent bounded to his feet then, throwing Jason's handkerchief back at him. "I hear 'em yelling. Break time is over."

Jason picked up their water bucket and ladles and trotted after Trent, more thoughts crowding his mind. The mysteries Trent brought up were interesting, but not as immediate as his own problem. He'd brought the Dark Hand to Haven. He needed to either find a way to send them back, harmless, or find a way to fight them here. Either sounded nearly impossible. If Gavan hesitated, what chance did Jason have?

But then, he had something Gavan didn't. He had nothing to lose. The Dark Hand did not, yet, hold anything dear to him that would stop him. If he went in, it would be up to the others behind him, Gavan, Trent, and the rest to get Eleanora back safely. His only targets would be Isabella and Jon and those despicable Leucators. Maybe dividing would be the only way they could conquer their enemies.

Heavy in thought, Jason hardly noticed the weight of the lumber he was being tossed and told to hammer in place as the afternoon wore on.

Despite the shimmering ribbon of water that was the Gulf of Arabia, Tomaz could feel the desert heat and dryness with every breath he took, even as the sun sank into a glowing red sunset. On the fringe of the great metropolis of Dubai, skyscrapers and city lights at his back, he could almost feel the likeness to his own Arizona sands as he walked down the street, hearing the soft call of foreign voices to one another. He found the tea shop he had been told to go to, and stepped inside.

No need to announce he was a stranger there. His looks, his clothes, spoke for him. Unlike Dubai itself, where every person seemed foreign and where the city teemed with those who came from all over the world to trade and make deals and even just visit, in this outskirts suburb, he stood out.

The owner came to greet him, with a nod and smile, and pointed Tomaz to a curtained alcove. Inside, as the drapes were lowered behind him, to shut him away from curious eyes in the small shop, he found nothing luxurious, just a basic wooden café table and a few nicely upholstered chairs. In moments, the owner returned, carrying a tray and cups and the alcove filled with the smell of hot tea, steaming milk, cinnamon, and honey. He set it down and left before Tomaz could ask him where Khalil was or when he would be expected.

The draperies stirred again when a young woman entered, her face modestly veiled and her body hidden in slender robes. She put a tray of sweets and cookies on the small tabletop and gave him a smile that even the veil could not quite hide before darting out. Reminded for a moment of Ting, Tomaz chuckled and poured himself a drink and tried to decide which of the pastries he might sample.

The curtains fluttered with a hint of evening breeze, and Khalil came in, wearing desert robes as he usually did, and with a broad smile upon his face. He clasped Tomaz's hand tightly before sitting down. "My friend, it is good to see you even though I trust you are not here just with good news." Briskly, he fixed his own cup of tea, adding milk and cinnamon and honey in good measure before stirring it and sitting back, dark eyes watching Tomaz keenly.

"Good to see you as well. Not all the news is bad. We have the academy almost finished. I would say that when spring breaks in Haven, we can take students."

"Truly? That is wonderful!" Khalil's eyes gleamed with his joy. He drank his tea cautiously, careful to keep his neatly trimmed beard from catching drips. He looked at the desserts. "All are excellent here, made by my friend's wife. From not too sweet, this one . . . to brimming with taste, these." His hand swept over the food indicating as he recommended. "I have students, of course, who are eager to see Haven, and to have classes as we'd hoped." He put his cup down. "And Eleanora?"

Tomaz quirked his head slightly. "What do your senses tell of Eleanora?" It had been Khalil's Talent that put her to sleep for a while, and perhaps still, kept the dramatic effects of aging from ravaging her. None of the Magickers knew what caused it, or what could remedy it, but they'd seen several of their own die from it. It might even be a side effect of Magick itself.

Khalil considered that. "I barely sense her at all. I think she has thrown off most of the effects of my warding her. But she lives still, if that is what you are asking."

He breathed out in relief and realized he had been holding his breath, waiting for Khalil's answer. It was, indeed, based on Gavan's fear.

Khalil nodded. "Then that answers another of my questions. You have not recovered her and FireAnn yet. A hostage situation is a very nasty knot to unravel."

"It colors most of what we try to do in Haven, every day. It is like walking a tightrope." Tomaz broke off long enough to choose a small pastry and devour it. Its flavor filled his mouth with almonds, honey, and butter, and perhaps a tang of exotic spices for which he had no name. His tongue warmed happily with the tastes. Not a man for desserts, he still appreciated the goodness. Perhaps he would try to order a tray or two to take back with him, for the children. He thought of the dancing excitement in Bailey's and Ting's eyes if he could.

"How can I help?"

"By telling what you will of wolfjackals. Our friends

seem to be using them in some way again, and although I do not think the wolfjackals an enemy, I do think they may be a most unfortunate pawn in the hands of Brennard's lot."

Khalil let out a long sigh and sat back in his wooden chair, stretching his long legs out in front of him. "It's come to that, then."

"Some secrets are not meant to be kept."

Khalil tapped his hand on his cup. Unlike many Magickers who were scholars more than craftsmen, Khalil was weathered, his hands callused. He worked hard in his desert stronghold, in many ways. His face was much like that of the desert hawk, and his senses just as keen. Tomaz held his silence, knowing that if it was going to be broken, it would be by Khalil.

Moments stretched. Then Khalil nodded, as if reaching an agreement within himself. "I will tell you this, which you know already. Wolfjackals are not of any world you and I walk. They are bound to Chaos and they seek it when it's unleashed, hoping to go back to the lands from which they were torn. Magick worked by us and the Dark Hand unleashes Chaos. It draws them. They feed on it, and in the case of Brennard's people, they have formed an alliance. None of them have succeeded in returning, but still they hope. They feed and yet are not fed. They are more than spirits, less than actual flesh. They are intelligent, to a degree, like wolves, and they are merciless in that the only way they know to get home is to take what they can."

"The Dark Hand offers them hope."

"The Dark Hand offers them Chaos, and in that is hope. We seek a balance, so we have less to offer them, knowingly. But—" And with this Khalil stared darkly into Tomaz's eyes. "We have a Gatekeeper."

"I won't dangle Jason as bait for wolfjackals or anyone else."

Khalil shook his head vigorously. "Not as bait, as hope. It's their only option, I think, to return. When he's trained enough, he should be able to sense their home and find the Gate to it. It may take decades, however, and they are bestial enough that tomorrow is too far away. They cannot plan for decades."

"So what have we to offer them?"

"Nothing, unless you think as they do, as wolves do. Fresh meat today, security tonight, a new hunt tomorrow. We can deal with them as Brennard's lot does. Offer them Chaos, Tomaz, and you'll bring them to you. Once brought to you, you can gradually show them that tomorrows do exist, and they can afford to wait."

"Tame a wolfjackal?"

"You ran with their packs once. If anyone can do it, you can."

Tomaz gave a short laugh. "They tolerated me. I think I amused them."

"Make no mistake on this." Khalil leaned forward, his expression intense. "They don't have to tolerate anyone. They smelled the power in you, like a predator smells the blood running just below the skin. They couldn't find a use for you, nor you for them, but the tie is still there. You can find a way to communicate with them, and help them. Or . . ." He paused.

"Or?"

"The Dark Hand will destroy them utterly, to their advantage."

"How so?" Tomaz picked up his cup again and found it had cooled as they talked.

"Think of the wolfjackals as a reservoir of Chaos. They hold it within themselves. They are storing the extra they can glean from our Magick workings, and they are made of it, to some extent. They are like a walking bomb, Tomaz. If Isabella can but figure out how to ignite them, she will. Does she think of doing it?" Khalil stood, gathering his desert robes about him. "If I think of it, what would keep her from thinking of it?"

With that, the Magicker left, the draperies of the alcove shivering as if a great wind had passed through them, leaving Tomaz with cup in hand and an iciness in his heart as though a knife had been plunged into him. Only words had been spoken, but what words!

Jon did not find time till nearly the end of daylight to retire and look over the journals. He had them hidden in a corner of his room with a ward on them, subtle, because anything stronger would attract Isabella's attention instead of turning it away, the opposite of what he needed. This was a dislike-and-ignore warding, and anyone touching it off would veer away from the items, rather like a disagreeable pair of stinky socks. He lit a candle rather than open his room's shutters, and pulled out the books. Both had been filled from cover to cover with his father's writing. It would be difficult reading, for all that he knew his father's hand, because this had been written as it would have been hundreds of years ago, with different lettering, and flowery script, and even different spelling. He was not hundreds of years old, but he had had practice reading such documents. His father had tutored him on old, handwritten treatises on magic and the makeup of the world.

In those years, he hadn't known who his mother was. She didn't try to seek him out till he was nearly eleven years old and she had done so secretly then, telling him his father must not know. He hadn't particularly wanted a mother, but Isabella was no ordinary mother. Tall and strong and carrying herself like nobility, she was more powerful than most men. It was the power that attracted him. It came from her intellect and force of will as well as her mastery of her own Magick. That, to him, had been like nectar to a bee. To have two in his life carrying power that could only be imagined by most, and to have both offer to him the same power . . . ah, yes. Irresistible.

Still, in their relationships with him, and later in their renewed relationship with each other, much remained unsaid and a mystery.

A little afraid and much disturbed, Jonnard opened the journal that appeared to be the oldest. Antoine Brennard had to have been in Haven, but when . . . and why and how? And would the answer be unlocked with mere words? Pages crackled as he turned them carefully.

20

Threats

HENRY SAT AT THE MONITOR, staring so intently he forgot to blink for long minutes until finally his eyes began to sting. He rubbed his eyes then, and ordered a printout. Trent would whoop when he saw this article, he thought, and quickly tiptapped a few keys to go to another reference source that the search engine had recommended. Most sources had little information, but he'd spent many of the last days dutifully printing out every scrap. What he thought unimportant might mean something very different to Trent.

The used bookstore had only yielded one prize, a tattered and very old book named *Little Known Myths.* He'd swooped down on that one and carefully wrapped it up and tied it with string, as it honestly looked like it might fall apart into two hundred ragged pages at any moment. It had cost less than a dollar so that wasn't the point; the point was he thought Trent would really really think the book was cool. He wanted to at least get it back to Haven in one piece, and what happened from there would definitely not be his fault. Not that anyone would blame him. Henry had a habit of blaming himself. His Talent so difficult to control and erratic, and after having had Jon suck a lot of it away and having gone without for nearly a year . . . he shuddered. He'd given up Magicking once; he had no intention of being forced to do it again. So, unlike the others, he stammered and stuttered his way through his lessons, a step forward cautiously was better than two steps forward and a disaster backward.

No way did he want to go through any of that again. Henry inhaled, leaned forward, and sifted through the various sentences coming up on the monitor. As if panning for gold nuggets, he tossed out the sites he'd already visited, and the ones that really didn't have anything to do with the subject although they'd come up anyway . . . how did that always happen? He didn't know, but it did . . . he smiled grimly and found two more web sites that would be worth hitting for Trent. Then home and chores. Strange. He didn't mind doing chores for the few days when he was home.

The library light flickered behind him. Henry glanced up, frowning. He pushed his glasses back into place, and then squirmed about in his chair. He had an eerie feeling for a moment that someone looked over his shoulder. The back of his neck itched, so he rubbed it briskly. Two more web sites and then home, for sure!

Both had little or nothing which seemed of interest to him, but he printed everything out anyway. He added a few quick commands to delete the history of his search engine then slid his card out of the charge slot to end his session. Gathering everything up and storing it away in his backpack, he had almost finished clearing the area when shadow fell across him again. Henry glanced up, and a tall man leaned over, smiling.

It was the vice principal from his old school. "Mr. Winchell!"

"Well, Henry Squibb. I thought that might be you. I am pleased you remember me." The man smiled. He had a face that wrinkled easily, and his expression fell into the many lines and almost disappeared. "Still doing home schooling?"

"Yes, sir. My brother has the computer tied up for a project, so I have to use the library." Also, he didn't want evidence on the family computer's hard drive as to what he'd been researching. Here, it would just sink into the overall picture of all the research everyone was doing and hopefully not be noticed.

"I see. Doing well, are you?"

Henry tried not to fidget under the man's long stare. "Grades seem to be okay." Having Winchell watch him reminded him of a discussion he'd once had with Jason over Jason's dragon: you argue with the dragon, thinking that he is wrong, and the dragon thinks you are dinner. Did Winchell think he was dinner? There was a reason none of the Magickers were still in school, and strangely curious men like this one headed the list.

"We were all disappointed you did not go on to the high school. We thought you were science team material."

Yes, that was it. The educator definitely looked at him as if he might be dinner. Or at least fodder for the very prestigious and hard-working science team. "M . . . maybe someday," Henry managed.

"Good, good! Well, then, give my regards to your mother and father. I look forward to your siblings entering middle school. All hard working, I trust."

"Yup." And none of the others were Magickers, thank goodness. At least, none that he knew of. He reached out and pulled his backpack up. "I need to go."

"Yes, of course." Winchell watched as he stood and shouldered the bag. "I take it your friends are doing all right, as well?"

"F . . . friends?"

"So many of you dropped out at once and went to home schooling, yet you all seemed to know one another." Winchell drew a little closer, his brows sharpening. His smile had completely disappeared into the wrinkled mask of his face.

"I don't know how their grades are, but I see 'em, sometimes."

"Yes, yes. Well, you know, the educational system tracks them. We feel responsible, at home or at school. You might let them know that." Winchell touched his shoulder lightly before moving away, and Henry gave off a little shudder as he did.

He scurried out of the library, got his bike, and headed for home, thoughts in a whirl. What had Winchell meant by that? He didn't know. It didn't sound good. Maybe his mom could decipher it. Adults sometimes spoke in riddles and sometimes they meant exactly what they said.

He didn't think it had been good.

After the dinner hour, when he was left to himself again, Jon put his journals away, still no closer to understanding why his father had been in Haven hundreds of years ago, nor why he had left the journals to be found only by one with Talent such as himself, although the how of Antoine Brennard's coming seemed to be emerging, page by page. It was that how which drew Jonnard in now. Was there a hidden Talent running through the veins of father and son? It was not as if he could ask Isabella; her knowledge of Antoine was even less than his own. No, if anyone had the key to the working of Antoine's mind, it was himself. Or perhaps Gregory the Gray, the lost mentor of most Magickers alive today. Teacher, guide, nemesis, who had been so wrong in his perception of magic and had lost his life for it.

Impatiently, Jon pushed away from his reading desk. His heels scarred the rough flooring as he did so, and the crystal hanging from the chain on his waist warmed to an angry glow so hot it burned through the cloth of his trousers.

Dropping a hand to it in defense to shield himself, he felt Isabella's irate and frantic call vibrating through the crystal. Jon surged to his feet. The chair tumbled over from his abrupt movement and fell clattering on its side to the floor, but he was already out the door, running, as it did so. The sense of Isabella amid the Leucators hung in his mind like the loud, ringing echo of an alarm bell, so it was that way he ran.

Thundering down the stairs in haste, he burst through the dungeon's innermost doors, skidding to a stop just short of running down Isabella who stood, her throat contorted in an angry, stifled wail, her hands knotted in the sapphire silk of her sweeping dress, her face contorted in fury.

"What is it?"

She pointed with a knotted fist. "There." She turned her face away, her tall body rigid.

Two Leucators lay limp upon the floor, looking more like sun-dried raisins than the golem twins of people she'd known and re-created. Jon's heart thumped at adrenaline-driven speed that slowed as he looked upon the sight.

Drained, drained beyond all usefulness and recovery. How could she? Not dead, but as good as, and with a sweep of his hand and a guttural word, bloody light shining out of his crystal, he brought their lives to an end. It was not so much a mercy killing as a necessity because the other Leucators would catch and amplify their pitiful state, and Jon enjoyed a quiet night's sleep, which would be nearly impossible if they started shrieking.

He took a step back, as weakness from the Magick working hit him hard, and his heart slowed to a crawl. He backed to the doorway and let it support him for a moment. With a growl, Isabella swept her fist back and the two bodies went up in a crackle of white flame, then turned to ash, in a matter of minutes.

She put her chin up then and looked at him.

"Isabella." His voice sounded weak, so he paused and took a breath, and forced it deeper. "How could you do that?"

"Me? Me? You think I did that?" The white of her face flushed with a different anger. "How dare you! What makes you think I'd be that kind of fool?"

He would have taken a step back in self-defense, but it was not wise to show weakness in front of her. Instead, he narrowed his eyes. "You didn't drain them . . . but if not you, who did?"

"Nor did I think you were raised to be a fool." Isabella swept past him at the door's threshold, her hems brushing him. "I don't know who did it." She pushed her hands into her hair, pulling it back from her face and then twisting it into a thick knot at the back of her neck. "It could only be one of them, and how they managed a draw from here, or at this distance, I do not know. But it means they have learned that Magick here drains, and drains permanently, and they are just as desperate as we are."

She thought one of Gavan's Magickers had done that? He looked at the two ashy-oily spots of residue on the dungeon floor, shackles lying empty. No. He shook his head. "I don't think so."

"Or them above." Isabella tilted her head to shoot an accusatory glance at the fortress overhead.

"If they could have done such a thing, they would have escaped us long ago."

"Find an answer, then, whelp, and quit arguing with me. It was done, and it's up to you to find out how."

He could have back traced the power drain, perhaps, if she hadn't been so quick to flash burn the bodies. He ground his teeth on his own sharp reply. She was tired, more so every day, and her anger flared often.

He put his hand out, palm up. "I will not only find out who and how, but I will bring you new reserves."

Isabella paused for a very long moment then, and the fear in her eyes drained slowly, to be replaced by a sparkle. "Will you, indeed?"

"You know I will." He waited.

Finally, she placed her hand in his. "I believe you will. The answers you seek, Jonnard, may well cement our position in ruling this world, as well as others."

The same thought had occurred to him. He let her lean on him as he escorted her upstairs. More mysteries to solve, and this one most urgently.

21

Happy Birthday, Happy Birthday—Happy Birthday!

"THE ROOF IS DONE! The roof is done!" Bailey's and Ting's voices rang out in unison as they raced through the building and down the back stairs to the makeshift lumberyard where the others stood with the downstairs crew of wanderers, intent on making siding, window framing, and shutters. They skidded to a halt, Bailey's ponytailed hair bouncing as it echoed her excitement.

"At last," breathed Rich. He gave a huge, lopsided grin, and paused, his shirtsleeves rolled up in spite of the fog which seemed to hang over the Iron Mountains that day. Stef thumped him in the ribs, grunted, and indicated the piece of siding he was shaping and sanding as if to say there was plenty of work left to do. Dokr and his workmen winked at each other behind Stefan's back, nodding in agreement.

Gavan, however, stood quietly. He flexed his shoulders with a weary sigh and looked at the girls with a tiny tilt to the corner of his mouth. "That is good news indeed. Looks like we should have a celebration in a few days. Dokr, we'll be done on the exterior . . . when?"

The head wanderer paused in contemplation, then

counted out on his hand, six fingers wiggling. "Four days at the most, barring rain. Then two weeks on the interior, finishing, but rain will not stop us there. In good time we must hurry, though, for we must get to our winter camps soon."

"A good job, then." Gavan smiled at him. "A very good job. We had hoped to just get half built before bad weather hit, and here we are, nearly finished." He wiped his forehead with the back of his hand. "Jason, think you can bring everyone home tomorrow for a party?"

Jason had paused, working in a team with Trent on storm shutter sets, his hand filled with nails and a hammer. "Should be able to. I imagine they're listening for me."

Trent reached over to pluck a few nails and tapped them into his framework while Ting and Bailey let out another shout of excitement.

"All right, then, I declare the day after tomorrow a free day."

Stef grumbled something under his breath and went back to work as if disinterested. Gavan raised an eyebrow and watched the well-muscled Magicker wrestle his siding onto the worktables as Stef seemed to ignore him further.

Rich shrugged in apology. "It's not a free day if he can't go where he wants," the redhead offered.

"Ah." Gavan tucked the crystals he'd been working with away in the inside pocket of his cape. Faint purplish bruise marks of fatigue underscored his eyes as he then took a handkerchief and polished the Herkimer diamond in the jaws of his wolfhead cane, before looking up at Rich. "Perhaps we can arrange a field trip—if Tomaz accompanies you? He'll be back then. It's not that I want to stop the lessons altogether, but we can't keep everyone safe if we're all scattered."

"A chaperone?" Rich looked interested.

"I don't need a stinking chaperone." Stef straightened up, gripping his shaper so tightly his knuckles showed white against his deeply tanned skin.

Something flickered in Gavan's eyes, but he responded mildly, "Not so much that, I have business in Naria that Tomaz could be doing. But he'd be within distance for help if anyone needed him. Then you all could head back for the celebration."

"You're not kidding?"

"No," Gavan shook his head slowly at Stef. "I'm not kidding. You've worked hard, all of you, and you deserve a break. Madame Qi has talked to me on your behalf, as well. She reminded me that not all must walk the same Path to be on a good Road. Or something Confucian like that."

A wide grin slowly spread across Stefan's face, and it was like the sun had broken through the cloud and fog hanging over the Iron Mountains and the tiny valley. His mouth worked for a moment, then he said, "Thank you," before bending back to his work, this time with an enthusiasm that matched his brute strength. Wood shavings curled up and flew to the ground at his feet in fine, feathery onion skins.

Rich flashed Gavan a thankful look, before tending to his carpentry as well. In moments, the air filled again with the sound of saws, hammers, and the noise of wood being shaped to finish the academy, accompanied by soft singing from Ting and Bailey and punctuated by an occasional squeak from Lacey as she ran around underfoot, helpfully finding lost nails and other shiny bits of interest.

Henry laced his backpacks shut tightly, pausing for a look of pride at their bulging sides. He had a hiking backpack for each shoulder! In addition, he had huge burlap bags of staples requested by the cooks—rice, beans, flour and more—and a few additional surprises like thermal blankets and winter items knitted by his mom and older sister that ought to make everyone very happy as well as warmer. He'd tied them together, as anything on him or being held by him would go through the Gate when he went. The trick, he'd discovered, was to hitch everything together tightly. As long as he had a firm grip on the ropes, the Gate seemed to consider it as part of him, and Jason could pull him through. They'd discovered that the first time or two he'd made a trip back for provisions, and left bundles on the floor about him, and had to wait weeks before he could return and get the rest.

He ticked off the items on his mental list. Books and notes for Trent. Letters from all the families for everyone. Chocolate for Ting and Bailey, and everyone else, really. The sewing items. Food in bulk. Recent newspapers, photocopied and condensed for those interested in the world they'd left behind. He'd gotten everything they wanted and more, feeling slightly heroic about his own efforts. He'd even found some things for the wanderers, an assortment of items Gavan had quietly told him might make some nice rewards for the crew for the work they'd done on the academy. Nothing that would be terribly out of place on Haven but things that might make their lot a bit easier. A warmth filled him at the anticipation of his friends going through his many sacks of goodies. A few days ago, he was reluctant to think about going back to Haven, now he could hardly wait. It was as though he'd had his fill of being home, and needed to go back where he was more than a son, he was a Magicker.

More than that, he and his parents had discussed the schooling issue. No trouble had yet reared its ugly head, but the warning Winchell had given hung over them all. No one wanted any questions being asked that would lead to trouble for the families. The sooner he got back to tell Gavan and Tomaz and the others, to figure out what might happen and how to head it off, the sooner he'd be happy.

Downstairs, he could smell something delicious in the oven. All he needed now, was a sending from Jason to let him know a Gate would be opening soon. He scratched his head. A faint feeling of being watched over his shoulder made him twirl on one heel to find . . . no one looking into his room.

Henry frowned. He swept a searching gaze over the corners of his room, so familiar and yet now strange in some ways. It seemed the academy, even with its roughness and unfinished quality, felt more and more like home to him. Maybe that was why he felt uneasy in his old room now, as if he didn't belong there and someone might be watching him. The back of his neck felt all creepy crawly and he knew it wasn't Jason. Jason had never felt like some kind of squirmy bug that ought to be brushed off and *squished* as soon as possible.

Henry shifted uneasily and looked about again, finding nothing as he figured he would. He'd had that trouble once before when Jonnard had been Linked with him and he hadn't even known it, but that link was severed at the great battle of opening the Dragon Gate, freeing him. Things were different now and a lot better. When he'd found out that Jon could spy through him, he'd nearly died of the humiliation. He'd been a traitor and not even known about it until far too late! Stuff like that shouldn't happen to anyone.

Nerves. He was getting nerves. If he didn't stop it, pretty soon he'd be as jumpy as fidgety old Rich! That would be pretty fidgety. Rich, with all his allergies and his hypochondria, could be darn difficult to be around sometimes. The first few months in Haven, Rich had them all in stitches over his imagined ailments about the new foods and herbs and, well, nearly everything that existed in the other world. Much to his own surprise, Rich seemed much healthier in Haven. Still, that didn't keep him from fussing like some old lady over everything. Henry imagined himself getting all twitchy. That made him laugh at himself, if a little sheepishly, before heading downstairs.

"Mom!" he called out, thumping down the steps. "What smells so good?"

The smell of vanilla and sugar permeated the air about him as he sat, nearly drowsing at his writing desk, and the aroma sank into the pounding of his temples. It refreshed him, filling his senses with a hint of an idyllic youth he himself had never had, Jon rifted his chin. His attempts to back trace the drainer of the Leucators had failed, time and again, but this attempt ... hmmm ... yes, interesting. Just when his failure seemed deepest and darkest and most bitter to report to Isabella, this sweetness had enveloped him.

He'd done it almost idly, not thinking it would ever be revived, but it seemed Henry Squibb had come within his range again. Jon decided to follow up on a tentative sensing of someone or something and had not been sure it was Squibb, but now he knew for a certainty that he had a hold on the round-faced Magicker once again. It did not solve the problem of the Leucators, but it might hold other possibilities of its own, and at least he felt somewhat reassured at his abilities. The defeat of one problem was softened a little by unexpected success here.

Jon smiled at the pleasantness of the contact. Squibb seemed to be at home, as the warmth of a kitchen and bakery goods filled Jonnard's senses. How like Squibb to be surrounded by ... what was it? Cupcakes? Something of the sort. He decided not to grasp for a better understanding. The link between them stayed fuzzy and indistinct and although Jon knew he could sharpen it, he did not wish to do so. That might alert Henry as to the return of his soul to Jonnard's hold.

And that would be a tragedy. So many delightful things could be accomplished with Henry within his grasp again.

Jon sat up to rest his elbows on his desk. Should he tell Isabella of this accomplishment? Not yet, perhaps. Things should fall into place a little more, he decided. A world of possibilities could open up. He closed his eyes and let his mind drift into the vanilla-scented world of Henry Squibb where he sat and ate something sweet and iced, and worried with his mother over school, and if the authorities were tring to track down the whereabouts of the other Magicker Henry worried, it seemed, that attention was being drawn to the Magickers who had fled to Haven. Bureaucrats and red tape could be very damaging.

Oh, yes. That could be something *very* useful. Trouble brewing at home could make Jason Adrian very vulnerable.

Looking asleep but with his scheming mind very wide awake, Jonnard leaned his chin on his hands and enjoyed spying. His reverie jarred to a halt moments later as Isabella called out for him, her voice sharp with command. He collected himself before finding her in what she called the audience room. The Havenite mercenary called Fremmler stood at the far end of the room, his hat in one hand. He dressed a little finer than others of his ilk, could read and write skillfully and had the ability to talk a duck out of its feathers, but Jonnard trusted him no more than any of the other mercenaries despite his education. Perhaps it was the scarred and obliterated tattooing across his hand, signifying the loss of his Trade Guild status and honor.

Isabella gestured to Jonnard to sit, and so he did.

"I have asked Fremmler to join us for a few moments as I have an assignment for him."

"Indeed." Jonnard looked the man over quickly. Fremmler was one of the many disgruntled outlaws who'd joined them fast enough when given the opportunity to raid the society he'd been forced away from. He seemed no more aware of what Isabella wanted from him than Jon was. Jon steepled his fingers and eyed his mother, unsure of what she had in mind.

"We have an abundance of stores, and it is my understanding that many villages here about are a bit short, despite the bountiful harvest. Therefore, I am preparing to send Fremmler to the city to broker sales to those in need."

Fremmler's heavy jaw dropped in undisguised surprise.

Jon laughed. "Mother dear, that takes balls indeed, to sell them back what we have stolen from them."

Isabella smiled tightly at him. "We cannot live by grain alone. Why let it spoil if they need it? Fremmler here was a trader in good standing not too long ago." Her sharp gaze resettled on him. "I take it you still have contacts in the guild?"

"A few." He cleared his throat. "Milady, I am no longer a trader."

"You are my trader if I say you are. If they want stores, it's you they'll have to deal with. Is that understood?"

"Understood, indeed. How long have I to make the deals you want? And how do I get your acceptance of the terms I negotiate?" Fremmler quickly dropped his roughness and slid into the smooth, assured role he'd been born and educated to fill.

"I'll make arrangements for you to communicate, have no fear of that." Isabella tapped a citrine crystal shard lying on a nearby table. It glittered and shifted under her touch.

Fremmler looked a bit wary, but bowed again.

"Don't worry," said Jon with a huge grin. "That one won't cast Lightning."

"Good. Very good." And Fremmler looked a bit happier.

"As to what I want . . ." Isabella leaned forward and began to rattle off what she considered acceptable amounts to buy and deliver the shipments of goods she was willing to sell, while Jon sat and watched his mother with undisguised amusement and admiration. When she had finished and dismissed Fremmler with his crystal, she waited until the audience room door shut firmly and the sound of retreating footfalls disappeared entirely.

"You will, of course, follow and ensure his . . . safety," Isabella murmured.

Jon nodded as he stood. The prospect of getting out of the fortress for a bit beckoned welcomingly to him, and there were a few things in his father's journals he could now investigate without her questioning his journey to Naria.

Isabella raised her chin. "As for the other . . ."

"I have found a small thread, a faint contact, that I am trailing, Mother. In a few days, interrupted by this task, I shall have a most satisfactory answer for you."

She put her hand up and touched his cheek fleetingly. "Excellent. Most excellent."

He nodded as he took his leave for the evening. Her fingers on his skin had been as cold as ice.

Jason found Tomaz standing on a desert hill in Arizona, his arms outstretched to a setting sun although he'd sent him through to Dubai on the Gulf of Arabia, it seemed his Magicker elder had wandered far on his own. As he touched, and brought him through, the two crows on his forearms bated their wings and cawed harshly at him. He startled at the birds.

"Tomaz, I'm sorry! Let me send them back."

"No, no. They wished to accompany me. This is Midnight, and his mate, Snowheart." Tomaz bent a finger to the second crow and rubbed her chest where a tiny white blaze of feathers marked her. He raised both arms, sending the crows into the air, where they spread their wings and circled high in the Haven sky. Tomaz nodded, as if satisfied, then turned to Jason and grasped his arm in greeting. "Good work, as always."

Touching Tomaz filled him with a brief surge of energy, refreshing after the tiredness which had been haunting him lately. He let the warmth surge through him gratefully.

"Henry back yet?"

Jason shook his head. "I'm having a little trouble reaching him. I'll rest and try again in a bit. Gavan wants everyone home. The roof is done, and we're celebrating."

"Indeed! That is good news. Come with me and we'll find Gavan."

His knees almost felt too wobbly to walk, but Jason swallowed that down, and found that he felt better with every step he took, stretching his legs to keep up with Tomaz as they crossed the vale. Early morning's bright sunlight bathed them, giving a lie to the time of year, and the Iron Mountains stood in rusty, jagged relief behind the academy.

Overhead, the two crows dove at them, cawing in what seemed to be avian humor as they swooped low, barely clearing their heads. Tomaz waved them off with a string of Navajo in a jovial voice.

Jason found Ting and Bailey trying to string loops of netted crystal shards about the trees close to the outdoor kitchens, in spite of the fact the sun shone brightly. He reached up and tied the strands at the branches each pointed him to, although both often talked at once, confusing everyone, till they finally got the job finished and both girls sat down laughing and shoving at each other. Lacey ran up with a squeak, dropped something in Bailey's lap and scampered off again. Jason watched the little pack rat disappear into the undergrowth with a flip of her tufted tail.

"Aren't you afraid she's going to wander off?"

Bailey shook her head. "Not anymore. We have this rapport, now, and she feels I'm her home. I do worry that something might snap her up, though. She's not as nocturnal as she used to be, and thank goodness for that. I worry about owls!"

"She will be fine," Tomaz reassured, hugging both girls in one embrace and making them laugh even harder, before wandering off in search of Gavan who was evidently taking another ward check with Trent about the academy.

Ting took a deep breath, waggled a finger, and all her tiny crystal shards lit up. The trees sparkled with a dancing light effect. "Oooooh!" breathed Bailey. "It looks even better than we thought it would."

Ting leaned back, her face paling. She looked at Bailey, then gave a tiny shake of her head, and Bailey grew quiet.

Jason realized something between them had just gone unsaid, and he wondered what it was, but if they wanted him to know, it *would* have been said. He reached up and tightened one last bit of light strand. "Stef and Rich ready to go to Naria?"

"Gavan put that off till this evening, but he said they could stay over. Stef thought that was great, he gets two lessons that way, it seems. Anyway, we're about ready, just waiting for Henry."

"Then," stated Jason, "I'd better get him." With a wave, he went off to the small, quiet glade in the valley where he could concentrate best, often talked to the Dragon about things, and could be alone to do what he needed to do. Sitting on the small boulder and finding it pleasantly warmed by the sun, he crossed his legs and composed himself, and thought about Henry and the Dragon Gate carved into the side of the Iron Mountain. Henry with his pleasant face, usually smiling behind his glasses unless he was looking befuddled over the effect of some Magick he'd just tried that had gone wrong, Henry with his ability to talk tech and Magick with the best of them, Henry who ranked among the best of best friends and who loved his family wholeheartedly....

He caught the sense of him then, a glow of welcome, followed by a tinge of sadness as Henry felt his touch and no doubt began shouting his good-byes to his family. There came that moment when, like looking into a pool of water, he could feel himself looking at someone/something *else,* then that solidified into looking at Henry, all trussed up like a pack mule and hanging onto a chain of packages and burlap sacks, with one free hand to hold out to Jason. He grabbed Henry's hand as he swung the energies of the Dragon Gate open wide. He could feel the power surge of both worlds, like an immense tidal wave coming in, even as the other came in as well, both meeting with a tremendous clash and the archway of those energies a doorway through which he pulled Henry back to Haven.

Henry fell on him with a grunt and the weight of a collapsing grocery store. Jason slid off his boulder onto the soft, browning autumn grass, surrounded by cargo of every imaginable size, shape, and weight, and prayed nothing was heavy enough to break bones.

He sat up carefully, reaching out to right Henry who appeared about to disappear forever among his own bundles. "Good grief. Now I know what a ton of bricks feels like. Did you bring the kitchen sink back, too?"

"I brought back anything anyone could ever want or even think of!" Henry said proudly, if a bit out of breath, as he got to his knees, then clambered to his feet. "No kitchen sink, though, 'cause Gavan says we won't have real indoor plumbing for a while. He doesn't want to interfere with the natural technological growth of Haven."

"Right." Jason dusted himself off as he stood and stepped around the tangle of knotted ropes that linked Henry to all his cargo. He had to grin, he couldn't help it, Henry had managed to bring back package after package of . . . well, he couldn't begin to guess what it all was. *Stuff.*

Two pink rectangular boxes tied together with string dangled from his left wrist and smelled delightfully like . . . like . . . Jason reached for them.

"Ah-ah!" Henry cried and danced away from him. "That's a surprise."

"This whole mess is a surprise."

"Well, this is surprise-er," Henry declared. He let out a whoop then as the sound of running feet descended on them, and an academy of Magickers fell on both of them. "Mind the boxes!" Henry yelled just before the welcoming crowd overwhelmed him.

"This," declared Ting proudly, "is courtesy of Laura Squibb, Henry's mom, who remembered that Jason's birthday is right about now, give or take a few days."

Everyone gathered close, their mouths beginning to water at the smell of the goodies inside, their plates and napkins in hand, waiting.

"And so," Bailey finished up, waving a cake knife about, as she stood over the big opened pink boxes, one proudly displaying a vanilla cake with fine gold-and-green balloons and sprinkles all over and a second chocolate cake with marshmallow crystals all over it, "in honor not only of Jason's thirteenth birthday but in view of the fact that he is growing as if he's raced through fourteen and straight into fifteen . . . Happy Birthday, Happy Birthday—and Happy Birthday!"

A resounding cheer echoed around the academy as Bailey began to slice up the cakes and serve everyone eagerly lining up for their share.

Narian Nights

SO, THEN TRENT SAYS, for about the fifth time, 'Did anyone else notice that the trading capital is called Naria, almost like the mystic country Narnia from the C. S. Lewis books?' and Stefan growls at him, 'Yes, and if you point that out one more time and I don't get to go, you're going to spend the rest of your days here twisted up like a pretzel and thrown in the bottom of some wardrobe.'" Jason laughed as he licked some frosting off his already incredibly sticky fingers, and the Dragon let out an appreciative chuff of white smoke, not quite a laugh, more like a little chuckle, but that was all right.

"And this Narnia. A dangerous place?"

"Always, and steeped in wonder. Trent's point, of course, was that he thinks the writer C. S. Lewis might have somehow peeked into *here* and used his visits as a basis for his books, but I think that's far-fetched, and even if he had, it wouldn't have anything to do with Stefan. Nor did the books mention anything Like the people and places we've met."

"I see." The dragon took another dainty nibble off his huge slab of birthday cake and tried to ignore Jason's sidelong glances as if he might still be a bit hungry. In fact, he cupped his taloned paw about the plate and slid it a bit closer to his chest, hoarding it. "And then what did you all do?"

"Oh, we goofed off. Trent and I got into our favorite sword fight, from the pirates movie—ah—play that we love . . . there's a bit . . ." Jason jumped to his feet, picking up a long branch from the ground to brandish like a sword. "One guy is the honest young hero, and the other is the pirate Captain Jack Sparrow, who is a bit crazy and very sneaky. So they're fighting away, and it's a good fight. Our hero is a very good swordsman, but Sparrow seems to be a bit better, and a little surprised by his opponent. Anyway, the hero doesn't like pirates and is trying to bring Jack to justice and Jack is trying to escape, but doesn't really want to hurt the hero. So it goes like this—" And Jason acted out the swordplay bits he'd memorized, his muscles stretching in forms taught him by Madame Qi and his own efforts. "Then Sparrow does this, which is totally punk, and he has the hero up against the blade, and the hero says, 'Cheating!' and Sparrow looks at him, and shrugs and says, 'Pirate!' which of course he is, meaning that naturally he'll lie and cheat, that's what pirates *do* so it's not really cheating, it should be expected . . . and the two guys kinda look at each other, shrug and grin, and go back to fighting." Jason laughed as he dropped his willowy stick and plopped back on the ground.

"You admire this pirate?"

"Yes and no. He's very smart and he tricks everyone, so I couldn't live like that, but it's his wits that keep him alive. And, in the end, he helps everyone out."

The dragon's forked tongue flickered out and he took another small nibble of the cake. "Seems you admire him a bit, though."

"I think Trent does more than I do, but, really, he's just a character in a movie . . . ah, play." Jason leaned back, lacing his fingers behind his head. "I think he's interesting. He makes a point of teaching that: one—not everyone is really what we expect them to be, so you shouldn't be labeling them; but at the same time, two—if they have a certain nature, you can't be expecting them to be anything else."

"Ah." The dragon let out a soft, rumbling purr which

might be because of what Jason had just voiced, or might be because of the velvety goodness now melting in his mouth. "Still . . ." and he paused to roll his tongue about his large mouth, savoring the bite of cake. "A play is more than just entertainment, it often has life truths buried in it. You seem to be pondering a few in this favorite of yours."

"In a way. It proves there are good and bad people in all walks of life, and you have to look at each person separately, you know? You can't just lump 'em together and say, everyone who wears a hat is evil or something like that. Then, too, it says something about the basic soul of a person. We have a fable about that . . . it goes something like this." Jason stopped. "Do you know what scorpions are?"

The dragon dipped his head. "I have met them in my travels. Nasssty creatures."

"Exactly. Well, spring rains have been heavy and every place is flooding and the only safety for this group of animals is to get to high ground, but to do it, they must swim a river. Most of the animals make it, after a struggle, and the strong, agile fox helps many by taking them over on his back. Finally, all that's left is the fox and a scorpion. The scorpion has been pleading for help, but none of the other animals would take it over. The fox is his only chance and he begs the fox to swim him over. 'Don't do it,' the fox's friends advise him from the other side of the river, but the scorpion says, 'Don't listen to them. I promise not to sting you and I want to live!' After a few moments' hesitation, with the river rising higher and higher, the fox agrees, for it is a smart but helpful beast. So the scorpion hops on and they dive into the water. The river is raging and the fox is nearly exhausted as he swims close to the other side. Suddenly, the scorpion lashes his tail out and stings him . . . once! Twice! Thrice! And the fox feels the poison burn through him, and begins to die, sinking into the waters. 'Why, oh why,' he cries to the scorpion. 'Now we shall both die.' And as the river takes them, the scorpion says, 'But it is my nature to sting and you knew that, foolish fox.'" Jason looked up at the sky as it darkened toward night. Somewhere below, Tomaz was escorting Rich and Stefan to Naria, and everyone was preparing for nightfall.

"A wise man who wrote that play."

"Very. It reminds me of Isabella and Jonnard."

The dragon rumbled lowly. "Ah. Now I have some sense of the train of your thoughts."

"Do you?"

"Your enemies bother you."

He nodded slowly. "I guess they do. I think I'm fairly certain of their natures, though."

"The problem then becomes . . ."

Jason unlaced his hands and sat up, looking intently at his draconian friend. "I think it's me I'm unsure of."

"Part of the infinite process of living, for many people." The dragon flipped his tail barb slightly. "It is a worthy pursuit to know oneself, one that many fear to understand and most never quite achieve."

"I think I need to know the answer a lot quicker than that," Jason said dryly.

"As long as you understand the answer is flexible. Perhaps not flexible but . . . evolving. Yes. The answer evolves as you do. Sometimes for better and sometimes for worse."

"That makes sense." Jason got to his feet.

"You don't seem comforted by it, though."

"Not yet." He smiled slowly. "I'll let you know."

"Do that." The dragon let his spiny face whiskers rattle as he drew his head down and nudged Jason slightly. "Again, thank you for the cake."

"Welcome. I'm glad you enjoyed it."

"Very much so, though it is not the sort of thing I would normally eat. I much prefer a nice charbroiled haunch of red meat, but it is good. As for the other quandary in your life, I might suggest patience. I have been called very patient by my colleagues. I can stalk prey for a very, very long time before I decide to attack."

Jason shifted uneasily. "I'm not sure knowing that makes me feel better."

The dragon laughed then, a real rumbling, thundering laugh, finishing in a spout of steam out his nostrils. "I am not stalking *you,* dear boy! But if I were, you wouldn't know it." The dragon dropped one scaled eyelid in a slow wink that unnerved Jason altogether.

He fished out his crystal and cupped it. "I think it is definitely time to go," he told the dragon and before they could exchange another word, he had Crystaled himself to the academy grounds. Jason let out a soft sigh of relief. He didn't want his friend reading any more of his thoughts that night, particularly the ones where he had almost decided he would have to break his vows of being a Guardian for Haven. It was *not* in his nature to lie.

Renart stretched his back and flexed his hands as he reached to light another lantern, the shadows in his office cubby growing darker and the papers he scribed on getting a bit harder to read. As the wick took and flared, and he positioned the lantern, the office glowed brighter. He took stock of his work. Only, what ... three more journals to copy and his work in here would be finished. For the month, anyway, when caravans would bring in their goods and their own ledgers. He might, yes, he might actually be able to wheedle a small five or six days to himself, which would give him ample time to visit Avenha and take a look at its rebuilding and, with any luck at all, see Pyra again as well. Although she hadn't invited him as a suitor, neither had she thrown him out, and he hoped he sensed a certain liking for her part. Upon his return to the Trader Guild's offices and warehouse, it seemed Mantor had spoken well of him, for his load had lightened a bit and the other traders were no longer so openly disdainful. Perhaps his days of being disbarred were drawing to a close!

He flexed his fingers yet again, as he reached for a new pen. In the muted corridor beyond, the hustle and bustle of the junior clerks and the trading ambassadors had grown quiet, for it was the dinner hour, and many had gone to the inns, or the sumptuous dining room for esteemed higher traders at the other side of the guild offices. Being more eager to finish his work for the night and remain ahead of the pace, Renart had elected to skip his own dinner, and the interruptions of the others as well.

Downstairs, he could hear the chime at the guild's front door. The lobby noise often did not filter up to him, but it being so quiet now ... Renart paused a moment to eavesdrop as a young apprentice scampered to the door and, panting faintly, pulled it open with a small squeak of its huge bronze hinges.

"Trader Fremmler here, to speak to the Trader Guild masters with an offering."

Renart dropped his pen on the desk and grabbed it

before its newly inked nib point could splatter ink everywhere on his neat ledger pages. Fremmler! That blackheart? The man had been cast out for life! What could he be doing here? Even if he hadn't known of Fremmler before, his own exploits had been thrown into his face as if he were following in the man's corrupt footsteps. According to the guild, Fremmler's trading habits had been as bad as murder. Yet he sounded as if he were proposing a trade!

Renart got to his feet slowly, well aware that the lumber joints in the massive, old building tended to creak with every movement. Yet, this was information he had to hear and if the apprentice did his job, he would lead Fremmler into the small antechamber for audiences and summon a master trader, one of the Guild Leaders, to talk to him. It would be up to the master to throw Fremmler out, or summon town guards to jail him for his audacity. Either way, Renart itched with curiosity to know what was going on.

He slipped off his boots and crept in stockinged feet to the small storage cupboard down the hall, where paper, ledgers, pens, nibs, ink, and the Spirit knew what else were stored by the shelf full, closed the door, and lay down on the floor. Here, he'd learned as a young apprentice himself, here things could often be heard through the flooring of what transpired in that antechamber. Sure enough, he heard the youngling downstairs usher Fremmler in, offer him a drink against the dust of his travels, and ask him to have a seat while he announced Fremmler's arrival. Moments passed but not many. Renart fought to keep the dust from irritating his nose. He scrubbed at his nostrils twice against persistent tickles.

Heavy boot steps announced the arrival of not one, but two trade ministers! The moment the first spoke, Renart knew which two it had to be, the Guild leader and his assistant. One Renart thought well of, as he'd served him several years as an apprentice, but the old gent, Shmor, he thought of warily. Shmor had all the power, and it was he who'd demanded Renart's disbarment. Now Renart realized it was because his actions had left Shmor out of the exchange and powerless over the Magickers. Renart took a long, slow breath and pressed his ear closer to hear all the better as Shmor made noises of outrage at the unwanted guest.

"Fremmler! Your presence was never to darken the Guild offices again. Must I summon the guards?"

"Shmor, Gammen." Fremmler sounded composed, even a bit amused. "I may no longer be a trader in standing with your guild, but I am here, nonetheless, representing a deal."

"Deal? Deal? What position are you in to offer a deal? You are disbarred!" Shmor's gravelly voice rattled and vibrated through the very timber of the floor Renart lay upon listening.

Gammen coughed. It was the dry cough of his many lectures, a sound Renart smiled at in memory. "It would be wise, Fremmler, if you left now. Otherwise, there are consequences. Your tattoos are branded and your standing dismissed."

"I am well aware of the consequences. However, I represent a party who could care less about the Trader Guild and its petty rules. I have a deal. Listen or not. There is always the smugglers' market where one can make a profit." Shoe leather squeaked, as if Fremmler pivoted on one heel to walk away.

Another cough. "We are all well versed in your acquaintance with the thieves' market. So, considering the stake, why have you come to us first?"

Renart smiled. Leave it to Gammen to cut to the chase ahead of Shmor who might talk in circles for days as if negotiating a great treaty and trying to leave the details so vague that no one but he would quite understand all the ramifications. No, Gammen was direct.

"My Principal requested that I come here first."

"Then you are handling the interests of another. Why would they choose an outcast to deal for them?"

"Do they not know better, you mean?" Fremmler let out a snorting laugh. "They know very well what they do."

Shmor let out a grumbling sound and ended up saying, "I would hear this deal, then. But make it quick, for you tread on very thin ice."

"The deal is this . . . we have goods to sell, foodstuffs, against the coming winter. Grains, cured meats, the usual gourds and fruits that can be laid down in cellars. We know that some of your towns and villages have meager stores due to misfortunes." Fremmler sounded intensely bored.

A dust curl seemed to be inching Renart's way and he shifted to pull a fine linen handkerchief out of his pocket and lay it over his face. A sneeze now would nearly be fatal.

"It seems your Principal is well versed in our needs."

Shmor let out another grumble, overriding whatever else Gammen might have been saying, at least to Renart's hearing. "Let us dispense with whatever pretense to pleasantries we might throw at each other. Who is your Principal?"

"Such a disclosure is not always required."

"In this case it is."

Gammen coughed faintly. If his old teacher said something under it, again Renart could not catch it.

"Lady Isabella of the Dark Hand," answered Fremmler to Shmor's challenge.

"Outrage!"

Gammen coughed in earnest, as if choking on his words, and for long moments, Renart could hear nothing clear or of any worth. He got to his feet reluctantly. Whether they dealt with him or not, he knew now what Fremmler wanted. What brass the woman had, to steal from them, and then sell the goods back. Yet it would be bought. It had to be. Their people needed their harvest against the oncoming hard seasons.

Back in his tiny office, he pulled on his boots, thinking. He'd send word to the Magickers of this new ploy. There was nothing that could be done and it would likely not win Isabella any new allies other than the outlaws she'd already drawn to her side. But it might. Yes, with enough cunning, it could be twisted, and Shmor probably would not stop the rumors for it would look just as bad for the traders to be dealing with what amounted to blackmailers. No, Shmor would want as good a light as he could cast on it. He might even say that he'd found a generous benefactor who agreed to help them in their time of need. The common people would never know the difference.

Renart frowned. He'd tell Pyra, too, and Mantor, of course, and the chieftain would, no doubt, have ideas of his own.

Renart stood up quietly, easing both feet deeper into his boots. He had much to do after hours tonight, and here he'd hoped for a good rest! Sitting down, he dove into the account ledgers once more, copying with a swift but legible hand, his mind scarcely taking in the task he did.

Oil in his lantern had sputtered more than once, signaling being close to having burned out when he finally put down his pen, swept away the used nibs into a small cup where they would be repaired or given to schoolchildren for their lessons, and closed the drawer on his paper. The hubbub of returning diners had come and gone and he was nearly the only person still in the building, or at least the only one working. Master traders might still sit in the back, in the lounge, partaking of a good brandy and chatting in front of the fireplace, mulling over Fremmler's latest audacity and the signs of a harsh winter headed their way. Some might even be talking of philosophy and the Spirit, and others might be snoring quietly, their day finished.

Downstairs the chime rang again as Renart stood, reaching for his cloak, and settling it about his shoulders, then put out his lanterns. If Fremmler's showing up hadn't been strange enough, now here was another visitor at an extremely late hour. He gathered his scribe case and trotted down the hall to the stairs. He was thinking of ducking out the back way just as the apprentice of the hour came round the corner and then gave a relieved smile.

"Renart! So you *are* still here! You have a guest."

"Me? The name?"

"Oh. Oh." Flustered, the apprentice bowed in apology. "Tomaz Crowfeather is waiting to see you."

Tomaz! Another bold surprise, but convenient. "Good," answered Renart. He renewed his grip on his scribe's case and made his way to the front door, where Tomaz stood haloed by the light of the sconces and the fading moon.

"Well met!" cried Renart and reached out for the other's hand. "Have you business here or have you come just to see me?"

"You, I think," answered Tomaz slowly, as if considering his words before saying them.

"Good. I feel the need of a hot meal and a good drink, and I have things to discuss with you. Many things."

"Hmmmm. Perhaps it is fortunate I stopped, then. Lead the way." But Tomaz seemed a bit preoccupied, and looked around the shadowed street a moment before catching up with Renart.

He touched Renart's wrist lightly, and whispered in a voice the trader almost did not catch. "Did you know Jonnard was hereabouts, and watching the guild?"

Renart shook his head quickly.

"Then it is indeed fortunate I am here. Find a quiet inn, with private corners, will you?"

And so what Renart had thought to be an early evening now looked as if it would be a long, and startling, night.

More Night

RENART SCARCELY DARED utter a word till he found a curtained alcove at The Turkey's Wing, and sat down with Tomaz, the heavy drapery certain to muffle whatever they said. Tomaz took a crystal out of a vest pocket and laid it on the scarred wooden table, spoke a word, and a dull orange glow flowed out of it and mingled with the light from the oil sconces on the wall.

"We won't be heard," the Magicker told him.

Renart nodded, feeling nervous but trying not to show it. "If you saw Jonnard, then surely he saw you."

"I doubt it. I take precautions when traveling here. Our welcome is still uncertain." Tomaz gave a smile that was barely more than a faint curve of his mouth, but his eyes warmed. "Why were you not surprised? Alarmed, but not surprised."

"I was leaving work and knew I would have to contact one of you as soon as I could. Isabella sent a disbarred trader, an outlaw named Fremmler, to the guild early tonight. He came with a deal. She intends to sell back much of what they've stolen, it seems."

Tomaz let out a low grunt. He traced a knife mark cut

into the wood of the table under his hand. "Enterprising of her."

"Very. She might even turn it into good propaganda, if people never understand she stole the goods in the first place. Without those stores, there are villages who will suffer terrible deprivations this winter. It will cost them to buy it back, but it is better than facing starvation." Renart shrugged off his cloak onto the back of his chair, and waited as the serving lad brought a tray in with the food and drinks they'd ordered at the counter. The meat pies smelled good and their gravies poured out through the crust onto the plates, and the bread loaf was warm as if just pulled from the oven. He took a mug of Narian tea and pulled it to him. "Is that why Jonnard was here, do you think? Isabella not quite trusting Fremmler to set up everything to her specifications?"

"That's the most likely explanation."

"Do you intend to stop it?"

Tomaz shook his head. "If I would stop anything, it would be the raiding. It would be a fool's attempt to stop a trade deal, however. Wheels within wheels and all that." He traced the knife mark again.

"If you didn't know about Jonnard, why are you here?"

"I'm escorting some of the younger Magickers on a town trip, and I thought I would stop in to see you." Tomaz leaned forward. "I have need of an old map, a copy. It doesn't have to be the artifact itself, but a reliable copy."

"What map?"

"One that shows the fortresses along the boundary of the old kingdom."

Renart's heart relaxed enough to give a normal beat. At least he wasn't being asked for the impossible, dangerous, or unwise. He lifted his spoon and made a vent in the crust of his pie, letting delicious smelling steam gush out. "I can give that to you tonight. I'd have to return to the guild house, though."

"Tomorrow morning, then. Best not to give Jonnard a reason to wonder at your comings and goings any more than he does. I am certain he remembers your dealings with us."

Renart shivered at the memory. He nodded. "All right, then. I can procure what you need early . . . but how to get it to you?"

"Where are the closest windows to your workplace?"

"Windows?" Renart had to think on that. He *was* on an outer wall, as well as the corridor. He swept his memory over the area. No, no, nothing so cheerful as a window . . . wait. Yes! A small oval near the ceiling, almost hidden by the overstuffed set of bookcases. It was hardly bigger than his head, however. "Small one," he answered.

"Show me."

Renart traced the remembered outline with his hand.

"Good. Open it for a bit of morning sun when you get into your office. Get the chart, roll it up. I'll have my crow there within fifteen marks of your entering the building."

"Crow?"

Tomaz nodded. "Make sure the chart is protected, their claws can be hard on paper."

"All right. Give me thirty marks, in case I have to trace a rendering first. The map I feel you want should have copies, but if not, I'll have to make one."

"Done." Tomaz took up his own spoon and began to chop the golden-brown crust down into the meat and its gravy, and for a long time neither said anything as they ate, and enjoyed, and thought difficult thoughts. When they both had pushed away their plates, he said, "I have places to go yet."

"Sleep for me, with much work facing me in the morning."

Tomaz smiled as he stood, and leaned over, and shook Renart's hand. "You've been a good friend."

"How could I be otherwise? You are good people." Renart gave a crooked smile before pulling his coat about him, fading into the evening crowd, and disappearing.

Tomaz scooped up the crystal, frowning then, as its glow had been nearly extinguished. He tossed the small object from one palm to another, pondering it before pocketing it. It should not have dimmed in the time they were there. He would have to stow away that knowledge with other, equally odd, observations.

Crossing town by the back ways, of which there were many, steeply shadowed in what was now the deepest part of the evening, Tomaz felt a prickling across the back of his shoulders. Without seeming to, he angled toward the buildings and looked around when he could, but nothing met his keen glance. Still, his senses told him that it was too quiet about the alleys. The small critters of the dark that always frequented such places, to catch what bits and pieces of food they could, were gone. There was something that startled them besides himself. Tomaz did not like the idea he was being followed.

He knew ways to confound whoever it was, though, and changed his pattern of movement only a little, headed toward the forger and arena where Stefan learned his sword work. The coyote had given him many lessons in stealth and trickery and Tomaz did not worry.

Torchlight flickered at the edge of the arena despite the time of night, and he could see Stef's big, square body, sword in hand, as he went through a series of positions and strike exercises, a slender girl watching him with the keen eyes of a hawk and barking out corrections as Stef took advantage of every moment of his time. Tomaz let himself grin at the sight, an expression which he would smooth away when Stef could actually see him as well. The boy who was not quite a man was sensitive and might misunderstand the humor in seeing someone so large carefully mind the orders of someone so slight. Yet it was true that the most slender of daggers was often also the most deadly.

Looking at the swordsmith's daughter, Tomaz could also easily understand why Stefan wanted his lessons. She was handsome more than beautiful, her expression intent as she watched, her jaw set, a large, heavy sword swinging easily from one hand as if it held little weight at all. Her long hair was pulled back by a beaded headband, and she wore an armored vest cut away from her shoulders to leave her arms free. Her leather breeches showed scuff marks and scarring from the impact of dulled blades.

He swept the shadows behind him one last time, then brushed his fingertips across his crystal, checking for presences he might have missed as he began to step out into the open. She sensed his movement as he did so, raising a hand to her in welcome. Stef swung about with a grunt of effort, as Tomaz let the grin drop from his face and searched for a more appropriate smile.

Something moved behind him even as his crystal flickered in meager warning. He started to swing about . . . too late, as heaviness crashed down on his head, and everything went dark.

Stef saw Beryl's intense gaze move away from him, and across the dirt arena to the darkened city behind the pole fencing. He wondered if her father had come to get them, declaring an end to the long night of lessons. Every muscle he had and a few he must have borrowed ached beyond reason and he felt thankful for a short break in her attention. Rich, legs stretched out in front of him and crossed at the ankle, had gone to sleep long ago in the shed at the arena's back which connected to the forge. The forge itself was banked for the night, fires down to a glow, but always present, never cold. He took a deep breath, then swung about to see what had attracted Beryl's attention.

Tomaz moved into the barest of illumination from a still bright moon though the Hunter's Moon was now days ago. Hand raised in greeting to them, he did not see the shadow rising from behind him, cloaked in billowing darkness, nor the sliver of silver that cut through it.

"Hey!" bellowed Stef. He ran toward the arena fencing as Tomaz dropped with a heavy thud into the street.

The cloaked figure stood over the fallen Magicker a moment, then turned toward Stef. He dropped the hood to his shoulders, revealing Jonnard's cruelly smiling face, and gave an ironic salute with his saber.

Stef launched himself over the fence with a roar and went after Jonnard. He could feel the bear cub rippling through his muscles as he yelled. "Rich! Rich, get out here, Tomaz is hurt!" He didn't know if he could be heard as he lowered his head and charged toward Jonnard. Alley dirt felt gritty under his feet.

Jon turned to face him with an ironic laugh. "And what do you think you can do?"

Stef bared his teeth as he brought up his blade, into a move Beryl had drilled into him only hours before, and it felt good. Without answering, he parried, then thrust at the other.

Jon met his blow, and stepped back, gathering himself. "You'll have to do better than that. A lot better!" He turned slightly and began his attack, the swords ringing off each other, even as the sound of people running toward them punctuated it. With a harsh laugh, Jon pivoted around and sprang away down the alley.

Stef followed without a second thought. Hot blood steamed through his tired body, and nothing mattered but catching Jonnard. Catching him and wiping that snotty expression off his face. Behind him, both Rich and Beryl called, and he heard it though his ears rang with the trumpeting of his own pulse and anger. The bear cub struggled inside of him to burst free.

No bear! A bear couldn't hold a sword blade or run the streets after Jon. He fought back, zigzagging after Jon's path. He turned a sharp corner into a smelly, dank mouth of an alley, and Jon sprang at him.

He accidentally parried the blow, and the vibration of it stung his forearm, but he forced Jon back onto his heels with a grunt. Stef righted himself and tried a jab which nearly got through the other's guard. A look flickered over Jonnard's face, quickly replaced by a curl of his lip.

"Think you've learned a bit?" Jon laughed sharply. He swung his blade easily and countered Stef with a series of moves that clashed heavily between them. Stef couldn't touch Jon, but neither could Jon break through Stef's defense. Jon tossed his head. "You are tired and your sweat stinks of bear."

Stef growled in response. He charged, not quite ready to attack, but his body flung itself forward and he had to go with it, fighting himself as well as the other. His body rumbled with the need to change. His crystal rested on a thick leather choker about his neck, a collar even the bear couldn't burst, and he dropped his chin to touch it better, reaching for aid.

His senses skittered away and then latched onto a Magicker, but not the Rich he expected, the Rich who'd always been there to help him. Rich had his hands full tending Tomaz. He only caught the barest glimpse of his friend. In need, his mind filled with another Magicker, surprising him. Instead, he found Jason. He reached out, pleading silently for help to stay himself in his own skin, to be centered. It was as if they had clasped hands. Without hesitation, Jason poured strength into him, steadying, his own anger fueling him, but with a cool concentration, as if he had . . . well, opened a Gate into Stefan. He let himself be filled with the other's confidence and encouragement.

He snarled as Jon saw him hesitate in that connecting moment and darted out of the blind alley, out of the stink and the fight. Stef went after him. He could feel Jason's pulse drumming inside his. He pounded after the dark billowing cloud of Jonnard's cloak, drawing nearer and nearer. *Go, go, go, get him!* Not built for speed, never built for speed, he lowered his head as he neared, and flung himself after Jon in a diving tackle.

They hit. Jon went down, sliding across the rough and broken paving of the alleyway under him, both grunting, and their blades shining like lightning bolts in the darkness. Stef rolled off the other and hauled him to his feet, panting, resisting a howl of triumph. Jon's foot lashed out, and pain shot through Stef s knee. Reeling back, he lost his grip on the other, and Jon shoved him back farther, bringing up his saber.

"Now," he said. "Face a master."

"Gladly!" Stef brought his guard up, feeling Jason still with him, anchoring him, and filling his mind with the moves that Madame Qi had taught him, as she'd tried to teach Stefan. No longer afraid the bear would rule him, he tapped into its strength as well, and a blend of himself and Magicker, he faced Jonnard.

Blades slashed and met one another, struck and countered, parried and stung the air. They rang and clashed off each other's blows, and Jonnard frowned as Stef met him cut for cut. It wasn't pretty or smooth, but neither did Jon outmatch him as he'd intended. Stef found himself grinning in a kind of fierce joy. Right blow, left, up, down, his blade answered Jon's.

He knew a lot of the flow came from Jason. He could feel it running through his mind and memory, Jason in Ninjalike combat with the Dark Hand, flowing through hand and feet and sword. He did not mind. This was what his body was meant to do, had been training to do. He couldn't master it yet, but he *would,* someday and when he did, this was how he would fight!

Stef threw his head back in a gleeful roar as Jonnard stepped back, sword arm trembling with effort.

"Freak," snarled Jon.

"And proud of it!" He raised his sword for another blow, strength still in his arms, and fury coursing through him for what Jon had done, and intended to do.

Jon broke. He grasped his crystal and disappeared in a flash of light.

Stef stood for a moment, anger still at high tide in him, and faced nothingness. He lowered his blade reluctantly. Jason's presence inside him began to fade away, leaving only the softest touch inside him, a congratulation for doing well, and then the other Magicker was gone as well.

Stef took a deep breath. He swung about, getting his bearings in the city, and then trotted back to the forge. Tiredness hit him like a falling tree, and he shook it off with a bearlike growl. By the time he found the streets he needed, he was staggering and laughing at himself.

Rich and Beryl met him.

"How's Tomaz?"

"Thickheaded, like you. Jon clubbed him with the sword hilt. How are you?" Rich swept his hands over him quickly.

"Nothing a good night's sleep won't cure."

Beryl eyed him, her face hiding its concern after a quick look. "Then I suggest you get that sleep. Tomorrow's lesson will be on gauging your opponent and knowing when to retreat!" She slapped his sword arm, not lightly, before walking away.

Rich said, "I think I agree. That was stupid going after him."

"Oh, yeah? Well I caught him and guess what? Bear and I made him run!" Stef let out a growling laugh. The night might be late, but it was good!

"Are you sorry we didn't get to go anywhere?" Ting spoke softly into the darkness of their room.

"There's time. I'm just glad Stef got to go. I mean, there's not much he asks for, you know? So, it's his turn to be Cinderella."

"Only he doesn't turn into a pumpkin at midnight, he turns into a bear!" Ting giggled softly, her voice almost like a wind chime.

Bailey grinned into the night. "Besides," she said. "We still have that map."

"True! We'll have to plan that out very carefully."

"Do you think our theory is correct?"

"I think that we are definitely losing power quicker than we did at home, and we're slower getting it back. That's not good."

"It sure isn't." Bailey turned onto her side. As her eyes adjusted to the gloom, she could almost see Ting's slender figure curled on her cot across the room. "We can't prove anything yet."

"I'm not sure if it's the kind of thing we *can* prove."

"It's likely," Bailey said quietly, "they already know and have decided not to tell us."

"You think?"

"It wouldn't be the first time. The question is . . . will it be really important at just the wrong time?"

"Yeah," breathed Ting.

Neither said another word, and after a long moment, Bailey realized Ting had slipped into sleep. She pulled her blankets closer about her, one of them brand new from Laura Squibb, and snuggled in as well. Just before she drifted off, she felt the tentative, tiny movements of Lacey climbing in as well and curling up close to her ear. Bailey fell asleep smiling.

"Good morning," Rich said cheerfully as he slid into the hot mineral waters, and sank down with a blissful look on his face. His fair, pale skin immediately pinked from the heat, his freckles standing out, and his red hair began to curl into a mat of frizz, but it was obvious he could care less.

"Isn't morning. Still night from what I can see."

"That's what you get for all the gallivanting around. And wait till Tomaz gets up. Even with that headache of his, I think you're going to catch it from him." Rich peered at Stef. About all of Stef that showed was the top half of his head, his nose barely clearing the bubbling pool of water. "If you can see anything through the steam."

"I can see." Stef jammed a thumb up at the shed's roof, where the sky could still be seen as dark. "Nighttime."

"The sun is on the horizon and Tomaz will be here any minute." Rich paused. "I'm sorry we have to go home early. At least you got some sword work in last night. Urm-mmm . . ." He reached out and touched Stef's shoulder under the water. "Wow. That's some welt. She must pack a punch."

Stef emerged a bit and gave a proud grin. "Yeah, she's good with that sword, dull or not. Really good."

"Maybe we can convince Gavan to let us come back regularly, like we were doing before."

"I hope so! She says," and Stefan cleared his throat, "she says her dad is forging a real sword for me. Special one. The hilt is this rearing bear, like."

Rich whistled. "You're kidding."

"Nope."

"That's, wow, that's some sword."

Stef looked intently at his friend. "You know I don't talk about myself, right?"

"Yeah, I know, buddy."

"Beryl thinks I could be, well, like a hero. Her father says, the lands are gonna need a few. He says the Spirit is getting weak. No one wants to talk about it or admit it, but he can't protect them like he did. If he could, the Dark Hand wouldn't have done what they've done. Jonnard coming into the city last night like he did just reinforced that."

"So the old guy believes in this Spirit, huh?"

"They all do. From what I heard, Rich, it exists. The Warlord existed, and he left this mighty Spirit behind to keep his people safe. But he's a Spirit, see, and he's not meant to go on forever. The other side is pulling on him, wants to make his soul whole. He's thinning out, and some day, the Spirit will be gone."

"What then?"

"Heroes." Stef nodded grimly. "They're going to need warriors to stand up for 'em. I'm not saying I fit into that, you know. I think I could help, though. That, I could do. This strength I get from the bear, this fearlessness. Sometimes that's what it takes."

"Stef—" For a moment, Rich felt very cold, in spite of the hot water of the pool.

"Don't worry, I'm not going to do anything stupid like I did last night. I met Jon, okay? But he's far better and I know it. Still, I like learning the sword. It makes my muscles work, like football used to, and my mind work in a different way. Magick stuff drives me kinda crazy sometimes, you know? I miss football. If I got mad at anything, I could just push it into there. Now, it's got no place to go and that isn't good for me."

"Gavan's just looking out for all of us."

"I know that. Doesn't mean he's doing the right thing, though, for everyone." Stefan stood up, water cascading off his stocky body, and wrapped a towel about himself. Rich could see three good-sized welts on his torso and a couple of purpling bruises on his legs. He wouldn't ask whether the training or the encounter with Jon had made them.

Rich had been a trainer for the football team, and he'd seen Stefan all bruised up any number of times. That had never bothered the big guy. What had bothered him was trying to do his best for the team.

His best for this team, Stef seemed to feel, did not lie in his Magick. Rich began to understand that. He made up his mind to talk with Gavan and Tomaz and the other elders and see if he could make them understand that, as well.

Stef had dressed completely and Rich had gotten most of his clothes on when Tomaz appeared at the shed door.

"Good. It looks as if you are ready." Tomaz nodded in approval, even as he lifted a finger and scratched the small white diamond on the chest of the otherwise glossy black crow on his shoulder.

"Who's that?"

"Snowheart," Tomaz told him. "She came back with me, as did her mate. I do not know if this world will accept them, but I needed them. We must hurry. After last night's retreat, I don't want Jon coming back to test our weakness." He rubbed the back of his neck ruefully. "He might have tried more if it hadn't been for Stefan."

"I'm ready for more!"

Rich thumped his shoulder. "This ain't the time, big guy. You yourself said you weren't quite ready yet."

"Yeah, yeah." Stef's face wrinkled up in disappointment, but he stepped back in agreement. Instead, he gathered up his things and Rich's herb bags.

"There will be a time," Tomaz told them both. "And let us hope it is a time we can be prepared for." Snowheart cawed sharply at his words, punctuating them.

Ghostwalking

JASON WOKE IN THE EARLY dawn, warmer than usual, and feeling it was darker than usual as he looked up and saw the roof overhead. He reached over and touched a fingertip to the crystal lantern, setting off its glow, and the reflector behind it broadcast light throughout the room. Trent's deep breathing indicated he wasn't even close to waking yet, and Jason wondered what it was that had awakened him.

A sensation prickled over him, something unfamiliar and possibly unpleasant, but he wasn't quite sure. Gooseflesh rose on his arms and the back of his neck, and he looked about without seeing anything. He rubbed his arms. He didn't like feeling spooked. What could intrude, with all the wards they had laid into the very wood and stone of the academy?

Jason shifted uneasily, then got up and dressed. Downstairs, in the kitchen, he found no one about but Madame Qi, leaning on her bamboo cane while shaking tea leaves into a china pot. She smiled as she poured steaming water into it.

"Henry brought back some truly excellent Chinese tea."

She smiled, her seamed face breaking into many wrinkles, as she took a deep breath and inhaled the aroma. "Have some with me?"

"That would be great." He sat down on one of the three-legged stools, leaving a sturdy chair for her. She said nothing, and he said little more, as she busied herself fixing their drinks and putting biscuits with jam out on a plate. The biscuits had to be from yesterday, but that was all right; they'd be good dunked. Jason waited politely for Ting's grandmother to sit and pour him a cup. It was then he noticed the goose bumps had slowly gone away, although the feeling that something had been watching him was still there.

"Jason, my student, always the quiet one and yet even quieter today. What brings you so early in the morning?"

He pulled the delicate, handleless cup close to him, the heat of the tea warming his fingers through the china. She had not been trained as a Magicker, yet she had told all of them stories of her grandfather who was a Chinese magician in his time, and who had undoubtedly had some kind of Talent as did she, and certainly Ting, her granddaughter.

She did not watch him as she gathered her own drink and biscuit, as if giving him a break from her sharp eyes. Otherwise, she always seemed to see more than others.

"Did you feel it," he asked then. "Something odd."

"We live in a world other than our own, where a dragon comes to talk with you, and someone offers you a six-fingered hand in welcome . . . and you ask if I feel something odd?" She sat back with a chuckle.

He cleared his throat, feeling very awkward. "I don't know how else to put it. It's as though I woke up and something had been watching me."

She nodded then, holding her teacup at chin level. "That, young man, is precisely what woke me. Whatever it is, the wards do not seem to bother it."

"Then I'm not the only one who felt it!"

"Even if you were, would you doubt it had happened?"

He thought a moment before shaking his head. "No. No, something was stirring. I don't know what, but I felt it."

"Like a ghost walking over your grave."

"Exactly!"

"And then, perhaps it was. Here, they speak of the Spirit often enough."

Jason sipped his tea. It was strong and slightly smoky flavored, with a bite. He wished he'd had some sugar for it, but they used sugar sparingly. It was hard to store and had become a luxury. "The Spirit. Looking us all over? I wonder."

"Wonder more if Gavan and Tomaz did not feel it. Has it cloaked itself against them? Will it test us? What is it looking for in us, and will we pass? Many questions to wonder about."

"I'm the one to ask them?"

"So it seems. Do you mind?"

He thought about it. "Well, I'm not happy about it, but— I guess not."

"Good. You have been a good student." She pushed the jam jar toward him and continued with her breakfast, silent now, her wizened face curved in a pleased expression.

Things like this always seemed to start so simply and end up so complicated, he thought to himself, as he measured some strawberry preserves onto a biscuit gone stiff as a hockey puck, and then dunked it in his tea until it was soft enough to eat. Messy, but good, and on the whole, worth getting up earlier than usual for. When he was done, he cleaned up the fixings briskly but couldn't avoid Madame Qi as she tapped her cane and sent him out on a long, early morning training run, just when he'd hoped she'd forgotten about his exercises.

The sound of his running had barely faded from her hearing when the quieter, softer steps of her granddaughter entering the kitchen stirred Madame Qi from her thoughts. Ting fixed her own cup of tea before sitting with a natural grace that warmed Madame Qi to watch. So much her mother's daughter, so much of her own family she could see in Ting. Life did indeed circle, if one only knew where to look. But Ting looked far from content that morning, an uncharacteristic frown settled on her face.

"There is trouble in you today?" Madame Qi probed gently, sitting back a little on her stool, and preparing to listen.

Ting stared into her teacup. "Not trouble," she answered slowly. "Exactly. But something." She looked up. "Everyone else seems to have a real idea of where their Talent might lead them. Jason is a Gatekeeper, Rich a healer, Stef a shapeshifter."

"Everyone?" echoed Qi. "Even Trent?"

"Well." Ting shifted. "Not Trent, no. And not me. I mean, I make nice little enchantments that last maybe a few hours or a few days or weeks, but I can't see that it's really, well . . . a Talent." She looked at her grandmother with questioning eyes. "Do you understand?"

"I do. I have no answer for that except to say that the world turns slowly, and in its own way, under the revealing light of the sun. What is hidden on one side, will eventually be revealed, as it turns."

Unhappiness winged across Ting's face.

Madame Qi stretched out her hand and patted her granddaughter's shoulder. "Because it is something from within you, it has to be discovered that way, too, I fear."

Ting nodded slowly. She turned her cup in her slender, agile fingers. "I also dreamed about home last night."

"Ah." Madame Qi nodded. "Missing everyone?"

"Not that home. Yours. And the house dragon."

"Indeed." Sudden intent interest flared inside Madame Qi, even more interest than that of helping Ting through a difficult day. "What of my house dragon?"

She missed her home in the San Francisco Bay area, with its bronze weather vane of a Chinese dragon upon it, the guardian of her family for many many years now. That bronze sculpture had been forged in their ancestral China and brought over to reign over their homes in America. Of all things in her old life she'd given up without regret, that was perhaps the only irreplaceable object. The Chrysanthemum Dragon, with its brilliant coat of enamel paint, and its long sinuously curling body, moving about slowly in occasional gusts of wind, had always been more than just a weather vane.

"I dreamed it was unhappy at being left behind, and that it wished to be here, with you. Upon the academy roof." Ting's gaze flickered up briefly as if mentally picturing it there.

Madame Qi smiled slowly. "It has its own duties for others, now. Yet it spoke to you, Granddaughter?"

"It did." Ting finished her tea and put her cup down carefully on the table. "Remember when it spoke? Remember when it hissed 'Jason' at us?"

"I do indeed."

"I didn't just imagine that."

"I don't think either of us did." Madame Qi leaned forward on her elbows, quilted jacket rustling about her wizened frame. "Many, many years ago, my grandfather was a magician in old China."

Ting's face took on a faint glow as she leaned forward in anticipation. "I remember."

Qi nodded. "I have told you some of the old tales. Not, however, all." She laid a finger alongside her nose, indicating that Ting should listen. "In the old tradition, a Chinese magician was a master of many things. An acrobat, an actor, singer, performer, with tricks of voice and illusion, and in my grandfather's case, tricks of Magick. Nothing remains from those days. The letters and journals he left were destroyed by war and purging, but there are still memories." She tapped her finger to her temple. "He could make paper chrysanthemums appear from thin air, while tumbling through burning hoops of fire. And he could make a dragon appear, from smoke and mist, as if bidden by his very call. It is that dragon that was cast in bronze, as a symbol and guardian for our home.

"A traveling magician, in those days, could earn much money from the families and weddings he entertained, but there were always bandits on the road eager to obtain his earnings. Sometimes my grandfather traveled with the family, oftentimes alone. I remember, however, the stories told of the dragon who would appear to chase away would-be robbers. A dragon whose strength would pull the wagon out of muddy ditches or rivers swollen with floodwaters. A dragon whose breath would be like the most reassuring campfire on wintry mornings. A dragon who . . . strangely enough . . . was there to help my grandfather even when my grandfather had mysteriously disappeared from the scene."

Ting blinked. "What?"

Madame Qi nodded slowly. "One never saw my grandfather and the dragon at the same time."

"But. . . what did that mean?"

Qi leaned forward, smiling softly, and whispered, "We were never sure. I always thought my grandfather *was* the dragon. He had the same long curling mustache, thin and sinuous as a river eel. Nothing ever frightened him, not even the Boxer Rebellion or the great wars which followed. When I knew him, of course, age had bowed and molded him, as it does me now, and his mustache had turned snowy white, instead of the glossy ebony in old posters he used to show me. He always wore a great pearl about his neck, not jewelry, but a beautiful object he prized. One day, he told me, it would be mine."

Ting had never seen that pearl. "Did you leave it behind?"

Madame Qi shook her head. "It disappeared when he grew ill and we all knew he had begun to die."

Ting gasped. "Someone took it?"

"In our family? Never!" Qi shook her finger at Ting for suggesting such a terrible thing. "No. It was thought he hid it somewhere. No one knows where. He was a clever man, my grandfather."

Ting looked at her grandmother with an expression of admiration. "I wish I could have known him, too."

"He would have been most proud. Many generations have passed without his magic showing, but it does reside in you, and you will discover more and more. You will not be an echo of him, but a fine magician in your own right." Qi reached out again and squeezed her hand tightly. "Never doubt that. Impatience will only slow you down."

Ting sighed. "I know, Grandmother." She stood, and flipped her hair back over her shoulder. "I'd better go wake Bailey. Lots to do today. Leave the dishes, I will clear them." She kissed her grandmother's brow and left.

Madame Qi gazed after her. Yes, her grandfather would have been most proud to see his blood still ran strong in his family. She poured herself a second cup of tea and warmed her hands about it, lost in memories.

Jonnard woke at the first touch of dawn and got up quietly, knowing that Isabella would sleep late. She slept later and later each day as her activities and the turning of the season took its toll. She was old, he knew, far older than he who had slept when thrown through the centuries after the battle of Brennard and Gregory the Gray, while she had lived, and even her own magic and that of the Leucators now seemed to be losing ground in keeping back the natural tides of Time. Still, he had hopes of not waking her.

He'd learned much in Naria, and she would be eagerly after him when she did awake. He would be able to tell her then that Fremmler had done as hoped, and more. The trade would make them wealthy as well as feared, and the first holds she wanted to establish over the cities and provinces of Haven had begun to be well anchored. All this, and more, would please her greatly later. Now was his time for himself.

He drew his father's journals out of their warded safekeeping, and laid them out. So many hints he had read over the days since finding them. To think that this man had raised and taught him, and never said a word about what he'd found in the journals.

Jonnard put a fingertip to one page. It crackled faintly under his touch, not with aging of paper, but with power, an energy he recognized well. He traced the words inked there.

I have found the place of repose of Gregory the Gray. He sleeps a sleep from which none of us could awaken him, nor would I wish to. He did all that he could to kill me, as I did all I could in kind. I could kill him yet; however, his mind walks on planes which none of us could see otherwise and when he awakens, he may be of use to me. So I will leave him be and let the guardian who watches over him think the secret well kept.

Jon lifted his hand. Well kept, indeed, for that information had gone to the grave with Brennard. He inhaled slowly. Even if he had it, he would be wise to think as his father had, and that Gregory might know something useful when he did awaken, and how vulnerable he would be in such a weakened state. When he had first read those words, he'd done the only thing he could, which was to focus a crystal and target it toward the sensing of Gregory if and when he ever rose from his Magick-driven sleep. Then Jon would be upon him.

The journals held other treasures in them. It was rather like sitting in front of a jewelry box and being able to dip his outspread hands deep into the contents, letting each gem shift and play upon his fingers. But what he desired most to know, how Brennard had come to Haven and why, could not be found.

It had to be written within. It had to be!

Jon sat back, puzzling over it, biting his lower lip in

thought until the sudden sting and taste of blood filled his mouth. He then sucked a moment at the smarting wound.

He picked up the books and studied the embossed leather, but the pattern imprinted seemed to be only a pretty design and totally at random. Suns and stars and moons in their phases studded the covers. Nice but nothing helpful. Jon closed each journal, holding it tightly in his hand. His ears buzzed with faint power.

"Damn."

He dropped the books and stared at them. His morning time was nearly spent, and he'd learned nothing useful. Perhaps he should turn them over to Isabella and let her work at them.

That idea stuck in him, though. This was *his* heritage and almost all he had, and the thought of giving it to her to shred in her pursuit of knowledge that would benefit her made him dig in his heels against doing it. The journals stared upward at him from the desktop. Years buried in the ground in the casket had done little to them, although the cover of the first book had suffered some damage, its fine-grained leather thickening and bubbling a bit.

Jon picked it up. He rubbed his hand upon it, feeling again the buzz of energy. Then he shut his eyes tightly. "Jonnard Albrite, you are an idiot." His eyes snapped open, and he slid a long thin knife from his boot. Working it carefully around the cover, he separated the leather from the book itself, and it fell off in his hands as though he'd skinned an animal.

Power blazed up at him, revealed, inscribed carefully on the hidden true cover of the journal, and it took his breath away. He read it slowly, whispering the words to himself, and it seemed as if the very room danced in the blaze, like the sun shimmering in a mirage off boiling desert sands. It filled him with a heady energy. "Gatekeeper," he breathed outwardly, and drew it nearer to read and learn it better.

Deep in the stronghold, in the dungeon of golems, the Leucators stirred in their chains, their graying flesh feeling the touch of warmth filtering down to them, as if someone had unleashed a summer sun. They rattled their chains and shackles and stood, with heads thrown back, and sucked in the feeling with a soft, keening moan. About them, in the very stone foundation of the fortress, another being moved through the earth as if it did not exist. It touched each of the Leucators, a fleeting shadow, then passed through wood and rock to other layers of the fortress, searching.

FireAnn woke. She felt a prickling over her skin, and she threw up her hand, crabbed from arthritis, and she moved to lean over the still sleeping Eleanora, to protect her however meagerly she could. She swatted at the prickling, the searcher, the irritant, cursing in the Irish tongue of her youth. Like bees stirred angrily from a hive, the thing stung at her. Here, there, here again, darting off to another place, then buzzing back in. FireAnn's eyes filled with angry tears.

"Off with you, foul Banshee! Ye'll not have my Eleanora this day!" She gestured as if she could still hold a crystal and send power shooting in attack, and the buzzing stopped a moment.

It crept back, and her whole body quivered as something unseen seemed to take their measure. The sting marks became fiery hot, as did the tears of frustration on her cheek, and Eleanora's body twitched under her, as the stings marked her as well.

"No! Git, bully lad. Ye'll not have her today or any other day, as long as I've breath in my lungs!" FireAnn leaped to her feet then, swinging about blindly at bees of power she was unable to see but could feel. She howled with frustration and her body jerked with each bolt from the attacker, and she wept with the pain and fear of it, a torture she could not prevent or answer . . . and worse, she feared, withstand.

After long moments, it withdrew, and FireAnn sank to her knees, hugged herself, and wept softly. Eleanora in her exhausted sleep, wept in echo.

Myths of Time

"W HEN DO YOU find time to read all this stuff, any-way?" Jason paused to wipe his hands on his pants, then eyed the wall sconce he had just fastened to the in-ner passage. Trent had been regaling him with information since they'd gone to work, throughout lunch hour, and now the evening dinner seemed to be approaching fast. Not that Jason minded listening to Trent, but he'd only been half lis-tening this time.

"Whenever I can. Sometimes I wake up and read af-ter you're asleep, so the lantern won't bother you." Trent flashed him a grin and went back to assembling the sconces they had yet to install. His nimble fingers worked to fit the metal parts together quickly, with the oil reservoir and re-flector and other pieces. "So, anyway, the point is, there are hundreds of creation myths from home. Every tribe has a story explaining where they came from. Some have several and argue about them; it's the beginning of religion, so they would, but anyway . . . not here. Everyone agrees on one thing. They fell in."

"Fell in?"

"Yup. They fell into Haven. Well, not everyone today,

there are families and they had children, and *they* got here the normal way, but I'm talking way back when everything started. They fell in."

Jason turned the yardstick in his hands as he prepared to mark off the next placement. "No wonder they didn't think it was too odd we all showed up. You think they . . . what . . . came through a Gate, too?"

"Most of the houses that have a record, or a storyteller to tell the tale . . . even the wanderers agree on this . . . talk about a great war on their lands before they fell. It's been different wars, not everyone got here at once, it's been over centuries and centuries, though." Trent finished assembling a sconce lantern and stacked it next to the other two he had done. "It's as if the energy of a war punches them through."

"A hole in the fabric of time?"

"More like a hole through the universes, I think."

"Not ours, though, we don't have six fingers. Or, it's very very rare."

Trent nodded. He stood, dusted off his hands, and came over to help Jason mark the wall. "There are a few tales about boats of sleepers being found, way, way back in the early times. They had six fingers. Must be a strong genetic trait."

"What do you think they meant about sleepers?"

"Boats of people asleep? Refugees maybe? People in some sort of hibernation? Lifeboats? I couldn't say, but it makes me wonder about the old science fiction thing, is there life on other planets, 'cause these people came from somewhere, and I don't think they came from Earth. But this world is used to taking in the survivors of disasters, so they didn't view us harshly. I think, though . . ." Trent drummed his fingers on the wall, a bit uneasy. "Those holes. I think they're Chaos related."

"Hmmmm. But we don't have stories like that at home, right, people appearing?"

"Nothing too close to it. People disappear mysteriously, but whole families don't just appear."

"Trent . . ." Jason paused, trying to put his question together. "When you go through the rest of that stuff, look and see if wolfjackals are mentioned."

Trent raised an eyebrow, and Jason knew he'd connected

on the Gate energy thought running, through his own head. .
"Which came first, the chicken or the egg?"

He shrugged. "Something like that. I'm just curious."

"Sure thing." Trent bent over to grab a wall sconce. "Don't
we need to get this passage finished before dinner?"

"Four and we're done." Jason dodged around Trent, letting him finish the one he held, while he moved to the next
measured location. There was a logic to Trent's interests,
and his knowledge of mythology had gotten them out of
fixes before. What if his study on Haven were right? What if
every one of them had fallen through a hole in the universe
to get here? What did that say about Gates, and Gatekeeping . . . and universes?

A chill ran down the back of his neck. What did it say
about Chaos and wolfjackals, as well? Is that what the wolfjackal who'd scarred him so very long ago before he even
knew he was a Magicker meant when it had growled at him,
"You are mine?" It had marked him because of his Talent
to Gate, bringing Chaos, which in turn fed the wolfjackals.
Or had it meant something even darker?

"Jase? Jason? Wohoo? Watching videos in your head?"

He shook his head vigorously. "Just thinking. I know, I
know, why start now?" He bumped his shoulder into Trent
before Trent could tease him, and went back to work, trying
to chase away disturbing thoughts.

Lacey scrabbled along the windowed wall, something shiny
in her grasp as she hopped up to Bailey's toe and then made
her awkward way up to the cuff. Bailey leaned down and
took the nail from her, as she lifted her up. The little pack rat
immediately dove into the pocket in the soft golden-brown
suede bodice Bailey wore, and made a little chirruping noise
as she groomed her whiskers. Bailey gently massaged the
back of the creature's head. "She's sleepy," Bailey said to
Ting. "Good Lacey, good girl, look what you found!"

"Why don't you put her back in the room to sleep?"
Ting paused, and opened and shut the inner shutters carefully, making sure they swung smoothly. Her face creased
with proud joy as they worked perfectly.

Bailey shrugged. "She says it's too noisy with everyone
pounding. I think when the school is finished, she's probably going to sleep a whole week!"

Ting laughed. "Must be rough on a day sleeper, huh?"
She stood back, with her hands on her hips. "I think we're
done in here, Bailey."

"Great. Only . . . twenty more rooms to go!"

Ting nudged her. "Don't be like that! Look at what
we've done."

Bailey's pony tail swung as she looked around, then
nodded. "I know, I know. Somehow, it's almost all built."
She stroked Lacey one last time, before tucking the pack
rat's tail into the pocket with the rest of her, and saying,
"Mom wants to go home."

"Both of you?"

"No. Just her. For a while." A troubled expression settled on her face.

"She'd leave you alone? She can't do that! She's like . . .
like . . . like your best friend!"

"I know."

"Did she say why?"

Bailey shook her head again. "Parents are like that, you
know? They have these reasons for things that they never
tell you about till later when it's all said and done, and you
think . . . I could have helped, but they never asked. Or
explained."

"It's a parent thing," Ting said in understanding.

"Exactly. Plus, I don't think she figured the Gate would
be closed all the time. I think she thought it would be open
and we would go to school here and go home at night or
something. I don't know." Bailey finished with a shrug that
elicited a sleepy cheep from within her bodice. That made
both of them giggle a bit. They picked up their work tools
and buckets and headed to the next room where sunlight
slanted low and faintly through shutterless windows, and
they knew their workday was almost done.

Ting pulled her hair over her shoulder, braiding its long
blue-black strands thoughtfully. "I've been watching everyone's crystals," she noted. "And I think our conclusion is
right. We're losing more power than ever before, and by
day's end, Gavan seems nearly exhausted. This can't be
good."

"I know. The question is why hasn't he told us or warned
us?" Bailey dropped her work bucket, nails rattling, and
picked up a set of shutters leaning against the wall, waiting

to be nailed and hinged into place. "I can't believe he hasn't noticed."

"Maybe he's maintaining so much, he expects the drain. But not the rest of us."

"I think we should talk to him tonight."

Ting came to mark the window frame, leaning in and around Bailey. "Not yet. I just want to be sure, you know? Another day or two."

"All right. We should watch Tomaz if we can, although he's hardly around."

"Good idea!" Ting brightened. She lowered her pencil. "Ready for you."

Heads together, sometimes giggling and sometimes yelling because of bruised thumbs, they went back to work.

At dinner, Gavan and Tomaz finished their meal quickly and retired to a crystal-lit corner, where they pored over a chart rolled out onto their table and weighed down carefully with crystals. The opportunity to look couldn't possibly have been better as both Ting and Bailey took them mugs of tea and coffee but did not linger as both men waved them off quickly.

Bailey nibbled on her lower lip. As they drew away, she whispered to Ting, "Even the crystal on Tomaz's bracelet looked dim. We need to know about Jason."

"But Jason's been Gating and we know that takes a lot out of him."

"A day or two more rest, then. We're going to have to ask somebody soon." She rubbed Ting's shoulder. "Look, remember what they told us when we first started learning. There's no such thing as a stupid question, all right?"

"Right." After all, if Bailey had asked one when she first became a Magicker, she wouldn't have been locked in her own crystal for days, almost to the point of never getting free.

Lacey poked her head out, nose twitching, and Bailey fed her a crumb of bread. The little beast took it and dove back in, making her bodice pocket ripple and move about busily.

Trent leaned in. "What're they looking at over there?"

"Some kind of map. Looks like Havenite work," Bailey offered, then shut her mouth firmly, not wanting to reveal that she had a Haven map of her own.

"No kidding?" Trent looked interested, nudged Jason, and the two drifted toward the elder Magickers.

Tomaz looked up as they came near the table, but Gavan barely noticed their presence. Jason and Trent peered down at the paper pinned to the table. "Fortress locations?" Jason ventured, hoping he recognized what he thought he did.

"Aye," muttered Gavan. He tapped the yellowing paper. "The Trader Guild keeps a good record of the boundary, because a main trading route developed along here."

"Makes sense. They'd have military protection, then," Trent said.

"Exactly. So one of these is likely to be Isabella's stronghold. This one," and Gavan pointed, "is the ruins near Mantor's village, where we went and had a look."

"But it doesn't look like ruins to us."

"Right." Gavan nodded to Jason. "Smoke and mirrors, magickal illusion at its best."

Trent leaned over closer, gaze narrowing intently. He put out a hand, as one might stretch a palm to a warming fire. Jason watched him and held his next words, afraid to break the trance his friend seemed to be slipping into. The dull and opaque crystal clipped to Trent's belt seemed to glow briefly. Tomaz also noticed and put his hand on Gavan's, stilling the other's indrawn breath, and everyone at the table went very quiet for a few moments.

Trent breathed. He put his hand down, covering an inky sketch. "Here," he said. "It feels like here. I can't tell you why or how, but the map is warm, right here."

Tomaz and Gavan traded looks as Trent lifted his hand. Gavan stared down at the mountainous spot. A little farther away, but well within range of all the villages which had been raided. Tomaz grunted faintly.

"It looks logical."

"It does indeed." Gavan appraised Trent. "Nothing more than a feeling. A vision, perhaps?"

Trent shifted uneasily. "I can't do that, and you know it."

"I know you couldn't. I also know that your Talent is a very difficult and stubborn one and is unfolding with agonizing slowness." Gavan smiled to take the edge off his words. "We'll take a look here first, then. Tomaz and I have found two other forts which they may have seized, but I have to admit this may be the best possibility." He frowned then. "I overlooked it. You, Tomaz?"

Tomaz nodded. He put out his own hand, turquoise-and-silver bracelet rattling a little. "My eyes slid right over it. I'd say there is an aversion warding to it, powerful enough that it even reflects on maps. Isabella is stronger than we feared."

"Not her. She uses the Leucators. She may even be drawing off Eleanora." Gavan swallowed hard. He reached out and briskly rolled up the map. "We'll let you know," he said to Trent, "when we scout it."

"Can we come with you?"

"Not for scouting. Later, yes." Gavan stored the map in its oilskin tube and tucked it away inside his cape.

Jason hid a fidget, hoping that later would not be too late.

A shout outside from the wanderers at the back of the kitchen door drew everyone out as a bonfire blazed and the workers gave a cry for dancers and stories, while night settled darkly about the academy and the Magickers. Trent and Jason followed the others out slowly.

Trent could not hide the gleam in his eyes, nor could Jason hide the heaviness in his heart. Isabella touched everywhere, like a black plague on Haven, and it was he who had brought her in.

It would have to be he who took her out again. The dragon had asked him if he were a guardian or a warrior and he'd chosen guardian in order to open the Dragon Gate. Now, he realized, he had chosen wrongly.

Only a warrior could cut through the tangle he'd made.

26

Oops

HOW COULD YOU let this happen? How? Did I give no idea that it was important not to let the others get a foothold here? Everything we've striven for, gone, worthless!"

Saying nothing in retaliation, Jonnard stared at Isabella as she paced the floor angrily in front of him, her long gown swishing and sounding like the sea driven by a high and maddened wind. He had expected nothing less than having to bear the brunt of her displeasure when he delivered the news he'd gathered while trailing Fremmler at Naria. He'd waited a day or so to tell her, knowing that she would explode in fury. He knew word of the Magickers and their academy would distress her beyond measure. He could only stand quietly until it passed. She had been raging for the better part of thirty minutes, however, and he had begun to tire of it.

"All our devices will be for nothing. Our work. We cut off their supplies, I thought! You were to see to that. The building was never to have been begun, let alone finished, and now you bring me this news." Her eyes flashed as she looked at him, her dark hair tangled about her face as it had fallen from the gem-studded combs holding it.

He waited.

"Our bribes were in place at the Trader Guild?"

He nodded.

"Useless. Absolutely useless to me!" Isabella glared at Jonnard. He felt a muscle along his jawline jump as he kept his teeth clenched. Another moment or two of anger, and he would break, and both of them would likely to be sorry. His fingers twitched as he fought not to curl them into a fist.

She took a deep breath. "How did this happen?" Then, lifting the hem of her skirt slightly, she sat down, her back ramrod stiff, and let the elegant folds of material fall into place about her ankles. "Talk."

"Our influence got Renart disbarred temporarily, as planned, and he was unable to procure supplies for them, as we agreed. We were also given access to the libraries for my studies, and I took advantage of warding the maps, as directed. Our locations remain undetectable. I hardly call that useless. As for the building of the academy, it appears that they hired wanderers, Gypsies if you will, who needed the work desperately. No matter what disbarment from the guilds, what whispers they heard, the wanderers are independent sorts and would judge for themselves, and evidently found a bargain to their liking. As for how they gathered their supplies, there is a black market, an underground, for almost any need, anywhere. If anyone could have tapped into it, it would have been the wanderers." He shrugged at that. "We planned well, Mother, and I see no fault in it. The use of the wanderers can be twisted to our advantage, for the people here are suspicious of the Spirit and those who disbelieve. The wanderers are outcast for their disbelief, and the Magickers, too, I think we can still turn it to our advantage."

"I haven't time." Isabella raised her hands and quickly upswept her hair, replacing her combs. She looked tired, and for the most fleeting of movements, well, old. He turned his gaze away before she could catch him staring.

"I'm not saying we must restructure. Our contacts are in place, and they're doing what we hoped. The Magickers have no idea what has been working against them. It is sheer luck they've countered us despite the hostages we hold. I suggest we consider a more direct strike as well."

Isabella lifted her chin. "Such as?"

"Wood burns."

A hungry realization flared in her eyes. "And winter draws near."

"A delay which even luck cannot put off."

She lifted a hand. "Very well, then. See to it. I will not need you when we take the caravan to Naria. Fremmler can handle that."

Jonnard gave a slight bow. He left her apartments then, and not until he was downstairs did he take a long, slow, steadying breath. Did she know how close she'd come to his answering her challenge? Did she even care?

He was not quite ready to battle her for leadership.

Not quite yet.

Downstairs, he assembled a group of five, veterans used to being Crystaled to a destination on horseback, and then raiding from there. He gave them their instructions, and told them when to prepare, before leaving them. They would be ready. He'd seen the hard lights in their eyes. They lived for mayhem. It served him now, but he made note of their names. It was never too late to plan or be wary for the future.

He would not examine the journals this night, for he had a feeling Isabella was watching him. His day would come.

Jason stirred restlessly on his cot, with the feeling of whispering inside his head, like an annoying insect. He got up quietly, observing Trent to see if his roommate were reading late, but the bundle of blankets suggested that his friend had burrowed into a sound sleep. He stood, shivered a bit with the cold seeping through the building, and pulled a blanket off the cot to wrap it about himself. The fireplace and chimney structures would be operating soon, yet not soon enough for those Magickers with thin blood unused to winters that could bring frost and even snow soon. He padded out of the room, thinking a bit of food might help drop him back into sleep. He always seemed to be a bit hungry these days. Growing spurts, he thought. When he crept downstairs, the buzz in his head grew louder, and Jason went outside in search of it, hearing hushed words. He drew back against the side of the building.

Peeking around it, he saw Rainwater and Crowfeather, and he sensed the tension then, as well as the quiet. He started to pull back, then held very still to listen, instead.

"You should be resting," Tomaz remarked quietly.

"I know. The days should be getting shorter, but they feel longer and longer." Gavan shrugged into his cape and rubbed his palm over the pewter wolfhead of his cane, as if settling in his mind what he wanted to say next. "I wanted to do this now, when everyone is asleep, in case there are problems."

Tomaz squatted by the fire which had burned to gray ashes and red glowing undercoals. He stirred it up a bit, setting flames to licking upward from within the broken stone ring. The orange illumination gave his face the look of ancient gold. He did not try to hide his worry. "I do not think this a wise thing."

"We can do it this way, or we can spend days, weeks, combing the countryside by horseback." Gavan scrubbed a hand wearily over his face. "I don't think Eleanora can last weeks longer."

"We know nothing for sure. Let me send Snowheart after her."

Gavan shook his head. "I know you can sometimes see through the eyes of your crows, Tomaz, but I need to know for certain what we find, what we can expect."

"You cannot Crystal to a place none of us has actually seen."

Gavan put his hand on the map tube inside his cape. "I think I can find it by the landmarks."

"Even stone changes, given enough time." Tomaz stood. His silver-disk belt flashed as he hooked his thumbs in it and stood, legs balanced. "Even anchored to me, I cannot help if you materialize locked in granite."

"I know." He fetched out the tube, handing it to Tomaz. "Each fortress had a distinctive guard tower. The one we want is studded with obsidian and the picture of it is fairly good. I should be able to Crystal near it."

"If the fortress is manned the way its illusion showed it, you could appear in a tent camp of armed men, Gavan."

"Let's hope I don't Crystal that close."

Tomaz took the map with a sigh. "I shouldn't let you

go, but I agree that time is no longer on our side." He put his other hand on Gavan's shoulder. "Don't let the coyote blind you."

Gavan gave Tomaz a lopsided smile. He rubbed his cane again, and the Herkimer diamond inside the wolf's jaws sparkled dully. He grasped it in his palm, and then was gone.

Jason lost his breath at the suddenness of it, and clenched his teeth hoping the noise hadn't been heard, but Tomaz seemed very intent as if he listened to the absence of the other. Jason wondered if he would ever see Gavan again.

As a lad, he'd grown up knowing how to Crystal almost from the moment he could walk. He had memories of using it to cross the moors when frigid howling winds seemed to chase him, and of Crystaling down the Thames to where the grand country estates near Windsor Castle held docks on the water, and of jumping across the London bridge in wild games of crystal tag, back in the days when getting caught might mean being prosecuted for being a witch. He had never known fear. Gavan reflected there were times when he probably should have, although none more than now.

He kept the image of the obsidian tower in his head, flint-edged rock studding a gray stone tower, overlooking the rills of a rocky pass with a verdant valley down below. The pass and valley were unimportant now, and with autumn hard upon them, might already be browned by frost, but it was the tower upon which he needed to keep his inner focus. The tower and Eleanora, for he hadn't told Tomaz that she would be his anchor there, even as Crowfeather would anchor him to the academy, holding his soulstrings if he himself should fail.

Crystaling should be near instantaneous, but he hung in the coldness of *between* for many heartbeats until his bones felt the absence of the life of the world and he wondered if he had emerged already and been sunk into the stone as Tomaz warned. Yet he lived. His heart struggled to beat one more time; his lungs ached for air, and the crimson veil of blood behind his eyes fluttered as if reminding him he could look inward as well as outward.

When his body screamed silently for a breath of air, then

and only then, he tumbled outward, onto the ground, hard stone smacking into his knees and palms, and he gasped, trying to breathe. He threw his head back and looked up, and saw the sharp tower not far away, as he'd pictured it but . . . in the thin gray dawn of morning.

Gavan got to his feet slowly, dusting off his hands and stowing his cane away. What had he done? He'd left at night. Now it was dawn. The inference made him shiver. He'd passed through time as well as distance. No wonder he'd nearly died *between*. He'd never known anyone who'd done it and lived. Was it the day before or the day after? No way to tell. He focused inward, felt the thread of Tomaz tied to him, and tugged it gently to let Tomaz know he lived. His only answering response was a faint warm glow inside himself, but he knew it was an acknowledgment from the other.

Thin plumes of smoke from morning fires drifted into the air from the fortress across from him. No doubt filled him now. Trent had identified this as the stronghold, and he had been right. This was the rebuilt and fully manned fortification whose image they had seen. How Trent had known it, Gavan could not say. No one in his history of Magicking had the Talent, or lack of it, or confusion of it, that that boy had. There was no naming of it, and no way to depend upon it except through blind trust.

He sank back to the ground, finding a broken boulder to shelter him, and tried to commit all that he saw to memory. He could see the trade road below, running through a pass cut by a river, for it was fringed with trees and brush, all glowing red and yellow and orange with color, thinning branches showing through as the leaf fall had already begun. The Dark Hand would take that road to Naria, and he traced the route in his mind. Waylaying the caravan too close to the fortress would be foolhardy; taking on the Dark Hand could be dangerous at best and murderous at worse. He would have to send Tomaz's crows over the trade road to get a better look at the terrain.

Gavan felt his nose and ears grow cold as he watched the fortress. He wanted to be closer. His heart and soul ached to be closer. The morning seemed so new that few walked yet, and sound seemed all muffled and hushed. He began to pick his way through prickly shrubs and broken rock, a hardscrabble of a hilltop upon which this stronghold had been built. He moved slowly, foxlike, across the ground, willing himself to be unseen, unnoticed, unheard.

For once, being chilled gladdened him, for his breath stayed invisible on the early morning air. He pulled his cape close and willed himself still as he crawled ever nearer until he could hear the raiders clearly, the first few up as they tended to the horses and built up the cook fires. His nerves tingled as he sensed the beginning of the ward lines laid down, and he knew he dare not creep closer though his eyes were drawn to a heavily shuttered window on the second floor of the stronghold itself. She had to be there. He could *feel* it.

Gavan lay there for a very long moment. The sensation pulled at him, as it had when as a young sixteen-year-old lad he'd first met the daughter of Gregory the Gray. She'd been five or six years older, a world away from him, it seemed, and all he could ever hope for was an occasional glance from her eyes or a view of her slender body as she passed by the study where her father taught Magick. To listen to her play an instrument was like listening to your own heart being drawn out and made to express itself. He had fallen hopelessly, forever, in love with Eleanora. She had noticed, of course, who wouldn't? She had the grace to neither tease nor flaunt his feelings for her. Gregory had tolerated it, saying little until, near the end, although neither of them had known it was near the end for Gregory and all those in those times, he had said to Gavan that if he had patience, eventually the age difference between them would mean little.

Gavan had taken it as a sign of encouragement, though he needed none. After seeing Eleanora, no one else could even be considered, and as long as she remained single, he'd have hopes. Then the great battle of wills happened between the rogue student Brennard, who by then was a master in his own right, and Gregory, and the power backlash from that encounter had killed many outright, throwing the others into comas and even through time. When they'd awakened, Gregory's prophecy had proved true. Time had equalized them. He'd awakened first, matured, grown, and, upon finding her, was no longer the love-struck youth he'd been. Young still, but someone adept in the modern world, finding and restoring Magickers wherever he could when, miracle of miracles, he'd found her.

He would not lose her again. Not to anything less than death itself, and even that he was not certain would keep them apart.

On the other hand, dying was something he'd rather avoid. Gavan took a long slow breath. He could see her if he Crystaled in. A whisper of power from this distance, little more. He had skills honed by years of playing hide and seek with his abilities. Sometimes those games had meant his own hide, literally. He wanted to see her. He had to know how she fared. If she could wait till they played their game out with the trading caravan.

He rubbed his crystal out of habit, concentrated on her essence, and with a movement like a silken wind barely stirring the air was *inside*.

His eyelids fluttered as stink and dank air struck him, and he staggered back a step. Chains and moans and a soft wailing greeted him. He pushed at his Crystal and brought the lantern light up, and then saw where he had landed.

A sea of Leucator flesh surrounded him. He was nowhere even close to his beloved Eleanora.

A ghoulish hand locked about his ankle and began to tug at him, icy fingers tightening.

Chains

GAVAN FOUGHT A MOMENT of panic as he backed up farther and the Leucator crawled along with him, mewling softly, its hand curling ever tighter upon his ankle. Picking his way among the graying flesh of the other creatures, he found a clear spot where none of the others could get to him, but this one seemed to have a longer lead on its chain than most and began to get up on its knees, free hand clawing the air at him.

It was not his own Leucator or it would have been on his throat in a flash, desperate to meld their bodies and souls and be whole again, although it would kill them both in the effort. Gavan felt a moment of shame that he could not identify this creature. If it had ever resembled a Magicker at one time, he either had never known the person or had forgotten who it could have been. It might have recognized him, for it cooed as it grew closer, but perhaps it just craved contact, warmth, fuel, of a sort. He could not even have said if it were meant to be male or female.

The others only seemed a little aware of him, thankfully. When aroused, they would set off a keening, a wailing, that would alert everyone to his presence in the stronghold, something he most certainly did not wish to give away. Foiled for now, when he returned, he intended it to be a surprise.

He shook his leg, hoping to deter the Leucator. It tilted its head, a few strands of stringy black hair flying into its eyes as it did, its clothing mere scraps of moldy fabric about its gaunt body. Its red gash of a mouth opened and closed. Its fingers kneaded his leg like a cat kneading a favorite blanket. He felt a moment of pity for the construct.

The moment fled as the Leucator struck, snakelike, angling its mouth to his leg, where its grasping hand had forced up his trouser, baring a patch of skin above his boot top. Like a sucker it fastened and he could feel it bite deep into the warmth of his flesh. Blood spurted as the Leucator gave a moan of happiness and latched onto him. He muted a scream of pain and shook with it. He raised his cane like a great sword.

Gavan gestured, brilliant white light from his crystal wavering, then dying out altogether, and with it he felt the total absence of power as the focus went black. Panic chilled him. Then he lowered his cane across the back of the creature, hitting hard, with all the strength he could muster.

The Leucator let out a muffled shriek of pain and fell back. Loose, Gavan lunged back out of its reach, his back to the dungeon wall, pain shooting through his leg. Hot blood trickled down into the boot. The other Leucators would smell it and begin their wailing. Injured, and well and truly trapped, he stood in a sea of undead flesh and pondered his options.

Jason stayed around the corner, pressed to the outside of the academy and wondered whether to blunder in or sneak away. Long moments stretched by the campfire, with Tomaz immobile, then he stood and stretched with an impatient mutter. The elder Magicker stared into the evening sky as if he could trace the route Gavan had taken, his shoulders squared back. Jason decided to back away as quietly as he could, knowing that Tomaz and his bottomless barrel of patience could stand and wait all night if he had to.

He made no sound, he swore he did not, but Tomaz spoke quietly.

"Stay, Jason, I think I will need your help."

He swallowed at being caught and moved toward the fire sheepishly. "I . . . I . . ."

Tomaz waved a hand. "It doesn't matter. I remember your days in camp, when you were often about at night, curious." Without turning around, he took the map tube, opened it, and shook the map out. "He's been gone far too long for a quick look, and yet I know he arrived safely, because I felt him. So . . . like you . . . he's gotten curious."

"Trouble?"

"I'm not certain. The contact is not quite right. Yet, this is Haven, where many things are not quite right." Turning, then, he drew both Jason and the map to the last dying light of the fire. "Study that."

Jason did so, his eyes sweeping the well-inked map, taking in all that he could, most especially the stronghold Trent had picked out. When he knew it well, he lifted his gaze to Tomaz who quickly rolled up and put the map away again. "Now we wait."

"Till when?"

"Till he returns or calls for aid, or I decide to go get him." Tomaz threw his head back and faced into the night wind, his broad face set into the nonexpression he often wore, his thoughts unknowable.

Jason fought off a shiver and edged closer into the fading warmth of the fire. He wondered if Gavan had sensed him also, then decided probably not. Still, being busted at all embarrassed him. He shoved his hands into the waistband of his trousers and wished he'd brought a winter cloak down with him. Coats were far more sensible, he thought, duster-length if they could be found, closer to the legs and knees, but capes and cloaks were the style here, even if the wind found its way inside most inconveniently. He'd rather have a good hoodie under a coat any day, and realized those days might be gone forever. Never going back? He couldn't quite comprehend that. There was too much to see here, though! Places the dragon had hinted about that he itched to see, when the time was right. How far did the land of the Warlord's Spirit stretch? What was beyond the emerald sea?

He rubbed his hands together. The fire stirred and sifted down to little more than hot ashes, yet Tomaz did not move to add fuel to it. They never let a fire burn all night without a watch on it. He came from a land of dry hills and wild-fires and knew the danger. Still, Jason wished he could be warmer, or at least, inside.

Curiosity had led him there and, he reminded himself, it wasn't keeping him warm. Another reason to think first next time. He wrapped his arms about himself and tried to remember playing soccer in the mud and rain, where sheer body warmth came from the action itself and the joy of playing. If he thought it would warm him, he was wrong as the edges of his ears began to turn cold.

Tomaz made an impatient movement. "I've waited long enough."

"What can you do?"

"Pull him back whether he wills it or not. If he's try-ing to find Eleanora," Tomaz grimaced, "he'll be more than angry, so stand clear." Tomaz reached out and gripped his hand in his strong one, and Jason could feel the power surging through both of them. Jason had anchored before, so he knew what to do without Tomaz asking him. Tomaz would be going after Gavan, although not quite . . . what the Magicker had planned was even more dangerous, for he would use himself as a bridge in between, neither here nor there, and with only Jason to bring him back safely, if Gavan were in danger.

"Now," said Tomaz quietly, as he made a gesture and ut-tered a word of Navajo that Jason thought was probably a blessing because he'd heard it before, though only when Tomaz needed great will or strength. Then, also he held his friend's hand and he felt Tomaz just sort of *go*.

The wind gusted wildly, buffeting them, seeming to blow through Tomaz's insubstantial form. Trent should see this, Jason thought. He'd know where the mythology of spirits came from. He shivered and held tight, more with thoughts and hope than by holding hands to nothingness which threatened to fade from his fingers.

He dug in his heels and clung to the essence of Tomaz. Patience as timeless as the sandy land he grew up in, con-fidence as strong as the sun beating down on the south-west, faith in his friends about him as far-reaching as the never ending bowl of sky overhead . . . these things beat like wings about Jason's head. Then he inched his head back and looked and saw the two crows gliding about, the black-as-black one, and the other with a patch of snowy white upon her chest. He'd called on them, too.

Wherever Gavan was, whatever he was doing, it would take nothing less than all they had to get him back!

He found himself holding his breath, and forced himself to breathe, even as he took his second hand and clasped it over his other, near empty hold on Tomaz. The figure of the Magicker stretched as little more than a mirage, face frowning in intensity, one hand outstretched to the heavens.

"Hold tight," murmured Tomaz more in his thoughts than aloud. "He is not only somewhere, but somewhen. . . ."

He had only a moment for surprise before gritting his teeth and promising himself that he'd never let go, never, no matter what. No matter if a pack of wolfjackals growled at his back or if . . .

Leucators!

Jason's mouth dropped open in revulsion and he fought not to jerk back in utter terror. They sensed him even though he was not really there and he heard their screeching begin deep inside his skull. They clawed at his thoughts, their own as slimy as the touch of their decaying flesh and he jerked and twitched as if he could dance away from them, but he fought to hold onto Tomaz. Don't let go! No matter what!

They wanted him. They wailed for the chance to devour him, body and soul, till nothing remained of him, not a thought or memory or drop of blood. He would be as gone as if he'd never existed! No!

Jason clenched his hands tighter to that which he knew was Tomaz. His spine bowed with the effort not to run screaming to save himself. Don't let go!

Tomaz gasped. His spirit image shivered on the air, then began to grow solid, and Jason pulled. He fell back on his butt, pulling slow and steady as if he needed to uproot a stubborn tree from the earth, his arms aching and his ears filled with the crying of the Leucators.

Suddenly, the noise stopped, and he felt weight in his hands. As he yanked, two heavy bodies hurtled out of the night and dog-piled onto him. Jason lay panting for air, flattened, Gavan's gasping in one ear, and Tomaz's deep rumbling chuckle in the other.

They sorted themselves out and sat up, Gavan leaning on Tomaz. He peered at Jason through the night, his rainwater-blue eyes narrowed.

"Up past bedtime, are we?"

Jason flashed a grin. "And you'd better thank your booty I am!"

"Indeed, indeed." Gavan started to get to his feet and fell back, and decided to stay sitting in the ashes of the fire, looking a bit like Cinderella as the soot drifted around him. He rolled up his pants leg over one boot, exposing a nasty looking bite.

"Someone was hungry," Tomaz remarked. "I'll get a paste on that. Looks bad, we don't want infection."

Gavan winced as he poked a finger at it, then nodded. "The wages of curiosity." He glanced at Jason to see if he was listening.

"Find her?"

He shook his head. "Her Leucator called to me, so I found myself in Isabella's dungeon. Unpleasant surprise, all around. But she's there, upstairs I'd say, and she lives." He smiled ruefully. "At least I've that much."

Tomaz stood and put a hand out, and drew Gavan to his feet. "Now the only question I have is ... were you there yesterday morning or tomorrow morning?"

Gavan's face twisted a little as he put weight on his leg. "Noticed that, did you?"

"I could hardly not. We've no anchoring through time, Gavan. At least, I wouldn't have said so until tonight."

The other nodded. He pointed at Jason. "This is definitely not for you to try. It nearly killed me." He palmed his cane, and the absence of any response from the crystal Herkimer diamond held there shocked Jason. "If not for the two of you, I would be dead. Or worse."

As the dragon had said, there were worse things than death. Jason thought he might have just glimpsed them, although he wasn't sure. He shivered. He didn't want to know.

28

Tightrope

DAWN CAME WITH A FLASH of lightning, long before he was ready for it. Jason sat bolt upright in his bed, the cot creaking dangerously under him as if it might collapse ... as Stef's already had, under the bulk of his weight, so he slept on the floor in a nearby room. Trent let out a muffled curse as he came awake, already on his feet, shrugging off blankets. He pulled on his jeans, torn and ragged but still mostly in one piece, and cursed again as Jason threw a shirt at him.

Boots, pants, shirts on but otherwise unready for the cold morning, they raced down the stairs as thunder shook the academy, its wooden sides booming and reverberating like the bass on the loudest boom box in the world, and they all collided into one another in the kitchen. Rich's pale face stood out as everyone reached for their crystals, but before a single Lantern spell could be focused, the inside of the kitchen lit with a brilliant flash. They all stood revealed in white-hot light. Outside the windows, black shapes on horseback flew by in silhouette.

"That's no storm," Jason cried out. "We're under attack!" He threw the door open, his body illuminated by glaring light, and they could all hear the beat of horses' hooves and the whistles of raiders as they circled the building. The smell of crystal Lightning stung their nostrils and the academy flickered with tongues of flame.

Stef grabbed Ting and Bailey by the elbows. "Out, out," he cried. "Everyone out!" His voice growled ever deeper as his words ended and dropped into a low roar as the bear in him fought to emerge. "*Now!*" and he lost his human voice and body altogether as he pushed the girls out of the burning building.

Bailey linked an elbow with Ting as they ran out, trying to keep their feet under them, propelled by Stefan's berserker strength. The bear loped past them, charging at two horsemen as they rode in, their hands filled with burning torches. The horses screamed in fear, their riders shouting and sawing at the reins to control the plunging beasts as Stefan reared in front of them, bear roars filling the night. His paws boxed at them, horses reeling back under the blows.

"Grandmother!" Ting called out in dismay, as Bailey guided her into the sheltering woods. She struggled and pointed at the school. Bailey narrowed her eyes, peering back at the academy as raiders and flashes of crystal Lightning flashed by again and again. She saw two figures then. "Mom has her," she yelled to Ting, drawing her back under a low branch where they could see but not be seen.

Rebecca Landau made her way around the corner of the building, her arms about Madame Qi who seemed very bent and fragile, hunched over her cane. Horsemen thundered near, and the tiny woman straightened in a heartbeat, her cane lashing out, bashing one rider in the leg. The man wheeled his horse away, yelping in pain and anger. Bailey let out a piercing whistle the way only Bailey could, and her mother's head jerked up, a smile cutting across the worried expression on her face. She guided them both toward safety, the two women scuttling quickly before the raiders decided to make another charge.

Ting's teeth chattered with cold and nerves, but she managed to say, "You absolutely have to teach me how to do that."

"Tomorrow," promised Bailey. She watched her mother and Ting's grandmother inch across the open ground, dodging raiders and Magickers as Trent and Jason both took up crystal Shields and two by fours, whatever they could wield, as the raiders closed in. Henry's crystal knocked a rider from his seat, tumbling him off his saddle, but he held onto the headstall and managed to drag himself back onto his mount while Henry danced around in excitement.

Dokr and two of his men circled Rebecca and Madame Qi to hustle them in under the trees, before the wanderer's leader said quietly, "I go to make my own people safe," and disappeared in the shadows as silently as he'd appeared.

Ting wrapped her arms about her grandmother to provide some protection against the cold, and held her tightly, while all of them stared at the fight in the courtyard.

The academy danced in flames, and the sting of smoke and fire crackled, as the raiders now ringed about Stefan and Rich, Henry, and Jason and Trent. Bailey could see Jonnard in the foreground as his crystal shot forth another shrieking lightning bolt of fire and damage and the edge of the rooftop splintered, giving way. Wrapped all in dark cloth and cape, only Jonnard's face and hands revealed who he was, but they all knew. Isabella could not be seen. Stefan's bear mumbled and growled, swiping at the horsemen, his eyes white with anger and ursine fear of the fiery torches in their hands.

Gavan and Tomaz emerged from the building last, and as they did, Jonnard pulled his horse into a rear, then pivoted it and shouted out a command that snapped through the air. All retreated then, the horsemen plunging about and galloping off, their taste for conflict gone. Jonnard's cape snapped in the wind as he put his heels to his horse and led the retreat. The night went deadly quiet except for the noise of flames. Gavan spoke a tired word, and the fires licking about the academy went out as if they'd never existed.

Bailey crept out from the trees first and went to one of the sooty spots on the wall where fire had just been. She put a hand out cautiously. Warm, yes, hot to the touch, but the wood barely showed a mark. She let out a whoop.

"We did it!"

Gavan smiled tiredly, and rubbed his hand across his face, leaving a charcoal smear over his eyebrow like a salute. "Good warding."

Tomaz held up his crystal and let its Lantern light spill out as he examined the structure, striding the length of the wall. "Morning will show us how good, but I suspect other than a corner of roofing, we'll see little damage." He shook his crystal in triumph before letting out a howl of victory, sounding rather like a desert coyote.

Dokr emerged from the shadows, too, his face folded into worry and curiosity. He trotted about at Tomaz's heels. "It was burning, was it not?"

"A little. Like green wood, Dokr, some flame, some smoke, but not really catching."

"That is good." He tilted his head. "It is a spell? Magick?"

"It is a treatment of the wood," Gavan answered firmly. He caught up with Tomaz, his expression guarded, and Tomaz nodded in agreement.

"It would be good to know such a thing," the wanderer said.

"Perhaps some day I can teach it to you and your workmen."

Dokr hid his disappointment, bowing. "Some day, then." He waved his crew back to camp. "When the sun rises fully, we shall begin repairs."

Rich sat with Stefan, who slowly began to quiet, his growls muffling as his friend rubbed his ears. His change back might take time. "I've got bear cub for a while," Rich said. He poked his feet under the thickly muscled body for warmth. "I'll sit out here with him."

"Want company?" Henry nervously pushed his glasses back to the bridge of his nose.

"Sure! Hey, you knocked that one guy off his horse!"

Henry's face flushed. "I did, didn't I? Too bad he got right back up."

"We wouldn't know what to do with him anyway," Bailey laughed.

"I would," said Jason quietly, and he did not laugh. He shoved his hands in his pockets, filling each with a crystal, and took another walk around the academy despite the darkness of the night which had barely begun to give way to dawn.

"What's eating him?" Ting looked after Jason, puzzled.

"It's hard to fight back with your hands tied," Trent

answered her. "Well, I'm for more sleep unless someone wants to fix breakfast?" He looked about eagerly, and no one answered. He shrugged good-naturedly then and headed back inside, true to his word.

Jason trotted about slowly, shining his crystal wherever he thought he saw smoke stains, but Tomaz and Gavan seemed right. The warding had kept the wood from truly catching and whatever burning had happened, was little more than surface charring which could easily be sanded off. He should be happy about the victory, small as it was. Jonnard had intended heavy damage, perhaps even total destruction of the academy. He'd no doubt about that. What were they supposed to do? Take it? They had no choice.

He stood in the shadows between the Iron Mountains and their Academy, his hands shoved deep in his trouser pockets now, cradling his crystals, and staring at the ground in thought.

Part of the mountain's foot seemed to flow toward him, glowing like molten volcanic lava in the night, rising up and wrapping itself close, reflecting the heat of the earth. It took shape with a graceful stretch and arranged its curving bulk about Jason.

"Early morning, is it not?"

Jason wrinkled his nose at the dragon as he opened his eyes wide and then settled down on his forepaws, watching him. "Does dawn come," Jason asked the vast beast, "when the sun rises or when the soul realizes a great truth?"

"My. Early for philosophy!" The dragon stretched a paw out, unsheathed his glittering black talons and admired them. "I'd say you just realized one, Gatekeeper."

"I've lied to you," Jason said simply. "I didn't mean to, but I have, and that's that."

"Oh?"

"When I passed the trial to open the Gate here, you asked me to choose. I chose guardian. I lied. I realize now I should have chosen warrior. I'm fighting back." He gazed down the valley, along the path of the raiders' retreat. "I'm not going to stand by and take this."

"Do you think guardians just stand and watch?"

"I don't know what they do. I only know what I'm going to do. I brought them here, now I'm going to take them out." Jason shifted weight. "Gavan has some plan to get Eleanora and FireAnn back, as a ransom. It might work, but it probably won't."

"And your plan will?"

"If it takes everything I have, it will." Jason stared at the dragon, into his large gold-and-amber eyes, and stood fast.

"I cannot help you."

"I didn't ask you to."

"Yet you apologize?"

"I don't like to lie," Jason answered.

"That, I know well." The dragon sheathed his talons, his orange-red scales rippling. The coming morning light began to dance upon his body, tiny motes of white fire upon molten red. "You may find yourself surprised, Jason Adrian."

Jason took his hands out of his pockets. His clear crystal, laced with bands of gold and lapis filled one, the lavender crystal of Gregory the Gray's was in the other. Both glowed with power. "As long as I don't fail."

29

Chaos and Order

BEFORE JASON COULD SAY more, or even blink, the dragon withdrew into the mountain or wherever it was he disappeared to, with as little noise as he'd made appearing, taking his warmth and smell of copper with him. Jason waited a moment to be polite before leaving, wondering if he had done right or wrong and knowing that he wouldn't know until the end of it all—if even then. That was the way of some decisions, he thought uneasily.

He put his crystals back, and his left hand began to ache and sting across the old scar; he smoothed the puckered skin down. The old Shakespearean quote, "By the pricking of my thumbs, something wicked this way comes" ran through his mind, but it was not through his thumbs, it was always the scar. He twisted about in the dawn where black shadow still streaked heavily, and light had barely started to part the night.

They only howled twice. The first hung in the air like a questioning wail, and the second, sharp and loud, answered. Then the noise of galloping, of paws covering the ground, drawing nearer, and the sound of panting as long-toothed jaws bit at the cold and tongues lolled out to scent

492

what lingered on the air. From the very clouds that hugged the valley wolfjackals spawned, one, two, three, five, seven, a pack, ranging down on the academy, their eyes glowing green. Their silver-and-black fur quivered as they circled the building, snapping at the air, swallowing the traces of the Magick fire that had burst all around.

Drinking Chaos, Tomaz would say. Jason stood still and watched them, the scar on his hand pulsing as they loped by. They took little notice of him save for the last one, a great-shouldered, hulking beast of a wolfjackal who paused and stared at him, black-and-silver mask unreadable even for an animal, save for the showing of sharp ivory fangs. After a long breath or two as if he recognized Jason by look scent or scar, the beast galloped off after his pack mate and they encircled the academy one last time before disappearing into the woods, much like any wild wolf pack.

It took a few moments longer for his scar to stop throbbing painfully. Then and only then did he enter the school. Upstairs, Trent could not be seen under the hump of blankets. Jason lay down on his cot and took out his lavender crystal, staring at it.

Found on a world seemingly populated by wolfjackals, and sometimes filled with an image of the elder Magicker who'd taught many of them, the crystal was his and yet not his. It had come to him, he supposed, because he was the only one who could carry it back, but carry it to whom? No one else wished it. Why was it where the wolfjackals roamed? Had Gregory been thrown there when Magick exploded? Or had he gone there purposely, and left a clue as to his passage? Was he a Gatekeeper, too, among his many Talents, or was Jason the only one left?

He pulled out the faintly lavender crystal and stared into it, his eyes adjusting to the dark, but his mind carrying the image more than the actual sight. It was a totally transparent gem, unlike his which had a band or two of rock embedded in it, and he could see into and through it. On more than one occasion, he'd seen Gregory the Gray within it. Never had the image acknowledged him, so he did not think it living. But he couldn't know, for sure. He only knew that Gregory was not trapped inside the crystal and that, once, it had been bonded to the great Magicker.

It warmed inside his fingertips. All good crystals did, as

if they had a life of their own. Gavan said they vibrated faintly with the energy charged throughout them. Supposedly, that resonance also held the elder Magicker although Jason often thought there was more to it than that. Jason rubbed it. He could feel a hum through the object. The more he rubbed it, the louder the hum got.

Although everyone thought Gregory had died in the great conflict between himself and Brennard, Jason had become more and more certain the man had not. He felt him. Where and how, he did not know, and the crystal certainly wasn't telling him. That didn't keep him from trying, though. It hadn't fallen at his feet by accident!

Something stirred inside the crystal. Jason gripped it tightly. Imagination, or had he felt the humming change, grow more intense? He cupped it, staring into it, trying to delve into its depths. Without pouring himself into it, he tried to reach as far as he could, not wanting his own power to flood the power that seemed to be blossoming in the stone.

The gem crackled with heat. He held it together, fearing that it might fracture from the inside out, shattering itself with the strain. Instead, a white snowflake bloomed inside it, and in a moment or two, the optical illusion rearranged itself into a face he knew as Gregory the Gray. The room glowed with the crystal's power, a soft blue yet somehow a warm light, and he could see the wide-browed, strong visage of the man as clearly as if he stood next to him.

He expected it to speak to him. Gregory seemed to look into his eyes, into him, much as he looked into the crystal. Jason's hand shook a little. The heat of the gem burned but there was not enough heat to force him to drop it.

A thought reached him, slow and quiet as if coming from the bottom of a great ocean somewhere, as if it took much effort and came out of great depths. *I sleep, and must sleep. If you find me, do not awaken me. I have promises to keep in my sleep. Those promises keep you all safe, and the oath must be met.*

What oath? Jason closed his hands tightly about the searing gemstone. Where . . . why?

Nothing else stirred through his mind. No echo, no sigh, no other feeling of support as though the effort to send that much had cost Gregory dearly.

Jason let out his breath, slowly, and released the crystal. Its warmth fled as he did so. Gregory lived, somewhere, somewhen. He knew they were all there, and somehow, he held his energy to ward them. Knowing that would have to be enough. Should he tell the others?

Eleanora should know. It would comfort her, he thought. When Eleanora was freed and she was ready, he would tell her.

The more he learned, the more bewildering questions he seemed to have. For now, though, the only one left to really dig at him was ... if he attacked the Dark Hand's stronghold, would the wolfjackals fight with or against him? Or would they merely rise for the Chaos which would ensue? He would not know till too late, so he decided to prepare against all possibilities.

Somewhere, deep in his thoughts, he fell back asleep as well, not to awaken till Trent opened their shutters and the full-blown sun's rays glared at him.

"That does it," said Ting firmly. "The crystals are definitely draining much faster than they should. Dormant, charged crystals seemed to be only a little faster, but charged ones in use ... well, look at this." She waved her hand over the table they had covered with bits and pieces of gemstones and quartzes and other crystals, as well as the larger ones they used every day.

"But what does it mean?"

"It means something outside is drawing on them, because they lose power even when we're not using them. And when we do use them, it's as if ... how do I say it ..." Ting wrinkled her nose. "It's like opening up a can of soda with four or five straws and everyone having a drink at once. Only, we didn't invite anyone to share."

"Isabella!" Bailey smacked one hand into the other, sharply, and the retort made little Lacey jump on her shoulder. She let out a resentful chitter before running down Bailey's sleeve, leaping to the floor, and scurrying off to her nest for some peace and quiet.

"Maybe. That, I don't know. I can't find a way to trace where the Magick goes, just that it does. Trent might be able to; Jason says he can see it."

"He has, a few times. Traps and such. I wouldn't count on it, though. It seems to be erratic with him. Jason says they're not even sure if it is a Talent or just a quirk." Bailey tapped the tabletop, setting the crystals to dancing slightly. "When are we going to tell them?"

"Now. We can't wait. Suppose a crystal failed entirely?"

Bailey stood, drawing Ting to her feet as well. "Let's go face the music and tell them the dancing slippers have serious holes in them."

"Ummm," Ting answered as she trailed after Bailey. "Right."

The two girls found Gavan outside in a serious discussion with the wanderer Dokr who seemed to be taking his leave. They hesitated at the fire ring, unsure if they were intruding or not, but Rainwater gave them a quick smile before clasping Dokr's hands.

"May your roads be smooth and lead always to home," he said, and the wanderer beamed at that.

"We will return in the spring," Dokr promised, with a short bow. "To do repairs and finish other projects you may wish."

"That is a deal. And, if you need anything through the winter, you have only to let us know."

Dokr smiled. "We are self-sufficient as we have learned to depend on ourselves. Not depending on a Spirit to guide us or watch over us, we have had to be." He stepped back, then hesitated. "We are outcast because of our beliefs."

Gavan inclined his head. "As I have known and respected. So are we."

Dokr gestured. "No, that is not what I mean. I know you understand who we are, but not why, perhaps. The Spirit exists. We feel it. Others says we cannot feel it, so we reject it, but that is not our way. We *can* feel it. That is why we do not follow it." Dokr took a deep breath as if trying to keep his words from stumbling. He thumbed the crystal on his belt loop that translated his words for him. "The Warlord was a great man, but his time is gone. Like all of us, there is another place for him now, yet he resists and stays. To stay, Gavan Rainwater, he must take from all of us. I say that giving up a bit of my own soul each day is too big a price to pay for his watching over us. So I say to you, in warning, the Spirit takes. It gives, but it takes." Dokr put his hands together then, and bowed deeply, touching them to his forehead, before disappearing into the grove. After a few moments, the sound of the wagons departing could be heard, wheels rolling as hooves paced steadily pulling the loads, and the soft shouts of the children calling back in farewell.

Gavan looked after them, with a strange expression on his face.

"Whoosh," said Bailey, finally. "Maybe that explains it."

"Explains what?"

"Ting and I have been doing experiments. Our crystals are failing. Kaput. Zip. Null and void."

"Indeed?" Gavan raised one eyebrow. He sat down on a stump, stirring up the morning ashes of a nearly burned out fire. "We all grow tired. If I have taught you one thing, it's that the magic you have, you draw from within you. Crystals are only a focus, and sometimes a reservoir."

"And sometimes a leaky faucet." Bailey and Ting plunked down across from Gavan.

"Pardon me?"

"Maybe that's not what I mean. It's more like . . . there's a hole in the bucket."

Gavan leaned forward, propped on the tree branch he'd been using as a poker. "What are you talking about?"

"It's like this," Ting rushed in. "We've been testing crystals for days. Dormant ones fade a little, even though they're not being used. They shouldn't. Nothing draws on them. Charged crystals lose power at four times the rate they should when being used. So, it's not like we're drawing that much power out by ourselves. It's as if power is rushing out of them, like a full bucket that has a hole in it, when it isn't supposed to."

"Indeed." Gavan sat up, dropped his branch and brought out his cane. The wolfhead cane's crystal looked unfamiliarly dark. "We've all been working very hard. I think it would be normal to need recharging, don't you?"

Ting and Bailey shook their heads. "Not like this!" Bailey shot back. "It's like burning the candle at both ends, but we didn't light the fire to do it."

Ting shot Bailey a look, then said quietly, "Something is drawing the power off besides ourselves. We thought it might be the Dark Hand somehow, that they've learned to tap into us. But after listening to Dokr, could it be something else?"

"And that's not even what matters," Bailey interrupted. "The point is, all of us are going to reach for our crystals sooner or later and find them dead. We're going to need them and they're going to fail us when we need them most, if we're not careful."

Gavan's mouth worked a moment before he said, "I'll take this into consideration. Discuss it with Tomaz, and see if we can find a way to test it ourselves. I appreciate your efforts." He stood then, rubbing his palm over his cane. The crystal nickered as if it tried to warm and could not. He closed his hand over it, hiding it from their sight. "I'll spread the word to conserve until we have a better idea." He left Bailey and Ting at the dwindling fire.

Bailey watched a coal break in two, both halves bright orange and then cooling quickly to gray ashes as she watched. "Think he believed us?"

"Yes and no. If we're right, it could mean a lot of trouble. I don't think we need any more trouble right now," Ting finished miserably.

"The thing about trouble," Bailey said positively, "is that there's always a pot of gold to be found when it's over." She pushed rocks from the fire ring into place with the toe of her boot, banking the last of the fire carefully.

" 'Zat right?"

"Of course it is."

"Oh-kay."

Silently, they watched the fire burn down, and the yard fill with noise as the boys awoke and came out to exercise with Ting's grandmother in military control.

Planning

THE ACADEMY SEEMED very still with the wanderers gone, and the incessant work on the building slowed considerably without them. It wasn't finished yet, but the work left they could do themselves over the winter, interior work and, as Bailey put it, "Hopefully, warm showers." Hot showers would have been a bit too much to expect.

Tomaz sent them outside to enjoy a warm, bright autumn day, with baskets of crystals to charge, as well as their own. They swapped looks at each other in anticipation, and Jason seemed grimly satisfied.

"Do you think," Henry began in a half whisper to him, but Jason didn't let him finish, answering, "I sure hope so."

They worked quickly, exchanging crystals and gemstones among themselves, for they all seemed to have preferences as to the color and composition of the crystal that worked best for them. Trent could not help. Instead he began to sketch a map of the magical lines as he'd perceived them from dragonback, and listened to their banter, his mouth twisted in a crooked almost wistful smile when he looked up every now and then.

Tomaz came by, Midnight on his forearm. "Good work.

Put the crystals up, and wait inside for a bit. I have to talk to Gavan, and then we'll let you know what's going on."

"Words, words, words," complained Trent, throwing himself at the kitchen table. "They're going to talk themselves to death before anything gets done."

"Plans have to be made."

Trent's fingers drummed on the table. "Talk, talk, talk."

"You're ready, then?"

"I don't know about that, but I know it's time to do *something*. Anyone can see that. Grab a sword and let's go spank these guys!"

"Swinging a sword isn't easy," argued Rich. He pointed at Stef. "Bear boy, here, can tell you that much."

"Sword work," Stefan said gravely, "is complicated and demanding, and is nothing like the swashbuckling movies you've seen. Forget any sword fight you think you've seen. They're faked. Choreographed and with anything but real weapons. Real blades are a lot heavier, for one, and one or two hits can bleed you of the strength you need to keep swinging. The moves might be similar, but the ability to carry them out is different. Beryl says my muscles are too old to remember some of it. Real blade users start when young, just like any athlete."

Rich let out a low whistle. "I think that's the most I've ever heard you say in a lifetime."

Stef reached out and cuffed the top of Rich's head. "Listen up, carrot top, this is serious stuff!"

"Yeah, yeah, big guy, you gash 'em and I'll stitch 'em up." Rich snorted and combed his hair back into place, freckles dancing in animation across his nose and cheekbones as he grimaced at Stef.

Bailey shrugged. "What do we do, then?"

"Run?"

Bailey threw an empty basket at Trent's head. Although he ducked, her aim had accounted for that and it still flew off the side of his face.

"Good shot!" Stef's face lit up in appreciation and Bailey took a bow. Trent rolled on the floor, laughing before sitting up and sticking his tongue out at her.

"I guess you can throw stuff and then run," he said, crossing his legs and leaning back.

"My suggestion is that you fight them with your strength,

not theirs. These guys can ride, and they can use a short sword. They're used to crystal attacks around them, but they can't use Magick themselves, so there's a lot you can do to hit them and hit them hard." Stef folded bulky arms. "That's all the advice I have."

"Seriously, bro, I am impressed."

"I just want everybody to know that this ain't a toy." Stefan rubbed at his nose, heavily embarrassed and said not another word but stepped back, holding his sword.

"That's all right by you guys," Trent spoke into the silence. "I'd like to swing a light saber myself like the rest of you, but there's no way I can manage that, and it looks like the real thing is out for me. So where do I fit in?"

"You will probably be the guy who keeps the rest of us from getting killed. You can see the wards as they're laying them. You can spot the spells as they throw them at us. Anything Magick that comes through the air to hit, hamper, or hurt us, you're going to see. If this works at all, Trent, it'll be because of you," Jason told him.

Bailey swung her head. "And some of us have to stay home, probably, whether we can throw and run or not."

"We might not have any way of getting back if you three can't pull us, you know that." Jason looked at her.

She sighed heavily. "I know, I know, but I wanted to have fun, too."

Rich patted her on the arm. "You can have fun with me after we get back, putting all the bandages on."

"Not *that* kind of fun."

"Why not? It's fun to me."

"Well, you're strange." Bailey edged away from him.

Rich put his hands on his chest. "Wounded! And mortally, too, I think."

Ting giggled as Rich staggered back and leaned dramatically against a kitchen counter before adding breathlessly, "I agree with Bailey, though. I hate being left behind."

Heavy footsteps sounded in the hallway. "There's a reason for that," Gavan told her, as he and Tomaz entered. "They already have two of our more precious Magickers. We don't intend to hand them two more."

"I can take care of myself!" Bailey tossed her head again, ponytail swinging from side to side.

"We don't want to take that chance, and our lives are

going to depend on the three of you. I don't see Henry complaining."

Henry looked up, round face emphasized by his round glasses. "It—it's just that I goof up, and I know I do. I'm better off here, out of the way." He gestured, and his brown hair seemed to go in every direction as he did.

"You don't goof up, but your Talent of Fire is pretty powerful and still needs training. None of us wants to go up in a puff of smoke." He patted Henry's shoulder. "Be that as it may," Gavan said. "Tomaz and I are finished talking. And this is what we've decided. The pieces we've been waiting for are in place, Midnight carried a message from Renart." He paused, looking over the table at each of them, one by one. "We move tomorrow. I've already sent to Avenha, asking for mounts, and they should arrive in the morning."

Stef let out a whoop. He jabbed a fist at the air. Gavan shook his head slowly at them.

"This is a dangerous situation. It may be a pitched battle like we fought at the opening of the Dragon Gate."

"And we're more ready for it than ever," Trent said evenly. "We've all been training. We know what Jonnard and the crew are capable of. Besides," and he flashed a grin. "Madame Qi has been running our butts off."

That drew a chuckle from Tomaz despite his solemn expression. He hooked his thumb in his turquoise-and-silver belt. "You are all nearly as tall as I am now," he said, glancing at all of them. "But that does not mean I'm ready to let you take shots I should be taking. That being said, Gavan and I have talked. If anything happens, our primary instruction is to fall back to the academy and have Jason reach Khalil. We know the other Council members, we know that of all of them, even Aunt Freyah, Khalil is the most capable of handling matters here. So, protect yourselves, protect Jason. If we lose our Gatekeeper, we are trapped here."

"We all go in," stated Stefan, "we all come out."

"Hopefully." Gavan took out his map tube, and unrolled his map, laying it out in front of them. "Look it over, memorize what you can of it, so you can Crystal safely. Remember the basic rules so that no one ends up where they don't want to be." He tapped the map. "The obsidian-marked tower is the basic landmark and it's not changed much, but we don't want the fortress. We want this valley pass here, about a quarter of a day's travel from the fortress. This outcropping of rock and grove are fairly visual, plus they have an advantage of being good cover for an ambush. Midnight and Snowheart have scouted it, so Tomaz has a good mental picture of it. He'll be leading us in, but you have to remember it on your own, just in case." Gavan tapped another corner of the map. "They'll be out of reach from their own horsemen for immediate aid, and not so far that we can't regroup and get the caravan to the warehouse Renart has secured for us. It's not going to be a hand-to-hand combat, it's going to be crystal to crystal." He lifted his chin to Ting and Bailey. "On that note, let me warn you. Our young ladies here have been looking into some matters and have some statistics which indicate that crystals being used are drained of their focusing power and any magic we have charged into them about four times faster than they should be. We don't know why or, more importantly, how, but someone's tapped into the energy. Be careful. Don't overextend yourself or depend on a reservoir of charge that may not be there. Back each other up and stay in communication." He lifted his hands and let the map roll up naturally, restoring it to its tube. "Any questions?"

"Just one." Jason shifted his weight. "What if it fails?"

"If it fails, we go after Eleanora and FireAnn. And we don't look back."

"You're sure?"

Something undefinable passed through Gavan's clear blue eyes. "I've never been more sure of anything in my life."

"Good enough." He put his hand out. "Team shake."

The Magickers pushed close around the table to slap their hands on his. Jason felt the briefest moment of knowing something he had never realized before, of the unity of all of them, something he told himself time and again, but for the first time really *felt* as they all touched. Their hands dipped down on his and rose upward, as they shouted, "Magickers!"

He could not answer for anyone but himself, but he was ready.

31

Sting Like a Bee

IF ANY OF THEM SLEPT AT ALL, the before-dawn pounding at the front doors, accompanied by the wailing of the alarms woke them. Jason and Trent threw themselves downstairs, having slept in all but their boots, but they didn't beat Gavan who threw the door open in welcome. The others stampeded in behind them, crowding the threshold as it opened.

Pyra stood at the academy steps, her face tilted up toward them, her father's second-in-command, Flameg, at her flank. Both looked armed to the teeth and ready for anything, as she said quietly, "My father sent me in response to your call for aid."

"That can't be good," Rich muttered, then blushed to the roots of his red hair as she fixed a stare at his forehead.

"Do you question my ability?"

"No, no," Gavan interjected smoothly. "Your father does us much honor by sending his best. Rich means, I think, that . . . well, knowing of Renart's . . . hmmm . . . feelings for you, we are obliged to take good care of you."

Pyra's face glowed for a moment, and she swapped the longbow from one hand to another. "It is I who shall take care of you." She gestured a hand behind her. "We brought horses, as requested. I know only that you have a raid planned?"

"Indeed, we do. Come, sit, have tea with us, and Tomaz will sketch out the plans."

Tomaz had been standing quietly with the others, listening, but as his name was mentioned, he cast the crow he carried on his wrist skyward, freeing it for the moment, and nodded gravely in the direction of the Avenhans. "We have a plan," he said. "Any thoughts you have regarding it will be appreciated as we make ready."

"And haste is needed. The sun is barely up, but the convoy should be sent out soon."

Pyra's eyebrow lifted. "Convoy?"

"Come and we'll tell you."

In the end, it was all of them putting in suggestions, hurriedly, even as they dressed in the gear they'd put together, and Pyra left off sitting and drinking tea to help Stef affix his weapons belt and to show Rich how to tie his herb bags so they would not affect his movements. Tomaz had Jason and Trent outside going over the horses to check the length of the stirrups and the tightness of the girths, and then inspecting the hooves for small stones.

Flameg nodded at Gavan. "A bold move, but one that should set them back." A man trained for such action, his eyes shone with approval and the anticipation of a fight. This was why Mantor had sent for the Magickers. This was the reckoning for the damage to his village and others. He tightened his baldric as he spoke, in readiness.

"So we determine."

He stood, eying Pyra with the same approval. "Your women fight as ours do?"

Bailey put her chin up. "Sometimes! Today we fight from here."

Pyra said softly, "Magic has different boundaries," as if defending that decision.

Flameg gave a curt bow. "Well enough, then."

Gavan touched Ting's and Bailey's hands, and repeated his words of the evening, as if to take the sting out of leaving them behind. "The moment you feel the crystals going, reach us. Without time to test your ideas, all we can do is rely on you two. You five here are our anchors, our backup." His gaze swept Rebecca, Madame Qi, and Henry as well as the girls.

They nodded solemnly.

"Let's go, then."

"I hope you've got a horse big enough for me," muttered Stefan as they headed out the door.

"Oh, we do. I made sure I brought the fattest, sturdiest pony in the herd." Pyra's mouth twitched.

Stef grunted, and the Avenhan gave in to the laughter shaking her shoulders as he stomped past, and she threw Bailey and Ting a merry wink before following him.

Bailey reached for Ting's hand as she watched the last of them go out the door. As it shut, and she heard the muffled sounds of horses being mounted and then ridden off, leaving them behind, she noted, "I must be growing up. This is the first time ever I've been truly afraid to see anyone go . . . worried that they might not come back."

Ting squeezed her hand. "Me, too."

Ting's grandmother spoke from the other side of the kitchen where her presence had not been noted, and her voice startled them a little. "With age and experience comes the ability to know sorrow and regret. It is our hope that, with our help, every generation knows less and less of it."

Rebecca entered then, holding Lacey by the scruff of the little rodent's neck. Lacey's tufted tail hung down dejectedly.

"This little pack rat is going to highly regret coming into my room if she's not careful!"

"Oh! You found her! I wondered where she'd scampered off to."

"She was pillaging my jewelry box."

"Lacey!" scolded Bailey, as she liberated her from her mother's hold. "That's a bad rodent!" Lacey managed an indignant chirp as if protesting her innocence as Bailey stuffed her in her pocket.

Rebecca sat down at the table and poured a cup of tea, making a face as she drank it. "Lukewarm," she explained. "Everyone is gone, then?"

Ting nodded as she seated her grandmother at the table.

"Then," said Bailey's mom, looking eerily like an adult

echo of her daughter, with her golden-brown hair in a ponytail. "Our real work begins."

"Mom?"

She looked at all of them. "Madame Qi has been teaching me a little of the Hidden Ways, and I'm here to help as well. I can do much more than be a den mother to all of you." She reached out and tweaked Bailey's nose. "Do you think that Talent in your veins just sprang up out of nowhere? I think it's run in our family for a long time, and although you got the lion's share, I am here to offer whatever I can."

Henry looked at her with unabashed admiration in his round face. "Wish my mom could say something like that."

"She probably has, Henry. You just have to know when to listen."

"Each generation builds on the other." Madame Qi nodded in agreement to her own words. "Nothing flowers that does not come from the seed of another blossom, sometime, somewhere." She laid her bamboo cane down on the table. "Now. We need to organize." In a few short moments, she had assigned watchers for the crystals, Henry to keep an eye on the academy and the Iron Mountains, and herself and Rebecca to boil water and make other preparations for wounded and to keep an eye on Bailey and Ting as they anchored. "And now," she finished. "We wait."

The Havenites from Avenha proved to have quite a sense of humor. Rich's borrowed horse was as tall and skinny and bony as Stef's was short, broad, and sturdy. He frowned at Pyra's back as she rode in front of him, her own mount sleek, well-groomed, and trained, while his seemed to jolt with every step, and even the saddle could not keep from bruising him. It was a good thing they would Crystal most of the ride. He said as much to Stef.

"At least you don't have to ride with your legs looking like a turkey wishbone being pulled in two directions!" His legs stuck out from his pony's girth, one foot headed west, the other east.

Rich shot him a wide grin. "Don't be falling off!"

"The head handles are the only things I have to hold onto." And, true to his words, Stef held one hand tightly wrapped in his pony's black wiry mane as he bounced along and the other in the reins, unable to bend his legs well enough to grip with them. He glared at Pyra's back as she rode ahead of them, her head bowed in serious discussion with Gavan and Tomaz, but he could swear her shoulders still shook now and then with laughter.

They rode just far enough to get out of the valley, beyond their own warding system, to avoid any backlash from the magical energies they planned, then Gavan circled them up, and they linked. Tomaz thought of the lands his crows had scouted. Jason got a swooping vision of dark green trees springing abundantly beside a deeply cut brook that must swell with rainwater in the early spring, the rock bed holding it was so deeply etched. He drew the crows' eye view of the site deeply inside of him to be his own guide should either Gavan or Tomaz fail to Crystal the journey.

He thought of Bailey's and Ting's warnings, tightened his own grip on his mount's reins, and then they were *between*. Frightened, the horses thrashed a bit, and around him, he could hear the very, very faint calls of each rider to calm them, and then the *between* opened into the grove, and the sound of rushing water filled his ears.

"Very good," murmured Tomaz. He dismounted immediately and led his horse around a bit to steady him. He glanced up at Gavan, adding, "We may have to fight on foot. These horses aren't used to it, while the Dark Hand has been raiding for months."

"That's a thought. We don't need to fight the horses as well. Everyone dismount, and we'll tie them off."

"I'll show you how to do breakaway ties. If anything happens to us, or the wolfjackals hit, the horse can slip the knot with enough pulling and free itself." Tomaz held up one creased hand, and they followed him, watching how he twisted the reins into a clever knot about a fallen sapling.

Then Pyra led them to the edge of the small grove, pointing down the pass, and they crouched, waiting for their prey. Above them came a low caw. Jason tilted his head back and saw a dark crow in the treetops above Tomaz, its own eyes sharply scanning the pass.

They would see the trading caravan long before it spotted them.

Unless, of course, there was magic at work.

*   *   *

Jonnard woke to the sounds of the harness jingling and shouts at stubborn horses and the creak of wagons being rolled into position. He lay on his bed, contemplating the day. With Isabella gone, he could delve into his father's journals again. He thought he had the full sense of what his father had done and what he could duplicate. The only problem seemed to be the draw of power. He had no wish to burn himself out, which meant he would have to steal. Nor would his uncertain ties to Henry Squibb serve the purpose. No, he would have to consider how to get the magic he needed, because it would have to be done deftly and ruthlessly.

He stood and had just finished dressing when his mother's voice rang down the hall. "Jonnard! Are you up and awake?"

He left his room, calling back, "Both, Isabella."

"Good. I've changed my mind. You're to come with us."

He shoved the disappointment out of his mind and expression, giving a short bow from the waist. "As you wish."

Isabella straightened as he joined her, and he could not help but notice the drawn look on her face and the heavy dark circles under her eyes. More aging. Every day now seemed to wear on her, and he knew she was no closer to finding the answer. Would she escalate every moment until she became a white-haired crone, as befit her actual age? Was Magick holding her back or hurtling her forward? He could not answer any more than she could, but he saw the fear in her eyes, an emotion she quickly shuttered away as she raised her chin firmly.

"I think both of us may be needed to keep the drivers in line. I would not put it past Fremmler and the others to think of hijacking these wagons for themselves. If only one of us is there it may tempt them to think they can actually do it."

"Understood. I'll be ready to leave when you are, then." He took her hand and kissed the back of it, in the old European way, and she smiled faintly, pleased, as he took his leave.

When the time came, Jon saw that Fremmler had dressed in finer clothes, as befit the trader he'd once been, and found a razor to scrape over his face, reducing his looks from grizzled to merely scraggly. He made a note to himself of the man's reaction to being promoted somewhat, as it could be useful to both reward and keep him in line, in the future.

He mounted the bay he used for a second horse, and his mother took the wagon seat on the first, lighter caravan. Then, at her gesture, the fortress gates swung open and they set out into the early day. Dew sparkled the grass and rock rills heavily, and a coldness lay upon the earth that the sun would have to work hard to dispel later. Seasons turned here, as they did at home. Jon put up the hood on his cape, seeking a bit more warmth until that selfsame sun rose higher in the sky.

The road to Naria led down off the butte where the fortress held high ground over the river valley, and wound its way beside that river. Wagon wheel ruts lay heavily grooved into the road of dirt, and Isabella sat, jolted side to side, as the caravans made their ungainly way forward. Jon rode his horse with a grim satisfaction that he had the easy going of it from the saddle as opposed to the wagon. They were nearly two hours out of the fortress, and with the sun finally high enough he paused to drop his hood.

Isabella crooked her hand, motioning for him to come and ride by her. She squinted across the landscape.

He recognized that alert look of hers, almost hawkish. "What is it, Mother?"

"Too quiet. Altogether too quiet." She unfastened the lacy cuff of her blouse, releasing her crystal bracelet to her touch.

"Shall I ride ahead and scout?"

"I am not sure." Her fingertips ran lightly over her crystals, brilliant gemstones of incomparable worth, as well as worth their weight in Magick.

Trees lined the nearby river here, and crowded the road through the passes ahead. He saw nothing suspicious nor did he feel anything, but he readied himself to put heels to his horse's flanks to calm her worry.

A caw rang out over the quiet morning air.

"Crow!" Isabella flung up her hand, startling Jon's horse. He wheeled it in a tight circle to keep it in hand as she added, "There are no crows in Haven!"

Crystal light flared, white-hot against the brilliantly blue autumn sky. It shattered as it met lances of light from the groves, and with shouts, the Magickers attacked.

Jon's eyes picked them out. Grown from the boys he'd first met at summer camp years ago, he still knew them. He kicked his horse forward, his own crystal blade coming up as Isabella shouted orders to the raiders driving the caravan behind him. He knew the Magickers well enough to know the weaknesses that would get them killed. He bore down on the big-shouldered Stefan. Frighten the bear out of him and the animal would flee, uncontrollable. Stefan would be the first to go.

Divide and conquer.

32

Power!

STEF SAW HIM COMING. Words from Beryl ran
through his head. *The best way to meet a blade on horseback is to unhorse him or go for the legs.* Reluctance to cut
down an animal made him hesitate, as he felt his friends
group at his back, Rich off to his right side, putting up a
Shield for both of them. Jon shouted something, beckoning
at a raider, even as he drew his sword clear, riding down
hard at Stef.

The other rode without hands. Steel shone in his right
hand and crystal flared in his left. It took Stefan aback for
a second to see that, to see the mastery in the dark-cloaked
figure. He knew how difficult it would be to face him on
foot, now this! His bear self roared inside of him in challenge as his crystal Shield shattered under the first blow.
Rich fell to one knee with a grunt, but cried out to Stef,
"I'm okay, I'll have it up in a second!"

He had, but in that second, as horse hooves drummed
down on him. Jon swerved at Stef, steel swinging low. He
parried. The blows met, with the blades singing out in a
low, hard *Thrummm!* Stef stepped back into position, and
brought his blade into guard, his shoulders aching with the

vibration. Jon dug a heel hard into his horse's flank, pivoting around on one hoof and charging right at him. Stef stood his ground. He bit his cheek until he could taste the blood seeping out, trying to keep the bear down, but his chest swelled with a contained roar of fury.

Something thwoshed through the air, so near it would have sliced him if he'd so much as flinched, and Jon veered his horse with a curse as arrows—one, two, three—slashed past. They hit the ground, burying themselves deeply, their shafts quivering. Jon glanced over one shoulder, then looked back at Stefan.

Then he laughed.

A cold, chilling laughter that infuriated Stefan.

"Archers! Return fire!" Jon waved his blade, wheeling his horse about.

Stefan realized he was about as big a target as he could be. He swiped his hand across his crystal to call up his own Shield. It came up and settled about him like a mirage over the desert sand, a shimmering of light. He heard the thunk, thunk of two arrows hitting close by, and a muffled cry.

Rich toppled over, doubled in pain, an arrow shaft buried deeply in his thigh as Stefan turned to look. Pyra grabbed Rich by the collar and dragged him back as Stef stood in absolute confusion for a moment. "Keep fighting!" she ordered. "I've got him!"

Keep fighting! He roared, and with that poured out all his anger and frustration, and the bear prepared to charge through after.

Jon bared his teeth in a humorless grin. "Send your bearskin after me, boy. He's more of a coward than you are!"

Stefan threw his head back, bellowing in anger. He charged after Jon. He would pull him down from that horse and pull him limb from limb! His head nearly exploded with the beating of his heart and his skin pulled, and pulled, until he knew it would split apart, and the bear would come roaring out.

In mid-stride, Jason's cool voice caught him. From the inside, not the out. The Magick coursed through him. *Center on me, Stefan. Keep the bear asleep. Focus on me!*

Stef let the voice sink through him. It cooled the fiery-hot lava of the blood drumming through him, and his skin stopped tearing. He wrapped both hands about his sword hilt and leaped at Jon with all his might. His heavy body arced into the air as if weight meant nothing. He swung.

His blade met Magick. The air shrieked with the clash of it, steel against crystal. The shrill keening sound of it tore at his ears. He came down, all his weight on the blow, felt it sliding away noisily, even as Jon let out an *ooof* and gave way.

As Stefan hit the ground with both feet again, knees bent, pulling his sword back to parry, he saw Jon with one arm out, flailing to stay aboard his mount. Unbalanced, he began to slowly topple to the ground, and he took his horse with him, pulling it about awkwardly as he grabbed its neck with one arm. Stefan scrambled back as the horse fell with a terrified whinny, legs thrashing as it immediately tried to right itself. Before Stefan could blink or gather himself to go after Jonnard, the crystal winked and both Jon and the fallen mount disappeared, to reappear on the far side of the caravan.

Stef let loose a howl of both triumph and disappointment. He fell back to the edge of the trees, searching for Rich and Pyra. He found them where the horses were tied, Rich lying on his back, propped up on one elbow, a shred of shirt wrapped about his upper thigh, his herb bag on the ground and lying open next to him.

A frown marred Pyra's oval face. She shook her head slightly at Stefan. "He won't bleed much, but that's not the worry here." She pointed at the arrow lying on the ground beside them. "That greenish tinge on the arrowhead . . . it's blackmarrow poison."

Rich threw Stefan a slight grin. "Not to worry, big guy. It's only a little poison."

Stefan wiped his forehead with the back of his hand. He seemed to be seeing everything with a red veil over it, his heart still pounding loudly in his ears. It faded slowly. He stood over Rich, not quite understanding.

"The arrow's out, right."

"Yes, but don't touch it. There's still poison on it." Pyra pulled a small vial from her own herb pouch, tapping it into the water cup Rich held. She had to lean over and hold Rich's hand to keep it steady. "Drink that. It will stave off the worst effects for a while."

Rich drained the wooden cup in three gulps and shud-

dered, making a horrible face. Stef could only imagine how
bad the stuff must taste. "How long a while?" Rich's red
hair was the only thing of color about him. Shock had sent
him as pale as Stef had ever seen him.

"Long enough," Pyra answered tersely. She closed her
herb pouch and picked up her bow. "Stay awake and don't
let anyone handle that," she ordered. "Stefan. They're still
fighting out there."

"But, Rich—"

"I'll be right here. You'll have to come to me when ya
get hurt, I can't crawl all that fast." Rich tried to screw his
face into a smile, but he just looked all the more pained.

"Not funny."

"Yeah." Rich met his eyes. He nodded slowly. "They
need you, big guy. Get out of here. I'll be waiting and I want
to know what's happening!"

"Okay," said Stefan slowly. Something knotted in his
stomach.

Rich put his hand up. "I'll link my crystal to yours, give
you an extra kick."

Stefan didn't intend to let Jonnard get far, Magick or
not. "That's a deal." He broke into a lumbering run, heading back to the righting field.

Jason felt and heard Stefan nearing the edge, but he could
not spare a look. The touch he'd braided into Stef grew
fainter and fainter, like an insubstantial rope drawn thinner
and thinner until nothing was left but a slight wisp. Reality
replaced touch as Stef thumped him on the shoulder, saying, "Thanks."

"How's Rich?"

"Okay, but not good." Stef gave a bewildered grunt as if
to emphasize his words, but Jason had no time to ask him
for more. The Dark Hand hit him with all their consider-
able might and he reeled back into the other's arms. He
shook the stun off as he straightened.

"Just keep hitting 'em. They'll break, there's only two,
and then we've got the caravan! But watch your crystal,
don't drain it out."

Stef rubbed his nose. He sheathed his sword. "Gotcha."

Jason narrowed his eyes and brought up both hands,
each filled with his crystals. The lavender one seemed

warmer than ever, and he wondered if it was because it had already been through a war of wizards and magic. It knew the devastation.

Trent wiggled his way next to Jason. He rubbed his eyes. "They've got Tomaz and Gavan pinned down, but I think I got them out of the webbing."

"Pretty bad?"

"It was." Trent scanned the trampled meadow in front of them. "I'd say they're trying the same on you." He traced lines only he could see through thin air. "Net isn't closed yet, but they're trying."

"Show me where, one string at a time, and I'll cut it." Jason's eyes sparkled with the idea. "The game here is to run their defenses into the ground, and then take the wagons. Once the crystals are gone, they haven't much chance if ours hold out."

"Let's play follow the leader, then." Trent sketched across the sky. Jason followed the movement of his hand, and swept a crystal blade through it, like trying to cut an invisible thread. A triumphant whoop from Trent told him he'd done it.

Trent's hands hopscotched across his field of vision, plucking and pulling at lines of magic Jason could only barely sense. Sometimes it took four or five attempts to bring down one casting, but more often he could get it in one or two tries. The fighting around him seemed to retreat to slow-moving visions that he barely saw as he concentrated. A look to one side showed Stefan with Shield up, and crystal in his knobby fist, blond face streaked with dirt and frown, growling at raiders as they attempted to close on them, and he drove them back.

A knot of fighters bore down on Gavan. He stood in a swirl of his cape, crystal Lightning in his hand. Flameg nocked an arrow to his bow and moved in on his flank protectively. Gavan loosened his Lightning and two men dropped. The third one he met hand to hand, while the fourth went after Flameg. He got his arrow off and it hit deep into the raider's leg, but even the cry of pain as it hit did not slow the swing of the outlaw's blade. It hit Flameg square, and the Avenhan fell to his knees, then sagged to the ground in a spray of blood. Jason looked aside, afraid of being sick. He barely caught the sense of what Trent said, flustered, and managed to focus on the last of the web about him.

The last thread of magic ensnarement cut, Jason rose to his feet, and grabbed Trent by the arm.

"We're going after Jonnard."

"Now?"

Jason looked at him. "There's a better time? We press him; either he'll drain his power or she will trying to save him. We haven't much left ourselves."

Thwoosh. Trent dodged an arrow, spun about on one heel, and shrugged. "I guess not!"

Jason threw up a Shield and locked arms with Trent. He gestured at Tomaz, indicating which way they were heading. The elder Magicker hesitated, then gave an agreeing nod. They zigzagged their way through the fighting. Raiders had fallen and lay silent, their bodies stunned by crystal shock or pierced by arrows. Jonnard saw them coming. He reined his horse back sharply, and the horse went back on his haunches, one hoof pawing the air in protest.

Jason struck. He did not wait for fairness or for Jon to acknowledge the duel or anything else. Their fight had started long before this one.

Crystal stroke met crystal in a blaze of sparks, the air sizzling with the noise and sheer impact of it. Jason did not wait to take a breath before striking again, hard, and again the Magicks met in an explosion of energy. Let the Dark Hand think he would kill Jonnard if he could. He knew the other had no such doubts.

His crystals cooled slightly in his hands. Ruthlessly, he reached back along their anchors, back to Ting and Bailey and Henry to tap their resources.

"Jason." Trent put his hand on his arm. "Jason! I can see it . . . Jon is tied into Henry again. He's draining him. You can't do it, too. You'll kill him."

"Show me!"

Trent gulped. His hands swung about aimlessly in front of him, as though signing an impossible message, then, "Here! I've got it!" He held his hands out as though the string were woven through them.

Jason reached out with one crystal, blading it, and swung the edge through Trent's hands. A zzzzt and then a sense of letting go as the strand parted. He had it! He knew it without Trent telling him. Poor Henry, ensnared again, and without even knowing it!

Jonnard let out a curse of frustration and savagely reined his horse around, wheeling to the far side of the first wagon, leaving Jason to look up into Isabella's haughty and furious expression. The rubies and other gemstones at her wrists and neck blazed with her anger. Here and there, a blackened stone hung in its setting, ruined and lost to her Magick. She raised her hand and pointed at Jason.

"Uh-oh," said Trent in his ear. "Incoming!"

Jason pulled Trent to his knees, and dropped himself, shifting all his energy to a defensive Shield. Fire and rage poured down on them as though dragonfire spewed from her hands, beating down until Jason's whole body trembled in the effort to keep the Shield up to protect them. He held the shimmering buckler up out of sheer will, and watched her drain herself. Then she cried out harsh words, and in the blink of an eye, Jonnard disappeared.

Jonnard stood inside the threshold to the dungeon. The air stank of the Leucators, filling his lungs for a moment, his pulse racing with the adrenaline of the fight and Isabella's hoarse cry in his ears to do something. A weakness tremored through his body. His link to Henry severed, that mongrel pup Jason sapping him . . . He palmed his crystal, centering his thoughts. If he did nothing, they would lose the caravan and the defeat alone might set the raiders against them.

Now or never, and if it were to be done, it would be better to be done quickly. Jonnard smiled grimly at the words of the old Bard of Avon running through his head. His father had told him, once, that Shakespeare had seen him do Magick and often wondered if Oberon were based on that sight.

The Leucators got to their feet, chains and shackles rattling eerily, like a crashing wave of metal upon metal. They eyed him hungrily. If they only knew what he had planned for them. They alone had the reservoir he needed.

He grasped their essence with his mind. He pulled on the magickal energies they held within themselves, mere shadows of the people from whom they'd been cloned, but still potent to a degree. They filled him with a fiery glow.

Like the rush of water from a broken dam, they poured into him. He'd miscalculated how much they had to offer. He felt the power growing inside of him until his own skin felt too tight, and he thought he must burst with the sheer frenetic energy of it. His hand about the crystal shook as he fought to contain what he took from them.

This, then, was their secret. Spawned by Brennard and Isabella, they were themselves what he sought. As he held them, he knew them.

He mastered them. The Leucators sank to their knees as he drained them, pulled all he wanted from them, and left them with precious little. Magick fountained inside of him, and he raised both hands then, reaching for what he wanted, seeing it, placing it.

Then, with a deep breath, Jonnard summoned it. He felt the sudden, shocking emptiness of Magick exploding out of it, the icy coldness of its absence, the harsh shock wave lashing back at him. It slammed him back on his heels, throwing him into the wooden frame of the dungeon door. He let out a gasp of pain as his shoulder crunched, but the doorjamb kept him from falling entirely, as his body went limp.

His mind reeled. It tumbled over and over with emptiness, with thoughts that bloomed and fled too quickly for him to comprehend them. They tore through his mind, a thousand possibilities and more, and he felt as helpless as a leaf in a hurricane. Then all came to a halt. Quiet, and trembling. In that moment, he felt as weak as a newborn, as though he'd touched time itself.

Jonnard straightened. He dropped his hands. His skin, always pale, seemed ashen. He flipped one hand through his hair, pushing it off his brow.

Had he done what he thought? If not ... what had he done? He took an unsteady step forward, realizing the fortress walls were gone. The sound of the river and the wind washed over him, but the battlefield was gone, left behind or left ahead, he could not be certain where. The wagons creaked in restless movement, and the living watched him fearfully.

He had moved the caravan. That much, he'd accomplished. The horses whinnied and shuddered in their harnesses, eyes rolling whitely, as the drivers held onto their headstalls and tried to calm them. Isabella dismounted, her eyes narrowing. "What have you done?" She gestured across the field.

His gaze followed her hand wave. There, in a hollow of ground, a maelstrom of darkness and fog boiled up. He'd brought the whole scene with him, bodies and all, and the dead slid across the ground and disappeared into the pit. It pulled at him, and he took a step closer, even as Isabella grabbed his elbow with a warning cry. "Don't."

"Look. Look at that!"

"What have you done?" She toyed with the necklace about her throat, unaware that most of the priceless gems upon it were now blackened and useless. She stared at him.

"It's a Gate. I've opened you a Gate." And he shook her off impatiently, eager to see the handiwork he'd wrought. A wind wailed down through the small valley, carrying what seemed to be voices on it. He neared it. It knew him, as he knew it. Where it went, he did not know. The sheer force of opening it had drawn the convoy to its mouth, and it yearned for them, yawned for them. Even as he neared it, he felt instinctively what Isabella had. The veil over it parted, torn by its seething inner action, and he saw it clearly then, a dark gash into the earth filled with bones and skulls, tumbling about as if caught in a maelstrom. The Leucators thrashed inside of it, disappearing and re-forming. He stared at it in fascination, unsure of it.

Chaos poured out of it. "Drink of that, my mother," he said to Isabella. "And our power here will never pale."

"Only if I dare."

"I dare," he said. He put his hand out, palm outward and drew upon that which he had made. Just a touch of it jolted him, and he shut off the contact quickly, composing himself. It held a Magick unlike any he'd ever felt before, and he was wise enough to know he might not be the master of it. Caution, then, until he learned the Gate well. He stepped back to Isabella's side.

She stared at the Gate of Bones for a long moment, then caught the hem of her skirt in one hand.

"I want the Magickers punished for their impudence."

"Of course." Jonnard bowed in her direction. "I will see to it."

She mounted a free horse and reined him off eastward

after a moment's contemplation of her crystal. The convoy bumped and jolted into movement after her.

Jonnard's mouth twitched.

She had not dared to drink of the power as he had. She could sense it as he could, and she'd been afraid she could not master it at all.

His time was nearing.

33

Aftershock

THE BLAST SLAMMED Jason on his back, knocking the wind clean out of him. He lay gasping, staring up at the sky, feeling the Magick roar around him in utter Chaos, then it was sucked back and . . . Gone. He rolled to his side, clawing for air, his body frozen, not breathing and screaming for it. All around him was . . . nothing. Every shrub or tree, every blade of grass for a hundred-yard radius about him lay flattened.

Not a wagon, horse, or person, dead or alive, could be seen except for Trent at his feet who lay making guppy noises. What had happened? His body fought to breathe, chasing thoughts away except for the weakness that seeped through him, and the wonder of it. Opening a Gate could feel like this. But he hadn't done it. So why? And why had the Magick smacked him down? And what had it done with the Dark Hand? Were they . . . gone?

Jason finally squeaked down a sliver of air and sat up. He nudged Trent's shoulder with his boot toe. "Relax." He couldn't say much more than that, but he'd had the wind knocked out of him before and knew that once the solar plexus relaxed, they'd both be breathing again. It was the hit, the shock of it, that sent the body into temporary paralysis.

That didn't make it any more fun. He hung his head over, whooped a few times, and finally got the circulation going. Jason wobbled to his feet. Trent flopped over like a hooked fish. After a splutter, he managed a long gasp of air.

"Smackdown," he muttered. "What the hell was that?"

"I don't know. Yet." Jason looked around, unable to believe what he could not see. Perhaps the whole convoy had been Crystaled, but it would never have created a backlash like the one they'd felt. It was as if Jonnard or Isabella had loosed a magickal atomic bomb or something. Or they had. Did Gavan dare to use resources the others never suspected? He scrubbed a hand through his hair, and resettled his headband into place.

A wail of mourning sounded behind him and Jason turned about. Figures rising slowly from beside the river and the band of trees along it where they had begun their ambush. The devastation ended there, as if the countryside had withstood it, or perhaps the Magickers' presence inside it had protected it. Pyra went to one knee, gathering up the shattered remains of Flameg's longbow from the autumn-burned grasses. Her voice wailed with primal grief. She clutched the broken weapon to her chest and stifled her cry to one soft murmur, then silence. She looked up, her face streaked with tears.

"Not even his body! How can I bury him? How can we honor him?"

"We will make sure he is remembered. We can do no less for a friend and ally!" Gavan's voice rang out reassuringly across the devastation. He and Tomaz emerged from the grove, each with a fistful of reins, leading nervous horses onto the battlefield. Though no bodies remained, their nostrils widened at the smell of blood and ruin. "We'd best get out of here before the wolfjackals show. I don't want another fight, just yet," Gavan added, weariness wavering his voice slightly.

"Eleanora? They're gone, right? They whacked themselves." Trent rubbed the flat of his stomach ruefully as he found words.

"What did happen?"

Gavan looked at Jason, then shook his head slightly.

"We don't know what happened here. If they'd destroyed themselves, I would feel Eleanora immediately, and I can't. Whatever that was that happened, we didn't do it, so I have to assume they did. I can't, I *won't,* leave her. If it's to be war here, regardless of the price to be paid, I'll free her first. We need to go in with full power, and surprise. If they retreated, then they still have their deal to carry out. They have a day or two to get that caravan into Naria, and negotiate and sell. We have a day, then, to act." He swung up.

Stefan approached them, half carrying, half supporting Rich who limped heavily and seemed to find each step a painful, gasping effort. His face looked deadly pale.

Pyra stowed the only remains she had of her old friend and teacher. "He needs to see Kektl, as soon as possible. That's blackmarrow poison in him, and what I gave him will help, but—" she paused. Then she repeated emphatically, "He must see Kektl as soon as possible."

"How bad is it?"

"Arrow wound," said Rich through pinched lips. "I'd like to say, 'tis but a flesh wound, but it feels like my blood's on fire."

"Tomaz, you can get him to Kektl? I have to meet with Renart and get Pyra back to Avenha."

Stefan said stoutly, "Rich isn't going anywhere without me." He shot an accusing glance at Pyra. "He isn't going to die, is he?"

"No," she answered. "Not yet." She would not meet anyone's glance at that, looking aside. Stef grunted.

"Nothing is gonna happen to you, Rich. I'm like . . . like Samwise."

Rich managed a chuckle. "Big guy, you look like almost anything but a hobbit gardener." He sucked his breath in sharply then, both hands going to his leg and knotting, as if he could grip the pain away.

"No time to waste." Gavan motioned Jason and Trent to his side. "Stay with me." Then, in a shimmering of crystal fire, the two groups went their separate ways.

Every bone in Rich's body ached and throbbed, and he could feel every single pulse of his heartbeat, for it swelled and exploded in pain, and he knew he must be sweating like Niagara Falls. Every movement, jolt, thought, touch echoed violently through his tall, thin frame. Even Stefan's hold keeping him upright was almost more than he could bear. Blackmarrow poison—what Pyra had called it—sounded bad. Really bad. Ironic. All his life he'd been taught to be afraid of getting sick and having allergies, and it was a poison that had gotten him.

They touched down in Kektl's Narian backyard, where the shed and pool rested, and Stefan gently put him down on one of the stump chairs, while he and Tomaz went to find the healer. Rich stared at the bloody tear in his pants, thinking that it hadn't really been much of a wound. Luckily it wasn't deep enough to sever anything major or bleed him to death, and nothing that muscle couldn't heal later. He wondered if he poured a bottle of hydrogen peroxide on it, how badly it would fizz. He wasn't sure if poison would set off the peroxide. It seemed to react mainly to surface contamination, but it was fun to watch.

Rich sighed and immediately groaned. There wasn't a spot inside or outside of his body that didn't ache fiercely. He leaned back against the small fence that surrounded Kektl's little home and garden and wished that Stef would hurry back.

Quickly.

The little garden grew blurry and danced about him, and then slowly he sagged down on the tree stump and everything slipped away.

He came to, sputtering, as someone poured the most disgusting drink he'd ever tasted in his life down his throat.

"Easy, easy now," came Kektl's stern but soft voice. "Drink it, and to the last drop."

Rich found he had little choice as Kektl's hand closed upon his mouth and insistently poured in the awful goo. He swallowed it all and waved both hands in protest as he did, unable to see much beyond the healer's face, although he could hear Stefan's low rumbling protest off to the side somewhere and Tomaz's dry laugh.

Kektl let go.

"Gah!" Rich sat up like a drowning man breaking the surface of the water that tried to claim him. "What *is* that stuff?"

"An acquired taste, and, I fear, what will keep you alive the rest of your days. Three times a day, I prescribe."

Rich shuddered over and over as the cold, sickeningly sweet thick stuff penetrated his body. "Ugh. I think I'd rather die."

"Don't say that!" Stefan thumped the side of his head.

Rich gave one last, hard shudder. "You taste it, then see if you agree." He blinked several times. The pain and burning in his body began to recede as if nothing could stand up to the awful taste of the potion. Kektl eyed him curiously. "Feeling any better?"

"Well. . . ah . . . actually. Yes."

"Good." Kektl sat, putting his hands on his bony knees, and staring into Rich's face. "There isn't any cure for black-marrow poison that I am aware of. All I can do is keep it at bay, make sure it does as little damage every day as I can. You take that potion regularly, and you will live a long life yet. In the meantime, herbalists such as I will dabble and test, and perhaps come up with something better."

"I say we take him home."

Kektl sat back. "If you can return to such a place, perhaps. I am not one for the crossing of worlds, so I cannot tell you if the poison will get better or worse elsewhere. I can only tell you what I can do here."

Tomaz shifted his weight and approached Rich. He put his thick, callused hand on his forehead, checking for temperature. He nodded to Rich. "You look better. How difficult is it to make this potion up?"

"Not difficult. Few of us know the ingredients, but as I am the one who devised it—" Kektl grinned slyly. "I think we can make accommodations. The herbs are easily gathered, although an unlikely brew. You, Rich, show much skill and aptitude. I hate to lose a student untimely."

"He can't just drink something all the time to stay alive!"

Kektl gave Stefan a mild look. "And why not? I do."

"But . . . but . . ."

Kektl inclined his head. "Who should know blackmarrow poison better than one who carries it within him?" He leaned forward and patted Rich on the knee. "From time to time, you may have to take more of the potion, or less. Your body will tell you. And, if the spirit graces us, we'll find a better antidote." He stood. "For now, I'll leave you with your friends, while I make up a batch and ready a scroll for you on how to prepare it yourself."

Tomaz murmured, "We thank you, healer," as Kektl moved past him. The Havenite smiled and shook Tomaz's hand in encouragement.

Stefan sputtered in barely contained frustration. "Are you going to put up with that?"

"I feel better. Why should I argue?" Rich slowly got to his feet. His leg sent a sharp pain through him, reminding him that there was a wound there, even if the poison had receded greatly. He leaned on Stef's stout, square frame. "See this house? The gardens? The pool? Kektl has this nice little place because he's a good healer. He can help when no one else can."

"I still think we should get you home."

Rich nodded. "We will. Just remember what can happen when: one—my body is tested for an absolutely unknown poison induced by an obvious wound suffered in some kind of warfare, and two—my body also tests for odd mental powers which can't be accounted for."

"Unfortunately, he's right," noted Tomaz.

"But, Rich—"

"No buts, big guy. Going home could be more lethal than drinking that awful stuff a few times a day." Rich poked him in the ribs. "I don't want to be anybody's lab experiment, do you?"

"No, but still . . ." Stef took a big breath, and shut his mouth, his expression screwed into a grumpy mask.

Rich scooped up the empty mug. "Here . . . try a drop."

Stef's nose wrinkled. "No way."

Rich laughed. "Sometimes you're just no fun!"

"Me?" Stef started to protest, then looked up and saw Kektl headed toward them from the rear of his cottage, his hands filled with what appeared to be a doctoring kit. "Looks like the fun is about to start again."

Kektl gestured at him. "That wound has to be cleansed and stitched. Let's get started."

Rich paled again and sat down abruptly at the sight of needles and thread. Stef crossed his arms over his broad chest in satisfaction.

"Pyra!" Renart darted out of the warehouse door, his face glowing with surprise and happiness, and he caught up the girl in an immense hug and swung her around. Protesting faintly, her face all a-blush, she pushed him away, saying, "Renart! Custom, please!"

"Ah." He cleared his throat and dusted himself off, straightening his dignity, reminding Jason ever so much of an embarrassed cat grooming itself to regain composure. "It's just that it's so good to see you." He took a second look, and then saw the dirt streaks and grime and disarray on them all. "Pyra?" He shot a worried look at her. She turned her face away. "No caravan, and it does not look like it went well."

"It did not," Gavan told him.

He wrung his hands once. "What happened?"

"They slipped our grasp. We are not sure how, but they're bound to come looking for revenge."

"Understood. Losses?"

"Six raiders." Pyra's voice choked slightly. "Flameg. And one of the boys, poisoned."

Renart frowned heavily. "Flameg? Dead?"

She nodded.

"I'll arrange a cart for the body."

"There is no body."

His eyebrows fluttered. "But—" He paced. "All right, then. I'll make sure you've an escort to Avenha, Pyra. I won't let you travel alone at a time like this."

She clenched her jaw. "I will see them dead for this!"

"No. No, a sight like that is too awful for any of us to see. There will be vengeance in its own time. In the meanwhile, you have to make sure Flameg is remembered in the village." He touched her wrist briefly.

She put a hand to her bag, where the shattered remains of Flameg's longbow had been stowed. "He won't be forgotten."

Gavan shifted his weight. "You need to cover your own tracks, Renart. Isabella is shrewd. Once she has gotten her deal, she will begin to sift for any who've helped us. She'll know the ambush was planned. You didn't rent this warehouse openly?"

"No, of course not. Tomaz and I discussed that. I should not be implicated." Renart took his eyes from Pyra and looked at Jason and Trent, then Gavan. "You're the ones who will feel her anger."

"I'm prepared for that. You'll get Pyra home?"

Renart touched her hand again. "If she allows me."

Pyra tried to smile. "Some company would be good."

"Done, then. Go with the Spirit watching, Gavan friend, and I will ask him to keep the Dark Hand from your door."

Gavan made a wry face. "If only it were that easy." He lifted his hand, as he nodded to the boys.

No, Henry!

THE MOMENTS CREPT by, and sitting at the table
helping Ting make crystal jewelry didn't seem to help,
even with Henry telling them both tales of home—good
and bad—and trying to ease the waiting. All of them could
sense the slow drag on their own Talents as the others
tapped them for a bit of oomph now and then, but they
couldn't tell what was happening! Bailey kicked an impatient foot against the table leg.

"I feel like the blind man with a racehorse!" Bailey
complained.

Henry pushed up his glasses to consider her. "I think
that's the blind men with the elephant," he said slowly. "If
you're talking about perceptions and how deceiving they
can be. You know, one of them feels the tail and thinks the
elephant is thin as a rope, another feels a leg and says, no,
he's big as a tree, and the other feels the trunk and says, no,
he's wiggly as a snake . . ."

She tossed her head. "I'm talking about being ready to
ride off, but I can't see where I'm going!"

"Oh. Okay, then." Henry reached down and exchanged
a wire cutter for a long-nosed pair of pliers, so he could

imitate Ting's quick movements and twist a wire cage into place about the crystal shard he held.

"I just don't think it's fair to get left behind," Ting said. She put a bracelet down in front of her and jangled the crystals, making a pleasant chime. They warmed at her slight touch. "I feel like I never get to help."

"These are helping." Henry swept his hand over the table at all the translucent stones they had imbued with power. "They need us to anchor, too."

"They were already charged. We're just sitting here doing monkey work! We should be out there, helping."

Henry shifted uneasily. "I don't know. I mean, Gavan's right, he doesn't want everyone out there, he doesn't want Isabella to have any more hostages. And . . . and . . . well, for myself . . . I don't trust myself."

Ting's almond-shaped eyes fixed on him. "What do you mean?"

"I mean that sometimes, I think . . . I'm afraid that Jonnard can still link with me. Sometimes I get this awful feeling. It's like getting slimed. I worry that he can get to me again, and know everything we're doing, and I won't be able to stop him."

"Henry, we'd never let that happen to you again."

"I don't think it's anything we can stop," he said sadly. He put the final twist on a cage holding a gemstone and examined it.

"We might not be able to stop his trying, but the minute you know he's doing it, we can stop that. We can." Ting folded her hand over the top of his and squeezed.

Henry turned bright red—from her words and touch—and blinked hard once or twice before sliding his hand away from hers.

Bailey opened her mouth as if to say something, then shut it. Instead, she swung her head, bouncing her ponytail from side to side. She stopped abruptly. "They're pulling on my power," she announced quietly.

Ting and Henry nodded. They began to sort through other objects and start a new bracelet to assemble, their fingers busy even as their minds dealt with the feeling of something at the edges nibbling away at them. Suddenly, Ting dropped everything.

"It's just so not fair. Jason has his dragon. We ought to have something, too."

"Or at least be able to have the dragon when he doesn't. If we had the dragon here, helping us defend the academy, no one would dare try anything. He wouldn't even have to do anything, just sit up and look dragonish."

"He would be awesome, wouldn't he?" Ting stood up on hearing Henry's words. "I'm going to go find him."

"Ting, we're on duty here."

"By the time something awful happens, it'll be too late to go get help. Why wait? We know he's around somewhere."

"I don't know," answered Bailey slowly. "I'm always the one who gets in trouble, but I don't think this is a good idea."

Ting looked stubborn. "I can't ignore it. I've been dreaming of our house dragon, and he's long gone, away in another world, but I know we've a dragon here, and that must mean something. It could be important, Bailey, as important as anything you're always going after."

"This is true." Henry looked from Ting to Bailey and back again.

Bailey sighed. "I know. But . . ." She shook her head. "It just feels *wrong.*"

"You won't go with me to help look?"

"Nope."

"I'll go!" Henry jumped to his feet. His glasses slid almost off his nose as he did, and he hastily rearranged them.

"I can't believe you won't come."

The two girls stared at each other a long moment. Bailey shifted uneasily in her chair. "I can't either," she said finally, "but I won't. I'll stay here."

"If I find him, and he agrees to help, can I call you a big wuss?"

Bailey gave a lopsided grin at that. "Sure! As long as you're okay."

"Deal, then." Ting turned to Henry. "Come on. I know just where Jason climbs up on the Iron Mountain, sometimes. We should find him there."

Henry shadowed her out the door, saying, "What are you going to do?"

"Not sure yet, but I'll think of something!"

Their voices got faint as they disappeared outside, around a corner of the academy. Bailey stared out the kitchen door, then bit her lip thoughtfully. She had to go with her gut feeling, and that told her to stay put. She shuffled her boots under the kitchen table, and bent her head over the crystals, arranging them back and forth, feeling rather odd.

Outside, gray clouds scuttled in and hung close about the Iron Mountains and the academy. It would rain in a day or two or maybe even late that evening. Ting and Henry could feel the pressure building in the air. Tilting her face up, she pointed out the area of the mountain range where Jason often climbed, and started up. Henry, puffing a bit and paling more every moment, took a deep breath before following after her. Halfway up, she realized that Henry was nowhere near her. Ting looked under her elbow. He clung to a small boulder a good half a city block behind her, panting for breath.

"Are you all right?"

"I'm really tired." His face stayed pale, though she could see his chest heaving as he struggled to breathe.

"Stay there, then. It's just a tiny bit farther. I can shout if I need help."

He nodded and brought up the edge of his shirt to pat his face dry of sweat. Poor Henry. They must be tapping his power faster than hers. Still, by the time she gained the flat top of the hill, she was breathing hard, too, and had to stand for a moment to catch her own breath. Then she wondered how she planned to catch the dragon's attention.

It seemed undignified to shout, "Here, dragon!" nor did she think he'd respond to it. And, after all, it was Jason's dragon, if a dragon could truly be said to belong to anyone at all. This one couldn't. He came and went as he pleased and, if anything, Jason belonged to him, rather than the other way around. She tucked a long, dark wing of hair behind her ear. What to do?

"How does one call a dragon?" she said aloud, to no one but herself, and wished she'd insisted on Bailey coming along. Bailey would be full of ideas, even if most of them would be wrong, she was bound to have the right one stuffed in there somewhere. Bailey was like that.

"That depends on how polite you are," rumbled a deep voice behind her.

Ting turned around with a gasp, caught her heel on a

stubborn bit of rock, and went down on her rump. The dragon lay down on his stomach to look at her closer, asking, "All right, are you? Did I scare you?"

"Of course you scared me! How can someone so ... large ... sneak up so quietly?"

The dragon chuckled. It sounded like faraway thunder on a hot summer night, and rather smelled like it, too. Faraway lightning, or something. He wiggled his whiskers at her. "Jason told you I considered young adventurers as appetizers, I see."

"He's mentioned it once or twice. In case he never comes back."

"I am astounded." The dragon, however, looked far from astounded, although he did look a wee bit curious as Ting clambered to her feet and dusted herself off. "If he did, then you must have risked a lot to climb up looking for me. What is the occasion, may I ask?"

"Help. Defense, actually," and Ting pointed down off the plateau at the academy below them.

"Are you under attack? I rather got the impression it was the other way around, that your lot was off attacking someone else."

"No, and yes, and well, they deserved it."

"Mmmmmm." The dragon let out a long, rumbling purr of thought. Then he said flatly, "No."

"No what?"

"No, I will not come to your defense."

Ting stared at him. "Why not?"

"First of all, it should be obvious that you're not under attack. At the moment, anyway. Secondly, and this is a bit more difficult to explain, I have a truce with this world. I come and go as I please, but I do not meddle. I rarely allow myself to be seen, and I do not use my powers in any way at all, if I can help it."

"But you're our friend! Jason's friend. How can you do this?"

The dragon sat up, and laced his long claws together. He said mildly, in his very deep bass voice, "I do not need to explain myself to you."

"Yes! Yes, you do!" Ting cried. "The Dark Hand is a terrible, awful group of people. They've been raiding and killing for months, and we're the only ones who can stand up to them, and if that doesn't deserve your help, then I don't know what does!"

"Ting," called a raspy voice behind her. "Please don't shout at the dragon." Henry staggered onto the edge of the plateau, his face absolutely gray with effort.

"Very good advice," observed the beast in question. "But, here, I feel obligated to explain myself although I normally do not have to. It's a matter of treaty, and negotiation, and tradition. I am not the Power of the world, so I am here by sufferance. I am friends with the Powers that be here, but I neither help nor hinder them. Surely you have friends like that in your old world?"

Ting's mouth worked soundlessly for a moment or two, trying to understand just what the dragon meant, when Henry said, "Switzerland."

"Switzerland?" Ting repeated incredulously.

"Yeah. They've been neutral for centuries. Everyone respects that." Henry staggered up to stand with her. He fought for breath as he did so, and wiped his face with his hand.

"So . . . Jason's dragon is like Switzerland?"

"He is, if he says he is." Henry nodded emphatically.

"There," said the dragon. "I do hope that explanation is satisfactory."

Ting stared at one and then the other, and realized she was getting no place. "Not really," she answered him. "But I guess it will have to do. It doesn't explain at all why I keep dreaming about my house dragon, and what it all has to do with me. I was so sure it meant I was supposed to talk you into helping." Ting gestured in frustration and bewilderment.

"Ahhhhh," rumbled the dragon. "You dream, do you?"

"We all dream. Just sometimes it seems really important, and it's nearly impossible to understand."

"Well," the dragon murmured, dipping his snout close to Ting, and lowering his great voice as if talking to her and her alone, although Henry plainly stood at her elbow. "These things come from within, don't you think?"

"I think—" Ting began, just as Henry let out a loud whimper and crashed to the ground at her feet. "Henry? Henry!"

He gasped, "Jonnard," as his eyes rolled up in his head and he passed out cold. Ting screamed.

35

Gate of Dread

IT FIGURES," mourned Bailey. "The one time I don't go with you, and something really interesting happens. I've always wanted to travel by dragon. It seems so much faster."

Ting was hanging from one claw, and Henry's limp body from the other, while Bailey looked up at them, hands on her hips, the dragon treading air as though he were in a swimming pool, his wings fluttering above them. Ting thought she was going to hurl from the bouncing, the uneven bobbing up and down. "That's not helping any," she moaned.

Bailey spread her hands out. "I can't catch you both. I say jump, and we'll both catch Henry."

Ting moved around inside the dragon's clutch and he loosened his grip a little. She crouched, looking at the ground which seemed a lot farther away than she wanted it to be. "Okay. Ready." She swallowed. The dragon opened his claws and she jumped.

He released Henry at nearly the same time, his limp body tumbling through the air, and both of them collided with Bailey. The three of them went down with an ooof and

536

a grunt and a groan. For a moment, Ting wasn't sure where she ended and the other two began. Bailey began to laugh as she tried to crawl out from under them.

"What . . . is . . . so . . . funny?" Ting pulled her long hair away from her face with both hands.

"I'm not sure," Bailey told her. "It just *is*. It's about time someone else got in trouble!" She dug Henry out as well. "He's out like a light. What happened?"

"I'm not sure. He seemed weaker and weaker, and then he collapsed, talking about Jonnard." Gently, Ting took Henry's glasses off his face. "Think Jon got to him again?"

"Maybe." Bailey put two fingers to her mouth and let out a piercing whistle. "We've got to do something. The crystals are all muddied, though." She frowned as the dragon landed nearby, following Ting's lead.

"Dragon," Ting stated as she felt Henry's too cold face. "This is the kind of thing they do. They take over your thoughts, your mind. They don't care what they do to anyone!"

"I can see that," the great beast said. His voice sounded a bit sorrowful amidst its low boom. "That does not change the pact I have agreed to. I will not interfere."

"If you're not with us, then you're against us," Bailey said harshly. She flipped her ponytail back and tried to haul Henry's limp body into a more comfortable position.

The dragon considered Bailey closely, and Bailey had the grace to blush a little. "Well," she said defensively, "you know what I mean."

"Unfortunately, I do. I leave you with this, then . . ." And he put out a talon that sizzled as if hot and etched Ting's open hand. "A key to be used for that you need most, Ting, if you've the courage to use it. As they like to say in those epic stories Jason talks about, use it when things seem darkest."

Ting jumped as if burned or branded, and closed her hand tightly, staring at the great dragon. Rebecca and Madame Qi hurried out of the academy in answer to Bailey's piercing whistle, both women letting out sounds of worry as they saw Henry lying on the ground.

"What happened?"

"He collapsed. He was being drained, and he just . . . fell over."

Rebecca knelt beside him, her hand on the boy's neck. "He seems all right now, though very weak. I can't believe Gavan would let anyone draw off Henry like this."

"Jonnard would," Bailey said bitterly.

Madame Qi knelt by Rebecca and Henry's still form. "There are many forces at work here," she said in her quiet way. "Not to hurry to a decision." She lifted Henry by the ankles. "Help me, Ting, and you two get the heavy end." She paused, and gave the dragon a respectful bow.

The dragon inclined his snout back. Then, with a great leap, and a powerful beat of his wings, he flew skyward.

Henry seemed far heavier than he looked, as the four of them wrestled him inside, and then up to the dorm wing where the boys slept. He had his own room, a pie-shaped place at the edge of the dorm, and it seemed to fit him in more ways than one. They laid him on his cot as gently as they could, although it was almost more of a case of all four of them losing their grip at once. Ting flexed her hand a few times where the dragon had touched her, as if in a little pain, but she kept her hand hidden every time Bailey tried to catch a glimpse.

"I shall stay with him," Madame Qi announced, and plunked herself down on a stool. She leaned forward to rest her chin on her cane.

Bailey's mom made a frustrated motion. "You two girls are better off downstairs, watching those crystals. Everything seems to be dimming. Any word on what's happening?"

Ting and Bailey shook their heads in unison. "They're fighting. More than that I can't tell," Bailey added.

Rebecca Landau made a face that emphasized the small lines at the corners of her eyes. "I don't like not knowing!"

As they went downstairs, Ting nudged Bailey. "So like you!"

Bailey muttered. "I know, it's scary." She waited till they got around a corner before grabbing Ting's hand and opening it.

A jagged red mark met her eyes, a fiery mark looking like a flying snake dragon, remarkably like the red enamel weather vane dragon that rested on Ting's grandmother's home, or at least the way she'd described it to Bailey many times. "Whoa," she breathed. "That must hurt."

"It does." Ting snatched her hand back. "And I have no idea what to do about it!"

"Then things can't be that dark. Yet." Bailey finished ominously.

They limped back to the academy. Trent referred to it as leapfrogging, since neither Gavan nor Jason could Crystal a significant distance. They relied on small landmarks from memory, viewed by dragonback or horseback from days ago. It took time as they shared their vision among the three of them, to make sure that they had details correct, and then rested, and then tried to decide on the next hop. Jason relied as little as possible on his lavender crystal, counting on his main crystal, the one he'd bonded to first, although its warmth and light seemed to waver badly every time he focused. Twice, Trent helped him find a ley line of natural energy that boosted his own weak energy, and still they staggered home as though tied together in a three-legged race.

Gavan made a fist about his watch fob crystal, the one in his cane still not having recovered, and they jumped. They landed on grass slick with dew as evening grew close, and they all grabbed each other to stay upright.

Jason felt a cold chill start down the back of his neck and on down his spine. He chafed his arms. "We've doubled back. We're near the Dark Hand fortress."

Gavan swore and rubbed his eyes. "My fault. I'm tired." As the two of them cast about for their bearings, Trent stared at the ground. He said quietly, "I know I don't feel things the way you two do, but . . . did you feel pulled here? Somehow?"

"Pulled?" Gavan arched an eyebrow. He rubbed his crystal fob.

"We're nearly exhausted. I can feel it, clearly. And while we were Crystaling, I could feel something, I don't know, tugging at us." Trent shrugged. "Can't explain it better than that."

"I feel," Jason added slowly, "watched." Slowly, he turned about in a circle, looking into the late afternoon light, when the sun slanted low across the land and shadows seemed to be multiplying everywhere. It felt damp, too, as though the skies would be gathering storm clouds when nightfall truly hit.

Trent danced his fingers through the air. "It feels like something over there." He found an invisible string and turned to tug on it.

"Watch it, lads." Gavan frowned.

"Think it's a ward or trap?"

"More than likely. Even likelier, if it is, it could be lethal."

"I need to look."

Gavan and Jason stared at each other a moment. Then Gavan sighed. "I suppose we all do."

"You felt it, too, then?"

"I did. What it was, I didn't know." He signaled to them. "Be quiet, and stay close. Trent, keep that Sight of yours alert."

They moved through the edge of a forested land, thin because they were already in the highlands, wiry shrubs with stubborn barbed thorns grabbing at them from time to time. The land opened up into a canyon or cove, and they all came to a sudden halt.

Shadows had a life of their own here. A gash in the ground opened like a yawning mouth, biting at the world about it. Darkness boiled around it. Jason caught a glimpse of a skull being tossed back and forth through the ebony chasm. Dry clinks and rattles issued forth, along with a low moaning as though wind escaped from the fissure as well, accompanied by the clatter of bones.

"What is that?"

"I don't know, and I don't want us getting any closer."

But Jason said, "I'm not sure," echoing Gavan. The gaping hole both drew him and repelled him.

"We need to get out of here. We'll talk about this later, but I don't want either of you coming back to take a look. Is that clear?"

"No argument here," Trent agreed.

Jason only nodded his head, as the elder Magicker took their arms and pulled them away from whatever it was. The one thing he could be certain of was that he did not believe it had existed before that morning.

In the clear, Gavan took a deep breath. "Home, then, however long it takes us."

They linked and Crystaled again, the moments *between* growing colder and longer as their powers faded.

*   *   *

Lanterns hung from the academy's corner eaves glowed as they touched down in the yard. Gavan staggered and almost fell over. Trent caught him by one elbow and Jason by the other. Looking down, Jason saw the cuff of Rainwater's trousers soaked in dark liquid that must have been blood.

"You're hurt! Help me get him inside!"

"No, no, it's nothing." Gavan hastily pulled the edges of his cloak together, trying to hide his legs from view. "That's not from today. A little bleeding is good. It'll help clean it out."

Trent looked at the shadow pooling around Gavan's boot heel. "Then I'd say a major leak like that must be fantastic." He rolled his eyes. "C'mon, man." He put his shoulder under Gavan's arm and with Jason's help, muscled the headmaster into the kitchen doorway. Once inside, Jason propped Gavan's leg on a stool while Trent stuck his head into the corridor, letting out a cheerful, "Halllloooo, we're home."

Great kettles of hot water steamed in the fire pit, and Jason grabbed up a torn rag from a waiting pile. "Looks like they were ready to bandage an army."

"Either that or they took up mummification while we were gone." Trent pulled a stool up next to Gavan and looked at the ankle wound in fascination as Gavan gingerly peeled his trousers away from it. "That is a bite, and a nasty looking one. Not from . . . there?"

"Indeed it is, and no. I didn't get any closer than you two did."

Trent nodded at Jason as he lowered rags and a bowl of hot water onto the table. "He's going to need a rabies shot."

"I most certainly am not!"

Trent sat back with a wicked laugh as Gavan, frowning, grabbed a rag and made a hot compress from it, laying it over the green-and-purple, jagged wound.

"That does look bad."

"It festered, but now it's bleeding cleanly and it will be fine."

Jason rubbed his left hand. "That's not a wolfjackal bite."

"No. It's from a Leucator."

Both boys whistled sharply at that. Then both spoke at once, Trent saying, "When'd you get that?" while Jason said, "That came the other night, then. You were looking for Eleanora."

Gavan closed his mouth stubbornly and answered neither, wincing as the heat settled into tender flesh. "Without success," he said finally. "And I don't want any discussion on the other until I've talked with Tomaz and others first. Agreed?"

Trent drummed his hand on the table, nodding, but Bailey and Ting, and the older women burst into the kitchen before he could say anything.

"What other," demanded Bailey.

"Nothing important. Is Tomaz back yet?"

"No, but he sent to us. They're staying the night in Naria." Bailey plunked herself down on a stool next to Gavan. "Ew!" She eyed his ankle.

"Ugly, isn't it? Good thing FireAnn can't see it. She'd have my hide." Gavan took up a clean cloth and wrapped it tightly, then tied it into place. "All right. How about a cup of hot tea and stories all around? Who wants to know what happened today?"

"We do! And we have something of our own to tell you."

"Good enough. Where's Henry?"

"He's upstairs resting," Ting said softly. "And he's part of it."

"Hmmm. Well. Rome wasn't built in a day, nor the Dark Hand defeated in one, it seems." Gavan tried a smile that did not quite work.

"What he means is, back to the drawing board, I think," Bailey said smugly, and laced her fingers around one knee as she drew close to listen. That brought fond laughter from everyone else much to her puzzlement. "What? I thought I got that one right!"

Rebecca kissed her daughter's forehead. "Yes, dear, you did. You got it absolutely right."

36

Aunt Freyah

HE WAS TIRED ENOUGH to sleep like a log, but he couldn't. Trying not to think about Rich and the black-marrow poison and Tomaz's warnings of it didn't help. The more you tried not to think of something, the more you thought of it. Logic told him that it wasn't his fault. He hadn't invented Haven or the raiders or the poison one of them had decided to use—and that didn't help either. Tomaz said the healer Kektl told him the rare poison came from a very difficult to grow flower and very few people could prepare it. Yet someone had and now Rich would have it infecting his system for the rest of his life, however long that might be!

Jason turned and thumped his flat pillow. Not his fault!

Still. He buried his nose in the rough sheeting of the bed and squinched his eyes shut. That was when he felt it.

He'd felt it before, but the strangeness of it chased the very last edge of sleepiness from him as it tickled along every nerve in his body. Very quietly he pulled out his crystals from under the makeshift pillow. They glowed faintly in answer to his touch, the clear gold-and-lapis banded quartz and the lavender gemstone. As he did so, he could feel the immediate attention of whatever it was that walked unseen, unheard through the academy. A shivering like a pool of water passed over him and as it did, both crystals dimmed. He could feel and see them growing cooler, weaker, in his hands.

Whatever passed over him was sucking off the reservoir of energy he'd put in them and, from the prickling of his skin, from himself as well! What the—

Jason rolled over angrily. He stared into the dim room, sweeping it for sight of something, anything—Jonnard in his black cloak, Isabella in one of her extravagant European dance gowns sweeping past—anything at all. The thing shivered away from him as he reached for it.

Trent murmured something in his sleep and kicked a bare foot out from under the homespun blankets.

Jason tilted his head, listening, feeling, searching with senses he hardly knew he had, for something magickal stalking the academy halls. He found it, and it evaporated from his grasp almost the moment he touched it.

Jason recoiled. He didn't know what it was, but he knew it wasn't the Dark Hand. Still unseen and unstoppable, it passed beyond the walls and his ability to reach for it again, and then was gone.

The lavender crystal cut into his palm. He looked down at it, its glow flickering like an ember trying to stay lit and alive. For a moment, he saw Gregory's countenance, so familiar and yet not, and then, he saw Aunt Freyah's. The vision looked distressed, but it reached out for him.

So independent and defiant and now utterly alone, she held a hand out to him. He had to go to her.

He dressed silently and slipped out of the room, leaving Trent behind. Halfway down the main stairs, a step groaned behind him. He turned and saw Bailey, rubbing an eye sleepily, Lacey tucked away in her other hand.

"Going somewhere?"

"You know me. I always seem to take a walk in the middle of the night."

Bailey had dressed, too. She yawned. He hesitated. "I think . . . I think I have a rescue mission or something."

She grew alert. "Really? Where?"

"Aunt Freyah."

"I'm going with you!"

It seemed like a good idea. He took her hand, and then thought of Aunt Freyah's little kingdom and her cozy cottage, and they Crystaled there.

Time always changed when they went to Freyah's. Jason anticipated that. What he never expected was the sight that greeted him. Her country cottage looked as if a bomb had struck it. Only two walls stood and a third of the roof still clung to them. The picket fence had fallen like loose sticks to the ground and the lawn and gardens were rampant with weeds and unruly thorn-bushes. The place was wrecked.

"It's falling down," breathed Bailey as if one loud word might add to the disaster. She moved cautiously across the weed-infested lawn.

"No kidding." He was surprised, and not surprised. He'd expected to see worse, but had hoped he wouldn't see anything like this at all. He was often wrong and wished this had been one of those times. He held out a warning hand. "Don't touch anything."

"No way." Bailey put her hand up to her bodice pocket and repeated the caution to Lacey. "Not even with a whisker," she added. "No wine cellar trips this time either. I don't know what you find so fascinating in her wine cellar, but you stay with me!" Her pocket squeaked back at her.

They approached the cottage door hesitantly, and Jason raised a hand to knock, stopping, because it looked like the only thing that wasn't falling over. Two walls and a door . . . surely she heard or saw them coming? He made a fist.

The door swung open. Aunt Freyah looked out, eyes snapping, silvery hair in bouncy ringlets. "Well, well! Come in, come in, have lunch or breakfast or whatever time it is out there."

"Midnight snack," supplied Bailey helpfully.

"Mmm. A challenge! Come in, then, before something falls on your head." Freyah turned away briskly and snapped her fingers, calling for her picnic hamper. It shuffled in with a grunt and a moan, as she led them to the parlor. Bits of plaster and roofing drifted down from above like a tree shedding brown-and-red leaves. Bailey sneezed and rubbed at her nose. "I apologize for the dust, dear, but it seems inevitable."

George, the serving tray, came galloping around the

corner and skidded to a halt in front of them. It shook in delight to see them, or perhaps it was in terror. Jason studied the long-legged tray. Difficult to tell with an animated inanimate object, frankly. George could have been either.

"George," said Freyah. "Do a good job. These are likely to be our last guests." She sat back with a sigh and looked about the ruins of her comfortable abode, her own bit of a haven. George sidled up between Bailey and Jason, its tray filled with a steaming pot of hot chocolate and two big empty mugs waiting to be filled and a small bowl of marshmallows. The hamper, pouting a bit, bumped Jason's knee as it popped its lid, releasing delicious smells of freshly baked muffins.

He did as expected, dishing out the muffins to everyone while Bailey poured the hot chocolate. Freyah had a steaming cup of café au lait by her chair, which she'd evidently been drinking before they'd arrived. Time sometimes got muddled that way in Freyah's home. As politely as he could, he bolted the blueberry muffin down to its last crumb before starting on business. Bailey was at least half a muffin behind him, even with Lacey's help, when he said, "Aunt Freyah, you can't stay here. It's why we came. I thought something might be wrong."

A ceiling tile hanging by one corner crashed down at his feet, covering his boots in dust and debris. Jason looked down at it and cleared his throat.

"Whatever makes you say that, dear?" asked Aunt Freyah.

Bailey finished her muffin, folding the paper cup it had come in, and dusting the last crumbs onto her knee for Lacey. "We really want you to come to the academy. It's dangerous here for you and George and everybody."

Freyah gave her a piercing but not unkind look. "I am touched that you both have come. But I can't leave. This is, or was, my life. As you two are keenly aware, I've been at odds for many years with Gavan about finding and educating you younger Magickers. It's left me out here, alone and isolated. It's only fair that I'm hoist with my own petard, isn't it?"

Bailey's mouth opened and she looked sideways at Jason. "She means," he interpreted, "she's suffering the consequences of her action."

"Aha. And people think *I* talk funny."

Freyah laughed, and waved a hand at the two of them, but her smile faded, and she looked as if she were almost in tears. "I can't come with you. I'd ask you how you knew I was in trouble, Jason, dear boy, but since you are responsible, we both know how—"

"Me? Responsible? I couldn't have done this!"

"It's all right. I don't blame you. It's all in the training." Freyah sat up straighter, holding her coffee cup and saucer on her knee. George tiptoed back to her side as if worried. "You've done very well, all things considering."

"I would never, could never . . ." He stopped in mid sentence, thinking of how his Dragon Gate had brought disaster to Haven. "Not on purpose, anyway," he finished lamely.

"You really don't know, do you?" Freyah tilted her plump face at him curiously.

"Not really."

"When you manipulate great energies, Jason, there can be great backlashes. For every action there is an opposite and equal reaction."

"Elementary physics," put in Bailey.

"Exactly." Freyah pointed her chin at Jason. "This . . ." and she glanced around at the wreckage of her cottage, "began about a day and a half ago, by my reckoning."

He drew in his breath sharply. The attack on the convoy and Jonnard's actions! "That wasn't me, but that was Magick. Jonnard did something, we're still not sure what. It was like a bomb blast."

She looked sharply at him. "No other effects?"

"One we're investigating. Like an abyss or something that opened, we don't know if it's related yet or not, but it feels like it."

Freyah shuddered. She dropped her coffee cup onto George, his tray ringing as he caught it. "So it begins." She stood. "You absolutely can't stay, then, children. Not for another moment. There won't be but a smidgen left of this place soon, and I . . . have things to do."

"You're coming with us. You and George and the hamper and anything else we can carry!" Bailey leaped to her feet.

Freyah shook her head. "No, dear. It's too late for that."

"We've lots of room. There is no way the academy couldn't use you for a teacher, and if you disagree with Gavan, so much the better. We're all different, and we need a lot of different teachers," Jason told her.

"It's not just that." She hesitated. "If you didn't cause this power surge, then how did you wonder about me?"

"This." Jason lifted his lavender crystal.

Freyah's mouth lighted into a sad curve, for she knew her brother's magical gemstone well. "I see."

"It's not just etched with his likeness. Sometimes I get feelings from it."

"It sent you this way?"

"It made me think I should see you, yes."

Freyah let her breath out, then shook her head. "What's done is done."

The far wall of the cottage began to creak and groan. It leaned away from them all, slowly, and then began to topple as if some great weight pushed it over, and it crashed to the garden grounds. They all stood in amazement for a moment. Only one exterior wall and the door remained at the front. Jason had never seen anything like it outside of his stepfather's construction business. He had seen something remotely similar with a great demolition down to one last wall which would be kept so that, technically, the new building could be called a "remodel." McIntire didn't like bending rules like that, but he'd done it that time because the remaining wall had a hand-painted mural on it that was irreplaceable by any means, and worth saving. The wall then had been propped up to keep it in place. There was no way a few timbers could prop up what was left of Freyah's cottage.

He picked up George under one arm, and the hamper under the other. "Freyah," he said firmly, in his deep-sounding new voice. "You are coming with us. There's no time to take no for an answer."

Freyah raised her hand, ring sparkling, her chin up. "Jason. Put my things down, and step away, or I will send you away, and with as much power as I have left, I am not exactly sure where you'll end up."

"Aunt Freyah!" Bailey took a step toward her, hands outstretched to block any crystal beam, and Lacey took off squeaking, across the floor, through the rubble and down the hall, headed toward Freyah's wine cellar. "Not again!" Bailey twisted about.

"Leave her." Jason stood rooted in place, determination running through every fiber of his being. The last remaining wall groaned and shivered a bit. "Please come with us."

"I can't." Freyah's voice dropped to a strained whisper, and she swayed as well, as if time and strength were a wind that moved her body, at last.

"What is it?"

Bailey let out a yip. "It's not a what . . . it's a who! Jason!" She grabbed at his hands, enveloping the lavender crystal. "Isn't it, Aunt Freyah? Tell him!"

The elder Magicker swayed again, and her shoulders drooped. "I'm so tired." She fell into her chair and gestured weakly.

"Come with me!" Bailey tugged on Jason. "Drop that."

He set George and the hamper down carefully, and shot a glance at Freyah. "Don't move."

"As if I could."

"Well, if something is going to fall on you, move then, but wait for us!"

Freyah nodded slowly.

Bailey shot through the dusty inner hallway, after the little rodent hopping and making running tracks in the plaster dust. She pointed. "There . . . the wine cellar stairs."

"And . . ."

"Look for yourself. You'll never believe me. I saw it last time she ran away, but it didn't hit home. And then I kind of forgot about it, although I imagine Freyah made me forget, I don't know. But go down and look. That's why Freyah won't leave."

Carefully, Jason moved down the old, worn wooden stairs. It would have been rather dark, but with most of the ground floor above it disintegrating, light from the crystal sconces above found its way through in streaks and rays. There, in the corner behind a nearly empty wine rack, was a long, long heavy wooden table and on top of it, a sarcophagus. A crystal window revealed the face of the occupant, and Jason came to a halt, wordless.

He looked at Gregory the Gray.

Footsteps paused behind him. "When Lacey finds a treasure, she finds a treasure," Bailey commented.

"I don't think he's dead," whispered Jason.

She shook her head. "If he were, I don't think Freyah would insist on staying. She means to move him somewhere safe."

"He can't be awakened. He's told me that. I don't know why, but he can't be. Not yet." He looked around the wine cellar and thought of the cottage and its gardens, the pocket of safety Freyah had spent an entire lifetime guarding. He took Bailey by the elbow and guided her back upstairs. She paused long enough to sweep up Lacey who had found something in a corner and stuffed it in her cheek pouch, instead of eluding capture.

Freyah had her face in her hands as they approached. She looked up.

"So," Jason said cheerfully. "We'll have more to move than I thought we would." He glanced at the hamper. "How much can you pack in that?"

"Almost everything important."

"And I can get the sleeper downstairs, and between the three of us, we should be able to Crystal out of here easily."

"I'd be bringing Gavan a world of trouble." Freyah stood and dusted herself off. A window frame off the front wall had gone while they were in the cellar, its paint flakes falling like snow.

"As if he doesn't already have one!" Bailey scoffed. "Besides. We need you, Aunt Freyah."

"You need me."

"You bet we do," Jason reinforced Bailey's statement. "We always have."

"Well, then. George and I never refuse a challenge." She fluffed out her hair. "Quickly, then! Pack up the essentials." She tapped George and the hamper. "You know who to gather. I'll get a satchel for my clothes. You two. Finish the muffins."

The hamper spit out a plate of muffins which Jason leaped for and caught in midair, George's job usually, but the tray was scampering off to the corners of the ruined cottage, doing Freyah's bidding.

Before the two of them had finished their cherry crisp muffins, everyone had come back. The hamper waddled laboriously as if weighed down, and George's surface was stacked with books and picture frames. His legs bowed under the burden.

"All right. You two be ready. I'll be downstairs with Gregory. On the count of twenty, we're headed for the academy kitchen. Right?" He stared at Bailey.

"Absolutely."

As Jason made his way down the creaking wine cellar stairs a second time, he could hear Bailey saying, "Now the main thing you have to do is convince my mom it's okay to have a casket with an almost-dead-looking man in it lying around. Other than that, it'll be a piece of cake."

It struck him as funny and he was still laughing when they landed in the academy.

37

Isabella's Fury

THE SHRILL SCREAM echoed throughout the fortress, beating at his eardrums. Jonnard took the dungeon stairs at breakneck pace, letting gravity give him speed that his tired, aching body could not. Every fiber of his being screamed in echo as he skidded to a halt, the dungeon doors thrown open, framing Isabella by torchlight.

She swung on him, her hand clawing the air. "The Leucators! My Leucators, gone, all gone. What have you done?"

Jonnard stared into the filthy, stinking depths of the cavern. Not a being could be seen, although the debris of their presence littered the area. Scraps of bone and food here and there, dirty strands of clothing. But the Leucators had vanished, their chains and shackles with them, and he shut his jaw quickly lest his mother see his own surprise.

He leaned a shoulder against the wall. "Well, of course. Did you expect anything different?"

"You fool. You idiot. Do you have any idea what you've condemned me to?"

"Mother." He kept his voice mild, even as hers strained higher and higher in rage and despair, while his thoughts raced ahead for an answer. He thought he found one. "I've condemned you to nothing. I showed you the Gate, did you not see?"

"I saw a miasma of Chaos." Isabella turned her head then, away from him, away from the stink of the dungeon. Her shoulders slumped. Her voice lowered to a hoarse whisper. "Oh, Jonnard. What have you done?"

"Nothing." He reached out and took her hand. "Nothing but good in the long run. Come upstairs, and sit."

She shook her head.

"You must," he said firmly. "Listen to me. You formed the Leucators out of the Chaos of a would-be Gate. It is a Gate my father almost dared open, but could never quite finish, but he taught you how to manipulate its energies and create the soul hunters we call Leucators. Now the Gate is opened, and the Leucators have returned to their elements. You can still draw on them. Even better," and he stroked her hand in his as he began to lead her upstairs, although she shrank back from him a little. "Even better, you can draw on the stuff of the Gate itself. This place has been draining us, slowly, and now we're invincible."

She stared up at him, the torches on the stone walls reflecting her face in harsh, strong planes. "You don't know what you dare."

"No, I don't. Not yet." He spoke not another word till he had her in her apartments, where the walls had been soundproofed, and no one could hear their voices. He sat her down at her desk, her place of power.

She seemed to regain her composure in the brightly lit room, its paneled walls and furniture a world away from the dungeon. "The Leucators are no longer bound, and we're all in danger here."

"Not all of us."

"They hunger for flesh, soul, and Magick, and we, above all, have to fear that."

"For right now, I can hold them. That's all that counts."

"For now? For now?" Isabella looked down her nose at him. Jonnard fought the instinct to grit his teeth. His intention of reassuring her evolved into one of withstanding her recovering scorn and outrage. "What about later?"

"Now is all that counts."

"How can you say that? How can you even *think* it?" She slapped a hand down on her writing desk. The furniture shivered under the blow, but he did not move a muscle except to answer her.

"How can I not? Did you think any further when you created the Leucators?"

She met his stare. Long moments passed in which he said nothing more, silently daring her to answer. Then, finally, her gaze flicked away. "It came out of necessity."

"We have an advantage. This Gate generates a Magick we can bend to our uses. It also creates fear, and we can use that as well. The obvious, you don't seem to have grasped. I am a Gatekeeper, Isabella." Jon leaned forward intently. "I've done it once, I can do it again."

"That is a Gate we dare not pass."

"Perhaps. We haven't tried yet, have we?" He sat back in his chair, stretching his long legs out in front of him, crossing his boots at the ankles.

"You can't be serious!"

"Can't I? You asked me for a bloody miracle, and you got one! But am I given credit? No. When did you get old, Mother? When did you grow so cautious?"

"Silence!"

Jonnard held back his next words, watching Isabella's face. Handsome rather than pretty, strong features, strong nose, lustrous dark hair that now showed a single strand here and there of silvery cast. But she'd lived centuries longer than he, and he knew she hadn't done it by accident. She'd done it by sheer power of her will and her intelligence as well as her Magick, even though the toll had begun to catch up with her.

She stirred, with a rustle of the fine satin of her gown. He wondered how many gowns she'd packed away when they'd fled to Haven, and how long her finery would last her on this rustic world. She tapped one fingertip upon the highly polished sheen of her desk. "What you have done is remarkable, Jonnard, I give you that."

He inclined his head at her acknowledgment. "But . . ."

"Yes, but. That is the crux of it. We have no idea of the consequences of what you've done, other than the initial outcome, and I'm not inclined to want to investigate. It may take resources we don't have, and it may bring to pass things we cannot handle."

"Or it may not. Look here. I am not forgetting who

you are or what you've accomplished, and I know you are speaking from experience. Still, we have an opportunity here, and I am excited by it. I will be cautious, but I expect to be able to use this to consolidate our position here as well as elsewhere."

"Then study it, but cautiously. You are of no use to me dead, Jonnard."

He sprang to his feet and then paused in her doorway. "Thank you for both the permission and concern, Isabella." Hiding his grin, he left her stewing in her study.

38

Who's Been Sleeping in My Coffin?

"THERE'S A BODY in my kitchen!" Rebecca Landau let out a shriek, and her voice wailed throughout the academy, from floor to floor, waking anyone who wasn't already awake and drifting down wondering what might be happening this morning.

It was, Bailey would say later, a scream loud enough to wake the dead, except, of course, it wasn't, for Gregory the Gray continued to sleep peacefully right through it, even as Magickers stampeded down to the kitchen in response to Rebecca's terrified yell. Bailey and Jason stumbled down to the kitchen last, her hair looking a wee bit like a pack rat's nest, and his eyes all bleary as he rubbed them and looked upon the sight. Even stiff-legged Rich made it to the scene of the crime before they did.

All Gavan could say was, "Good lord," and he sat down abruptly on a nearby stool, staring through the translucent part of the coffin at the face of his old teacher long thought to be dead and gone in the mists of time.

Rebecca took a deep breath. "Gavan Rainwater. I've put up with a lot. You came to me and said, 'May we teach your daughter sorcery,' and I said, 'Well, okay, if that's what

556

she really wants.' You say, 'She has to go to another world to be safe,' and I say, 'Well, all right.' You say, 'You've got to come, too,' and I say, 'Well, if I have to,' and you say, 'There's nothing for you to do here but be a glorified kitchen maid,' and I say, 'Well, as long as I'm helping,' but This! This!" And she pointed a trembling hand at the sarcophagus. "I draw the line at this!"

"Mom," said Bailey, catching her hand. "Chill."

Jason shot a look at her. "I thought you were going to sit with him."

"I did. He didn't do anything, and I got sleepy, so I went to bed." Bailey wrinkled her nose at Jason. "I planned on being up before anyone else." She shrugged.

Gavan swiveled around on his stool, his clear blue eye staring at them. "You two knew about this?"

"We found him," Bailey stated proudly.

Jason shook his head. "We knew, but we didn't really find him. That is, he's never actually been lost. He, ummm," and Jason cleared his throat uncertainly. He always found it difficult to tell anything remotely like an untruth. Rich, still pale and a little uneasy on his leg, watched him, while Stef paced back and forth, rolling an eye now and then at the seemingly dead man. He looked as though his grip on his bear self had reached the breaking point.

"I had him, Gavan," snapped Freyah from the doorway. She looked at him from her tiny height, silver hair practically sparking about her face. "I will leave immediately if we're not wanted."

"Not wanted? How could you be not wanted?" Gavan's mouth moved a few more times, soundlessly, and he turned to Tomaz whose solid body filled the doorway to the outside, a crow perched on each shoulder. He waved soundlessly at Tomaz.

"I think he means we're honored and moved at the sacrifice you've made all these years to keep watch on Gregory. It is a burden we'll gladly share with you now," Tomaz said humbly.

Freyah's indignant expression immediately melted, and she gathered her robes about her, with a sniffle.

Gavan cleared his throat. "Right. Exactly that." He reached out and touched the coffin. "This looks familiar."

Freyah colored slightly. "Hmm. Well, um. It might. I do

believe that was the ancestral coffin meant for you someday, Gavan. I, hmmm, borrowed it, rather."

Gavan blinked. He stroked the side of the chiseled artifact. "Well done."

"Do you think so? Your family didn't mind. I paid them
well for it. I suppose they thought it was for you, after all,
having lost you so young to Magicking."

Gavan nodded. In those days, Magickers walked away
from their families to avoid political and religious troubles. He'd been little more than an orphan, studying under
Gregory. He stood up slowly. His fingers went to the latches
covering the translucent part of the coffin.

"No!" Jason leaped forward. He charged toward Gavan. "You can't wake him. Not yet. I don't know why, I just
know you can't."

Freyah crossed the room swiftly, backing up Jason. "The
lad is right. My brother left specific instructions no one was
to wake him. He sleeps, but it is a part of some bargain, and
he'll wake when his time is due."

"Bargains," muttered Gavan. "Some good, some bad.
Who is to know? But I gather waking a sleeping wizard is
even more unwise than waking a sleeping dog. So." He patted the latches back down firmly into place. "He stays."

"That is good." Madame Qi, who'd been standing quietly, leaning a little on Ting, tapped her cane. "One less
mouth to feed at the moment."

"What kind of bargain could he have made? And with
whom?"

Freyah shook her head. "Even if I knew, Rainwater, I
couldn't tell you. It is his wish. Not even Eleanora is to know."
She frowned, dark eyes snapping. "Not got her back yet?"

"No. Not yet." Gavan ran his hand through his hair.

"What's keeping you?"

"At the moment? Finding someone sleeping in my coffin, in my kitchen." He made a distracted gesture. "We'll
have to find someplace to put you, someplace that Isabella
with all her wiles can't detect." His brow arched. "Ah, and I
might have just the spot."

"Ooooh," breathed Bailey, in recognition. "Just don't
trip the trapdoor!"

"I do not like small places," Freyah stated. "Cozy, yes,
small and confining, no."

Tomaz shook his crows off into the morning sky, and came fully into the kitchen. "It is best."

She eyed him. Then Freyah gave a little sigh. "All right, but only until I find another cottage. You, and you, accompany me. You have Talent and absolutely no schooling or discipline," Freyah pointed at Rebecca whose only response was to stutter a denial, and then she pointed at Madame Qi, "while you have discipline but not much flexibility. If I'm going to be bored, I might as well be teaching."

Madame Qi bowed from her waist. "I shall be honored."

The men and boys took up the weight of the sarcophagus and followed Gavan through the academy to the silent hallway where Bailey had found herself imprisoned. They left the doors standing open, and took their breakfast in there, and let Freyah know of the plans to attack the Dark Hand fortress and all that had happened to each of them since she saw them last. George trotted from Magicker to Magicker like a happy pup, just to nudge them and say hello. So the day began.

High Noon.

They crouched at the foot of the inner stair, Gavan gesturing warningly behind him to Jason and Trent, stilling them. Not that they needed that. The fortress was not empty as they'd hoped. Worse, Jonnard and Isabella seemed to be about.

"It's not now or never," Jason whispered. "But now is better."

They'd split into two groups, Tomaz taking Stef and Rich as a decoy from their movements inside the fortress. Henry stayed, frowning, with Freyah and the others at the academy. His job was to distract Jonnard if Jon should try to draw from him again, giving him false ideas of what might be going on. The look on his face had been one of extreme unhappiness as they'd Crystaled out.

Now he might be one of their only hopes to Crystal back safely. None of them alone could anchor; all were too tapped out, just as none of them dared attack alone. They would succeed together or not at all, but only failure would meet those acting alone.

Jason felt his pulse pound in his throat as he waited for Gavan to signal their progress upstairs. Behind him, Trent put a hand on his back, fingers drumming to an unheard tempo. He could feel the tension in Trent as easily as he felt it in himself. Gavan looked over his shoulder, making a motion that looked as if he were plucking harp strings in the air with his hand. He was asking Trent if he saw any sign of magic streaming their way.

Trent shook his head slowly, but held his hand up, and indicated an invisible line down the stairway. Not for them specifically but built into the fortress, much as they'd warded the academy. Gavan made a sign that he understood, and beckoned them up the stair, staying well away from the warding. As near as Jason could tell, it would act like a laser beam on an alarm system . . . touch it and it would trip. What sort of trap, exactly, it could spring, they had no idea. Knowing Jonnard, it was bound to be nasty.

Gavan paused. In a whisper pitched so low that they could barely catch it, he said, "That way are Leucators. Stay here. I'm going to check something."

Jason sat down on the step, his back to the safe wall. His body shook slightly, with eagerness and adrenaline, and he could feel the same emotions running through Trent. Trent looked at him, then checked back the way they'd come. He motioned with his hands at the web of enchantments they'd crept through, indicating the holes were getting bigger and bigger.

Jason decided it was because they approached the living floors of the fort and they couldn't have people setting off alarms all the time, could they? He mimicked foot traffic by walking his fingers about, and Trent grinned. He either agreed with Jason or thought he'd suddenly gone crazy. Jason laughed silently back, ducking his head.

Gavan returned after long moments. He drew the boys close, his face grave. "The Leucators are gone."

"What?

"Nothing left but their stench. Stay close to me. I don't dare leave anyone behind."

Trent shook his head emphatically at Jason. Isabella drew energy from Leucators like vampires drink blood from their victims. As despicable as Leucators were, they held great value to Isabella. Where were they, then, and why? The two got to their feet, and followed on Gavan's heels.

On the second landing, he slowed, casting about for any sign of Eleanora that he could catch. Boot steps thudded down the hall, and he pulled both Trent and Jason to him, throwing a dark shadow over the three of them. They held their breaths as Jason watched the raiders disappear into the stairwell. Trent blinked. He stepped out of the cloak and saluted Gavan. Then he leaned over as if picking a piece of lint off the ground. He held it between his thumb and forefinger.

"Music," he said quietly. "It's a strand of music. Don't ask me how."

"Eleanora!" Gavan said fiercely, his voice pitched low but intense. "They've got her blocked, but they couldn't block that. Lead on!"

Trent took up that which only he could see. Jason stayed at the rear, alert, ready to fight or do whatever else was necessary.

They entered a dank, dark wing, one built where the sunlight would never filter, its walls and doors old and stout and scarred. It spoke of misery, much as a dungeon would, telling of prisoners from the past that were treated a little bit better than those shackled down in the stony cellars, but not much. Gavan put his hands to the wood of one massive double door. There, guided by Trent's quick gestures, he cut the cords of enchantment holding the door shut, one crystal knife edge at a time, while Jason listened for interruptions headed their way.

The door fell open. Gavan stood for a moment on the threshold as if uncertain whether to enter. Trent leaned in and waved a hand signifying all clear. The three entered an ill-lit room that smelled like an old attic, musty and closed up. Slowly, Trent turned in a circle, indicating all the walls. Indeed, rather like the closed-in corridor and Magick-proofed room in the academy, Magick here was meant to neither enter nor leave. Nor were its occupants.

The entry room looked sparse and worn, almost devoid of all furniture and heat and warmth. A broken lute sat in the corner, as if leaned there with as much care as could be given an instrument with missing strings and a soundboard punched out far more than it should be. Somehow Jason thought she might have played it anyway, setting it across her lap, and trying to coax some sort of music from its remaining strings. Eleanora was like that. Gavan caught him looking at the instruments, and his mouth quirked bitterly. He must have thought nearly the same thing.

"Tormentors!" A low, hoarse whisper came from the dark room beyond. "Banshees!"

"FireAnn." Gavan stepped into the second room carefully, his eyes narrowed, peering into the permanent twilight. A rustle of clothing, and then he fell back, with a wild woman howling and clawing at his throat. Gavan wrestled with her. Jason kicked the outer door shut, muffling the noise, while Trent jumped in, calling the redhead's name, over and over.

Gavan wrestled her down to her knees, his hands on her wrists. FireAnn growled in disappointment, hot tears welling in her eyes. Her hands, misshapen from arthritis, curled into claws as if she would fight him yet. "Now, now," he murmured softly. "It's Gavan, FireAnn. It's me, finally. We've come to get you."

"She doesn't know us," Trent said numbly.

Jason bit his lip. In the long weeks, her hair had gone from copper-red to silvery-red though a kerchief still tamed her unruly natural curls, and her eyes of emerald green glared dully at them. He took one arm from Gavan and signaled for Trent to hold the other. "Go find Eleanora."

The other did not hesitate. He bolted past them, his cloak sweeping over them as he did. FireAnn threw back her head and looked around, owllike, as if totally dazed. Jason stroked her wrist soothingly, but kept a firm grip as he felt muscles still wiry and strong.

She squinted at him. "Jason, lad, is that ye?"

"Nobody else but."

The camp cook and chief Magicker herbalist stared hard and long at him. "And how do I know this, lad? There's nobody but tricksters around."

Jason leaned close. "I'll eat anything you cook but red Jello." He shuddered a little at that, having had all he could stomach of the red fruity flavor when very young.

She gasped. "Lad! But ye canna stay! There's traps everywhere. Take your friends and flee whilst ye can. Do ye hear me? Afore the banshees and others know ye're here."

"We know," he said softly, quietly, firmly. "It'll be all right."

"No, no, no." She shook her head vigorously, curls bouncing under her faded scarf. "The boy is as mean as the devil himself and he'll come for ye, he'll come for Eleanora. The lass can't take much more. She thought she felt Gavan the other day, thought he'd come for us, and it near broke her heart."

"FireAnn. He has come for you, and this time we won't leave without you. But you must be quiet, and help us."

"Hist! Quiet, he says. All right, then, quiet I'll be." FireAnn twisted her arm in his grasp. "She did this. Her and her Leucators, taking the very life out of my bones. And that other, the watcher, he drinks of what we hold all the time, small sips, and thinks I canna tell!"

"I know." It hurt him to see her half-crazed and twisted as she was. Jason heard heavy steps and looked up. Gavan stood, a slender figure bundled in a wretched-looking blanket in his arms, but she wept, and held her arms about his neck, and it was indeed Eleanora. He straightened his shoulders. "Get us out of here, *now.*"

Trent and Jason drew FireAnn to her feet, and they linked together, Jason cupping his crystal, as Trent kicked the outside door open. It was then the scream hit, a wailing of banshees woven together, piercing their eardrums with anger and dismay. Rebecca's scream of terror from that morning couldn't hold a candle to this decibel-challenging screech.

They shrank back, discovered.

Webs

"R^{UN!"}

"Run?" Jason looked at Gavan.

"We can't Crystal out from here without Tomaz and the others. I haven't enough strength to jump to him and then out. We have to get to him on foot. So, *run.*"

"No!" Trent threw his free arm out, blocking them. "It's like a spiderweb down there. We'll be caught for sure. We can't run. Creep out, maybe, the way we came in."

Gavan stood stock-still, listening, cradling Eleanora tightly to his chest. He tilted his chin to Jason. "Find out if that was his diversion and if not, tell Tomaz to stay low and quiet."

Jason ran his hand over his crystal of quartz and gold and lapis, and made the link. Tomaz seemed as baffled as they were about the screaming, but agreed to lay low for the moment although he indicated urgently that they should get out. Jason repeated that to Gavan.

The fortress fell silent. Gavan shifted his weight. "It is possible that was no alarm. Isabella is known for her temper. We've no way of knowing what set it off."

"Then I say we get to Tomaz, link up, and get out." Trent tapped his feet on the hallway floor in impatience.

"Trent in front. Jason, behind me." Gavan took a slow breath. "I am counting on you both, lads."

Trent led FireAnn behind him, saying, "Not far to go."

She put a crooked finger to her lips in answer. Told to be quiet, it seemed she would. She stumbled along behind Trent, trying to pick her way as he did. Jason watched anxiously. Gavan followed, moving as though carrying Eleanora was no burden at all to him, and perhaps she wasn't.

Jason raised a Shield for the rear and tried to keep track of Trent in front. The stairs sounded with every one of their steps upon it. No matter how quiet and cautious they tried to be, the old wood complained. Every slow step they took was with Trent guiding them through it as if they were climbing through barbed wire. It looked odd. He unwove webs they could not see, although they sensed the magic all about them, malevolent and harsh, a mirror image of the power they used, and as they went farther, the more tangled it got. Jason felt the shivering of the power as it shrugged past, seeking and missing him time after time. It gave him the same creepy crawlies as bugs did.

At last they reached a door to the outside compound, and it swung open invitingly, the haze of afternoon struggling to shine through it.

At the sight of daylight, cloudy though it was, FireAnn broke away from Trent. She staggered out of the fort and into the compound yard with her hands in the air, and did a wobbling Irish jig of joy. "Free," she cried in a cracking voice and then sank to the ground. Trent grabbed her up, shushing her. She nodded and began to cry, softly, brokenly.

It pierced Jason's heart to hear her. A murmur came from Gavan's bundle. Gavan dipped slightly in answer so that Eleanora could put her hand out and comfort FireAnn. Little could be seen of her but the frayed blanket and one terribly thin arm. His eyes and heart filled with the drama of the scene, but his ears heard a noise behind him. He turned.

Jonnard smiled thinly from the fortress door. "I thought I heard mice scurrying about."

"Difficult to hear with Isabella ranting."

"Sad but true." He came out of the doorway.

Jason raised his Shield between them. He called Tomaz to them, his hand over his crystal and added, "Now," to

Gavan and Trent. "Or never, I think." He could feel the
power welling up in Jonnard. They had gambled the Dark
Hand would be as drained as they.

Gambled, and lost.

Tomaz, Stef, and Rich appeared in a shimmer. Jonnard
dropped his shoulder and Jason instantly sensed the gathering and focusing. He charged forward, dropping into a
sliding tackle, Shield up, and drove Jonnard off his feet
gasping. Trent was the one who linked them all, as Gavan
stood, dazed, and tried to protest, and Trent told Tomaz,
"Now, now, go now!" amid the dazzle of crystal energy.
The last thing Jason heard was Trent's thin voice from out
of the nothingness vow, "I'll be back!" Then they were
gone.

For one quick moment, he cursed himself for not going
with them. All would stand or all would fall, but he knew
better. They had a good chance of getting out, and he had a
good chance of keeping Jonnard from blocking them.

Jason rolled and got up. "That," he said, "was soccer."

Jon spat dirt from his mouth. He dredged his crystal out
of the ground behind him, and did not even try to stand
before focusing a blade and slinging it at Jason, intent on
cutting him in two. Jason danced away as blade hit Shield,
and sparks flew, and Magick hummed angrily like a hor-
net's nest greatly disturbed.

Jonnard leaped to his feet. He wiped the back of his
hand over his mouth, then spit aside one last time. "You
never cease to amaze me," the young man said, circling Jason warily. "Although I would rather you just *cease.*"

"Oh, I can't do that." Jason kept his power up, just as
cautious. "I have friends who depend on me."

Jonnard swapped hands, crystal blade sparkling, and
then he had a blade in each, and dropped into a stance the
other recognized all too well. Jason took half a step back,
turning his foot on a large rock on the stony fort courtyard.
It saved his head, as he bobbed suddenly, and the blade cut
through the air so close, the ends of his hair sizzled.

Jason spun away. "Another duel?" he said as he straightened up, dancing a little from foot to foot, loosening himself up, just as he would before a soccer match. His boots
weren't as limber, but his muscles felt good. Not all of him
was mind and Magick! Madame Qi's long runs, and hard

work and exercises, had seen to that. "I don't always win, but I seldom lose."

Jon showed white teeth in a wolfjackal snarl. "I will see you finished off."

"Not if I can help it." Jason dodged again, as Jon's hands moved in a slash of light, crisscrossing. He went to the ground, rolled, and came up, not knowing how close it had been, only knowing he hadn't been hit. That was what counted. He laughed. "How about a bet? If I win this time, you and the rest of the Dark Hand go back."

"Go back? Back there? You must be kidding. If there is one thing that you and I agree upon, it is that going back means becoming someone's laboratory experiment. Going back will never be an option." Jonnard moved with dangerous grace. Magick fire seemed to outline his entire form, dazzling Jason's sight of him. His name, after all, was Jonnard Albrite, despite the dark nature and every intent of his birthright. "And you have nothing to wager that I value. Anything you have, I can take from you."

Jason hesitated. Just for a moment, his mind taking stock of what he had that he valued, the faces of his friends and family flickering through his thoughts, and in that instant, his foe struck.

The blade sank deep. He reeled back in white-hot pain, his arm on fire with the hurt of it, wrenching away, feeling the blood fountain up. He put his hand to it, still holding the crystal, and as blood washed over the quartz, it seared him a second time. Jason cried out. He held the gaping wound shut, still moving, not giving Jon a chance to hit him again, and wondering if he could get the blood to stop.

He gasped with the torture of it, once, twice, narrowing his eyes, trying not to howl or cry, shaking with the effort. His crystal hummed loudly and grew searingly warm and he pulled it away to see . . .

Nothing.

Yet, not nothing, but an angry white seam of a scar showing through his torn sleeve where before there had been a gash of bloody flesh. It ached and throbbed in fresh pain still, every pulsing ebbing a little as though his body could not realize it had just been healed, nerves still yowling with being freshly cut. His finger traced the ropy scar.

He'd done that. But how?

"Well, well. Blooded your crystal." Jon made a *tsking* noise, circling around him. "Not a good thing to do."

Jason shook it off, gathering his scattered thoughts. "What are you talking about?"

"Blooding your crystal. They didn't tell you? Alas, your education is sorely lacking. It might be the death of you." Jon slashed again, lightning quick, but Jason saw it coming this time.

Arm still sore, it was his feet that reacted. He kicked out, curved instep meeting that round rock that had nearly tripped him earlier, half the size and probably twice the weight of a soccer ball. His foot met it squarely. It felt like one of the best kicks he'd ever taken as a forward. The rock shot through the air, arcing like a cannonball at Jonnard's head. The young man ducked away, and it caromed off his shoulder with a solid, sickening thump of rock against flesh. Jon let out a cry, going to his knees.

"Someone," Jason observed, "is going to be very upset you let her captives get loose." He gripped both crystals tightly and felt them answer to him. Shield or flee, and he decided that fleeing would be best for now. Home, he thought, picturing the academy, and felt the chill of *between* take him. Jonnard's shout of pure hatred and anger pieced the void as he went.

Even then, he wouldn't have made it. He stayed *between* long enough to know that, the chill creeping into his bones, when he should have Crystaled here to there in the twinkling of an eye. Nothingness numbed him and the longer he stayed, the more paralyzed he would become, until the end. He wrapped his arms about himself and felt a webbing of power in the abyss, tiny threads of those he loved and who had been in his last thoughts. He clung to them, Bailey's amethyst thread and Ting's of vibrant pink, and Trent's punk blue and Gavan's pewter gray, and Henry's flaming red, and all the others, a rainbow of strands that he could knot around his hand and pull himself. . . .

Home.

40

Sanctuary

I'M MAD AS a hatter," FireAnn remarked cheerfully. "Yes, dear," Aunt Freyah told her, patting her on the shoulder as she passed by, steaming teapot in hand. "We all know that. Hopefully we'll know even more, in time."

FireAnn cackled to herself and sat back in her chair, near the cooking fire pit, enjoying the warmth of the banked fire. Dancing flames reflected in her wild copper hair. The promise of rain was finally fulfilled at nightfall and the sound of drizzle could be heard against the academy walls.

Rich held Jason's arm across one knee and looked at it for the tenth time or so. "I'd say it's healed," he finally said, reluctantly. "Not neatly, and there may be some nerve regeneration needs to be done. That was quite a slice. It's numb here and there?"

"Part of it still stings and, yes, part of it's numb. Weird."

"You're lucky you've got full mobility." Rich shook his head in wonderment. "I don't know how you did it."

"Neither do I." Jason rolled down his sleeve, watching Gavan, still waiting for an answer on his earlier question of, "What did Jonnard mean by blooding a crystal." Gavan hadn't responded yet, but stirred as he sensed Jason's attention.

The Magicker flicked a finger against his mug. "As for your question, I haven't a clue," he said, reading Jason's mind.

"Doesn't ring a bell? Nothing? Even something Brennard or the Dark Hand might have done that we think is forbidden?"

Gavan shook his head, adding, "Although it sounds as if you have the right of it there. Any kind of blood ritual sounds like their portion rather than ours." He stood. "It's been an exceedingly long day. I'm going to check on Eleanora and turn in."

Freyah perched on one of the stools. "Wait a moment, Gavan."

He paused.

"I can't stay here. I think we need to discuss moving Eleanora, FireAnn, me, and my brother."

"And where would you suggest?" Although weary, his voice took on an edge. Jason didn't blame him. He'd just gotten Eleanora back; now Freyah wanted to move her away. "And how would you protect yourselves?"

"I'd go with her," Rebecca said quietly.

"And I." Madame Qi tapped her cane firmly on the floor. "She cannot take care of everyone by herself, and I would not lose a good teacher. At my age," and she flashed a wrinkled grin, "classes are not to be wasted."

"Grandmother," said Ting, moving close to her, and putting an arm over her shoulders affectionately.

"This earth is good to me. Yet my days do not stretch forever in front of me." Madame Qi nodded.

"That does not answer my concern. Where would I send you? Where could you be safe?" Gavan frowned and his jaw tightened before he could say more.

"We have drawn attention here," Tomaz said mildly. "You know that. Freyah is right, they should be moved. The where of it, we'll have to consider."

"Avenha? It's almost rebuilt for the winter."

"Perhaps," Tomaz replied to Henry. "Much to think about." He stood. "Isabella won't be happy."

"Even more reason for us all to rest well, while we can." Gavan tipped his fingers to his brow in a wry salute and went up the stairs to the rooms given to Eleanora and FireAnn. Freyah watched him leave, then released a tiny sigh.

She stared into the fire's flames for such a very long time, she did not seem to notice as everyone else, even FireAnn, said good night and drifted away. George stirred then, and came to her side and butted her, as her drooping fingers nearly dropped her teacup and saucer. She patted the tray. "Thank you, George. Deep thoughts on a deep subject nearly put me into a very deep sleep." She rose and followed after.

"I have killed people for lesser failures," Isabella intoned.

"As I have, for lesser insults and reprimands." Jon raised a defiant eyebrow. He stood his ground.

"The Leucators are gone, now the hostages. How do you expect me to make a stand on this world?"

"I don't think I need to point out that your coin purses are quite full now."

"But my fortress is empty." Isabella paced angrily, turning her back on him, another insult. If she respected him at all, she'd be afraid to show him her back. Jon stared at her, his eyes gone steely hard. His shoulder ached, marked deeply black and blue from the rock blow, and his anger grew icy deep inside him. He would take out the Magickers, one by one or all at once. He no longer cared if they had power they could contribute or if they could be subverted by him. They would be his and regret the moment they became so. Fools with Magick were still just fools.

"Your fortress stands, as does your Gate."

"The Gate. Where would an abyss like that lead?"

"It doesn't matter."

She swung on him. "Doesn't matter! Listen to yourself."

"No, listen to you." Jonnard leaned forward. "I opened one Gate, I can open another. Did that possibility escape you? Or did you think it a fluke? Did you think I tripped and flicked a finger, and a Gate flew open by accident?"

An expression glanced across her face that he couldn't read. Had that indeed been what she thought of him? Jon contained himself though he wanted to shake in anger and continue shaking till the building dropped in rubble about them, but he did not let himself. He clenched a fist until the sore wound of his shoulder throbbed with the force of it. He moved for the door.

"Where are you going?"

"Out," he grated through clenched teeth. "In case you've forgotten, someone knew we were moving our goods for sale. Someone in the Trader Guild betrayed us, and I intend to find out who. They won't do it again." He left before she could deny him the right to go although he almost hoped she would try to stop him.

He rode the bay. The horse took to Crystaling well, and did not mind being ridden in the light rain, although both were soaked by the time they reached Naria's outskirts. Smoldering lights tried to brighten the night when he dismounted at the Trader Guild and turned the horse's reins over to a stammering stableboy who may or may not have recognized him. An apprentice let him in the front door, immediately bowing and bolting off for one of the senior guildsmen. Jon did not care who answered his call, as long as someone did. He stripped off his riding gloves and stamped his boots, shedding drops of rain.

"Master Jonnard! I am honored, honored." Presumptuous, overdressed as much as his flesh was overstuffed, and smelling of vinegary wine, Guild Leader Shmor himself came to press his hand. He still had a cloth napkin stuffed in his waistband, obviously interrupted at dinner. "What can I do for you? The deal is done? Problems?" Shmor shifted uneasily, and his body wobbled.

"Done, yes." Jonnard released the sweating hand as Shmor let out a long breath of relief. "Well done, no. Part of our negotiation concerned the need for utmost secrecy. I thought we had your assurance on that." Jonnard drew his gloves slowly between his fingers.

"You had! You have!" Shmor rumbled indignantly. "I don't understand."

"Let me make you understand, then." Jon stepped in, neat and clean, his hand to the trader's throat. Loose skin and wattle pooled about his fingers as he began to close them. "We were compromised, Shmor. Compromised badly enough that we almost had no deal to make, and I know that no one on my end was foolish enough to wag his tongue. That leaves your end."

Shmor began to turn red. "No, no, no! None of my people." He gargled a bit for breath and Jon loosed his hand just a touch. "I assure you. In the old days, I would have pointed to your man Fremmler, but I doubt that now. He seems quite loyal to you. Believe me, Master Jonnard, I know of no one who would be stupid enough to go against the guild or Isabella of the Dark Hand." He panted, his fat throat undulating against Jon's grip. "Our deal stands, and we hope to make many more. No one in the Trader Guild would run afoul of that."

"Someone did."

The trader gestured wildly. "I will make inquiries! I will leave no stone unturned finding out what I may!" Shmor gargled again.

Unpleasant as the man was, Jonnard believed him. He let go. Shmor hastily took a step back, rubbing at his throat. "I will not rest until I find out who, and turn him over to your tender mercies." He bowed heavily at the waist.

"Don't throw me a crumb," Jonnard warned. "Don't set up some poor fool to make me happy. I want the truth, and I'll know it when I see it."

"Understood, Master Jonnard. Well understood!" Shmor cleared his throat with a fruity noise. "Have you, ermm, dined yet?"

The last thing he wanted to do was share a table with the man. "I'll find an inn."

Relief flooded Shmor's face. "Well, then. May I recommend The Hot Spit? It's a block over. Clean, plain food, good brewery."

"I look forward to hearing from you soon."

Shmor brought his napkin up to his mouth. He looked as if he might be trying to stifle tears. "And I, I look forward to answering your inquiry." He bowed but did not leave till Jonnard himself did.

He thought he heard a muffled sob as the door closed on his heels.

Unheeding, Jon made his way inside the establishment which smelled of straw and the wetness being tracked inside, beer, and sausages crackling on spits. The beer tasted like beer of old, thick and rich, not the swill served in many modern-day bars, and the sausages were not quite like any he'd ever had before, but he did not care, they filled his stomach. He sat at the table by himself, his five-fingered hands wrapped about a crude mug and endured the stares of passersby who marked him for his difference.

After two mugs of the beer, he decided he was ready to go home. He'd rattled the traders enough, something would shake out or not, although he wanted someone he could settle the score against now. The beer soothed his temper a bit. He'd have to bide his time. He dropped a coin on the table, a hand-stamped metal of unknown origin that passed for precious on Haven and drew his feet under him to stand. A sopping wet bundle of rags dashed up against him.

"Sir! Sir! A coin for a street lad? I'll clean yer boots, sir!"

Jon grabbed the small boy by the scruff of the neck. Muddy and stinking, the child struggled a bit, then went limp. "How did you get in here?"

"They let me in, sir. I clean boots. I sing, sometimes. And I draw pictures. Look, look!" Dangling from Jon's fist, the urchin still managed to open his cloak and from within his shirt, he took out a fistful of papers. He scattered them on the table's edge.

They caught Jon's eye. Drawn in firestick charcoal, they showed a bit of talent. He recognized streets of Naria, peopled by various characters, going about their lives. He picked out one. It showed fat Shmor on the Trader Guild steps, thumb in his vest, talking with a hapless apprentice. Jon peered closely. Upstairs, on the second story, a crow perched at a window. Plainly, a crow.

But crows did not inhabit Haven.

"What's this?"

"Oh, that one, sir. The Head Trader, sir."

"I know who he is. This," and Jon stabbed a finger at the crow.

"A great dark bird, sir. Ne'er seen anything like it, I have. It comes and goes sometimes."

"From that window?"

The boy looked at him shrewdly and pressed his lips firmly together. Jon let him drop. He flipped him a coin. "From that window?"

"Always, sir. None other."

Jon took the sketch and put it in his own pocket. "You know nothing."

"Never did, sir. It's why I'm poor." The lad scrambled together his other art, and dashed off, stowing them away, zigzagging through the inn and off into the rain.

He had to fetch his horse from the guild stables anyway. Jon put up his cloak hood against the rain which had tailed off to a fine mist, and slowed as he came upon the building. He paced the street till he saw the unusual window from the urchin's sketch. He thought he had an idea where it might be on the second floor.

The apprentice let him inside again, and hesitated. Jonnard pressed a few coins in his palm. "No need to disturb Shmor again. I think I left something up on the second floor. I'll just be a moment."

"Well and good, Master Jonnard. Shall I wait for you here?"

"Good idea." Jonnard took the steps cat-quick, before the apprentice could decide the bribe was too little and told someone of his presence anyway. The small offices upstairs all seemed to be dark. He lit a crystal, passing door by door. He nearly missed the one he wanted, and back stepped. Lantern light from his hand filled the small office. Stacks of papers met his gaze, an unremarkable clerk's office. Racks of books, scrolls, and maps lined the wall. The one window seemed high, but a small ladder to reach the bookshelves stood in the corner. Jonnard paused at the desk, and sifted through the top layer, trying to determine who sat there and who signed the documents.

He did not know the written language yet, but he recognized the signature, nonetheless. Renart.

Of course. He should have known.

Jon tilted his head at the window again. He knew where the crows had come from, and now he knew who they'd come for. He no longer needed Shmor's help, although he would give the trader credit if he confirmed it. Jon shuttered his Lantern spell and withdrew. A knit scarf hung on a chair by the door. He took it with him.

A little something for the wolfjackals to remember Renart by.

Warm with accomplishment, he Crystaled to his Gate instead of going directly to the fort. He dismounted a distance away, as the animal became skittish at the turmoil of energy, and left the horse tied to a shrub. He would go to bed full, in more ways than one, he decided. Jon approached it, the moon lowered in the sky and barely illuminating the night, and he could hear the skeletons rattling about in an ever circling movement of Chaos. He extended his hand to drink of the Magick it contained. It drew him closer. It held everything he wanted or needed. It flowed into him warmer than sunlight, more bracing than any drink, and it *knew* him. He swore that as it filled him to overflowing. Jonnard broke it off at the moment when it seemed he would become more it than he was himself, and the Gate seemed to sigh as he did.

He pulled his hand back, wiping it on his pants leg. Shadows boiled. Figures began to emerge, watching him with baleful eyes as they solidified. They took a step toward him. He should have felt fear, but did not.

A whisper in the night. *Let usssss hunt.*

Jonnard considered that. What would they hunt? Dare he ask? Did he want to know? Leucators had come from this stuff combined with some human essence, and now they'd returned to it. He knew how Leucators hunted.

On the other hand, he had a lesson to be taught.

Jonnard withdrew the scarf from his cloak and dropped it on the ground. "Hunt that one, then," he said.

Shadows rippled and whirled about the scarf and in moments it was shredded into nothing more than bits of yarn as if devoured. The Gate shimmied. Jonnard backed up a step.

"Hunt no other," he commanded.

Yessss.

He did not turn his back on the Gate and the fiends as he left. He would find out soon how much a master of it he was. It could be useful.

Or it could be disaster.

41

Hunting

"THE REPAIR WORK is going well," Renart said, pulling back the reins and drawing his cart to a halt. Avenha was absolutely bursting with construction as they drove in past the new gates. He jumped down to put a hand out to Pyra, but she had already vaulted over the seat, two strides ahead of him.

"Many hands," she shouted back at him, before dashing off to her father's gatehouse.

Fresh wood gleamed in the afternoon air, and the sound of industry filled the morning. The stench of burned wood and death was gone, cleaned out by wind and rain and hard work as the villagers had hauled out the past. He knew the proverb she quoted, about many hands making a village, and indeed it did, whether building from the ground up or in day-to-day living. He steadied the carriage horse with a pat to the neck before following after Pyra. He would give her a decent amount of time to break the ill news to her father.

The horse, on the other hand, puzzled him. The beast, one of the fine Trader Guild stock, had been skittish the whole trip, as though something trailed them. Once or twice, Renart thought he had seen something loping off the road behind them as well, but few animals could keep up with the sustained trot of a carriage horse bred for stamina. They'd camped overnight, with a bright fire, just to keep the horse quiet although the animal had slept fitfully, ears flicking back and forth and whickering nervously now and then. They'd taken the road slower this morning because the horse had seemed tired. The horse roiled an eye at him now, before dipping his head and shifting his weight and relaxing a bit. A stabling lass approached them, and Renart handed her the reins, and a coin. She bobbed in thanks and led the animal and cart off, chatting cheerfully to the horse in the way that good hands with livestock do, and the horse rubbed his muzzle on her sleeve looking for a treat.

Pyra had not seemed to notice either his nerves or the horse's, her mind filled with worry and grief. Mantor and Flameg had been close, she'd told him on the ride. It would be like losing a brother, and worse, she could not even bring his body back so his bones and ashes could be blended in with the dirt of the village which would mourn him. Renart straightened his clothing, and set off after her.

He entered the gatehouse to hear Mantor let out a guttural sound, the deep-throated noise a man makes who seldom cries and cannot do it even though he needs to. Renart hung back a step or two, hearing that, and feeling his own throat tighten. They all dealt with loss. Some came shockingly quick, some in its own good time, and some never in time enough to prevent suffering. It was the way of all life, but it did not make it any easier to realize that. He straightened his jacket a second time before rounding the threshold.

Mantor sat, his great, scarred hands holding the leather pouch with the only remains of his guardsman. His fingers tightened as he stood. "What is done, is done. He lived well and died well. We will burn his remains with honor and till them into the soil, to return to the living. The Spirit knows his name and will not forget it."

Pyra looked down quietly. Her shoulders shook a few times. Renart stepped immediately to her side and slipped an arm about her as Mantor looked at him. "Thank you for bringing them home."

"I couldn't do any less," he told the chieftain.

The smallest corner of Mantor's mouth quirked slightly, as he observed Renart, and the trader felt himself warm a bit, as though the chieftain could see right through him and how he felt about Pyra. Mantor said nothing, however, except to slap him heartily on the shoulder as he strode past with Flameg's remains. He wondered if the chieftain's daughter was as perceptive. He waited till she stopped crying silently, then stepped away a little, giving her space. She cleared her throat and composed herself, giving thought to the business of the future.

"You will stay the night? To rest the horse, if nothing else."

He bowed his head. "Of course."

"Good. We'll be putting Flameg to rest at sunset. It would be nice . . ." She paused, as if searching for words. "It would be nice to have you there."

His heart soared. Did his feet leave the ground? He hoped not. She had quiet ways and he had no wish to scare her off even though he now wanted to shout from the rooftops. She brushed past him, saying, "Let me show you where you can rest."

Pyra halted in the doorway, her eyes sparkling. "You're quite flushed, Renart. Perhaps you should wear a hat more often, the sun seems to have burned you a bit." She ducked out then, and he thought he heard her chuckle as she led him on.

He dozed after lunch, though he meant not to, but having stood watch during the night left him drowsy and he slipped into a light sleep despite his intentions. He woke to the sound of voices raised in greeting.

Jason poked his face around the corner. "Hey, sleepyhead! Pyra said I'd find you here."

"Jason! You are well, then?" Renart sat up hastily, and grabbed for his boots, tugging them on.

"We're wonderful. We've got Eleanora and FireAnn back."

Renart beamed at the Magicker. "Incredible news! But I thought our endeavor went badly?"

"That part did, but we don't give up easily."

He joined Jason in the gatehouse hall and noticed that the boy had grown again, and now stood a bit taller than he was. Jason jostled him good-naturedly before wincing slightly, and gripping his right forearm with his left hand.

"Something wrong?"

"Nah. It's healing, just smarted a bit. Tomaz wants me to bring you in. We may have some negotiating to do."

"Oh? What about?" Renart's eyebrows raised, intrigued.

"You'll see."

Tomaz sat opposite Mantor who had reined in his emotions of the morning and now sat with his customary, stoic expression. Pyra was dipping out cups of cooled cider and passing them around. The air smelled of the pressing, crisp and sweet like the apples it came from, and Renart took a cup eagerly. Was it his imagination or did her fingers linger on his hand as he did?

His thoughts whirled as he seated himself at the other end of the table, neither with nor against either of the two men already sitting, his trader training working even before his conscious thoughts could gather.

"You ask a lot of us, even as you honor us," Mantor noted. "I will return Flameg to the ground which birthed him tonight."

Tomaz inclined his head. "We know this. There aren't enough words to thank you for his help, or comfort you for his loss." Jason slipped up to the table and sat quietly next to the elder Magicker, his glance darting about, placing and weighing everyone. Renart had a quick thought of what a trader that one would make, before turning his own mind to the negotiations at hand.

Mantor said to him, "Tomaz has asked us to take in a group and keep them secured, quiet, hidden from the Dark Hand."

"Who?"

"The rescued hostages, and a few caretakers. Such a thing could be done. However, it would not be secret within the village. That could not be kept. Knowing this, then, every Avenhan would be opposing the Dark Hand and the risk is shared by all. We've already paid a price, but I also know that the Dark Hand won't consider that."

"We wouldn't ask, Mantor, but we know that our academy will be the main target. I'd like to see Eleanora and FireAnn get the rest and care they need without facing that hazard," Tomaz said evenly.

Jason looked to the outside wall, restlessly, and this time his right hand went to his left hand and rubbed it without his seeming aware of it. Renart, trained to note the movements of everyone at a negotiating table, did. However, it seemed to have nothing to do with the current matter.

"What are the compensations for such a risk?" he asked.

"We can offer lanterns that require no flame to keep lit. Our aid when needed. Training in certain technologies that you might find useful."

Mantor looked at Tomaz, then at Renart, before commenting, "We need your aid because of your very presence. This would only compound it."

"You had no bandits before the Dark Hand?"

"The world has always known bandits." The chieftain smiled wryly, indicating he understood Tomaz's point. He nodded to Renart. "I'm not inclined to say yes or no, understand this. I am only asking if there is a way to conceal this, for the sakes of my people."

Tomaz tapped his finger on the table. "The Dark Hand won't know of this. I'll ensure that."

Mantor gave a low laugh. "Spies and greed are as old as bandits. You can't keep an entire village quiet."

Leaning forward, Tomaz said softly, "I could, but my methods would be no less despicable than those we call enemy, and I won't do it. Have you suggestions, then?"

"I can perhaps find kinsmen who would consider it, outlying farmers or shepherds, that we can support quietly."

Jason twitched again. His hand rubbed the other once more, a glancing movement that he scarcely seemed to note.

"Hmmmm." Tomaz scratched a thumbnail along the edge of his jaw. "A possibility."

Jason opened his mouth and shut it. Renart looked toward him. "Something to add?"

"Kind of. I think I know where to place them, but they'd need Avenha's help."

"Put it on the table, then," Renart told him.

"The wanderers would take them in. But, through the winter, having extra people around and stuff might be a hardship. They'd need supplies and things like that, help."

"The wanderers have chosen their own course." Mantor's gaze rested lightly on Jason.

"Oh, I know. I understand, and all that. But they're good people, too, and they'd be eager for the lantern lights and such, and I bet the Dark Hand wouldn't even know where to find them."

"For that matter, where would we?" Pyra set down her cider cup, tilting her head slightly with interest.

"I can find them," Jason told her confidently.

From anyone else, Renart would have thought it a ploy to shame the Avenhans to take in the Magickers, but from Jason, he knew it was a sincere communication. Mantor shoved back from the table a little, his brows lowering in consideration.

"It might be done."

"Father?"

"It might be done," the chieftain repeated, "without breaking their self-imposed exile. We would be aiding the others, not the wanderers, and the Spirit has always guided us to help where we can. This one world is like a great ship on a voyage, and we are all but passengers. To not aid is to impede the voyage for everyone."

"Right. So it's a deal?" Jason asked eagerly.

Renart coughed. Tomaz leaned slightly, pressing his heavy shoulder into Jason as if to squelch him a bit.

"There are details to work out, not the least of which is finding the wanderers and asking Dokr if he wishes to do this." Renart began making mental notes.

Jason's head turned away from them, and he frowned, as if noticing his fidgeting for the first time. He got to his feet, still awkward in his lanky body and height. "I'm not sure," he said, "we have much time."

"What's wrong?"

"Something . . . is coming."

"Show me!" Pyra grabbed up her longbow from the rack on the opposite wall, and the two sprinted out of the gatehouse meeting room. The men scrambled to their feet, close on their heels, Renart last of all despite his youth, his fighting instincts not quite as sharp as his trading ones.

The guardswoman let out a piercing whistle. Heads jerked around, and then people rushed to the gates, preparing to close them, as she led Jason up onto the catwalk so they could look down the valley and the approach to the village. Workers on the outside streamed inward quickly, slipping through the gates before they slammed shut and the great bar dropped into place.

Pyra nocked an arrow in the longbow as the others joined the two of them on the catwalk. "What do you see?"

"Nothing, yet."

Mantor laid his hands on the top of the wall which surrounded Avenha. His nostrils flared slightly as if he could scent an invader. He shook his head.

"It doesn't matter," Jason said tersely. "I know it's coming."

Tomaz rubbed his crystals. "Not far away either," he said. As if in answer to him, two crows arrowed through the sky toward them from the trees lining the valley's edge, their caws demanding shrill attention. Midnight and Snowheart dove at his head, before circling and taking up a post on the gatehouse roof.

"There." Jason pointed at the under shadows of the faraway grove. Something loped to a stop, and melted behind a tree trunk, but they all saw the movement.

"Wild animal." Renart tried to sound hopeful.

"Not a wolfjackal. It looks to be standing upright."

"Bandits would ride in, would they not?" Pyra sighted down her arrow at the trees, far too distant for a shot, but keeping ready.

"Aye, Daughter, that they would. Quickly in, damage what they can, grab what they can, quickly out."

"What, then?"

No one had an answer. Mantor drew his own bow, and readied it. They stared along the cleared ground and down the road. After long moments, the shadow separated itself from the tree and began to cross the expanse. Other shadows grouped behind it, staying half hidden.

Mantor stared. "Hold your fire! Hold it!"

Pyra breathed in disbelief, "It's Flameg."

Rénart blinked as he stared down. The figure moved in an oddly fluid way that seemed wrong somehow.

"No, it's not," said Jason.

"Hold your peace, boy. I know that man like my own brother. He's managed to get home." Mantor turned away from him. "Open the gates!"

Jason swung on Tomaz, grabbing his arm. "It's not him, believe me. He's dead, think about it. Don't let him in!"

Tomaz stared down at Jason, but it was Renart who moved. He leaped off the catwalk, and flung himself against the gate, as they unlatched the great bar and began to tug it open. It inched wider despite his efforts. Jason jumped to the ground next to him, straightening, his hands filling with a white fire.

"Don't let it in!"

Renart swung about. He could hear the snarling. He turned and saw the ... thing ... running at him, charging at the gap between the gateposts. If it had been Flameg once, it wasn't now. He didn't know what he faced if it wasn't the living dead. His heart froze.

Jason shouldered him aside. The air sizzled with white heat, and the thing stumbled, then rolled to its knees. It got up with a growling noise from a throat that had been ripped open. It kept coming.

"It's a Leucator! Or ... something," Jason shouted up. Villagers jostled him, hurrying to close the gate again, as the terrible thing threw itself toward them, and other things began to break out of the forest, howling.

They got the gates closed. They fought from the catwalk. Some of the attackers had flesh, but some were little more than bone and gore. They pounded at the walls, mewling and howling. They took blows from arrows, reeling back, and then coming on again.

Only fire seemed to deter them. Three of the fiends fell in crystal fire and flame, and the pack fell back to the forests and disappeared.

Renart helped stand the watch until late in the evening, but the things did not return. They burned Flameg's longbow anyway, although the thing that might have been him had run off, and none of them knew if their neighbor and friend would have peace or not.

When it was done, Mantor turned to Tomaz. "Whatever needs to be done, will be. If the wanderers agree." He walked away without waiting for an answer, his heavy shoulders bowed.

42

Desperate Times

IF I NEVER HEAR the words, 'Are you the Magickers and are you going to help us?' again, it will be too soon," Stefan said wearily before collapsing onto the floor, his legs folded up under him. He scrubbed at reddened eyes, not caring that he'd missed a chair entirely.

"Well, it *is* our fault," Henry said mildly. He leaned on the table, his head propped in his hands as if he couldn't hold it up any other way. His glasses sat askew on his face, one of the lenses sooty and smeared.

"How do we know that? How?" Rich pulled himself up a stool, got his flask out and measured a draught of his medicine. He quaffed it quickly, making a terrible face, then closed his flask.

"Okay, guys, listen up." Trent leaned over the group. "Bailey, give me that map tube I gave you earlier."

With a smothered yawn, she fetched it out of her ragged backpack and handed it over. With a quick twist, he liberated the map inside. He unrolled it and smoothed it out on the table. He grabbed one of Henry's hands and slapped it down on a corner, took one of Rich's and did the same, and Ting put her own down, taking the hint.

"This is how they used to do it in big city police departments. Watch closely." Trent fished a pencil out of the billowing sleeve of his shirt. "Attacks have been here, here, here, and tonight, here." He marked the map starting with Avenha and going to the different villages, including the city of Naria. "Now. We know these things don't ride, animals can't stand the sight or smell of 'em. They move on foot. They're faster than we are, 'cause they don't need to rest or eat or breathe, but they're still on foot. So . . ." He drew a circle connecting the targets. "It suggests that they radiate from somewhere within this circle. Look familiar? I think it does."

They all stared at Trent's map. "The Dark Hand."

"Has to be."

"The abyss they opened."

Trent nodded. "A given, I think."

"That confirms it." Jason took a deep breath, shaking his head slowly. "I didn't think Jonnard could be that stupid."

Gavan and Tomaz came in, their steps heavy. "Jonnard is far from stupid, give him that," Crowfeather stated.

Rich snorted. "I wouldn't give him the time of day."

"Underestimating your foe gives him the first strike against you. Remember."

Jason stared at the map until the lines blurred. "If he's directing the bone fiends, what's he got in mind? It's no longer looting. It just seems to be terrorizing."

"It has to be more than that, he wouldn't waste resources. What do the villages have in common? And what about Naria? That's a pretty big city to attack."

Tomaz tapped the bright star that indicated Naria. "My understanding is that the Trader Guild was hit. There weren't enough fiends to infiltrate more than that."

"Renart was here." Jason put his finger on Avenha. "Here." He touched Naria. "And here, I think," indicating the small village of Missail. The hills beyond Missail was where Jason's dragon told him the wanderers often wintered, and Renart had gone there in search of Dokr. "Coincidence?"

"Probably not, but the other two, then?"

Gavan said quietly, "Who says Jonnard is in complete control? These are more than Leucators. They're taking dead with them."

"He's opened something he doesn't know how to deal with?"

"Possibly."

"Then how can we expect to?"

"That, lad, is something I don't know. Yet." He slapped Jason on the back. "You all need a shower and sleep, I think."

Ting shivered. "No hot water!"

"Someday," Gavan promised. "In the meantime . . ."

"We know, we know." They got to their feet, the kitchen filled with the sounds of chairs and stools scraping. Sleep while they could, while it was still peaceful.

"I promise you, it will be exhilarating. You will feel omnipotent when you're done." Jonnard patted Isabella's hand as he led her over the landscape carefully, darkness masking her face and eyes from him, but her ragged breathing betraying her fear. That and the coldness of her hands in his. "It'll be fine."

"I have little choice." She faltered a step, and he righted her. He could feel a frailness in her body that he'd never felt before, Isabella of the iron will and temper. He wasn't sure that he didn't enjoy the weakness, but he shuttered that feeling away. He needed her, for now. He tightened his hand on her elbow.

A pack of wolfjackals circled uneasily about the Gate as they neared it. Their eyes caught the light from the sickle moon overhead, and glowed an eerie green as they trotted around the two of them. They growled, low and nearly muted, but still defiant.

"There was a time," Isabella said bitterly, "when they didn't dare snarl at me."

"That will return. All things will bow to you."

"Even you, Jonnard?"

He did not answer. She cursed in French, then laughed. He recognized only the word serpent in her fluid muttering, and decided not to answer. Instead he tugged her forward faster, harshly, over the foreign ground, uncaring if she stumbled, making their way to the Gate. The wolfjackals slunk away, looking back over their shoulders, eyes flashing like hot emeralds in the dark as they did.

He stopped. Isabella said quietly, "What do I do?"

"Hold your hand out, dip it into the shadow, and drink of the energy. Stay wary of getting any closer, though. It is an abyss and a fall."

"We wouldn't want that, would we?"

"Actually, no," he answered flatly.

That seemed to mollify her a bit. She brushed her hair from her face, resetting her jeweled combs, and then put her long-fingered hand out, just touching the swirling edge of darkness. The Gate immediately let out a low moan, as ghastly as any haunted house could issue, and she shivered but did not stir. He could see in the dim light, the bones tumbling about, and the black aura of the power within.

Isabella hissed a long breath inward. "How powerful!"

"Drink deeply. You'll see."

"Jonnard," she murmured softly, entranced, not seeing him, her whole concentration fixed now on the Gate. She almost glowed with it as it filled her. He knew what she felt, and he smiled to himself.

When she was done, he could feel the iron in her again. She drew herself up, and turned to look at him. "Now," she said. "For the price."

"Price?"

"There is always a price to be paid."

He could never put anything past her. He drew her aside. "Not by us." It took but a moment, and then ghouls began to spill out of the Gate. Whole flesh and broken flesh, bone linked by sinew and little else, and the bone fiends gathered.

We hunt.

No longer a question asking permission of him. They told him they were going. Jonnard gave a bow, and the hunters went forth, their feet whispering swiftly across frost-burned ground.

"What do they hunt?"

"Whatever they wish. Not us."

She waited until they stood alone. Then, she said, "This cannot be."

"For a while, Mother. Only for a while. It has its purposes. How long has it been since you felt this good?"

"Do you control them?"

Jonnard thought of several answers, discarded them, and answered, "No."

"Then it cannot be. If you're a Gatekeeper, open us another Gate. We'll drink of purer, safer energy. Escape to another world if this one is corrupted by them."

He shifted weight. He'd been studying in the days since he'd opened this Gate.

Isabella arched an eyebrow.

"I can't open a Gate as long as this one is open. One at a time, it seems."

"Then shut this one."

"It won't be shut."

"No?"

"Not without every ounce of power I have. It would consume me."

She considered him for a very long time. Then she said, "It needs to devour a Gatekeeper to close?"

"So it seems," he said reluctantly.

"Why, Jonnard, the answer is simple. Give it a Gatekeeper. Give it the Magicker Jason Adrian."

"He has one weakness he can't protect from me," Jon stated. "His friends. Even Jason cannot be everywhere, all the time."

43

Desperate Measures

A TAP, TAP, TAP DREW Rich's attention as he huddled in a blanket, teeth chattering and sweating off some of what he'd come to call blackmarrow fever. It came and went, and he knew it was his body trying to throw off the poison. It gave him some hope that he might do it someday, that his constitution was different enough that a cure could happen.

Tap, tap, tap. Rich blinked. That was definitely not his teeth. He shrugged off the wrap and got to his feet. A black crow fluttered by the window, and he quickly opened it for Tomaz's Midnight. The creature cawed at him and swiped his beak across Rich's hand as if chiding him for taking so long. It took two tries with shaking hands for him to untie the message scroll. As soon as the weight left his leg, the crow hopped off the table and winged outside, in search of whatever crows went in search of. He supposed roadkill could be found just about anywhere.

He decided the object of search ought to be Tomaz and found him giving Stef a lesson in bear lore, which the big guy seemed to be only half absorbing. Both seemed relieved when Rich interrupted by handing Tomaz the scroll.

Tomaz shook it at Stef's nose. "Think about what I told you. The bear is a powerful creature but an unthinking one. You need to learn to use the power without letting the animal take over."

Without waiting for an answer, he unfastened the scroll.

"Where's it from?"

"I left Midnight at Avenha, so it should be from Mantor or Pyra." Tomaz unrolled the small bit of paper. He ran a crystal over it, frowning, deciphering what he could of the writing. Talker crystals worked much better, although Renart had been giving them books from which to try to build a Writer crystal. "It's from Pyra. Renart is missing. Another attack while . . . I think she means the wanderers . . . trying to finish his mission with them. The wording is not exact, but that seems to be what she's trying to get across."

"No! Not Renart."

Tomaz ran his crystal over the scroll again. "Missing," he repeated, although his voice sounded disheartened.

"Not as bad as dead."

"Bad enough." He twisted the scroll in his hands. "I need to find Gavan." Without another word, he walked off, and Rich and Stef traded looks.

"Not good."

"Definitely not good," Rich agreed. He shuddered, and his teeth chattered violently.

"You don't look good either."

"Thanks." Rich stomped off, headed back inside in search of his blanket and solitude. Stef made a puzzled snuffling noise as he went.

He felt no warmer despite the fever boiling off him and not much better when Bailey came strolling by the door. She poked her head in. "Rich?"

He nodded miserably.

She took a hesitant step in. "You want me to get someone?"

"N–no. My fault. I didn't take enough stuff yesterday." He clenched his jaw shut for a minute.

"Take more?"

"I did." He looked down at the floor miserably. He'd

dropped his waterskin, and the thick liquid pooled around his feet.

"Oh, Rich."

"I've got s—some more. Somewhere."

Bailey picked up an old shirt in the corner and tried to wipe the mess up. "Ugh. This just smells sickly sweet."

"Tastes good, too," he said sarcastically. "I'll brew more up tomorrow."

"Ting and I can help. What do you need?"

"Dried keffelberries and thane grass. I've got the berries. Thane grass is that stinging, needlelike grass down by the river. It grows here and there. And water, gotta boil it all day."

"That's easy enough." She bounced to her feet. "You go ahead and drink what you need, we'll brew up more, okay?"

Rich heaved a sigh. "Thanks, Bailey."

"Don't be so stubborn. If you need help, ask for it."

"I have to learn how to deal with this." He shook again.

"We all do," Bailey told him solemnly. "Today it's you, tomorrow it could be any one of us, okay?"

It chilled him even more to realize she could be right. He watched her miserably as she ran out to find Ting.

Ting got gathering pouches for both of them, while Bailey tried to explain what it was they were looking for. Finally Ting said, "Ooohhh! Those awful grass things by the rocks."

"Right. Thane grass, looks like a blade, and if you're not careful, you'll slice your fingers up good on 'em, and they sting like crazy."

"Gotcha. I haven't seen any by the pool lately. I think we're going to have to follow the river down a little."

"He says it boils down so if we both get a bagful, that should make at least one batch, don't you think?"

"It should." Ting fretted.

"What?"

"Let's stay close, just in case."

"No problem. I don't want to go outside the wards anyhow. You start here, and I'll walk down the river. Any problems, go for the crystal."

Ting nodded and began to search the edge of the deep water pool. Bailey followed the river, skirting the rocky shore carefully.

* * *

Having been there once, it was no problem to get inside the wards a second time. Rainwater lacked a certain finesse and strategy for subterfuge, Jon thought, as he guided his horse through the intricacies of the alarms. He wanted to get close enough to observe, though not close enough to be observed. The key to Jason was the sense of obligation he felt to others, and if he was going to trap Jason, that would be the way. They'd taken the wrong person in taking Eleanora, he thought. One of the girls would have been better. The slender, almond-eyed Ting or the vibrant Bailey. Gavan had stayed cool over Eleanora despite his feelings for her. But the younger ones, they did not have the experience or the maturity. He could have broken them over the girls. He knew each of them well enough to know how they would react to one of their own being in trouble.

The sound of running water covered his movement through the woods as he let the horse pick a cautious way closer to the academy building. He sensed it, more than saw it, for it had its own aura and he knew that Gavan and Tomaz had imbued the place with a great deal of energy.

The bay put his ears forward in curiosity, listening. Jon reined him back, and pitched his senses as well.

When he recognized her voice, he thought it must be a moment of wishful thinking.

"All right, all right, down you go. You see if you can find the stupid grass." And there was a Bailey laugh when a series of indignant squeaks and chirps answered.

Jon leaned forward, peering keenly through the foliage. A slow smile broke across his face. If it was an illusion, it was the one he most hoped to see. And alone, although no Magick worker was ever alone, if they used their senses properly. No, he would have to isolate her. He'd lost one chance to do that, he wouldn't do it again. Coax her to come with him willingly. He sat for long moments, considering, remembering, sifting through the times he'd lived among them and they'd not known him for what he was. Then he thought he had it.

Bailey watched Lacey scurry off, whiskers flattened to her cheek pouches, little tufted tail snapping now and then in irritation. She let the rodent scamper across the mossy rocks, picking up glistening pebbles here and there that shone prettily in the partial sunlight of a day where there were as many clouds as not. The thought of thane grass flitted through the kangaroo rat's mind and left, but Bailey let her go. Lacey had been, after all, a wild thing, and sometimes Bailey wondered if she should ever have bonded with the small creature. It had happened suddenly, though, without either really knowing.

Lacey ran right through a patch of brilliantly green blades, her body barely bending them as she twisted through, intent on something she saw and coveted with her pack rat mind.

"You found it!" Bailey went to her knees. A sawlike edge whipped through her touch. "Ow!" If she'd had any doubt this was the stuff, it fled. Wryly, she pulled out a pocket knife and began cutting the blades down, cautiously putting each one in the pouch as though it were a thorny rose stem. Even so, she found herself sucking on a cut finger every few minutes. She'd quit, but this patch was a treasure trove, enough to fill her gathering pouch and more, and she could get back to Ting. Next time, gloves!

Faintly. "Bailey."

She looked around. "Mom?"

"Where are you, hon? Bailey?"

Anyone else could Crystal for her. She got to her feet, wondering where Ting had gotten to.

"Bailey, I need you."

She sounded hurt. Fear rushed through Bailey. "Mom?" She whirled about, trying to catch the direction. "Where are you?"

"Here. This way . . ."

Bailey walked toward the overhanging trees. She left the pouch and Lacey behind.

She stopped dead in her tracks. "You!"

"Not another word. To anyone, by any way. Think on it carefully."

She stared at Jonnard. "What are you doing here?"

"I came to help, actually. I need you for that, though, Bailey." He crossed his hands on his horse's neck, his clothing all in black like the shadows he stayed half hidden in.

"Like I believe that."

"If you want to or not, it's of little matter to me." Jon

leaned forward, the expression on his pale but handsome face very intent. "Warfare between us will destroy Haven. It opened the abyss, and it will spread the contamination until that chasm devours all of us."

Bailey shivered. "You're lying."

"Am I? I was alive when Gregory and Brennard fought. I know what Magick, when it explodes, can do. You, of all people, should know that as well. You're a Magicker. Why do you think Gavan and I don't just go toe to toe and end it all, for once? Because after that once, it became the single, unthinkable thing to do. Our hatred for each other is great, but not great enough to destroy an entire world for it."

Bailey breathed out. "You are serious."

"I am."

"Then what are you doing here?"

"I came for help. It will take two of us to close the abyss. Myself and one of you."

"You're sneaking in."

Jonnard gave a crooked, dry smile. "I think my reception probably warrants that, don't you? The need to avoid conflict is great, however. With every attack between us, the abyss widens, and gets more powerful."

"My mother—"

"A trick, one I apologize for. I wanted to draw you close enough to have a chance to tell you the truth, to convince you . . . I need help." Jon's voice trailed off. "Desperate times mean desperate measures." He leaned forward, extending a gloved hand. "Will you come with me, Bailey, and mend the abyss?"

How could she not? She took his hand reluctantly. "All right. But if you're lying to me, Jonnard, there'll be hell to pay."

He laughed as he pulled her up on horseback. "How could I doubt that?"

The thing was as gruesome as she'd heard. It made her sick to look at it. Jonnard reined to a halt, putting away his crystal, and dismounting. He put his hands to her waist and helped her down as well. They'd ridden and Crystaled, so she knew they'd come a distance, but she also had a good idea where they must be.

"What do we do?"

"We get as close as we dare," Jonnard said. He took her hand reassuringly. "You'll feel it, Bailey, it has an energy all its own. It'll fill you as much as you let it."

Bailey took a step closer, but Jonnard's hand was tight on her and pulled her even nearer. Then, his other hand whipped out and he began tracing his crystal through the air. She saw lines of light falling about her, caging her, disappearing almost before she even realized she saw them. Her feet froze to the ground. Her arms would not work. She looked at Jonnard, stricken. Words failed her.

"Yes," he said. "It is a trap. I have you where I want you." He ran a gloved finger through a strand of hair that had fallen loose across her forehead. "If he doesn't come in time, then the bones will take you, and you'll still be mine. If he comes in time, then I'll have him. Either way, it's a win-win for me."

He hesitated, his fingers on her cheek. "Of course, it doesn't have to be that way. I have been watching you grow. Blossom. I can wait for you a little longer, if I knew you would join with me."

She glared at him. "You must be crazy!"

Jon sighed sadly. "Not yet. Although that day is probably coming. I take it your answer is no."

He traced his hand across her mouth then. "One scream I'll give you, then silence." Jonnard smiled thinly.

It burst from her throat. She heard it ring through the air and through her crystal. "Jason! Help me please!" Then her mouth sealed shut and it was all she could do to even breathe. The ground began to sink under her feet as the abyss yawned wider to swallow her.

Jon backed away from her slowly, still smiling, swung aboard his horse and began to ride away. She saw him pull it into shadow and sit there to watch her, his pale face an oval moon, just out of reach.

She struggled. Every slight movement pulled the cage closer and tighter about her. She could feel hot tears of fear sliding down her face. She could sense the abyss aching for her and she thought her heart was going to jump right out of her chest.

Wolfjackals came. Their howling filled the air, joining in chorus with the howling of the Gate of Bones. Their green eyes caught the light, flashing, as they circled, tails lowered, teeth gleaming. Watching her, they came nearer and nearer. Bailey fought just to breathe. Swallowed by the abyss or torn by wolfjackals? What was her fate?

A wolfjackal broke away from the pack, all silvery and black, with a white throat. It paced near, nostrils flared, sniffing, voice in a low warning snarl. Then it reached for her hand with ivory fangs. Closed its mouth upon her wrist, gently, and pulled. A second wolfjackal trotted up, licked her other hand, its tongue hot as flame, grasped her in its massive jaws and pulled as well.

Their gentle tugs did not move her, and the wolfjackals whined anxiously. They milled around, talking to one another in low growls and yips. Two or three pawed at her boots, digging, and then yelped as the shadow and fog rolling out of the Gate touched them.

Jonnard raised his arm. He spoke a harsh word, and whipped the air with crystal Fire, lashing the pack with ropes of power. They snapped at him, backed away, tails down, eyes slitted. Then the leader gave a yipping howl as the pack formed about him, and they raced off.

Bailey knew something important had happened, but she was not quite sure what. She took a very careful, long slow breath, as if sipping the air, for it was the only way she could breathe now, as the cage of power tightened again, and the abyss began to pull her feet out from under her.

Jason! Anyone, please!

Tomaz frowned over the scroll. "It doesn't mean we've lost Renart, only that Renart is lost."

"We should have given him Snowheart. A crystal. Anything he could have relied on if there were trouble." Gavan paced back and forth. Henry, Trent, and Jason watched.

"I think we don't give him enough credit," Henry said, pulling his glasses into place.

The two men stopped arguing.

"I mean," Henry said apologetically. "He's done a lot of trading. You should hear his stories about caravanning through flash floods, and clan wars, and stuff. He's a resourceful guy."

Gavan flicked the edge of his cape back. "True enough." He took a deep breath. "Pyra will undoubtedly be scouting the area."

"Undoubtedly."

"She could use help."

Tomaz nodded. "I'll offer."

"All right. And the rest of you. We're going to have to watch each other's backs from here on, carefully. The attacks are spreading. We have to be a target, sooner or later. Stay close. No one wander off."

Doing laundry could hardly be called wandering off, Jason told Trent, as they hiked down to the pool. "Although if you wear those jeans one more day, I think they could stand on their own."

"Hey, hey! These are vintage jeans. Holes and all."

"Henry's offered to buy you new ones."

"They take time to break in." Trent's expression looked serious. "Do you think I want to wear stiff, scratchy new denim? Give me soft, old, worn denim any day!"

"I think you just don't want to let go."

"Maybe not. Just like Bailey wears that old watch of hers, even though it's never kept time here." Trent dumped his bag on a rock ledge. "Looks like Ting beat us down here."

Ting rounded the water, a muddy smear across her nose, and a full pouch of greenery bulging on one hip. "Either of you seen Bailey?"

"No. Better watch yourself going in, Gavan's put the word out no one is to go off alone."

"Too little too late, I think." Ting stood on one foot and then the other. "I can't find Bailey."

Jason dropped his laundry bag next to Trent's. "Leave that, we'll find her, you go on."

"Okay. Don't get her in trouble, all right? We're gathering Rich's potion stuff for him. She said she'd go downriver."

"Understood. I'll give you a holler when we find her."

Trent matched Jason's long strides down the stream. "Think she's in trouble? Fell in or something?"

"Bailey is so stubborn if she fell in, she'd float upstream. She just got involved, probably. Or Lacey ran off again." They ducked under the cooling overhang of the forest's edge. Trent picked out a fresh boot print in the soft shore of the river. "She went this way."

They had gotten deep into the forest when the shout hit Jason and drove him to his knees. He doubled over, gasping with Bailey's pain and terror.

"Jason! Jeez, man, what is it?"

"Trouble. Big trouble." He grabbed Trent's hand and Crystaled without warning or thinking. Cold *between* rushed past them both.

He felt it the moment they touched ground. He jumped to his feet, still linked with Trent. Bailey's mouth opened in a silent scream and she reached for them as the Bone Gate roared wide open behind her. He could feel its pull, its yearning for him, for her, for Trent.

"She's caged!" Trent yelled over the moaning and wailing of the Gate.

"Show me!"

He reached for Bailey, tracing the bonds that held her, and Jason's crystal flared about his neck as he grabbed her hand and held on. The Gate pulled her and she hung in the air between them. He cut her loose strand by strand, but the Gate sucked all three in. Bones crackled underfoot and he gagged at the stench of rotting things. It glowed as if it could feed off them, its darkness lightening to the color of gangrene.

"Don't. Let. Go." Bailey mouthed to them.

"Hang on!" Jason yelled at her. He dug in his heels. The Gate promised him things, whispering in his ear of undying life, power. He wanted nothing but the three of them out and safe.

Trent cried out, "That's the last rope!"

Jason lifted his hand, crystal Fire streaming from his fingers, the pendant on his chest so hot it felt as if it could burn through his shirt.

And then they had her, pulling her toward them, out of the abyss, out of the Gate of Bones, and it wailed in frustration and grief at losing its prey.

44

Frying Pans and Fire

WHAT WERE YOU thinking?" Rebecca waved a
hand. "If we had a dungeon, I'd throw you in it for a
few days." She paced in front of the girls. Bailey opened her
mouth, and her mother jabbed a finger in the air. "I'm not
done talking, young lady!"

Gavan said aside to Tomaz, "I'd punish them myself,
but I think a mother's wrath is probably worse." Tomaz
chuckled, his hand covering his face. Both men cleared
their throats and quieted when Rebecca gave them a look
as well.

She swung back on Ting and Bailey. "I could have—we
could have—lost you. There's no excuse for going off alone.
Latrine duty for a month. Darning duty. Laundry duty."

Bailey shuffled her feet. Finally, spent, Rebecca dropped
her hands, eyes red, and she said, "Don't ever, ever, ever do
that again!"

"Yes, ma'am," both girls echoed each other.

Rebecca gathered them up in a massive hug, hiding her
face against them for a moment. Tomaz stirred, and dropped
a leather gathering pouch in Bailey's lap. It fell open, to reveal not only the harvest of thane grass, but a tightly curled

up furball who woke from sleep long enough to twitch her tufted tail. Bailey beamed at Tomaz, and hugged the pouch to her chest.

Gavan waited respectfully for a few minutes before saying quietly, "Be that as it may. We need to know what you can tell us. All three of you."

Rebecca let go, retreating to the corner, where Madame Qi sat, her back straight, her face lined not only with her age but great worry. She took Rebecca's hand and held it for a few moments.

Bailey said defensively, "He told me the abyss was caused by our Magick warring, like what happened between Gregory and Brennard. He said we were all creating it, and it would take two of us, one from each side, to heal it. That's why I went."

"Did you not think of who he was?"

"Of course I did!" Bailey looked up defiantly. "But if something could be done, we'd do it, wouldn't we? We'd do what we could to stop that thing. I thought he meant what he said. Even if he didn't mean to heal it, he could still be right."

Gavan leaned on his cane, wolfhead gleaming. Bailey looked at it and thought of the wolfjackals. "Even the wolfjackals are afraid of it."

Tomaz took a step forward. "You saw them?"

"A pack. They ran in, and circled me."

"Chaos draws them, we know that. They need it."

She shook her head at Tomaz. "It wasn't like that. I thought I was going to die, one way or the other. But then, one of them crept close and took my hand and tried to pull me free. A few of the others came to help. They dug at my boots, but nothing they did could move me. Jonnard drove them away."

Tomaz inclined his head slowly. "They are not tied to the Dark Hand, though they serve it sometimes. They are like what they sprang from, Chaos. I can't predict them."

"Sounds like they were just saving dinner, to me." Trent waved a hand.

Gavan faced him. "What did you feel?"

"Jonnard had her all spun up. It took us a bit to cut her free. The thing itself—" He shrugged, his face tightening. "It is like a nasty pit of slime. I can't explain it better than that."

"Negative energy?"

"The most negative energy I could imagine." Trent crossed his arms over his chest, as if protecting himself.

"Jason?"

Jason had been studying the floor, listening. He looked up. "It's definitely a Gate. How it opened, I don't know, but it knew me, knew my powers." He rubbed his hands together lightly.

"Could Jonnard have spoken truly?"

Jason shifted uneasily. "There's a lot I don't know about Gates, but I don't think so. I do know, it's opening still. It's devouring. It could take everything with it and still be hungry." *And it wanted him. It wanted him the most.*

"Could you close it?" Gavan looked him in the eyes, and Jason met it, unflinching.

"Maybe."

"Did you Open it? Somehow, without knowing?"

Jason shook his head violently. "Never! Not something like that!"

"I had to ask."

"Did you?" He stared back, and after a moment, Gavan did look away.

Rich took out his flask and took a drink, shuddered, and capped it, putting it away. "What do we do now? Is anybody but me bothered that the only one who heard Bailey through the crystal was Jason?" He swept his red hair from his forehead. "Has Jonnard got that kind of power?"

Gavan cursed. Words spilled from his mouth that would have made Shakespeare blush, and he stamped his cane into the floor, driving a dent into the wooden boards. "Is this true? No one else heard?" He pointed the cane at all of them, sweeping about the room.

Trent spread his hands. "I'm deaf to those things, I never hear anyone."

"N-not a thing," answered Henry. He took his glasses off, cleaned them, and set them back on.

Everyone else just shook their heads.

Tomaz tapped his fingers on his silver-and-turquoise belt. "If he had that kind of power to tap, we wouldn't be in this struggle. We'd have been swept away already."

"Maybe he's just learning. Maybe the Gate feeds him."

"If it does, then we've no choice but to do everything

we can to stop him, and close the Gate." Gavan stamped his cane again. "We can't afford any weaknesses if we're going to strike at the Dark Hand." He pointed at the boys one by one. "Search party. Ting and Bailey will hold the academy."

"What are we looking for?"

"Renart. Safety. An answer to the Gate of Bones. Whatever it takes," Gavan answered.

The academy went deathly quiet after the search party left. Ting dragged her feet as they started their chores and finally Bailey nudged her, hard. "We got off easy."

"Maybe. But at least you got to do something, even if it was wrong." Ting sighed. "I feel absolutely useless."

"Don't. I think that's why Jonnard keeps failing. He's picking on us one at a time. Henry. Stefan. Jason. But we're more than that, we're all of us. You can't bring us down one at a time."

Ting considered her. "I don't know. Maybe you're right, maybe not."

Bailey hugged her. "Of course I am! I'm always right except when I'm wrong."

Ting laughed in spite of herself. She pushed Bailey away gently, about to say something else, when the academy lanterns flickered. One by one, the crystals dimmed to the lowest of lights and even though the sun shone outside, the great building grew dark.

From upstairs came a shriek. "Death! Death and disaster! Banshees!"

FireAnn appeared at the top of the stairs, her hair unbound, red-and-silver curls wild about her head, her hands upraised. "The banshees come!" Cackling, she tottered down the stairs, grasping the banister for dear life.

"Jonnard's back!" Bailey swung around wildly, dashing to the front door to drop the guard bolts in place.

Madame Qi came out of the kitchen, the wooden spoon she was holding fragrant with the aroma of Rich's potion, its sweetness permeating the air. "Something is here." She gestured. "Feel it, Ting?"

"I've felt it before," Ting answered slowly. "It's settled over the whole place."

"Demon."

"Banshee!" FireAnn reached the landing and grabbed for Bailey. "Protect Eleanora! Go to her, lass!"

Bailey unwrapped FireAnn's twisted hands from her arm carefully, saying, "Stay here." She took the stairs two at a time, leaping upward to the third floor where Eleanora rested. The door was thrown open, and a coverlet lay on the floor. Eleanora swayed by the side of her father's coffin. She turned to Bailey.

"It's come for Father."

"What has?"

"I'm not sure. Can you feel it?"

Bailey spun on one heel. Defeated, she shook her head.

From the doorway, Ting said quietly, "I can. It's dampening everything. I can't reach Gavan or Jason or anyone."

"It's Jonnard!"

"No," breathed Eleanora. "It's not Jonnard." She looked up. "It's not one of us, it's something beyond."

"We need to get out." Bailey took Ting's and Eleanora's hands, pulling them from the room.

"Gregory!"

Freyah burst in. "Get her away from here." Her voice snapped briskly. "I'm staying with him. I've kept him this long, I can keep him a bit longer."

Bailey looked at the sarcophagus and the feisty silver-haired woman as she sat on it, and crossed her arms. "I think he's probably as safe as he's gonna get. Come on!"

She and Ting had to draw Eleanora with them. Still weakened, she struggled gamely to keep up with the girls, her breathing growing ragged. Madame Qi and Rebecca were trying to soothe FireAnn as they arrived downstairs.

"Is it an attack?"

"Only one way to tell. I'm taking a look." Bailey took a deep breath, stepping to the front door. She unbolted it, then drew it back. Or tried to. The door stayed firmly shut in its frame. She braced her heels, pulling on the handle with all of her might. It wouldn't open.

"Kitchen door." Ting raced Bailey to the side door, reaching it first. She tried to yank it open, and nearly fell, as it refused to yield.

Every window in the kitchen refused to open as if hammered close. She and Bailey rounded the big room, pounding on the frames.

They tried every exit they could think of, one by one. The academy stayed shut. They returned to the others.

"We're locked in."

"Is it the Gate? What's happened to the others?"

Bailey shook her head. "I don't know." She shivered. "I don't know!"

Madame Qi drew herself up. "My grandfather fought demons," she said. She looked at Ting. Ting swallowed. She opened her hand and looked at her palm. The fiery red dragon mark seemed to wink at her.

"This may be our only way out." She traced the mark.

A hot wind swept the room, filling it. Ting jumped back, startled, her hair streaming behind her. FireAnn fell to the floor weeping in fear, and Eleanora went to her knees to comfort her. As Ting and Bailey stared, a fiery ring opened up, like a great eye.

"Go," urged Madame Qi. "Hurry!"

Ting gulped. She tugged on Bailey. "After you!"

45

Pearls of Wisdom

"ARE YOU SURE this is the darkest time?" Bailey asked, wrinkling her nose. "I mean, it's desperate all right, but somehow things always turn out and I really wonder if one bad Gate a day isn't enough—"

"If you don't move, I'm going to kick you in the rump myself," Ting said firmly. "Now go!"

"Jeez. When did you get so bossy?"

"Since . . . since I met you! Now move!" Ting waved her arms wildly, startling Bailey into jumping through the fiery aperture, Ting on her heels. The fire ring hung in midair a moment with the roar of flames, then disappeared.

Instantly, the world changed. The silence of Haven disappeared and they could hear the once familiar sounds of auto traffic, the buzz of electricity in the air, the drone of an airplane passing by, although all seemed muffled in silvery fog. From far away, a foghorn sounded forlornly.

"Where are we?"

"Home, I think." Ting brushed her hair from one eye, looking about. "Grandmother's home, that is. I think we're in San Francisco."

"So it really is foggy." Bailey peered through the soft,

billowing ground-hugging clouds, unable to see almost anything except Ting as she flashed an embarrassed smile.

"Only sometimes. I like it, though." Ting took a deep breath. For a moment, all her troubles seemed to drop away. "The funny thing is, if you're on one of the hills, often only some areas have fog. It's like part of the city is gift-wrapped. I like to sit in Grandmother's courtyard and watch it drape the house." Ting tilted her face up. She took a few steps forward across short-trimmed grass that was as wet with the fog as heavy rain, her shoes making whispery sounds as she crossed it. "Bailey," she said softly. "I *am* home. Look." And she pointed at the house beginning to emerge, walkway by corner by roof eave from the silvery fog, and the proud enamel red Chinese dragon gracing its roof tiles.

Bailey looked up. "So you think your great grandfather really enchanted that."

"It seems logical. It could be our only help now. I have to bring it back!"

Bailey stared at her friend. "Nothing about Magick is logical. It's all wondrously improbable but possible. So. How do we get this dragon down? Climb a rain gutter?"

"I was thinking garden ladder."

"What if someone sees us?"

"That," Ting said solemnly, "is an excellent question, and I have no idea. Family still lives here, but I'm not sure I want to wake anyone up. I think it's early morning."

"Very early." Bailey stumbled. "Streetlights are still on, if anyone can see them. Note to self: try not to walk into one, they are tall and solid and hurt." She rubbed her kneecap ruefully. "Where is that ladder?"

"This way." Ting slipped through a side courtyard, opening the gate latch as quietly as she could, and guiding Bailey past a koi pond where brightly colored fish slithered lazily through the water, themselves looking as if they were only half awake.

"No alarms?"

"We've never needed any." Ting looked guilty. "They might now, if we take the house dragon. I should leave them a note."

Bailey put a hand on the back of her wrist. "I think someone stealing it is probably enough of a hint."

"Oh. True."

Fog had barely filtered into the back courtyard, although its dampness dappled the flagstone and left rainlike drops on the many flowers and plants. Ting found the ladder and she and Bailey managed to somewhat quietly carry it to the mostly likely corner and place it. By silent agreement, Bailey held the foot of the ladder while Ting climbed up. It was, after all, her dragon.

The fog seemed to follow her up as she climbed. It curled about the ladder rung by rung until when she emerged, she could see the roof but not the street or anywhere else around. She stepped cautiously upon the red-clay tiles curving like ocean waves under her feet. The Chrysanthemum Dragon stayed motionless on its weather vane, facing her, metalwork even more beautiful and fantastical than she'd always seen from the ground.

The long and sinuous body of a Chinese dragon was accented by the large head with wire whiskers, and a curling tail. It ran on three feet, the fourth one curled with a reaching step, as though the artisan had caught the dragon in a gallop or perhaps frisking through midair. The vane was made to turn in the wind, but she had never seen it do more than circle gracefully no matter how forceful the breeze, as though it was beyond a dragon's dignity to whirl crazily about. Up close, she could tell it was half as long as she was tall, or maybe even slightly bigger than that. She hoped it wasn't too heavy for her to carry, at least as far as the ladder and Bailey's aid.

She reached it in three more cautious steps. It slowly swung about to face her, although she couldn't feel a breeze. The fog did not stir at all.

She put her hand on it. "We need you," she explained, "at Haven. I need you, and Grandmother Qi, and Eleanora and Freyah and FireAnn. I know it's been your job to guard here, but I'm hoping you'll come with me, at least for a little while."

The enameled metal felt warm to her touch, surprising her, for the San Francisco morning seemed very cold yet. She bent over, examining the structure. It appeared all she had to do was lift the dragon from its post, the one sleeve slipped into the other. The rest of the dragon would rotate and swing freely about the post. If she could lift it, that is. She reached down.

The dragon swung away.

Ting frowned. She moved into a better position and reached again to grasp and lift it. It spun in the other direction, coming about so quickly it knocked her off her feet. Ting ducked and dug her hands into the tiles suddenly afraid of slipping, as the dragon swung about.

"What are you doing up there?"

She could hear but not see Bailey. "I'm trying," she said, "to get it loose."

"I think somebody is awake down here. I hear a tea-kettle whistling."

That was the last thing she wanted to hear. Ting carefully stood up, balancing on the curved tiles. Did she remember a story her mother used to tell, about a workman come to paint the dragon once? A high wind spun it around and around, eluding every stroke of the paintbrush until he finally came down off the roof, ranting in rapid Chinese about demons and tricks and refused to do the work. Grandmother Qi finally hired an art student to enamel the vane, and he had sat patiently, day after day, doing a true craftsman's job and never once did the dragon move.

"Please," pleaded Ting. "I need your help!" She grasped the dragon along its spine with both hands and pulled up.

It snapped its head around with a hiss. "Ssssstaying!" As it exhaled, fire and smoke spewed out, swirling away into a huge ring, just like the one that had brought them there. Its free paw uncurled to swipe at her hand, and as it spun about, it knocked Ting clean off the roof toward the fiery portal. Her ears roared with the lick of flames, and as she flew past Bailey toward it, she reached out and caught her friend by the sleeve. Together they went tumbling through air and fire.

She landed on her back, Bailey across her legs. The impact hurt, as if she had fallen from the roof and she didn't move for a while. She wiggled a foot first. Then an arm. Nothing seemed to be broken, just squished.

"I can't believe it."

Bailey groaned and crawled off Ting's other leg, sitting up. "It didn't work."

"It wouldn't come. What did I do wrong?" Ting put her hand to her face in dismay and something fell out. She stared at the ground. A great opalescent pink pearl rolled to a stop near her knee, a delicate gold chain trailing behind it.

"Wow," breathed Bailey. "Where did that come from?"

"I don't know!" But she did. Ting sat up. The house dragon had had that front paw curled up tightly for decades since being cast. Had the pearl been in its clutch all that time? It must have been. She picked it up reverently. "This is great grandfather's pearl. It has to be!"

"The one you told me about? The one he wore?"

"I had the wrong dragon. This must be the one." Ting cupped the huge pearl, its colors swirled from creamy white to blushing pink. "He summoned it with this. Or this became it."

"Either way. What are you waiting for?" Bailey gave her a hand up.

"I don't know what I'm doing, that's what."

"That's never stopped me!" declared Bailey.

Ting laughed at her, wrinkling her nose a little, then looked down at the pearl in concentration. "I should ask Grandmother."

"But she'd never seen the pearl either, right?"

"No, just heard stories of it." Ting cradled the object. "If I focus on it, I should be able to tell if it has any Magick at all. Then we can figure out what to do."

"That sounds like a plan."

Ting felt the pearl warm in her hands, the gold chain dangling from it. It was not made as a showpiece of jewelry, although the object could be worth a king's ransom. It had been worn as a pendant, perhaps, or a talisman. She let her eyes and attention be drawn into its richness of color, the play of the opalescent sheen over it, the essence of the pearl itself, a seed of possibility held within an oyster once upon a time before being worn about the neck of her ancestor—

POOF!

Pink smoke exploded everywhere. "Holy moly!" Bailey jumped and let out a shriek. Magick slammed through her, knocking her off her feet and onto her duff. It had been that kind of day, she decided, and just sat where she was rather than get up again. When the smoke cleared, she began to laugh and looked around for Ting.

"Ting! Ting? Here's your dragon. Well, I think it's a dragon. I don't know if we can use it for a guardian, though. It . . . it's kinda small." Bailey got on her knees and looked at the beast, Chinese in every aspect, like the weather vane creature, but this one was a blushing pink from tiny whiskers to sinuous tail. "It's not really a dragon, I think. About the size of your average cat. Smallish."

"I know," said Ting, very muffled.

"Where are you? Come see this. It seems a little . . . frightened." Bailey looked about, bewildered, then held a finger out to the dragon. It hissed. "Heh. It's spunky, though. Okay, I can't call anything this small a dragon. I mean, it's like . . . garden-sized. It would get lost in a hedge. That's it. There's hedge wizards. This is a hedgedragon."

Ting sighed. The hedgedragon let out a long, corresponding steamy *sssssssss*.

Bailey peered at it. It stared back at her, whiskers drooping.

"Oh, no." She leaned down. "Ting?"

The hedgedragon sniffled.

"Oh. My."

46

Face-to-Face

I'M NOT RESPONSIBLE for this mess."

Hedgedragon and Magicker stared at each other. The beast wiggled its nose, fine kitteny whiskers waving as it sniffled again. A big golden tear formed on a lower eyelid and ran down the delicately scaled face. "Okay, okay." Bailey reached out and gathered the hedgedragon into a hug. "We'll do something. I don't know what, but something." The pearl bumped against her chin. The hedgedragon now wore the object around its neck. Her neck. The dragon was Ting. "You'll change back."

"But when?" Ting's voice sounded very, very far away, and wrapped in tissue paper. "We have to do something *now.*"

Bailey looked around, having been far too busy and bewildered to note where they had returned. They sat in the academy courtyard. "At least we're outside," she pointed out.

"I don't think I can face any demons like this!" And the hedgedragon wailed pitifully. Not only was it a pitiful sound, but a pretty poor attempt at wailing, Bailey thought. It was more like a squeaky yodel. She reached down and scratched the hedgedragon's floppy ear to comfort her.

"Oooh," murmured Ting. "That feels *good*. No wonder cats like it." Her eyes closed to slits.

Bailey looked up. And up. She stopped scratching, saying in a distracted voice, "That's good. I'll do more later. After."

"After what?"

"After we find out what that is." Bailey stretched an arm out, pointing at the huge apparition that stood over the academy, vaguely man-shaped, draped in body armor, with a helmet on, reminding Bailey of an ancient warrior knight or maybe a shogun. She thought of standing, and decided it wouldn't make her tall enough to make any difference, nor would getting to her feet help running away any. She touched her crystal, but it remained cold and mute. "We're face-to-face . . . um . . . snout . . . with the demon."

The hedgedragon turned about in Bailey's lap and then froze. A string of sounds burst from her that sounded Chinese, although Bailey had never really heard Ting speak it. She didn't know if Ting even actually knew Chinese. The hedgedragon put up a curled paw, then flexed it, and talons snapped out, like a cat putting out claws. It might have been impressive if the hedgedragon was anywhere near the size of the other.

The thing leaned down to peer at them. "Who are you?" it said, the man's voice as thin and hard to describe as the wind. "You who throw ancient curses at me?"

"I am Ting!"

"You guard this house and all who dwell inside?"

"I do!" The hedgedragon punctuated that with another few words in Chinese.

"Do you know who I am?"

The hedgedragon let out a low hiss. Stalling, Bailey thought, or bluffing. Ting whipped her curling tail about, looking fierce. "Is that wise?" Bailey asked in a low whisper.

"I protect," Ting declared, "what is mine."

"As do I." The being, which had been leaning over peering at them, now stood and stretched. It raised its arms and looked as if it could hold up the sky with them even as insubstantial a ghost as it seemed to be. "This is mine." With a gesture, the being indicated everywhere about them. Its eyes gazed down at them again to see if they understood.

A terrible idea struck Bailey. She pulled on one of Ting's wings to get her attention. "Ting. Ting, I think that's—"

The hedgedragon let out a boiling hiss of warning as the being reached toward them. It paused, and its body moved as if it might have been shaking with laughter, though not a sound reached them.

"Ting, do you think that could be—"

The hedgedragon swung her tail around, whapping Bailey right in the mouth. "Ow!" Startled, she put her hand to her lips.

Ting put her ears flat, and uncurled all her talons, arching her back. "Touch us if you dare."

"A dragon is a dragon is a dragon, it seems." The hand that had begun to extend downward withdrew.

"A pact is a pact. We are both guardians in this place."

"So you know me, then."

"I do. You take from all so that you can protect all."

"A balance is reached."

Ting's whiskers wiggled. Her ears flicked up alertly. "You've overstepped here."

The being crossed his arms. "You mistake my powers, small dragon. I take a little, to guard a little, to guide. That is all I can do now." It made a sad noise, like waves crashing upon a seashore, and then withdrawing. "The one who takes much now lies inside, asleep."

"Gregory!" muttered Bailey, then immediately clapped her hands over her face again, wary of the hedgedragon's snappy tail.

"It is disturbed. There is much imbalance here," and the being looked across the valley, toward the faraway hills and the Dark Hand's fortress. "I have calmed the sleeper, but know this. We are entangled, he and I, from centuries ago when we walked together in this land, and we learned much from each other. He draws from you to live, as I draw from my people to stay in this existence, and we learned this together. There is nothing that exists without balance or it ceases altogether." It inhaled, a great sucking in of air, and the very forest moved and shivered with it. "He tried to awaken, but there is not enough power he can draw to do so without harming you. He wanted to defend you against that which has opened, but he is helpless. As I am helpless."

Ting made a sound in her throat.

"You are not helpless. Yet. Time is running out . . ." The apparition began to grow wispy and shred, like an insubstantial cloud on a windy day, and then it was gone.

Bailey leaped to her feet, dumping the hedgedragon to the ground. "That," she said, "was the Warlord Spirit!"

Ting shook herself off, scales making a fine, chiming noise. "I know."

"You knew?"

"Inside me. Something dragonisssssh."

Bailey's crystal bracelet began to warm, very slightly. She sighed in relief. "It's coming back."

"Good. I think." Ting scrubbed a paw at her whiskered snout. "I can't go in like this. I can't!"

A roar sounded from the Iron Mountains, a roar that carried the scent of hot copper and magic with it. Bailey cringed. "We may not have to. I think we've been summoned."

47

Dragons and Dungeons

"EXPLAIN TO ME AGAIN why I'm carrying you up this mountain."

"Becausssse," hissed Ting, "I hafffft to meet Jason's dragon to find out what'ssss going on."

"No, no. I've got that part," Bailey said, as she shifted the hedgedragon from arm to arm. "I meant, why do I have to *carry* you. You may be as small as the average cat, but you weigh as much as a big dog. Why aren't you flying? Dragons do fly, don't they?"

The hedgedragon ruffled its wings, then said sadly, "I don't know howwwww."

"Oh, sure, like that's a good excuse that's gonna hold. I think I'll try that at home. I don't know how to make my bed or wash the dishes. How long is that going to work, hmmmm?" A little out of breath, Bailey paused, swapping Ting from side to side again, as climbing took all her attention. For long moments she clambered up the side of the Iron Mountain until she reached a plateau.

Ting let out a hissing sigh. "Do you think this is easssssy?"

"Look, sister, I don't know how you cut it, but being carried up this mountain has got to be easier than climbing it one-handed with a heavy reptile in the other!" Bailey put the hedgedragon down. "All right, call up the big guy."

The hedgedragon curled up and ducked its head inside its wings. "Don't want to," Ting said sulkily.

Bailey looked around. Besides the slope they had climbed, leading down to the academy and the pool of water of the small valley, and the grove, the other side of the plateau had a steep drop-off. "I wonder how dragons learn to fly," she observed. "I wonder if they have that 'kicked out of the nest' first lesson, like falling off the side of a cliff." She leaned her head to look off the steep side, then looked back at Ting.

"Nooooo!" The hedgedragon scuttled away from her, and Ting's words evaporated into high-pitched dragon squeals.

"Oh, jeez, I was just kidding. Lighten up, Ting. This isn't easy for anybody. It's not every day your best friend turns into a dragon, you know?" Bailey sat down and crossed her legs, and made a coaxing sound like she made to Lacey whenever the pack rat was being stubborn.

A great shadow fell over the two of them. "Well. And well, well. I didn't believe it when I sensed it."

Jason's dragon hunkered down on his forelegs, and looked the two of them over curiously. "Yet, here you are. We don't have a cutoff to qualify for dragons, but if we did, I'm not sure you'd make it." The large beast rumbled in gentle laughter.

"Both of you!" Ting huffed and puffed, and a tiny bit of blue-gray smoke came out her nostrils. "Ewwww! That ssstings."

"What is it you called her?"

"A hedgedragon," said Bailey firmly.

"Yes, indeed. Most appropriate, I think." The dragon put out a claw to poke Ting. "I am not an expert, but I think it could grow to some size, given enough time."

"I'm . . . sssstuck like thissss?" Ting curled up again, wings over her whiskered face, and wailed.

"No, no, little one. And do show some dragon dignity. We do not wail in public. Or," the dragon coughed. "Ever." He shook himself. "You'll return to yourself when ready. With enough lessons, you'll become adept at going back and forth."

"Like Stefan-bear!"

"Yes, well, rather like that, although one hopes with a bit more aplomb and less angst."

"Whatever." Bailey reached out and gathered up Ting, scratching behind one scaly ear. "See?"

"Will I fly?"

"Eventually. Think of it as swimming, that will help." Jason's dragon pulled back to sit on his haunches. "You have a great deal to learn about yourself, young Ting."

"So it seemsssss." Ting rested her chin on Bailey's shoulder.

"Let me say this. A guardian's ability is not always in its size or its fierceness. You learned that earlier, however, did you not?" The dragon looked her over. "I think you'll do."

"I will?"

"Let us hope. Now off with you two." Jason's dragon curved his talon and gave Bailey a nudge back the way they had come.

"But—but . . . we're not done," Bailey spluttered.

"Of course you are."

"We have more questions."

"But I," the dragon intoned deeply, bass voice rolling out of his chest, "have no more answers."

"One more, one more, pleassssse!" Ting fluttered anxiously.

"Perhaps one."

"How do I change back?"

"By the pearl, naturally, although why you would want to, I can't begin to guess. Being a dragon is so much better."

"But I'm not a dragon."

"Only sometimes. One last word of advice. Never eat a friend. It can cause all sorts of disconcerting trouble you can't imagine, and simply isn't worth it."

Bailey paled. Ting dipped her head saying, "I'll remember."

"Now off with you. There is some worrying going on downhill, and you've some explaining to do."

Bailey picked Ting up. Both of them called out thank yous to the dragon, even as it lay back and melded into the great mountains, its brilliant red-orange color dulling until it became one with its background and they could not tell where the dragon ended and the mountain began.

As for the dungeon, Bailey expected they were both going to end up in one after all, for the trouble they'd put everyone through.

Freyah was stunned when they told her about Gregory. They finally went upstairs to tell her, after watching Ting POOF in and out of dragon form a few times, to everyone else's amazement and delight. She grew tired of it, though, and hungry.

The hedgedragon beat Lacey to a cricket and gobbled it up. Then, POOF! As the pink smoke cleared, Ting put her hand to her stomach. "I can't believe I did that! Ew! Bailey! You let me eat a bug."

"Not only did you eat it, but you beat a famished pack rat to it. There was no one here going to stop you." Bailey coaxed Lacey over and gave the little rodent a bit of very stale biscuit.

"Grandfather used to carry a sign with him," Madame Qi said. "It read, Don't Feed the Dragon. He kept it for many, many years after he retired. I used to ask him why. He told me, it was a reminder that the dragon must feed him, not he the dragon. It was a matter of discipline and control. You may be very wise to remember that, Ting, and not feed as the dragon lest its instincts overcome your own."

"That sounds like a good idea. Plus, I'm not sure I can handle any weird meals."

Bailey glanced at Ting. "Are you stable now?"

"Stable?"

"No more POOFing?"

"I hope so."

"Good." Bailey looked upstairs. "We need to talk to her."

Freyah had moved to a chair, sitting near the sarcophagus, knitting needles and something made of fluffy yarn in her lap, with George patiently at her side holding the ball of yarn on his tray. "I can't believe my brother would draw on us like that, jeopardize all of us."

"I don't think he meant to. From what I can tell, he absorbed most of the explosive energy of the war between himself and Brennard. He expended that, keeping everyone safe, but it left him no reserves. You've been keeping him alive and asleep, Aunt Freyah, ever since. Now he feels the imbalance, the jeopardy, and wanted to awaken to help, but he needs that energy back just to do it." Ting held her hands like scales. "Energy in, energy out, energy in. He had to draw from us and yet, when he realized it could damage us all, he couldn't stop. The Warlord felt the imbalance and stepped in. He can't awaken yet. We just don't have the input to give him."

"That makes sense, in the magickal equation, for our side." Freyah told her. "And it seems the Warlord's Spirit has been tapping all of us a little, capping our abilities, to keep his own world in balance, but he's failed with the Dark Hand."

"There's nobody to stop the Dark Hand but us, and I'm not so sure about us." Bailey rubbed her eyes in worry.

Freyah started knitting again, needles clicking quickly. "Sometimes great sacrifices have to be made." Smiling wistfully, her gaze fell on her brother's motionless face and stayed there.

The girls left quietly.

The search party came home in the middle of the night. While they ate and rested, Stef wouldn't be satisfied till Ting had POOFed for him in and out of hedgedragon form at least three times. His hand wrapped about a huge sandwich, which he then consumed in three bites, he managed to say, "Wow. Does that hurt? It does me, sometimes. Not like they show werewolves in movies or anything, but my bones and muscles ache."

"I get heartburn." Ting coughed, and a little puff of pink smoke came out. She blinked in surprise.

Trent and Stefan nearly fell down laughing, and she shrank back, her mouth in a small pout.

"Be that as it may, we had as busy a day as you did."

"Did you find Renart?"

"Possibly. Packs of wolfjackals are roaming the countryside. We've identified at least three. Some attacks have been quite hostile, and some are merely coming in after bone fiends, as we know wolfjackals will do. Renart appears to be one step ahead of one of the packs. As Henry said, give him credit. He seems to be quite resourceful and hmmm . . ." Gavan grinned tiredly. "Fleet."

"So we have much hope in him yet," Tomaz added. He stood. "I'll see you all in the morning."

Slowly, they all drew away. Bailey and Ting went up the stairs last. At the top, Bailey turned around and looked down.

"What is it?"

"Did you ever look at something and realize it'll never be the same again?"

She'd felt that in the moments she stood in the fog. She nodded solemnly. They hooked arms together.

"Things change. They always do."

"Sometimes they change too fast."

48

A Helping Hand

"IF A TRAP WON'T work," Isabella mused, "then perhaps the direct approach."

"You would recommend what?" Jonnard sat, charging a handful of crystals on the table in front of him, their gemstone transparency gleaming with an inner fire, bursting with the power he put into them. Eyes still dazzled a bit, he narrowed them as she caught his attention.

"I think we need to talk to the Council. Convince them we can be quite helpful."

"I'm not following you, Isabella."

"That, my son, is why I still lead." She rose. "Get a carriage ready. We have a trip to make. Naria, I believe, before the storms move in and the roads get muddy. I don't know how long it will take these people to make a decision and do something, so we had better make haste now."

Jonnard swept up his crystals and pocketed them in his cape, his mouth twisted in a swallowed word. His failure with Bailey and Jason had not earned him any respect from her. The day would come. Soon.

* * *

"Rich doesn't look good again."

"Did he take his medicine?"

"Yup." Stefan shifted his weight uncomfortably. "I think we should take him to see Kektl. I know you think it's 'cause I want to see Beryl, and I do, but that's not it."

"I know it's not," said Gavan, not unkindly. "Let me take a look at him." He let Stef lead the way, noting that despite his lumbering size, the young man had developed a kind of grace. Most certainly his body had gone to muscle now, instead of just largeness, and it was obvious the sword work had done him a lot of good.

Rich huddled on his cot, covered with all of his blankets and most of Stefan's. Still, he shivered and shook, and a cold film pooled over his forehead. Gavan let out a deep breath. "All right, then. You take Rich. I'll get Jason and let the others know, and we're off."

Rich rolled an eye at them. "I'll be fine. Really. Once the Ice Age goes away."

Stef pulled him out of bed and hoisted him over his shoulders. "Nice sense of humor. Don't give up your day job."

"Shivering *is* my day job."

Jason joined them outside. "He's really that sick?"

"I don't know. Yes, he's feeling badly, but if it's the blackmarrow or if he's picked up something, I can't tell. It's a new world, we could all be exposed to something we have no immunity to."

"Oh, joy," Rich mumbled from somewhere around Stef's armpit. "A hypochondriac's paradise."

"Then you should be happy."

"I'm giving it up," he said. "It takes too much of my time." He stopped talking to shiver and groan as Gavan took them *between*.

Kektl looked a little startled as they all appeared before the outer doorway of his home and practice. He looked up from the leg and ankle of his young patient, eyes widened at the sight of Rich, and motioned to them. "Please. I won't make you wait long."

Stef rolled Rich onto a chair. He promptly drew his knees up under his chin and tucked all the blankets he had brought with him around himself. The young lad Kektl bandaged shot him a wide-eyed look.

"I had ten stitches," the boy told Rich. "I didn't cry once."

"I cry all the time," Rich fired back. "It gets me attention."

The boy edged away, drawing a curt word from Kektl who calmly straightened his bandaging out and then finished. To Rich, he said, "Don't tease the lad."

"Right. I'm sorry." Rich sat up, shedding his blankets. "That was pretty brave, actually. And keep it clean!" He called after the lad who sprinted away as soon as Kektl said, "You're finished."

The healer washed his hands in a minty smelling basin, then came over. "Let's have a look at you."

Anticipating the question, Rich muttered, "Yes, I've been taking my medicine." His teeth chattered and he gritted them between every word.

"How much and how often?"

"Four times a day. A swig from the flask."

Kektl pursed his lips critically. "Actually, I told you three. Four if three didn't work, and I said to take a ladling spoonful. A swig can be more or less, and in your case," Kektl took Rich's hand in his and eyed the thumbnails and then looked at his eyelids. "I'd say you took even more than that. The good news is he's overmedicating."

"But he looks worse than ever," Gavan responded.

"Because thane grass is, in itself, a poison. That's why the doses have to be worked out and carefully administered. I'll give you a spoon, and I want it used." Kektl turned to a small, carved bureau, with legs like paws, opened a drawer, and fished out a flat-bottomed spoon with a hole in the handle. "I suggest you tie it to the flask. Three times a day, absolutely no more. Two times tomorrow and no more today at all. You need to work that out of your system."

"You're giving him a poison?"

"Thane grass is much milder, really an irritant, but it counteracts the blackmarrow. It's the best I can do, for now." Kektl smiled sympathetically. He went to the basin and washed his hands again. "How is everyone else?"

"Fine."

"That bite?"

"Clean and healing well." Gavan bent over and rubbed his ankle as if checking. He nodded. He dropped a few coins in the dish on the bureau provided for payment, and Kektl gave a deep bow.

"Would you care to stay the day and night?"

Stef looked hopeful, and his face fell as Gavan shook his head. "Much to do before winter sets in."

"I remember those days well." Kektl made a sign of gratitude, his six-fingered hand flashing gracefully. A commotion in the street outside drew everyone's attention.

Kektl bowed and went out to see who hailed him. He returned, a little drawn, and made another bow. "It is discovered you are here. The Council has sent for you. You may leave if you wish, but . . ."

"Council? Is that the same one that meets with the guidance of the Spirit?" Jason had been quietly watching, brought along only to help Gavan in case of fatigue, but the words went through him with a disturbing ripple.

Kektl nodded at him. He started to tell Gavan no, but the headmaster had already begun answering, "Perhaps we should meet them."

"I will tell them you'll be along, but you have a sick member who needs to remain in my care." Kektl glanced at Rich. "He should stay quiet for a while."

"All right. Then it's the three of us, and I suggest you two listen and learn."

Jason murmured a vague word of agreement. When the escort came for them, and took them to a great house, with tall arched doors, the sinking feeling of a dream come true hit him.

The Council stood in robes at the far end of the hall. Most of the finer details didn't match his foreboding at all, except a group of people waiting for them, and to the side stood Isabella and Jonnard. If he had felt better about that for a moment, it fled.

"We are here at the Council's behest," Isabella said. "Come to give them a helping hand, as it were. How fortunate to find you here today, although we've been here several days, in discussion. Troubles have beset our lands."

"And ours. Strange that the trouble seems to be quite close to your borders."

"It comes, brethren dear, from strikes made against us. I've told the Council of everything that falls between us. We're all agreed." She reached out and put her hands on the railing before her. "The warring must stop."

Stef made a low growl in his throat, only to find Gavan

striking his cane across his chest as if to hold him back from anything further. Gavan tilted his head toward the speaker of the Council. "Are you mediating, then?"

"We will if we have to, but we prefer you make your own terms with each other."

Gavan absorbed that. "Very well." He faced Isabella. "Close the Gate. It is an abomination."

"Of that, we're also agreed. However," and her glance flickered. "We didn't open it, so we have no control over it. There is only one we know of who can be called Gate-keeper." She looked past Gavan to Jason. "It is a Gate of the dead. The only thing that can close it is . . . a life."

Jason only half heard her. His dream played loudly in his mind, muting the sounds around him. He heard Gavan make an exclamation, then a denial, and then, with a flash of his hand, he Crystaled them out of there, before Jason could blink and Isabella's words could sink in.

Gavan paused at Kektl's to gather up Rich and then brought them home, so angry he said scarcely a word to anyone.

If it was a dream, it was a very bad one.

They gathered at the worktables, and Ting's quick fingers braided a thong for Rich's spoon and attached it to the flask while Jason related as much as he remembered of the Council meeting.

Trent frowned. His fingers drummed the table in agitation. "You couldn't have heard her right."

"Well, I'm baffled." Stef scrubbed a hand over the top of his head. "Isabella got snotty, Gavan got angry, and we got yanked out of there. That's all I know."

Jason's mouth drew tight. "Think about it, Stef. That Gate is rogue. It will take everything a Gatekeeper has to close it. Everything." He shoved away from the table and left them all sitting there.

Ting looked after the disappearing back of Jason, her forehead creasing in bewilderment. She swung around to Trent. "What is he talking about?"

Trent said nothing. He looked down at an invisible spot on the table and appeared to study it intently.

Stefan slapped his heavy hand over the imaginary target. "Come on, you know, so give it up!"

They traded looks all the way around the table. The

sound of Rich scuffling his boots filled the otherwise quiet room.

Stef frowned heavily. "Come on, guys. I may not be the sharpest knife in the drawer—" He paused. "Well, actually, now with all my training, I *might* be that, but you know what I mean! What's Jason talking about?"

Trent cleared his throat, then took a long, slow breath, and sat back with a squaring of his shoulders. "He hasn't said it directly, no one has, but everything seems to point toward it. Closing the Bone Gate will require a sacrifice. Not just any sacrifice, but the ultimate one."

"Oh, no." Bailey paled. She reached out and took Ting's hand in her own, and both girls trembled slightly.

Stefan kept his steady gaze fixed on Trent's face, waiting for more.

"That's all I think I know. It'll take a life to close the Gate."

"You have to tell someone!"

Trent shook his head. "I think almost everyone knows, they're just not talking about it. And neither should we."

"I almost . . . I was *there* . . ." Bailey gulped. "If you two hadn't pulled me out, who knows. . ."

"And that's probably how he knows. He felt it. He knows what lies in there." Trent's words fell heavily among them.

Stuck on You

HEAVY RAINS BROUGHT a few days of rest and peace. The bone fiends quieted as if even the undead could not face nature's fury. The Magickers all concentrated on patching the roof, which inevitably had a few leaks, or tossing Ting off the stairwell banister in her hedgedragon form to teach her how to fly and a myriad of other duties and classes. Some assignments seemed a lot more fun than others.

Jason grew increasingly restless. He woke early on a gray morning which found the sun breaking through again, and had barely dressed when alarms began to shrill. He roused Trent and ran outside to find the valley awash with wolfjackals and two crows.

Snowheart swooped through the air, her shrill cries ahead of the alarms, sharp beak and talons plucking at the invaders with a nip here and a rip there, attacking as only a crow can do, with speed and agility. All she could do was harass and tease the wolfjackals, but she kept them dodging and yowling from her, distracting the beasts as they circled the academy. Midnight joined her, his smaller, more muscular body weaving patterns in and out with hers, the two birds turning an entire pack of wolfjackals despite their flashing jaws. Yet for all their effort, the wolfjackals only altered their course to another path, bearing down on the academy.

For all their help, the crows of Tomaz also hindered. No one dared send a crystal flash at the wolfjackal pack for fear of hitting one of the birds. Instead, they concentrated on circling the academy as Gavan and Tomaz shouted orders, and the Magickers ran to their posts. Blushing, Ting poofed into her hedgedragon form, pearlescent scales glittering in the late afternoon light, flying not nearly as well as the crows. Twice she bumped into either Bailey or the corner of the academy eaves, letting out a tiny cloud of pink smoke as she did, her tiny dragonish ouch of pain. She flitted and darted at the wolfjackals as they circled past Bailey, her little dragonish talons extended, her Chinese body curling and uncurling as she hissed and spit in hedgedragon fierceness at them.

Bailey bit her lip to keep from laughing, for Ting was hardly as fierce as she thought she was, although the wolfjackals swerved away from them as they galloped past, their howls on the air. Bailey kept ducking away from her as she bopped up and down, still trying to get the hang of flying in hedgedragon form.

Stef stepped out boldly, his sword in hand, and Rich took up a position at his back, crystals in his. Stef's big square body dwarfed Rich's in width, but both were of a height, and the wolfjackals slowed as they neared them, foam splashing from their teeth as they gnashed and snarled at the boys. Stef turned his broadsword slowly hand over hand. "Come and get me," he said.

Jason and Trent nodded at each other and took up similar stances, although Trent's weapon was more of a basher than a blade. He hooked one elbow with Jason, as the crystals in Jason's hands flared, and Gavan spoke to all of them through their gems.

Stay close to the building, use it to guard your back. Take them out as they come through.

Jason repeated it aloud for Trent who set his jaw in answer. The pack circling them was huge, the biggest he'd ever seen, and the first time he'd noted young cubs running with them, wolfjackals probably still young enough to be nursing. He frowned.

Bailey let out a shriek. Jason peered around the corner of the building to see the hedgedragon caught in Bailey's hair. Well, no, not caught—Ting seemed to be determinedly yanking at Bailey's golden ponytail with all of her hedge-dragon strength, all the while spitting and hissing. Bailey bounced on one foot.

"Get her off, get her off!" She stopped bouncing for a moment, frowned, then yelled, "Get Madame Qi! I can't un-derstand a word she's saying, it's all in Chinese, I think!"

The hedgedragon let go of Bailey's ponytail and let out a teakettle whistle and began to fly around Bailey in ex-cited circles, tail lashing.

Jason gestured to the academy, alerting Henry inside, asking for his aid. Eyes nearly as round as his face, Henry darted out, helping Madame Qi through the makeshift bar-ricade. She put her palms in the air.

"Granddaughter, Granddaughter, slow down. I have not heard this dialect in many a decade." Qi tilted her wizened head and listened intently as the hedgedragon perched on her wrist, rather like a dragonish bird of prey. The exchange had gone silent, mind-to-mind. Qi's face frowned in con-centration, and then she put her chin up. "Everyone stop! Ting says the wolfjackals are here to help, not harm! Please note, she says, wolfjackals have always come after an attack before, to absorb the Chaos. Or they have attacked with the Dark Hand. But this is a family pack, see the cubs? They are here to help."

Tomaz loped from the far end of the academy, the sil-ver roundels at his wrist and belt flashing in the late after-noon sun. The wolfjackals stopped circling and came to a halt, still growling, teeth bared, enough of them to ring the building. The ones facing them lowered their heads warily, tails stiff behind them. The elder Magicker paced toward an enormous male wolfjackal, likely to be an alpha mem-ber in any pack, his hand held out.

"He's gonna lose that hand," muttered Stefan.

The hedgedragon swam clumsily through the air and made a slow circle about Tomaz as Tomaz continued to ap-proach. The wolfjackal peeled his lips back in a long, slow, continuous snarl. But he did not snap nor did he back up as Tomaz drew within range.

"She's sensed something," Tomaz said calmly. "This pack is different. I have run with one or two, not all are savage."

The wolfjackal male scratched at the ground. He looked over his shoulder with brilliant green eyes, as if he could see into the distance.

Gavan's voice flared from Jason's crystal, and he could hear a dim echo from other nearby crystals. *Are they here to help? If so, aid against what?*

Snowheart flew overhead, diving down and then drawing away, her white diamond chest skimming the trees leading from the valley. Tomaz tilted his head as he followed her flight with his mind.

"Raiders," he said. "Raiders riding hard."

The wolfjackal growled low in his throat and shifted restlessly. Then, as if making up his mind, he put his muzzle to Tomaz's hand in canine entreaty.

Jason had never seen a wolfjackal act like that. Ting made a giddy circle about Tomaz, whistling in delight. Tomaz said, "I think we have allies. Asked for or not."

The circle of wolfjackals drew close. Jason felt the hair on the back of his neck and his arms rise, as one of the beasts brushed by him, fur grazing his leg. He'd never been so close to one not focused on killing him. He swallowed tightly. Before he had much more time to think on the strange partners, war whoops filled the air, with the thunder of hooves, and the crackle of crystal energy, as raiders charged through the grove.

Henry took Madame Qi by the elbow as she brandished her cane with her free arm, her voice ringing out in a high-pitched Chinese phrase that sent the blood drumming through all of them. Reluctantly, Ting's grandmother returned inside the more secure academy, Henry Crystaling the doorframe as he moved through it, restoring the door's strength and locks. Sparkles danced along the wood before sinking into its very fiber.

Jason turned to face the raiders, and as soon as he saw them, his stomach clenched and shrank inside him, and he let out a wordless sound.

Trent shuddered beside him, and the two backed up a step in disbelief. These riders bearing down on them now came from the jaws of the Gate of Bones itself. With ashen-gray faces, bloodless wounds still gaping open on them, the raiders were echoes of all the battles they'd fought in other villages over the last weeks. Stef let out a low rumbling in disbelief, "I killed that lead rider last week."

Fiends from the Gate of Bones rode down on them as if seeking the very life inside them. They whipped and spurred the horses under them, and the poor beasts trembled with every jump as if they could not bear to carry the riders on their backs, their flanks heaving with ragged breaths and foam. No longer afoot, the undead could range as far as a horse could go before it dropped.

Tomaz made a gesture with his hand as if warding himself. He sent both his crows back into the air with a shout, and his hand came down with a blade of crystal light, slicing across the horde of fiends.

Jason raised his own hands, feeling Gregory's crystal as well as his own grow heated in answer to his need. Let them last, let them give until the fight was over. . . .

And he understood why the wolfjackals had come. Chaos drew them, they fed on it as if it were air itself, and the fiends of the Gate of Bones were Chaos itself. Yet their corruption roiled about them like filthy boiling water, and it stank, and he realized that the aura they gave off was as deadly to the wolfjackals as poison. They had come as much to save themselves as to save the Magickers.

He had no more time for thought than that as the raiders closed on them, and they fought for their lives. What he could not get with crystal, Trent got with his shovel, and what they could not get with either, wolfjackals tore from their sides, growling and snarling and pawing at their muzzles after as if the touch of the bone fiends disgusted them.

Gavan set flash fires on the cleared ground about the academy. The wolfjackals and horses sprang over them, but Stef and Rich dragged raiders' bodies into them as soon as one could be unhorsed. The stench of burning filled the air. The afternoon sun nearly spent, Jason found himself fighting shadows as often as a dead raider in dark shrouds.

He swung his crystal blade and Shielded until his arms ached and he did not think he could stand, and he backed up, leaning on an object for strength. The object, a panting wolfjackal, leaned back on him and for a moment they drew power from each other.

A horse veered past, eyes wild, rearing at the scent of fire and smell of death. Its rider bailed, landing on his feet, and he bared his teeth at Jason in a grin. "You are mine," the dead man said. "Gatekeeper." He gave a low hoarse sound that might have been meant for laughter. He stalked toward Jason. He bore himself with the ease of a fighter, and Jason recognized a man who in life had been the second headman of Avenha. Pyra had mourned Flameg, but this . . . thing . . . resembled him only vaguely.

Trent swung around, shovel in hand. The raider grabbed it and pulled Trent to his knees, then clubbed him with the back of his hand. Trent went down, stone cold.

Stef growled, but he and Rich struggled with their own fight, too far away to help. It was just Jason and the wolfjackal as the dead man stalked closer. Flameg drew a short, curved blade from his waistband. The last, lowering rays of the sun glinted off it. The old, crescent-shaped scar on the back of Jason's left hand throbbed with a painful stabbing.

The wolfjackal sprang. Jason stumbled as the beast launched past him, with a growl and a snarl. He did not stop growling even as the sword blade impaled his body, and the heaviness of his weight brought the raider to his knees. Jason blinked. He brought his crystal up, and took the dead man's head off before he could think about it twice.

For a moment, the raider's body stayed upright, on his knees, and Jason wondered if there was a way the things could be killed. Then it toppled, taking the wolfjackal with it.

Pain creased Jason as the animal let out a low groan, and then, a gasping whine. He went to it, but he could see nothing could be done. The beast whimpered a moment, then put his muzzle to the back of Jason's hand and his tongue gave a slow, hot lick. The light of knowing fled from his bright green eyes, and the wolfjackal died.

Wetness stung Jason's eyes. He swung about, with a remembered cry. "Trent!"

Trent lay on his back, staring upward, but his chest moved and then he kicked a foot out with a moan. He sat up, with Jason's help. "What hit me?"

"Never mind. Are you . . . you're all right, right?"

"Sure. My head is probably the best place on my whole body to get hit." Nonetheless, Trent wobbled as he stood, face pale.

It took Jason a moment to realize they stood in relative quiet. The fiends, or what was left of them, had fled into the shadows, their weary mounts stumbling off. Wolfjackals, what was left of the pack, lay on the ground, panting. Magickers, all of them, took a step back, exhausted, their crystals going dim one by one.

Gavan came out, as did Henry. Henry lifted his crystal solemnly after all the bodies had been rolled into the front fires. His Talent of Fire roared as he raised his crystal high and the flames answered, shooting skyward with a brilliant hot fury that almost instantly seemed to burn away the dead raiders. When the fires died down, no one spoke for a long moment.

Jason didn't see Bailey. He swung around on one heel, in the smoke, feeling panicked for a moment.

"Bailey? Bailey!"

Had they lost her somehow? But how?

A whimper answered him. Frowning across the fires and haze, he saw her seated at the corner of the academy, a fur bundle across her knees. She looked up, tears streaking her face. A wolfjackal pup huddled in her arms. "His mom . . . his dad . . ." she said, slowly.

Jason nodded then, understanding. Tomaz moved across the ground, and stood with Jason, hand on his shoulder, watching Bailey.

"He's . . . he's stuck," she said.

"Hurt? I mean . . ." Jason tried not to think of the wolfjackal who'd saved him, impaled on a sword blade.

"No. In my head. We're—" Bailey took a deep breath. "I think we're bonded."

The pup let out another whimper and laid his head on her shoulder, shoving his snout into the curve of her neck. An outraged squeak greeted him, as Lacey pushed her way out of Bailey's pocket and glared at the newcomer. The wolfjackal turned his silver-streaked mask quickly, snuffling at the rodent who chirped and dove headfirst back into the safety of Bailey's pocket. The interested pup tried to shove his nose after, but Bailey thumped him. "Stop that!"

The pup chuffed and buried his face on her shoulder again. Bailey stood, holding the animal in her arms, its legs dangling. Ting, still in hedgedragon form, came to ground.

"I think we won," Trent remarked.

"This time," Gavan replied. He signaled to Henry to snuff the fires. "Only this time."

The wolfjackals got to their feet, put their noses to the sky, and let out a series of mournful wails. Then they faded into the forest as well, not a one of them looking back after the orphan Bailey carried. "Hey!" she called. "Hey! Hey! You can't just leave him."

"I think they already have," Tomaz told her.

She hugged the furry pup closer.

In quiet time, Trent worked on his maps of what he'd seen on dragonback, using a purloined copy of one of Renart's maps to help him. Jason came into the study after him.

"Bedtime."

"I'm almost ready. I'll be able to give this to Gavan soon." Trent raised an eyebrow at him. "You're up late."

"Been thinking."

"Gate raiders?"

"I think I was their target."

"Couldn't prove it by me, I think I was out cold at the time." Trent's voice trailed off, as he saw the serious look on Jason's face.

Jason said quietly, "I've looked at this from all the angles I can think of, and there's only one way I can be sure will close the Gate of Bones."

Trent paused in his sketching, and flicked a look at Jason in disbelief to which Jason shrugged, adding, "I think the Dark Hand is correct about this one."

"You're kidding me, right?"

"Wish I were. Think about it. In all your beloved myths and legends, this boils down to it . . . someone's gotta go slay that dragon, so to speak."

"No. I refuse to believe that. The only solution they've come up with is a human sacrifice. And not just any human, they've elected you, Jason. I don't think they care whether or not it *works*, they just want you out of the way."

"I know."

Trent dropped his drawing pencil and lifted both hands. The sheet of paper he'd been mapping upon began to roll up slowly, as if cringing and hiding. "This is crazy. You're walking right into their trap. Without a fight?"

"No. I've been thinking and thinking." Jason dropped

onto the stool next to Trent so he could look eye to eye with his friend. "Jonnard isn't a real Gatekeeper, but he opened that one. It doesn't swing open and shut like a normal Gate, and as near as I can tell, it doesn't portal like a normal Gate. It doesn't lead from place to place. I think it . . . well, I'm not sure, but I think it leads from existence to existence. From life to death, from good to evil, or something like that. Whatever it is, it doesn't belong here, and it's corrupting everything every moment it stays open."

"And your point is . . ."

"I can't allow it to stay open, and I think it will take all of a Gatekeeper's power to shut it."

"All of their power?"

"All."

Trent shoved back from the table as if rejecting everything he said. "No way!"

"I need you to trust me on this."

"Trust you? When you've gone insane or something?"

Jason took a short breath. "If I've learned one thing—make that two things—since becoming a Magicker, it's to trust when I look inside myself, and to trust in my friends when I reach out to them. I can do this, Trent, but I can't do it without you. I don't want anyone else to know what I'm planning, but if you think you can help, then let me know. Either way, I know what it is I have to do." He stood. Without another word, he left the study, and behind him he could hear muffled words that sounded like Trent muttering, "Oh, maaaaaan."

Trent watched Jason walk out of the study and rocked his stool back on two stubby rear feet, balancing himself precariously. His fingers drummed the edge of the tabletop in time with his thoughts as they galloped through his mind. Although he'd come to the same conclusion, he hadn't voiced it to Jason, and he hadn't thought Jason would ever come to believe in it, too. No way would Jason say, all right, Jonnard is the big kahuna and he's right, and I'm gonna go throw myself in the volcano for everyone's sake. No way.

But he just had, in so many words.

Trent syncopated his tapping fingers and mind through every myth he could think of, without finding a way out, and finally let his stool sink back to the floor on all fours.

He needed ammo if he was going to talk Jason out of anything, and he couldn't come up with it. If anything, old stories and tales and religions tended to reinforce what Jason intended to do.

There was no way Trent would let that happen. And he couldn't think that Jason would just give up that easily, not the Jason he knew, not the friend he'd come to depend upon.

For that matter, why had Jason come to him, and not to all of them? They were all in this together, always had been. There was no doubt the two of them, though, had shared thoughts with each other that no one else knew. Jason had opened up to him about things Trent knew he would never tell another soul, unwilling to vent anything that could hurt anyone else. Trent had listened to him when Jason feared he could tell no one else. Then, why his cryptic last words? Why would Jason possibly think he'd help do something so rash?

Trent blinked.

Because . . . possibly . . . Trent was the only one who *could* help.

"I'm an idiot," he said, and got to his feet. He reached for his crystal. He couldn't find Jason through it the way the others seemed to find each other by talking and seeing, but there was no way he was going to run through the academy yelling at the top of his lungs. If, as Gavan had hinted, the walls might well have unfriendly ears, there was ample reason Jason hadn't come right out and said what he meant.

But he had his own ways of finding people, and as he held his crystal, his mind cleared a bit and he could see through the doorway a faint aura-colored pathway trailing after the way Jason had gone. Magick leads Magick, he thought, and went in search of the other.

50

The Decision

A HEAVY HAND THUMPED on the academy's front door. Gavan opened it, Jason at his elbow. Rain had come and gone again, but more clouds threatened on the horizon. It did not, however, dampen their pleasure at seeing who stood there, as the other Magickers raced downstairs and crowded around.

Dokr stood there, hat off. "A bargain has been made," he said. "I have come to help." A faint smile creased the man's face.

Henry whooped behind them. "Renart did it!"

The wanderer gave a slight bow. "He has given us seed for fields and seedlings for orchards, and land for us to hold. We would make him king for that, but he tells us it is your doing. I'm here for fulfilling the bargain."

They hurried to get everyone packed and ready, while the wanderers stood by with the same uncurious, patient look they had held while building the academy. Gavan brought them all together.

He held Eleanora in his arms, but she sat up, smiling, looking far better than she had days ago, her hair brushed softly about her face. He kissed her temple lightly before aying, "We're never alone, as Magickers, you all know that. But we can't use the crystals to stay in touch, not right now. There is a chance, however slight, that the Dark Hand might overhear us at these distances. So, our correspondence will be as the crow flies. Snowheart or Midnight will be taking small messages back and forth when needed. We won't be far apart, or for long."

Tomaz held up a forefinger. "Small messages," he repeated. "And only as absolutely necessary. Crows are not jet planes."

"Everyone ready?"

"I am staying," Madame Qi stated firmly. "Otherwise, I think all are ready."

"Staying?"

She nodded at Gavan and said nothing more.

"Then let's go. I don't want to attract attention to wanderers on the road this late in the year." Gavan carried Eleanora out first, murmuring something none of the others could hear in her ear. She laughed and pinched his ear back tightly, bringing a flush to his face.

Dokr seemed unfazed by the invalid Eleanora being loaded onto the first wagon, or even FireAnn who cackled and either blessed or hexed in her Irish brogue the teams of horses hitched to the wagons, but he did give pause as they loaded Gregory in his sarcophagus.

"He is dead, no?"

"He is dead, no. I mean, no, he's not dead. Just sleeping. For a very, very long time." Jason faltered in his explanation.

The wanderer stared as they stowed the coffin in the cargo bin of the wagon. "Very well," he said to Jason finally, with a shrug. "I have seen stranger things, I believe."

Freyah tapped him on the shoulder. "We're all in, young man. Time to move out."

Ting leaned against her grandmother. "Are you sorry you're not going?"

Her grandmother smiled, her face breaking into a thousand wise wrinkles. "There is something here I must finish first. Let Rebecca get the first lessons, she has much more to learn."

Jason watched as Rebecca and Bailey hugged each other fiercely.

"Stay out of trouble," mother told daughter as daughter burst out, "I'll try to stay out of trouble!" They laughed at each other. Then Dokr gave orders to his drivers and the three wagons pulled out to the slap of harness and sharp whistles urging the horses, leathers creaking and wheels jolting. Eventually, they all turned away but Gavan and Bailey.

Jason watched from the doorway as Gavan leaned over and hugged Bailey tightly. Jason listened as he made her no promises, though. They might be safe for now, they might never be safe, as long as the Dark Hand valued power more than life. He turned away, thinking that this was as good a time as any. He and Trent exchanged looks, and he gave a nod.

Trent frowned and nodded back.

He tidied his bed and few things. He took his crystals, the one in his pocket, and the one he often wore on the chain about his neck, his old soccer shirt twisted into a headband and sundry other items that meant something to him. His other things he left in a neat bundle at the foot of the bed. He did not say goodbye to anyone, not until he Crystaled to the edge of Dark Hand holdings.

Wolfjackals surged toward him, snarling and yipping, a wave of fur and flashing eyes, the first alarm of intruders on the land. He waved a hand, and they stilled. He rubbed the scar on the back of his left hand, the scar he had carried since before he had even known he was a Magicker, the scar a wolfjackal had marked him with, and he said, "I am yours."

They parted to let him through. He strode across the outer boundary of the hills until he reached the blackened valley where the abyss broke through, and there he waited.

In a few brief moments, Isabella and Jonnard appeared. She was dressed in midnight-blue satin, her gown sweeping the winter grass of brown and sand, while he was all in black, as usual. "What are you doing here, Magicker?"

"I've come to close the Gate."

Jon's eyes flashed in triumph. Isabella raised a hand. "You're agreeing to do whatever is necessary?"

"That's why I'm here. In case you're doubting me, I

rought a witness. Someone so there won't be any trouble later, no blame for whatever happens." Jason turned, quirked a finger, and Trent loped up behind him.

Jonnard's mouth curled. "The Magicker without Magick."

Isabella put her hand on his, stilling him, saying, "I think that's wise. A witness is an excellent idea."

Jason looked at the Gate, and took a deep breath. It sensed him, its voices growing louder, calling incoherently for him, for the power he carried. A moment of regret filled him. He wouldn't see his families again, either one. He hadn't told the dragon what he intended to do. And he'd dragged Trent into this. He turned around. "You don't have to stay," he said to his friend.

"There is no way you're getting me to leave."

He put his hand out. "Whatever happens, then." Trent took his handshake, then pulled him in for a hug. In his ear, fiercely, Trent whispered, "Never alone!" before letting go and moving back.

"The Gate is quiet," Jonnard pointed out. "It would be wise to do whatever you're going to do before the fiends start emerging. Their taste for flesh is . . . not pleasant."

"I don't need encouragement," he answered flatly. He took Gregory's crystal, warm to his touch, out of his pocket. He thought about it a second, then passed it to Trent. "See Eleanora gets that."

"But—"

He shook his head quickly. "I won't need it."

Trent whistled softly. "All right." He tucked it away, his own crystal swinging from its chain on his belt loop.

Without any more thoughts, he stepped into the whirling edge of the Gate, into the mists at the lip of its abyss, bones snapping underfoot, and a skull caught in the maelstrom of its movement bobbing around in vacant-eyed mockery of him. Power licked at him like cold green flame. It wanted to crawl inside of him, but he thrust it away. He didn't want any part of it or its false promises. He looked up and saw Trent's tense face, watching him, and he smiled. With a hand to his crystal, he began to do that which he could do best.

He learned the Gate. Without taking its powers, he learned its fury and its weakness, its purposes and its

ending, and he began to deny it pulse by pulse. Jonnard
leaned close. He had to shout to be heard over the whirl
wind and the moaning.

"What are you doing?"

Jason smiled at him. "Closing the Gate. What I came to
do."

"Fool. You're doing nothing. Step inside it!"

"It will devour what it wishes," Jason told him calmly
He continued to set up his matrix, and for a moment, he
thought he could do it, actually do it, and survive. He drew
on himself, and he drew on the Chaos of the wolfjackals
circling the Gate, their eyes glittering with hope and anger
at the nearness of their freedom.

Then the Gate awoke. Like a great beast that sensed
prey within its grasp, it truly awoke. A thousand Magicks
erupted inside of it, bathing Jason, dragging him back and
down. He thought he felt hands on his ankles, Leucator
flesh, grasping him. Jonnard licked his lips.

"Power," he said. He leaned closer.

Jason felt the Gate open him up, atom by atom, tast-
ing him, deciding how it would devour him. Stricken, he
stared at Trent, his plans evaporating. He thought he knew
it because he'd taken Bailey from it. He realized now that
nothing the Gate truly wanted would ever escape. He lost
his grip on the earth. The maelstrom of energy bore him
upward and then began to drag him back into the mists and
carnage, back into its throat of an abyss.

Jonnard reached out. He grabbed Jason's outflung hand
crying, "Give it to me!"

Jason hung between the two of them, Jonnard and
the Gate of Bones, power draining in both directions, his
life flowing out, a candle burning wildly at both ends. So
quickly! He thought he might have more time. . . .

Trent moved. He reached out and grasped Jason's forearm, his other hand untangling line after line of magical
force only he could see. The Gate groaned and wailed as
its strands snapped one after another, and Jason could feel
himself flowing back. He gripped Trent tightly. Then, he
pulled Jonnard in with his right hand.

The Gate seized them both. Jonnard yelled in fury and
thrashed about. Jason anchored on Trent and let himself be
pulled out, even as he continued to shut down the Gate, its

attention fastened on Jonnard. It had him by the throat. His cries ceased, but his thrashing grew wilder.

Isabella flung herself at her son and heir. Whether she intended to push him in, or pull him out, no one could tell. Jonnard grabbed her fiercely, his face in a snarl, even as she screamed at him to let go and just feel the power.

Trent hauled Jason out, hand over hand, and the Gate snapped shut with a tremendous roar. It sucked itself inward, imploding, with a sound and fury that deafened them. Like a land sink, it filled itself in and the two had to scramble for it, dirt collapsing into a tremendous crater and they running to keep from being sucked down into it after all.

No sight could be seen of Isabella or Jonnard whatsoever.

The wolfjackals lifted their heads to the sky in a long, triumphant howl. They whirled about. Lightning crackled off their silvery-black forms, and the clouds gathering opened up to take them in, as the two stared.

The quiet lasted only a moment. Then their crystals burst with voices, and Jason leaned back, listening to the Magickers, and he laughed.

And as a special bonus feature,
here is a brand-new *Magickers* tale
written especially for this volume.

AFTER GATE

HE HAD A BAD FEELING. Everything should be over but Jason had this—feeling—no, not a feeling because it wasn't that definite. It was more like a tug. He mused over it and Trent caught him because musing for Jason often meant chewing on his lip and knotting his face into a frown. In short, it was hard to miss.

"What's up?"

"Nothing."

Trent stared at him.

"Really. Nothing."

More staring.

"Really. Empty air." Jason pointed at his head. "Nothing I can explain."

Trent crossed his eyes.

"Fine. It's like something pulling at me. Almost like someone has a hand wrapped around my ankle but that's just stupid. Even more stupid, it feels, no, it tastes like Jonnard."

"He has a flavor? Dude. That's just gross. He went through the Bones. If he isn't dead, he's just chopped up like hamburger or something." For emphasis, Trent put his

647

hands on Jason's shoulders. "Ain't nobody coming back from that. We barely got out and we're the good guys."

"I know, I know." Jason struggled out of Trent's hold. "It makes no sense. But then—" He waved a hand indicating their fortress home, the valley where it was located, and all of Haven. "None of this makes a lot of sense."

"Okay." Trent straightened up. "I've only got one cure for you. Go talk to your dragon. He'll either fix your head or bite it off."

Jason let out a half snort. "Too true." He lifted and dropped a shoulder in a farewell shrug before leaving the balcony to make his way down the stairs. It wasn't his dragon, anyway. It was THE Dragon, a wise but terrible teacher. Jason had no doubt that a time would come when the dragon would tire of instructing his backward pupil and leave him to struggle on his own. Maybe even look upon him as a morsel ripened for dinner. He didn't think things would progress in that direction but he knew the dragon was a meat eater and he was, well, meat. He couldn't seem to convince his friends of that rather sticky part of his relationship with the dragon. The great creature, however, had certainly convinced *him*.

Trent cut ahead of him going down the stairs. A good thing, too, because when Bailey charged around the corner at the bottom step, it was Trent she nearly knocked heels over teakettle instead of him. A second good thing was that her wolfjackal pup had not barreled in on her heels as he usually did, closer to Bailey than most shadows could get. But Jason ran out of good luck when Ting rammed into him as he tried to sort the other two out.

In seconds the four of them had gotten more tangled up than a whole party's worth of people playing Twister. If they still played Twister back on Earth. Jason hoped they did. He remembered it being a lot of fun and as embarrassing as his current situation. Though he refused to look, he was pretty sure that Bailey's rump was smothering his face. And he didn't want to think about where his hand had ended up.

Stefan walked in as they strove to untangle themselves, a goal that got harder and harder to accomplish as first Ting, then Bailey, began to giggle and then laugh helplessly until both girls went as limp as rag dolls. While it made things impossible for the four of them, Stefan merely stepped in with a growl and began to lift them free one by one. Both the girls dangled from his large hands like kittens held by the scruff of their necks.

They'd all had growth spurts but Stefan's was a colossal one. The effort of hauling them apart seemed like nothing to him.

Stefan frowned heavily, glaring at Bailey and Ting. "I thought I told you it was important. Rich is dying."

That took even longer to sort out than all their sprawled bodies.

"What I said was, I could be dying and no one would notice," Rich repeated slowly.

"I could swear I heard you say that you *were* dying! Besides, look at you, pale as the sheets." Stefan scratched at his head.

"I'm a redhead, Stef. I don't tan; I freckle. I was born pasty! You riled up everyone blundering through the place just like you were in bearskin—"

"And both of you just as unreasonable. Listen to your caterwauling."

The group of Magickers parted at the gruff, commanding voice sounding through the Chaos. Tomas stood in the doorway to the boys' dorm, his arms folded across his chest, his face creased in an expression that none of them were used to: disappointment. The silver conchos on his belt flashed in the daylight as he moved, echoing the glint in the elder Magicker's eyes. He pointed a thumb at Rich. "You know exactly what you said and why. There's no doubt you're carrying a burden none of the rest of us would want, but pulling the strings of our concern for you is a foolish and dangerous gesture."

Rich folded his arms across his chest, unconsciously imitating Tomas' posture. His nose flared as he did so; otherwise, he kept silent.

Tomas raked his gaze over the others. "As for the rest of you, you let him throw you off stride like this? How would this help if he had been in trouble? We've been through enough together, I think, that we know better."

Rich's hand twitched and it was only then that Jason saw he held a letter. "What's that all about then?" He jerked his thumb at the pieces of paper, an item even more precious to an ordinary citizen of Haven than to one of them. Paper, dearly made and dearly used. Whoever sent the letter, had sent something important.

Rich traded a look with Tomas, perhaps seeking permission to speak, before unfolding it. "This is what I was complaining about. Reeve Bailey sent a letter, and a map, to ask for our help. This is the second time he asks, he says, and he promises an ample harvest of my herbs in return. My herbs," Rich repeated, and he rattled the pages in the air at them. "Who ignored his first letter? This could be a year's worth of antidotes for me."

Their Bailey put her shoulders back. "I can't say what happened to the first one. If any of us had seen it, you know we would have been all over it. Anything to keep your medicine in stock. But now we have this one, and a stitch in time means better first aid." She snatched the papers from his fingers, darting away before he could grab it back. Her eyes went wide as she read it for herself.

"He's right. There's a map and everything. Just one little problem Reeve Richard of the Bailey wants us to take care of first." She lowered the letter. "He has a dragon in the way."

Henry had come to the door just in time to hear Bailey's comment, standing in the threshold with Tomas, and listening. "I thought that wasn't possible. First of all, there aren't any dragons native to this world. There's your dragon, Jason, and there's Ting who's not exactly a dragon, more of a shapeshifter, really, but any other dragons would be highly unlikely, not to mention uncommon. . . ."

"He's not MY dragon," Jason said stubbornly. "He just has metaphysical ties to the main gate here. But you're right. There shouldn't be another dragon here. Not without his knowledge or permission, because it affects the whole physical makeup of Haven. I think I'm going to have to have a talk with him."

"One of the more sensible things I've heard yet," Tomas told him.

Jason smiled weakly. "Glad you think so. Anyone want to volunteer for backup? The news isn't going to make him happy."

No one spoke up. In addition to being big and extremely dragonish, Jason's friend had a legendary temper.

Finally, Ting said in her quietest voice, "I guess I could go." Bailey, standing next to her, could sense the tension and fear hiding in her friend's body. Ting was anything but calm.

Henry made a move with one hand, as if reacting to Ting's distress, and hoping to protect her from it. "First thing we should ask ourselves is whether this meeting is even necessary. What do we know of this Reeve Richard of the Bailey?"

That dropped like a lead weight into the silence.

"I know he's not a relative," said their Bailey. "At least, not that I know about."

Trent stirred. "He wrote us for help, so there's a good chance we might know him, right. He knows about us. The name sounds familiar." He elbowed Bailey. "I'll be back." Trent bounded off while Bailey searched for a reply and failed to come up with one.

"Where's he headed?"

Tomas had the advantage of still being taller than most of them. Only Stefan seemed likely to pass his height soon. He looked over the heads of everyone to remark, "Headed to the library, I believe. Another good choice." And he leaned a shoulder to the wall, to wait with the patience of his Native American background, as his ancestors had waited in centuries past.

The recess turned out to be only slightly longer than moments. Trent returned with one of their journals from their early days in Haven. He flipped it open with Henry's help. "Here we go. Reeve . . . that's kind of a rural headman, Reeve Richard of Bailey, a farmer, carpenter, and stonemason. Particularly well known for his carpentry. Hey, this is the guy who made Eleanora's dulcimer. A great guy, now that I remember him. He did a lot of work on the fortress early on."

"That's right," Stefan added. "Big ol' gruff guy, strong and smart but gentle. He has a son and daughter, householders themselves. He did a lot of work around here, and then left us with some good crews. I'd take his word any day."

Tomas inclined his head. "I recall him as well, although

we called him Dick. If he wrote us, then there is indeed trouble, and we should answer."

"Oh-kay," said Jason. "I guess I take the next step then. And, Ting, you don't have to go if you don't want to."

Bailey hooked her arm through Ting's. "*We* want to," she declared firmly.

Ting gave him a shaky look that may or may not have agreed.

So the three of them went to talk to the biggest and deadliest conversationalist they had ever or would ever meet.

The dragon roared. The sound reverberated through the stone and hills and cliffs like a runaway freight train, shaking the very ground under their feet. Like a massive, hurtful wave, it pounded against their eardrums even with their hands clasped firmly over their ears.

Jason thought his ears might actually be bleeding, and there was a slight chance his bones were going to vibrate into mush. Next to him, both Bailey and Ting had collapsed to the ground. When the roar finally passed away—a receding tide of sound and terror echoing in the distance—the dragon's throat swelled as if he might roar again. His great eyes rolled a bit, taking them in. Then the dragon lowered his head and licked his lips a few times.

"Well then. I do not like this news you have brought me, Jason Adrian. However, it explains a few things. Have you not felt a disturbance that should not be occurring?"

Bailey's nose wrinkled and Jason could hear her mutter, "Is there a disturbance in the force, oh scaled obi-wan kenobi?" He cleared his throat loudly to cover her words.

Then he agreed. "Actually, something's been, well, nagging at me. Not sure what it was till we heard about this mysterious dragon."

"That would be it. Not only is this Unwanted trespassing on MY territory, it has disturbed the balance. Haven is a world in which many forces are delicately balanced to coexist." The dragon directed his amber gaze to Bailey and Ting. "We'll need that pup of yours."

Surprise immediately chased any other expression from Bailey's face. "You will?"

"Yes. He eats Chaos, does he not? Just as he sups on

meat. As for Pearl, she will be needed to distract the Unwanted."

The two girls helped each other to their feet. Ting shut her eyes tightly then opened them again, as though trying to screw up her courage. "Bait. You want me to be bait for another dragon."

The dragon snorted. "Think you that I value you and fledgling Pearl so little? I should show you my teeth for letting that cross your mind. No, not bait. You will be instrumental in fooling our Unwanted so that our trap might be sprung properly. Without you, Bailey, and you, Ting . . . this cannot succeed." The dragon put his paw out, releasing his claws, each talon looking like a mighty silver samurai sword. "I'm not to be trifled with! I thank you, my servants and pupils, for bringing this to my attention. I will devise a plan that will bring this Unwanted down and then flush it from our world. You have my leave to go now." And the dragon clenched his paw tightly before curling his huge, scaly body away from them in dismissal.

But not before dropping one eyelid in a wink only Jason could see.

Jason trotted down the cliff-side path behind Bailey and Ting who had begun talking excitedly halfway down, whatever effect the dragon had had on them fading, while Jason's ears still rang from the creature's anger and his own puzzlement. He cupped his crystal, letting its response to his touch comfort him a bit. The dragon had been both startled and angered by the news. Yet the wink bothered him. Did the dragon know or suspect how the others wanted Jason to use him the way one might use a well-trained dog or a saddle horse? Was this a test for them? Did the devious dragon plan much more than simply getting rid of the trespasser? And as for the reward of finding a treasure store of herbs for Rich—well, who knew if Reeve Dick could supply what he promised, growing things being as chancy as it could be. Who could guarantee a wild crop? Jason let out a sigh and nearly ran headlong into the duo standing at the bottom of the trail.

Ting staggered back a step. "Jason. Weren't you even listening?"

Why pretend? "No, not really. I was thinking we need Trent along on this, whatever the plan is."

Bailey flipped her head, ponytail cascading down onto her shoulders. "Good idea."

"Because I—what?"

"Good idea. In fact, I think all of us should go. And Tomas, too. He said once the dragon was a great power but that he could be like the Trickster Coyote in Native American fables. Powerful but not always reliable."

"I dunno about that, but sometimes he has different endings in mind."

"Exactly. And he was suddenly just too eager to stick all of us into his scheme. Not that we think he wants to eat us or anything, but . . . " Bailey slowed a moment and traded looks with Ting. "We just think he might be teaching us a lesson we haven't asked him for."

Ting nodded in agreement.

"What do you think?"

"I'm not sure," Jason admitted. "But I kinda came to the same conclusion."

"Good. Then it's agreed. We won't look a gift horse in the mouth but we won't get on it and just go riding without training wheels either!" She and Ting marched off to the fort leaving Jason in their wake trying to decipher what Bailey had just said as opposed to what she probably meant.

Tomas whittled down the rescue party to himself, Trent, Jason, Bailey, and Ting, and then added the wolfjackal pup by dragon request. Rich protested, saying they would need his healing skills. Stefan, of course, growled and stomped about, saying his swordsmanship would be called for, as well as his bear self. But the Magicker told them and Henry that they were needed at the fort, alert and guarding while all the others were away. It seemed to be a plan. Rich still didn't like it.

"You'll be nearly three weeks away by horseback. How can we get to you if you need help?"

"The dragon has made plans for that, no doubt." Tomas patted his shoulder. "Remember your poisoning is one of the reasons we're going on this rescue mission and although you could undoubtedly be of help, your own condition is weakened."

A dark look flashed over Rich's face as he turned away.

Stefan hunkered down silently next to his friend as Henry scurried off to see if he could help Ting pack.

In the end, though, it was the dragon that decided who went and who stayed when they trooped up to his plateau. After a moment or two of hushed discussion with Tomas, done in low rumbling tones which Jason tried his best to overhear and could not, Tomas stepped back.

"I won't be going. My brand of Magick conflicts with the dragon's. I'll be little or no help at all under those circumstances. Trent may go by virtue of his unique abilities. The wolfjackal will go in the harness you two rigged for him. The rest of you will all ride where told or you will be left behind. Understood?"

If Tomas standing with a stern look on his face wasn't enough, the huge crimson-scaled beast towering behind him was. The four of them gulped and nodded almost as one. Bailey's pup sat on his rump and scratched at one ear determinedly, seemingly unaware of any tension.

Tomas then grasped each of them by the shoulders as he said good-bye.

Jason watched him hike back down the trail, trying to tell from the way he walked whether Tomas expected to see any of them again in one piece. He couldn't read the body language but knew that Tomas would be with them if he could. None of the Magickers ever let the others go it alone.

There was a time when he'd thought differently, but he'd learned his lesson. Jason's mouth crooked. No Magicker was ever truly alone. He'd learned a lot since picking up his crystal.

"Attention," the dragon commanded. "Mount where I tell you, hold tightly to the harness straps I will have you place, and use your crystal to put up a shield. The pup I will carry in his sack with my claws."

Bailey's face squinched up but before she could protest, the dragon added, "The animal will be fine." She clamped her jaws shut.

"The plan?" Jason ventured.

"You ride. I fly. Shields up. We will attack out of the setting sun without warning. He is a trespasser and he knows what he has incurred, and what the penalty for his actions will be. Ting becomes Pearl and goes for the soft underscales of his throat. Bailey, you will guard Ting and direct your pup toward the spill of Chaos all our magicks should release when the two of us clash. Keep close watch on that pup and on Pearl. Our hedgedragon will need to be nimble and cowardly."

"Cowardly?" Ting narrowed her eyes as if that was unthinkable.

"Yes, cowardly. You will be outmatched. I am the true menace. All I need is for the Unwanted to forget it for the barest of moments. Are we all in agreement?"

They all answered. Even the pup let out a little bark as he rolled over on his back to wave his paws at Bailey. Jason and Trent leaned over to wrestle him into the backpack harness Henry had fashioned for him. The furry little guy tried to gnaw on their fingers and then his straps until Bailey went to one knee, took his head between her hands, and said a few things to him in a language of soft sounds along with words and even a wolfish growl or two. The pup immediately sat on his haunches and his ears perked in wolfish attention.

Trent cleared his throat. The dragon flicked an ear at him. "Something not to your liking, friend of Jason?"

"It's the plan. It seems well . . . it seems a little thin to me."

"Thin?"

"Lacking in details."

"Ah. Well, I should imagine the heat of battle will provide what you feel is missing. Get aboard or be left behind!"

The Magickers scrambled to do his bidding.

Jason had flown before but he could never grow used to the way the dragon took off. A lumbering run and then a plunge off the top of the cliff, the bottom of the valley hurtling at them until he was certain he would be smashed. Now, as then, the dragon waited until the last moment before filling his wings and sailing upward, up until he was higher than the cliffs and his great wings ruled the sky. Behind Jason, Trent had been reduced to muttering and Bailey's thin scream had faded away. Ting had bent over, burying her face against her hands while gripping the harness as tightly as she could. The wolfjackal, barely visible, hung his head out of his harness, reminding Jason of a dog with his head out a car window, enjoying the trip without any idea of its true implications. Trent raised his voice loud enough to say, "Don't you dare get sick, Ting."

No answer.

Even if there had been, the dragon picked up speed slowly but surely until talking, or even thinking, seem impossible with the rush of the wind against their faces.

When the sun began to dip low across the hills, Jason shaded his eyes as he realized they had to be nearing their destination. Indeed, below them, he could see organized fields and orchards, the line of ground tamed and worked. The dragon let out a trumpeting call and dropped low over the farm, circling, until people exploded from the various outbuildings: sheds and barns and workshops. He saw the broad-shouldered and somewhat portly man he knew to be Reeve Dick of the Bailey come running out, pitchfork in his capable hands.

"Come defend your family and lands," the dragon called before sailing away.

Jason craned his neck to see the Reeve drop his pitchfork and wave his arm, shouting orders. Men scrambled in response though a few stood at the farm's lane and watched them all with pale faces.

And then they were gone, away from the farmstead, the Reeve left on his own if he wished to catch up with the battle. They dipped over a velvety green hillside and the dragon came in for a landing, like an airplane on just one wheel, for he kept his bundle of wolfjackal up in the air as he put his belly down. They scrambled off his body without urging, Ting bailing first, her dark hair tangled about her, her brown eyes wide in her astonished face. Bailey lunged past her to retrieve her pup while Trent and Jason both jumped feet first on legs that felt a little rubbery. Trent stretched his hands out. "He's woven a web of magick about these hills."

"And?"

Trent grinned. "I begin unweaving."

Jason threw up a shield to protect Trent while he worked, a shield that would stay in place even if Jason moved away, or Trent did. Bailey freed her pup then tapped Ting on the shoulder.

"Time for Pearl."

"I know." Ting took a deep breath. She threw her arms around Bailey to hug her tightly. "Promise you won't let her eat any bugs?"

"I'll try. You know a young dragon gets hungry!"

Ting reached inside her jacket to pull up her necklace and the beautiful, large pearl pendant it held. She cupped it, her face creasing in intense concentration. Jason glanced at Trent whose hands moved as if untangling threads on the air only he could see (which was probably pretty much the truth), a shimmering cloaking him. When he looked back, the small dog-sized pink and pearlescent dragon that was Ting's alter ego stood between the great dragon's clawed feet. Her ears and spines were pricked all over in both fear and eagerness. The dragon lowered his head and whuffed over Pearl.

She spread her wings, ready to go.

But not in time.

A blast knocked Jason off his feet and tore at his concentration. While heat licked over his body, the shielding surrounding Trent trembled and shook as if it would tear into wisps and blow away, even as Jason tumbled, ending up on his stomach. Bailey lay flat as well, anchored by her wolfjackal pup. But as Jason took a deep breath through a throat that felt scalded, Pearl took off. Like a dart, she hit the air and arrowed down the mountain, her objective a dark shadow that curled and uncurled as it reared up and up in the valley below. It was, Jason realized, the other dragon.

He didn't know what he'd expected. The trespasser was another dragon, that he'd been told. But he had never expected a dragon greater in size than his dragon. Greater, with power and the stink of dark magick rolling off him like a fog, with silvery eyes whose depths were shining ruby lights, and who could easily swallow Pearl in one tiny mouthful.

Jason yelled to bring her back. His voice was lost in the roar of one dragon challenging the other. Suddenly everything that could go wrong went wrong in a blast of dragon magick.

Pearl disappeared. Bailey threw herself down the hillside, the wolfjackal bounding after her. Trent, shield and all, was snatched up by the red dragon with one great swoop of his taloned feet as their dragon launched himself downward at his ebony foe.

And Jason was left standing alone.

All alone as the black dragon leaped over the red, raking with his claws as he did so, opening a raw, bloody streak and knocking the red dragon off his feet and rolling.

His heart in his throat, Jason did the only thing he could. He redoubled his shield around Trent to protect him as the dragons collided heavily with a sound like mountains falling. Even as the black dragon bounded free and headed for him, the ruby depths of his silvery eyes lit up with a volcanic glow. Suddenly Jason knew he would be the first to die.

Or not. Feisty Pearl hadn't forgotten her part in the scheme and dove at the black dragon's sooty gray throat, where the obsidian scales had not yet hardened and would never entirely lest the dragon's throat close down. Her slight, pearlescent form pricked at its underside, tumbling over and winging out of reach not once, but three times before darting away, the black dragon snarling in frustration, magick and acid saliva pouring out of his jaws and searing the ground below. He swung at Pearl, missing her, but the force of his blow created a wind stream that sent her desperately bobbing away. And all around them, a sickly green mist boiled out, roiling over the ground and the dragons like a kind of poison. Lightning sparked and thunder rumbled, echoed by the growls of the beasts. Below the circling dragons, Jason could see Bailey and the wolfjackal making their way along the fallen rock and burned grasses, the pup snuffling the mist as eagerly as he would a bowl of dog kibble. Static surrounded Bailey and the wolfjackal, making their hair turn bluish and stand on end, sparks running the length of their limbs. She had more than she could handle between the pup and the Chaos, Jason realized suddenly. Bailey couldn't possibly be shielding Pearl.

He jumped down to the nearest outcropping of rock and flung a shield of his making about the small dragon. She buzzed up and down at first, and then settled as she identified Jason's magick. She came to a perch on another jagged bit of stone, her head held proudly. His own ears rang with the effort of guarding Trent and Pearl but he could do it. He knew he could. Down below, the black dragon knocked the crimson one across the landscape and the red beast lay limply as if mortally wounded. His paws flexed, releasing Trent from his cagelike hold. Trent crawled a few lengths' away before his hands resumed their unweaving patterns.

Chaos crept up on Trent, slithering over his ankles and pulsating, like a heavy dense mist shot through with electricity of the sparking, high voltage kind. Trent yelped at the sharpness of its touch, dancing on one foot and then the other in pain. He attempted to kick it off, but the mist reacted by tightening around his feet, the way a python squeezes its prey. If it withdrew at all, it did so with a dragging motion, threatening to pull Trent along with it, in a path leading toward the massive black dragon. He staggered in an effort to stay on his feet, arms and hands waving madly for balance, jerked away from his pattern of unweaving.

Jason could feel the beat of the black dragon's energies and the chill of the Chaos the beast shed. A gate hung on the verge of being opened, so powerful was the energy, and Jason feared that more than almost anything. The rift along the colliding energies of Haven and the abyss stank of Jonnard, of hatred, and of awful, terrible things. Truly the dark side of Haven itself, shocking him to his core. It shouldn't be opened; he couldn't let it be opened. Jonnard—alive? Lost behind that rancid gateway? He shuddered and retreated.

He stumbled backward, his heart thudding and then stuttering deep in his chest. He *felt* Jonnard. Worse, awareness leaped, and he thought . . . he thought . . . Jonnard felt him. This was no echo of energies beyond the physical world that had been left behind by their battle at the Gate of Bones. This was— faint though it was—real. Happening now. What had he and Trent and Bailey done to Jonnard?

Before another thought dared tick through his mind, Chaos flooded toward Jason. It flew at him as if magnetically attracted and unavoidable. Even as Trent let out another sharp yelp of pain, Chaos struck Jason with an overwhelming impact.

Sudden cold bit at him and with every freezing gnaw, the mist drained his power. The rapid, frightened beat of his heart weakened at an alarming rate. His shields flickered. He not only couldn't go on the offensive to help his dragon and the others, he could not longer defend his friends. Jason forced words out of a throat going numb.

"Watch . . . yourselves. I'm losing it."

"I've got you," Bailey cried in answer, jumping over stones and shrubs, racing uphill toward him, her wolfjackal pup at her heels. But who had her? Trent was as trapped as a fly in a spider's sticky web.

Serpent quick, the black dragon twisted about and struck at Bailey. His teeth snapped, jaws rattling, his spines shivering with the sound of iron wind chimes clashing. He missed Bailey only because her feet slipped on the bruised and beaten grass, slick as snot, under her. She went to one knee; the snapping jaws closed right where she had been, but no longer was.

Bailey flung herself forward on her stomach and rolled out of reach as the wolfjackal spun about with a loud yip and snarl. The black dragon recoiled for another strike but as he did, the crimson dragon wrapped tightly about his haunches, hauling him back a little. Ever so little, but enough that Bailey got to her feet and sprang free. She grabbed her pup by the scruff of the neck, and the amethyst clenched in her free hand began to glow. Her power shot out, hurtling her and the pup completely out of the dragon's way, throwing her up into the thick mist attacking Jason.

The mist shredded before the onslaught of the pup as he lowered his head, biting and chewing at Chaos as if tearing into a delicious hamburger. His eyes glowed avidly and he bounded here and there, looking for a better bite, before he ran into Jason whose entire body began folding like a wet noodle. He could feel himself toppling. Then, in a snap, the horrid cold and numbness fled. His brain felt as though it was enveloped in an ice cream freeze inside and out, throbbing in agony that slowly faded away. The taste of Jonnard that had filled the back of his throat evaporated. Gone. That quickly. But the danger did not snuff out even though Chaos left. The strength—the anger and will—of the black-as-deepest-night dragon doubled.

They could all feel it gather new power, Jason realized as he looked to Trent and Bailey and saw the same awareness flood their faces. Pearl dragonette faltered in her flight and landed on a momentary perch out of the way as if the same feeling pierced her all the way through to Ting inside.

How could they save each other? How could they grab some kind of victory out of this losing battle? Jason didn't know if he had enough left in him to do it.

Bailey caught his hand. Her pup leaned upon her knee, panting happily, tail wagging and oblivious to the awful moment.

Jason's dragon groaned. His body rippled with the effort of keeping the black dragon anchored as his moan sounded through the valley, an expression of extreme effort and, yes, even desperation. Hearing that cry raised the hair on the back of Jason's neck, and Bailey let out a deep sigh. Pearl fluttered her wings weakly in response, but she had no energy left to fly back into the dragons' battle.

"We've got to stop it." Bailey looked at him, eyes brimming.

"I know."

Her hand tightened around his. "Ting can't last much longer either."

As if hearing them, Jason's dragon angled his head toward them, one luminous amber eye fixed on Jason. He spoke. "Remember. The young do not know their strength." Whatever else he might have said was lost as the black dragon wrapped a front paw about his neck and squeezed.

But, Jason realized, the dragon was wrong. They did know their strength. They'd been through a lot together. Jason's mouth tightened.

A clatter arose at the head of the valley. He looked up to see horsemen riding in. They'd never live without the aid of the Magickers.

Jason hauled Bailey with him to join Trent on his rocky stand. "Lend me whatever you can. We'll let the Reeve distract him."

"And then?"

Jason looked hard at them. "And then my charged crystal goes down his throat just before it explodes."

"Your crystal?"

"Without you attached to it," Trent added to Bailey's gasp.

"Whatever it takes. My crystal goes or we all die here." Jason dropped Bailey's hand to grip his focus crystal in both of his. This bit of rock was what made him a Magicker. Or did it? He'd bonded with it, but had he merely bonded with talent inside himself he hadn't known he had before? Was he a Magicker with or without his crystal? This seemed a bad, and yet, the only time to find out. The object bound to him might take him with it when it was destroyed.

So be it.

At the foot of the valley, Jason could spy three horsemen riding in, Reeve Dick in the front, an enormous sword in his hand. He took a deep breath, throwing a bit of a guard over them, but he couldn't spare much more than that. They were protected, a little, if the black dragon found the time or a way to throw flame or spit acid, but Jason couldn't save them from the lethal, snapping jaws or swiping talons.

Jason's dragon went to battle again with a muted roar. They met like two great, immovable titans, rearing up against each other with a furious noise, the crash of avalanches meeting. Even as Jason strained to hold his guardian shields over his friends and the farmers, the crimson dragon broke. His bulk slid away and he tumbled downhill, to lie belly up and vulnerable, great body shaking with fatigue.

Jason had never thought of his dragon as old and maybe over the hill. Not before this moment, anyway. He stopped and then clasped his crystal tightly in his hand. One more shield. And not just any shield, but one great and tough enough to protect a dragon. He took a deep breath and spun it out, spun it farther and wider than anything he had ever attempted before even as the black dragon rose in triumph, his claws ready to gut his fallen foe.

Pearl dashed in at his throat. Trent bounded to his feet, throwing his hands in the air, shouting, "Done! The web is gone!"

The black dragon faltered a moment before dipping his head to breathe in the sickly mist about his body—but too late, for the wolfjackal had been lapping at it steadily, leaving little but tiny wisps. The dragon swiped at Pearl in irritation and caught her, not directly but the wind of his blow lifting her up and tossing her aside.

For all their magick and all their plans, nothing seemed to work.

Past little Pearl panting on the ground, past Bailey and her wiggling wolfjackal, past Trent and his now empty hands, Reeve Dick came galloping. He carried his great silver sword like a lance and he never hesitated nor did his draft horse slow as they bore down on the two dragons. Jason's dragon flailed about with a groan and encircled the black dragon's hindquarters as he turned to snarl at the farmer.

Too late. Reeve Dick of the Bailey's sword sank into the sooty gray softness where chest met throat, plunging down into the heart of the black dragon.

The beast let out a great screech and keening of pain, falling backward, tearing the sword from the Reeve's hold but not ripping the blade out. He died, with the farmer standing over him and his crimson opponent wrapped tightly about his lower body, all his biting and thrashing bouncing harmlessly off Jason's shield.

Like Twister, it took a while to unwind all of them, reap the promised reward of rare herbs, and limp their way home, the dragon protesting he could only fly a bit at a time because he was, after all, wounded and no one was too eager to have a wildly unsteady flight as it was.

Jason waited a few days for his friend to heal before he went to check on the massive beast. He sat on a nearby knoll while the dragon soaked in the sun. Finally the dragon pretended to suddenly notice him.

"We won," Jason said.

"That we did. Did you have any doubts?"

"A few. Your fighting method was a trifle ... unorthodox. And what if the Reeve had not shown up?"

"How could he not? He did not ask for you to solve his problem for him, only for your help."

Jason absorbed that a moment.

The great dragon appeared to smile. "The black dragon died from overconfidence. He thought he could take whatever he wanted from us. The Unwanted lost because he made the fatal mistake of trying to measure us by our weaknesses. Me supposedly burdened by trying to protect you lesser ones, the Reeve Dick by his mortality." The dragon lowered his head to better look Jason in the eyes. "You Magickers are not my burden or my weakness. You, with your joy and enthusiasm and new ideas, are most definitely a gift to me in my ....hrmmm ... older years. As for the Reeve Dick, his very knowledge of death as a foe to meet and accept, particularly to defend his family and his lands—well, that's a courage and motivation the Unwanted could never have understood or anticipated."

"He's a hero, isn't he?" Jason asked slowly.

"Yes, my boy, but he's a hero because he gets up and faces death and adversity every day and does his work to better the lives of his children and his community. Every single day is his battle and, more often than not, it's a quiet victory." The dragon dropped one eyelid in another of his deliberate winks. "May you have many such victories and may your Magick never fade."

Warmth flooded Jason's face as he heard this. Could it be a blessing from the dragon? "Why, thank you," he began, but a deep rumbling purr interrupted what else he might have said. Jason looked closely and saw that both of the dragon's eyes were shut as his snores grew louder. Jason opened his mouth and closed it again. Had he even heard that last sentence from the weary, battle-scarred old beast? He decided he had, and grinned.

MERCEDES LACKEY
Reserved for the Cat

In 1910, in an alternate Paris, Ninette Dupond, a penni-
less young dancer, recently dismissed from the Paris
Opera, thinks she has gone mad when she finds herself in
a conversation with a skinny tomcat. However, Ninette is
desperate—and hungry—enough to try anything. She
follows the cat's advice and travels to Blackpool,
England, where she is to impersonate a famous Russian
ballerina and dance, not in the opera, but in the finest of
Blackpool's music halls. With her natural talent for dancing, and her magic for enthralling an audience, it looks as
if Ninette will gain the fame and fortune the cat has
promised. But the real Nina Tchereslavsky is not as far
away as St. Petersburg...and she's not as human as she
appears...   978-0-7564-0488-8

The Elemental Masters Series
And don't miss the first four books of
The Elemental Masters:

The Serpent's Shadow	978-0-7564-0061-9
The Gates of Sleep	978-0-7564-0101-1
Phoenix and Ashes	978-0-7564-0272-7
The Wizard of London	978-0-7564-0363-4

To Order Call: 1-800-788-6262
www.dawbooks.com